D1106606

The
Torch Bearers

A NOVEL BY

BERNARD V. DRYER

SIMON AND SCHUSTER • NEW YORK

THE TIMES AND PLACES of this book are real, but the people in it are not. All the characters in the story are invented. If any of them seems to resemble you or someone you know, or anyone else, or any place elsewhere, that's by chance alone.

The private tempo of the fictional people's pulses so often differs from the actual recorded public heartbeat that occasional small liberties have been taken with the calendar, the map, and governmental organizations. For example: an airline flies where, in fact, it does not; a law officer with a fictional title has been given imaginary authority over a jurisdiction which does not exist; real political titles have been given to completely invented characters; a nonexistent hospital and fictional medical personnel treat fictional patients; some recent history has been compressed or expanded simply because time is experienced more flexibly than clocks admit.

*To my daughters
these intimations of immortality*

CONTENTS

BOOK I

CARIBBEAN:
Dr. Dionisio Mayoso Martí

1 Mayoso balanced his massive frame astride a cane stool beside the roughhewn table and concentrated fiercely on scratching medical notes into his journal with a dip pen. A powerful eight-band transoceanic radio on the table was on shortwave, tuned to the 7510-kilocycle band, so that Mayoso could receive the government's rural network in Camagüey province.

". . . milk rations to nursing mothers and to preschool children," the shortwave from Cuba announced, "will be limited, el Máximo Líder explained in his new decree, because our valiant sugar cane workers, the foundation of our economy—"

El Máximo limited, Mayoso said drily to the radio without pausing in his medical scrawl and cut off the voice with a rotary flick of the dial to a Miami station. A famous woman refugee's voice, self-assured, fluent in English despite the Spanish accent, brimmed over the radio: "A Soviet-built PT boat based at Victoria de Playa Girón—"

Mayoso interrupted her without raising his head from his writing: No, cara, based at Caibarién.

". . . was attacked over the past weekend in Siguanea Bay off the Isle of Pines. Fidel's Radio Rebelde, monitored here in Miami, reported the anti-Castro boat used a large-caliber North American demolition weapon in the action . . ."

Wrong, Mayoso said. Finnish. Helsinki's surplus, via New Jersey. He half ignored the radio. She was an intelligent girl there in Miami, with very good sources and doing a difficult job with skill—but instant news, like instant anything, was never quite right.

The tropical storm belt, he wrote in his leatherbound journal, lies in a loose casual loop girdling our amiable Caribbean, innocent-looking as a lover's knot, sun-bright where sea meets sky, coiled to tighten like a hangman's noose each hurricane season.

Qué? he said, caught off guard by the radio, and dialed the volume higher.

". . . from San Juan," the Miami news announcer was saying calmly, "through the joint spokesman for several refugee groups including the Students Movement for Recovery, La Hermandad de Cubanos Radicales Democraticos, and the Commando Zero Zero. The spokesman, unidentified by name, said that Dr. Dionisio Mayoso Martí, formerly Professor of Obstetrics and Gynecology at the University of Havana School of Medicine, now practicing in Puerto Rico—"

I don't have to practice, he growled. I know how—

"—will be offered a centralized leadership post as a gesture of unity in exile among the many—"

Click. He shut off the set. Heroics. Castles-in-Spain pipedreams. Quixotism. They suffer from sincerity. They had sworn secrecy, and now this broadcast to the four winds. Those pipsqueak El Máximos! He jabbed the steel point of his pen into the inkwell, but, instead of continuing his notes, he doodled absently on the envelope containing his plane ticket to Caracas, curling his bare toes in his huaraches, humming *Lamento Borinqueño*, until he realized his pen had traced a chain of zeroes.

Zeroes.

Arab astronomers had invented zero, he thought, a brilliant achievement for them but a dirty trick for the rest of us. As abrasive as discovering anti-matter. Diagnosis?—zero minus anti-matter. Therapy?—count upward, round well-fed plus numbers only. Pro-matter. Survive. Prognosis?—guarded, but hopeful.

He laid his wooden dip pen across the two bent nail supports and locked his fingers together in a sling behind his head as he rested back to stare out at the straits where the Caribbean and the Atlantic met. Broad shafts of tropical sunlight slanted down between the clouds, and, where the beams struck the sea, the surface threw back the light with the fragmented gleam of hammered silver.

Out there, far out over the water, he watched a single cormorant soaring upward, solitary against great cumulous masses of clouds above the ocean, dipping its wingtips, drifting in lazy circles downward below the horizon line.

He stood up and stretched mightily in the doorway, filling its height and most of its width. A torn fringe of mosquito netting tacked along the upper doorframe reminded him to duck his head as he leaned against the peeled, but unhewn, wooden supports. He was still wearing the white cotton shirt and faded blue jeans he had worn while fishing during the night; only the unique gold seal ring on his finger and his unusual height made his appearance different from all the *jíbaros* who were his neighbors in these Puerto Rican hills overlooking the sea.

His pet macaw waddled toward him, using a sailor's rolling gait, turning her great panache beak and iridescent featherduster body from side to side as she searched for her breakfast of finger-size niño bananas. When the sunlight ignited her she became a tropic blaze of greens, yellows, blues, golds, a clown's white circles around her eyes. Because of her curved beak he had named her with sardonic Spanish humor after one of the most esteemed noses in history.

"Buenos días, Nefertiti," Mayoso said to her.

"Días," the bird croaked, giving herself a little shiver.

"No bananas today." He pointed upward at a lemur-eyed capuchin monkey sitting atop a flamboyante tree gorging herself on bananas. "Ché-ché stole them," he said. "If you weren't such a fancy señora you'd get up earlier like everybody else."

High over the Caribbean an arrowhead speck broke off from parallel stratospheric contrails and descended in the direction of the International Airport at Isla Verde. A jet en route to Caracas?

He sat himself down on the woven-cane stool and absentmindedly wiped the nib of his pen on a stained square of chamois. He dipped the point thoughtfully into the inkwell, and continued writing the lecture he believed he would again give, some future day, at the medical school of the University of Havana.

The mother of hurricanes is the big-bellied anvil-top cloud, secretly married to the warm tropic sea, seeded inside by nothing more than droplets and air, her crown hammered flat and forged by the cold stratosphere. Each mother cloud swells as it rises awesomely into the thinning upper windstream, strong, beautiful, flickering internally with forked heat lightning, the blood-warmth of its womb mounting to oven heat as it creates a charged electrical life of its own. When these individual mother formations surge and swirl together they no longer live as single structures but as a fertile community, a great expanding wheel one or two hundred miles in diameter. The outer rim of the wheel is studded with heavy lashing downpours which drum furiously at waterproofs and drench the skin as if the air had turned to water. As it births the hurricane the entire system whirls faster and faster, beyond the highest human weather dial markings, gale force 12, howling with violent banshee winds, gyrating with the energy of a dozen boiling suns, raging to batter down the land's breakwaters.

Natural laws vanish. Gravity is suspended. In the suffocating shrieking hell, the human spirit crawls back into its original cave, shrinking before such incredible vengeful gods. As if it were a paper target, a concrete wall is pierced by a wind-driven broomstick. A comically flying soda straw, sucked suddenly aloft and hurled through a window, slivers through a man's skull as easily as a steel spear.

The green angry whirlpools race outward, a volcanic churning; sea combers rotate gyroscopically into moving mountains, spraying spume from their crests with the velocity of bullets. Avalanches of ocean water crash down like rockslides onto land borders, burying believers and beachcombers alike. Not even a hydrogen bomb dropped squarely into the eye of a hurricane can contain the torrent of unimaginable power born amazingly from the fusion of pinpoint droplets and air.

With time and scientific study the anvil-top mother may yield to under-

standing so that she may bear life-bringing rain instead of mindless destruction.

He raised his head from the page. The air was slaked with heat shimmers, crickets persistent in the thatched roof overhead, the frangipani tree beside the door alive with scent so sweet he was filled with unfathomable nostalgia.

And the plane tickets to Caracas smoldering beside the inkwell.

The tassels of cane on the slope up from the sea rippled smokily as a hesitant breeze moved inland and faintly touched his face.

Caracas.

Finish, finish this lecture of yours, and be done. He dipped his pen and carefully tapped the excess ink from the point on the inner glass lip while he read over the last words he had written.

Mindless destruction.

Aie, Caracas.

He drew a thin wavering uncertain line through all the zeroes he had doodled on his plane ticket. Wonders are many, and none more wonderful than man, saith that ancient Greek physician who wrote plays. Only against death, Sophocles had concluded, shall he call for aid in vain. But from baffling maladies he hath devised escapes.

Well. Conclude your own homily, Doctor.

Shading his eyes with one hand, Mayoso drove his pen with an urgent obstinacy.

Through the diamond lens of your mind, see the coming together of ice nuclei and airborne water droplets as if this were the joining of human sperm and human ovum. Imagine a great swelling mother cloud as pregnant with life. Let your imaginary omnipotent eye see a global procession, like a weather system, and you barely begin to glimpse what the elemental human ability to create new life can do in the world.

2   THE IBERIA FLIGHT from San Juan to Caracas winged upward over the palm fringe of Isla Verde and banked south over the Atlantic. Mayoso sat in the first-class section with his medical bag on the floor between his feet. He looked down at the green island of Puerto Rico falling away below the climbing plane. Will I come back? I thought I had learned to live with myself and these departures, but I have not. How I envy men who can accustom themselves to

fear. Hell is paved with frightened men and as a man who has made more than one trek through hell, I know. I know about fear in my bones, which is where knowledge counts.

But a reasonable estimate of difficulty is not fright, he assured himself. After all, my doing the surgery may be illegal, but if there will be no complications it will go like one two three. All right, let's not call it fright; it's too late, because here you are on this plane, and you're on your way to Caracas. No, something rational and clear-sighted in him said: not dishonorable fright. Just honorable fear. How admirable and therapeutic, the mind's rational ability to delude itself with complete confidence.

To his left, seen obliquely as the plane tilted, a knotted ribbon of beaches wavered and stretched toward the distant jumble of upthrust hotels and office buildings which now fenced in the narrow cobblestone streets of old San Juan. To his right, the palms raced past his window as the plane leveled off. Thatched bohíos huddled between the green spiky tree-crowns, looking primitive as African huts from this height. Inside, the bohíos were papered with covers from *Life* and *Look*. Outside, swarms of shirtless boys practiced big-league beisbol pitching with rocks, and barefooted schoolgirls in starched Sunday crinoline dresses swayed like apprentice Hawaiian dancers, a perpetual motion of plastic hula hoops spinning around their nubile waists.

To their sometime-working mothers and often unemployed fathers, Mayoso thought, to the parents who produced the children in an annual crop of hungry infants, the method of limiting them to a smaller number who could be fed was as astronomically remote as the far-off world of wealthy sophisticates of old San Juan: the fashionable Spanish-speaking men and women who scanned table-size luncheon menus written in French; the tanned tourist world of Condado Beach, bikini-bare ladies lolling on cashmere sands daydreaming of languorous Latin love, ladies who knew about pills, sheaths, devices to open or close the door of life. To the breeding families in the bohíos, a few miles away, that San Juan world was as distant as the planet named for Venus.

Dr. Dionisio Mayoso Martí had had only a few hours of sleep before dawn; he had planned to use this weightless time aloft to catch up on the rest he needed before he reached Caracas. The operation would be a simple one, but so many small things could go wrong, especially the bleeding, that it was only common sense to rest now while he could. Just as he closed his eyes, the music of *Bésame Mucho* blasted from the loudspeaker mounted in the ceiling overhead, then modulated itself to a more reasonable level. Everywhere I go, he thought wearily, I hear that unofficial Latin anthem. Last week in Miami. Now here.

A rolling bar cart appeared and the stewardess' voice asked, "Beverage? Doctor Mayoso Martí—cocktail for you?"

Dr. Mayoso shook his head. He did not like her using the formal Spanish style of address, linking both Mayoso and Martí, because he did not know who might overhear her. His patronym, Martí, was as loaded a name in Caribbean politics as Kennedy in the States; he preferred the everyday Mayoso. "No, thank you," he said in English.

The woman in the seat next to him said brightly to the stewardess, "I thought you'd never get here. I'm dying of thirst."

"You can have a double, señora," the stewardess said. "Sherry?"

"No. A martini. Double."

Señora Dolores Valdez del Sevillano took two quick ladylike swallows from the chilled glass handed to her, then turned to Dr. Mayoso to pick up the conversation she had begun before takeoff. She was a former patient, she was talkative, and, Mayoso had already decided, she wanted companionship.

"What hotel will you stay at in Caracas, Doctor Mayoso?" she asked him.

"With friends," the doctor said. Friends. Again, the nick of fear.

"That's nicer for the first day or two." She sipped her martini. "But after that"—she waved one jeweled hand with beautifully manicured nails—"you get tied down to your host's family routine, no? I like the freedom of a hotel. You disturb nobody, and nobody disturbs you."

"That's true, señora," Dr. Mayoso said. "You can come and go." A swift arrival, he thought, but a swifter departure.

"Exactly. Don't you feel Caracas is a wide-awake town? The way Havana used to be." She rotated the liquid in her glass, then drank some slowly. "It's alive," she said as she put the glass down on the flat surface they shared between their seats. "Even the shoeshine boys in the plazas give you the old-fashioned Spanish eye, you know, the Andalusian *piropo*. Is it virility or vulgarity, this custom of ogling women and talking to them on the street?" She did not wait for his answer. "Vulgarity, I think. A man, very good-looking, followed me half a block from my hotel. I could feel his eyes on my back. 'Señorita,' he said from behind me, 'now that I have seen you I will pay anything to buy the biggest American foam-rubber mattress just for us together. Meet me tonight.'"

She was so transparent that he was amused. "Did you speak, señora?"

"On the hotel steps I turned and crushed him. 'You,' I said, 'sound uneducated.'"

He kept a straight face. "He must have been shattered. It all sounds like the old Havana."

Years ago she and her husband had escaped from Cuba on a patched fishing boat whose engine was broken. That was before Castro's decree that even fishing boats must carry a guard, so she and her husband had managed to smuggle aboard what they judged to be vital for escape: two canteens of water and a small suede-lined leather case of gems. Now their jewelry shop on Calle Cristo was the most fashionable *joyería* in San Juan, fronted by tall double bronze filigree doors imported from Madrid, hushed by specially designed V'Soske rugs. During their first four years in San Juan, Señora Dolores Valdez del Sevillano had had three babies, and last year, with the camaraderie of one Cuban refugee visiting another, she had come to ask him for the *operación*.

"What can I do?" she had said last year, sitting in his clinic office. "The Ogino rhythm method, my Americano neighbor lady calls it Vatican roulette." She had smiled intimately. "My sister in Madrid, with six children, calls her last three accidental *oginitos*." She had sighed. "Contraceptives? You don't know my confessor, Father Gofredo Möttl." She made a tight, delicate fist. "Strict. He's from Spain, strict as a convent teacher. He would make me spend my life on my raw knees for using the pills or those rubber things."

"I've seen Father Gofredo on San Juan television. He speaks very well."

"A brilliant man. A Franciscan, with the, the"—she shook her fist, then exploded her fingers outward—"the *incendio* of a Jesuit. A burning bush. I admire his unshakable faith, even surrounded by a faithless world."

"Ah," Mayoso had said, settling deeper in his office chair.

"How can a confessor like that understand me, Doctor? Before Cuba my family was Andalusian, but he's from the cold northern mountains, the Basque country, or Galicia. A southerner like me is as strange as an Oriental to a northerner like him. In the south with our *piropo,* our guitars, our warm nights, our aromatic gardens of orange trees in Córdoba and Granada—to a stern northerner like Father Gofredo that's all a pagan heritage from the Moorish days of the Alhambra. Even Saint Teresa could not pray with her whole heart in Seville, Father Gofredo told me a month ago at a meeting of The Holy Trinity Court of Catholic Daughters. Imagine! A saint, and she was tempted! The seductive power of the carnal southern cult of voluptuousness is satanic. Even rural priests have been known to lose their celibate vows in amor loco and end up with their own children greeting them in the streets as Señor Tío.

"So I said, Father, can't there be beauty, even with physical love? He said that sensual beauty for its own sake could be the greatest seduction of all."

"Ah, how Castilian," Mayoso had said.

"How like Father Gofredo."

Sitting at his clinic desk he had said to her, "Señora, the complications of biology are my profession, not the complications of theology."

"No," she had said as she had lighted a corktipped English cigarette. "And I am not the convent girl of my mother's generation Father Gofredo thinks I should be. I am more European—"

"But Spain is part of Europe."

"Since when? Galicia is the north, closer to Europe, maybe even a little bit Germanic. My friends say that Father Gofredo's father was high in the Nazi hierarchy, so high that his family had to flee from Germany after the war while he was still a boy. To Galicia, not Castilla. So, they say, he grew up twice as Spanish as any Spanish priest." She had squinted across the upcurling smoke of her cigarette at him. "What can you say to a confessor who pronounces that to enjoy the act of love is sinful?"

"Father Gofredo is your confessor, señora. It is not for me to judge."

"But he judges physicians all the time."

He had shrugged with polite dignity. "Perhaps he was trained to judge. Speaking medically, what can I do for you?"

She had ground out the newly lighted cigarette in the ashtray on his desk and had come to the point. "My friends say that you can tie a woman's tubes closed inside, pff." She had washed her hands in the air. "Finished. Safe. No need for birth control, so no need to confess."

"So simple?" he had asked. "Just pff?"

"They say that with your skill you do the surgery in seventeen minutes. A lady can sit up and play bridge the same evening."

"One is nimble from experience. One can learn to remove an eye in seventeen minutes."

Her large black eyes had looked directly at him. For centuries, he had thought, such eyes as these have gazed like this at men until now it is folklore: promise them heaven, but first get what you want on earth. Even the flamenco was a duel.

"I remember your father in the Havana days, Doctor. A fine man. My father trusted nobody when we settled in Cuba, but he trusted your father. Your father advised him on his estate, his will, everything. He said to do business in your father's law office was like swearing on the Bible. Now, I see, you combine your father's legal talent with your medicine."

"Only to caution you, señora. To tie off your Fallopian tubes—that's almost like taking out an eye. You can't put reproductive ability back later."

"I've heard of operations to open the tubes later."

"True, true. Exceptions. Rare, but true. Now aren't you the lawyer?" She had frowned. "You know what I think? I think you're prejudiced."

"I am, señora. But each prejudice comes only after much experience. I'm covered with scars."

"Ah, Doctor, don't be ironic." Her eyes had narrowed. "We two are from old families. We can speak frankly."

"Frankly," he said, "does your husband know you want to have a sterilization operación?"

"Of course."

"He agrees?"

"Completely."

"Good. I always ask for the husband's signed consent."

"What for? If it's the woman's idea—if it's her own body—"

"I'm afraid it's my turn to be legal. For a woman to have her tubes tied off, or a man to have a vasectomy, deprives them both of future parenthood. If one of them is against the idea, then a sterilization operation can become grounds for what the law calls constructive desertion—"

"Ah—"

"—or cruelty. So your husband's consent—"

"I'm sure you've guessed already—my husband knows nothing about this."

"I know only what you tell me."

She lifted both hands toward him lightly, a delicate begging, a plea to reason. "Spanish men are mostly sensitive boys, no? But you, you're a man. A guerrilla hero. You left the comfortable university faculty to go fight in the mountains. Yet here we are—even you, you're insulted because you think I want to hire you like a plumber, to fix a pipe." She sighed. "My friends warned me you are prejudiced against the rich."

"I'm not. Money's a tool, a utensil, like a hammer or a spoon. I'm not prejudiced against money, believe me."

"They say you have the big fees deposited to the committee for the refugees."

"Yes. They need all the tools they can get."

"Would it be better, would you be more willing to say yes, if I came here like a woman of poverty, with my hair a mess, dressed in a sack, nursing a baby and crying about eight hungry kids in a row and one more on the way?"

"I salute you, señora. You have just described all of Latin America in ten seconds."

She had raised her handsome eyes theatrically to his office ceiling. "Aie, Dios mío. I sit with my heart breaking and he talks geography." She had crossed her silken legs. "Nothing can persuade you as much as starving children?"

"I would be more willing to do the surgery, of course," he had said. "But this way? What if something happened to your children, and you wanted more? What if something happened to your husband? What if you wanted children in a new marriage?"

"All men are the same," she had said, twisting her rings back and forth. "In back of a man's big stiff *macho completo,* he is a prosecuting attorney. And in back of that, he is a judge." She had appealed to his neutral face. "Doctor Mayoso, your name, your family name, Martí—it always stood for freedom."

"You know," he had told her, "even if I sound like a newspaper editorial, freedom is the hardest responsibility of them all."

Her dark eyes hardened. "Words!" she had cried. "Spanish men! Their poetry and their philosophy and their words! What do the words have to do with how people live?"

"Could it be," he tried to say kindly, "that it's how you live, not la operación, that you should think about?"

"Ah, how I live. I think about nothing else." She had raised her lacquered head angrily. "I know what you think. I'm spoiled. I'm idle. I think only of myself. Only of pleasure."

"Who says so?"

"Father Gofredo."

"Is he right?"

"Perhaps. But everyday life is so different from what I thought it would be. I don't know how to change things for the better."

"Your children make demands?" he had asked. "Your husband is married to his business and keeps a girl friend? You're gaining weight, and soon you'll be thirty, and one of your husband's best friends wants you to go to bed with him?"

Her mouth had opened slightly. "Dios mío, who told you?"

"Señora, you are young. Many things can happen in your life. I've tried to explain you should not have the operation which will make a permanent change."

"I'm willing to pay any amount, directly to the refugee committee if you say so—"

"Please, money has its place, but not here, not with such a question. We're talking about your life as a woman, not a purchase. You should not try to buy your way into the operating room, señora. For you, as an individual, you would not be buying an operation, you would be buying a mutilation. Believe me. I've seen this many times before."

She had stood up. "I can go someplace else."

"Of course you can. And I can only advise you the best I can."

"How does it feel to play God, Doctor Mayoso?"

"I don't know, señora. I've never tried. Qué va! It's difficult enough to be a man."

As the stewardess came up the aisle of the plane, the señora raised her empty glass above her head. "My motor needs another tank of gas, please."

The stewardess took the glass. "Martini? A double?"

"Of course," she said. "What good is single anything?"

The stewardess went off toward the galley. The woman was silent until the stewardess returned with a fresh martini on a tray. "I put in an extra olive," she said as she held the tray forward.

"You're an angel of mercy, señorita." The woman turned to Mayoso and raised her glass. "*Salud*, Doctor. *Pesetas y amor.*"

"*Salud.*"

She swallowed a mouthful, then said, "The *pesetas*, that's simple. The *amor*, that's complicated, no?" When he said nothing, she giggled. "Oh, such a discreet professional silence. The owl and the pussycat. You know, you may think it's only the martini talking but I must tell you one thing about yourself. Frankly—"

He waited. She will now say more about herself than about me.

"—with that white hair you look older than you are. You look the way I remember your father looked in Havana."

"We were all much younger in Havana, señora."

"But we felt older," she cried. "I worked, Doctor. Hard. My fingernails were trimmed short as a stenographer's. I was one of the *Damas Auxiliares* in your own University Hospital. I gave to the charities, enough for an award, a Cruz de la Beneficencia." She sat up straighter. "And the taxes? To pay crooks to steal more? Casino licenses on sale to syndicate gangsters. There are men in Miami this minute who stole millions. Dollars, not pesos! Expensive welfare programs? For girls with one illegitimate baby after another? For men who won't work unless an overseer sits there on a horse and watches all day?"

"Señora—"

"Doctor, let's be frank. You're a fine man and you carry a noble name. You and your father were professors," she said. "But our income was from land, sugar cane. Washington made the laws and Wall Street decided the prices. But what can you know of such practical things in medicine?"

"There's much to know. You don't have to be a doctor to know. The results of despair are as bad as the results of disease, no? People become sick in the outside world, not in the medical offices. Nobody can live feeling life is a tunnel with a dead end."

"God helps those who help themselves."

"And those who cannot?"

"For the faithful, Doctor, there is life everlasting."

"But this life comes first, no?"

She waggled a finger at him. "Ah. Ah. Your father's son. Now you're the lawyer again."

Dr. Mayoso motioned to the stewardess who was undulating down the aisle. She bent toward him. "Señor?"

"I need to write a letter, please."

"Un momentito, señor."

Mayoso turned to the woman beside him. "Will you excuse me?"

"You don't have to be so polite, Doctor. I don't mean to nag you into letter-writing. I know you feel very strongly on these things."

"It's a simple matter," he said. "Fewer babies or more bread. Simple survival."

"Survival is not so simple, Doctor. Bread and schools, not so easy. You should know."

How well I know, he thought. I'm one of the world's survivors.

"Survival." She sighed. "The word has the sound of apes."

"By itself," he said, "maybe it does."

"After, after how much time is it?—fifty thousand years?—we should be able to come down from the trees and out of the caves and plant mushrooms in the bomb shelters."

"Yes," he said.

"We're still animals. Not the martinis, but I say so."

"Señora—such *mea culpa*? Here?"

"It's true. An airplane can be a confessional. Let us confess, Doctor. We are animals."

"But human animals, señora. A little difference that makes a difference."

"But animals. Who knows better than our Cuban generation? When Batista's SIM storm troopers picked up a university student from the Avenida Quinta on suspicion he was an underground courier, did they care, courier or not, guilty or not? No. No matter. Hold him incommunicado. Use him as a warning anyway. Send one of his eyes to his mother. Break both arms and both legs before shooting him. Throw his body like a sack on the university steps."

Her eyes were wet with pain and fury. They sat not speaking, then she said angrily, "And you say human animals are different? No wonder the first families, the professionals, even the big American companies, all gave Fidel money in those days. My father gave to Fidel's 26th of July Movement. We gave to the Segundo Frente de Escambray, to the Organización Auténtico. I used to count stacks of money so new that the edges cut my fingers. What fools we were! Who would dream that Fidel, the idealistic young lawyer, and el Ché, the idealistic young doctor from Argentina— who would dream what they would do later? The blood baths! That scream! *Al paredón!* Even over television, to hear thousands scream *To the wall!* at a prisoner. My skin crawls just to remember. If all that can happen in a great civilized city of Hispanic culture, Havana, it can happen anywhere. Rio, Buenos Aires, Caracas."

He said nothing. With two double martinis, neither her voice nor her anger would stop now.

"And what of your own father, Doctor? A famous professor of legal history and ethics, the man they turned on like a light when they wanted Cuba to shine. Did the noble name Martí protect him?" When Mayoso did not answer, she said, "Havana and San Juan are small gossipy towns for people like us. I heard one of Batista's kangaroo courts sent him to hard labor in the Zapata swamps."

Actually, his father had finally been imprisoned in La Cabaña. In the hills at guerrilla headquarters Mayoso had received a message: Call the Batista headquarters about your father. Call from any telephone, any time. Say your father's name and you will be able to talk to him. Trap or not, he had to try. A squad of *barbudos* went with him to an isolated sugar mill from which he had telephoned directly to the top, to the big white concrete SIM headquarters, Campo Columbia, outside Havana. The Batista lieutenant at the other end had been very tense, very quick. "Call back in half an hour!" he had shouted over the phone. To avoid an ambush Mayoso and his squad had driven like maniacs, bouncing over ruts, risking their necks as well as a broken axle, to reach a different telephone in the next town. When Mayoso called this time, the Batista police put his father on the phone. A wave of relief ran through him when he heard his father's voice.

"Papá, how are they treating you?"

"As one expects. The blindfold keeps me from reading. It's good to hear your voice. Your fighting goes?"

"It goes, Papá. Can you hold out?"

"I will try. They are convinced I am some kind of underground *jefe.*"

"Only tell them no. The simple truth, Papá."

"I try to remember what that is."

"Tell them. They want me, not you. Explain that your son is not you."

A heavy military voice had broken into the conversation. "Mayoso, listen. Your father is sentenced for execution tonight. Mayoso, you hear me?"

A freezing disbelief seized him. He managed to choke out, "Dios! Don't punish him. I'm the one!"

"He can live, and you too, if you leave Cuba. Just bring us a list of the underground cells in Havana and you can take him out of La Cabaña tomorrow, free."

He had been completely unable to speak. His entire body shook. His father's voice came on the line. "Take care of your mother and sister. Goodbye, my son."

"Papá, Papá—"

"What can we do? I kiss you goodbye, my son."

He had staggered out of the phone booth, stumbling, blinded by a rising wall of tears.

"Yes," he said to the woman passenger in the airplane seat beside him. "Life changed in our family."

"He never came back?"

"No." One way or another, none of us ever came back, he thought. In one generation we have become so brutalized that suffering means as little as dirt. Or maybe we only pretend so, because to do otherwise would make the pain unbearable.

"You went early into the underground, didn't you, then?"

"Yes," he said. "Many university people did."

"I heard you were with the attack on Moncada Barracks with Fidel."

"Yes."

"Then Mexico? One of the first *barbudos*."

"Yes."

"And each night Radio Havana kept broadcasting it was a true proletarian revolution, a peasant uprising."

"I know," he said. "But it wasn't that way. The peasants in the country came into the fight late. When we fought Batista, we totaled twenty thousand casualties. One thousand were killed in the countryside. The other nineteen thousand were killed in the cities."

"My aunt told me your sister became a courier at that time, until the Batistianos caught her. She was a Joan of Arc, your sister. And your fiancée, wasn't she also caught?"

"Yes." His sister caged and desolate in Guanajay. And his fiancée, that last terror-breathing afternoon. "Please," he said. "I know how these things still burn inside. But I—I mean, my sister, my family, your brother, let's not talk of a past we cannot change."

"You're wrong," she said. "It's better to talk."

Talk? he asked himself. Some things I can never talk about. How can I talk about Boniato?

When I was in solitary in the coffin-size *cabañita* of Boniato prison, naked and up to my armpits in water slimy with body wastes, upright, unable to crouch, they kept the bare bulb overhead protected by a wire mesh cover to prevent prisoners like me from breaking the glass and using the glass slivers in the only useful way one can use broken glass in such solitary confinement. The fiery electric light bulb blazing, burning, no darkness ever, no night, no day, only the burning homicidal bulb, and on my wrist the chevron of the civilized world, a wristwatch. A twentieth-century man, entirely naked in a torture box, dressed insanely in a wristwatch. I would say in my head: Thou. Keep me sane. Bless thy cogs and wheels and scientific clock face. When Copernicus dreamed the soul-wrenching dream of a heliocentric universe, when Galileo crouched on his begging knees before the Inquisition of the Holy Office to whisper, *Epur si muove*, did they ever dream their solar universe would be captured in thee, little tinplated cogwheeled watch that connects me to the great astronomic world of day and night?

Until even this clutch at sanity fails, and time becomes biologic, peristaltic, salivary, and one returns to the period before sundials or seasons, before the Cro-Magnons, the era of ants and dinosaurs, and one marks with bleeding fingertips the passage of eternity on the raw concrete *cabañita* wall. To make small talk about this is impossible.

"Señora," Mayoso said, "you will forgive me if I disagree with you. We are not the same people we were in the past."

"It's easy for you to say that. Doctors are not very sensitive people. But when I think of our garden back home, or my father sitting in our library just looking out the window with his finger between the pages of a book to mark his place"—she shook her head—"oh, I get such an ache in my heart." She sighed, then said, "I'm sorry. This is no way to talk on a holiday to Caracas. And you have an important letter to write."

"Yes," he said quickly, "I actually do have to finish a letter before we land."

She tried to smile, clinging to the protocol of gracefulness. "So urgent? Oh là là. That sounds like desperation or romance."

He pretended to smile back. Only the former sign language of a black lace fan was missing. "There's so little time for either, no?"

"You know," she said, "you're a strange man. Everybody talks about you but no one knows you. The stories. The stories! You're a gunrunner. You're this, you're that. You're a secret adviser on birth control—or should I say population?—to the Governor. You have a beautiful mistress in Miami. You live in a thatched bohío in the hills like a barefoot *jíbaro*."

He spread his hands slightly and shrugged to her. "I've heard those silly stories. As you said, our families were well known. People talk. Actually, I'm just another doctor."

Be careful, he told himself. I don't like so much curiosity. After all that talk, could she be a Fidelista agent? Being blackmailed into service?

Again, the sting of fear: What if I don't come back from Caracas? You'll come back from Caracas, he told himself.

All right. But speaking calmly and statistically, on a fifty-fifty basis. What if you don't come back?

You'll come back, amigo. Twenty minutes of surgery. Not too fast, because there will be no plasma or blood for transfusion. Barring complications, making allowances for the tricky details, that's not such a big thing.

But twenty minutes of surgery is only the in-between. What my chess-player friend Governor Roque would describe as the middle game. The opening moves are to get there, the end game is to survive.

You have a talent for survival, he told himself. You'll come back to San Juan. The surgery in Caracas is what Americans call hit-and-run. Twenty minutes, thirty at the most. The instruments in the bag are already sterilized, even the rubber gloves. A military precision. One, two, three. Then zip back home to San Juan on the next flight out of Caracas.

Creo que sí. But who knows?

You have the talent, he told himself contemptuously. Ah, others die, your own father died, but you have the survival talent of one of those matadors who are gored time and again by the point, *el diamante*, but always live. Lazarus, weren't you good as dead those times, in Boniato, in La Cabaña? The execution squad aims, you look into the business end of gun barrels, the sergeant throws down his cigarette, ready to bark, *"Fuego!"* Now your hair is white and you know each day is part gift, part miracle.

Creo que sí? How long can a man live until the law of averages says: stop. You made a fatal mistake.

But to do nothing? he asked himself. A comfortable nothing? To do nothing is an action, the worst action of all. The fighting is terrible, but not to fight is even worse. It's the same decision as surgery to prolong life in a terminal illness. You're damned if you do, damned if you don't. Women are wiser. They are on the side of life. They carry the water from the well. Maybe that's why I became the kind of doctor I am. An inheritance from my lost father, a belief in life.

He was annoyed with himself for allowing the woman beside him to open this locked door in his memory.

For the past two days he had pretended to ignore the time running out before his departure from San Juan for Caracas. Forget the trip to Caracas, he kept telling himself. When you get there you'll be there. Until then do your work.

Yesterday he had paced himself through a heavy hospital clinic schedule. He knew if he kept busy enough he would stop counting the hours before he had to leave. In his preoccupation with his last patient of the afternoon he had been able to disregard his foreboding of ambush and doublecross in Caracas. Like most pregnant young women, his patient was healthy and had needed only a routine check-up. "It's my Lorenzo," she had said as she ran her fingers over the head of her six year old son. "He's cranky. He doesn't eat."

"Well—" Mayoso had said noncommittally. I'm not a pediatrician, he had thought, and it's been a long day.

"Maybe," his pregnant patient had said, "Lorenzo maybe has some fever." As she bent and pressed her lips against the boy's forehead Mayoso realized she had come to the clinic not for herself, but for the boy. "Sí, sí," she said calmly, "fever."

"And you?" Mayoso had asked. He glanced at her chart on his desk. "Your temperature is normal." She watched him patiently. He knew the look. It was four hundred years old. We are the people, the look said, but you have the books. "Lorenzo," he asked, "do you go to school?"

The boy did not answer. This white-haired doctor in the strange white coat towered above him. Mayoso guessed the boy's feeling and crouched down beside him.

"Tell me, Lorenzo," he said gently at the boy's own eye level, "for your mother, I need to know if any of the children in your schoolroom are sick."

The boy said nothing. The mother prodded her son's shoulder.

"Lorenzo," she said, "tell Doctor Mayoso."

"Only Rosita," the boy said shyly.

"How do you know?" Mayoso asked.

His mother nudged the boy again. "Tell the doctor. How do you know Rosita is sick?"

"She sits next to me—" he began, then stopped.

"Ah," Mayoso prompted. "Rosita sits next to you."

"But her seat is empty. She's sick."

So was Lorenzo. Within ten minutes Mayoso had found that the boy had an elevated temperature, palpable lymph nodes in his neck, a barely visible rash, and no Koplik spots. The clinical diagnosis was rubella. For Lorenzo's mother, perhaps for many of the women in this clinic today, this was very dangerous.

"German measles," he had explained to her. "You know the three-day measles? Your son Lorenzo almost surely has German measles."

German measles was highly infectious. As gently as he could, he told her she would have to be tested. He did not tell her that German measles during early pregnancy often damaged the developing fetus. He also did not tell her that he had to consider the less likely diagnoses: a drug rash, scarlet fever, secondary syphilis, and infectious mononucleosis.

The problem stayed with him all evening. Was his clinical diagnosis correct? Laboratory confirmation, even with the new virus isolation technique, would take time. And not only Lorenzo's mother but other women in the waiting room had been exposed. The medical journals had reported widespread German measles in the United States. Had the virus spread here, to the island?

The Health Department had to be notified; the obstetricians on the staff, the pediatricians, the other doctors in town, the nurses who made home visits, the neighborhood pharmacists to whom the people of the *barrios* brought their symptoms. Isolation or quarantine of his patient was not as simple as it sounded; the disease seemed so mild, one had to see, months later, the infants born underweight, with cataracts or damaged hearts, to believe what the rubella virus did to human embryonic tissue.

If the diagnosis of German measles was correct, therapeutic abortion must be offered to the patient. The hospital might or might not cooperate. Nurses of religious conviction might refuse to function in the operating room. I'll do the abortion—if it's needed—in my office clinic if I have to, he had decided. In the meantime the pregnant woman would have to be given human gamma globulin as soon as possible; its worth was not proven, but if she refused therapeutic abortion, the child she was carrying needed every possible treatment which might help.

Caracas was put out of mind as he drove the back-country horseshoe roads to his bohío in the hills.

At home, he tried to draft the beginning of another lecture in his big leather notebook, but nothing he wrote seemed right. The annoying pulse-beat had begun tapping again, less less less time until tomorrow. In the soft humid night, the blotter under his hand was damp with sweat. Insects buzzed suicidally against the screens. The thousand-throated chirpings of *coquís* all around the bohío changed from the earth's rhythmic tempo to an irritable cricket cacophony. He threw his pen down impatiently. On the table lay his ticket to Caracas. There was still time to tear it in half and cancel his flight. But he had promised Filho he would be there; the possibility of not doing what he had said he would do was not acceptable. His entire idea of himself was that he would keep his word.

He tried to rest inertly on his bunk but he kept seeing Filho's haggard face at their last meeting. Pity, Filho had said, the fatal mistake that killed even God. Aie, he thought as he tossed, another wrung-out sleepless night for me. Damn Filho, damn promises, damn Caracas, and damn fools like me who say yes because of pity.

He got up and walked to the door. Why pace the floor all night? That was no good. He threw on his fishing clothes, a cotton shirt and denim pants, and drove back into San Juan to search among the *juego de dados* games in the *cafetines* to find his friend Tranquilino.

Tranquilino was a short dark-skinned man with a barrel chest, a 65th Infantry veteran of Korea who still wore a broken-visor army cap. By Mayoso's estimate, Tranquilino was the best fisherman in San Juan, a man who always did what he said he would do.

Together they had rowed out into San Juan harbor. The immense dark bowl of Antillean night curved high over their small rowboat. A half-dreaming ease melted through his veins. The irritating twitches and tugs of making a decision about Caracas, yes or no, go or stay, keep the promise or break it—all this faded as he had known it would.

The remote scattered stars were so limitless. The stone ramparts of El Morro, and the few lights of La Fortaleza, seen through a tracery of palms, were diminished as toys, their massive walls reduced to a child's sand castle on the great sea's edge. Ballooning tropical towers of cumulus clouds puffed upward more than two miles, their moon-washed whiteness shining upon whiteness with a pale bulbous ghostliness over the whisper of the Atlantic waters. When the highriding Caribe moon broke through, he and Tranquilino could make out the conical landmark of the Devil's Sentry Box of San Cristóbal jutting from its low rocky bastion of battle-broken walls.

The depthless galaxies rotated beyond Orion's pursuit of the Pleiades; the sea rose and fell gently, the slow-breathing bosom of the world: his yesterday, his today, his tomorrow, all the war dance that had circled him, now washed away by this hypnotic marine metronome. Time was the fourth dimension of the mind, a fugue, a simultaneous future, present, past; here, he lived in all three at once.

An unanchored strangeness, a moonraking abstraction, always drugged him as they drifted slowly with the harbor current, a kind of oceanic narcosis. Yesterday's green gardens now brown and vacant, the wrought-iron gates locked, the house of his childhood shadedrawn and shuttered, his father's voice stilled.

The youthful fighting in Sierra Maestra, later the betrayals in Havana, the sleepy-eyed execution squad before dawn. Ten years later: Operation Pluto in the Bay of Pigs, his helpless furious agony while the men on shore fell exhausted into the meatgrinder of Castro's heavy Soviet tanks and 122-mm. howitzers while Mayoso watched from his medical aid station on

the destroyer U.S.S. *Eaton* in international waters; the voice of a Brigade
tank officer with whom he had trained in Puerto Rico now crackling
through static from a walkie-talkie: *The Fidelistas are closing in around
us! We're desperate for air cover over Blue Beach! Where the hell is
promised air?* . . . The radio contact broke, then, when the shipboard
operator picked up the signal again, the voice on shore, though fainter, was
shouting: *Left flank critical! Stalin tanks! Are you bastards abandoning
us?* Voiceless voices dampened out here in the harbor by the healing
hush of time.

Time, beneficent time, blanketed the waters. Beneath him, he phan-
tomed other men-at-arms foundered amid encrusted shipwrecks strewn
throughout the curving archipelago of the Windward and Leeward Islands, a submarine trail, fouled anchors of the New World; fat-bottomed
Spanish galleons creaking with Peruvian gold and Mexican silver stretching their seabreeze canvas for San Juan Bay, a halfway port garrisoned
with loyal troops, a hundred cannon, an island of fresh meat and water;
rakish blackbirders from the Slave Coast, built for speed to deliver perishable African cargo to the wholesale flesh markets of Havana and New
Orleans, the black men and women packed together on shallow wood
shelves like spoons, chained belly to buttock, rack upon rack, stinking
downwind with Arab traders' rot and New Englanders' profiteering sea-
manship. In this bay they opened hatchways to hose down the living, toss
overboard the dead, unaware that they too would settle at the bottom
someday, silted over, guarded only by a watch of razortoothed jack-o'-
lantern faces with yard-long antennae and skeletons of drowned slaves;
Venezuelan frigates manned by rebel crews commissioned with letters of
marque signed by Bolívar the Liberator to sweep the Caribbean of
Spanish men-o'-war sent by Madrid to smother his brushfire replica of
George Washington's revolution.

A continual gunsmoke had blurred the blooddrenched history with hallucinatory colonial splendors and demented cruelties, yet even now, entire
countries lay as flaccidly asprawl the new industrial century as peasant
women ravished by marauding seafarers from all Europe.

The armed brigantines and seadogs long gone, Mayoso thought, fathoms deep, but this whole watery world is still awash with crosstides of
overlapping centuries, waves of hungering religions, freebooters and fortune hunters disemboweling these lands beneath the horizon's arc.

A part of him knew his half sleep was rounded by time's mesmerism,
yesterday becoming today. Whenever he illusioned the ocean filled with
lost cities, a chimera surfaced in his mind's eye—not the engulfed world
of history, but the shadowed Havana of his own life.

His childhood, his lost family, his tortured fiancée, the metallic clang of prison memories in his barred skull—all fell like pebbles into the huge encirclement of liquid space, glimpsed then gone, sinking down down down to the bottom with all the rest, so that now all that remained was the slow wash of waves against the battlements of El Morro, rippling outward, running eastward toward the stepping-stone island world of the Virgins just over the horizon, toward Cuba to the west, toward the Norteamericano continent as nearby as Miami.

"Doctor," Tranquilino had said quietly, "you need more bait?"

"What?" Mayoso had asked sleepily. He had been catching quick little catnaps, half asleep with the plastic fishing line tied around his finger until a grouper might hit the hook and he could yank it with a surgically precise snap of the wrist into the boat.

"Bait? You need more?"

"No."

Mayoso fished as Tranquilino did, casting the line from the boat with nothing more than a baited hook and lead sinker. His forefinger was his pole. Tranquilino had asked him about that one night.

"Doctor," he had said, "if you hurt that finger, how can you do la operación?"

"It's a strong finger."

"But if you hurt it?"

"I could still operate, amigo."

"That's true?"

"Sí. I could." But I could not tie ligatures very well, Mayoso had thought. And la operación has become a sociological necessity. I fill a public need. If I really damaged that finger I could not go from the first incision through the abdominal layers down to the Fallopian tubes and back out to skin sutures again, all in less than twenty minutes.

"Tranquilino," he had said, "maybe you're right. Maybe I should use my ring finger."

"It's up to you, Doctor. I only don't want the responsibility. Maybe I should bait the hook."

"Hah?"

"Maybe I should bait the hook."

"Tranquilino, my friend, I'm twice as big as you are and you want to baby me?"

"No baby, Doctor. The world has a big investment in somebody like you." He tapped his chest. "Me? Men like me all over. You can go down the Paseo de la Princesa any morning while they all stand there by the fish-cleaning table. You can find another fisherman just by saying buenos días, but another you is not so easy to find."

That had been several weeks ago. Since then Dr. Mayoso had used his

ring finger, not really for himself, but because he respected Tranquilino
and he did not want him to be on edge while they fished between midnight and dawn. Anyway, he had told himself, I am not a fisherman fishing for fish.

"Tranquilino," he had said last night in the rowboat, "let's go for some
red snappers."

Tranquilino had leaned back on his oars and had looked up at the
vaulting sky. "No snappers tonight. Too calm. You want to go out past
Buoy 2 El Morro for snappers? It's choppy out there."

"I don't mind the choppiness," Mayoso had said. "But we should stay
in close. I have to go home early to pack for a trip."

"Up to Miami?"

"No."

"To Washington?"

"No."

"That's good. I worry when you travel for those Cuban refugee committees."

"There's nothing to worry, amigo."

"You should not go alone. You always go by yourself."

"It's easier. Faster. No disagreements. Less attention from authorities."

"Ah, Doctor, those committees. Ya ya ya, talk talk talk. Debate clubs.
Acción? Only to fight each other for military supplies. Worse, they all
want you."

"Not me. They want my name."

"That's your trouble, Doctor. When you carry a big name like Martí it's
like a family duty, no? Even for money those *agrupaciones* could never
buy such a historical name."

"They're coming together," Mayoso said slowly. "The refugee groups
are combining. They cooperate. It becomes more efficient."

Except for the old Batista crowd, he thought. The worshipers of anonymous Swiss bank accounts and twenty per cent loans. The heavy-fingered
money-money hacendados, absentee landlords shod in alligator shoes,
their girls all peacock swank and diamonds. The private swaggerers training separately in some hidden Guatemalan valley or on Key West for
future hit-and-run raids on Cuban sugar mills. The overfed ones fighting
a publicity war over Cuba Libre cocktails from elegant refugee clubs like
Les Violins in Miami.

At a money-raising dinner in Les Violins last week, he had been surrounded by singing waiters; just as the room lights dimmed so the famous
multicolor phosphorescent violins could glow more brightly, someone had
tugged urgently at his sleeve. *Bésame mucho,* sang the shining violins,

while the voice whispered hoarsely beside him, "Teléfono, Doctor. Quick. Maybe a message from Ruiz Street."

Ruiz Street, near the corner of Ponce de Leon, was the Coral Gables address of the Medical Committee for Cuban Exiles, so he had politely excused himself to his host and had hurried to take the phone call. Under cloud cover another Cuban refugee boat had slipped past the Castro hunter planes from the San Antonio de los Baños air base. The U.S. Coast Guard Albatross patrols out of Key West had missed the refugees and now they had drifted ashore on Key Largo. One of the refugee women was pregnant, gasping as hungrily for air as a landed fish on the dark beach, laboring to give birth. Can you hurry? the girl at the switchboard had asked.

After a wild drive, he had stumbled behind his guide's flashlight along a deserted shoreline to the refugees' landing point. The group had crossed the strait from Cuba in a rotting sailboat, towing a crude raft of roped and patched truck-tire tubes loaded with an old fisherman, his two sons, five women and a baby. In the three days at sea, with little drinking water and no food after the first day, the fisherman's sons had disappeared from the wet bobbing raft somewhere amid the circling sharks. The *novia* of one of the sons had begun to drink seawater yesterday until she convulsed and had fallen over the side. The fisherman had rationed the final cup of their drinking water to the pregnant woman and her last-year's nursing infant in her arms, but the child had become lethargic, then comatose, then dead. She continued to hold the child, and now, as Mayoso found her lying at the base of a coconut palm, she arched her back in a tetanic spasm, her heels dug into sand, dying in her body, then her lungs, then brain, then heart. Dead.

The refugee world of chilled champagne and pressed duck *à l'orange* and eight phosphorescent violins throbbing *Bésame Mucho* was very far off—the world of the new well-to-do, the courtly manners, the dignified protocols, the aristocratic myths of benevolent paternalism for the dirt-covered poor, the well-meaning ineffectual charity, the shrugging fatalism, the costume parties on All Souls' Day when the young swinging set wore white makeup and dressed as ghouls in black shrouds.

What a schoolboy joke it once had been in Havana, Mayoso remembered as he knelt beside the woman, to wisecrack at some fashionable All Souls' Day Miramar party: Death, where is thy sting?

Here, he thought. On this shore. On this earth.

□ □ □

Sometimes his patients were badly wounded men.

Two nights before the Key Largo episode he had been at the 23rd Street house where some underground exiles kept a twenty-four-hour monitor on the 40-meter radio band. A coded distress call had come in before midnight. The assistant duty officer had revved up the launch which had been loaned to their commando group and had run Mayoso out of the harbor toward the open sea within ten minutes of the first distress call. They ran at top speed. In the darkness, with their running lights off, their trim black-painted launch was invisible.

Within a half hour they rendezvoused with the commando, a converted PT boat. Mayoso had tied a short length of line through the handles of his surgical kit and taken several turns around his wrist, just to make sure that when he made the tricky jump from the launch to the boarding ladder on the bigger boat he would not lose his equipment. As soon as he waved to the duty officer on the launch to show that he had transferred safely, the smaller boat had swung outward cautiously until there was enough clearance, then picked up speed quickly for the run back to its berth in Miami.

The night had a warm affectionate softness. It was not a time to die. In the distance lay the thin glitter of luxury hotel lights along Miami Beach: out here, in the international waters at the edge of the Gulf Stream, the darkness under the heavy swollen clouds covered them as closely as a black tent. Their low profile was protective. Only when a high white moon drifted through a torn space in the clouds could their boat be seen in silhouette.

In their bow, a 20-mm. Finnish automatic cannon rested its six-foot gun barrel on a steel support bolted down to both the port and starboard rails. A thick steel recoil spring, which held the breech of the cannon to the reinforced planking of the foredeck, creaked slightly as the commando boat made headway. She lay low in the water under the load of rusty thirty-gallon drums of gasoline and the stacked cans of homemade guerrilla fire bombs containing gasoline mixed with baby-soap flakes.

The converted PT nosed ahead slowly, its powerful engines throttled back to the point of just ticking over, bubbling softly, all running lights turned off so that no Coast Guard cutter nor one of the Grumman Albatross search planes could spot them. After the Bay of Pigs, the Coast Guard had become very strict about the exiles' hit-and-run raids against Castro.

Some of the young riflemen on deck were asleep, exhausted, their backs against the rail, their knees drawn up to their chests, their heads fallen forward onto their crossed arms. In the faint offshore breeze the Cuban ensign fluttered limply from their radio mast. The sea rippled with silky lightness along their high-speed hull as their small bow wave rose and fell.

Inside the cabin all the curtains had been drawn and sealed tight with strips of electrician's tape. Mayoso, bending over the wounded man in the iron-pipe bunk, finished his injection, withdrew the needle, then used his free hand to take the flashlight from its awkward place between his elbow and side. He turned to the skipper at the wheel. "Do you have a carbide lamp on board? I need more light. Steady light."

The skipper shook his head. He was wearing a black scuba diver's suit which was split down one leg, with blood streaked and caked the entire length of the tear. On the deck at his feet lay a clutter of breakaway gear: empty food cartons, a fishing line, a roll of toilet paper, a water canteen, spent ammunition casings. Bullet holes had splintered the wheelhouse woodwork. Both forward windshields and an aft stanchion were shattered; even the glass over the gyrocompass was cobwebbed with cracks.

Mayoso turned back to the wounded man. "The pain will be easier in a few minutes, Mateo. Understand? The injection I gave you will make you feel sleepy."

The wounded man began to nod, then squeezed his eyes tightly, wincing with pain. He had been hit at the side of the neck. "Madre," he grunted. "It feels like a hot iron spike under my ear." Even in the cool air, he was shiny with sweat.

"They brought me out here as fast as they could," the big white-haired doctor said apologetically. That bullet has to come out, he thought. Soon. But the surgery he needs is impossible here.

"Funny," Mateo said weakly. "Those bastards caught me in the neck but I can still talk." A spasm of pain forced his head back against the foam-rubber bunk mattress. "Ahhh. Ahhh. Mother of God. Don't let me die."

"We'll fix you up," Mayoso said. After six hours, infected wounds flared outward. Only six hours from the time of injury until the little reddish lines of blood poisoning begin to streak the skin. "How much time since he was hit, Captain?"

Without turning, the skipper at the wheel said, "Plenty. We keep feeding him penicillin tablets. Aspirin. Water"—then, with a quietly smoldering rage—"We kept having trouble with our goddam gas filters. Losing speed all the time. The Fidelistas caught up with us in Nikolás Channel, you know those chunky Russian patrol boats? Pain of Jesus, like the nails going in. We're hung up. They have a searchlight. Radar. In the water, when their lights find us, they think we're a fisherman. We hove to, so it looks like cooperation. Madre, my hands." He shook them ironically. "Casta-nets. I keep dropping the goddam spare gas filter. The boys lay low. Mateo stands up in the light with a net, like a fisherman. We hold our fire. They throttle down to come alongside, but we ease our bow a little starboard so our cannon will fire line of sight the minute Mateo whips off the can-vas. I work like hell on the gas filter. Christ in His sorrow, my fingers don't do what I want! If that patrol boat captain pulls astern and radios for a MIG to fly over us, we're a sitting duck. But he closes in. At fifty yards we let loose. Everything. Cannon. Rifles. Even our grenade launcher. Aie, *bendito!* A miracle! We hit their gasoline. Caramba, how they jumped overboard when that gas fire exploded." He looked back over his shoulder at the doctor. "What I would give for a searchlight at such a time. Just to spot those Fidelistas in the water. Like you shoot fish in a barrel."

From the galley a boy came into the cabin holding two tin cups. "Café Cubano?" he said, offering one to the skipper and the other to the doctor. He wiped his hands along the seat of his pants. "How's Mateo?"

Mayoso drank some coffee thoughtfully, slurping it to cool the hot brew, then said, "I found the bullet, but the neck is full of complicated anatomy and it's hard to see with a flashlight on a rocking boat."

The skipper grunted. "Rocky? This tide is gentle as a baby in a cradle. You should have seen us when I got that gasoline filter fixed and throttled those two big overhead cam Kermaths up to 35 knots. We could hear a plane circling overhead. But thanks to God, when he drops flares, they're miles astern. We run hot all the way to Cayo Anguillo. Dios, I pray, don't let that goddam British destroyer *Decoy* catch us now." He jerked his head at the coffee boy. "Here, take the wheel, Admiral. Hold her steady as she goes." He poked the doctor's shoulder and swiveled his thumb to indicate going out the double doors.

As the doctor painfully straightened from his cramped position, the skipper said to the boy, "Turn off the flashlight. Doctor Mayoso and I are going on deck. After I close the doors just run with the gyrocompass light."

"Okay," the boy said. "Leave it to me."

When they came up on the deck the doctor took a deep breath of fresh air and rubbed his back.

"What's the matter, Doctor Mayoso?" the skipper asked.

"My aching military back."

"No, I mean, what's the matter you don't do something? They didn't run you all the way out here, three miles offshore, just to drink coffee with us."

"You're right," Mayoso said. "I can get this same lousy seagoing galley coffee at home."

"Oh. The doctor is insulted. To remove a bullet is not such a big surgery, no?"

Don't let him pick a fight with you, Mayoso thought. He considers it sport to shoot drowning men. He's been hurt, they got caught before he completed his mission, and now he's a wounded bull. Don't fight back. Just go along and explain things. "You're right," Mayoso said. "Not such big surgery. Not in an operating room, with lights to see by, no. With sterile instruments, with enough blood available, no."

"Blood?"

"The bullet is lying in the muscle that goes from the collarbone up under the jaw and behind the ear. Under that muscle is the carotid artery to his brain. As much as I can see, the bullet is just nicking the artery. Fooling with that bullet out here—hell, it's like putting a Bandaid over a shell hole in your hull."

"An artery to the brain? You mean he could bleed to death, no?"

"If he's lucky. If I move the bullet a fraction of an inch, he bleeds. If I tie off the artery to stop bleeding, I stop the blood to one side of his brain. Then he will be paralyzed on one side. You see? The bullet has to come out and the hole in the artery sewn up with very fine stitches that don't leak."

The skipper peered past the shadowy bulk of the tall doctor; beyond the lighted shore of Miami Beach lay the world of hospitals, ambulances, operating rooms, electric light, blood banks. "We have strict orders," he said, "not to come ashore. If just one boat breaks security, the Americanos crack down."

"Strict orders? This is not something for first aid. If the Coast Guard stops us, I'll talk to them. You have to land Mateo, and damn soon."

"Listen, Doctor, my orders are strict. Ever since one of our boats put a torpedo into that Russian freighter *Vaku* everything is political. The crackdown. Now even the British keep watch for us."

Quietly the doctor said, "Talk to them in Coral Gables."

"Talk to who?"

"To Acme Shipping Company." Slowly he gave the telephone number of the CIA in the Miami suburbs. "Let the Americanos slug it out with their own people in the Coast Guard."

"I just told you, Doctor. That could begin a very political thing."

"The hell with that. Mateo is not exactly in political shape."

"Doctor, I know you have a big name in the underground. I see you know the Miami cover of the CIA. You give a medical lecture in town, then it's easy for you to fly back to your house in Puerto Rico. But I have to follow my orders in this little tin can."

The doctor calmly began to swear. Then he said, "Damn it, these speed-boat raids have to stop. You blow up a sugar mill in Puerto Pilón. You machinegun the Havana waterfront and knock out a few lights maybe. You kill a couple of country boys wearing *miliciano* uniforms too big for them. What the hell good do you do?"

"To hear such surrender talk from Mayoso Martí? Who would believe it?"

"This is commonsense talk. We pay a big price and we get back nothing."

The skipper grasped the edge of his torn scuba suit and ripped it up to the thigh. "Nothing? Look at this, Doctor." His voice was tight. "How much do you think you can pay me for this nothing? God burden me, I do it for what I believe, not for your stinking lousy money pay."

"We all do it for what we believe. I don't question your bravery. But what to us is a big mission, a heroic attack, it's only a mosquito bite for Castro. The cost of one grave could feed refugee kids for a year." The doctor motioned toward the cabin. "Mateo. A thousand boys like him. How long can I keep patching you boys up without asking what for?"

"Listen," the skipper said. "I don't like how you sound. An accident could happen to you."

"Don't be a horse's ass."

"If I didn't know how much fighting you did, Doctor, how hard you work for us all the time, I swear you could fall overboard right now."

"Aie," the doctor said wearily. "Two Cubans. And already a civil war."

Furiously the skipper banged his fist against his own chest. "Jesus Mary and Joseph! What the hell you want me to do?"

"Head for your marina at Key Largo while it's still dark. You can smuggle Mateo into a boat motel while I collect some surgical operating equipment and a few bottles of plasma from Coral Gables."

When the skipper did not move, Dr. Mayoso said, "You asked me, so I told you. What do you think happens to guerrilla morale when your men know they will be abandoned?"

"Shove that. The men knew the score when they shipped out with us. They know the risks, Doctor."

"Knowing is one thing. Dying is something else."

The skipper spat over the side. "How can I do it? A boat motel. Jesus save me. Like a whore's abortion. What kind of military dignity does that have?"

"The wounded piss on dignity. They feel their own pain. You should know—you're a wounded man." He paused cautiously. "In fact, your wound is so bad that you have told me to take command before a loss of blood makes you unconscious." He paused again. "Understand? You have orders, but you are bleeding. Terrible. Before you go out, you command me to take over."

In the darkness the skipper stared at him and said "Ha!" Mayoso held his breath, then they began to laugh together. "Aye, aye, sir," the skipper said.

Remembering, sitting in Tranquilino's boat, Mayoso shifted uncomfortably. That skipper had been a brave bull, but stubborn.

Tranquilino rowed powerfully with his easy effortless stroke. Like all the other two-oar white boats, theirs carried no lights. On their bow, as lucky weather lookouts after last August's hurricane, Tranquilino had painted two flat Byzantine eyes. The oars in the loops of hemp oarlocks made so little sound that from a distance they were only a tiny passing whiteness sliding silently between sea and sky.

Mayoso had thought: I must write another letter to David Sommers in Connecticut. Tomorrow, on the plane, I'll have time to write.

"Tomorrow, Doctor?" Tranquilino had asked. "You travel by the plane?"

"Yes."

"Jet?"

"Jet. Primera clase."

"Far?"

"Caracas." Last night Mayoso's transistor set had picked up both Radio Rebelde and Radio Progreso boasting on the short wave from Havana. The Castro underground in Caracas would soon take over the city. Viva Castro! Viva the FALN underground! Death to the Yanqui imperialists! And their final salute: *Venceremos!* We shall conquer. As he had snapped off the radio, Mayoso had thought: the promises, forever promises, genuine grievances twisted as always into pie in the sky.

"Politics in Caracas?" Tranquilino asked. "For the Cuban refugees?"

"For surgery."

Silence. Only the sound of water slipping beneath their boat, then Tranquilino said, "You have a license to do surgery in Caracas?"

"No."

"So. You do illegal surgery. You travel first class. Somebody must pay plenty."

"Yes."

"And the money goes to the Cuban refugees?"

"Yes."

"This of being a grandson of the historical Martí family is like a cross on your back, no?"

"Don't be an old fool. In Caracas they are willing to pay a very big price, and right now the central committee needs money."

"What do they do with so much money, Doctor? Eat it?"

"Everything costs. We picked up an arms shipment two weeks ago in Haiti. From the cost, you would believe the mortars were made of gold."

"Aie, Doctor. You exposed yourself to the *barbudos* in Port-au-Prince?"

"No, no. I don't take foolish risks in town. We flew around Cap-à-Foux, followed the shoreline of Ile de la Gonâve, then turned due east over that little fishing village—"

"Anse-à-Galets—"

"Sí, sí. Then we skipped over the sugar cane fields to a plantation with a landing strip cut out of the *zafra*."

"Aie. I remember one of those weapon hideaways. You can be killed just by landing across the ruts from the cane carts. Those iron rims cut deep. I remember landing. Like jumping out of a window onto a fence." He shook his head. "Very dangerous. Very unhealthy."

Mayoso grunted. "Tell me about health, Professor Tranquilino. What is not dangerous?"

"To stay in San Juan is not dangerous," the old man said hopefully.

"San Juan?" Mayoso pointed at the shoreline. "Right over there, last week, the body of Armando Gómez. Six slugs, all .45's, in the belly. Probably done with a silencer right in town. So don't give me any health lectures."

"Money, money. Your damn committee runs you day and night like a money machine."

"Tranquilino, you know what we paid for mortars in Haiti last week? I mean good arms, prime, packed in Cosmoline, with no cheating on the case count. Take a guess."

"I don't want to guess."

"You were talking about money."

"Aie, Doctor, what kind of dignity can a man like you find in money?"

"The dignity of paying bills for the arms we need. It costs more than a bottle of Hatuey beer. A mortar costs six hundred dollars."

"*One* mortar!"

"One. Tube, bipod, and base plate. And ammo, ten rounds to a box, a bargain. Fifteen dollars a round. A hundred mortars. Add it up, Tranquilino. Subtract the dangers to health of the takeoff or landing, or a doublecross. Just add a few more dollars for the pilot, the bribes, delivery costs. And you talk about money."

"Terrible," Tranquilino said. "Terrible. A whole town could live a year at such a cost. And build a school, make electric light, or give away shoes."

"You're right. I hate all of it." After a moment Mayoso said, "But to get the committee to change—"

"Please, Doctor. I'm not blaming you."

"I know, I only want to tell you you're right. We should stop buying weapons and spend the money on the Cuban families getting settled in the States, like Ybor City or right here on the island."

"That's a good idea if you help them get settled and keep them off city welfare—"

"I've already told the committee—now they're worried. They're afraid I'm surrendering. Or maybe changing sides."

"Doctor, when you keep even one kid from going on city welfare, you save a lot of pride."

"Ah. Pride."

"I know how you make fun of Spanish pride, Doctor. But listen, you can't always buy bread, but pride is free, no? You can always have pride."

"A feeling of independence, amigo. That's the best kind of pride. All the immigrants to the States, the Germans, the Italians, the Irish, all the rest, they all stick together and take care of their own."

"You've been sticking with your own. Your classes in Miami to teach Cuban doctors the medical English—"

"That's only a handful, Tranquilino. What about the thousands all over the States? The ones far from Miami?"

"Some of those committee boys," Tranquilino said, "those compañeros, they think pride is only in the shooting. What if your committee over-rules you and votes to spend money only on more weapons?"

"No," Mayoso said, "it's like chess and I hold checkmate. If I earn the money, I can ask the Governor to set up a public board of trustees to run a new refugee resettlement fund."

Tranquilino chuckled. "Aie, Doctor." He tapped his old army cap. "I always knew education was good for something."

Then they were silent. Mayoso looked up at the astronomic wheel of time turning around him. In the dark there was no sky, but only galaxies lying beyond the unimaginable cosmic spaces. Mayoso remembered the tale about time told by his father, about the two memo boxes on Franco's administrative desk in Pardo Palace. The incoming box carried the legend: Problems time will solve. The other, the outgoing box, read: Problems time has solved. His father had doubted the story was true, but that did not matter because, in a Spanish story, the factual truth was not so important. Only the spiritual truth counted.

After ten minutes, Tranquilino shifted on his seat and spoke quietly and stubbornly. "Stop your charity patients. Then you can have the money without taking chances on illegal surgery in a shaky place like Caracas. Why take such risk? The FALN guns people down in the street. Lots of nervous trigger fingers in Caracas."

"Stop the charity patients? You serious, Tranquilino? You think a mother from El Fanguito with seven kids should be turned away? You think a pregnant woman with German measles should be told to have a baby she doesn't want? With maybe a fifty-fifty chance of the baby being born with something wrong? Listen, there's something called preventive medicine, amigo."

"But who pays you to prevent? Not this pregnant señorita with measles. That's charity, Doctor."

"No, it's common sense. The cost of trying to fix up a malformed child —harelip, heart surgery, spina bifida—that costs a lot more. And not just money."

"Doctor, listen. Caracas. For you to go to Caracas, that's putting your head in the lion's mouth."

"In every circus, that's the highest-paid man."

"Listen, Doctor, I know what I say." Tranquilino wiggled his fingers in the air to suggest the ability to compromise. "Better to stop charity work in San Juan than to fly primera clase to Caracas for illegal surgery. If one of the Cuban refugees is hurt, let his committee bring him to the hospital there."

"This," Mayoso said quietly, "is not the committee."

Tranquilino held his oars. "No? The surgery is not for a refugee?"

"No. The other side."

"A Comunista?"

"Yes."

"Seriously?"

"Yes."

Tranquilino's voice changed. "You do this surgery on a Comunista for money?"

"I think it's funny. The Partido Comunista will pay directly to the refugee committee."

"Does hell pay heaven?" Tranquilino asked. "You sure this is true?"

"It's true. Also funny, no?"

"No," Tranquilino said. "It means they need you bad. Maybe for politics, not surgery. That worries me. They would never give money to their enemies if they don't need somebody very bad."

"You're right. The surgery is special."

"They also have special ways to handle people. You forgot your happy days and nights in Castillo del Principe? Galera 14, remember? More than anybody, you should remember from Cuba, Doctor."

"I remember." I came out here to forget, damn it, Mayoso thought. When the hook goes down in the dark, let it be only a penny fishhook on a line, and let the dark be only water. This kind of talk never helps, it only makes people nervous. How did this damn talk begin?

"You remember, Doctor, how in La Cabaña they take you to the first-aid room to donate one or two liters of blood to their blood bank before they take you out to be shot?"

"Let's get to shore," Mayoso said. "I have to go home and pack for the Caracas trip."

"You go alone again?"

"Of course." After a silence, Mayoso added, "You worried? You think maybe I changed sides? They bought me with money?"

"Madre mía, no!" Tranquilino crossed himself briefly. "God forgive such an idea. Who can buy a Martí?"

"Nobody. But this surgery is for money."

"But why should you risk yourself in Caracas? Make the money here in San Juan. Make your donation here. That refugee committee, they burn your money like cigars."

"But we need a bucketful of cash. I can make a month or two of cash in just one day. So I'll do the surgery in Caracas and come back."

"If you come back."

"I'll come back."

"To take such a risk? Must be much money."

"Yes."

"Send another Cuban refugee doctor."

"Impossible. The Partido Comunista wants only me."

"Only you? Not one other doctor in all of Caracas?" He shook his head. "The biggest hospital in South America is in Caracas, but it must be you and you alone?"

"They have a reason. They said it must be me."

"It's a trap. How can you walk with open eyes into a trap after what they did to you in Cuba?"

Dr. Mayoso Martí answered warily. "So? If it's a trap, what kind of fish can they catch? One used-up, beat-up surgeon, good for not much."

"Good for propaganda. That Martí. A name good as Abraham Lincoln. Who else alive is like you? With your family name on statues all over Cuba?"

"Sometimes," Mayoso said, "taking a chance, there's no other way."

Tranquilino shook his head. "Aie," he said, "don't you remember what they did to you?"

"For the love of God, yes. Drop the subject. Let's get ashore."

Tranquilino had pulled back angrily on his starboard oar and they had swung hard toward the Paseo de la Princesa, only the painted eyes on their bow gazing immovably at the dark approaching waters.

The carefully made-up eyes of Señora Valdez were smiling at him over her martini. "We're almost there. We should have cocktails together in Caracas." Unexpectedly she laughed out loud. "As they say, let me show you my operation."

The stewardess leaned in across her from the aisle and handed Mayoso the letter portfolio he had requested. "The ball-point pen is inside," she said. "Envelopes, too." She gave him the wide universal airline hostess smile. "Everything but the stamps, señor."

"Gracias, señorita. The stamps can wait. There's no hurry."

That was not true. The letter to David Sommers was long overdue, and if he did not write it immediately, before landing in Caracas, who knew when he would find another chance to write? So much to say. The old quip: I don't have time to write you a short letter.

He opened the letter portfolio on his lap, placed a thin airmail envelope on the blotter side, and began to address it to David Sommers, M.D., Associate Professor of Obstetrics and Gynecology, Metropolitan Hospital, New Haven, Connecticut, U.S.A.

He wrote slowly at first, then faster and faster. No time to write a short letter. His memory-provoking conversation with the señora beside him? Or only something he wanted to capture in his own mind before landing? The condemned man wrote a hearty last letter. The words poured from his pen in a fast looping scrawl.

If you will understand, David, that this letter comes from a man strad-dling a bullet in flight, you will forgive my tone of hurry and my awful handwriting. In those days at Yale, when your father was my Chief of Ob-Gyn, and I was his galley-slave resident, he used to read my hand-written clinical charts upside down to demonstrate the impossibility of deciphering my scrawl.

I am en route to Caracas, and you in your laboratory there in Connecti-cut will surely think that this Caribbean city is as far away as sunshine from snow. But Caracas is your next-door neighbor, David, just like Lon-don or Bonn, Saigon or Tokyo. I often think how much we are like moun-tain climbers, all roped together, as we inch up the rocky slope of this damned and blessed century.

When the President appointed your mother to the Population Council of the United Nations, I thought, at last there is hope. At last a woman

*will speak at the highest levels about world balances between children
and food, schools and living conditions—subjects which have always been
legislated by men whenever they had spare time between wars and fornication.
She did me the great honor of asking me to come to her Blair
House meeting in Washington this week to help plan her recommendations
to the President. I wanted very much to go. The last time I saw you
and your rocket-propelled brother was during those upside-down negotiations
in Havana, so it would be the pause that refreshes to see you and
your brother and your extraordinary mother under the benign eye of the
American Eagle in Washington.*

*But I cannot go. Your mother has never taken no for an answer, so
you must defend my case for me.*

*I have a rendezvous in Caracas which cannot be changed or avoided.
Since I left Cuba I have felt compelled to engage myself in many activities
which a North American physician—who is usually separated from public
political life—would find it hard to understand. Your father (who is as
wise as my father was, which means a large Sophoclean wisdom) said to
me: Mayoso, why in blazes do you always have to be in front of where
the battle is? Can't you find a more reasonable outlet, like fencing or boxing?
I said: Wait, my reasonable New England American Protestant Dr.
Sommers. When the battle comes down your reasonable street to your
reasonable house you will know why.*

*We now enter the decade of the big oversimplified opposites. Life or
death, Capitalism or Communism—and, where I am going, the Castro
slogan Patria o Muerte. Fatherland or Death. Leaves little margin for error,
eh?*

*I embrace the Sommers family—your father, my Chief, and your
mother, my inspiration—your brother DeWitt and his wife Betsy, the
Goddess—and you and Alice and your children. From my years in New
Haven I know that Latin emotion embarrasses you New Englanders, but
I refuse to apologize. I embrace you all. Pray that I will not lose my little
margin for error.*

The intercom speaker overhead began to crackle and he stopped his
rush of words as the pilot's voice broke in. "Ladies and gentlemen, we
are beginning the final leg of our descent to Caracas. The control tower
at Maiquetía Airport has just radioed that a terrorist explosion in the
luggage room will slow normal entry procedures. This is no cause for
alarm."

That means some very nervous surveillance by both the police and the
plainclothes Digepol while going through customs, Mayoso thought. His
feet tightened against the medical bag on the floor. Could the bag be

carried through, unopened, by dignity alone? Not very likely. Those Digepol boys were like all secret police: careful.

"Please have your passports, vaccination certificates, and luggage keys
ready at hand to facilitate prompt handling. I repeat, there is no cause for
alarm. No delay in estimated time of arrival. We have tower clearance
to land on schedule."

Mayoso found himself straining forward stiffly. He forced himself to
ease back in his seat.

Señora Valdez pressed against his elbow on the armrest between them
and whispered, "You think the pilot's announcement is true? Or maybe
it's like last year, the beginning of a big putsch in the streets?"

He spread his hands and discovered he was holding the unfinished letter. I'll finish it later, he thought as he began to fold the airmail sheets
carefully. "Probably an isolated episode," he said. "Some hothead students.
It happens all the time."

"Of all times! My husband goes to Paris on a buying trip once a year.
Once a year I have time to catch my breath and take a little vacation. Now
this! Why are you smiling?" Her voice dropped. "Are *you* one of them?"

"No," he said. "There's nothing to laugh about."

Her complaint had just reminded him of the story of the man who lived
in a village outside Paris. During the Revolution he met a friend who came
from Paris and asked what was happening. It's terrible, terrible, his friend
said. They're cutting off heads by the thousands. Sacré Dieu, the villager
had cried. Surely not heads! Why, I'm a hatter!

Señora Valdez del Sevillano reached out, trembling slightly, and
grasped his wrist with chilled, jeweled fingers. "I'm afraid. I don't like
the sound of it—" Her voice was taut.

"Don't worry, señora. A little incident—"

"But if it's a *big* incident—"

"Then stay in your hotel."

"Madre," she whispered hoarsely. "Last year the airport closed down
for a month when the fighting started. My husband will be home next
week. How I could make use of another martini!" Her tense grip tightened. "Please, after customs, will you escort me into the bar? I can't go
in alone." She shook his wrist gently. "Please. My heart's in my throat—"
When she saw him hesitate, she dropped his wrist. "A doctor. You
don't even know how fear feels, do you?"

He looked into her urgent unhappy eyes and shook his head reassuringly. "I do know," he said. "I'll order two martinis. One for you, one
for me."

Overhead the tape-recorded music came full circle. The rhythmic rattling gourds and the cuatros began to repeat Bésame Mucho: "Love me

a little and say that you'll always be mine—" the mariachi voices sang huskily.

The descent sound of the engines changed as the plane banked into its landing pattern. The sky wheeled past Mayoso's window and the mist-crowned mountain ring around Caracas seemed to thrust upward like a half-open hand grasping at him.

BOOK II
CONNECTICUT AND WASHINGTON: The Sommers

3 DIONISIO MAYOSO MARTÍ, M.D. was the name engraved on the small brass plate fixed above the seal of the University of Havana which was painted on the back of the walnut captain's chair.

Side by side stood more than two dozen identical captain's chairs, all made of walnut, none softened by upholstery, each emblazoned with a different university seal and brass nameplate. They circled a long conference table in a room adjoining the office of Dr. Benjamin Nathaniel Sommers in Metropolitan Hospital, New Haven, Connecticut. Each chair represented a man or woman who had been the chief resident under Dr. Sommers during his tenure as Chairman of the Department of Obstetrics and Gynecology of Metropolitan Hospital. Benjamin Sommers had reached compulsory retirement age several years ago, and now the men and women sitting around the table were themselves chiefs of departments around the world. The roll call of university seals, the sonorous Hebrew and pithy Latin mottoes expressing unquiet faith in man's mind as an instrument to grapple with the world, and unquestioning faith that the university was the world's instrument to grapple with the universe—all these summarized within the twenty-foot conference room the brief centuries of human inquiry since Erasmus kept his balance on the schism between the Roman Church and Martin Luther, and Voltaire sabered down the fanatics with a goosequill pen.

Every two years the men and women whose names were engraved, each on his own chair, assembled in this conference room under their old Chief to take a global view of advances and changes in obstetrics and gynecology, and, during the coffee break and cocktail hour, to exchange names of younger physicians with the characteristics to become tomorrow's departmental chiefs: young people with research ideas, preferably in molecular biology; some ability to teach, although this was negotiable, not vital; an observance of at least the minor decencies of social exchange; and a major belief that the intellectual rewards of academic medicine would make up for the steep drop in income they would receive when compared with their colleagues in full-time private practice.

Columbia was there, the University of Florida on his left, Duke on his right; the newer medical centers were across the table—Connecticut, Arizona, Hawaii, Ceylon, Hebrew University of Jerusalem. Some old schools were there too: Maudsley's and Guy's Hospital of London, Edinburgh, McGill, Freiburg, and the oldest, Salerno.

The only chair which was empty was the University of Havana.

By midmorning the corridor outside Dr. Benjamin Nathaniel Sommers'
conference room was crowded with young technicians pushing wheeled
stainless-steel laboratory carts filled with shining glassware and mouse
cages of the clever new stacking design. The aroma of instant coffee boiling in Pyrex flasks drifted through the hallways. Most of the girl technicians skipped breakfast at home and had coffee in their labs. Each
morning they tossed ten cents into a kitty to pay for one doughnut out
of the bagful from the street vendor, which someone smuggled upstairs
in a mail basket. Most of them had majored in the biological sciences
and ignored their knowledge of nutrition in order to do their hair and
get to work less than a half hour late.

Many of the young men with whom they worked wore brown laboratory coats to indicate they were fundamental researchers and not among
the sleek white-coated clinicians who dealt with the fuzzy confusions of
a biological system called the human patient.

Baggy flannels and beards were currently the badges worn by free intellectual minds; their fiercely ritualized concentration on the tiny details
of coming and going in their daily lives made them the direct descendants of the learned medieval monks. But the monks' hand-lettered
illuminated parchment manuscripts had been replaced by computer print-
out sheets and the gatefold pinup section of *Playboy* magazine; the vows
of poverty, chastity and obedience had now narrowed to poverty alone—
a poverty in which each man had only one pre-doctoral fellowship, occupied one apartment, owned one Volkswagen or MG, and pointedly did
not own a boob-tube television set. They splurged instead on a transistor-
ized stereophonic phonograph and music to copulate by which was re-
puted to modify the mating behavior of the girl technicians in a unilateral
biologic direction. Some said they were committed, *engagé*, or pained
by existential angst. Some, the stronger ones, were. Each considered himself or herself free; all identically so.

They were bound invisibly to Oxford, Cambridge, the Sorbonne, Hei-
delberg, Bologna, Madrid, Caracas; even Moscow University shared some
of their jazz, their clothes and hair styles. They felt an unbridgeable gulf
between themselves and the adult world.

Metropolitan Hospital was affiliated with the University; on the floors below Benjamin Sommers' conference room an army of students marched
through the hallways in squad-size groups. Medical students in short white
jackets wore their shiny new stethoscopes draped casually out of a side
pocket while dogging the attending physician, the ward resident physi-

cian, the ward intern, and the ward supervising nurse, always hurrying from one interesting case to the next.

One senior medical student trailed behind the group casually. He had a bright boyish face with an alert clear-eyed way of keeping his eyes directly on anyone who spoke to him, creating a faint me-and-thee intimacy even in casual conversation. As he moved from bed to bed with the fluent grace of a crown prince visiting a battlefield hospital, he asked small questions and got small grateful replies. Even the ward aides offered him vital bits of information—"Mrs. Wilson, in Number Three, she just don't take her fluids like she ought," or "Mr. Lary, in Seven, his daughter sneaks him his old cortisone pills from home, y'know?"—so that Gerald Morton Roone could often explain symptoms which the visitant, who made rounds in an hour or two, could not.

Roone stood next to one of the ward windows, looking down at the hospital parking lot four floors below. Betsy Sommers was just parking her green Jaguar convertible and, as she swung out of the low seat with her knees held chastely together, he enjoyed both the silken look of her legs and the dancer's way she handled them. He watched her unwind the long green chiffon scarf she wore, smiling a little to himself as the unseen omnipotent observer who knew all about her: She checked into the hospital volunteers' office this time of day each week and then walked to the coffee shop a block away for brunch before she began her duties in Pediatrics. He could tell by her manner, and little things she said, that she hardly lifted a finger at home. Yet she worked hard with the child patients. The lady protests too much, Roone thought. Maybe I should specialize in diseases of the rich.

In the nurses' central stations, the endless river of clinical information was being handled, not as information but as colored pieces of paper to be added in chromatic layers to hospital charts by professional nurses when they were not otherwise busy telling their nonprofessional aides how to do their nursing work. Student nurses in candy-striped uniform blouses hurried brightly down the halls, healthy, hopeful, still bemused about last night's television episode—called "Man in White"—in which the young intern had pinned a nurse helplessly against the shelves of the linen closet.

Platoons of students crisscrossed—the occupational therapists and the physical therapists, the psychologists and radiology technologists—and social-worker students grouped around coffee percolators and plates of chocolate-chip cookies busily exchanged calories for gossip about municipal pay scales and criticism about snooty med students' problems with ego identity and libidinal cathexis.

On the floor below, the corridor of one wing had been painted ivory, instead of the hospital's usual eye-ease green, and the floor was paved with a special linoleum imported from England because its twenty-seven per cent cork content softened the harsh sounds of the doctors' shoes. Here was the suite of offices of Dr. Anthony Hale Douglass, Administrator of Metropolitan Hospital.

The administrative departments, the library, the medical records room, were busy digging mine shafts between mountains of paper, while their supervisors wrote begging memoranda to the Administrator's Office pleading for more assistants, more space, more pay, more typewriters, and more paper. Anthony Hale Douglass hoped to solve the problem with a new computer, if only Washington would approve the self-sacrificing budget requested in his last grant application.

In the Administrator's Office, Edwina Hawthorne, Administrative Assistant to Doctor Anthony Hale Douglass, slit each memo envelope with a flick of her monogrammed sterling silver letter opener, relishing her ability to discard six memoranda per minute in the brass wastepaper basket beside her vestal ankles. She had a physical distaste for clutter, and incoming memos she classified as clutter.

Anthony Hale Douglass sat enthroned in his private office behind an antique rosewood desk, a classic of the Federal period. His desk inspired confidence, he was sure, by its look of traditional status and inherited good taste. On the visitors' side of the desk stood a delicate fence: a silver bud vase with a single rose which Edwina Hawthorne supplied daily; a cut-glass inkwell; and a pewter tankard, bearing the Yale seal in Latin, from which pencils stood as stiffly as his maiden aunts.

An unimpressed visitor was the district attorney, who looked over the desk of Dr. Douglass with the tonic smoke of battle rising in him.

The district attorney crossed one knee over the other and tapped his toe lightly in the air. Their small talk was over, and he could move toward his target, Dr. David Sommers.

"Just remember," his right-hand man had said at the morning staff meeting, "that Sommers *filius* has a Sommers *pater*. The old man, Benjamin Nathaniel Sommers, is the one trustee of the hospital who picks up the tab for the annual deficit no matter how many zillions. And Sommers' *mater—*"

"Stop the law-school Latin, pal," the district attorney had said. "Think what God could do if he had money."

"They wear old clothes, you know, the whole bass-ackward New England simplicity bit. But when the Sommers talk, nobody interrupts."

"Roger," the district attorney had said. "I'll make it a hospital condolence call. I won't fire till I see the whites of their eyes."

The district attorney moved his head slightly. The silver rosebud vase was in his direct line of vision to Anthony Hale Douglass. Pressure, he thought. Just the right amount of pressure and this Yankee gentleman administrator will cave in. But too much pressure and the whole crowd will close ranks to protect brother David and sure as God made little green apples I'll hear a scream from the Statehouse bunch. So, how much pressure is too much pressure?

In the Cardiology Department, on the floor below, two visiting Soviet scientists and two visiting British scientists refused the offer of midmorning coffee from their American host so they could continue their intense debate about whether human psychologic factors could modify lipids in the blood stream to contribute to coronary atherosclerosis. In any case, the Soviet physicians preferred the direct surgical attack to bypass plugged arteries, while the British doctors kept reminding the Soviets and the Americans in the room that coronary disease was a pie of many slices so to speak, human ecology and all that, and if the National Institutes of Health in Washington would spend some of its annual billion-dollar budget abroad, studies leading toward a solution might possibly be viewed as perhaps leading to a tentative approach which might possibly make some small contribution to an ad hoc solution.

In all the comings and goings, the teaching and the learning, the ringing of telephones, clatter of typewriters, the muted voices of Telepage speakers calling doctors' names, the opening and closing of the metal doors of elevators, the jostling of delivery trucks in reverse gear as they backed up to unload food crates at the cafeteria dock—at the core of this humming wheelworks, capable of delivering the best medical knowledge in the world, there were the almost forgotten sounds—the moan, the cry, the belch, the protesting gusto of the newly born, the quarrels, complaints and whispered prayers.

This was where Dr. David Sommers worked.

They stood in a tense triangle of confrontation in the surgical resident's office in the Emergency ward wing: Dr. David Sommers in a long white coat, with laboratory acid holes burned through it here and there; a silent young woman wearing a short white medical student's jacket during her two weeks' clerkship in E.W.; and the surgical resident, who was admissions officer for the day, in rumpled white jacket and white trousers.

The resident's jaw was dark with an unshaven stubble. He had been up most of the night covering the Emergency service and deciding which patients were admitted for hospital care and which were sent home, who needed what kinds of treatment, or consultation, or referral to other hospitals.

He stood facing Dr. Sommers, holding himself very stiffly in his yesterday-starched but now sagging house officer's white uniform. "Doctor Sommers," the surgical resident said with great formality, "it's my responsibility, not yours."

"That's right," David Sommers said. "And that's why I can't understand your refusal to admit this patient. She belongs in the hospital."

The younger doctor crossed his arms firmly. "In this whole hospital," he said, "if you check every damn ward, pavilion, wing, corridor, *every*-thing, there's only eight beds open. Five hundred beds, and just eight are open, and"—he nodded toward the Emergency ward—"the weekend crowd is just starting to come in."

The silent woman medical student looked from the older doctor to the younger, like a spectator at a tennis match.

"And?" David Sommers asked easily. "What are those eight precious beds open for, Doctor, if not for patients who need them?"

"But this is a *teaching* hospital!"

"Well now, as one of the teachers, Doctor Greene, I think she—"

"Doctor Sommers," the surgical resident said, "she can be treated here in Emergency and released to one of the hospital clinics or one of the doctors in town for follow-up. We'll admit complicated cases, but if I gave a valuable teaching bed to every little Spik girl who came in here bleeding with a potassium permanganate pill rammed up her twat—!"

"Doctor Greene, I know you're dog-tired and you don't want yakety-yak from me. Okay. So this is a teaching hospital." David Sommers turned and smiled very faintly at the quiet woman medical student. "They teach that barnyard nomenclature in your gynecology course, Helen?"

Helen shook her head no. She liked the surgical resident and she felt his bone-weary fatigue, but she decided to say not a word. The thin Puerto Rican girl who lay on the examining table in the emergency examining room across the hallway—admit her to a hospital bed? How would I decide, Helen thought. The hospital would drown if we took in everybody and became a first-aid station. The surgical resident was right. We're a scientific *teaching* hospital as he'd said, not the great big anonymous Family Doctor all the hurt and bruised and bewildered humanity insist they want us to be.

But Doctor Sommers was right, too. He was being awfully thoughtful.

"Please do me a favor, Doctor Sommers, spare me the shafting, and let's avoid the combat fatigue routine."

"Doctor Greene, you're as much on the teaching staff as I am, aren't you?"

"Sure. Sure. That's why I came to a teaching hospital."

"All right. Here's Helen Wilson, just a few months from graduation and her shiny new M.D. degree. That girl lying on the examining table across the hall doesn't have to be just another Emergency room case for Helen here. If you stick to your pitch about teaching hospitals, Doctor—just what are we teaching Helen about that girl?"

Dr. Greene dropped his arms resignedly. "Reverse twist, Doctor Sommers? You turning the heat on? Just to teach *me?*"

"No, I know your work. I respect it. You're a good scientific doctor. I'm trying to define the teaching hospital problem for all of us. Maybe mostly for Helen."

"Please, Doctor Sommers, I can't just stand here being academic!"

"But you're saving those eight empty beds for academic purposes, aren't you? Cool down, man. I'm with you. This *is* a teaching hospital, and we'd have to report to the Maternal Deaths Committee if this girl conks out." Dr. Sommers cocked an eye at the surgical resident. "It's your signature on the E.W. chart, Doctor Greene, but I have to write a consult note. So let's get together."

This Sommers may be a ball of fire in research gynecology, Dr. Greene thought, but I can't run my hunk of hospital like a basement branch of his goddam ivory tower lab. My signature on the chart, but his consult note. He's got me boxed in.

"Look," Dr. Greene said, "why don't we evaluate the señorita one more time, and then decide, okay?" The resident turned to the young woman medical student. "Any questions while we examine her, Helen, just sound off."

"But with discretion, Helen," Dr. Sommers said. "She's a kid, no more than maybe fifteen—"

"Seventeen," Helen said. "She told me. She's just thin-looking. On the vital signs, her temperature was 99 point 2. Her blood pressure is labile, from about 100 over 65 to 135 over 85. Respirations 20. On the lab, her hemoglobin was 7, hematocrit 30 per cent, total white count 14,000 with a normal range of distribution. Urinalysis 2 plus albumin, 1 plus bacteria, 3 to 6 leukocytes."

Dr. Greene reddened. "I'll scramble across the hall and check her again. I mean, while you're reviewing her as a teaching case."

"Thanks," David Sommers said. "We'll be with you in about four minutes."

Dr. Greene's rubber-soled white shoes squeaked with his irritation and hurry as he left, remembering, as he went, the hospital gag about Four

Seasons, Three Sommers, Two Services, One God . . . and He's related to the Sommers. The old Doctor Benjamin Sommers may have been a great pioneer, but his son David was an icky-picky research type.

"So," David Sommers said, taking up the thread as if there had been no debate, "equivocal lab data? Low hemoglobin goes with the bleeding. But malnutrition, too, maybe? We need more information, don't we? Is there hypochromic microcytic anemia? A Puerto Rican immigrant—anemia due to some rural parasitic disease? They still have schistosomiasis down there on the island, you know." He watched Helen's face change. "More than just a gynecology case, isn't she, when you consider it? By now you know that people don't come in with textbook chapter headings. The human body doesn't give a damn whether you heal it in the Department of Medicine or in the Department of Surgery. Take this girl's emotional status. Just plain and simple: how does she feel?"

Helen Wilson was puzzled. "How does she *feel?*"

David Sommers waited.

"Well, sir, she hurts."

"Okay, good. That handy-dandy observation is so simple we all forget how important it is, Helen. She hurts. Pain affects her splanchnic vessels, and vasodilatation would lower her pressure, particularly the critical diastolic pressure, right?"

"I forgot about that, Doctor."

"That's why this is worth going over in some detail. Ask your women patients about blood flow during their menses if they're under great emotional stress at the time. Family mix-up, fight with the boy friend—and the menstrual period gets out of tempo like a dropped clock. They flow like open spigots."

"But why?"

He smiled. "I don't know. We can make some good guesses, but we don't really know the whole story of how blood changes from a flowing liquid to a solid clot. That delicate liquid-solid balance, Helen, you take a crack at the molecular biology of that and the Nobel prize will be yours. So. To get back to the little lady. She hurts. That deep bellyache inside. Salpingitis, maybe. And she's scared stiff. Lying there on an uncomfortable table with her legs up in stirrups, all exposed, while strangers in white uniforms insert a metal speculum into the most sensitive orifice a woman has."

"Is that why you touched the speculum to her thigh first?"

"Yes. Never just put a cold metal speculum directly against the introitus. Touching the skin first gives her a chance to ease a bit. And remember, the closed metal surfaces go in at a slight angle."

"I know," Helen said. "I've had one or two slam-bam vaginal examinations myself."

"All right. You have to ask yourself where our patient's bleeding comes from. And distinguish fresh bleeding from oozing, or clots, or uterine or placental tissue."

"Well, those grayish clots in the basin looked placental, didn't they?"

"Did they? Why?"

"Well," she said anxiously, "first, the color, second, the spongy consistency. Oh, yes, the suggestion on the surface of chorionic villi."

"Good. You're using your eyes and your brain, not just your hand."

"I looked for a fetus, if there actually was one—"

"Strictly speaking, this early in pregnancy, any conceptus would be an embryo, not a fetus."

"But how can we even be sure she's pregnant, Doctor Sommers? Her bleeding might be, well, it might be the whole differential diagnosis of uterine bleeding."

He smiled again. "You're in the soup now. They'll surely ask it in your exam for state licensure. What's the differential diagnosis of uterine bleeding?"

Helen pushed both her hands into the pockets of her white jacket. "Well, ah, complication of pregnancy, endometriosis, neoplasm, hematologic disorder, fibroids, trauma, functional—"

"Fine. That's enough. Top of the class for you. But we're giving a provisional working diagnosis to this girl—what's her name?"

"I—well, I—"

"She's just another emergency case?"

"Sort of, yes, sir."

"But if you empathize with her vaginal examination, why not hold on to her name? My father always reminded us that statistics are people with the tears wiped off."

"Carmencita. That's her name. I just remembered the way the surgical intern printed it in block letters on the chart."

"Carmencita. Sound a bit flowery and operatic to you, Helen?"

"Well, she was really carrying on so emotionally, Doctor Sommers. While we were waiting for you she kept saying, 'I want to keel myself! I want to keel myself!' That's, well, if you want to call it something, that's operatic. Soap opera."

"But what if she really does want to kill herself? She must have paid ten or fifteen dollars for that two-cent permanganate pill. Frightened out of her wits by being pregnant, and flat broke."

"Doctor Sommers, this 'keel myself' routine. I've heard lots of jokes about so-called psychiatric indications to end pregnancy—"

"So-called?"

"Well, anybody can waltz into your office saying she wants to kill herself and try to stampede you."

"Helen, when a patient threatens suicide, even if she's acting, you ought to stop, look and listen. It's pretty hard to fake a combination of anguish, constant weeping, insomnia or nightmares, and a sharp loss of weight."

Helen's voice became milder. "She doesn't have hospital insurance, Doctor. And I'll bet there's no man around to lend a hand."

Dr. Sommers rubbed his chin with his thumb a moment. "That's an assumption about the patient's social history."

"I think it's a valid assumption, sir. In most illegitimate pregnancies, the man heads for the hills. Like the song says, it's the woman who pays and pays and pays."

His thoughtful expression did not change. "Illegitimate? There are no illegitimate babies, you know. Just the parents. Part of the importance of all this is in the size of the numbers of girls and women involved. Remember the statistics?"

"No, sir." She added quickly, "but it was a lot of people, I remember that much."

"Well, about a quarter of a million unmarried mothers last year. And that figure may go up as more of the girls of the postwar baby boom reach their reproductive years. If the fathers of these pregnancies don't pay the costs of maternity care, who will?" He could see that she had no interest nor experience in such questions. "Okay," he said, "we're really making a grand-rounds teaching case out of one young lady who probably tried to abort herself. So there she is across the hall with Doctor Greene checking her over. We believe that she inserted a corrosive chemical pill up against the cervical mucosa and kept it there until a painful inflammation began to spread. If both tubes are badly inflamed she'll have a hell of a time getting pregnant when she's married. The human factor in the dynamics of Gyn pathology, right? I'd guess she became frantic when no bleeding appeared, because there's a small laceration in the six-o'clock position of the entrance to the endocervical canal—"

"I didn't spot that—the tenaculum blocked my line of sight."

"Look again, in a minute. There's a definite laceration. Probably poked at herself with a crochet hook or a knitting needle. Means we have to worry about infection, maybe tetanus."

"Tetanus?" she asked. "I thought tetanus was practically wiped out, except for kids who step on rusty nails."

He shook his head. "Check the literature."

"When you think of the automobile accidents that come in here," Helen said, "the burns, the penetrating wounds—maybe we should order more passive immunization when they come in. But we don't. Are we wrong, Doctor Sommers?"

"How many things are all wrong or all right in medicine? We're the great compromisers. Lawyers like things right or wrong, yes or no, but we're stuck with the headaches of everlasting maybes."

Helen smiled faintly. "Stop the world. I want to get off."

"You're learning here under unfortunate pressures, Helen. You need to know enough about enough to make the best compromise choice out of a range of hard choices. Like the old joke about decisions, decisions." He pointed to the door the resident had hurried through a few minutes ago. "Let's say you're as busy and as tired and as rushed as Doctor Greene. What would you decide?"

She sighed. "Sometimes it's discouraging, really."

"Oh no. There's great encouragement."

"There is? What's the answer, sir?"

"You tell me, Helen."

"More research," she said firmly.

"Don't play the faculty finagle factor with me, Helen. Think. What's the answer?"

"I don't know, Doctor Sommers."

"Sure you do. I'm not examining you. We're just practicing thinking, that's all. The little kid across the hall, Carmencita, she's your stimulus to learn all you can before you yourself have the responsibility. Okay? Can we drop tetanus and get back to Carmencita?"

"Yes." This was great! A multi-discipline review. The subtle moves of medicine. The big picture, in 3-D. Sommers talked to her like a colleague. He was a dreamboat. Thorough, but no sweat, no threat. Not every faculty member reviewed the cases the way Sommers did. His New England manner of camouflaging a kind of missionary zeal with a calm off-handedness could fool you. Only by listening carefully to what he did and did not say could you get the whole message. She was lucky Dr. Greene had made such a big noisy deal about a teaching hospital.

As she and Dr. Sommers started to leave the resident's office for the treatment room across the hall, he stopped her at the door. "We agree the provisional etiologic diagnosis is pregnancy, incomplete abortion, don't we? The diagnosis of cervical and vaginal inflammation is obvious by inspection and history. But why—in the middle of all the different diagnoses this could be—why are we calling this pregnancy? If she were your responsibility, why would you write *Pregnancy* on the hospital chart and sign your name to it?"

She paused cautiously, then decided to say frankly, "Gosh, Doctor Sommers, you've got me up so high with the big picture I wish I knew why."

He ticked off the reasons on his fingers. "History. Her missing a period in an otherwise regular normal menstrual history. Inspection: the nature and extent of fresh bleeding and recent clots. Social pathology: the fashionably filthy permanganate pill. And the clincher: bimanual palpation of the body and fundus of the uterus. The height of the superior border of the uterus—instead of being the size of a small pear, it's up a bit, larger. A grapefruit, let's say. And much of the firmness gone at the neck of the uterus. Feels spongy. Got it? So medicine plays the biostatistics, the numbers game. With all these combinations of findings here in the E.W., what's the most probable working diagnosis of the many probabilities?"

"Pregnancy, of course."

"Just as long as you know what a wide range of observations go into that of course. Probable pregnancy, probable induced incomplete abortion, but keep in mind possible polyps, vaginitis, cervicitis, and cancer. They'd have to be ruled out." He stretched a little, and she realized that he was a tired man, not a white-coated teaching machine.

"All right, Helen," he said, "let's wind up the diagnostic side, shall we? Let's decide how to treat our young lady named Carmencita."

□ □ □

Upstairs, in the Administrator's Office, Dr. Anthony Hale Douglass pulled open a desk drawer to get one of his peptic ulcer antiacid pills. There was something disconcerting about the elaborate politeness of the district attorney and the mannered way in which he crossed one knee over the other, then carefully straightened the crease of his trouser leg.

Despite the chalk-tasting pill, Dr. Douglass felt the familiar burning pincers grip his duodenal loop as the district attorney's eyes measured him across the heirloom rosewood desk.

"Doctor Douglass," the district attorney said, "in the interest of saving your time as well as my own, I'll come right to the point. A doctor on your staff is doing illegal abortions in this hospital."

"Abortions?" Dr. Douglass was incredulous.

"I was just being colloquial, Doctor Douglass. Technically, criminally induced abortions."

"I can't believe it."

"Neither could we, downtown. Naturally, I checked this out personally with the witnesses to make sure of my facts."

"Witnesses? That's impossible. No such patient could even get a bed in this hospital."

"Doctor Douglass, Metropolitan Hospital is a pretty big place, right?"

"Five hundred beds, if that's what you mean."

"That's just what I mean, Doctor. Thousands of people coming and going twenty-four hours a day, seven days a week. Penthouse recreation areas and a dozen underground tunnels. Lots of nooks and crannies."

Dr. Douglass put one hand flat on the desk blotter before him, spread his fingers apart and studied the spaces between them, then closed his fingers into a fist. "I believe," he said without expression, "you said you'd come right to the point. You've made an extremely serious accusation. I could tell you I have witnesses who've heard you say you planned to run in the next election for state Attorney General, but without the facts, it would be unfair of me to accuse you of that motive, so I won't."

"Now that you have, Doctor, we can play quid pro quo. I won't accuse you of running a slack hospital."

"You mentioned witnesses."

"Never mind them, Doctor, I don't want any nurses getting their arms twisted and clamming up." He straightened his trouser seam again. "In this great big hospital, Doctor, you have fourteen research beds. Right?"

"I can't say I appreciate your tone. Perhaps I ought to call Mr. Terrence downtown. He's our hospital's attorney."

"You don't have to climb walls, Doctor. We're just having a conversation."

"How do I know, in this crazy day and age, whether you have a tape recorder running in that attaché case?"

The district attorney threw his head back and laughed. "See what television does?" He placed his tan leather attaché case on his lap and snapped open the locks. "There you are. Five proofs of my boy's graduation picture, a list of the lumber I have to pick up for a bookcase I'm making at home, and a copy of the *Law-Medicine Monthly Review*, which I won't have time to read."

"I beg your pardon, but in hospitals, we see some pretty strange things."

"Well, then, Doctor, you can add this item to your collection. Those fourteen research beds are not under your direct administrative control."

"Well, yes and no."

"Mostly no, I would say, because the doctors who get the research grants decide which patients occupy those beds."

"Of course. We can't let a small fraction, fourteen out of five hundred beds, hold up the medical machinery of the entire hospital."

The district attorney lowered his voice to a comradely prompting tone. "So it wouldn't be very hard to call a pregnant lady a research case, and slip her into one of those research beds, would it?"

"Theoretically, no. Actually, yes."

"Actually, Doctor, I have evidence that a pregnant teenage girl was admitted to the hospital six weeks ago, occupied one of your free and easy research beds and underwent a criminally induced abortion. When I told you this was just a conversation between us, I meant it. Now, do you want to talk about the details?"

"I believe," Dr. Douglass said, "that I'd better. Would you like a cup of tea as we go along?"

"Why, thank you, Doctor. I believe I would if your girls can brew it up strong enough to walk on."

Dr. Douglass pressed the button for Edwina Hawthorne, then rested his head back in the Windsor chair which he had inherited with his rosewood desk.

The hospital corridor which tunneled through the Emergency ward wing was filled with people, many of them the overflow from the waiting room. The nurses threaded their way coolly through the anxious knotted groups; the supervising nurse kept urging people to wait in the lobby; a man in dark grease-stained overalls with one arm in an improvised sling followed a young doctor into the fracture room; a two-year-old boy screamed in his mother's arms with blood running from both nostrils while his mother stood at the admitting desk to answer the secretary's questions for the admission forms.

One of the nurses stopped Dr. Sommers. "Oh, Doctor," she said loudly, above the noise in the hall, "did you get your page?"

"No—"

"They paged you about ten minutes ago. Your lab must have taken it for you and called the desk down here."

"Thanks, Claire," he said. "As long as my lab got it. I'll pick it up soon as I can."

The nurse glanced at Helen Wilson beside him. "If you want to see a stab wound of the chest with pneumothorax, Helen, there's one in Room Nine."

"Uh-uh," Helen Wilson said. "I'm going to stay with Doctor Sommers on this one."

The nurse shook her head. "That's what all the girls say. What have you got, Doctor Sommers, the others don't have?"

"Time," he said. "I'm Ol' Man River, jes' keeps rollin' along."

He held open the double-hinged swinging doors of the treatment room for Helen, an old-fashioned courtesy in this hospital setting.

Carmencita was lying on her back on a padded treatment table, her legs up in obstetrical stirrups. Dr. Greene sat on a white metal stool between her raised knees with a nurse adjusting a light behind his shoulder as he eased a stained gauze tamponade out of the girl's body into a steel emesis basin the nurse held with her free hand. He looked up at David Sommers, then his eyes slid toward the partly filled basin the nurse was holding. "The working diagnosis worked, Doctor," he said.

Dr. Sommers nodded and stepped beside the girl. He picked up her vital signs chart and scanned the sheet before he began to talk to her.

"Señorita," he said, "are you feeling better? *Como está usted?*"

The girl gripped the sides of the table with both hands. She was pale and sweating, her eyes enormous and dark as she rocked her head to blink up at him.

"*Me duele la cabeza. Tengo frío. Náuseas. Cuándo me sentiré mejor?*"

"*Lo más pronto posible.* If I speak English, can you understand? *Habla usted inglés?*"

A wave of pain struck her and she arched backward on the table. "*Dios mío!*"

Dr. Sommers untied a sterile pack of rubber surgical gloves and motioned for Helen to stand behind him. The nurse tilted the examination light so that Dr. Greene could swing off the white metal stool and let Dr. Sommers take his place. Dr. Greene peeled off his gloves and picked up the girl's chart to add some notes.

The medical student, holding her hands carefully behind her, watched over David Sommers' right shoulder while the nurse refocused the light over his left. The nurse reached for a vaginal speculum but he shook his head and indicated the next smaller size on the tray. Gently he inserted the instrument at a slight angle, rotated it to a straight position, expanded the blades and tightened the lockscrew to keep the mucosa of the canal and the cervix in the illuminated line of vision. He shifted sideways to give the medical student a chance to see the inflammation and the dark clots extruding from the cervical os.

He murmured quietly to the girl as he picked up a blunt forceps and eased a gelatinous clump forward into the nurse's emesis basin. "Only a moment more, Carmencita . . . a moment . . . *bueno* . . . *espere un momento* . . ."

"*Quiero hablar con un cura,*" Carmencita moaned.

Without turning, David Sommers said, "Did you call her pastor?"

"Yes, Doctor," the nurse said. "He was out. I left the message. And I asked the desk to phone St. Jude's. Father Tuohy is the curate there. He's only four blocks away. And the desk's trying to locate her sister at work someplace."

Dr. Sommers pointed to the clump in the stainless-steel basin, then flipped it over. Within a bubble smaller than a fingertip floated a quarter-inch whitish string, like a fragmentary clipped-off end of a strand of spaghetti. It had the shape and features of a month-old embryo: the tiny lump at one end, the beginning of a head, two dots of dark pigment pinpointing the future eyes, two diminutive millimeter-long flipperlike stumps which might have become arms, the snippet of umbilical cord to link this incomplete space voyager to his mother's oxygen universe; the almost indiscernible curlicue tail, evolutionary inheritance of prehuman oceans; the reddish miniature tube at the center, still primitive and two-chambered, enfolded upon itself to begin its ascent to become a heart.

The nurse raised her eyes to Dr. Sommers. "Should we wait for Father Tuohy?"

"It's up to us," he said quietly. "We don't even know if he's coming."

Her voice trailed off with uncertainty. "How old is the fetus, Doctor?"

"I'd guess at maybe four or five weeks, so it's not a fetus yet. Still an embryo. If there's biologic viability, which I doubt, it'll be gone in half a minute—"

Carmencita raised her head painfully. *"No es mi culpa*—a baby, no?"

David Sommers stood up. "No," he said, "not a baby." He pinched his thumb and forefinger to indicate something smaller than mere littleness. "Just the beginning of a beginning of one."

She dropped her head back and closed her eyes as she wept.

"Carmencita," David Sommers said, "I don't know when the priest will come. You understand? I am allowed to baptize if he is not here."

"Es muy tarde—"

"No, it's not too late. You want me to do it?"

"Por favor—"

Quickly, he loosened the lock screw on the speculum, then swung to Helen. "Will you get that flask of saline solution? Nurse—" He scanned her plastic oblong nameplate pinned to the upper pocket of her uniform. "Miss Klementz, will you hold the basin where the señorita can see this?" Then, to Helen, "Open the flask, and when I say *now,* pour about five c.c. over the embryo. Got it?"

Helen Wilson yanked the stopper out of the flask. Dr. Greene stood still, without expression. Carmencita watched the nurse raise the stainless-steel basin. Dr. Sommers lifted the spongy placental fragment and the fluid-filled amniotic bubble and broke the sac open with a quick pinch, exposing the pink embryonic tissue.

"Now," he said. "Pour the fluid directly on the embryo as I speak." The thin stream of water splashed lightly over the embryo while he intoned, "I baptize you in the name of the Father, and the Son, and the Holy Ghost."

Carmencita crossed herself. She touched her lips with her tongue, then whispered. "*Muy bien. Gracias.*"

Dr. Sommers sat down again on the round white metal stool, thinking: the words are ritual to me but real to the girl, as therapeutic as a blood transfusion. He opened the speculum again to continue his examination of the exposed cervix. The medical student behind him lowered herself, almost crouching as she peered over his shoulder.

"See the laceration?" he asked softly. "Six o'clock position, just where the vulnerable squamous epithelium begins?"

As she moved her head to see better, Dr. Sommers looked up to speak across the girl's supine body. "A priest is coming, Carmencita. But we will make you feel better, *sentirse mejor, pronto, lo más pronto posible.*"

The girl rolled her head back and forth. "*Es muy tarde . . .* aieee, *qué debo hacer . . .*"

"No, it is not too late. We took out the chemical pill . . . *lo saqué . . .* the *veneno . . .*" As he spoke he inserted a fresh gauze tamponade, then released the lock screw of the speculum and dropped the instrument into a basin. He threw his gloves into the same basin and stood up. "Better get her legs out of those stirrups," he told the nurse. He stepped beside the girl. "We're stopping the bleeding, Carmencita. I put in something like a *tampón.* Carmencita, *oiga.* Did you put a knitting needle into your body, Carmencita? *Aguja?*"

"No no no no—"

"Somebody did. Who did it?"

"No," she moaned. "*Nadie, nadie.*"

"That's what they all say," Dr. Greene said with quiet irritation. "We sure do a big slippery elm twig business in this shop."

Dr. Sommers picked up the chart with Dr. Greene's new notes on it. "You feel sick now, Carmencita, but we know how to make you feel better. One of the priests who come to the hospital will be here—"

"Padre Suarez—?"

"We'll keep trying to reach Padre Suarez on the telephone. And your sister, too."

"I want make confess—I can die . . ."

"No, you will live. You have pain now, but you will be better. I will tell the priest you are getting better. I will tell him you do not need Extreme Unction, because you are young and you will recover and feel better. You will live to be a mother of your family with your own husband and your own home. You understand, Carmencita?"

She rested her elbow across her eyes and began to sob so hard her body shook. Dr. Sommers touched her shoulder. "The nurse will stay with you. Just rest for now."

He stepped away from the table and motioned to the nurse. She understood immediately and carried the stainless-steel basin to a side shelf where the Path specimen jars were stored. Dr. Greene and Helen followed David single file out into the hubbub of the Emergency ward corridor.

"Helen," David said, "for your legal medicine exam, just remember that most of our laws prohibit removing even a nonliving embryo or fetus from the mother."

"Then we just broke the law!"

"Well, yes and no. Legal boundary lines are sort of hazy. Originally, the early laws protected the unborn child more than the mother. Prohibiting removal was supposed to deprive quacks of the defense that they were only taking out something already dead. About a hundred years ago the law began to show some concern for the mother's life."

While they were crossing the crowded hallway, Dr. Greene said, "There's a priest. Maybe he's the one the desk called."

David stopped and waited until the priest reached them. He looked young, and flushed with hurrying. In one hand he carried a small black satchel.

"Father Tuohy?" David asked.

The priest stopped. "Yes. I'm Father Tuohy. The lady at the desk—"

"I'm Doctor Sommers. Doctor Greene. And Doctor-in-training Helen Wilson."

"How do you do?" Father Tuohy said. "I came as fast as I could."

"The girl's resting a little more comfortably now," David said. "Could we chat in the resident's office for a minute?"

"But if she's in extremis, Doctor—"

"She isn't, Father. That's what I want to discuss with you."

Father Tuohy frowned slightly, then, as David moved toward the door to the resident's office, he joined the group. Dr. Greene held the door open for them—"Welcome to my broom closet"—then squeezed inside and closed the door after himself.

"Father," David Sommers asked, "may I ask if you've had much hospital experience?"

"Some, some. It's hardly a full-time pastoral duty, you know."

"I ask, Father, because I'm concerned about the patient if you give her Extreme Unction."

Father Tuohy's frown deepened and he shifted his small black satchel to his other hand. "Quite frankly," he said, "I don't see that as a medical problem, Doctor."

"I don't want to interfere in a religious matter, Father. If I thought for a minute she was dying, I'd ask you to hurry. But—"

"They told me on the phone she was in serious condition—"

"Yes, she is. But with modern blood replacement and antibiotics, especially in a young woman—"

Father Tuohy straightened. "Doctor," he said with dignity, "I don't even understand why we're having this time-consuming discussion. If you've taken care of the girl's medical needs, then I'll have to assure myself the Holy Viaticum and Extreme Unction are available to her spiritual needs."

"Of course," David said. "But this girl has a very labile blood pressure and—"

"What does that mean?"

"Her blood pressure rises and falls very easily in response to her feelings. A religious ritual to prepare her for death just might lower her pressure dangerously. I've seen it happen."

"Doctor, her spiritual welfare is more important than her physical well-being. The more humiliation or pain or sin she's suffered, the more she'll need—" He paused, then began again. "She has every right to the mercy and providence of God."

"Of course," David said. "But she believes she's going to die. She's overwhelmed by so many factors, infection, blood loss, pain, and obviously a lot of shame and guilt—my impression is that right now, this minute, she wants to die. That belief may profoundly affect a number of the body mechanisms that can help her live. D'you see my line of reasoning, Father?"

"I'm doing my best to follow you, Doctor. I believe you when you say she's in no critical danger this moment, else you wouldn't keep me here now—"

"Of course I wouldn't."

"But your biological attitude and my pastoral duty are different. Her soul is immortal. She *must* have confession and—"

"Father, confession will help her. It's the anointing and preparation for dying that I—"

"You can hardly understand, Doctor. These bring peace to a believer."

David turned to Dr. Greene. "What were the last few blood pressures you checked, Doctor?"

"All around 88 or 90 over 58 or 60. Then up to 96 over 66 after you baptized the embryo."

"You—*what?*" Father Tuohy asked. "You *baptized* it?"

"Why, yes. If there was biological life in it, that would be gone in a minute or two. We didn't know if or when or how soon you could come—and the baptismal sacrament is a lay ceremony, anyway, I believe."

"Sometimes, Doctor. Yes, sometimes—"

"And better a baptism, Father—and properly done—"

"You used water? Over the head of the infant?"

"Well, Father, water, yes. But there was no head, strictly speaking, but there is the head *end* of the—it's not an infant, you know—just a six-millimeter speck of embryo."

"Yes, with a living soul, Doctor."

"If you want the details, Father—the amniotic sac was broken so the water could touch directly on the head end. The words were pronounced during the pouring."

"The embryo was living?"

"At that moment, strictly biologically, I mean—there isn't even a skeletal structure at that embryonic stage, you know—no one could say there was or was not biological life."

"Then the baptism might be conditional, Doctor."

"Yes, but better than nothing at all. And a spiritual comfort to the girl lying there. And the embryo will not be cremated, if I recall the rules correctly."

Father Tuohy smiled faintly for the first time. "All this is very thoughtful of you, Doctor. One doesn't often come across such understanding. Who taught you all these important details?"

"A Doctor Mayoso. He was—oh, back quite awhile, years ago—he was chief resident in Ob-Gyn here. He knew all about Catholic doctrine."

"I confess I owe you an apology—"

"You figured: oh Lord, another Protestant bigot?"

Father Tuohy laughed. The charged air in the room had changed. "No, not the usual bigotry. But the more subtle secular sort of materialism."

"Now, there's a bit of a big subject for a rainy day's debate, I'll bet."

"I'd like to see the girl now, if I may."

"She's right across the hall."

Father Tuohy put out his hand. "Goodbye, and pleased to've met you. I assure you I'll consider everything twice before doing anything that might possibly scare her with some death-wish idolatry."

David Sommers shook his hand. "Thanks. I guess we all have our important details, don't we?"

The priest raised his hand, a fractional goodbye to all three medical people, a token blessing, then he went out.

Dr. Greene said, "I thought I'd heard everything. But *this—?*"

"You might as well learn it here," David said. "You never know when you'll need the details in your practice." He shouldered back against the wall of the cramped office and concentrated on Dr. Greene. "What have you decided?"

"They told me upstairs, Doctor Sommers: don't throw away that bed space—"

"I know, I know. The Administration upstairs has to run the whole show. Et cetera. But we see the patients. One at a time. We sign that bottom line on the chart. I'm just guessing, but young Carmencita may even be suicidal. I don't want to risk the couple of hours to get her to another hospital. She doesn't have her own doctor"—he waved his hand toward the noisy corridor beyond the door—"like most of these people. If you discharge her from E.W., I'm willing to write an explanatory consultation note on her chart and orders to transfer her to one of my research beds."

Dr. Greene stared at him. "A *research* bed?"

"Sure. I run my own research beds."

"Isn't that pitching a curved ball?"

David Sommers made a snorting sound. "Better than striking out while the patient's on third base."

Dr. Greene sized up the woman medical student. "You want to follow up this patient?"

"Yes. I've already learned a lot."

"Okay. She comes in. I'll write an admission note."

"After the first thousand cases, it's easy," David Sommers said quietly.

"What about Señorita Thousand-and-one? What about the police report? The criminal abortion?"

"But is it criminal?" David asked. "Septic, yes. But criminal? That can get to be a big word."

"Almost every septic abortion we see in here is criminal," Dr. Greene said. "Or am I wrong again, Doctor Sommers?"

"I think you're probably right, but the statistical boys who bug my research keep hollering that correlation doesn't prove causation. She certainly denied criminal intervention."

"They all do, Doctor. They play Let's Pretend I'm Virgin Mary. They screw like rabbits, then make believe they're lambs. It's like asking a stone wall to ask her who sold her the pill or inserted it. But I don't want to go fight City Hall, y'know."

"Well, as a matter of fact, I think I will," David Sommers said. "City Hall could use a little fresh air in the medicolegal department."

Dr. Greene scowled. "Count me out. I'm no crusader."

David Sommers eyed him. Our young Doctor Greene feels he's lost face, he decided. Tired, hurried, underpaid, frustrated, no breakfast, and now here I am, professorial, shaved, showered and well fed. "Let me buy you a drink sometime," he said. "We'll bend an elbow and ponder the ancient Greek oath of Hippocrates."

Dr. Greene rubbed his forehead with his fingertips. "The Greeks had a word for it, all right, all right. A four-letter word." He nodded briskly to the medical student. "Let me know how she comes along, will you?"

Helen Wilson asked gingerly, "What'll they do with the embryo?"

"Flush it," Dr. Greene said, and trudged out.

"Is he serious?"

"No, Helen, of course he's not. Any tissue removed from the body in this hospital has to go to Pathology."

"Tissue seems like a peculiar word, Doctor Sommers."

"Well, any organization of cells is called tissue."

"Aren't those two dark little pinpoints . . . eyes?"

"No," he said, "just the beginning of optic cups."

"I've never seen such a tiny speck of a human being," she said.

"Scientifically speaking, Helen, this embryo was not a human being."

"But you baptized it."

"For Carmencita's benefit, yes. Her church considers an embryo a human being. They call it human from the moment the sperm fertilizes the ovum, right up through blastula, gastrula, embryo, fetus, long before the obstetrical and legal stage with that quaint old name, quickening. Will you remind the desk to get in touch with Carmencita's pastor? He'll want to say a prayer for the dead, I'm sure."

"You mean, in Carmencita's religion, she's destroyed a human being?"

"Yes."

"But in legal medicine—"

"Not until the mother feels life. Until then it's an embryo. A fetus. The product of conception. Incredible, isn't it? Five hundred developing pairs of skeletal muscles, millions of sensory and motor neurons, the beginning of a brain that might someday go places—"

"Places like a home for unwed mothers with no way out—"

"Or go to medical school," David Sommers said, "and learn what a hell of a lot we don't know. I don't want to shut off any questions, Helen, but I've got to get going. Gynecology rounds are at five. Ask the resident to release you to come over and make rounds with us. Explore the idea that women are just like people."

She hardly had time to mutter, "Thanks," gravely and admiringly, before he was gone.

"Doctor Sommers," the Emergency ward secretary at the admissions desk said as he strode by, "did you get that call?"

He stopped short. "No," he said. "May I use one of your phones?"

"Sure thing. Take line four, Doctor."

As he dialed his laboratory he realized he had forgotten the nurse's message about the call. He could hear the buzz of his lab phone ringing at the other end. After the fifth or sixth ring he was about to hang up the receiver when a man's voice said, "Hello?"

"Dad?"

"Dave? Glad I decided to answer Mr. Bell's obnoxious invention."

"Sorry to disturb you, Dad. Where are the girls? Isn't there a note on the chalkboard?"

"Well, let's see now. *Be right back. Sally.*"

"That means she's grabbing a coffee break. Laboratory work on reproduction bores her. She prefers field experience."

"There are some more notes on the board, Dave. *Dr. Sommers. Call home.*"

"That's not urgent. Alice wants to remind me to pick up fresh flowers for the dinner party tonight."

"*Dr. Sommers. Call L.I.V.E. clinic.* I know what that is, Dave. Your mother has a new Spanish-speaking volunteer at the clinic. She wants you to give the lady a brief orientation course of preventive medicine and maternal health in about three minutes of well-chosen words."

"I'll be at the L.I.V.E. clinic after lunch. That call can wait."

"*Dr. Sommers. Garage called. Your Volkswagen fan belt replaced.* How do you feel with a new fan belt, Dave?"

"Less gassy. More pep."

Just a minute, Dave. Down at the bottom of the board it says: *Urgent. Call Administration.* What's up, Dave? You treating Doctor Douglass' edifice complex? Or have you been pinching nurses on rounds?"

"Not this morning, Dad. It's probably a lunch at the Faculty Club for some visiting Soviet and British doctors who want to go through the lab. Contraception by injection is a hot item."

"A lab tour? Today? The place is a mess, if I may say so."

"Organized chaos, Dad. We finally got the sperm-ovum experiment going yesterday. All that camera gear is time-lapse motion picture stuff to record the moment the sperm penetrates the ovum. Roone was up half the night keeping everything shipshape."

"Roone's always up half the night. Well, if you get hung up over there for lunch, Dave, let me know."

"I'd rather have lunch with you, Dad. Witt may place a conference call from Washington on that South American blowup. We could talk to him together."

"I'm too darn annoyed with your brother to talk to him on the telephone."

"Well then, talk to Mother. She's in Washington with Witt." Change the subject, David decided. Sometimes Dad sounds eccentric, like the newspapers make the Sommers family seem to be. "How'd the new chapter on Semmelweiss go this morning?"

"Not a word, Dave. Couldn't scribble a single blessed word. I've been sitting there in my office all morning, flat on my most contemplative coccygeal position, staring out the window."

"See anything?"

"Visions. Visions. I believe I'll resign from the human race, Dave."

"Can you wait till after lunch?"

"Reluctantly."

"It's a deal. I'll see you soon. 'Bye."

He was still smiling as he dialed Administration. His father was one of the last pinches of salt in the academic soup of conformity: he tapped the antique walnut case of the barometer in the hallway each morning and checked the *Farmer's Almanack*, forever pretending he was a latter-day Ben Franklin.

Actually, Dr. Benjamin Nathaniel Sommers had long been one of the country's best researchers on human reproduction. His idea of growing transplated segments of the lining of the uterus inside the chamber of a monkey's eye, and his achievement of the extraordinary delicate observations of the tides of menstruation as the visible tissue responded to hormones—all that had given medicine an understanding of menstruation in the female reproductive cycle, and had almost earned him the Nobel prize. His wife Marjorie, David's mother, had organized one of the first family planning and birth control clinics in Connecticut; these the local district attorneys and police had closed with the vigor and promptness of self-assured virtue.

"Adminis-*tray*-shun," a girl's voice said in his ear. "Miss Stone speaking."

"Doctor Sommers here, returning your call, Miss Stone."

"Doctor *Ben*jamin Sommers?"

"David Sommers."

"One moment, please. I'll check."

So, David thought, Administration tried to reach Dad, too. They don't know he's capable of ignoring a ringing phone and laughs out loud when he reads Aristophanes in Greek. Now, why would the super-busy Administrator try to reach both Dad and me at the same time?

A mature woman's voice, musically modulated as a flute, came on the line. "Doctor Sommers? Edwina Hawthorne here. Thanks awfully for calling us back. I know how busy you are."

"Did Doctor Douglass call me?" he asked bluntly.

He had learned never to play ring-around-the-rosy with Edwina. Her hand-painted bone china teacups and crocheted heirloom antimacassars and elaborately genteel voice disguised the Renaissance intricacy of the Administrator's Office. Dr. Anthony Hale Douglass was a Florentine dagger of a man, made as such medieval weapons were, a thin triangular blade with a sawtooth edge, designed so that a thrust in the dark would leave a spuriously tiny entrance wound which killed by massive bleeding inward, invisibly. He was the smiling Medici for whom Edwina fluted.

Edwina's teacups and antimacassars were decoys for faculty members who asked a bit too forcefully why the quintuplicate copies of their research grant applications sat piled on her desk so long. Edwina's young secretaries, in the wood-paneled outer office, were chosen by her to hang there as apples on the tree of knowledge, inviting the medical students to bite thereof. The girls were subtly trained to report back all information to Edwina; opinions about clinicians, scuttlebutt about staff amours, rumors about faculty offers from elsewhere, crumbs of backstairs flyspeckery. "Oh my dear," Edwina would say when the girl was warmed to confidence and intrigue across the midmorning teacups, "my dear, we really mustn't jump to conclusions. No laboratory could possibly keep two cases of beer hidden away in a research refrigerator!" The musical scale of ladylike laughter. "Two *bottles,* maybe. Not two whole cases! It's just hilarious enough to bear Doctor Douglass looking into it just a tiny little bit. What was the young man's name who told this to you?"

"No, Doctor Douglass did not call you, Doctor Sommers," Edwina said on the phone to David. "I did."

"Oh?"

"He wondered if you could come up to the office, Doctor Sommers."

"No cause for wonder," David said. "I can't."

"I checked your surgical schedule, Doctor, and that ovarian wedge resection is staff. Your department chief agreed to replace you. That should ease your time a bit, shouldn't it?"

"Edwina," he began, and stopped short. She had undoubtedly worked out her gambit to include his inevitable comment so that her next move would be checkmate. "Maybe you'd better let me talk to Doctor Douglass about the organization of my time."

"He's in conference, Doctor, and you know"—she chuckled warmly—"how wholeheartedly he gives of himself with visitors. But I'll query him . . . if you insist."

"I insist."

"This may take a minute. *Ne quittez pas,*" she said disarmingly, faintly conveying the implication that she knew he was the sort of man who would understand her la-de-da use of French, and that he could trust her, as a friend in high places, to handle his stubborn insistence on interrupting Dr. Anthony Hale Douglass.

Click. "David?" Voice of the Administrator, Dr. Anthony Hale Douglass.

"Hello, Doug," David said. "Sorry to interrupt—"

"Not at all, old man. Not at all. No life-threatening interruption. Just speaking about you, as a matter of fact."

"What's this about my surgical schedule?"

"I tried to get you about that, David, but they said you were down saving pregnant lives and instructing the young in E.W."

"The instruction part was true. What—?"

"David, could you waltz over to the nearest elevator like the gentleman and scholar you are, and ascend to this poor overburdened office? I'll prevail upon Edwina to give you a hot cup of tea, just to keep your electrolytes in balance."

"Doug, it's a helluva tight day for me—"

"For all of us, David, every single one of us. Tight is the exact word. But I confess this matter is a wee bit on the urgent side—"

"Something clinical, Doug?"

"Yes and no. Yes and no. The long and the short of it is that the District Attorney is in my office, and it would be an act of grace in the best tradition of your forebears if you'd help enlighten me about some of his, ah, viewpoints." In the pause which followed, David heard another man's voice, some distance from the telephone, say firmly, "Let's stop horsing around with him, Doctor Douglass. I don't have all day."

Rather quickly, Dr. Douglass added, "I tried to reach your esteemed father, David. He's in the office right next door to your lab, isn't he?"

"Yes."

"Well, there was no answer. Dave, quite candidly, even though your father is one of our trustees, there are occasional moments when he tries the patience of saints."

"Doug, you sound like my saintly mother."

"Your saintly mother is another Sommers I can't seem to reach by telephone."

"She's out of town. Washington."

"D'you know her phone number there, Dave?"

"No. Probably at Blair House, if this is all that urgent. She and Witt may be calling in here during the lunch hour."

"Oh?" Dr. Douglass' voice went up cautiously. "DeWitt's down there with her? May I ask, company business or government business?"

"Both, I think. A South American thing about Witt's pharmaceuticals. Everything crisscrosses into government policy, I suppose."

"Well now," Dr. Douglass said, "when it rains it pours. Same sort of problem here. A Marjorie Sommers L.I.V.E. birth control clinic is private until it crosses Connecticut laws. Doctor Benjamin Sommers is professor emeritus and trustee. Doctor David Sommers is on the staff here. DeWitt Sommers' company contributes generously to our research programs. One of our hospital volunteers, Mrs. DeWitt Sommers—"

"Leave Betsy out," David said more strongly than he had intended. "She just lives here. The Sommers family *works* here."

"Must we haggle about this on the telephone, David?"

"If it's something I can handle on the phone—" David said.

"One question you *can* answer, Dave—"

"Yes?"

"You don't have many teenage therapeutic abortions, so I imagine you'd recall whether you did a D and C on a teenage girl about six weeks ago?"

"Why, if it's the girl I think you mean, it's all in the hospital record room."

"In *writing?*"

"Sure. Fourteen-year-old kid. Raped by four boys."

After a silence, Dr. Douglass said, "Dave, please come up here, will you?"

"You're loud and clear, Doug. I'll be upstairs in a minute."

"Fine. No hurry, Dave. None at all. We'll expect you, if you don't mind a bit of Pentagonese, on or about the next five minutes."

The hospital elevator was crowded because everyone had squeezed to one side to make room for an old woman bent forward in a wheelchair. The nurse's aide beside the woman said cheerfully, "See? I told you they had all these doctors here to fix you good as new."

The old lady managed to twist her stiff arthritic neck. "No, thank you, ma'm. None of these for me. They're all too young. Go ahead," she said to the medical students and interns, "you can smirk at the bony old lady all you want. Don't matter." Her thin rheumy voice climbed. "Think the whole world's in them big books on your desk." She shook her head in a small painful arc. "Aaah, you don't even know what it's like to hurt so bad you want to die." She winked an eye at David. "You're not one of these young TV types. You look like *you* had a mother."

The starched white knot of students and interns laughed.

"Give 'em hell," David said. "I'm on your side, Grandma."

David got off the elevator on the Administration floor. Maybe she's right, he thought. Everything comes wrapped in plastic, supermarket style. Or maybe the students and interns are simply very young. The surgical resident in the E.W., Dr. Greene, may have been tired and partly right in refusing to admit Carmencita, but his legalistic harshness and his outraged adolescent dignity, his shrewd balancing of all the factors of hospital politics and my polite blackmail—all it meant was that Dr. Greene put the patient last instead of first.

Or, he thought as he turned from the corridor into the office under the discreet little suspended walnut sign ADMINISTRATION, or is it just that I'm thirty-nine and getting to be a crotchety old crock myself?

4 THE COFFEE SHOP was a block from the medical center, across the street where the streetcar tracks had run. After the urban renewal program had leveled all the delicatessens, the ever-hungry student nurses and medical students began dropping into the joint for what the owner called a cup of pizza and a slice of coffee, and the cash register rang like a church bell. Then came the liquor license, a new cash register, a remodeling job which sealed up the front with brick and a padded door modeled after Whisky-à-Go-Go in Paris, and a new neon sign suggested by one of the students: THE WOMB WITH A VIEW.

It was just what Betsy wanted before beginning what she thought of as her *hospital* days. At home she had put on the almost formless blue dress of the hospital volunteer uniform, always a little depressed by the mirrored sight of herself in such a *sack* and the reminder that her reputation for staggering beauty actually required every prop in the book, and this blue *bag* was not one of them. Last year she had had her dressmaker create a minor miracle by fitting the blue uniform with darts and tucks to demonstrate that a charitable volunteer hospital lady could also look like a *woman*. She had been on duty pushing a rolling magazine stand through the men's urological ward that day, in her specially tailored uniform, and afterward the nurse on G.U. duty had complained it was impossible to catheterize any of the men.

"Maybe it's the way you walk," Mrs. Crotty, the hospital's director of volunteers, had told Betsy in her office.

"What's wrong with the way I walk?"

"Now, Mrs. Sommers, I'm not criticizing, believe me. I'm only suggesting you stick to the regular uniform, like everyone else. And with Doctor Sommers as your original sponsor, maybe you'd like to change over to one of his obstetrical wards?"

She had wanted to quit on the spot, righteous with indignation: Why are women always against me? Why is it my fault if those sterilized nurses and interns have trouble with catheters? Saints above, such *panic* in the streets! How am I supposed to walk, on my hands and knees in front of your whole damn unattractive tasteless flat-heeled uncombed cotton-pickin' Mrs. Grundys?

But she knew David would hear of it, so she had said very brightly, "I'm here to do a job, Mrs. Crotty, and whatever you say is best for the hospital service, why, that's fine with me."

So now she wore the shapeless blue *tent,* but refused to wear low heels in public. She carried her hospital shoes in an elegant little Italian leather-and-wickerwork basket, and changed into them in the volunteers' dressing room at the last minute.

However she always stopped first at the Womb for a cup of tea and a last cigarette. It was a college bar, noisy as a kindergarten full of rabbits. She always felt younger there, but envious of the student nurses' and med students' blasé blend of long biological words and short vulgar ones which David had told her was the tribal lingo of the Medical Center. She took refuge in always sitting alone at the counter, or, preferably, in a booth, and letting a small, aloof, maternal smile sit on her face above the teacup.

"Mrs. S., good morning and bonjour to you."

"Good morning, Joe."

"To you I should say top o' the morning, eh?"

With his remodeled joint and new prosperity, Joe had decided to become mine host, convivial and witty. Betsy always humored him.

"Sure, an' ye should. Full house?"

"Not a seat, not a booth."

"Standing room only?"

"You know how it is, Mrs. S. These kids buy a cuppa coffee and set up housekeeping on the layaway plan. Ha, ha."

She turned to leave as the young man in the booth behind them got up and said, "Mrs. Sommers? You want to grab a seat with us? Lots of room."

"Oh, hello," she said.

"You know this boy?" Joe asked, very surprised.

"Down, boy, down," the young man said, just as she answered, "Oh yes. He's the student helping me paint a mural in the Pediatrics playroom."

"I'm Gunga Din, the water boy," the young man said to Joe, then ignored him. "Please join me and my friend, Mrs. Sommers."

She looked at the friend with the waist-length ponytail sitting in the booth, and decided immediately that the girl was no student of nursing or anything else. She was postgraduate everything. "Thanks, Roone," Betsy said. "Two's fun and three's a political convention."

"Oh no! No, don' say that," the girl in the booth said. "Tree's a lucky number. I jus plunked ten bucks on número tree inna daily double. Now you make me lose."

Betsy stared at her. "I what?"

"Out of the mouths of babes," Roone said. "Especially when they're half Gypsy."

"I'm not half, you *gajo*. Full-blood Romany back to the Pharaohs."

"Okay. Full. Up to here. Also a babe," Roone said.

"Whatever you say, Roone doll." She looked up at Betsy. "For Chrisake don' be such a lady-lady, lady. Siddown. You *gajo* ladies don' know how to sit down or lay down, nothin. Siddown, we'll make the bad luck you said go away."

Betsy sat down, delighted. The whole morning had come alive. Roone was about to sit down beside her, but the girl half stood to grab his sleeve and yanked him to her own side of the booth. "Ah, no white meat for you, Roone."

Roone grinned at Betsy. "She's like this all the time. Her name is Vulgar."

The girl laughed and punched his arm. "Volga. Volga." She smiled at Betsy. "He don' hit me back. Good thin I'm goodlookin, hah?" She lifted her half-filled beer glass. "Salud," she said, and drank it in a single gulp.

"Yes," Betsy said. She *was* good-looking. Her long black ponytail, her darker-than-tan skin, the piled red coral beads over the rainbow shirt—yes, she was. And the medical student, Roone, had always seemed such a blond and fairskinned churchgoing boy, so ingratiatingly polite and neat and intelligent in a nicelooking bland shirt-ad sort of way—here with this Romany creature with an incredible name? It would have all seemed a little unreal anywhere in New Haven except the Womb.

"You goodlookin, too," Volga said. "Roone tol me about you. All that black hair and them eyes. You got a Persian-kitten-in-the-rain look."

"Synchronize your watches, men," Roone said. "Here we go."

"You did tell me! You said you play widda goodlookin high-'ciety broad inna hospital."

"I said she was a volunteer in the Pediatrics ward, with the kids. What the kids call a Play Lady." His eyes met Betsy's and she saw for the first time a different Roone, with a bold, direct look she had never seen in the hospital. It was as if he had touched her face. "Out of the mouths of babes," he said. "Tell her you're a Play Lady."

Change the channel, Betsy thought. Right now. "Volga," she said. "What's a *gajo*?"

Joe stopped at their booth. "Those peons, they didn't take your order yet, Mrs. S.? I'll get it. The Darjeeling tea? Some melba toast?"

"Please. Thank you, Joe."

"Hey," Volga said. "You British?"

"Only when I laugh."

Roone smiled, because he knew the joke, but Volga said, "Who else drink tea in a mornin?"

"My father," Betsy said, surprised that she felt so quickly friendly, intimate, with these gamins. "He had tea every morning and every afternoon."

Roone said to Volga, "See? When she came in, you said she was Irish."

Volga shook her head. "When you tell fortunes for a livin, you gotta know things fast. With such black hair, an green eyes, an such skin? That's Irish."

"Okay, you lose," Roone said to Volga. "Payola, baby. The *bujo*—that's one time you don't score, Miss ESP."

"Who she?"

"Extrasensory perception." He held out his hand and snapped his fingers. "Pay, gypsy, pay."

"That was no bet. She walk in, you look at her widda hard-on look, so I make a joke. I say I bet a five-spot she's Irish, but only for a joke."

"You know what happens to people who don't pay off when they lose?"

Volga smiled with delight and leaned confidentially toward Betsy. "A tough kid, hah? Like a real *rom*, a real Gypsy man." She made a small red mouth at Roone. "Bet you beat me up, a real lover boy. Who bought you a French shirt to wear to the weddin down on Mott Street? Expensive English pants wit no belt and a zip fly big enough for a truck? Last night I come from *ofisa* straight here, I give you a wad, ninety-two buckaroos, now you wanna bang me for a lousy five-spot?" She swung to Betsy. "Gall, hah? An I don' mean his bladder, this student medico. If he had black hair an some right relative, this big blond bum Roone he could be better'n a con man. He could be an *agent*. A big one, the boys who score in the big G's and catch a jet to London before the bulls button their pants."

"Cut it out," Roone said. "You told the lady you would break the bad luck."

"Here comes her British tea. We see what the tea leaves say."

With the teacup before her, Betsy rummaged through her purse for cigarettes. "Got a cigarette?" she asked Roone.

"Volga finished my last one." He slid out of the booth and stood up. "I'll get some." He held out his hand to Volga. "A contribution, baby."

"Pay yourself for her cigarette."

Roone snapped his fingers again. "Pay-as-you-go plan, dark eyes. Pay or you go, ochichornye."

"Oh, please," Betsy said, opening her purse again. "I'll buy my—"

"Stop!" Volga threw up one hand. "A guest who pays? Never. My fodder would curse me." She reached into her brassiere with two fingers and pulled out a squashed bill. "Here," she said, dropping it into Roone's hand, "foldin money."

"A lousy *dollar?*" Roone said, and walked away.

Volga nosed across the table. Betsy caught a wave of very strong perfume. "You look surprise I give him money, ah?"

"Well, it's none of my business. I mean, he seems so different here. I've never seen him without his white lab jacket. Or even outside the hospital."

"Yes? Good! Because you come in here an I see his face. I wonner if he lays you on the side."

Betsy set her teacup down, amused. "No. No, no."

"One no would be enough, lady. He lays like a rug."

"I'm *married.* I have a wonderful husband and a home and a young son—"

"So? Upstairs between your legs, God made you diffren? Why you wear so much eye makeup?"

"I always have."

"One eye is more like green. An this side is more like blue. I never saw it before."

"The green is my father, the blue was my mother. I'm not really very pretty, so I use makeup where I've got something."

"You sure got somethin for Roone."

"Don't be silly. He's very young."

"An you? Old enough to vote?"

"I could almost be his mother."

"He likes a lot of mudder in bed. Tits, everythin."

Betsy stared at the girl. The frank talk she heard at dinner parties was often only sophisticated prurience. This was different; neither frank nor coy, but simple bread, the staff of life. She was a trifle ashamed of the sound of offended gentility in her own voice. "That's not what—"

"Okay. Okay. I only wanna know. I wan him to keep a hard on. A woman live for a man, ah? Cook for him. Steal for him so he can buy a best, wear nice clothes, give him enough money to feel like a real man, not a cheap bum. What else? Not like a *gajo.*"

A young man strolling past their booth stopped to stare at Betsy Sommers. Volga snickered. "Ha, look who got up for breakfess! Buenas tardes, Tabac."

Betsy looked up. The young man was dressed in an Italian-cut dark mohair suit, with a white damask tie sporting a black onyx tiepin. Even his eyes were onyx. He was short, thin, with pomaded hair and very white teeth. She found his stare so direct and insolent that she lowered her eyes immediately and became busy with her teacup.

"Buen' días, Volga," Tabac said. He nodded toward Betsy. "This I like. She just come in?" He hunched forward and put his fingertips under Betsy's chin to raise her face. "Nice stuff—" he began to say, just as Betsy muttered furiously, "Take your hands off!" He pulled his hand back.

Volga hooted. "She's a *guest*, Tabac. She don' *work* here." She rattled in Spanish, gesturing toward Betsy. The only word Betsy caught was señora. Tabac grinned slowly, saying "Sí . . . sí, sí . . ." as Volga spoke.

"You pardon me," he said to Betsy. "I tought you was a new girl." Betsy said nothing. He turned to Volga. "You guest don' talk? No tongue for a stranger? She need a polite introduction?"

Volga waggled her hand at him. "He's Tabac Gutiérrez."

"Mucho gusto," he said.

"Jus call him Tabac. *Macho*. A verr big cigar," Volga added, and hooted with laughter again. "You surprise him. Everrbody nice to Tabac. A big man in bolita lottery, numbers, you know, anytin that can walk nice and easy t'rough Customs in San Juan or N'Yok. Tabac is verr big business."

"Show biz," Tabac said. "Volga, you got a loose lip? Call it show biz, you dumb broad." He looked at Betsy. "You don' even know what we talk about. I can see that."

"I can guess." She managed to keep herself from smiling. All this was so *different. Mar*velous.

"I could show you, doll. Like to see a cockfight tonight? My guest."

"Whose cock?" Volga asked with her cigarette bobbing between her lips, coughing smoke and laughter.

Roone came back. "Hey, Tabac."

"Días, Doc. How's the sickness business?"

Roone glanced at Betsy, and nodded toward Tabac. "Is he giving you the *mucho macho* routine, Mrs. Sommers?"

"I don't know what *mucho macho* means," Betsy said, and Volga began laughing again.

"Man, oh man," Tabac said. "You got a babe fresh from a farm?" He turned to Betsy. "*Macho*, it's Spanish for a real man."

"A bi-i-i-g cockfight," Volga laughed, and made a gesture older than Rome.

"A *real* man," Tabac added.

"Okay," Roone said. "Okay, okay. Lay off the guest. She doesn't appreciate all this." He towered over Tabac, frowning.

"You hear?" Tabac asked Volga. "Hear what Doc says? Lay off." They grinned whitely at one another.

"Mrs. Sommers," Roone said carefully, "this Tabac is very big in the

Puerto Rican colony all around here. *Mucho macho.* Also a very big gentleman. A caballero, y'know? There is no gentleman who can outclass a Spanish gentleman, hey, Tabac?"

Tabac shrugged modestly and ran his fingertips delicately down his white damask tie, a gesture suggesting a small bow. "We got class, Doc."

"Exactly. But another man's party?"

"How do I know, Doc? They sit here alone."

"I just went for some butts."

"Reefers?"

"No, no, for Chrisake. No junk. Just cigarettes. Cellophane-wrapped bronchiolar carcinoma."

"Doc, you slay me. Them medical words. It ain't who you know, no more. It's what you know."

"Oh no, Tabac. It's what you know about who you know."

"Hey, you know your onions. *Al que come cebollas, se le para la polla.*"

"Come again?"

"It means the guy who bites the onion, he gets a hard on."

Roone winked at Betsy. "Folk wisdom, island style."

Tabac tapped Roone on the shoulder. "I lay you odds, compañero"—he spread three fingers—"tree to one. I can teach you Spanish in one mont."

"Impossible, pal. I'm just a dumb *anglo.*"

"Oh no. No no. You look all dumb blond outside, but inside you smart. Doc, a janitor in the hospital tol me there's a pile of sleep pills stashed away there. Civil Defense stuff from who knows when. Stuff they forgot. A smarr guy like you, you like to talk biz on a lil deal?"

"There's a time and a place, señor." Roone smiled, "It sounds very illegal." Betsy admired his adroitness. Roone sat down in the booth, conveying that the conversation was over. "I'll see you around, Tabac."

"Hasta luego, Doc." He ignored Volga and spoke to Betsy with elaborate politeness. "Nice to meet ya, doll." He and Roone gave each other a snappy hand flip, a slightly upraised palm.

"Peace, Straight Arrow," Roone said as Tabac strolled away. "Hey, hey," Roone said, "were you two having an argument while I was gone? You should see what you two looked like across the room." He tapped a cigarette out of the pack and offered it to Betsy, then, with lavish courtesy, a second to Volga. He scratched a match and held it in the circle of palm and fingers like a sailor.

"You're against three on a match?" Betsy asked. "Or just not smoking?"

"Heh!" Smoke exploded from Volga's mouth. "Funny taste." She made little spitting sounds. "Pfui! Like toilet paper. It ain't the Turkish."

"No," Roone said. "They're Players."

"Since when you cheap, Roone? Bargain stuff? Wit a lady-lady guest?"

"They're not cheap," Betsy said. "They're British."

"They cost more," Roone said to Volga. He glanced at Betsy. "I've seen you use these."

"Thanks," Betsy said.

"Okay, lovebirds, break it up. Break it up." Volga grasped Roone's wrist on the table. "She wants fancy British butts, let her buy um for *you*."

"Stop it, for Chrisake," Roone said. He pulled his wrist free. "You and your palaver. You can't even speak English straight. Spika da inglés. Once I thought it was cute."

"You mad about Tabac?"

"I'm mad at you. There's a time and a place."

"Hah! The time is always now. The place is always here. You read too many big books, Doc. The big doc. You don' know how to live, *gajo*." She swung to Betsy. "You like to drink tea, drink it." She stabbed her cigarette into the ashtray. "You like to smoke British, smoke."

Betsy was enjoying herself completely. She gave Volga the friendly smile of an older woman who has conquered a younger pretty one, without even trying. "But I know how you feel, Volga. I like to smoke Papistratos or Laurens Khedive."

"You do? Wit latakia?"

"Yes. If I had a Kairouan rug and bubble pipe, what do they call?—a narghile, isn't it?—I'd probably smoke that, too."

"Good, good. You got blood in you vein. You come to my *ofisa*. Rugs, all over. Even on walls. A narghile, you can smoke." She dropped her voice, and made an upward sinuous gesture, smoke curling. "What you want. Reefers? Goofballs? Cough medicine? Tabac gets me good stuff."

"Real joy-joy," Roone said. "Three puffs, you're on. You take a trip. Walk on the moon. Or Hong Kong style. Mandarin clouds."

Betsy was amazed. The polite thank-you-ma'am medical student who earned scholarship money by helping her in the Pediatrics ward was not this young man bending toward her with tousled wildfire blond hair and speaking a slang she had never heard. What luck! In a world of boredom, this is so alive.

"What's an *ofisa*?" she asked.

"You rent a store. Hang up rugs. Couple taborets, two poufs on the floor. A lil smoke. You tell fortune. You look for rich widow who farts aroun in her Cadillac tree times a week to a doctor. Pains here. Pains there. All over. Keeps movin. Money? Up to here. Love? *Nada*. Lonesome? Like a corpse. You sit wid her. You lissen. Agh, you lissen. A son-in-law, a law-yer? You drop her quick. He can put the bulls on you. Crazy, she hears voices? Her dead husband talks to her? Drop her. She's a real kook, not a half kook, an some downtown lady wit eyeglasses can catch onto her an send a hospital car. But a lady in-between, a *half* kook, lonesome, buys cha-cha lessons five nights a week on lifetime plan, expensive queen-bee jelly crap to change skin, December back to June, she believe it, she honest to God cross my heart believe it—you get a lady like so an you can make a verr big score. A real *bujo*."

Betsy sipped her tea to hide a smile. This girl is one in a million. I'm taking a trip. A walk on the moon. "That's what you do in an *ofisa?*"

Volga batted her eyelashes. "Sometime. A *bujo* is like when you go downtown to the big hotel bar. Tight dress, short, up to here. Wiggle you ass, *culipandeo*. Wear a merry widow to push you out, pointy, like a dairy queen. Ponytail, you look like you born yestiday. Some John pick you up an you play him like a call girl. No whore. Jus a nice girl like to be wit a nice guy, onny need a lil baksheesh for some expense, y'know? In taxi to *ofisa* you give um a big passion, he's so nice, m-m-m-, so everrtin, use you hands on him, play beat me daddy on um like a piano. You come to *ofisa* in taxi. Your *rom* steps out of a dark door. A *gaga*, he holler, you two-time *puda!* He crack you on face. OO-*ee!* You scream. Quick! Scram! You yell to the John in the taxi. Man, does he scram. *Fast.* No John want trouble. You an you *rom* sit in *ofisa* an laugh an count money from the John's wallet."

"His wallet?"

"Sure. He don' come back. Not even go to a cop. What can he *say?* What can he complain? A ponytail girl in a taxi? You touch a man skin wit one han, it's easy to take wallet wit *this* han."

Betsy took in Volga's enormous dark eyes and their confidential conspiratorial grin. Was Volga enjoying the corruption of an innocent, a lady-lady, or faintly suggesting shoptalk between a pro and a potential pro? I should be flattered I'm being recruited.

Roone made a thumbs-up gesture. "It's easy. Penis erectus non discriminatus est. Quote unquote."

His phony Latin did it. Betsy's sense of being subtly insulted by Volga vanished, and she burst out laughing. "Never! *Never*, absolutely *never*, not in all my born days! You make stealing sound like the most marvelous fun game in the world!"

"You would be good at it." Volga nodded. "I mean it. Cross my heart."

"Oh, go on, now. I *would?*"

"Wit that little English ladyface? No John would say no."

"See?" Roone said, sounding relieved. "Now you're on our beam. No John would say no. Sounds like a folksong. She's a poet and she don't know it."

"Look, she dunno what a John is."

"Of course I do." Betsy strummed an imaginary guitar and sang: *"Here*

I sit on Buttermilk Hill, who can blame me, cry my fill? Me-oh-my, I loved him so, Broke my heart to see him go. Only time can heal my woe. Johnny's gone for a soldier."

Volga clapped her hands. "Hey, a John ain't the same as Johnny, but it's nice. You should sing at night here. When all cats come."

"I'd love to come some night," Betsy said. "But only to watch. I'm too shy to perform."

"Irish ballad?" Roone asked. " 'The Irish Brigade,' wasn't it?"

She looked at him, pleased. "Yes."

"You're a lass with a delicate air. Where'd you learn it?"

"My mother," Betsy said. "She used to sing songs like that—I can hear it even now—or she'd hum a tune while she worked around the house, just sort of humming to herself. Did you ever hear the wild swans of the lake country hum?"

"Hum? Uh-uh. Swans are mute."

"Oh, the domesticated English swans are, sure, but the wild swans in Ireland hum like sad women singing. No hunter would lay a finger on them."

"Live and learn," Volga said. "Why it's sad?"

"Sad?" Betsy shook her head. "I didn't mean to sound sad." She could see Roone's diagnostic eyes studying hers. Hurriedly, defensively, she said, "It's not easy to explain."

I can't explain about my mother, how alone we were, how close we were. And her stories! The stories and the talk, country ballads and country songs, all easy as breathing, Mother whose voice is always with me like my own bones. *'Tis a short visit we pay to this world, so drink up friendly before a last shake-hands.*

"You're so quiet all of a sudden," Roone said.

"Oh—" She didn't trust her voice and shook her head again. Her throat had tightened. The noose of memory.

Ah, just calling to mind Mother's stories of Ireland: herself, Mother, as a slip of a girl surrounded by brothers and sisters of the MacDiarmada brood, every last one of them born near Spanish Gate in Galway, all of them gawking from their cottage doorway at the painted gypsy wagons lumbering over the hills of Connemara past the grapeskin-purple peaks of Twelve Bens and the bluegray loughs.

Explain this? In a joint named Womb with a View? To strangers? The inherited memory of gypsies making do for the night inside a circle of fires, their supper pans rattling from far off through the still air that smelled of smoke from handcut sods of burning turf and sea wrack left by the high tide, the spangled Romany women baking next day's bread in blackened pots under red coals of peat piled on their closed iron lids.

Mother's tales of umbrella-mending gypsy tinkers, the wild free singing, the campfire dancing to tambourines, striped skirts flaring, rainbow colors in a country of gray clouds. Oh Mother, Mother. I haven't remembered all this in years. Is that why my eyes ache with unshed tears?

Roone interrupted her daydream. "Knock, knock. Anybody home?"

She raised her eyes. "Don't knock it. Didn't you ever hear that life would be grand if only the English would talk and the Irish would listen?"

Volga dug her elbow at Roone. "See? I tol you! *Irish*." She put out her hand. "Pay, gypsy, pay."

"Pay hell. There was no bet, remember?"

She kissed his cheek. "Wunneful! You good as a con man. A real *agent*. If God gave you luck to grow up a Gypsy, you could be a real *agent*."

"Great. That's all I need. Thanks."

"I *mean* it, lover! I nevair lie. To take a lil sometin sometime, it's only to make a living. Gotta *live*, no? But to lie to a lover, that's a big sin."

"Okay, you sinner. But I'll stick to medicine, with the police on my side. Me, I'll make my big score legally."

"Ah, in you heart, you Gypsy. You know it. Jus like this nice Irish girl." She crossed her arms in a saintly pose and raised her eyes piously. "Two all-American kids, nice clothes from downtown department store. Clean Americanos from church, shiny teet. Cool, no sweat." She dropped her arms and grinned. "But in here, in you heart, it's a tambourine. Ta-ta-ta-*ta*. You like open sky. A big wingding dingdong daddy. Make you nature so hot you wanna die wit you two bellybuttons screwed in tight." She pointed at Betsy. "Look at you. I don' need a tea leaf to tell you fortune."

"I wish you would," Betsy said. "I love all the playacting, turning my cup upside down and full circle three times and back. Presto chango, hocus-pocus."

"Tell fortune youself."

"Me? That's funny. You don't know how funny that is. I couldn't foretell my way out of a tea bag. I'm just a here and now type."

"I see around you eyes, you whole life, glad an sad. Some tings verr sad. Up here lady-lady, yes? Down here a warm lil rabbit, likes to lay all over, no? But in here, inside you heart, a real Gypsy girl who jus wan her one man, true. True, true, true."

"Can I have another cigarette?" Betsy said to Roone.

As he gave one to her, Volga grabbed her hand, "See? Jumpy fingers."

Betsy pulled her hand free. "They shake a little all the time. Especially when I'm chilly. That's why I'm keeping my coat on."

"Oh no. I can see a blue hospital dress. You hate uniform. Makes you a nottin."

"You've got a pretty cloudy crystal ball, Volga."

Volga nudged her. "No insult. Jus true. Who cares? I can tell this blond *gajo* here, wit a beautiful face from all the icons painted for love, in his heart he's a true stealer, a true *rom*." She ran her fingers through his blond hair, then yanked it gently. "Lover boyyy."

Roone snorted, blowing cigarette smoke from both nostrils. "She means all that talk as a compliment, Mrs. Sommers."

"Mrs. Sommers sounds like somebody's grandmother." Betsy gave him a special smile to show she was offering a valuable gift. But casually. "Please call me Betsy."

He salaamed. "Okay. Betsy."

"On second thought, after all this, make it Alice in Wonderland. Certainly not in New Haven, Connecticut." She turned to Volga with the feeling that if she could keep herself talking she would work her way back to her own world of pleasant conversation, nothing threatening, nothing obscene, nothing *personal*. "How did you come to New Haven, Volga?"

"For the Puerto Ricans," Volga said, making it an explanation.

"Lots of Puerto Ricans migrated here, and to Hartford and Bridgeport," Roone said. "And upstate, the Connecticut Valley has the best shade-grown tobacco in the world. The cigar boom brings Puerto Rican tobacco farmers and Cuban refugee cigar makers up here for the wages. The men who know tobacco best."

"Like Tabac?"

"Up here," Volga broke in, "Tabac was a poor hungry kid. Skinny, a tootpick. Mad alla time, goddam Americanos. Now look, Mister Mafia."

"The triumph of evil over evil," Roone said to Betsy, grinning expectantly for her to appreciate his joke. Somehow she did not find it amusing.

"I've lived here for years," she said. "I never knew—"

"You live on another planet. Volga follows the immigrants like a fisherman follows fish. A lot of them are Catholic on Sunday, but on the side, Saturday night, there's a lot of spiritualism—"

Volga bobbed her head. "Ya. *Espiritismo.* You got a no-good boyfren? I fix it."

"How?" Betsy asked. She wasn't really curious, but any talk was better than the scrape of faraway Irish spellbindings.

"Take away a bad luck *salazón,* mix up *agua de Santa Marta* in some Florida Water, tree piece cinammon an sassfrass, a lil *culantro,* some money wish candles for in church, a lil gold Hand of Fátima you wear between you tits to keep a boyfren true."

"Expensive," Betsy said. "A Fátima charm in gold."

Volga rubbed a thumb and forefinger together. "Pays good, but in N'Yok I pay plenty for *haung* leave an passion flower."

Roone's touch of a tiny smile, as if he and Betsy shared a secret. "Better than *Macbeth,* isn't it? Root of hemlock digged in the dark. Scale of dragon. Tooth of wolf."

"Sounds like heap big powerful medicine, Doctor," Betsy said. "Sounds like easy money. Tabac and his show biz."

"Easy money," Volga said. "Always in a love biz. Women cry, beg, pay any price for good stuff. Special pills to stop pregnan and take out baby. *Una pérdida.*"

"What's that?"

"A loss," Roone said. "Spanish, polite for abortion. Dig?"

"You understand the—the?"

"Not all of the patois. Not the latest Romany. It's part orthodox religion, part Spanish. Part Brooklynese now, with some Main Street gloop and Harlem bebop mixed in to put on."

"Put *on?*"

"Special talk. Sounds like talk but has a corkscrew meaning. Baffles the squares. It's like a secret society. You can understand it only if you're on the in."

Secret society. Where had she heard that before? Gaelic? Had it been Witt grouching about Gaelic? She realized Roone was still talking, but now the held-back Irish undercurrent of years ago had unexpectedly surfaced—she and Witt bound for Ireland, the newly married Mr. and Mrs. DeWitt Sommers, dancing on deck, younger than springtime; their honeymoon trip, with their stayover in Dublin.

She tried wrenching herself back to the present, back to what Roone was explaining, but her inner ear caught Witt's voice as clearly as if he sat beside her—*See, Betts? You can go home again.* How underhanded of Witt, sneaking into my mind on the sly when I'm trying to detach myself from our disaster last night—it's Witt, not Ireland, I've been trying to hold back! The slap of insight flushed her face.

"Hey," Volga was saying, "why you blush?"

"Am I?" Yesterday's sluicegate opening now. All the morning's reminders swirling together, the Connemara gypsies of Mother's childhood, the put-on talk like a secret society—a flash flood, remembrance of things past.

Of course. Dublin! Where Witt had complained that feisty Gaelic talk baffled him.

In the bedroom of their hotel suite Witt had exploded. "What the hell is it, a secret society? The Sinn Fein? It's great at first, Betts, this talk talk talk, but now it's rubbing off on you."

She had just begun to undress, and paused, holding one shoe. "Rubbed off? I feel grand. I feel back home. There's no secret society, darling."

Two hours before, she had taken Witt to Neary's Pub, the actors' pub her father had frequented, just for a glass or two of stout.

"Oh, your father was the great one," the convivial barkeep had orated, ignoring DeWitt as a heathen, showering Betsy with wordage. "Camaraderie his middle name. Them Abbey actors had tongues like harpstrings, Gaelic or English, both. Playboys of the western world, they were. Your mother'd leave you at home, Betsy Mary—you don't mind an old friend of your da' usin' your baptismal name?—you bein' just a sweet babe in pampooties at that time, livin' over the Liffey bridge at Bachelors' Walk and O'Connell Street—and your mother'd come in through them doors all delicate and smilin' like she was on tippy-toe. Your father'd take the grand hint and wooze up steady on his feet, announcing to the company one an' all, 'I will arise an' go now, an' go to Innisfree. Off to my galley chains an' mulish burthens, lads. Neither a borrower nor a father be!' I admired the man. No tittle-tattle them days, Betsy Mary. They had tongues with the taste of honey and apples."

"Oh Witt," she had said tactfully in their hotel bedroom, "he was just an old man rememberin' old times with a pretty girl in a pub."

"But don't you realize how everybody else gets shut out? An invisible door. A family might have been in the States for generations, sure, red white and blue, but when it's handy with pretty girls or politics"—he snapped his fingers—"tsst, they're The Irish. The amateurs, the semipros, and pros who are more Irish than the Irish Irish. If you follow me."

"You feel shut out?"

"Damn right I do! One minute you speak English, then you meet one of these nonstop talkers, and there you go—through the looking glass."

She had really been surprised. "I'm just bein' friendly."

"Friendly? Betts, baby, our clocks run on different times. That was more than just friendly at Puck Fair in—in Kill-something—"

"Killorglin, County Kerry—the *kill* means church—"

"All those gypping gypsies crowding around you—"

"Witt, they're not gypsies."

"All right, tinkers, whatever they call themselves. Ready to rob you blind."

"Oh, Witt, the *fun* of it, though! They're the travelin' people, that's what they call themselves in those high covered wagons, just traveling like I wish we would on our only only honeymoon."

"Now you're getting sore!"

"Yes, by glory, I am! Ireland walks at a strolling pace, no hurry. My only honeymoon, a dream of a dream, none of this efficiency and timetable that just—if you'll excuse the language—gives me consti*pa*tion! I *loved* jabbering Romany talk with those tinkers at the fair. I *loved* being rich enough, with a purse full of pounds, to be cheated and overcharged on every little tinplate crucifix. I loved the—the—the ex*cite*ment and the gaiety of it! I *loved* the way they camp around the edges of the fair with those wonderful bright plaid shawls, always a baby under one arm—"

"Always the other hand out begging—"

"But with their pride still there. Poor but proud, and don't you ever forget *that.*"

"Take it easy, Betts. I never—"

"Oh yes you did, you Philistine! You felt shut out? You *were* shut out!"

"My God, Betts, you want to play gypsy?"

"Oh me, oh my." She rolled her eyes upward to call upon heaven. "And now we hear the Voice of Decency arise in the land?"

"There you go, Betts. I swear, I'll have to get you an old derby and a clay pipe. Sometimes you take their quare talk—"

"I do not!"

"Oh yes you do, you fake the Celtic blarney. Down with the bloody English and Protestant bigots. You're a dark-haired colleen with skin more fair than the white white rose." He spread his arms, pantomiming a bar-room tenor. "My wiyuld Irishhh rose, my rose of Tralee—"

She threw her shoe at him. "Stop! Stop stop. *Stop* it! I won't go on to Europe with you. I swear I'll catch the first boat back."

"I'll swim after you. You're so prim you'll be embarrassed as hell."

"Go ahead, joke."

"Because you look so fierce and stricken. I apologize."

"Oh, Witt. Why are we having our first real fight?"

He had grinned immediately, and she had loved him for it. "Because we were up all night, you hussy. You, with the smell of the hearth peat still in your hair. And marching over the moors, or the bogs, or the peat turf, or what the hell the picturesque stuff was we were marching around all day—"

"And you keep being shut out. It's true, darling. And I'm sorry. My mother said it comes from such a long time of bein' persecuted, cut down. And, my God, the breadcrumby poverty. Many's the woman who stretched potato peelin's for days to feed her kids. We're as ancient and proud and pushed into clannishness as the Jews, darling. They got The Book, my father used to say, an' we got The Harp. We remember every-thing. All the talk that shuts you out, all that talk does is to say to the other one, I remember the same as you. I know what *hungry* means. Even words that sound like oldtime sure-an'-begorra vaudeville, Witt, those words ring a bell inside."

"I know. When that handsome young gypsy made a pass at you yesterday"—he imitated the brogue—"oh the sweetest heather honey is atop the mountain"—his voice changed—"and I knew you were encouraging him—"

"Not him, not him, but only the way he spoke—and now the paddy talk's rubbin' off on you, Witt. And here we are in Dublin town, and you keepin' me standing here, only one shoe on—"

"On tippy-toe, all delicate and graceful—"

They fell laughing across the great white linen battlefield of the bed.

I've got to make him stay in Ireland, she had thought, as coolly and clearly as if she had said it aloud. Money talks. It can learn the brogue well as any other mother tongue.

"Put-on talk may sound like jabberwocky," Roone was saying, "but it's one way of telling the truth—"

Volga leered fondly. "I like how you talk, Roone. Educated."

Betsy arranged her face in a pretense of interest, but she was in Dublin.

"How else can you fight back?" Roone asked. "How else can you tell it like it is?"

"Well . . ." Betsy said vaguely. Her voice trailed off. She was barely listening. She was back in Dublin. . . .

The next day she and Witt had been drugged with lovemaking, but she had deliberately organized a caravan for two. Money talked. A car. Fishing gear. Across the lovely green land she had taken Witt, to Dingle Bay in County Kerry, a picnic lunch of crossmarked apple bread and jugged sweet milk and cheese, then a stop at Geohagen's Bar at the far end of Dingle where the Atlantic came up to the doorstep. "Ye're as far west as Europe goes," said a dour countryman wearing a tweedcloth cap and corduroys. "Ye're close to home."

"No," said the barman. "Cahirciveen is farther west."

"D'you want a geographical punch on your fat grog blossom of a nose, man? We're as close as a body can be to the States and still be standing on God's own Irish soil."

At dawn, the next day, Betsy had strolled along the miles of clean sandy shore: the beach was empty as a green moonscape, naked as the beginning of time on a lunar surface of endless mornings, the Atlantic's clear iron-blue world curling a crystalline glassiness in the shallows. A strangely exotic island lay seemingly a fingertip away, a unique place lapped by the Gulf Stream's warm Caribbean current, its fantastic shore spiky with palm trees.

Inland, the low molded pastel hills of heather shouldered up, swelling one beside the next, earthen breasts. Thin layers of mist scattered the dawning sun in a fine rain of light on their eastern slopes. Not a house, nor a tree nor man nor dog, not even a fisherman's tarred canvas currach on the sea, but only a solitary bird wheeling down the great blue bell of sky, flying so close overhead she heard its wingbeats.

She felt a lifting lyrical pulse. We'll have lots of kids, she thought. No child should grow up alone the way I did, alone and so much inside myself. She ran impulsively back to where Witt stood knee-deep in water, rubber-booted to the hips, fitting a feathery fly lure to the leader of a salmon-fishing line. My morningstar, she thought, the world well lost for him. And he stands there all unknowing in those clumping rubber boots. He's not one bit as buttoned-up and calm as he makes out, but if he wants to pretend, so can I.

She stood on the bank, with her arms crossed, hugging herself and watching him. He had found a sloping shelf where one of the three rivers ran into the bay, separated from the sea by a sandy spit, a position where the salmon entered the channel mouth. The tide was high, and just beyond him schools of salmon were flickering and thrashing to cross the invisible watery barrier where salt met fresh river water.

Witt grinned at her. "They pull like twenty-pounders. Real heavyweight champs," he said, then studied her carefully. "Hey," he said. "Look at you."

"Mm." She paused, then said, "You won't laugh at me if I quote Yeats?"

He had learned that nothing was really real to Betsy till she said it, named it, labeled and handled it. "Of course not."

She opened her arms to embrace the bay, the sky, the gentle hills, and declaimed, " 'And I shall have some peace there, for peace comes dropping slow—' "

"Nice. He must have been a fisherman."

"Why do they fight so hard, those fish?"

"They're coming in pairs to spawn."

"They twinkle like spinning silver spoons."

"Sure. Spin. Spoon. Spawn." He peered out over the rush and splash of the current. Several fish gleamed as they trimmed the edge of the bank into shallow pools, rippling above their fluid shadows. "All over the world, every year, they struggle and leap and jump and fight upstream with some overwhelming urge to mate and spawn." He finished exchanging the fly. "David said we all carry the ocean's salt in us, but they fight for fresh water for their spawning. After that, the fight's over, and they die."

"What noble fish."

"What a noble fisherman. I'm giving them all the breaks."

Betsy recognized his skillful cast. He placed it just right, letting the fly fall lightly to the water in a downstream curve, then drift and bob toward the fish ahead of leader and line. A riffle of water washed the fly to one side, so he reeled in and got ready to cast again. "You don't seem to be giving them the breaks," she said.

He held up his fishing tackle. "A light fly rod and a single-action reel."

"Me, I feel for the fish. Especially when they're gill to gill and fresh run from the sea. What's so sporting about your tackle?"

"There's no brake or drag on the reel. It's just me and the fish at each end. I have to use a finger as a brake. If I press too hard, blisters. Too light, and my reel overruns and tangles the monofilament line and the fish breaks free. And here, see this fly? A small single hook in a number-fourteen fly. The grip of this little hook is so light that landing these heavyweights on one is almost impossible."

"Then why do it the impossible way?"

"Because it's what you said. A noble fish. Catching it right is more important than catching it."

"Oh."

"A game fighter at the end of your line—you can feel every shiver while it fights and breaks water. Pull too hard, try too hard, one false move, and you lose the climax."

"Sounds sexual."

"Now there," he said, using brogue and winking, "don't go away thinkin' *that*." He contemplated her standing on the slope above him as she tried to hold her hair from whipping across her eyes in the breeze, somehow both seraphic and sturdy in that dazzling morning light.

She winked back. "I'm lost unless I holler loud for help." She opened her arms, "And that I surely won't do."

They made love on the beach, laughing like children, playful enough at first so that she put her hand down between his legs and said, "Ah, nothing better than a light fly rod—" but then more urgently, working with delight against one another as if it were the first and last time.

Later, at lunch, she had said, "I wonder why—"

"Why what?"

"The top and the bottom of human feelings. All Anglo-Saxon four-letter words."

"And a good thing," he said with the calm she admired, "that one of them is love."

Within a week she had found a thatched lime-washed cottage near a teacup harbor and a boat to keep moored beneath the nesting places of petrels and kittiwakes beyond Waterville. She waited cleverly a whole month to say, "Let's stay in Ireland, Witt. You're mad about it."

"You're the one who's mad mad mad. I just enjoy it."

"I've never been so happy as here with you."

He had put his arms around her. "How can I stay? Who'll run the business back home? Who'll take care of the store?"

"Sommers Pharmaceuticals can hire some bright Boston somebody from Harvard Business School—"

"And we'd be shirtsleeves to shirtsleeves in three generations, Betts. You love being the Cinderella who went off to the States and comes back as the queen. But the Sommers family is used to lots of pocket money and the business pays all our bills."

"I love the jingle of pocket money, too, Witt. After all, I grew up near here on potatoes and pawn tickets."

"I'll save you from being poor, Betts, if you'll save me from being rich. Is it a deal?"

She took his face between her hands, "Oh, Witt, if we go back you'll work at being big and successful, and I don't know how to be a big success."

"Be a small one, Betts."

"I don't know how, darling."

"I'll show you."

He did, and while they stayed in Ireland she had been both a big and a small success. But when they returned home to the States the honeymoon, just as she heard the worn phrase, was over.

"Another cup of tea?" Roone asked.

"Uh-uh. No, thanks." Betsy forced herself to fake checking her wristwatch. That time with Witt, whenever it bubbles up I'm left shaken and sorryish. Those fine wide beach sands that filled the hourglass, pinched to such a trickle through today's narrow stem. "I've got to move along." She began to slide out of the booth.

"You goin?" Volga sounded hopeful.

"Back to the trenches." On your feet, men. Keep moving, pal.

"It's early," Roone said. "What's the hurry?"

"I'm late for the hospital." She buttoned her coat firmly. I need to back away from these two jolly swagsmen. Whatever's footloose always tugs at me. I must be a heathen tinker at heart. "I've really got to rush." She snapped open her purse, but Volga held up one hand.

"Stop. You don' pay for lil cup tea." She modestly smoothed two long spitcurls from her sargasso sea of hair. "You a guest."

"Oh. Thank you very much."

Roone got up. "You working on the masterpiece in the playroom today?"

"No," she said. "The mural can wait. The paint I ordered hasn't come in yet. I'm giving the kids a puppet story hour. Hansel and Gretel, Aladdin, one of those." This was familiar hospital talk.

"I have Ob-Gyn clinic at one-thirty," he said. "And later I have to work in Doctor Sommers' lab."

"You have more odd jobs—"

"Food, clothing and shelter. And shish kebob. And med school tuition is going up another fifteen per cent."

"Doesn't hardly pay to be poor, Roone."

"You can say that again."

"Goodbye, Volga. Nice to meet you."

"Likewise, doll. Any boyfren trouble, you come see me."

Betsy found Roone watching her with uncomfortable intensity. Reaching for a casual joking lightness, she said, *"Mucho gusto."*

He nodded seriously. *"Igualmente,* Betsy. See you in church."

Outside, the street appeared strange for just a moment. The underwater murk of the Womb and the tropical fish like Volga and Tabac who swam through it were a heightened reality. They made the gray street and hurrying passersby even more sadly commonplace than usual, resembling a monotone Buffet painting. Each building: the liquor store, the self-service laundromat, the discount-sign-plastered corner pharmacy, the sagging rooming houses; how much excitement the neighbors are missing right *here!* Even the graceful old elms are blighted.

What *fabulous* luck, she thought as she hurried toward the tall buildings of the Medical Center. Who in the wide world would ever *dream* of such people only a block away? And Roone. How incredible. And yet, why not? All the other med students and interns and student nurses dropped in there. The Womb with a View was the only joint open into the wee hours after the hospital's basement cafeteria closed at midnight, a decompression chamber, part coffeehouse of Restoration England, part speakeasy of the twenties when the Yalies piled in swaddled with raccoon coats and chanting boola-boola.

What was it about Roone that made a feather stroke across her memory? His unusually long eyelashes? They made his eyes unattractively feminine. During each of the dozen times he had been assigned to help her redecorate the Pediatrics playroom, she had the fractional recognition of having met him before. More and more she discovered people of other times and places climbing rungs up to consciousness; the past mounted parallel with the present, like the other half of a ladder, past and present side by side. Sometimes she felt uncomfortable. As if I were ninety.

Second childhood! I'm alone too much, she thought. I have nobody to talk to, so I talk to myself and there's nobody to interrupt with what's real. All the yesterdays bridge over to right now.

Not until she took the shortcut across the hospital parking lot did she remember Mason. Mason, in Atlanta, so long ago. That high school vacation summer and the heated fumbling ecstatic girlishness. Mason, like Roone, blond, the same bulky athletic height with no hips at all, with a cocky muscular walk. She had not been able to recall Mason for many years. There was too much remembered pain instead of scar.

"Betts! Hello!"

"David! What a pleasant surprise!" She scanned his armload of medical journals, manila folders, books, and stacked groups of unanswered mail. From his right hand swung his car key; it dangled from Witt's Korean prison-camp identification bracelet which David used as a key chain. Why does David work so hard, she thought, when he could buy the whole place with the Sommers family pocket change? "You always look so dizzy-busy, David," she said.

"You look great," he said.

"Of course. I've just been talking to"—abruptly she recalled that Roone worked part time in David's laboratory—"to a Gypsy."

"A Gypsy?"

"Uh-huh. A real Gypsy-type Gypsy." She smiled charitably at the look on his face. "You think I'm stark raving, don't you?"

"Yes, I do. But in such unique and interesting ways. You're the champagne in our little coffeepot world."

"Oh David," she said, "now you've made me wish you could ask me to lunch. You could tell me how nice I am. You know I need admiration the way kids need vitamins."

"Oh no," he said, "I'm finished in the admiration department. You're high as a kite right now."

"Haven't had a drop."

"Sure, now. Just some Irish tea."

"Can you tell?"

"Look at a mirror, Betts. Mirror mirror on the wall."

"Oh David, if only you weren't such a stuffed shirt. You always look at me like a big brother who's proud of his cute kid sister."

"Stuffed shirt I am. Cute kid you ain't."

"Yes I am."

"Fifteen years ago, but not now. Now you're a beautiful woman, so when you talk to a stuffed shirt you mind your manners."

"Inside that stuffed shirt beats a solid-gold heart."

"In a wooden head. I know because I've just been banging it against the wall in Our Leader's administrative office."

"Oh, oh. I take back the stuffed shirt, David. Compared with Doctor Anthony Hale Douglass you're happy-go-lucky. What were you on the carpet for this time?"

He ignored her question. "How come you didn't go to Washington with Witt?"

She shook her head, her eyes dodging his, suddenly childlike. I'm not in Dublin town, one shoe off and one shoe on.

"Okay," David said. "The Court withdraws the question."

She glanced up at him quickly. "Washington?" She repeated fiercely. "Land of the free booze and home of the brave budget. Witt's always meeting somebody on a confidential something at the Coffeehouse Club. All those distinguished old backbones of the republic. David, that crowd your distinguished brother hangs around with is so constipated that going to the john becomes a State Occasion. I'll bet they have musical toilet seats that play the Marine Band's 'Hail to the Chief.' Go ahead, smirk. But if I'm going to fight my way into a girdle and some fancy clothes, I'm not going to waste it on the grandfathers of the nation."

"Oh Betts," he laughed, "you're impossible." He had never quite decided where her sensitive gentleness ended and the tea-cozy gentility began, and when the gentility became a Chekhovian charade of gay aristocracy momentarily out of funds. No one except Witt could keep up with her. Witt always makes fun of his oddball wife in the oddball Sommers clan, but when Betsy's not around we all miss her. Betsy and her brave silk flags flying for an army that was never there. "You're just what the stuffed-shirt Sommers clan needs."

"I wish you'd tell that to my husband, your stuffed-shirt brother. He was a mighty man of wrath last night when I told him, Yankee, sí, Washington, no."

They avoided the real reason why husband and wife hardly ever traveled together. Betsy and Witt had walked, then stumbled and then crawled through all the stations of the cross of those who want children but cannot have them. Even Dr. Mayoso, in the days of his University of Havana professorship, hadn't been able to help.

She fished her white-frame sunglasses out of her purse and slid them on. Usually she wore them everywhere out of doors. She believed the bright daylight hurt her eyes, but sometimes she suspected that the dark reflecting glasses were for her a one-way window on the world behind which she could look out with a green-eyed vagrant sexuality, secretive and safe. "All of a sudden I feel like a poor wayfaring stranger," she said. "I feel like crying."

"Just do what comes natural, Betts."

She flashed into laughter. "Ho! I've tried *that*. Nothin' but trouble that-away. David, you *sure* you can't ask me to lunch?"

"Sorry. No can do." He gestured vaguely toward the hospital's basement cafeteria. "Just had an early lunch in Ptomaine Tavern with Doctor Douglass and the District Attorney. Those two are no answer to the problem of hidden hunger."

"But if you took me to lunch, David, we could each have an ice-cold martini or two—two, *taboo*—rhymes, doesn't it?—and you could make a very civilized pass at me while I played ladylike and aloof and hard to get."

He swung his keychain in a flip-flopping arc around his finger. A whirling dervish, he thought. She's sore as hell at Witt.

"Well?" She struck a pose. "Half aloof is better than none."

"Ouch. Your weakness for puns."

She exaggerated the cadence of Irish speech. "Surely, en route to the scaffold I'd hang me head in shame."

"You ought to pitch a carnival tent and sell hootchy-kootchy tickets."

"I've got the nicest legs, David. Bit of shadow under the eyes, maybe, but in the leg department the Gallup Poll shows one hundred per cent."

"Betts, I've seen you in a bathing suit. I'll admit that whoever put all the parts together wanted a really nice model on the road."

She arched her eyebrows at him, then put one small foot up on the bumper of the nearest parked car and slid the borders of her coat and her volunteer uniform up high enough so that she could adjust the garter fastener on the hem of her stocking.

"Betts, you're higher'n a cockeyed kite. Pulling a striptease stunt like this, just for kicks?" A short groove of disapproval deepened between his eyebrows.

"Uh-huh." She reached under her thigh to fix the garter in back. "My secret ambition—all my *real* ambitions are secret—is to be a stripteaser." She stood up and dropped her coat back into place. "In Paris, when Witt and I were on our honeymoon, I sneaked off one Thursday—it's only on Thursdays—to a place near Boulevard de Clichy, Le Strip Tease Club. Ever hear of it? Le Concours International Amateurs *qui sera jugés par le public*. You pay three hundred francs' entrance fee with seven other amateurs. The lights go down, the music comes up, the M.C. with the slicked-down pompadour says Et *voilà*, Mademoiselle Bettsee, and there you are, on stage, practically blinded by the spotlight. He announces your measurements over the microphone. I was almost afraid he'd say *soixante-neuf*. You'd never guess. I'm eighty-six, sixty-five, eighty-six."

"Impossible."

"In centimeters."

"Now listen, Betts—"

"Never breathe a *word* of it, promise? The audience thought I was one of those barebreasted English girls from the Bluebells—you know they come only from very good English families, don't you? And go to work two by two and come home two by two, like a convent class?—and, David, I *wowed* 'em! Laid 'em in the aisles. Fan*tas*tic, David, up there all alone, with five hundred men crouching in the dark out there, and you can let 'em have it right between the eyes, and they can't do a thing."

"Step down," David said. "Next witness, please."

"You don't believe me?"

"You're a fabulist, Betts. All the world's a stage. You sure hate to tell the difference between what's on stage and what's in the audience. And the more forbidden the better, I suppose." Betsy's sham affectations that were real, he thought. Her realities that were affectations, her dance of the seven veils, her come-hither smile that promised—if you could only catch her—a thousand and one nights.

"You really don't believe me, do you?" she was saying. "Poor mad Betts. No facts, just fancy."

"What's the difference whether you did it or dreamt it?" He shifted his armload of books and papers. "Betts, you know I always enjoy passing the time of day with you, but duty calls."

"You think I'm crazy, don't you?"

"In a sort of pop-the-cork raise-high-the-toast sort of way, yes. Like I said, champagne in a coffeepot world."

"You worry when I get high this way, don't you?"

"A little." He mimicked her voice. "You just luh-ove to play with fire."

"But I'm on my way to be a Play Lady in the Pediatrics ward, then back back to my li'l ol' shack in New Haven, Connect-eye-cut. So all's well that ends well, isn't it?"

"Betts, sarcasm does not become you."

Before she could stop herself, she said, "If I don't have a man pretty soon—Davey, this is one of those days I'm a bit afraid of myself. I'm just awful, aren't I?"

"Don't be foolish, Betts. You need to have your own doctor, somebody you can talk to—"

"I can't talk to anybody but you—or your friend Mayoso. But you're both so far away."

"Betts, I can't be your doctor. It's impossible. And Mayoso lives in another world. There are a dozen good doctors here, and you need—"

"I need you for a friend, Davey. You never make a pass at me. You never judge me. I love *you*, taboo."

"Mad mad mad."

"When'll you get back from the L.I.V.E. clinic?"

"Fourish."

"And your Gyn rounds at four-thirtyish? I'll be finished in the play-room by then. Just about teatime. You can stir up some of that hot tur-pentine you call home-brewed genuine laboratory coffee."

He smiled. The slow Sommers smile, she thought swiftly, so kind, so incomplete, so understanding, so self-assured with money in the bank and more where *that* came from, and so ready to give you anything but them-selves. Witt carried that smile last night. Infuriating.

"It's a date, Betts. Home-brewed coffee at teatime. Dad'll be delighted to see you." He transferred the load of books to his other arm.

"You'd better go." Her voice faltered. "I apologize for holding up your parade." She pouted a little kiss in the air toward him and hurried away, her heels tapping on the parking lot pavement, staccato. She glanced back over her shoulder and saw him standing there, watching her go, a curious frown on his face. She stuck out the pink tip of her tongue at him. Oh hell, she thought, alone again, but I don't give a tinker's damn. The heather honey is always atop the mountain.

David admired her special high-heeled stride, her slender shoulders-back chin-up way of walking, the hair lifting back from her face.

"When I walk into a room," Betsy had once told him, "I want every-body to say *ah*."

"But when you walk out," he had asked her, "do you want them to say *aha?*"

Junior Miss on parade, he thought, as he turned and sidled between cars to where his Volkswagen was parked. That's what his wife Alice had said about Betsy. "She always struts as if she's on display, David. Miss Drum Majorette."

"I think she looks great," he had said. "If you don't mind."

"Well, a man would think so. She isn't natural. She shows up in a bath-ing suit, but never gets wet. She's like a model in Junior Miss sportswear or something."

"It's the something," he had said. "That universally appreciated little something. D'you expect her to go barefooted?"

Alice had sniggered. "You know what I mean, Casanova. She's like a selfconscious teenager. I don't know if those four-inch heels are for reach-ing up to a man's chin, or just to show off her doll-baby legs."

"Meow."

"Oh, I know I sound catty, David. I'll even admit it—I *am* catty. I sort of envy her. That color combination, black hair and outer-space eyes. She needs two hours just to get herself looking bandboxy glamorous. Like a Barbie doll, not wearing just clothes but an outfit. Every hair in place. She combs those wavy black tresses every hour on the hour."

"Alice, her being a glamour girl is as much her picture of herself as my being a doctor is me, or your raising a family is you."

"What's *that* profound pronouncement supposed to mean?"

"Simple. We generally behave like what we think we are, don't we?"

"The identity routine? Right out of ye olde textbooks?"

"Yes ma'm. The identity routine. Right out of the books."

"Listen, pal," his wife Alice had said, "you can't worry me with them there big words." She had stopped smiling. "But sometimes I do worry a bit about li'l ol' David playing on his li'l ol' harp. His li'l ol' Irish harpie."

"You're not kidding about this, are you, Alice?"

"No, I guess not. Not even one little bit. I should pretend to be very casual, I know, but I can't. I don't like the Lorelei act she puts on every time she sees you."

"You think Betsy has some kind of magic?"

"Well, I've seen grown men act like kids when she sits down, the way she sits down, and crosses those legs—especially those legs. Especially everything. And when she turns on the blarney—really, David, when she lights herself up like a candle, every man around flutters up to be burned. You've seen her. One day she's a poetic Irish faerie queen, the next day she's the cool Anglo-Irish aristocrat of the huntin' shootin' country gentry. One minute she's an intellectual, style of 1890, the next minute she's Cinderella sweeping the peat turf ashes off the cottage hearth."

"I knew you and Mother disliked her. But you detest her."

"No, I don't, David. She just worries me, that's all."

"Alice," he had said, "you've been fooled by the glossy façade. Everyone is. It's the old old story of the beautiful girl. She's the same as everybody else until she's forced to find out that nobody wants her when she's like everybody else. They want her to be different, a showoff possession. So the beauties show off."

"Oh, I know, I know—I've heard the same from your father. You and he believe she's just a sweet misunderstood pixie. A poor little lamb who's lost her way, baa-baa-baa."

"As a matter of fact, Alice, she has. Now don't get that look on your face. She's lonely and lost as a mermaid on dry land. All her big come-on—can't you tell she's counting on me never to take her seriously?"

"David," Alice had said, "have you any idea of how intelligent and at the same time upside-down you can sound?"

He had grasped both her shoulders. "Mind if I turn you upside down? Just to see how intelligent you are?"

He dumped his armload of books on the passenger side of his Volkswagen, then went around to edge into the driver's seat.

That Betsy. A mermaid on dry land. Thrashing around.

No wonder, he thought as he wheeled into the slow stream of traffic, the ancient Greeks blamed such agitation on *hystera,* the uterus. Women like her try to be up and down for men, both at the same time, and they become shaky. Even the doctors believed the Greeks far into our not so scientific age. In Freud's Vienna and Charcot's Paris and Osler's London there were surgeons removing the female uterus, absolutely certain that the innermost temple of demons was thereby cast out. Some women still believe it. And here I am, poking through town on my way to a maternity clinic to exorcise a few more demons.

A luminous neon halo over the varsity joint he was passing fluorescently spelled out A WOMB WITH A VIEW. Betsy's favorite hangout for a scuppa tea on her hospital volunteer days. The name flashed the new collegiate humor, biologic as always, only more so; the boisterous comic embraces changed to swinging haymakers. Strong men into the lifeboats first, women link arms on deck as the ship goes down.

"The saving grace of irony," his father had said yesterday at lunch. "You know, David, the classic definition of irony is the difference between things we profess and things as they really are. Well, in my declining years I do believe that even irony is gone because nobody knows how things really are."

I dismissed that yesterday, David thought as his car crept along. The academic summation, setting-up exercises for the professor emeritus at lunch. But somehow the idea lingers, its generality bumping into contradictory particulars. Such as Mayoso, years ago commenting ironically during one of the Sommers family Sunday afternoon dinners. Mayoso had balanced his long Havana cigar on the edge of an ashtray and had said to Father, "Irony, Doctor Sommers? When you have a bayonet shoved up to the rectosigmoid flexure the way Batista's boys are doing in Cuba, one may lose the philosophic stimulus to become ironic, no?"

Mayoso had written only once this year, from Puerto Rico, a card at Christmas—*los Tres Reyes* riding cardboard camels toward a paper star of Bethlehem—with an enigmatic valedictory scrawled on the inside fold: *The fight goes on. Tragic but necessary. One learns how easy it is to be crucified, but how hard it is to rise from the dead. I pray I may see all the Sommers family some time during the New Year. Muchas felicidades.*

Mayoso sticking to his guns, taking risks, in the Martí family tradition, David thought. Nothing ironic in his note. For a man named after Dionysus, much too sober, maybe grim. That's how things are with him.

And with me? Yes, we have no ironies today. Only a circle from the irrational to the unreasonable and back again. From tired young Dr. Greene to pussyfootin' old Dr. Douglass rapping my knuckles for the District Attorney. Carmencita's emergency-room prayers and Betsy's wacky parking-lot conversation. Witt's flying down to Washington, as always, corporate but alone. Dad's *visions, visions*. Life's one hell of a lot simpler in my lab. Causes have effects there. Effects have causes. Very little of this muddleheaded human rough-and-tumble. Bedlam.

Red light. David stepped automatically on the brake pedal, instantly obedient to the robot traffic control.

How things really are. With all of us, he thought, gentlemen and players. So, my researching friend, if you're so cottonpickin' smart, tell me: how are things?

5 DeWitt Sommers had slept with a guarded stiffness, like a wounded man lying on a stretcher. Night battles had marched through his head, leaving a ragged procession of stragglers, so that the touch of dawn slipping thinly through the venetian blinds awakened him suddenly in the narrow bed. One moment he dreamed through alarms and confusions; in the next he was awake and alert as a sentry.

But against what enemy? He felt annoyed with himself and combed his hair with his fingers. Fragments of the night were still with him: Betsy, during their stay in Ireland, a newborn morning, hills of heather in the vivid air. *What noble fish*, she had said in a strange spell-caught way. He had sighed in his sleep, defenseless against the pain of loss. Betsy, he thought, ready to reach out for her, but then, from nowhere, a meeting of the Board of Directors, with the chairman of the Finance Committee warning him angrily: *You'll destroy the company, Witt! You can't ride off in two directions at once. We cannot afford to expand in South America while the cost of our research doubles each year.* And the other voices, but whose? All warning voices, but about what?

He got up and tilted the blinds open, glazing the room with early morning light: the brown painted metal bed, the bookshelves empty except for a card which read: *Coffeehouse Club Members and Guests will please observe the* 3 p.m. *Checkout Time.* Above the dark stained chest of drawers hung a framed steel engraving of the Roman Forum balanced on the opposite walls by an engraving of the Parthenon and a sketch of the White House before the British burned it down in 1814. Beside him, on the small wooden student's desk, the dark green scabrous blotter had curled upward in its corners with fatigue; hieroglyphics of ink blots were scattered over it. Any one of the blots, Witt thought only half quizzically, might be another $E = MC^2$, because some of the world's most distinguished scientists visiting Washington had slept in this corridor of monkish rooms. Maybe that was why the place was so ascetically bare-ribbed and lean, like the low-rent rooms most of them had lived in during the Depression years of the thirties. In my company, our newer breed of scientists are younger, wearers of British tweeds and smokers of pipes, travelers on champagne jet flights as company consultants and in tourist class as government task-force advisers. But David and my father, Witt thought, both feel right at home here.

He shaved above the skimpy sink in the corner and examined himself in the small mirror which was screwed to the wall.

"You look like a man of distinction," Betsy had said brightly yesterday morning, at home. "Maybe I ought to dye a silver streak in my hair to keep up with you." Damn it, he had thought, why this everlasting game of Let's Pretend? Why does she believe she can live only by changing costumes and hair styles, like an actress in a repertory theater?

The harsh electric light above the mirror did not make him look like Betsy's man of distinction: the president of an international corporation who must be decisive at breakfast with his legal adviser, easy and unhurried for his meeting with his mother immediately afterward, and then relaxed and friendly with the new crowd over at the Food and Drug Administration who wanted more information from Sommers Pharmaceuticals about the company's clinical research with contraceptive pills.

From Massachusetts Avenue, on the other side of the Club, came the working noises of the Capital Transit buses stopping for passengers on the corner in front of the Club and then moving off in low gear. Through the faint hum of traffic tooted an occasional auto horn. The early morning butchers, bakers and candlestick makers, Witt thought. As a thin rim of sun glinted in the mirror, the memory of Betsy on the beach at Dingle Bay grazed him again for the last time before the day's agenda started. Another of his efficient visits to Washington had begun. Sunupmanship.

Witt walked down the curving stairs to the small lobby of the Coffeehouse Club. The Senegalese student who worked the morning shift to help pay his way through Georgetown University was just putting on a red coat like that of some Cossack general. He stared at Witt, surprised, and said brightly, "Early morning start, sir!"

"What's new from Dakar, Iban?" Witt asked.

"Don't ask me that thing, Mr. Sommers. I'm too hard study English and Fall of the Roman Empire history."

In the breakfast room, the pale sun through the large bay window made the floor of unoccupied tables beneath the pseudo-Spanish arches look empty as a deserted ship. Three waitresses and a busboy were setting out napkins and silverware precisely, turning water glasses upside down at each place, until one of the girls saw Witt in the doorway and called across the room, "Not till seven, sir!"

Witt wandered back through the corridor in which a wall of photographic portraits of members who were Pulitzer prize winners faced a wall of the pictures of Nobel prize laureates. In a toothy smiling public relations age, almost all were smiling. With time on his hands, Witt moved slowly down the line, reading the names of the non-smilers. They had the open-eyed acute stare of Dantesque sinners glimpsing the hells of nuclear war and mass starvation. Physicists or population experts, he decided. They've earned the right to be unfashionable non-smilers.

At the corner opposite the elevator he stopped to examine unhurriedly a different picture which had been hung at eye level. In it, two medieval monks raised their arms in a gesture of sending on his way a third monk departing down the church steps. Beneath the picture in an imitation of medieval script was the legend *Bene Dictum, Benedicte!* Witt glanced irritably at his wristwatch, then, to fill the time, he read the words of St. Benedict within the frame:

If any pilgrim monk find fault with anything, or expose it, reasonably, and with the humility of charity, the Abbot shall discuss it prudently, lest perchance God had sent him for this very thing. But, if he had been found gossipy and contumacious in the time of his sojourn as guest, it shall be said to him, honestly, that he must depart. If he does not go, let two stout monks, in the name of God, explain the matter to him.

Witt looked at his watch again, then idly scanned the roster of new members and their sponsors. In last month's group he spotted a name in capital letters: DIONISIO MAYOSO MARTÍ, M.D. Sponsors: Benjamin Nathaniel Sommers, M.D., and David Sommers, M.D. How now, pilgrim monks, Witt thought, and, for the first time that morning, he smiled.

He turned to the bulletin board opposite. A printed notice read: SCIENCE IN A WORLD OF WIDENING HORIZONS, a lecture by the chairman of the Atomic Energy Commission. Beside it, typewritten on Coffeehouse Club stationery, was the note: "The following question will come before the next meeting: Should the beams and panels of the library ceiling be painted a uniform light gray color?" Under this was a small sample card to illustrate how the members could sign up for reservations for a wine-tasting rendezvous of the Chevaliers de Tastevin.

A ruled-off oblong in the corner of the bulletin board was labeled, 75 YEARS AGO TODAY. Beneath it was a photomontage blending press clippings, fragments of official correspondence and photographs of bald men wearing bushy whiskers. Next to a small sepia-toned oval portrait of President Grover Cleveland was an excerpt from the New York *Telegraph*: MONROE DOCTRINE CHALLENGED. British Guiana frontier erupts. Venezuela asks U.S. aid. A fragment of an official note in curlicue script from a U.S. State Department official: "Willful aggression by the British upon Venezuela will be interpreted as a threat to the United States."

An excerpt from an article on sea power by Admiral Alfred T. Mahan: ". . . The Caribbean is a vital military crossroads . . ."

From a letter in the New York *Times*: "When E. L. Godkin, Editor of the *Nation*, opposes the Venezuela Message and calls red-blooded Americans a 'half-crazed public,' he speaks as a mad man and a Celtic immigrant. I say burn the *Nation*, horsewhip Godkin and ship him by the next boat back to his native peat bogs."

A sentence in a letter written by William James, Professor of Philosophy at Harvard University: "Of Venezuela, it is instructive to find how near the surface in all of us old fighting spirit lies and how slight an appeal will wake it up. Once *really* waked, there is no retreat."

A sentence from a letter written by Theodore Roosevelt to Admiral Mahan: "What fearful mental degeneracy results from reading the New York *Evening Post* or the *Nation* as a steady thing."

What a solid self-righteous bewhiskered time that was, Witt thought as he turned away from the bulletin board. The history of this country was a history of frontiers, up to and including the open-door policy in China. My plan for expansion in South America—good or bad? At what point do profits become exploitation? He strolled back into the lobby. The student in his splendid red coat was polishing the brassbound slot of the mahogany box into which members could drop suggestions to the House Committee.

"Care for the morning papers, Mr. Sommers?" the boy asked courteously.

"Thank you."

"New York *Times*, Manchester *Guardian* or the Washington *Post*?"

"All three, please."

Witt surveyed the headlines as he walked back up the curving carpeted stairs which led to the long gallery on the second floor. The *Times* reported BRITAIN'S STICKY WICKET: THE COMMON MARKET. In the next column,

POPE FORGIVES GALILEO. Witt smiled. Except for the accident of time, Galileo might be a member of the Club.

The President of Venezuela warns the OAS about terrorist infiltration in Caracas.

U.S.A. GHETTOS EXPLODE. Angry leaders reject birth control clinics as anti-Negro plot. Militants predict Saigon-type guerrilla underground in American cities. "Brothers in our worldwide struggle," says Castro.

Famine in India. In the Manchester *Guardian* the lead story was EAST OF SUEZ: YES OR NO? Alongside it was a story, datelined Paris, about the report of a French Minister to the Cabinet about his visit to Peking.

In the Washington *Post*, a headline about the Population Commission of the United Nations caught Witt's eye: U.N. DELEGATE SIDESTEPS PUERTO RICAN CHURCH-STATE CONFLICT. "Mrs. Marjorie Sommers, U.S. delegate to the United Nations Population Council, refused to comment last night on the absence of birth control legislation in Puerto Rico. 'Governor Santos Roque,' she said, 'is in a difficult position. . . .'"

His mother had been the overnight guest at the Vice President's house in Georgetown. Marjorie had telephoned him last night to answer the call he had placed to her in New Haven the day before.

She had laughed on the phone last night. "Silly, isn't it, Witt? We can meet so much easier here in Washington than we can back home."

The Vice President had come on the extension phone. "You have to work out some solution, Witt. The President wants your mother to continue to head up our delegation in the United Nations but it's damned embarrassing with her holding so much stock in a company that makes contraceptives."

Witt had felt himself frowning at the phone. "Mother has nothing to do with the policy-making and operations of our company," he said.

"I know that, Witt, and you know it and the President knows it, but how many people do you suppose would believe it?"

He folded the newspaper under his arm and lazed his way through the magazine room to the library. Marjorie had a birthday soon—who's counting, she liked to ask—but he knew she enjoyed getting presents, and if he could find a recent copy of *Rare and Valuable Books* from that London outfit on Marylebone High Street he might be able to find one of the old herbals she collected. The library was so dim that, as he turned on several lamps, he decided to cast his vote to paint the beams and ceilings a uniform light gray color.

In the bookcase labeled NEW BOOKS BY MEMBERS, there was a privately printed monograph on the *Toy Soldiers of Yesteryear* beside a heavy volume titled *China Today: Tomorrow the World.* Next to these some casual reader had put down a copy of *Ivory Hammer 3: The Year at Sotheby's and Parke-Bernet* and a slender clothbound book lettered along its spine: *The Defense of Terrorism—Trotsky.*

Witt's father, Dr. Benjamin Nathaniel Sommers, had enjoyed pointing out to him with a pretense of scholarly fussiness, only a month ago, that the leather-bound books were not being hand-rubbed with lanolin often enough.

He had shown Witt the book in a severely black morocco cover, written by Witt's grandfather in 1906, to convince doctors that contraceptive products under the Sommers label were always of the finest quality. "If our great surgeons such as Halstead and Cushing protect the patient during surgery," the old gentleman had written, "by using thin seamless rubber gloves which do not permit the passage of a single microorganism, then the same thin rubber material can be used as a sheath over the masculine generative organ to prevent conception."

A great idea, Witt had thought when he read his grandfather's book, so good that it almost bankrupted the growing company called Sommers Medicinal Tinctures. Hardly anyone wanted to limit having babies in 1906. The young country to which Ebenezer Philander Sommers had migrated believed that more people made more progress which made more prosperity, so the old gentleman had been forced to drop his neo-Malthusian broadsides. Today, he thought, we'd call it changing the company image. Within a single year, Ebenezer Sommers had changed the name of his new rubber condoms to FATIMA and had printed on the package a sultry odalisque in transparent silk pantaloons to invoke the veiled world of sultans surrounded by harem concubines. At first, because some research doctor in Europe named Ehrlich had discovered syphilis was caused by a germ, Ebenezer Sommers had emphasized that his rubber condoms protected men from social diseases. But safety did not sell; Sommers had quickly shifted to Pleasure *Plus* Protection.

"You see," Dr. Benjamin Sommers had told Witt, "your grandfather had to learn fast. He came off a leaky immigrant boat into New York without a penny in his pocket, not a stitch on his back. His first job was packing sausage skins. He used to watch the other men steal the skins to use as contraceptives, so he began to buy the skins and reprocess them. He sold them by mail at first. His slogan was: Thin Skins. Each One Wins. Can't you just *see* it? Gaslight, hoopskirts, Sin still spelled with a capital S, and people making a great to-do about the difference between a Lady and a Woman."

"Now it all sounds so innocent and a little comic," Witt had said to his father.

"Oh no," his father had said. "It was all dignity, high-button shoes and a gold watch chain over your vest. Your grandfather kept the Sabbath and everything else he could lay his hands on. When he started in business in 1885—that was two years before Merck opened its American branch—he gave away a free spermaceti candle—why do you look so odd?"

"Spermaceti candles?"

"They were the rage among the ladies, then. Every lady wanted her necklace and rings to shine by spermaceti candlelight. Free premiums of candles turned FATIMA into a moneymaker. Why, Witt, overnight your grandfather cleaned up. He bought the first Stanley Steamer in Connecticut, people in New Haven would set their clocks when his car steamed by in the morning. Everything he touched—laxatives, ointments, lotions, tinctures, medicinal wines—business boomed."

Dr. Benjamin Sommers had shaken his head admiringly. "How the doctors in those days believed in the B's! Big brown bottle, big spoon, bitter medicine. Your grandfather came out early with the new compressed pills to replace the horse-sized ones. He made his detail men wear top hats and white gloves and carry silver-plated hammers so they could demonstrate that their competitors' pills were hard as nails. He guaranteed pure products. He sent his best chemists to study in Germany. Sommers Medicinal Tinctures Company needed senna for laxatives so he started buying in Egypt. You think you've made Sommers international? He had an overseas branch just for essences: rosemary from Spain, sandalwood from India, attar of roses from Bulgaria. Then citronella from Ceylon, vanilla beans from Madagascar, licorice from Turkey. We even sold ant eggs as fish food! The year I began to lose my baby teeth, your grandfather figured out a way to hold false teeth in place with karaya gum and tragacanth." Dr. Sommers had paused, then said, "I remember walking with my father through our New York warehouse and calling off the items like a boy train conductor. Belladonna, mandrake, wild cherry bark and calumba root, golden seal and passion flower, spearmint and wintergreen. And my two favorites, bhang and ginseng, from Shanghai. People bought them as aphrodisiacs. Your grandfather shocked his British managers by establishing our London sales office for Fatima condoms on Maidenhead Lane. His British letterhead and cable address became famous. He knew P. T. Barnum in Bridgeport, and used to quote him to the staff. 'Don't care what they say about you so long as they *talk* about you!' Oh, Witt, I'll tell you, son, the sky was the limit for your grandfather! He became an Officer of the Venerable Order of the Hospital of St. John of Jerusalem. Honorary Freedom of the Society of Apothecaries. Légion d'Honneur. Honorary Correspondent of the Ancient College of Doctors in Madrid, the scroll presented by the great Professor Patric O'Brien Hernández himself."

"Madrid? Irish?"

"Well, practically Irish. Ever hear of the Celt-Iberians? The Spanish and the Irish. Heads and tails on the same coin. Ask Betsy, if you don't believe me. She thinks she's the unofficial ambassador from Dublin, doesn't she?"

"I'll have to remember that for my Rotary International speeches, in South America."

"Witt, you can tell them Sommers International opened its first permanent office in South America during World War Two. I designed a new kind of pyrethrum spray to kill malaria mosquitoes. Malaria was knocking out more men than the Japanese were. Remember my bringing you and David to the Pentagon after the war? That ceremony was to give me the Medal for Merit."

The Medal for Merit. The Pentagon. His father had accepted the medal, sounding oddly shy in this capital city of chesty assertion. As always, Dr. Sommers put a pinhole into a ballooning ceremony which had become pompous. "Can you spare another medal?" he had remarked. "I have those *two* boys of mine to decorate when we leave here."

Then lunch at the Coffeehouse Club, which at that time was in Lafayette Park diagonally across from the White House. After lunch, he and his brother David had walked briskly with their father across the park to Blair House where the President was staying while the White House was renovated.

"We're just going to say hello to the President for a few minutes," Dr. Sommers had said to Witt and David. "He's a very busy man, so don't pester him with a lot of questions." Witt remembered the guard outside Blair House tapping over them carefully for concealed weapons before allowing them under the canopy which shaded the flight of stairs up to the front hall. Some Puerto Rican Nacionalistas had tried to gun their way into Blair House. A guard had been killed.

"Your wife still trying to make Connecticut vote Republican?" the President had asked. "Can't you make her stay home, Ben, and take care of these two fine boys?" Witt remembered that on the President's desk was a sign lettered: THE BUCK STOPS HERE.

Years later, during the war in Korea, Witt had met his father and mother for lunch at the Club. He had wangled an overnight pass near the end of his Marine training at Camp Lejeune, and his father and mother had come down from New Haven to meet him about halfway, in Washington. He had survived Marine bootcamp training, the iron-gutted drill instructors, the sweat-drenched staggering marches of the USMC, Uncle Sam's Magnificent Crotch, close-order drill and march cadence, tromp stomp head up heels on the deck, *Hup!* Two! Three! Four! Come on, you raggedy-ass yardbird gyrenes, y'all look like you been shot at and missed, crapped on and hit, suck in them guts or I'll knock your ass off and piss on it. He had braved the wild gung-ho check-and-raise five-card stud with a dollar ante, pot limit, joker works aces, and the color of cash Marine green. Whadda ya mean, *tough?* You shoulda been here yestiday when it was *really* tough. One step outa line, you keep office hours in the brig and go Asiatic in private. So keep a tight hole, buddy, and send your heart home to Momma, your ass belongs to the Corps. He had endured and survived.

His parents had seemed like people from a strange far-off civilian planet when he had met them in Washington.

"Witt!" Marjorie had cried. "You're so *thin.*"

"But all muscle," his father prompted.

"I'm still alive," Witt said. "There were a couple of times I thought I'd never make it." His brother David had wanted to volunteer with him, but their parents had insisted one of the boys must stay home. Witt and David had tossed a coin to decide, and Witt had won. Or lost, he decided much later.

After a slow lunch at the Coffeehouse Club, carefully casual because the war news from Korea was so bad, they had stood talking on the small tree-shaded patio, putting off the time they would have to say goodbye.

His father had said, "You may see some of these trees when you get to Korea, Witt. They're ginkgos. Very rare outside of Asia. The only living things that are ten million years old."

Marjorie Sommers had slipped her hand under Witt's arm. "Your father," she said to Witt. "He's just trying to say that this too shall pass away."

Witt never knew how she had wept that night.

Finally Witt found the rare-book catalogue he had come into the Club library for, and, after flipping a few pages, running his finger down each list, he located a copy of *Hexandrian Plants, by Mrs. Edward Bury. A large folio engraved about 1831. Now available bound in contemporary half-green morocco.* Sounded just right for Marjorie's birthday—not the Mrs. Marjorie Sommers whom the President had appointed to the U.N. Population Council, not the brisk lady executive at ease with reporters, but the Marjorie of gardening gloves, pruning shears, tender nursemaid of flats of seedlings ripening in her greenhouse. Marie Antoinette, her husband called her. After this, the deluge.

Witt strolled out of the Club library slowly. It was a room of a world going, going, gone, even though his father insisted it was the cutting edge of the twentieth century. "Witt," his father had said only a month ago, "this is a congregation of the lay bishops of science. A new kind of synod. A Sanhedrin of the new power."

Witt had grinned at him affectionately. "If you need tranquilizers, Dad, I can get you some free samples."

"Go ahead, laugh at the old coot. When you and David were youngsters, Einstein couldn't get anybody to listen to him and Szilard about nuclear physics and atoms. He had to blast a path to the President. This new Club crowd, they just pick up the telephone."

Witt stopped before the tall French doors overlooking Massachusetts Avenue. Across the street was a formal mansion much like the one occupied by the Club. All stone, with a tall Romanesque gateway to the curved cobblestone drive. Beside it was the new Washington, a high-rise apartment house, mostly picture-window glass and red brick.

The morning traffic was heavier now, bumper to bumper. In the tree lawn along the street five elm trees made high green arches, just as they did on the lawn around his parents' house in Connecticut. Very different from ginkgos, Witt thought, looking out at them, still swimming in the flood of memories. His father's voice: *Very rare outside of Asia*—and his mother's: *He's trying to say this too shall pass away*.

Korea had not passed away. The frozen dark tunnel of fighting a rearguard action against the Chinese from Chosin Reservoir to evacuation beaches at Hungnam had not passed away. A retreat filled Chosin with wounded crying out as Chinese execution squads moved among them from shell hole to shell hole; the open-mouthed, gasping, infuriated Chinese soldier whose bayonet was deflected by Witt's armored vest so that, after one more blunted stab, he aimed his rifle point-blank as Witt lay holding his torn frozen leg muscles, firing point-blank but a fraction high. Witt's helmet had deflected the bullet just barely enough so that his scalp had been creased by fire, and he thereby lived to learn about the communality of men in prison camps and the educational benefits of hunger and horror. He often dreamed of the sentinel elm trees, graceful and brooding over their sunspecked shadows like great green ballet dancers circling his home, their upper branches creaking in the wind like ship's rigging, and his father's voice, trying hard to be casual about the Asiatic ginkgo which was ten million years old.

He had held this dream in his head when he was chosen by the Chinese to be one of the American soldiers who would voluntarily confess he had seen evidence of American germ warfare against helpless North Korean women and children. His body had never been harmed directly by any tool of torture, but he had been kept in a hole in the ground for two months, with no food on alternating days, ordered out to stand at attention until he fainted, and kept upright under a gushing downspout throughout the spring rains. The Chinese officers who questioned him while a guard pressed a gun barrel at the back of his head all seemed to believe genuinely that the Americans used germ warfare—how else could the sanitation-trained Chinese troops have louse-born typhus among them?—and through this Witt had burrowed deeper and deeper into his dream until the elm trees of home became twisted ginkgo shapes whose ten-million-year-old roots reached out toward his throat.

Korea had been the splintered hinge on which his entire life had turned. He was one of the battered raggedy-ass Ridgerunners who fought through the ambush tunnel from the Chosin Reservoir to Hagaru to Koto-ri and Chinhung-ni, carrying out their wounded, lugging their dead lashed beneath gun barrels, slugging every mile over a lunatic terrain.

The Marines had never been up against the Chinese infantry, not since the War of the Righteous Fists, called by Europeans the Boxer Rebellion; the trained men of the Chinese IX Army Group under General Sung Shin-lun were very different from the starved mobs of the 1900 war. Now these men served under professionals, graduates of Whampoa Military Academy, veterans of fighting Chiang Kai-shek and of the Long March under Mao Tse-tung. One hundred thousand had begun the trek, their Chang Cheng, from Kiangsi 6,000 miles to the safety of Yenan. Twenty thousand survivors reached Yenan one year later. Anyone who straggled or fell along the road was executed or abandoned. Ten years later, victory over the warlords and the Japanese. From such veterans came the Chinese career officers.

In Korea, General Sung had led the IX Army Group across the Yalu River and then over 150 miles of mountain terrain, a forced march in bitter winter, slogging through the snow, some wearing fur boots but most shod in canvas sneakers, living on Korean rice and powdered dried peas eaten in cold lumps when there was no time for cooking. In the beginning there was no time for cooking.

Sung, and his commander, General Lin Piao, chose night attacks when the American artillery and air support were blind. In the opaque cold darkness their infantrymen could reverse the heavy quilted greenish cotton Chinese uniforms into white snow covers, then creep forward, waddling on elbows and belly as close to the American positions as possible, and then, when their rah-tatata-TAH bugles and ear-piercing whistles commanded them across the frozen air, leaping up and charging into hand-to-hand combat screaming MAHLEEN DIE!

This was bayonet and grenade fighting, in which small Chinese units used their guerrilla experience to infiltrate United Nations' lines and claw apart platoons they succeeded in isolating. Chinese companies fanned out, using their tested Hachi Shiki V-shape formation to outflank the road-bound U.N. troops. In daylight fighting, Communist commanders exchanged their men's lives for bullets. Press-ganged South Korean conscripts were sent against U.N. positions. If conscripts were too few, crowds of refugees were rounded up and driven at bayonet point into zones of fire, then a second wave of recent North Korean recruits, a third wave of battle-tested infantry, and, by the time the fourth wave of veterans charged, the Americans, the British, the ROK's, the Turks, the French, were out of ammunition.

The hundred thousand Chinese infantrymen of the IX Army Group had been told by their commissars that the Oberbandit MacArthur had had to beg the Soviets to save him from Japan. Now, their Order of the Day said, the Hitlerite MacArthur was a Wall Street house dog. He had given the viciously brutal Marines orders to drench Korean soil with the tears and blood of Korean children, women, and aged patriots. Like the Hitlerite S.S., the yellow-leg Marines were indoctrinated savages trained to scorch the earth and rape the wives and sisters of men at the front. Afterward, the Marine running dogs would plunder the people's food and send home to America war loot packages of stolen rice.

The fighting had been terrible among the brittle cadaverous rocks of North Ridge and Fox Hill. Once they had been saved, Witt remembered, by the British Royal Marines' 41st Commandos, incredibly clean-shaven, wearing berets instead of helmets, leapfrogging through the ragged bitter encrusted Marines of George Company, 3rd Battalion, going up the hill against the Chinese, not running but insolently walking in formation through a rain of mortar shells.

Frozen Chosin had been cold beyond belief. Witt had learned how you can be brainless with cold, your brain a fistful of ice, shrunken and clanking inside your skull; your eyelids stiff and scratchy as wooden splinters, the sweat inside your shoepacs turning into ice and frostbite, your entrenching tools cracking like toothpicks, rations hard as bricks and rifles kept unoiled because even the oil became ice. Bullets ricocheted and pinged murderously from rock to rock with deceptive sounds of steel against steel. To receive a minor wound—and the specification of what was minor became heavier each day—was a magnificent experience because you would be brought briefly into a warming tent and given some hot food before being ordered back into the iron darkness, a darkness shuddering with explosions and point-blank gunfire.

Witt and his frozen Ridgerunners had slogged into Koto-ri, staggering in long wavering lines, crawling into the tents, slurping hot coffee into the chin space of their parka hoods while trying to hold the mugs between stiffened mittens, dropping off into a sleep deeper than the bottom of the world, relieved to know that finally they were out of the fighting.

Four hours later they were ordered out of the tents. On your goddam feet! The ironic snarl: *Gung ho. Let's go.*

They had marched back up north again, back up the road down which they had fought their way, marching back up because they knew the terrain and they knew somebody had to go out to rescue the battalion of trapped artillerymen and the handful of surrounded British Marines.

There, on the stone razor of a narrow highback, Witt had taken the skull wound just as a blizzard began. The cold had saved him from bleeding to death so that he could live the next few years in the prison camps of Chung Kang Djin, Ha Djang Nee, and the Valley Camp V near Pyotong, where he would learn how modest was Dante's medieval architecture of nine descending levels of Hell.

Not only the cold had saved him but also the military accident that he had been found unconscious, later, by a special Chinese platoon whose orders had been reversed: Now they were commanded to take as many American prisoners as possible and to treat them humanely for later interrogation and indoctrination. Instead of dying on the road to the interrogation camp at Suan, Witt had been put into a compound at Chung Kang Djin. He was racked by fever from the infected wound in his scalp and, one day, a mule cart pulled by shaggy Mongolian ponies had trundled him across the Yalu to a Chinese People's Hospital on the Manchurian side.

There a Chinese surgeon with a wispy white beard and nicotine-stained fingers had been very gentle and had carefully explained in fairly good English that Witt could be given only a limited amount of penicillin, because the drug was needed at the front. Also, no anesthesia was available except for chest and abdominal surgery. Would he like a glass of brandy before the metal splinters in his scalp were debrided? "You unstan my Engrish? I study at Pek-ing Union Medica' Co'ege."

The Chinese surgeon had copied Witt's name and serial number from his dog tags, then he had said jokingly that there was an amusing coincidence. A company in the United States, also named Sommers, manufactured penicillin and anesthetics, the drugs Witt needed.

"I know," Witt had said. "That's my family."

"So?" The Chinese surgeon had said nothing more, but picked up his writing brush. Witt saw him brush several boxy and looped Chinese characters on a sheet he added to the medical chart.

After that the surgeon had been friendly and said "Herro, comrade" during ward rounds. One day he returned Witt's dog tags and had warned Witt to hold on to them. They were in great demand among the Chinese troops as battle souvenirs. Also, he had found a little extra novocaine to infiltrate Witt's scalp, which was fortunate because the final surgery would be long and painstaking, close to bone.

The next day, Witt was given a meal which included chicken and daikon soup, instead of prison-camp cabbage leaves and corn mash. One week later, a young Chinese officer walked briskly up to his bed and said in very good English, "I am Captain Liu Keh-yu, liaison officer with the International Red Cross. I am here to establish your identification so that your family and next of kin can be notified." He had held out a box of English cigarettes and, after Witt took one, put the box on the bed beside Witt. "You are being treated well," the captain said, not as a question but as a statement.

His English sounded only a little stilted. He said Marine, not Mahleen, which Witt recognized as a practiced linguistic skill. Usually he was grammatically correct. Everything about the captain was correct; even his officer's coat was not the usual loose Chinese jacket, but had the padded shoulders and nipped-in waist of the North Korean version of the Russian uniform. Sometimes the captain wore a white gauze mask, just as most of the nurses and doctors did. When he smoked, he held the cigarette between his little finger and fourth finger, carefully avoiding inhaling. Witt guessed the captain smoked only as a technical courtesy. An interrogation skill. He was always very courteous, but also, as Witt quickly discovered, Captain Liu Keh-yu was very suspicious. Once Witt mistakenly mentioned that his toothbrush was gone, and that night he heard the nurse had been punished. Suspicion was the pivot of everything. Chinese prison sentences were open-ended. This was only humane, the captain explained, because prisoners who reached correct thinking sooner were released sooner.

"What happens to prisoners who don't learn correct thinking?" Witt asked.

"They need more time to learn. They stay in prison."

Outside, the grumbling sound of engines in low gear never stopped as thousands of Molotov trucks ground bumper to bumper toward the front across the river. There were times Witt thought he could hear American artillery approaching in the distance, the special booming of the 105's, but after a few days he realized he was imagining whatever he wanted to believe. There was no approaching American artillery across the Yalu and there was no bona fide international Red Cross liaison officer. There were only the never-ending Molotov trucks, day and night, and the visits of Captain Liu Keh-yu each afternoon.

The captain had come to the point unexpectedly. "You come from a prominent drug manufacturing company," he had said, squinting carefully at Witt through the curling smokescreen of his cigarette. "And your name is known like Dupont in chemicals or Michelin in tires. How is it you are an enlisted man?"

"I never had officer training."

"But from such a family you must be an officer."

"Back home," Witt said, "I'm not even old enough to vote."

"I think you are an officer who will try to make a resistance organization in the prison camps. That is why I think you are lying."

"And I think you are lying about the International Red Cross."

"We have the Lenient Policy. It amounts to the same thing. You are living better than the masses of Korean peasants lived, even before you began this war."

"We didn't begin it. The North Koreans crossed the 38th parallel and invaded the south."

Captain Liu Keh-yu waved his cigarette, a mild dismissal. "How can you know the truth, Sommers? You have only your own prostituted press and radio."

"Listen, Captain, you can buy Russian literature almost anywhere in the United States. I'll bet you can't do that in China."

"We have no need for outside literature, Sommers. Our newspapers tell only the truth." His eyes had narrowed. "The truth is that you people learned germ warfare from the Japanese. Now you use it on a defenseless people."

"You don't believe that, Captain."

"I believe it because we have proof. We have an International Scientific Commission. We have evidence. Bugs, lice, dead rats, beetles, many insects. Best, we have the confessions of your pilots."

"I don't believe it."

"I respect you to say so. After six thousand years of civilization it is hard for China to believe that even Wall Street aggressors would give such instructions." For the first time he showed anger. "Why do you smile at such terrible things?"

"I can't help it. It's the way you mention Wall Street."

Captain Liu Keh-yu said nothing. He had lost face. He simply left the room. The next day he came back wearing his gauze face mask and carrying what he called the evidence: photographs of bug jars, discolored leaves, and clippings from a dozen newspapers around the world. Then he upped the ante. "You are a young man," he said to Witt. "You have a life to live in front of you. If you will sign a cognition that you have seen this evidence we will put you on the radio so that your parents and some pretty American girl can know you are still alive."

Witt had known immediately that he could not serve the Chinese and, after one more day of trying, Captain Liu Keh-yu knew it also.

"You are worse than a soldier obeying orders to kill innocent farmers in a country which never did you harm. You are an enemy of the truth, Sommers. As an unconfessed war criminal you can be sentenced to execution. You can be buried without having your dog tags put in your mouth. Not even your own graves registration people could identify you. Your mother would never know what happened to you. I have told them to move you to another room to think over the difference between saying no and saying yes to a simple request from people who treat you with kindness."

That night Witt had been shackled and handcuffed in an unheated hut, about a half kilometer from the hospital. No food that evening. None the next. He had lain curled and shivering on a mat, both his legs pushed into one trouser leg to conserve body warmth, troubled by remembering the meals of chicken and soup and the bean sprouts with soy sauce. By the end of the next day, he understood in his bones and the lining of his stomach why a Korean farmer would take his child's pet dog, toss it into a sack, and swing it methodically against a wall for twenty minutes to tenderize the meat before cooking it.

For a time Witt had tried to count the individual Molotov trucks, but somewhere near the five-hundred mark there had burst upon him the importance of his signature to Captain Liu. A broadcast by the son of a well-known pharmaceutical manufacturer would seem to be one more proof of the Chinese germ warfare propaganda. Fear trickled through him. He could no longer count the trucks. This was only the beginning. His interrogation would become much worse.

As Witt turned away from the French doors which overlooked the elms in front of the Club on Massachusetts Avenue, he felt hungry and slid back the cuff over his wristwatch. Twenty minutes after seven. Saved at last, he thought, and hurried out through the carpeted hush and down the staircase to breakfast.

Terrence had taken a table for two beside the bay window overlooking the little garden. He was sipping coffee as he read a copy of the Washington *Post*.

"Good morning, Counselor," Witt said.

Terrence raised his bushy eyebrows as Witt took the chair across the table. "You're late, boss. You must have had as much trouble getting out of bed on time as I did. Last night was the night that was. A real swinger, one of the blond experts in something at the State Department. Legs with a grip of steel."

"Lucky Pierre," Witt said. "Sorry to be late."

Terrence tapped his copy of the Washington *Post*. "See the story on Marjorie? These Washington patriarchs used to ask for your blood, sweat and tears when you took a government post. Now they want your money too. Your mother would be very ill-advised to let them pressure her into divesting herself of Sommers stock by outright sale." He peeled back the *Post* to the editorial section and showed Witt the cartoon.

Marjorie Sommers had been drawn as the Statue of Liberty in New York harbor. On her spiked halo was printed: *United Nations Population Council*. The torch she held was labeled *Food*, and the book she clasped to her bosom carried the title *Birth Control, the Patrician Mission*. On a toy ocean liner steaming into the harbor stood a mustached caricature of Rafael de Jesús Cándido Santos Roque, Governor of Puerto Rico, surrounded by a swarm of immigrants. On Marjorie's shoulder a cynical old owl was hooting to a shrewd young pigeon. The caption read, "Now hear this! The rich get richer while the poor get children."

Witt handed the paper back. "Not bad," he said. "Marjorie will probably have the original framed and hung in her office by tomorrow night."

"It's a shrewd poke," Terrence said. "If your mother's money came from dog food or cracker jacks, nobody would give a damn. But contraceptives?" He rolled his eyes upward piously. "Saints preserve us!"

"I was counting on you and your staff to preserve us, Terrence. Where's that nationally famous legal eagle, the hope of widows and orphans?"

Terrence grimaced. "Watch your language, Witt. I've been an orphan for years. When will Marjorie get here?"

"Mother said right after breakfast, on her way to a meeting downtown at Blair House."

"Governor Santos Roque?"

"Yes."

"Great," Terrence said. "Just dandy. That gives me about all of ten and a half unhurried minutes to brief her on the details. Now just how do I do that?"

"Well," Witt said, "I thought you'd get into that last night."

"I did," Terrence said. "All the way. But not from a legal angle."

Whenever he traveled out of town, something fundamental changed in Terrence. He became frisky and goatish, a great surveyor of unescorted girls at bars. He had offered to teach Witt his faultless technique: the courteous introduction of himself, the first polite offer to buy a companionable drink, the niceties of closing in for the kill. "My legal retainer," he told Witt, "doesn't cover my free field testing of Sommers' famous products." Back home in New Haven, he was a stern and upright barrister. Any young woman in his office who was discovered leading his law clerks astray was summarily fired. But, Witt reminded himself, Sherwood Wilson Terrence was a brilliant attorney.

"If my old mother could only see me now," Terrence said. "A shanty-Irish kid breaking bread at the very heart of the Protestant Establishment."

Witt took a bite of toast. "Save it for after breakfast, will you, Terrence? I can get that Irish routine at home. I don't have to travel."

"See what I mean, Witt? You're one of them. Inhibited. You can't express your feelings."

"But you can, Counselor?"

"Darn right." Terrence looked around the room. Men were sitting at the dozen tables nearest the garden view; most of them had folded copies of the *Post* or the *Times* to fit beside their coffee. At the table beside them a white-haired man in naval uniform set his cup down hard and said loudly to the civilian across from him, "But what the hell do you suppose the Navy is *for?*"

"Witt," Terrence said, "you look a little peaked." When Witt did not answer him, Terrence said, "I'd lose a little sleep myself. When I think of your mother dropping her bundle of Sommers stock overboard just to hold an honorary position in a U.N. committee"—he jabbed himself lightly over his heart—"it gets me right here."

"Well," Witt said. "If she holds the stock, it's so easy to make a conflict of interest charge against her. How can she discuss population control in India, or Puerto Rico, or anywhere else, when she has an interest in a company selling millions of dollars' worth of contraceptives?"

"Go ahead," Terrence said. "You can afford to be casual about money. I can't. I work for a living."

"Not me," Witt said. "I have a rich father."

Terrence laughed. "Your New England sense of humor and Marjorie's orchid greenhouse and herb garden and your father's pretending he's just another bookworm professor, and your brother driving his old Volkswagen to the lab, where his research could any day kill your company's market position—sometimes I think the only sane, sensible thing the Sommers have done was not to try to stop you from marrying Betsy when you came home from Korea." He raised both hands. "Stop. Don't get sore."

"I'm not sore. But when we stand up, the fellow who kicks you will be me."

Terrence sighed. "What a thing of beauty and a joy forever a couple of million dollars must be."

"Listen, Terrence, we've known each other for a long time and all that, but right now would you mind sticking to business?"

"You sore because I mentioned Betsy?"

"Of course not."

"A beautiful girl like that, Witt—people mention her all the time. No offense intended."

"Of course." He signaled the waiter for more coffee. "Before Mother comes in to join us, let's get the other two items on the agenda out of the way."

Terrence pawed through the briefcase at his feet until he came up with a manila folder. "All this technical stuff on industrial security. You want to read the whole thing?"

"I read my copy on the plane coming down," Witt said. "Industrial security, hell. It sounds like spying on our own employees."

"How else can you protect yourself, Witt? Some of your best patents are turning up in Italy, and the attaché at the Italian Embassy says his government has no plans to pass laws protecting drug patents. Your losses in Europe in the last fiscal year were over ten million dollars."

Witt stirred in his chair. "It'll be higher this year."

"You can plug the leak in your lab for peanuts, Witt. These modern eavesdropping gadgets are no bigger than a dime. They can put a microphone inside the olive of a martini and transmit conversation from a toothpick. So they bug a couple of telephones. Tape-record all calls. Nobody's offended because nobody knows."

"Isn't wiretapping illegal?"

"Not on your own wires inside your own lab, Witt."

"But you'd be tapping telephone wires, too."

"That would be a technical accident. After we have the evidence we need, we could reprimand the electronics company very strongly for doing it. Cancel the contract."

"Spy stuff may be okay in the comic strips," Witt said. "But once you start, where do you stop? Makes me as uncomfortable as hell."

"Me, too, Witt. But we can keep it clean. Inside the law. A little discomfort and you save more than ten million dollars a year."

Witt pondered the ginkgo trees outside. No, the elm trees. Business was business, except that it was not. He felt a subtle anger that in one way or another he paid for Marjorie's high offices, his father's scholarship, more than half of David's research, and all of Betsy's games. Terrence was right. Valuable lab findings and proprietary formulas were being stolen from the company laboratory. There were no strings attached to the research grants made to David, and David's work—especially that once-a-year injection for men—might one day destroy the multimillion-dollar market for women's oral contraceptive pills. The mountain of confirmatory clinical data the government required before he could put a new drug on the market was forcing him to spend more time in Washington. And Betsy refused to come with him. Last night, on the plane, he had sensed she might agree to come along on the inspection trip to Puerto Rico and South America. He had remembered something else about Betsy this morning, some flicker of years ago, but when he tried to recapture it now it became a handful of smoke, gone.

Terrence's voice was saying, "If you decide it's no go, Witt—" When Witt turned from the window to look at him, Terrence added, "It's your decision."

The buck stops here, Witt thought. "We'll do it," he said. "But I want to review the contracts myself before we go into the private detective business."

"What kind of talk is that?" Terrence slid the manila folder on industrial espionage back into his briefcase. "You don't watch enough television. We're not the cloak-and-dagger type. We're just two men who have to work for a living."

"Thanks for the promotion, comrade," Witt said. "On this Italian patents problem, we need a more positive approach. Maybe we should concentrate on penetrating the Italian market for contraceptive pills. We could be number one. The market's wide open."

"Of course it's wide open, Witt. A few little legal items keep it that way. Would you believe Article 553 of the Italian penal code? Or Article 112 of the Public Security regulations? Even their medical journals hardly mention the subject."

"But some Italian women are using the pill."

"Sure, but only on prescription for female-disease therapy."

"There's the answer, Terrence. Damn it, I'd rather try to promote prescription sales in Italy than pay a bunch of electronic eavesdroppers to bug my own staff."

Terrence tugged at the braided gold watch fob which held his Phi Beta Kappa key and pulled out the nickel-plated Ingersoll watch everyone in his office joked about. Only Witt and David knew his mother had given it to him as a high school graduation present. "Looks like the Queen Mother Marjorie is late again, boss."

"Let me make a suggestion," Witt said. "You can't be late for that clambake over at Food and Drug, so why don't you give me a quick summary on the conflict of interest thing so that I can give Mother a brief fill-in? Then you can shove off and I'll come along to fight later on."

Terrence scratched an eyebrow thoughtfully. Whenever a client got the feeling that legal answers were easily come by, fees suffered.

"The legal details," Terrence said, "are a little bit on the intricate side."

"But there must be some basic idea—"

"Well, the basic idea is to put all your mother's stock interests into a trust, outside her control. She no longer serves on your Board of Directors, so that's taken care of. We simply divest her entirely of any self-serving or beneficial connection with Sommers Pharmaceuticals or Sommers International." He scowled; he had made it sound too easy. "You understand, Witt, there will be a few loose ends to tidy up, but you and I can work that out in New Haven."

The waitress stopped at their table. "More coffee, sir?"

"No thanks. Will you let me have both breakfast chits?"

"Yes, sir. I'll be back in a minute."

As they waited they heard the man in civilian clothes say to the uniformed naval officer, "You American chaps see things quite differently than we do in London. Your policy of expanding market sources while trying to build a nuclear picket fence around the whole bloody Eurasian land mass from Moscow to Peking—well, it simply won't work. You can send your Peace Corps chaps and foreign aid and missionaries in ahead of your salesmen, the way the Spanish used to send their priests in to pacify the natives while the conquistadores reached for the loot. And you'll end up being hated."

"The British never minded being hated," the Navy man said.

"Ah," Witt heard the Englishman laugh. "You Americans want to be loved."

The waitress came back and put both breakfast chits on the table. Witt scribbled his signature on them, then he and Terrence left the room. As they rounded the corner, Terrence said, "No wonder so many of us cross-got Irishers ran off in a kind of Diaspora. Only God can make an Englishman."

"If we didn't have them, we'd have to invent them," Witt said. "Too bad we're separated by a common language."

"Bloody right," Terrence said. "See you at FDA. My respects to Marjorie." He rammed his hat on at a swaggering nautical angle and launched himself into the turbulence of Massachusetts Avenue.

Witt sat down to wait for Marjorie. He drummed his fingers lightly on the arm of the uncomfortable chair. I don't mind Marjorie's being late, he thought, but she'll be much too hurried and haphazard to make important decisions. Iban came up to Witt and said smartly, "Someone's rung up for you, Mr. Sommers. You can take the call on the lobby telephone."

Marjorie was at her brightest most charming most hurried self. Witt could tell by the way the receiver sang, "I know I'm being terrible, dear, keeping you waiting, but we're just starting out. Get them to give you another cup of coffee, dear."

"Mother," he said, "I've already had some coffee."

"Have another cup, dear. Did you see the cartoon in this morning's *Post?*"

"Yes."

"Transcendental, wasn't it? I loved it. That Patrician Mission line. But it's going to make the conference with Governor Santos Roque quite sticky."

"Don't worry," Witt said. "His voters may all be Catholics but he's as pagan as Protestants like you and me." Who but Marjorie, he thought, would call a cartoon transcendental?"

"The man who sees this from all sides," Marjorie said, "is Mayoso. Governor Santos Roque would take Mayoso's advice about Puerto Rico before he'd take mine."

"Maybe so, Mother. Santos Roque and Mayoso have been chess partners for years."

"But Mayoso hasn't answered a single one of my letters or phone calls! Is he still playing hermit Buddha on top of that lovely mountain?"

"I don't know, Mother," Witt said. "He might be anyplace. Lecturing to refugee doctors in Miami, out fishing, on hospital rounds, maybe operating. For a hermit Buddha, you'd be surprised how much he gets around."

"Witt, you're being awfully sweet to be so patient with one of your own parents."

"Yes," he said. "But just you wait till I hang up."

She laughed lightly, "See you soon," but, at her pace, the phone clicked off before she finished the sentence.

Witt ambled back into the lobby and sat down opposite Iban, who was deep in study of *The Decline and Fall of the Roman Empire.*

When Marjorie Sommers strode into the small lobby of the Club, the air crackled, the porter stopped dusting, the telephone girl ignored the buzzes of her switchboard, and the gray-jacketed steward behind the desk paused in his sorting of the morning mail. Mrs. Marjorie Sommers was in her sixties but looked twenty years younger. Slender as a spear, two sharp blue eyes for spearpoints, a strong woman who accepted her inherited fortune as a social responsibility and believed without doubt that people everywhere would be happier by applying in their lives the Vigor and Intelligence she practiced in her own. Her mother had chained herself to a lamppost years ago, during the suffragette struggle for women's voting rights, and Marjorie Sommers kept the faded yellowing newspaper picture of the episode framed on her desk at the United Nations Headquarters Building. She had never had a headache, constipation, nor premenstrual tension; but she had gradually learned such ailments were commonplace and taught herself to be sympathetic.

Witt was pleased to see she was as elegant as usual. Years ago, Betsy had introduced her to the uniqueness of Irish fashions. The combination of deftly tailored simplicity, a silk-and-tweed two-ply sturdiness, was exactly what Marjorie Sommers wanted, and now Sibyl Connolly in Dublin designed everything she wore.

She kissed Witt lightly and said, "I'm awfully sorry, dear, I know how you hate waiting."

"This is one morning I didn't mind."

"Oh?"

"Well, in my old age, I'm becoming contemplative."

She raised her eyes in mock horror. "Oh Lord," she pretended to pray, "I have a contemplative husband and son already. Take not this one from me."

"Amen," Witt said. "How much time do we have?"

"Oh now, Witt, stop looking at your watch. Don't be one of those busy efficient Americans."

"Mother, you're the most marvelous fake in the world. How much time do we really have?"

"About sixteen minutes." She glanced up the curving carpeted stairs. "Doesn't the august membership of this Club permit females on the second floor? Or does the House Rules Committee suffer from hardening of the categories?"

Marjorie Sommers was certain inside her fine long bones that the world required only intelligent organization. "Men, money, and materiel," her U.N. speeches said. She had a fair enough view of her strengths and the weaknesses they caused in others, so she spoke of her deep feelings rarely, and then only with a faintly self-mocking humor. "I just don't like mushiness," Marjorie would admit, but would never say aloud that she mistrusted people who evaded direct muscular effort, who used electric toothbrushes, soaked in hot tubs aromatic with bath salts, drove to the near corner for a pack of cigarettes instead of walking, and paid masseurs to knead their passive muscles. She would walk over burning coals for her men—her husband, whom she alone in the world called Ben, and her sons David and DeWitt—although, while in the fire, she would demand information about the inefficiencies which led to such a blaze.

As they went up the stairs side by side she slid her hand under his arm. "You don't look contemplative to me, dear. You look pale, as if you need one of the patent medicines your grandfather made for tired blood. Indian Chief Tonic. Good for Man or Beast."

"Tired bones, not tired blood."

"Oh. Aren't the rooms comfortable here?"

"A narrow plank and custom-tailored hair shirt is all we visiting members get."

"You should rise above discomfort, Witt. No true-blue member of our family," she said satirically, "ever trusted a loose woman, champagne with meals, or a down mattress."

"Mother," he said, "how can you keep handing out that Spartan propaganda?"

"It's easy. Choose a rich father. Then a rich husband. Let others do the dishes. Bring up two smart boys. Keep your eyes and your pocketbook open, and always volunteer if the cause is worth it."

At the top of the steps she stopped and put one hand over her chest. "Oof! Why do they make steps longer each year?"

"Why do some people, no need to name names, try to squeeze some big decisions into sixteen minutes?"

"Oh, oh, oh," she said. They turned the corner into the carpeted lounge and moved toward the two small facing leather sofas which flanked the fireplace. "Now I've got your diagnosis."

"Sure. All doctors' wives practice medicine on the side without a license."

She reached out to put her hand lightly and affectionately on his shoulder. "You're *angry*. What's been happening with you?"

"Why only sixteen minutes?" he said evasively.

"Big doings at Blair House," she explained as they sat down facing each other in the quiet dimness. "Governor Roque is running for re-election in Puerto Rico, but this year the election is very special because the Church is moving in against him. He asked some of us to join him at a press conference this morning."

"And some of us includes you?"

"Oh, I'm just window dressing, dear. The lady who wears Eleanor Roosevelt's shoes and the Queen Mother's hats. I'm God's gift to the newspaper cartoonists' union." She clapped her palms together with a sudden idea. "Witt! When the Vice President picks me up, why don't you come along with us to Blair House?"

"Can't. I have a meeting at FDA."

She dismissed his meeting with a gesture. "We'll have more time if you come, Witt. And *you* can give good solid factual answers to all the inevitable questions about why I sell population control at the front door while I collect Sommers International profits at the back door. You know," she added, "Washington does something to newspaper people. They refuse to trust a word you say if they smell money. Honestly, I do believe most of them had very strict toilet training."

Witt threw his head back and laughed. "Mother, where did a nice girl like you learn language like that?"

"Don't blame me. Your brother David talks like that all the time."

"Doctors are allowed to talk dirty."

"Ha, you're telling *me?* I was married to a gynecologist before you were born."

"But when Dad talks dirty," Witt said, "he says it in Latin."

"That's because he's a show-off," his mother said. "I used to have to keep telling him he was a genius so that he could pretend that humility professors have to profess." She gave him one of her Brahmin smiles, unable to say: You're just like me with your light hair and blue eyes, a stubborn doer of the things of this world, while David is your father's son, black-haired and brown-eyed, a dreamer of dreams not of this world. When you were little you always climbed out of your playpen while David stayed inside content to count the wooden beads.

In that moment Marjorie understood why Witt hadn't slept well. Betsy. Of course. Witt had caught her rain of quicksilver in his hands, held it gleaming for four or five years, and now the shining liquid was slithering out between his fingers. Only Betsy could tip and tilt him so far out of balance. Marjorie was sure Witt did not understand that was why he had married her. As far back as their first engagement party, Marjorie had forecast Witt would be taking his directions from a weather vane while storm signals were flying.

"Betsy decided not to come down on this trip." It was a comment, not an inquiry, as Marjorie said it.

"No," he said, too quickly, defensive. "She's busy painting a mural in the playroom of the Pediatrics ward at the hospital, and she wants to finish it."

"I keep forgetting she's a Play Lady volunteer."

"Now, Mother, I know you're miffed because Betsy doesn't help you run your L.I.V.E. organization—"

"Not at all. After the police closed our Stamford clinic, Betsy smelled the smoke of battle and came to see me. Charged into my office ready to take the Queen's shilling and carry a rifle."

"Did she? She never told me."

"Husbands aren't for telling, dear."

"Why didn't you accept her when she volunteered?"

"I told her she was much too beautiful for the daily grind of a maternal health center. Pregnant women don't like coming in with their big bellies and baggy maternity dresses and seeing themselves with the most beautiful woman between New York and Boston." Her eyes met his. "And," she said, "I wasn't sure it would work out for Betsy."

"Now, Mother," he said. "Nobody ever gives Betsy credit for being a solid citizen."

"She's too decorative, Witt."

"Since when are good looks like leprosy?"

"She's attractive. That means she attracts."

"The men all cast her out because she won't lie down and wag her tail, and you women cast her out because you can't stand competition."

"You sure you've had breakfast?"

"Yes," he said. "Yes, yes, yes."

She tried to make a joke of his irritability, "In the United Nations, dear, four yeses equal one affirmative."

Sometimes, he thought savagely, one *no* is enough. The other night, in bed, when he had touched Betsy's shoulder and she had said no, that had been enough.

The evening had begun pleasantly. She had been playing a stack of new recordings, all folk songs, filled with lament and injustice and lost love.

"*Oh me, oh my,*" Betsy had sung with the phonograph, "*I loved him so . . . never dreamt he'd leave me, tho' . . .*"

Witt had been her audience from across the room. He enjoyed her ability to give herself so completely to the guitars and the young hurt voices. Betsy had lived all her life on thin slices and, during all these years she had been Mrs. DeWitt Sommers, she had learned to like the whole loaf, all or nothing, preferably all.

Not being able to have a child of our own must be a death of a thousand cuts, he had thought, each more painful than the last. What should have been the freedom and grace of love has become a kind of administrative biology. At first, years ago, it had seemed a little humorous that Sommers Pharmaceuticals earned millions every year from the manufacture and sale of the famous FATIMA line of condoms, Hol-Tite diaphragms, Estrogentle pills, and that the president of the company and his wife had no use whatever for these international products. Later, as the humor wore thin because Betsy never became pregnant, they had gone bravely to David for advice. He had explained that he could not be their physician—after all, they were too close—obstetricians never even delivered their own wives —so he had sent them to Dr. Dionisio Mayoso Martí, in Havana. Not that Dr. Mayoso held some magic no one else commanded, but Mayoso was first-class and Havana was far enough away to eliminate local gossip leaks and close enough to be a bit of a holiday.

Witt had hated some of the infertility tests. The invasions of the body as if it were a machine, the microscopic analysis of the size and shape and maturity of spermatazoa. He had not realized how strongly Betsy had felt because she had seemed to make a game of taking rectal temperatures every morning and hooting at mid-month, "Look, it's up a notch! It's ovulation time on the ol' stud farm!" But one morning, he had found her standing with bent beaten shoulders in the bathroom, her head lowered, refusing to answer him, with the little glassy stick of the clinical thermometer shattered in the washbasin before her.

What had been a humorous irony, then a temporary biological accident, then a tiresome necessity, slowly over the years became a silent monstrous wall. For years Betsy agreed with Witt's disapproval of artificial insemination. He never confessed his deepest reasons—that another man, even a stranger, should give his wife the pregnancy he could not—and he had tried to pretend his objections were rational and farsighted: the laws were not definite, he had said; someday there might be trouble if his will conveyed a large estate and an international company to a child who could be challenged as a bastard. She had been infuriated; wills, estate, stock, laws—the whole ponderous machinery was a money-grubbing gravestone where an open field should be. She made him feel like the blind tyrannical State; she was the lonely freedom fighter. Mayoso's very gently given suggestion that adoption of a child often helped conception of another set her off on an underground chase in the gray market for a baby.

Witt knew nothing whatever about the thousands of unwed girls who turned their unwanted newborn infants over to baby-selling operators who were as well organized as the meat-packing industry. He only knew that Betsy, who had strummed a gentle harp, was now a harsh twanger of guitar strings, swing high swing low, one for the road and two for the turnpike, you take the high road and I'll take that long long lonesome low road. Occasionally she tossed down a quick drink, just for the top o' the morning to you, and then stayed on top all day.

He had come home one day and had heard a baby crying upstairs. He had raced up the spiral staircase, two steps at a time, and had burst breathlessly into what had long been the empty nursery. Betsy was sitting there, in a completely outfitted room, holding a baby in her arms while she tried to burp him, holding him up against her, patting his little back and rubbing her face against his blond fuzz of hair.

He had never been so angry in his life. Not even his years in the North Korean prison camp had taught him to handle his own helpless fury. Under his storm, Betsy, soft sensitive gentle Betsy, became a rock. In the end, when he learned with whom she had dealt, what she had signed, and what she had paid, he was reduced to the childish embarrassment of a punitive gesture. He had canceled her bank and charge accounts.

Brian Boru had been the greatest Irish king, the first native Christian king. There was no greater name, Betsy said; she named the little boy

Brian Timothy. The child had grown with no trace of her black hair or green eyes, but amazingly, with Witt's tow hair and ruddiness.

Only years later Witt learned that King Brian Boru's beautiful wife had plotted with his Danish enemies against him, and when the Good Friday battle ended that ancient day in Clontarf, near Dublin, Brian was no longer king because he was dead.

And now, five years afterwards, some unspoken balance leveled between them, Betsy sat on the floor of the music room, cross-legged as a tailor, singing: *"Oh me, oh my, I loved him so . . ."*

Later, upstairs, he had heard her moving beside him in the double bed and said in the darkness, "What's the matter?"

She had sat up. "I think," she said lightly, "I'll tiptoe through the tulips and get me a small nightcap."

He sat himself up beside her. "Why don't I barrel downstairs and get one for each of us?"

"You're a gentleman and a scholar."

"Don't mention it, luv."

"You're also a lifesaver. My itsy-bitsy delicate feet are *freezing*."

He had come back upstairs with a bottle of champagne under his arm and carrying two glasses in which he rotated ice cubes.

"Pretty fancy," she had said. "Chilled glasses, just like downtown. If you persist, sir, you'll probably have to marry me."

The champagne glasses had chilled enough, so he carried them into the bathroom to toss the ice cubes into the washbasin. There, on the long tile surface, stood a small flexible plastic bottle, the kind travelers pack in their luggage, except that this bottle had no top on it. On an impulse, he bent and smelled it. Oh Lord, he thought, angrily and guiltily, she's begun to sneak Scotch into the upstairs john.

As he returned to the bedroom he was caught by her actions, feeling the first embarrassment of an observer who marks the unaware secret absorption of another. Betsy had the bottle of champagne between her knees and was expertly edging the cork out by using both thumbs to push. The cork popped orgiastically, and Witt felt a scratch of repulsion at her primitivism. The champagne foam spilled over her hands. She licked one palm, then the other, with a child's sensuality. He forced himself to smile as she poured the wine with such abandon that each glass overflowed. "And uh-one for you," she said happily, "and then uh-one for me and we'll have uh-one apiece for the both of us."

Betsy, he had wanted to say harshly, be what you are, one of the laughing sprites, one of the last of the lovely gamines of the world. Boozing it up is a bar-girl stunt and doesn't become you. Sneaky bathroom Scotch and spilled champagne don't mix. But her gaiety stopped him cold.

She tossed the champagne down the way a man might swallow a shot of whiskey, then kissed the bottom of her upturned glass like a Russian finishing his fourth toast.

"Don't just stand there," she said, "do something. Here," she added as she lifted the full glass from his hand and gave him her empty one in exchange, "I'll drink yours before it gets warm while you fill mine again."

"Hey," he said. "That's cold."

"What's cold?"

"You just spilled half a glass of champagne all over my pajamas."

"Oh," she giggled. "You get out of those wet things right this minute."

With a quick tug she pulled the cloth belt of his pajama trousers loose so that they fell comically to his ankles. She dropped her glass on the rug and threw her arms around him. "I don't want you to catch a chill," she laughed.

This is lopsided, he had thought as they had fallen across the bed. Nobody sober can keep up with rockets fueled with alcohol. She was all over him as she had not been for years, laughing spontaneously, no longer angry about the inserted tubes of gas or the daily clinical thermometer, but as free and flying now as they had been at their beginning.

"Me first," she chortled, her black hair flooding across his skin, "then you. All's fair in love and war."

Oh God, he thought, if only I could be drunk too. I'd give anything to be as high as a kite and flying.

Suddenly she stopped and pushed the tumbled black hair away from her eyes and stared at him. "What's the matter?" she whispered.

"Nothing," he said thickly.

She put both her hands on his chest and began to push herself away. "That's a grand brave soldier you've got there," she said angrily. "Dead as a doornail—"

"Betsy—"

"And me acting the fool."

"I don't know what happened."

"You can't say you're drooping with alcohol, can you? Not when you haven't even had a drop."

"But you have—"

"Oh Lord love a duck"—she began to snicker drunkenly—"a grand great big goddamn *duck!*"

Four hours later, as the silky light of dawn slid into the room and over his aching sleepless eyes, he turned to look at her, asleep on the pillow beside him. He reached out and touched her shoulder, then grasped the warm roundness of it and shook her gently. In the wide black fan of her hair her head moved slightly and, in her sleep, she muttered, "No."

"Witt," his mother was saying, "you still haven't given me your opinion."

"What?" *No*, she had said. In her sleep. He made an effort to focus on what his mother was saying. "I'm sorry, Mother. An opinion about what?"

"Oh, Witt. I don't believe you've been listening to me."

"I have," he said. "It's just that I'm thinking."

"Well," she said, "for years you've been talking about Sommers Pharmaceuticals going public, being listed on the Exchange, and all that."

He sat up straighter, back on solid ground. "Of course. The day of the tight little family-held company is over."

"But so many of the Europeans still have them."

"They don't have our tax laws. All the major American drug houses that started as family companies—Upjohn, Lilly, Searle, Johnson, Abbott —they've all gone public. For two years I've been trying to get you and David and Dad to listen to me, but you're all so busy uplifting the world, or drinking vodka with some visiting Russians or bargaining with some district attorney who wants to close one of your L.I.V.E. clinics—hell, Mother, I've never been able to get to first base with any of you, and without your controlling block of stock I'm just a hired hand."

She examined his face in a slow complex way and said quietly, "Witt, you seem to get so angry so easily these days."

"Do I?"

"Yes," she said. "It's becoming noticeable. Even your best friends won't tell you."

"I thought you were my best friend."

"I'm not," she said. "I'm your mother, that's why I'm telling you."

"You could have told me in Connecticut."

She sighed. "Connecticut? You're hardly ever home."

"Now you sound like Betsy."

"Well, Witt, it's true, isn't it? The name of the game is profits."

"Could be. But where you work, Mother, the name of the game is power."

"No. The name of the game is peace."

"Mother," he said, "I've seen you in action on television. You're better on camera."

"My, we're all salesmen, aren't we? Every one of us."

"Maybe," he said. "But this particular morning I'm not buying." *No*. And in her sleep.

"Witt," she said. "The Vice President is picking me up in a few minutes. We're going to meet Governor Santos Roque at Blair House—some sort of meet-the-press clambake—then lunch with the President."

"Mother," he said, "if you don't mind my saying so, the big global picture just isn't my dish of tea this particular morning. I've got to get back to Connecticut. If you'll excuse the vulgarity, I've got a payroll to meet."

"Witt," she said, with a new tone of concern in her voice, "I've never heard you talk like this before."

"Well, maybe I'm just tired this morning. Or under the gun too much. Or maybe I need a hobby." Damn it, he thought, there must be a better way to protect our research than plant espionage. He raised his head sharply. "D'you know what David's research costs? As a matter of fact, Mother, have you any idea what it is to keep your greenhouses going year-round, up there in Southport? Orchids need a good deal of moisture and warmth, even in the winter."

"Oh dear, this sudden cost accounting is very unlike you, dear. I was going to phone the gardener this afternoon to add a new wing for some Japanese mountain orchids." She smiled reassuringly. "I'll tell him to make it a very small wing."

"Mother, Japanese flower arranging may uplift the soul, but haven't you heard that so many American women are flying to Tokyo for abortions they call the planes the D-and-C-8?"

"Mmm. Modern jokes are so savage, aren't they?" She touched his arm. "When you were born, Witt, you were such a smiling butterball of a baby. So good-natured."

"I've aged."

"Don't smart-alec me, Witt. Something's wrong. Is it Betsy?"

"No," he said. *No,* she had said, and while in her sleep.

When one of the Club staff came in to say that the Vice President's car was waiting outside, Marjorie Sommers thanked him in her unhurried way and turned back to Witt. "This has been such a quickie, dear. Hurry, scurry. Hello, goodbye."

He stood up with her. "I'll walk out with you."

"I'm worried about you, Witt. I really am. I don't like that look around your eyes."

"You just don't recognize a man of distinction."

"What's distinctive," she asked as they moved toward the door, "about not being happy?"

For a moment he was ready to tell her how he felt, how he really felt whenever he stopped long enough to think about how he felt, but they were crossing the lobby now, and there was no time.

As they walked out the front door of the Club, the long black official car which had been kept back from the entrance rolled forward in the curving driveway. A secret service man in a dark blue raincoat sat beside the uniformed chauffeur. The Vice President jumped out before the car had stopped completely and bounced up the steps to meet them.

"Marjorie," he said, taking both her hands, "the only woman in the world on time! And how the hell are *you*, Witt? You look great. Just great. British tailor? How do you keep so slim and trim?"

Sommers Pharmaceuticals made a remarkably profitable dietary drink called Trim-'N-Slimmer, but Witt decided to sidestep the cue. "Fasting and prayer, Harry," he said. "Thanks for taking good care of Mother. She's a country girl and shy with big city slickers."

"Madmen," Marjorie Sommers said. "Have you two any idea of how you sound? Harry," she added, "can't we invite Witt to come along to the Blair House press conference?"

"Sure thing. How about it, Witt? Help me protect your mother from the city slickers like NBC and CBS and all the wire services from here to Timbuktu. Marjorie, they all like you, but don't the Girl Scouts have a motto, Be Prepared?"

"You just lost two million votes, Harry. That's the Boy Scouts."

"Those reporters are not Boy Scouts. This morning they'll show you no mercy."

"To a little white-haired old lady?" Marjorie Sommers opened her eyes as widely and innocently as possible. "What were they, test-tube babies? Don't they have mothers?"

"They play the old parlor game. Knives along the Potomac," the Vice President said.

"As they say in Washington, you're not communicating, Harry."

He stretched one arm toward the car. "I'll explain on the way downtown."

A military officer got out of the car and stood beside the open door. He was tall, young-looking for a man of senior rank, with a heavy bristling British military mustache.

"Marjorie," the Vice President said, "this is General Moshe Edin. General, Mrs. Marjorie Sommers and her son, Mr. DeWitt Sommers."

While they shook hands, Witt noted a paratrooper insignia on the General's tunic. The Vice President added, "General Edin was Chief of Staff of the Israeli forces."

Witt watched his mother raise her handsome head. She had caught the scent of a possibly useful ally. "I've read about you, General Edin," she said. "Your commando exploits with the British Legion and that fantastic story of capturing a whole regiment of Egyptians at Suez."

"Pure luck," General Edin said. His accent, like his military stance, was British. A one-sided grin slipped out from beneath his shaggy Sand-hurst mustache. "Lady Luck is a Hebrew goddess, you know."

"I've been wanting to meet you, General," Marjorie Sommers said. "You have something in Israel the United Nations Population Council needs very much."

"Surely," he said, "you can't mean the Torah or the Dead Sea Scrolls. And the Arabs have the oil, if you mean money."

"Doctors," she said. "We badly need doctors and yours is the only coun-try in the world with a surplus of them."

General Edin bent toward Witt. "And you're planning to expand your plant near Tel Aviv, aren't you?"

Ah, Witt thought, the Vice President is up to his famous informal meeting tricks again. Harry must have brought the General along pre-cisely for this. "Yes," Witt said. "Israel is stable, democratic, and English-speaking. Recruiting scientists is fairly easy. Some of your people at the Technion and Hadassah-Hebrew University Medical Center are doing research on fertility, and we're in that business."

"I'm sure General Edin is quite neutral about your plant expansion, Witt," Marjorie said. "Aren't you, General?"

"Of course, Mrs. Sommers. I must be neutral."

"My wife," Witt said, "has an old country saying: neutral, but on whose side?"

"I like that, Mr. Sommers. Frankly, I'm neutral against you."

"Are you willing to say why, General?"

"Just between us," the General said, "Israel needs more people, Mr. Sommers. Not fewer. If we could only persuade our rabbis to come out against contraception we could borrow the French laws. Our birthrate would climb. We need boys. Later on, we could stop drafting girls for our army." He faced Marjorie. "If you'll forgive my being so bloody blunt— we Israelis have the manners of frontiersmen, y'know, because we're sur-rounded by armed Arab frontiers. You want more of something, and we want less of something. Maybe we can arrange a fair exchange."

Marjorie Sommers stiffened. "I have absolutely nothing to do with the management of Sommers International."

"Ladies and gentlemen," the Vice President said skillfully, "this im-promptu curbstone conference has to be adjourned or we'll be late." He beamed at them in a circle, mission accomplished. "Hate to pick up our dolls and dishes just when the party gets interesting, but y'all had a chance to say how d'you do."

While the car rolled smoothly out of the private driveway into the traffic of Massachusetts Avenue, General Edin said, "Mr. Vice President, could you ask your driver to drop me off anyplace near the Pan American Bureau? I know you're in a hurry, and I can stretch my legs a bit."

"Didn't you want to come along and chat with Santos Roque before the press conference?"

"Thank you, no. After I make my swing around South America I'll catch up with him in Puerto Rico. They're doing some awfully good things there in converting solar energy to electricity."

"I'm due to visit our Puerto Rican plant soon," Witt said. "Where are you staying?"

"Damned if I know. If you'll be kind enough to ring me at Governor Roque's office in La Fortaleza, I'm sure you can zero in on me."

"Just watch out for Witt's wife," the Vice President said. "She's the prettiest girl between here and Jerusalem. An Irish brogue she turns on and off like a garden hose, and a way with her that could make even the Israeli army stop and dig in."

"So," the General said. "Now I know America's new secret weapon."

"General," Marjorie asked, "will Israel be neutral against us when the Population Council reports to the United Nations?"

"That's not for a soldier to say."

"But personally—?"

"Personally, you know and I know the Arabs will vote with you and go right on having hungry children in medieval circumstances. The Israelis might abstain, but they'll practice what you're preaching. Only as few children per family as can be raised decently."

The car stopped. "Here you are, General," the Vice President said. "The Pan American Bureau is right down the street there. Just far enough for a morning constitutional."

"A good word. Also, I like to walk around constitutional Washington at this time of year. Winter's ended. The college girls picketing the White House put on lipstick. Everything looks so hopeful." The General got out and touched the visor of his cap lightly, saluting them all. "Thanks for the lift. I'll look forward to seeing you in San Juan, Mr. Sommers. If your wife will teach me an old country jig, I promise to teach her an older country's *hora*."

"Fair exchange," Witt said.

The General looked as if he were trying not to smile. "You give a little," he said, "you get a little. Right? Otherwise we'll all have to learn to dance the kazatzki to Chinese music."

Marjorie stretched out her hand. "General, shalom."

"Shalom, lovely lady." He saluted them again and strode away.

"Now," Marjorie said as the car picked up speed, "you promised to brief me, Harry."

"It's complicated," the Vice President said. "One of those Chinese boxes within a box within a box."

"Can't we leave the Chinese out of this, Harry?" Witt asked.

"Hardly," the Vice President said. "If you don't believe me, ask your mother. They have seven hundred million people, they keep having floods and famine, and propagandizing birth control. And go right on producing as many children every year as half the population of the United States."

"I don't believe that figure is quite accurate, Harry," Marjorie began.

"Well," he said impatiently, "the point is accurate. Eighty per cent of their people are scattered all over the map, so that they say they're not afraid of a nuclear bomb the way we are in the West with our congested cities." He shook his head. "Don't get me started. I was going to tell you about Santos Roque. He's a first-class man, smart as they come but running scared for re-election because he took the traditional position of separating Church and State in a Spanish culture that has very little tradition of separating the two. No tax money for parochial school buses, or books or construction. He's dared to question tax exemptions to Church-owned business property."

"Courageous, maybe," Marjorie said, "but that could lose him the election."

"Wait. There's more. The island's biggest export has been people. He's an acrobat on the high wire between two cultures. And thousands of island women are on welfare, barely feeding their kids. They don't know the facts of life about conception, or contraception. We think Puerto Rico should be a showcase of American-style democracy for Latin America—more jobs, housing, food"—he made an inclusive gesture—"the whole package of personal self-respect. But a lot of his opposition, especially the old families with money invested abroad—Madrid apartment houses, Swiss banks, you know?—people who should know better, they keep telling him he's selling their souls for *piti-yanqui* pottage. Selling out to immoral high-bracketeers like Mr. DeWitt Sommers, who manufactures contraceptive devices and pills."

"I'm glad I had a big breakfast," Marjorie said. "I'm going to need my strength."

"Will the Latin American press be there?" Witt asked.

"Yes. You've been in Latin America for some time, haven't you?"

"Not Mexico," Witt said. "Syntex and some of the others have pretty well saturated things there. But we do have a packaging outfit in Caracas where we shift from bulk to retail shelf items. Plus a fairly large warehouse, of course, and a South American marketing staff."

"That's a good case in point," the Vice President said. "Let's say you're standing in front of the cameras right now and the man from *El Mundo* asks you how many Venezuelans are on your staff in Caracas, compared with the number of Yanqui managers."

"Harry, that's a loaded question."

"You don't say. But try it on for size. Keep the answer simple because the *Times* and Manchester *Guardian* will bother with the details."

"Witt," his mother said, "don't let Harry needle you. You're a private citizen and you don't have to say a word."

The Vice President swung to her. "All right, Marjorie. Let's say I'm a woman reporter trying to put a family handle on the story. I ask you, Mrs. Sommers, doesn't your family have a tradition of civil disobedience? Going back to when the suffragettes had to meet secretly after dark, in graveyards—"

"Yes. My mother—"

"Thank you very much. And didn't you begin an organization called L.I.V.E. which opened clinics in Connecticut to teach birth control during the years it was still illegal?"

"Yes and no. No, because we helped many women who were not fertile to have children. Yes, we operated openly illegally because the laws of Connecticut were archaic and needed to be tested in court. These tests took place, all the way up to the Supreme Court. It is now legal for married people to have access to birth control materials in my home state."

"Is it true, Mrs. Sommers, that you have a vested interest in the success of the products made by your son's company?"

Her bright blue eyes began to burn. She grasped the armrest beside her as their playacting became real. "Yes," she said. "I have a vested interest. So have you. Your draft-age sons. Your taxes. We've had death control all through history, but we cannot indulge in such primitively satisfying horrors again. To paraphrase Lincoln, the world can't endure two-thirds hungry and one-third well-fed. So we all have a vested interest in birth control."

"That's not good enough, Mother," Witt said. "Remember the old Anglican saying? You can get away with unorthodox doctrine or unorthodox behavior, but not both. You can't duck sideways about your stock ownership in our company. You'll have to explain that you have no voice in the policy or management of Sommers International—"

"And income?" the Vice President threw in quickly.

"And no income from the company for the duration of your appointment."

Marjorie's eyebrows went up. "Is that true, Witt?"

"As of right now," he said, "it's true. Terrence had a different idea in mind, but as of right now, now that I hear more of the intricacies of all this, he's going to have to work out a new package. You've got to be clean as a whistle."

"Can you prove it?" the Vice President asked. "Some of these reporters have seen the Indian rope trick too often. You can't just climb up and disappear into thin air."

"We'll be able to prove Mother is free of any conflict of interest by tomorrow noon, even if Terrence and his whole staff have to stay up all night working on it."

"Good. Better have photostats." The Vice President patted Marjorie's hand. "You're doing fine, but here come the hard ones. I represent *Le Matin.*" He had begun to enjoy his own performance. "Will you be kind enough to enlighten us, madame, on your views toward France?"

"Gladly. Speaking individually, monsieur, I believe France is barred by laws passed after the first World War which forbid contraception or abortion. Reliable French sources estimate about one million illegal abortions in France each year—about one abortion for every child born. And yet French medical students are not taught about contraceptive methods because they would break the law if they instructed women about contraception. Your government, monsieur, permits private family planning associations to function. But any woman who wants a diaphragm must import it from abroad, and she's never had a chance to learn they come in different sizes. Let me ask you to ask your paper to ask your readers one question: Which is more humane, to change a postwar law of long ago, or to live with such large numbers of desperate women and desperate abortions?"

Their tempo had quickened because time was running out before they reached Blair House.

"I'm from the Calcutta *Times,*" Witt said. "We Indians, Mrs. Sommers, need our children for farm labor. Why do you tell us to have not so many children when you have millions of tons of surplus food?"

"Insects and rodents eat twenty per cent of your food every year, sir. Rural electrification could not only ease your free hours at night, but also—turning on a single light at night works better than most contraceptives. If your men want to prove they are men, let them help their wives as strong men do and stop breeding hungry children for proof. How'm I doing, Harry?"

"Great. But don't be surprised if the State Department boils you in oil and breaks you on the rack before they shoot you between the eyes."

"Russia," Witt said. "I'm from *Tass.* Tell me, Marjorieskaya, why does your President say there are too many hungry people in the world? In actuality, does he not want to cut down the number of people with colored skin?"

"Ah," she said. "I'm glad you asked that question, tovarich. I've been told that everyone's newest form of psychological warfare is to put out misleading information. This is an example of Soviet *dezinformatsiya*. We in the United States have no monopoly on virtue, agreed? But we do have a great deal of food, knowledge, machinery, and fertilizers we've been sharing with the mostly nonwhite world. How much food has the Soviet Union shared with people who have darker skins than the Russians? Soviet delegates to the U.N. Population Commission have insisted that overpopulation was only a fruit of capitalism. Socialism could meet any increase of people, they said. But Russia and China, with all their farmers, have had to import food."

Their car began angling out of the Pennsylvania Avenue traffic flow toward the curb in front of Blair House. Under the canopy-covered steps Witt saw a group of photographers, each man draped with several cameras.

"Marjorie," the Vice President said, "don't ever try to be an ambassador. But anytime you want to run for President, let me know, hear?"

The car stopped precisely before the canopy and, immediately, the photographers went into action.

The paneled door under the graceful fanlight opened as they walked up the steps. Inside, under the antebellum black-and-gold chandelier, Governor Santos Roque stood ready to greet them. In the drawing room off the front hall Witt saw television and motion picture cameras, lights, cables, tape recorders. Poor Marjorie, Witt thought swiftly as the greetings began and the flashlights popped, she hasn't learned the fine art of the half-truth, the humble pretense, the deflection of responsibility.

"Witt," Governor Santos Roque said, "how did you come from thin air? Nobody told me they were going to land the Marines. Where's our friend Mayoso? I thought he was invited."

The Vice President leaned toward Santos Roque's ear. "Let's get this show on the road. The President will be coming across the street to join us for lunch."

"Very good news," Santos Roque said. "I need all the support he can give me."

Witt could see, as they moved into the long drawing room with the dining room just beyond it, that Marjorie was losing the taut look she'd had before they got out of the car.

The glass Regency chandeliers had been lighted in both rooms and all the vases were filled with fresh red roses, white chrysanthemums and lilies-of-the-valley. The Adams and Hepplewhite chairs had been pushed back, but caught enough light to glow with a subdued gold and blue. The pale yellow walls were just right for Marjorie. She became stately, Witt saw. Dignified, almost regal, with no trace of pomp. He watched her move with confident ease, talking graciously with the reporters as if this were her own historic home and they were her guests.

6 THE PEDIATRICS WING of Metropolitan Hospital in New Haven was a world with its own cribs, small beds, kitchens for mothers staying overnight, a television room, and a blackboard-lined schoolroom for long-term patients. For ambulatory patients of nursery school age, there was a playroom. The Play Lady in charge this afternoon was Betsy Sommers.

In the hospital volunteers' locker room, when she had combed her hair, she had been surprised to see herself faintly flushed and very bright-eyed. Those incredible vagabond jokers at the Womb with a View. It had been no more than two hours ago, sitting there in the booth opposite Roone and the girl, and already it seemed a week ago and not of this world. All that incredible chatter, *put-on talk* he had called it, put on for squares like me. Married ladies from the suburbs who came to the hospital to be Play Ladies.

Thank Heavens he's not scheduled to help out on the ward today, she thought. It would be embarrassing. Roone knew David Sommers; and he knew that she and David often had a cup of coffee together in David's lab. She had glimpsed Roone washing glassware in David's lab—it was one of Roone's innumerable odd jobs—and he might be embarrassed to think she would mention to David his unusual friend of his private life.

In the playroom she found herself smiling and laughing a great deal, and the children caught her mood immediately. She put on a puppet play for them: "Aladdin and the Magic Lamp."

Below it all, she thought: don't be a fool. No fool like an old fool; raised on loud talk and moonshine . . .

. . . Her father standing in the kitchen door in his undershirt, declaiming with pantomime, "What should I be but a prophet and a liar, whose mother was a leprechaun, whose father was a friar? Teethed on a crucifix and cradled under water"—and her mother's tart-tongued "Water? Pot whisky more likely!"—and his raised hand for silence: "What should I be but a fiend god's daughter? After all's said and all's done, what should I be but a harlot and a nun?" . . .

She made herself concentrate on the puppet draped over her left hand.

"New lamps for old! New lamps for old!" the puppet announced. The children in their hospital pajamas and robes, sitting in a circle of little chairs, two or three of them in wheelchairs, all hushed to see if the trick would fool Aladdin.

The performance ended. They all clapped before the aide began rounding them up to return to their beds.

A voice behind her said, "Who's that on your left hand, Mrs. Sommers?"

She swung around, startled. Roone was grinning slightly, dressed in a white student jacket, hair neatly combed. The very model of a modern medical student. And that *Mrs. Sommers.* Smart boy. She felt her cheeks become warm, and she was instantly annoyed. *He* should be the embarrassed one, not *me.*

"Oh, Roone. Are you scheduled for me today?" Damn it, I didn't say that right.

His politely calm expression did not change. "No, but the egg tree came in for the kids. It's pretty heavy, Mrs. Sommers, and I thought you'd need a helping hand." He pointed at the puppet on her left hand. "A helping left hand."

She raised it. "This is Aladdin." She stuck out the puppet's arm. "How do, Doctor Roone."

Roone shook hands gravely with the puppet. "How do. Praise Allah. The left hand is the dreamer."

She pulled her hand free of the puppet and nursed her thumb. "That hurt. You've got strong fingers."

He did not apologize. He rubbed his thumb and forefinger together in the universal money-counting sign language. "Lots of financial exercise."

"Counting Volga's money? I'm sorry, I shouldn't have said that. Is Volga really her name?"

"What's really anything?"

"That's an odd thing to say."

"I mean it."

"Is it her name?"

"No, her real name is Kishli, after her father's mother. She's only part Romany, but she makes a living being one hundred per cent Gypsy. The whole tea-leaves-and-tambourine bit. Show biz. Like you and the haughty-married-lady bit."

She stared at him. The polite, almost diffident smile, the pressed white shirt and dark tie, the very good-looking intelligent face. Indeed the very model of a modern medical student—and the obvious intimacy with someone actually named Kishli. The boy was a Dr. Jekyll and Mr. Hyde.

"I thought of the perfect gypsy name for you this afternoon," Roone said. "That's really why I delivered the egg tree."

"Where is it?"

"Out in the hall. Don't you want to hear the name?"

She didn't like this, but she made herself smile as an older woman does, tolerant of the young. "My raggle-taggle tinkers' gypsy name? So I can run off to Puck Fair and make a living?"

"Volga said she could get you a hundred dollars a night. Wait, wait, just don't get sore. She meant it as a compliment."

"Tell her thanks, but I don't want to change my husband's tax bracket." She picked up the box of puppets and began to turn away.

"Don't you want to hear it? It's better than Betsy."

"What's the matter with Betsy?"

"Sounds like frozen angel-food cake."

"Men usually say Betsy Ross and the American flag."

"Men are damn fools."

"The vote is unanimous. Lucky you're not a man."

"Sure I am, and you know it. And you yourself said you're no lady-lady."

"You're on awfully thin ice, Roone."

"You ought to watch me walk on water sometime."

"I could report you for this."

"You won't. You're all for the underdog. You're Irish. That's why I decided it would be Pat."

"Swell. Sounds real gypsy. Like almost, as we squares say."

He was smiling. "It's short for Patchouli." His eyes went over her slowly. She wanted to go, hurry off, get the egg tree, anything to end this sense of being, of being, being *handled*.

"There's patchouli in that perfume you use, Betsy. I've always liked that little whiff of Oriental pizzazz in your perfume. I've always liked everything about you, the way you look, the way you tool into the parking lot in your green Jag with your scarf blowing. Even the jazzy shoes you wear." He looked down at her feet. "Everything's different on you. What kind of shoes are those? Never saw anything like them."

"They're makassar."

"Is that a snakeskin?"

"Yes. Borneo."

"And dyed just right to go with a blue hospital uniform. That's what I mean about you. You must be rich."

"You must be poor."

He laughed. "That was last year. This year I'm poverty-stricken. See this shirt? Belongs to a buddy. His tie, too."

"Really?"

"I thought we decided nothing was really."

"I mean, are you serious?"

"It depends. Semi-starvation, that's serious."

She found herself looking him over as slowly as he had scanned her. "You don't look starved."

"Carbohydrate bloat. Carbohydrates are the cheapest food around. I cook up a mess of macaroni with meatless long-life sauce and live on it a week. Haven't tasted protein since nigh on Whitsuntide. Isn't nothing to laugh at!"

"I'm sorry. You talk so, so, *odd*, sort of. I'd never laugh at starvation. I worked for a living once, and I know."

"You? You *worked*?"

"You're damn right I did. As a model, in Chicago. If some gentleman didn't buy me a delicious nutritious steak once in a while, it was yesterday's hamburgers for li'l ol' Betts."

"That's what I need. A gentlewoman to buy me a steak."

"I saw that one coming. You've really, I mean, *a*ctually, you've been living on macaroni?"

"Cross my Achilles heart."

"Well, my little boy Timmy and I will be happy to feed you a protein diet tomorrow night. Maybe a steak, Gaelic style."

"You mean it? At your house?"

"Of course, you shrewd beggar."

"Thanks, Pat."

"Don't mention it, Mike. What *is* your name?"

"Your obedient servant, Gerald Morton Roone, ma'm."

"That's almost as yum-yum as Betsy. Your mother must have been devoted to the Oxford Dictionary of Christian Names."

"My mother was a slob."

"Ugh. Just like that?"

"Sure," he said. "It's a plain simple fact just like that."

"That's sad," she said.

"Why? Why should it make you sad?"

"Well, after all," she said, "your *mother*. What a thing to say. Mine was an angel."

"*That's* sad," he said. "Makes you sound ten years old and mid-Victorian. I'll do like the nice folks do and call you Little Eva."

"Well, I'll do as the Romans do and call you Roone."

He began to say something quietly just as one of the nurses came into the playroom, but changed immediately to an ordinary conversational tone. "Thanks, Mrs. Sommers. Regular hospital procedures are the best bet."

"That big box in the hall for you folks?" the nurse asked. "Against rules in the corridor like that. What if we had a fire?"

Betsy watched Roone become instantly polite, very faintly obsequious, anxious to please. "It's the egg tree for the kiddos. I'll bring it right in," he said. "We were just deciding which corner it ought to go in." He smiled deferentially at the nurse, inviting her judgment.

"Well, that's different," the nurse said. "The supervisor said you folks are going to paint a mural or something on the long wall."

"The special lead-free tempera paint hasn't come yet," Betsy said, feeling as if she had joined Roone in a conspiracy. "The Administrator's Office sent it back with a memo about why do we need itty-bitty paint."

The nurse nodded. "Wouldn't you know it? That Edwina Hawthorne writes more memos than she throws away." She surveyed the playroom. "Why don't you set the tree right up on top of the TV set in the corner? You'll be out of harm's way."

Somehow she thought of the nurse's phrase that night as she sat before the altar of her triptych bedroom mirror, slowly rubbing dabs of cleansing cream outward on her cheeks and forehead. She had had the mirror lined with bulbs, like the makeup mirror of an actress's dressing room; she could remove cosmetics as meticulously as she put them on, liner and mascara and lipstick first so that no color would be rubbed into the pores, then the eyebrows she kept unfashionably heavy to let their black accentuate her eyes, cleansing all the hairs beginning at the inner corner, no one would ever find her with unsightly color deposits at her eyebrow tips where most women skimped, then the slow creaming with an upward, outward stroke, watching the nightly ritual of her experienced hands and thinking: Look at you. Now who would even *think* that lass with a delicate air had been through so much hell?

The nurse had said: out of harm's way. A recognition of Roone's conversational intimacy? Or did he have a reputation with the nurses? Out of harm's way. That was it, of course. Be the maternal older woman. A hearty steak dinner for a lean and hungry student of medicine. Timmy would be happy to have a visitor to chatter with. Maybe instead of the Gaelic steak and fussing with pot whisky on watercress, maybe just grill the steak in the fireplace in a pleasantly casual, improvised way. Baked potatoes. And very cold ale in stoneware jugs. Checkered tablecloth, folksy and frontier and very masculine in a nice sort of way.

Her white bedroom phone rang quietly. She stared at it a moment. Only a few people had the unlisted telephone number. Witt? He called almost every night between midnight and one. Witt, coming home from Washington later than he had planned?

"Hel-lo?"

"Pat? That you?"

She saw her pulse beat visibly in her wrist. "Great saints, it's Roone!" She stopped just before adding: Extrasensory perception, Doc. I was just thinking about you.

"Your voice sounds so different, Betsy."

Betsy. This is your own damn-fool fault. You'd better go back to being *Mrs*. Sommers. "I thought it was somebody different," she said carefully.

"Who? Your husband?"

"Yes."

"So late?"

"He always calls late," she said lightly.

"Bed check?"

"Just to say hello." Why am I bothering to explain to *him*?

"But he's building pyramids in Washington or something, isn't he?"

"How did you know where he is?"

"I heard you tell one of the nurses."

Perceptive beast. "How did you get this phone number, Roone?"

"In Doctor Sommers' handy-dandy thumb-index address book. He keeps it in his desk drawer."

"You're *work*ing at the gynecology lab? Now? So late?"

"I'm one of the night people. I'm acquainted with the night, ma'm. Aren't you?"

"Don't blarney me. You gave me a real earful, today."

"No blarney. The straight scoop. I'm working heroically at the lab. Doctor Sommers has nice cuddly cells growing in the incubator, very delicate cells from some pregnant lady, constant temperature perfusions to make like in utero, and some midnight slave has to tuck them in—"

"His desk drawer? Doesn't he keep his desk locked?"

"I know the cabinet where he hides the key—"

"Roone—"

"And I really, see, now I'm talking like you?—I *really* wanted your personal just-you-nobody-else-but-you phone number."

"Something about tomorrow night? You can throw out the stale macaroni, Roone. We're having a thinking man's steak."

"I've got tomorrow tattooed on my corpus callosum. But that's a long way off. While I was tuckin' these cell cultures away for the night, I wondered who was tuckin' you in."

"I'll be saying goodnight, Roone."

"Just suddenly goodnight?"

"You sound a little tight."

"A drop of beer. The thirst was on me, lassie. I thought about you all afternoon long. My mouth's so dry I can hardly talk." He paused. She could hear him breathing while the wires hissed between them. In the triple mirror lined by makeup lights, she saw three of herself with an infuriating blushing pink rising up her throat. She heard his voice change.

"How about my coming over to tuck you in, Betsy? Nothin' like a good tuck."

"You're a child, a *nasty* one. The kind that drops four-letter words to see if they'll bounce."

"Slow down, Betsy. Cool off."

"You've got one hell of a nerve, Roone. A college kid playing big bad wolf—"

"Nothin' I like better'n a good fox. I'll lay you a wager, Betsy—"

She slammed the receiver down, shutting off his voice.

She tried smoothing the cold cream again, but her fingers were trembling with anger. She looked at herself furiously. All this from a simple offer to sit down in a booth and chitchat with someone over morning tea . . . the sudden feeling of being sixteen again, free and a little wild and off to Puck Fair with the raggle-taggle gypsy-o. Because of that and of being jealous of an earthy fortune-teller, Miss Rocking Pelvis at some flashy beauty queen contest at Savin Rock, probably, hardly able to speak decent English. And that long-lashed dropped-eyelids look Roone has, the look of that boy in Atlanta when out of pity my aunt invited me down to that Southern peachtree porchswing world, Atlanta. And the doctor's son, home from college, lifeguard at the pool, Mason, Mason, long-lost Mason who had saved my summer with his blondness and his tanned swimmer's body. And my daily dream of his marrying me, taking me away from the Chicago of dark fourth-floor walkup apartments, the old soapstone sink and greasy gas cooker I could never scrub clean. With a remote drunken man once the handsome talker, the prince of players once called Father rocking slowly by the airshaft window in the back bedroom. And the burning end of summer, the end of summer that cut to remember it even now. And this morning you walk into a New Haven joint and there across the table, incredibly, sits a young man more blond than Mason, better-looking than Mason, incredibly becoming the doctor Mason never ever did become, and out of all this and loneliness, and feeling young as green grass, you make the light touch of friendship, always a mistake with a man, and now a man, a *boy*, believes he can tumble you in the hay like some gypsy tinker just passing through Puck Fair.

Most of my life I've known this running and chasing, all tension and storms, thunder, and the great bluff of men. If Mother had lived, or if her pneumonia had come a year or two later when the newer antibiotic drugs could have saved her instead of her being carried out on a stretcher all flushed and delirious with fever and never coming back. Or if Father had kept up the loud talk and the walks along the lake and swimming off the rocks at 55th Street near the swank Chicago hotels. If he hadn't closed himself off—("Don't stand there Betsy Mary, with your damn lip quiverin' and snivelin' like some abandoned orphan! My own heart's full to burstin' and half buried in your mother's grave. You're a big girl now, too big to be cryin' for your ma. *I can not stand your pain!* Hear me? Now get on, Betsy Mary, and make yourself some supper." Reaching for his bottle. "I'm not hungry, so don't be waitin' for me.")—Oh God, if he hadn't closed himself off. Maybe I'd have stayed home nights without all that frantic clutching at fumbling boys in the back seats of cars, my being worried as a nun on Saturday nights that I'd be killed in traffic or something before confession next morning, ashamed if the ambulance picked my body off the street, the young doctor finding me in a torn slip, bra straps all frayed and held together crooked with safety pins, and no pants on like a really decent kid would have. From all those early morning hours lying in a frowzy bed unmade for weeks, the wet line of tears running into the lumpy pillow, from all that, the running and the chasing to this graceful elegant bedroom in New Haven, to this mirror.

But the mirror was the mirrored wall of her bathroom. She did not remember wiping off her cold cream or walking in here. A gap of time that came more often now. The scary gap of time lost and not accounted for, like walking into the pantry and trying to remember what she wanted there, or dialing, but forgetting her own telephone number. Sometimes she backed her car out of the garage, and abruptly she was parking in the volunteers' space in the Medical Center parking lot, wondering: how did I get here?

She let her negligee slip to the floor, and watched the slender girl in the mirror. She had always felt her breasts were small and inadequate until Witt had told her she had the ideal Parisienne *poitrine*. "But the Romans set the style now, Witt," she had said, "and every girl needs a blouseful of *mamma mia* goodies."

But she had been pleased by his admiration because she had discovered she constantly needed a man as a mirror. She needed to see a shining reflection of what Witt had once called her Wedgwood china-doll delicacy, the face small as a nun's under the black coif of hair, *whose mother was a leprechaun, whose father was a friar, what should I be but a harlot and a nun.* She needed the shining reflection she saw in a man. When she was alone she felt sad, absent from herself, but in a man's eyes she saw a lovely sprite with black hair, seraphic, chaste, uncaught, touching earth only if he learned to follow the twisting Ariadne thread to her secret self.

(Witt's laughter: "Awake and sing, Betts. That moony Isolde stuff goes with the old gag about chaste, chased, and chastened." . . . "Your idea of humor, Witt, honestly! Like a lead balloon. A few things are still *de-*

cent!" He had grinned, humming the opening bar of "Night and Day" while putting his arms around her.)

She took a deep breath, watching her girlish breasts rise, remembering the first time in Chicago one of the older models had shown her how to use Scotch tape as a bra. "Gives you that invisible up-'n-at-'em," the model had said. "But still *au naturel*. Guaranteed to knock 'em dead, or your money back."

I'll never get a wink of sleep like this. Remembering always ends up hurting, because long ago sometimes seems like only yesterday. I need a sleeping pill, a jug of wine, and thou beside me. The medicine cabinet shelves were a small drugstore of dozens of lipsticks, creams and lotions and powders, hair sprays and rinses, eye makeup and perfumed dusting powder. There were pills for tranquility, pills for pep, pills for sluggish stomach, gall bladder, duodenum and colon, pills for the same intestinal segments when overactive—but where oh where the hell did I put those pretty little red sleeping pills?

She found the travel-kit plastic bottle labeled MOUTH WASH and drank some of the Scotch in it. The whiskey burned, then mellowed. She surprised herself in the mirror, still with the day's pink brightness, the look of secret excitement. *I thought about you all afternoon long. My mouth's so dry I can hardly talk.* She smiled fuzzily at herself, eased by an instant woozy assurance: oh oh oh it's noddins and bobbins for our sleeping beauty, now, isn't it?

I don't look any older than he does. I used to hate being a slender junior-size brunette, but now I'm glad. Here and there I'm not a kid, but with a little bit of skill and a little bit o' luck, the heres and theres can be smoothed out, especially around the eyes. Mason, my Southe'n sho't-ribs cornpone smooth-talkin' watermelon-cuttin' down-by-the-crick lying lover boy, you're paunchy bald and prematurely gray now, and here I am with a beautiful bright boy after me like queen of your goddam white glove Mardi Gras. Drinking out of yo' daddy's silver hip flask, and when you came out on the country club porch because you wouldn't see Little Orphan Annie me *in*side and I told you crazy with worry my period was a week late, all you could say was *Now which one of the boys knocked you up like that? You better run on home to your ma, Betsy.* You killed me then, Mason.

She took another drink from the plastic flask, a deep one, without the burning sensation on the way down this time. She felt light-headed now and raised the flask again just as the phone rang. She lurched toward it, tripped and fell to her knees. Her head spun with pain and fury while the phone rang.

I'll tell him this time. He can't talk to me like some hot wiggly-ass co-ed on the town. No dinner for Roone tomorrow, no more being drawn into little intimacies of shared lying, like the cocky act with the nurse in the playroom, and that about the key to David's desk. No more feeling of pursuit, the small shames of wanting the chase, the subtle net of a slow smile, the unspoken beckoning come-hither in small evasions and silences.

A lonely self-re*spect,* she thought as she pulled herself up by grasping the edge of the tub. The saving grace of respect. That's better than this. How can I live without a little self-respect?

The phone rang shrilly, in long bursts. She tumbled toward it. It'll wake Timmy down the hall, she thought angrily as she snatched it upward. "*Yes?*"

"Betts? . . . Can you hear me okay, darling? . . . Hello? Hel*lo?*"

"Witt—" Her voice broke.

"You took so long to answer—"

"I was in the silly john—" Her heart was thudding in her chest. He can save me. I have no ma to run home to.

"How are you, Betts?"

"Lonesome as hell. When're you *ever* coming home?" She began pacing, wavering through the room, trailing the telephone cord, watching the triple reflection of herself, surprisingly nude, in her dressing table mirror.

"Say, have you been crying? Your voice sounds funny, Betts."

"Just finishing up here for the long day's journey into night. Can you come home soon?"

"You sound that eager, I'll fly home tonight."

"Wish you would."

"Somebody's birthday?"

"No. Just one more damn lonesome night."

"How's Timmy?"

"Fine. Learned how to count to ten in Spanish today. Like Edison discovering electric light. How's Washington going?"

"So-so."

"I saw the cartoon about Mother. How cruel."

"Mother," he said, "thought it was transcendental."

"I don't even know what that means."

"There was a big press conference at Blair House."

"Oh? Marjorie loves those. She thinks so well on her feet."

"I've never heard you at a loss for words yourself."

"Well," she said, "I think better on my back."

"There's that sound in your voice again."

"Wasn't there a song once—'All Alone by the Telephone'?"

"At least," he said evasively, "you're home."

"You in one of those monastery cells at the Club?"

"Having non-wonderful time. Wish you were here. I really do."

"Oh, Witt."

"It may be another day or two, Betts—Betts, you hear me? May be another—"

"I heard you the first time."

"With all the new rules and regulations over at the Food and Drug Administration—"

"Terrence is down there to handle all that, didn't you say—"

"Well, there's more, Betts. At Blair House today, Santos Roque told me it's blowing up a storm in Venezuela. Just got a most-urgent cable from our manager there. He wants me to fly down, pronto."

"From right here, that sounds pretty far away."

"Not anymore, Betts. We have a big investment in our Caracas warehouse."

"My," she said, "you sound like an international Fuller Brush salesman with a big brass-nozzle firehose."

A moment's silence, then, "Betts, you been lickin' at the dewdrops? Tappin' the old moonshine chug-a-lug?"

"I'll start drinking for sure any day now, if you keep this up."

"Sorry. Damn poor joke. But you do sound sort of hundred proof."

"It takes one to catch one, dear."

"Strictly teetotal, Betts."

"I was brushing my death, dear, so I sound fuzzy. Mouth fulla toothpaste."

"Okay. Okay."

"You sure you can't just pack up and leave Washington and be home tonight? I'll pick you up at the airport."

"You sound hotter'n a two-dollar pistol, Betts."

"Well, let's run it up the flagpole and see who salutes, as your hearty executive colleagues put it."

"I apologize. Just don't start getting sore—"

"I'm not. Zooming home on wings of song was your own grand gesture of an idea. Oh, the Irish tongue is a wonderful thing, my father used to say."

"Now Betts, it's not as though there's been a sudden death in the family—"

"No. Just a few little dyings. Horseman, pass by."

"Now what the hell does that mean? One more of your quote unquotes?"

"No. I don't know what I meant. I'm sleepy as a cradle. Witt, let's not quarrel long distance." She made an effort to change her voice. "Come home. We can quarrel for free."

"I will. Soon as I can." He paused.

In the silence, their years echoed. I pity him, she thought. Now that I have him contrite he'll become hearty, then cheerful. I pity us both.

"You know, Betts—if I have to fly to Caracas, you come with me. How does that sound? Maybe ski a little at Mérida or Espejo Pico. Some great trout fishing at Laguna Negra. Stop in San Juan on the way back. Make fiesta brava with Mayoso—"

"Well . . ." Not brava, she thought. Bravado.

He hurried on persuasively, offering her toys and games. "And there's a handsome Israeli general who promised that if you teach him the jig he'll teach you the *hora.*"

"The *what?* Sounds immoral!"

"Think it over, Betts—we need more time together—"

"When will you know about this, Witt?"

"I'll see how the ball bounces tomorrow. I'll phone you tomorrow night. Will you be home?"

"I'm home every night. You know that."

"Hasta luego, my sentiments in Spanglish." He grunted with distaste, and said, "My attempts at humor get worse and worse. Maybe I'd better just say goodnight, dear."

" 'Bye, Witt."

As she hung up she discovered the plastic bottle in her other hand. She emptied it with two long swallows, then dropped it on the white rug.

In the middle of the night she awakened at the bottom of the world, sleep-filled, turning over in the dark, blindly stretching out one hand, feeling the texture of one of her blue silk pillows: where am I?

She had dreamt strangely, a kaleidoscope of bizarre terrors plunging through the nightmare circles of hell. A faceless man in a hotel room. Chicago? Her clothes off, stockings thrown on the floor. Across the dark room he was fumbling for the belt on her dress over the back of a chair, saying with a grotesquely hoarse menace: All you girls deserve a good old-fashioned whupping. Then turning toward her angrily: A *cloth* belt! Smart, huh? All the angles. A pro, at your age, by God! Her skin crawled with his cold anger. She had come out of love. Who was he? *Who was he?*

Suddenly she was in two places at once, aware this could be only in a dream, yet somehow connected with the mysterious man and the hotel room, but the trick was money now, not just cash money on the bureau, the corner of a small pile of tens held down by a hotel ashtray, but the roundabout dodge of buying her an airplane ticket and an armload of outrageously fancy lingerie, but faceless clerks were refusing to give her cash for the canceled ticket and the return of the lingerie. Why? She needed money. Why? Upside down, now she was buying, *everything black* she told the clerk, *I'm a widow*. I like that new tie-on mini-bikini but you'll have to order it for me in black. And some black lace hankies. I'm a soldier's widow and I'm in mourning. No, the clerk said, your father's in mourning for your mother.

Suddenly the dream changed. Her head down, tilted back over the edge of a wide, terry-cloth-covered chaise. Her mother was gone. This was another time, another place, quietly threatening. Dark. No, a starlit darkness. The latticed beach cabana at the Sommers' shore house in Southport? Waves, the haunting Atlantic sound of eternity, the near ripple of waves along the pebbled Connecticut shore. Night swimming with Roone. Swimming nude with Roone. But he loomed over her in the shuttered cabana, while she lay with head straining far back, still tasting the salt on his skin, murmuring, Roone, no, no please, Witt may come back home tonight, no please. And Witt's voice approaching, talking to Timmy, fatherly but firm, saying: Now, Timmy, quit your fussing. We'll find your little ole piece of sleepytime blanket and you can go right back to sleep. Next time you take your nap out here. . . . The choking sensation as the double-shutter doors of the cabana opened, Roone frozen above her body, her upside-down view of Witt's incredulous face hovering whitely over his beach flashlight, Witt staring stupidly as he automatically completed the habitual gesture of clicking the light switch, pouring terrible exposing light on them all, blinding them. Then the sudden treasonable dark closed over them, and Timmy started to cry. And on the terry cloth where Timmy had napped after lunch, beneath her bare back, his small piece of blue blanket with its worn silk-bound edge, his bedtime pacifier.

In her nightmare, a freezing fear choked her so that when she screamed, no sound came.

She jolted up in her own bed, breathing hard, painfully recognizing her own darkened bedroom in the dim light sifting in from the bathroom. Dreams, dreaming, hands wet with sweat. She rubbed her palms irritably over the sheer blue coverlet with its insertions of lace. Blue, blue silk, blue blanket. Timmy! Crying? She slid hurriedly off the bed and discovered she was nude. Her negligee was lying in a soft heap on the bathroom floor. She threw it over herself and hurried down the hall to his bedroom, stopping only to flip on the hallway lights. The sudden glare struck her with a vague discomfort. She turned them all off but one, then tightened her negligee as she pattered along barefoot.

She had left Timmy's bedroom door ajar. Sometimes his floor was a minefield of scattered toys, log cabins, and airplane models, and the dim plastic Mickey Mouse night-light helped not at all.

He lay asprawl, as Witt always did, but his body reversed, his head at the foot of the bed, his blankets pushed aside. The night riders in this house, she thought. The son all over the bed and the mother all around the world between midnight and half four in the morning. The long stripe of light from the hallway glimmered across the sleeping boy's blond hair, so much like Witt's blond hair, so different from her own that even now she was surprised.

She tried to turn him gently to get him back under the cover, but he lay so heavily in her arms as she bent over him that she sat down on the corner of his bed and put his head in her lap. A slip of a boy.

In the thin elfin light edging past the door she touched his hair, cut so short it stood stiffly as a blond hairbrush. ("Oh Betsy Mary, ye'll be a mother someday yourself, and ye'll see. A son is a son till he gets him a wife, a daughter's a daughter all the days of her life. You need a green thumb with children, Betsy Mary. The tender heart of them don't bear some bruises.") Oh, Mother, she answered in her mind, I still hurt and there's no place to lay my head.

The Westminster chimes of the grandfather clock striking three on the lower stair landing came muffled from the hallway, making the quiet after it silent as sand. Beach sand in the hourglass. Three o'clock? I had thought it was almost five. The time in my head is so different from clocks. So much has happened today. This morning is twenty years ago, and twenty years ago seems like this morning. That crazy mix-up of a dream. All the terrible obscure hungers of being young, alone, a stranger in the stone city.

The sadness, the reptilian sadness that always lay curled in the shadowed far-down places where she never could bear to look, the sadness for which she spent all her bright coins of gaiety as blackmail to buy peace of mind, now, here, at the bottom hour of night, she had no strength to hold back. Up it came, the dark waters rising, her sense of loss so unbearable she needed to reach out to touch another face in the night, a stronger swimmer, before she sank beyond all grappling.

Where had the whole bright morning music of the world gone?

7 BETSY AWAKENED as she often did, lost for a moment in what seemed to be a stranger's silken room shuttered against the morning light. Some dream of love lay lightly in her memory. Her body felt so ready and warmly open that she reached out one arm for the always-reassuring kiss of a companion on the journey,

ready for the slow sensuous sprawling fitting-together, for stretching lazily, then curling length to length, ready to feel the friendliness and warmth as well as more of the same of the night before.

But no one was beside her. Only a smooth pillow, cold and unyielding as a gravestone, and this awakened her. The day opened with the sudden sickening drop of a trapdoor.

She sat up, bewildered, until the familiar iconography of the bedroom reached her: four small oval pictures of her mother spaced within one large silver frame, pictures such as no one photographed anymore. The pictures had all been taken by natural light and then sepia-toned. Her mother as a girl, fresh and warm as country milk, looking directly at you (actually at the photographer, who had just called out, "Say *prunes!*") with only the small corners of her mouth to show how easily the smiling came. The picture had been taken on a Dublin street, at their front door. Her mother had stood carefully beside two-year-old Betsy whom she had perched on the photographer's pony, her mother's dark head and oval face close to her own. They were as nearly alike as two coins, and now there they were, in a silver frame together, a tiny immortality.

And the picture on the ocean liner, the Statue of Liberty in the watery background, her father's cocky corner-boy's stance, exaggerated because he was making fun of himself; her mother in the pretty coat bought for the trip to America, and herself, a dark-haired chip off her mother, she was that much like her, small as a minute, proud as a pup in a belted coat and Mary Jane shoes.

When she went downstairs to her kitchen the sun came warmly through the windows from the luminous east, an omen that this would be a good day. She knew she was a modern woman in a scientific age, but silly as it might seem, there were times like omens when you could *tell*. This would be all sorts of a bright day. Too much poking around in the nighttime ashes of memory was so unnecessary. It was just good sense to be sensible. Like the man said, who needs it? Suddenly she felt lighter and spun on one toe, enjoying the ballerina's flare of her robe. To keep the day just right she poured a half shot of her best hundred-proof vodka into her breakfast tomato juice and turned on the stereo hi-fi phonograph. She was glad this was the morning for Barrett and Mrs. Barrett to take the station wagon into town for the week's marketing. This one morning could now be private, hers alone, until the day laundress came.

She found the morning newspaper on the hall table and settled down within the familiar domestic grooves of another day—breakfast with the paper, getting dressed slowly, then Timmy home for lunch, then the hairdresser. Another day.

The black newspaper headlines were imprinted with the chaos of the

outside world: airplane wrecks, burning buildings, incredible human angers unleashed as former lovers destroyed one another—how can people
behave that way, she wondered—another atomic bomb tested by China,
mixed-up fighting in South American streets between rebels and juntas
over issues she couldn't quite understand clearly and didn't care about
anyway except for Witt's business in those countries.

How orderly and safe the kitchen was. The Scandinavian yellow and
blue caught the neighborly sun and smiled back. Nice, Betsy thought. The
blue print above the breakfast table of Picasso's girl eating with a big
spoon from a wooden bowl, a napkin tied around her neck.

The Royal Tara bone-china teapot of her mother's which raised the
heart in her whenever she poured a simple life-restoring cup of tea. And
the tea, the tea. She enjoyed just looking at the soldierly ranks of Irish
baleen tea caddies, holding the pellets of gunpowder tea, shreds of Irish
tea so hearty you could walk on it, clear amber Darjeeling, fragrant evocative jasmine, the mint-tasting tea of Capri; and the rare East India teas
which Witt had arranged with Fortnum and Mason to ship to her from
London, and which, like an annual dividend, never stopped: Harts Horn,
and her favorite, Black Ginger and Broken Nutmegs. For others home and
hearth might be bread and salt, a glass of wine, a bowl of fruit. For her, it
was tea.

From the living room came mariachi music that made her raise her head
to listen. *Bésame Mucho.* She knew many of her friends considered it a
tired war-horse of what was usually called Latin Rhythm, but it had been
Our Song once, long ago, all through that rainbow-hued, star-scattered
seventeen-year-old summer in Atlanta. Everybody had one Our Song, and
for her and Mason ("the most posolutely absotively gorgeous hunk of lifeguard in the world," she had called him then) the song was a romantic
fable of clinging, swaying on the country club dance floor while a rotating
mirrored ball on the ceiling flashed colored darts of light through the dim
scented air.

She put the kettle to boil, remembering Mason as he had sat there on
his lifeguard tower like a bronze god, and the sun, bright as sheet lightning, making his honey-yellow hair look white.

When Roone knocked at the back door, she let him in, amazed. He
looked a trifle haggard, with a day's short stubble of beard, unlike the
crisp polite-looking medical student in the Pediatrics ward yesterday afternoon. Yesterday afternoon? Lord, it was very like a month ago. Even
last night seemed so long ago. How strange.

"Well," she said, determined to be unfriendly, even in the face of his
gaunt unfed look, "why aren't you in class? With all the other boys."

"Don't give me a hard time, Pat," he said. He zigzagged his fingers through his blond hair, the hair which somehow made him seem familiar, someone she had met before. "I've had a hard night. And I pawned my wristwatch to rent a car. Why do the rich always live so far out of town?"

"Won't something happen if you cut class?" She was immediately concerned. For her, living was full of unquestioned rules. Breaking them required strong feeling, love or anger, and a protective darkness.

"Class? It's a joke. Doctor Sommers never takes attendance. I mean the old man, Benjamin Sommers, with his song and dance about medical history. History! In one era and out the other."

"But he's always so interesting."

"What's so interesting about a bunch of old Greeks and Romans running around in their nightshirts? What's it got to do with the price of potatoes or modern medicine?"

"But he's a wonderful man, Roone, I could listen to him for hours."

"Well, I can give you his whole spiel by heart." He bent forward slightly and clasped his hands behind his back, immediately aping an elderly schoolmaster peering over the tops of his spectacles.

" 'In Rome, gentlemen,' " he said in an old man's voice, " 'many of the best, the most subtly skilled physicians, were Greek. That is to say, outside the direct mainstream of the Roman militaristic culture, hmmph, ah, just as many of our leading scientists in certain fields today—physics? mathematics? rarely in medicine?—come from cultures outside the, ah, ah, pioneer, ah, practical, Protestant, ah, ah, one may say, mercantile tradition hallowed by the Iroquois tribes of Princeton, Micmacs of Harvard, and the Mohawks of Yale.' "

"Wonderful! You sound just like him."

He raised his finger sternly. " 'The phy-si-cian of Rome, gentlemen, had patients who complained of poor sanitation, arthritis, overcrowding, poor help, noise, air and water pollution, ah, ah, ah, lewd fantasies, marital discord, borborygmus and flatulence. The most common prescriptions were for an epidemic disease: love trouble. The disease is known to medical students by the, uh, uh, somewhat Asiatic name, lackanooky. Prescriptions for love philters—' "

"For what?"

" 'Love medicines included many components, like modern-day monkey-gland cream and musk-ox perfumes, simple magic stuff such as marjoram, spikenard, frankincense, and powder from the desiccated ovaries of a pregnant goat.' "

Betsy applauded. "Terrific takeoff! You should have been an actor."

"No, thanks."

"Why not?" She bristled. "Acting is a fine profession."

"Well, acting an old man, that's easy." He rubbed his nose thoughtfully. "I feel age creeping up on me. It's my birthday."

"Oh, for heaven's sake, this is no way to start a birthday. Come in, sit down, pull a chair up by the fire."

"If I remember, you did sort of invite me for a broiled steak. Or if I read you right, you believe in strawberry-shortcake birthday cakes."

"For you? Devil's food, nothing else would fit." Did I actually invite him to come for dinner?

"Sure, an' the Irish Brigade is feelin' pretty chipper this mornin'."

"I do."

"You didn't last night."

"Last night?" She knew immediately what he meant, but decided not to say so.

"My God, Betsy. I phoned you last night."

"Oh, that's right. That naughty-little-boy talk." She smiled maturely. "I just forgot the whole thing and slept like a log." She liked her tone of maternal understanding and haughty dismissal of regretfully boyish behavior.

"What's that you're drinking?"

"A Bloody Shame."

"A what?"

"A Bloody Mary with the vodka left out." The smooth ease with which she lied gave her a sense of power. "Want some?"

He stared at her, then said harshly, "What the hell are we talking about? I've been thinking about you all night."

She did not know whether she was attracted or repelled by his intensity. No one she knew spoke intensely about sex. Of the world, the flesh and the devil, only the devil was ignored even though he was the most fetching of the three.

"Flattery will get you nowhere," she said lightly, "except a birthday cup of tea."

"Tea? In the morning?"

"Of course. I've just hot the pot for myself, and it's easy to pour another for you. Just don't stand there like a lost soul at a wake. Sit down," she said firmly, feeling confident and strong with him for the first time, a gently firm trainer with an intelligent bear. Vodka courage? Maybe. Whatever it is, stay with it.

She made much of the tea ritual, feeling his eyes on her as she moved in the sunlight between the stove and table. In her belted robe and slippers, her hair simply combed back, without lipstick, she felt domestic and intimate. Almost no man had ever seen her without preparations she made elaborate as a geisha's.

"I never tasted tea like this," Roone said.

"Like it?"

"I don't know." He sipped some experimentally.

"Exotic, isn't it?"

"Well, the word fits. So are you."

"Me?" She reached for ridicule. "In my flannel-lined sarong?"

"So once a week you're a sensible Play Lady."

"For sick children, yes."

"Well, I'm young enough, and I'm not feeling well, and it's my birthday. So why don't you play with me?"

"I am." She looked him in the eyes, Mason's blue eyes, Mason's honey hair, Mason's muscular bulk and arrogance, and she felt the old angers stir. "D'you think I have breakfast with any unshaven bum who knocks on my back door?"

"You sound different today, Betsy."

"Because I know you, now. I know all about you, buster."

He lifted his cup. "A nice friendly cup of tea. The domestic bit. And now a spit in the eye?"

"You asked for it, Roone. That play-with-me routine. Someone ought to fetch you a great clout."

"That's pretty cold, cruel talk, Pat."

"Well, Mike, for a little while it can be your birthday, if you behave."

"Do you know what you sound like? Queen Victoria."

"Of course I do. That's exactly what I should sound like."

"Yesterday you sounded different."

"This is my house. Yesterday was the Womb with a View."

He looked around the kitchen. "Some womb. Try and get pregnant here." He leaned toward her. "I knew that'd make you laugh."

"Honestly," she said, shaking her head in mock helplessness.

"There's nothing honest about you, Betsy. You're acting every minute, even to yourself."

"Nobody invited you here, Roone. As a matter of fact, I believe your fubsy welcome's worn out, now that we've drunk a *cuineas* to your birthday."

"There you go again. That Irish talk."

"The tea reminds me. It always reminds me. The tea brings back a hundred and one remembrances. Oh, you could never imagine how one small sip of tea brings back so much."

"You really believe in sweetness and light, don't you?"

"Ah, no son of Ireland would ask that rude a question." She threw out one arm theatrically, and, as her father used to do in the kitchen back home, she declaimed, "Instead of dirt and poison we have rather chosen to fill our hives with honey and wax, thus furnishing mankind with the two noblest things: sweetness and light."

She couldn't help bending with laughter at his incredulous face. "Oh, oh," she choked, then coughed and patted her chest for air. "Oh, look at the man's face."

"I got the feeling this morning that today would be different," he said. "But this isn't different. This is way out, like crazy."

"I sympathize with you. I felt the same way yesterday in the booth with you and that gypsy girl."

"Like crazy?"

She nodded. "Like wild. Ah, there I go, talkin' like you."

"If we're both crazy, maybe we better declare peace. Hands across the sea," he said, and held his hand out across the table.

She took his hand, expecting to shake it, then found he would not let go. "Your hand is so cold," she said.

"You look nice and warm inside that robe."

"I thought we just declared peace."

"Right. Nothing like a good piece."

She drew her hand back angrily. "Enough is enough, Roone. You'd better go."

He raised his head. "Music? Where from?"

"The living room." She pointed up to the ceiling speaker. "It's piped into here."

"That piano. Listen to that pi-an-o. Sounds like real." He cocked one ear and listened carefully. "Thelonious Monk?" He leaned back, closed his eyes abstractedly, and ran his fingers up and down an invisible piano keyboard. "Oh, man. You jus' let your right hand stay in that mellow mel-oh-dy groove while your left hand goes downtown."

She had never seen anyone like this before. He spoke several kinds of English, classroom, collegiate, medical, put-on jive, shifting from one to the other as easily as a sports-car driver. He ignored her anger as if gravity had ended and there was no point in dropping anything, leaving her suspended. He was completely unresponsive to any of the social behavior cues she had all her life considered automatic between men and women who were—well, nice. Or decent. Words like that were as pointless to apply to him as to a hawk.

"La-dee-da-da-*dum*," he sang with the complex harmonies and oddly voiced chords, "dum-*da*-dum-*da*-dum-deedee—oh man, tremble that note an' stomp it inna grave." He rocked his head, snapping it downward in tempo, keeping his eyes hooded with a mystical sleepiness. "Play, man, play. It's always night or we wouldn' need the light. Oh ho, oh ho-ho, it's always night or we wouldn' need the light." The music changed meter, blending into a waggish old-time stride piano style, then slid sideways and ended.

Roone opened his eyes. "I knew this was the day. I told you I knew it. He plays that piano like he's telling the truth."

"If I had known you liked him, I would have played his"—she made a small circle in the air with her finger to include their cups—" 'Tea for Two.' "

"Have you got it? On the Criss-Cross recording?"

"Got it? I love it."

"You mean it?"

"Of course I mean it."

"You'll play it?"

"Of course I will. Just for your birthday."

"Betsy, I knew you had the right vibrations. We click, like that honey and wax."

"Don't click me, Roone. You boys are all like TV commercials for Eversharp blades. Push-pull, click-click. Just remember I'm seven or eight years older than you, my boy."

"Twelve years," he said calmly. "I looked up your health record."

"All right. Dr. Jekyll. Twelve. It feels like a hundred." She meant to stop, but she was beginning to feel encircled by his easy blunting of her every defensive thrust, by his omnipotent access to her medical record. How? Hospital records were kept so carefully, David always said. Another of David's well-to-do, decent items of ignorance? And now, Roone's having caught her in a childish, womanish lie about her age stung her. "Hit and run," she found herself saying, "that's all you kids know. Wham bam, thank you ma'm, and hippity-hoppity off to mount the next cottontail bunny."

"You're no bunny, Betsy. You're a lady. A face on you like a fallen angel."

"Gee, Dad, thanks." Oh Lord, now I'm imitating *his* talk.

"You're the first lady I've met. You're a lass with a delicate air, Betsy. A little kooky maybe, but in a real ladylike way."

"Columbus discovers America. Hooray, I'm a lady."

"A Play Lady."

"And you. A toy tiger?"

He bared his remarkably white, even, smiling teeth. "A real tiger. The lady and the tiger. Wanna ride? You'll jus' love bein' in the saddle."

"Don't be ridiculous. This whole thing is ridiculous."

He shook his head. "Uh-uh. No, ma'm. I'm for real." He waved his hand, taking in her kitchen, her home, her neighborhood, her world. "*This* is ridiculous. There're at least three different revolutions going on right now in the United States, and I guess maybe three times three all over the world. All over, things are cookin' on gas on all the burners, but around here everything is far away and long ago." He snorted. "You drive up this tree-lined street to this tree-shaded house and what do you see?"

"I know what I see, and I like it." Ah, now she was stage center again, an embattled heroine. She liked the firm sound of her voice. She wished she could pour herself another Bloody Mary without losing dignity. One more, and the pipes of Pan would begin to play and the birches would bend like harps. They would grapple, but intellectually. *Marvelous!* Now she was interested. "What do you see, Roone?"

He grasped his jaw between thumb and forefinger and shook it, saying, "Br-r-r. Now I can feel those bennies. Tom-toms in the thalamus."

"Bennies?" His unexpected conversational shift made her feel off-balance again. What would he say next? Which of his different Englishes would he use?

"Benzedrine," he said. "No sleep, so I hooked me a capsule."

She remembered the gypsy put-on talk in the booth yesterday. Heroin. Mandarin clouds. Her voice dropped. "You take *drugs?*"

"Oh, knock it off, Queenie. Aspirin is drugs. Sleeping pills are drugs. Whiskey is alcohol, and that's the most popular drug. Didn't you ever hear the song 'Who Put the Benzedrine in Mrs. Murphy's Ovaltine'? Bennies are pep-up pills, that's all."

"Just to stay awake?"

"I told you. No beauty rest for the wicked. I didn't sleep."

"Poor thing. Why not?"

"Can't you knock it off, Queenie? You know damn well why not. Y'know, there's a coy lace-curtain-Irish streak in you. It's phony and it's unattractive as hell. I couldn't sleep because I kept taking you apart and putting you back together again. A construction job. My erector set was working the night shift."

"So you hooked a bennie and hocked your watch and rumbled all the way out to this tree-lined lace-curtain street"—her voice was rising now—"for an unattractive phony Irish biddy twelve years older than you are?"

He shrugged. "I'm just as surprised as you are. You really pressed that red alert button, my hot line. It's like bein' kicked in the balls."

"Why can't you just plain ordinary cut out the dirty-little-boy words?"

"Welcome to the twentieth century, Queenie."

"I don't care for your twentieth century, Dr. Jekyll."

"And your eighteenth century is all gone, Betsy." He waved his hand again at her whole world. "You mortgaged all your castles in the air, beautiful dreamer. Now the po' folks' bank is gonna foreclose."

"I don't know what on earth—"

"You know what I mean. This is dreamland. Every house around here has at least ten acres to keep out young couples and their million kids. It's municipal birth control by zoning laws. Let 'em eat cake, but not on these weed-free lawns. Your neighbor, no, the one this side—the one with the pink painted *hitching* post where their drive begins."

"Well, I'll buy that, Roone. I'll agree with you there. That's ridiculous."

"And down thataway? That little metal statue at the driveway? A toy Negro groom."

Betsy nodded. "I'll buy that, too. Very bad taste."

"Bad taste? For Chrisake, Betsy, get the picture? A little statue of a slave? A phony British love of horses? Crap all over, but not a horse within miles." He bent forward. "And you? You've got a lamppost with a gas lantern in front of your house."

"I happen to like gaslight at night."

"Romantic as all get out."

"No," she said. "It's just that Witt's away a good deal. We've been robbed once. I need a night-light in front of the house, and one over the garage in back."

"*Gaslight?*" He snapped his fingers toward the invisible orchestra in the living room. "Music, maestro. The Merry Widow Waltz."

"Oh," she said, defending herself again, "gaslight just brings back remembrance of things past."

Dublin. My mother standing in the doorway, lifting a shawl over her dark head. Half my heart, she thought with a stab, buried in the grave. She tilted her cup and swirled the tea in it, searching down the tiny liquid funnel as if her childhood lay at the bottom.

"Things past?"

"Myself. Sitting on a photographer's pony for a picture out on the street."

"So now you're crying?"

She raised her head fiercely. "I'm not."

"Okay. Shiny nostalgic tear or two."

"Well, you said: be yourself. I'm soft as Christmas pudding. I'm actually a very sentimental sort, tough guy."

"Me, Betsy? You don't begin to know what *tough* means. I'm not tough."

"I keep forgetting. You med students prefer words like *realistic.*"

"You scored that time. We do."

"Oh," she said, "I know you, all of you in those short white gloopy-looking jackets. I've heard you boys talking in the coffee shop. Your diseases never hurt like hell—oh no, your diseases are just *interesting*. Pain? That's just a note on your chart. Fever? A little red line."

"Irish? A curvy green line."

"Don't blarney me, boy. You're a great bluff. You barge in here, un-invited, hopped up on bennies, talkin' up a great revolutionary storm—by God, I'm fed up with your—your—"

"Crap?" he suggested mildly.

"Yes! Crap!"

"See, Betsy? You can learn real words."

"Oh crap," she said.

"Say orgasm. Go ahead. Try it."

"I can't. I've never said it in my life."

"There's always a first time. Grow up. It's easy. Just say it."

"No."

"Lady, we're talking about the heart of darkness. The reason for gods. You afraid of black magic? It's only one little word."

"I know. Let's skip it."

He shook his head with exaggerated sadness. "Superstition. The ancient Hebrews never pronounced the true name of God. Live and learn, Betsy. We're talking about the big connection, your trip around the world, the big O."

"Oh," she said.

"Not bad for a growing girl. Now once more for good luck."

"Orgasm," she said. "Now do I win the stethoscope?"

He spread his hands. "See how easy it is? Why stay in the wrong century?"

She pushed her chair aside and made a move to go.

Roone's eyebrows went up. "Running away?"

"Upstairs. I've got to get dressed."

"I make you uncomfortable?"

She pointed at the kitchen clock. "It's late. Min will be here any minute. Timmy comes home for lunch." She frowned at him. "And it's my house. I don't have to run away."

"Except from Dublin."

"Oh please. Please, Svengali. Maybe your mind-reading act impresses the nursing students, but not me. I've seen you working in Doctor Sommers' lab and helping out in Pediatrics, and butter wouldn't melt in your polite yes-sir, no-sir mouth. You're a Dr. Jekyll-Hyde character who needs Witt to come home and fetch you a great clout."

"If he tried it, I'd kick him in the crotch."

"Sure. But Witt fights with his fists. He fights fair."

"Okay. So I'm not a hero like DeWitt Sommers. Jeesuzz, what a phony Dutch name."

She was incredulous. "You know Witt?"

"He's in your medical history, Betsy. Your two marriages. First the boy who was killed in Korea, and then DeWitt after the war. Throw in the usual premarital screwing and some country club two-ships-that-pass-in-the-night, and I'd say you've been up and down like a beautiful yo-yo."

She was choking. Shame and anger gripped her windpipe. A knot of debasement tightened in her stomach. Her life, a public turnstile? Cut down into two or three surgical notations? The bare foundation exposed like dirt, the whole house-of-living complexity brushed aside in a heap? This was worse than standing naked in a terror dream, naked under a downpour of lights. Fury pumped the blood out of her heart, flushing her face and throat. She trembled, completely unable to speak.

"Betsy," he was saying hurriedly, "don't take it so hard. A coupla lines in a medical file, that's all. Take it easy. I didn't mean to hurt your feelings."

She tried to walk toward the door, but her knees had become puppet-hinged, collapsible, ready to tip her over. He stepped forward quickly, beginning to hold out a hand to help her, but when he touched her elbow she slapped him with all her strength.

He rested his long fingers along the red splotch on his face, touching it carefully without changing his expression. "Congratulations," he said. "There's life in the teacup, after all. The sleeping beauty wakes up with a bang."

"I'm up, all right! Just you watch your tongue."

He smiled slowly. "Hallelujah, baby! That wallop must have felt mighty good."

"Yes and no. Now my hand hurts." Her anger was draining away in his calmness, so she said as harshly as she could, "And you *eat* with that mouth?"

"I really didn't mean to hurt your feelings, Betsy."

"Yesterday you said nothing was *really*."

"You remember yesterday, after all."

"Yes. Damn you." She felt off balance each time he outflanked her.

"Then what's all the big fuss, Betts? You enjoyed it, yesterday."

"I did. But now you've spoiled it, Roone."

"How? I said something stupid, so I apologize. But nothing—nothing, ah, like vol*can*ic—has happened, has it?"

"You'd never understand." Yesterday, she thought, I was practically in heat, with a swollen pelvic feeling and that pressing in my back, something he could never ever conceive.

"I'm just another unshaven damn kid?"

For the first time he sounded hollow, uncertain, his mask as a swaggerer had slipped, and she knew her own picture of him was betraying the anger she needed. "No," she said, as if she owed him reassurance, "you're a man. But very young. Really, Roone."

He grinned, "Great song title. Really Roone." He plucked at an imaginary guitar, singing, "Really Roone, really Roone—" He stopped. "What rhymes with Roone?"

She felt herself smiling, too. "Loony," she said. "Doesn't anybody ever call you by your Christian name?"

"Betsy, do you expect me to believe in a Christian name? Or God? Or Jehovah, or Yang and Yin, or the little green leprechauns of th' ould sod?"

"My, I really touched the red alert button that time, didn't I?"

"With you, you can touch anything you want, including my red alert button. But nobody calls me by my childhood name except"—and he used his vaudeville accent again—"me wee gray mither."

"Yes. I remember your mentioning her so pleasantly. Didn't she ever have any *living* children? And isn't there a wee gray father?"

"Father?" he asked. "My fah-hah-ther? Yes, there was one. Biologically, yes. Every other way, no. A forked radish."

"Oh my," she said mildly, determined now not to let him see her offended. "I keep forgetting your generation blames everything on its parents."

"My father believed God made the world in six days, and saved Saturday for on the town and Sunday for watching television in his undershirt, with the top of his pants unbuttoned, drinking beer." His voice had begun to rise. "My father believed women were delicate things who thought only clean thoughts except for nine minutes on Saturday nights and, other than that, cooked and cleaned, packed your lunch, fed the kids, and took a beating before or after the nine minutes on Saturday night. He made a pile after the war, his hole-in-the-wall hardware store is a chain of Handy Home Helper Centers now, and he still sits around in his undershirt, only it's silk and monogrammed now." He shrugged. "He's living it up. I'm living it down."

She was genuinely shocked. "What a way to talk!" She felt a chill, and clutched the edges of the collar of her robe together at the neck with one hand. Not me, she decided. *He's* the one, awake now, and singing. Not the polite clean-cut medical student nor the groovy hipster of jazz joints. Just another familiar, angry, self-pitying, anxious-to-prove-himself young man who prowled up and down the dark streets of his desires like all the rest. Just a young cub scrounging for scraps here and there. All he needs is a hot meal and a warm girlfriend, she thought sympathetically—then, amazed at her simple discovery—and I was beginning to be a little afraid of him!

"My father," he was saying, "ran booze in the twenties. In the thirties he was in the soup lines or rakin' leaves for the WPA. In the forties he faked himself a section-eight discharge from the Army. He faked a whip-lash injury on the factory assembly line and poked along on workmen's compensation checks and started his hardware store. You had enough?"

"Yes. You've killed him completely."

"Oh, no. Not that tough ol' crotch-scratchin' buzzard. He used to send me checks in college to stay away. Just to stay the hell away. Two years ago the check had my name spelled wrong so I tore it in half and sent it back. So guess what?"

"What?"

"No more checks. The sink-or-swim bit, y'know? Makes you want to vomit, doesn't it?"

"Yes." She meant it. A nauseating distaste of everything which crawled beneath the rocks of the world, the seedy tattered dirty-fingernail sweaty-armpit torn-underwear swarm of the world, all balled together into a lump of distaste. I've spent my whole life running away from it, Chicago and that railroad flat and the drunken prince of players in the back bed-room, and now Roone drags it into this shining kitchen. She stared at him with hate, but only until he dropped his head slightly and said, "Happy birthday to friends, Romans, countrymen. Me, I just work here."

"You're hungry, aren't you?"

"More or less."

"Mostly more."

He grinned, and she noticed his even teeth, again feeling the twitch of a faint familiarity. "Shucks now, ma'm," he said, sticking his thumbs into his belt and bowing his legs like a cowhand, "jes' don' y'all trouble yore purty li'l haid 'bout us'n hired hands."

She held her nose. "What an accent."

"Gotta ride tall in the saddle, missus."

"Okay, enough of that talk, thank you. I'll go up and get dressed and then make you an honest-to-goodness birthday breakfast."

He reached out and touched her arm gently. "You're not sore, Betts?"

"I don't know. I just don't know what I am. You're a circus. Three rings and a high-wire act. How can I be sore at a circus? You're a daring young man on a flying trapeze, and I'm sure you'll break your neck some-day."

"You're very ambivalent, Betts."

"Watch it, boy. I think I know what that means."

"To hell with it. Like the Frenchman said to a Vassar girl: Enough of this talk. Let's go."

"Go? Go where?"

"To New York."

"To New *York?*" She felt the ground tilt slightly. His carrousel was beginning to rotate again.

"Sure!" He flung one arm toward the window. "Beautiful day. I've been invited to a veddy veddy smashing going-away party on the—the—whatever they call that big Swedish ocean liner."

"Ocean liner?" The carrousel was turning faster now.

"The S.S. *Smorgasbord,* or *Aquavit,* or whatever it is. Caribbean cruise. Fun in the sun. Lay your troubles aside."

"You know?" she said. "Sometimes I have a little trouble following your train of thought."

"It's simple, Simon. Tabac—you remember him?"

"Of course."

"Well, he's taking the boat as far as San Juan. Maybe a little stopover in Fort Lauderdale."

"Fort Lauderdale? I thought that was only for white-haired Republican ladies and their husbands' tax-deductible yacht-ta-ta-ing."

"At Belle Glade they import experienced field hands from Puerto Rico for the sugar cane. Sometimes Volga goes with Tabac to pick up a big *bujo.*"

"I didn't know you two were fortune-telling buddies."

"We're not. But where he is, that's where the action is. With Tabac on deck, can rum be far behind? And those Puerto Rican girls who come down to see him off, Tabac calls 'em *cañas dulces*—that's sweet sugar cane." He drew a sinuous, voluptuous line in the air. "When they start that cha-cha, man, they shimmy an' they shake, crawl on they belly like a snake."

She was both amused and annoyed. "With all that snaky sugar cane around, why do you need some New Haven hausfrau as your date?" *Date* wasn't the right word, but what other word was there? There was something youthful about *date* which was missing from the usual faintly derogatory words like babe and dame, and others which sounded worse. Why did men use such words for women?

"You'd knock 'em stone-cold dead, Betsy. You've got that black black hair, but those two green—or are they blue?—eyes. Here, let me take a good look." He swiveled her chin toward him with one finger.

She held herself stiffly while he peered directly into her eyes. Just as she had not wanted to look at him before, now she did not want to look away. His finger was warm on her skin now, not the icy feel of when they had shaken hands across the table. First he inspected one eye, then the other. His face was professionally noncommittal. When he spoke again, he used what she had begun to recognize as his medical English. "Interesting. Dilated pupils—is that why you wear dark glasses so much? This eye's blue-green. That one's green-blue. Like two different people."

"Of course. There's a blue me and a green me."

"You must have very interesting genes."

"Blue jeans," she said, straight-faced. Puns like that were popular in the old-fashioned Sommers family, but not elsewhere.

"You're beautiful," he said seriously. "You are one beautiful cookie."

"Yes, I know," she said, still keeping her face straight. "Emerald eyes. Nose like the prow of an ancient Greek ship. Shall I go on?"

"No," he said. "You can stop."

"But it'd save time. You a legs man? Shall we discuss legs? There's a rumor I have gorgeous legs."

"No. I get the idea."

"Good. Hold onto it. And please spare me the doll-baby line."

"Who ever heard of a woman getting sore because you tell her she's beautiful?"

"Well, now you've heard of it. I know how I look. I know very well how I look, and it's brought me nothing but one headache after another."

"I know, Betsy. All gift wrapping and no box. You want to be respected and appreciated for what's inside, right?"

She watched him, suspicious of double-talk. "More or less," she said. "Corny as it sounds, that's the idea."

"Then just let me inside, so I can respect and appreciate you. You following my train of thought?"

"You don't have a train, Roone. Just an unwashed little red caboose on one track."

"Hey, great, Betts. You're better'n instant Zen. I bow to Hon'able Missy Banzai."

"Oh, stop jabbering like a fool."

"I mean it. You're a real geisha."

"You just want to trump Tabac's dark-haired playmates with a gift-wrapped box of your own."

He put his thumb under his upper lip and flipped it forward. "Ts*sah!* It'll be a great party, believe me. A brawl. An insurrection. I'll bring my guit-tar"—he plunked his fingers in the air—"play 'The Irish Brigade' just for you."

"In tango tempo?"

"Betsy, no kiddin', you'd enjoy it. Nothing homogenized, repressed, or depressed about these people. Natural as breathing. Fountain of Youth."

"And I'm the Girl Most Likely?"

He smiled a long slow lazy smile. "Betts," he said, "you're veddy hip, sometimes. Like a bit of all right. You're what's happening, baby."

"I happen to have to stay at home, Roone. I'm expecting an important phone call from my husband. He may ask me to pack for a quick trip abroad with only an hour's notice."

"But New York's only about an hour down the pike. We could zip down and back before dark. I believe in nursery book rules. Like early to bed."

She enjoyed his put-on talk, and tried to match it. She had grown up among people who used words the way gamblers use roulette chips. She liked the spinning of the wheel, phony but fun.

"Fun in the sun?" She kept ridicule out of her voice.

He nodded. "Veddy avant-gaudy. Lots of fairy grandfathers."

"Sin now, pay later?"

"Be my guest, Betts."

"Not so fast. It's hard to eat on an empty credit card."

"Don't be a Mother, Betts. You gotta have a queen's confidence. Go anywhere, anytime, in your chemise."

She snapped her fingers at him, as he had done at Volga yesterday. "Play, gypsy, play."

He caught her game and laughed, decided to ride with it, and threw his head back to address the invisible gods of the kitchen ceiling. "She's got it! I think she's got it!"

"Forget it," Betsy said. "She's done forgot it."

He raised his elbows and executed a quick heel-rattling Spanish dance step. "A tango with a mango, señorita? *Cañas dulces*. Raise a li'l Cain in the sweetes' sugah cane?"

Betsy heard footsteps on the driveway beside the house. She dropped her hands to her sides. "Children's Hour is over, Roone. Time to stop this collegiate chitchat and get my weary bones dressed."

"Ah, now, Betsy—you got me burning on a short fuse—"

The footsteps were coming up the back porch steps now. "Stop it!" she whispered fiercely. "Here comes Min!" She heard the back door open.

Min had come to work for Betsy as a Thursday laundress, and it was a year before she told Betsy that Dr. David Sommers was her hospital clinic doctor. She had been surprised to find in Betsy a person easy to talk to, very different from most of the other wealthy women she had worked for before, and sensed that Betsy—like herself—had a vulnerability which needed help, domestic and personal. Min had made it clear that she did not need to work, her husband had a good civil service job at the New Haven post office, but the fact that she was childless made her nervous. Dr. David Sommers had told her in the clinic that she should not sit around worrying and stewing in her apartment, but should work at something active while the clinic tried to help her begin a family. She was sure her job at Betsy's house was a good idea. "Missus," she would say, "I swear, sometimes you make me feel like I'm a mother an' you the chile."

Min tramped into the kitchen heartily.

"Mornin', mornin'," she said. "That damn 32-B bus was late again this mornin'. I swear, nothin' runs right these days."

"Ain't it the truth?" Betsy said, and they both laughed at their familiar nose-thumbing at the untruthful facts of life. Min looked at Roone, and Betsy suddenly saw him through Min's eyes: unshaven, no tie, the surplus-government-property Air Force jacket, beltless pipestem chino pants stiff enough to stand alone, heavy white gym socks and sneakers.

"This is Mr. Gerald Roone, Min," she said hurriedly. "Mrs. Mildred Curtis."

Min nodded. "Hi."

"Pleased to meet you," Roone said politely.

"Mr. Roone is the medical student who's helping me at the hospital." Betsy found she was talking too fast, and tried to speak more casually. "You remember? Painting that mural in the Pediatrics playroom. He's brought me some, ah, brushes out this morning."

"Oh, sure, I remember." Now Min smiled at him. "I thought you looked like somebody I met before someplace."

"Min is one of Doctor Sommers' patients," Betsy explained to Roone. The simple introduction had now become stickier than flypaper. "She's in the fertility clinic."

"I'm due for another test next week," Min said. "Where they put that little tube in to see if you nature is workin' okay."

"The Rubin test? Gas through the Fallopian tubes?"

Min pointed at him. "That's where I seen you. In the clinic. That desk where they give out them little paper packages of birth control pills. You sure look different without a shave an' a white jacket."

Roone rubbed his jaw with the back of his hand.

Yesterday Betsy would have believed the gesture was boyish embarrassment. What a clever actor!

Roone nodded to Min. "No time to shave. Up all night with a sick man."

"Ohhh." Min's voice slid down, sympathetically. "World's fulla troubles. How's he now?"

"Stiff." His face was grave, but now Betsy detected the wild goat-hoofed far-off laughter in it. "He needs to be laid out for his reward."

"Too bad." Min shook her head. "Dust to dust. The Lord gives, then He takes away."

"True, true," he said. "It's a long long lonesome road to the bosom of Abraham. Or any other. But every man has to cross over the Jordan to lay his burden down."

"Amen to that," Min said. "Preacher says when your knees knock, kneel on 'em."

"Just look!" Betsy said quickly, before he might carry his blarney further into cruelty. "Look at the time! Timmy'll be home any minute. The Barretts are out marketing. Min, while I throw something on, will you heat some tomato soup?"

Min chuckled. "We've got food'll stick to his ribs better'n hot soup. Hot beef san'wich? How's that sound?"

Roone put his hand over his heart. "Right here. You're gettin' to me."

"Oh, my," Min said, "you're a sketch. You talk like TV."

"It's his birthday," Betsy said, unsure which way Roone's winds would blow. "Do we have a cake in the freezer?"

"I'll find somethin'. How 'bout a vanilla cupcake?"

"Don't bother, please," Roone said.

"No bother." Min started toward the refrigerator. "I'll have it all fixed, time you dress, Missus Sommers."

"Time you dress?" Roone sounded surprised. "We're not going to the opera, madame. Just a quick run down to New York."

Min stopped. "Oh?" She eyed Betsy. "Want me to stay on late? Ain't this the Barretts' night off?"

"No—" Betsy began, but Roone interrupted her.

"A vanilla cupcake with no candles on it? What kind of hospitality is that?"

"Honestly," Min said. "Hard to know when you're jokin'. You're a real trouper. How many candles you require, Doctor?"

"Jus' one, please, ma'm. One for good luck."

"Ho-ho! Rest don't count, now, do they?"

"No, they don't," Roone said, "'less you can burn them at both ends." He raised one finger in the air and intoned, "Better to light one candle at both ends than to curse the dark."

Betsy looked from one to the other. "You two comedians don't need any interruptions from me. I'll just run along."

"Okay," Roone said. "You just do that little thing. Don't bother wearing your heart. Jus' slip into somethin' comfortable."

Behind her, as she left the kitchen, Betsy heard Min call after her in a voice beginning to float on Roone's tide and burble into laughter, "Hasta la vista!"

While Betsy was in the shower, she heard the door slam downstairs. Brian Timothy. The young master of the house cometh. She soaped herself quickly. Duty calls. I should have been up and going hours ago. If only that wild grinning young man, half innocence, half lust—she stopped. Her nipples had hardened into points with a sudden, unexpected traitorous life of their own. No, she thought fiercely, and turned the shower to a needle spray so cold and punishing she gasped. His pitter-patter vaudeville routine, barely saved from banality because he scoffed at it and himself.

He sidestepped everything so smoothly, doffing his jester's cap and bells —my, even the way he had sweet-talked past Min's shrewd appraisal. The artful dodger. That candid open gaze. Then the shooting glance, mocking. A ball of mercury, that boy. The kind that chase girls only when it's downhill. Really, it wasn't very funny at all. Then why does he make me feel ready to laugh? As he'd said: What's real? What's really? It's as if he'd discovered some great forbidden joke on the world and shared it only with me, both of us shaking with secret, silent laughter. My old problem: how to have my cheesecake and eat it, too. That's how he'd say it, I'm sure.

Ah, it takes one to know one, her mother's voice said—or was it Witt who had said it?—and there's a world's difference between a comical mischief and all the tumbling vices. You'll never fall off the roof by standin' on the ground. Oh, Mother, from a penitential world of corseted rockbound respectability; of gentlewomen coughing daintily into the backs of their wrists, watchful for sin, each carrying her life delicately in one hand like a bridal missal, ready to swallow poison before facing a whisper of wrongdoing or any public shame from the neighbors. Oh, Mother, the world's changing so fast, even the nuns go out in shorter skirts now.

While she began drying herself in her terry-cloth robe, spinning out the cobwebby voice of her mother in her mind, Timmy knocked on the door. "Hey, Mom! You in there?"

"No," she called. "I'm not." Thank God for him, my one unquestioning, unquestioned, anchor of love. He's small, Mother would say, but daily growing. She heard him giggle.

The door opened an inch or two. "Phew! Steamy! Can't see you, Mom!"

"I can see *you*."

"No, you can't. How?"

"In the mirror, silly."

"I'm Jack. The teacher said so."

"Jack what, darling?"

"In the play. The beanstalk."

"Jack and the Beanstalk? That's *wonderful*, Timmy."

"The Giant gets to say ho-ho-ho."

"But you get the pot of gold? And bring it home for your mother?"

"I sure do!" he shouted. "And kill the giant!"

Actor's genes, she thought. The prince of players. She felt her love for the boy rush through her. She ran to open the door and put her arms around him. "Oh you peanut pie," she said as she kissed him.

"Mom! You're all drippy." He wrinkled his eyes at her, Witt's shrewd wheeler-dealer eyes, Witt's chunky squared-off shoulders. "Hey, Mom—"

"You look like someone who wants to make a deal, Jack."

Timmy lowered his voice. "The man downstairs said he'll get me an ax to cut down the beanstalk."

"Oh, he did, did he?" That Roone, she thought. I'll strangle the surgical monster. "I'm not so sure your teacher will appreciate a real, live ax in school."

"But he said—"

"Never mind what *he* said. It's what I say. Now why don't you have your lunch while I get dressed?"

From downstairs came the muted sound of the kitchen telephone.

"It's his birthday, Mom."

"I know, darling. We all know. He's riding it to a fare-thee-well."

"He said I could share it with him. He said the ax was a present to me."

"Missus Sommers," Min called from downstairs. "Can I talk to you a minute?"

Betsy kept her arm around the boy's shoulders as they walked out into the upstairs hallway. She leaned over the banister. "Yes?"

Min was craning up at her from the bottom of the steps. "Missus Crotty from the hospital. Can you volunteer today? I tol' her you in a shower, then you goin' down to New York. Wanna talk to her?"

"Yes. She'll think I'm uppity if I don't. Oh, Min, what's this talk about an *ax?*"

"Oh, jus' a little rubber toy one. Kinda cute, huh? Come on down, Timmy honey, and have some lunch."

Betsy patted Timmy's bottom lightly to steer him toward the stairs. "Munch-crunch lunch, Mr. Jack," she said, and then went into her bedroom to take the call.

"Oh, Mrs. Sommers!" Mrs. Crotty sounded breathless and effusive on the phone. "Please don't feel I'm drafting you for slave labor, but we're so shorthanded in the snack bar today that it's pitiful, honestly! Can you help us out just for a few hours this afternoon?"

"I'm so sorry. I've got a really unbreakable bon-voyage party date in New York today," Betsy said effortlessly. "These are old family friends. The date was made months ago and they'd be upset if I didn't come to say goodbye."

She marveled at the genuine tone of regret in her voice. As always when she lied with successfully instant ease, she felt a victorious on-top strength replace the constant discomfort of her introspective pin-scratches. Easing that inner invisible itch, she had decided long ago, was the reason men fought life so fiercely, competed for shiny brassplated prizes, placed chesty fists-up ads in papers AGGRESSIVE PROMOTION-MINDED YOUNG MAN SEEKS POSITION IN PET SHOP and lied to women with the round-and-round repetition of a stuck phonograph needle.

At least we women never lie unless we have to, she thought as she put down the phone. And when we do, it's to save somebody from hurt feelings, especially when the somebody is oneself.

She saw herself in the long mirror. Her mouth wore a tiny understanding smile beneath the green eye smiling at the blue one. The princess of players. Oh, you're a fine bluff of an actress, you are. Lying even to yourself. You were not going bucketing around New York. Definitely not. You're forever saying you won't go near the water, not a single step, oh maybe just one small step just to dip a toe or two in some comical mischief, and always the forbidden waters rise in a flood and there you are, drowning again, clutching at some man, some lifeguard, some companion. For a fleeting second she saw a terrified stranger stare out of the mirror and she turned away from the brutal glass to begin dressing.

The scratch of uncertainty had come back, as always, but another hail Bloody Mary full of grace and a wee drop of vodka would heal *that*.

She found herself opening the bathroom wall cabinet for her Chanel dusting powder and her hair spray, but it was the wrong cabinet. What am I looking for? Forgetful. This cabinet had on its bottom shelf the modernistic white plastic case emblazoned with a stylized golden sea horse in the shape of the letter S—the Sommers trademark—and a miniature circle of letters: *Sommers Pharmaceutical Company*. Inside the plastic case was an unused diaphragm. Her friends considered the device an old-fashioned item of sporting equipment, but as much a household necessity as a raincoat or umbrella. What Olympian irony, that she and Witt knew they were among the statistical select, the one couple in every ten who never needed the products of the family's company. We happy few, she thought, the women who don't get pregnant no matter how hard they try. And try. Mayoso had explained her sterility several years ago. Some undiscovered something in the vaginal fluid was lethal for sperm. Like an allergy. No one's *fault*. One woman in twenty. Research, maybe David's research. You and Witt should keep trying. Sometimes pregnancy . . .

Me. Of all people. One of Mother Nature's pitless peaches. Lethal something for sperm. A killer-diller. Ugh.

She banged the cabinet door shut as her skin broke into the sensation of a heat rash. Men! Damn them all, the long and the short and the tall.

I know Witt. He'll be wondering all day today about how I sounded on the long-distance phone last night.

A hard obstinate knot of annoyance tightened as she hurried expertly through her makeup, concentrating on her eyes. She knew the look she wanted, all bones and brightness, green eyes under unfashionably heavy black eyebrows.

As her hairbrush moved skillfully, she swished her hair over one eye. No, that's trying too hard. Too much Portofino and St. Tropez. We want the freshly scrubbed all-American look, the clean-cut jeune fille, athletic, hair pulled together at the nape with a heavy silver buckle, there, like that, an upward touch with the black eyebrow pencil and a trace of lipstick. Nice. Outdoorsy. *Très sportif.*

She considered her clothes, calculating choices. Avant-gaudy, he'd said. For a moment she paused over the idea of linen-weave Pucci stretch pants and sandals, proof she hadn't bothered to dress up, yet revealing enough to look naughty nicely. No, she decided. I want something simple, flawless, something that'll *stun* him. Dress to kill. Quickly, enjoying the game more each minute, she chose her never-failing ensemble of green: pale green lace girdle, matching bra—no, she threw the bra aside, no need for the bra with the loose emerald silk-ribbon-knit traveling dress—very sheer stockings and high heels to match. Earrings? No. The green dress was enough. Just right. And there we are, luv, musing into the mirror again, all eyes, jade-green and secret-smiling as a cat queen of the Nile.

She swept confidently toward the door, tasting triumph ahead, momentarily mythologic, nymph and huntress.

Roone's alchemy had turned an everyday lunch into fool's gold. He made pennies disappear from his hand and pop out behind Timmy's ear. He folded a paper airplane, and, when Timmy left to return to school, Roone sailed it across the back porch for him. Roone assured Min pontifically that the world was indeed upside down when those who wanted children couldn't produce them. For Betsy's benefit, when Min brought him his hot beef sandwich, he bowed his head and delivered what he called Scottish grace.

"Soom hae meat but canna eat, 'nd soom wad eat that want it; but we hae meat 'nd we can eat, so let th' Lorrd be thank' it."

Min shook her head admiringly. *"Hon*estly!" She went out, and a little later the high domesticated whine of the laundry machine reached them in the living room.

"You should've been Irish," Betsy said.

"The Ancient Order of Hibernians would niver iver have me, lass."

"Oh, sure, with that farfetched tart tongue of yours, they'd make you an honorary Irishman."

"No," Roone said. "I know them. I grew up with them. Went to parochial school with them. The Protestant Prod, they called me. A very big hoo-ha. They used to tell me, like boasting, they were just natural poor, natural proud, and natural poetic. Me, I'm just artificially poor."

Betsy answered more intensely than she intended, "Oh, they *have* to dream. Don't you understand that? Their poetry isn't fancy stuff to be printed. It's spoken, natural as talking, common as good manners."

"Good manners? Which Ireland you talking about? I've been there, dead-broke in Dublin. You need to hear some Dublin medical students whisper about the big money they make doing abortions in basements. Zero birth control—b'gorra, the curate'll fry your soul in hell, but do you know how much infanticide there is?"

She raised her shoulders, a self-protective shrinking. "D'you always see only the ugly? You and your brainer-than-thou bit. You never met the Dublin I grew up in, full of decent people. Full of sorrow after so many years of being treated as serfs. Doing without. My first go-to-school blouse was made from the cloth off a torn umbrella. Can you believe it? My mother used to buy coal for the stove, one lump at a time, the coal man weighin' it on a little brass scale in the alley behind the house, the two of them discussing the price of each lump polite as saying Scripture for the dead."

"There you go with the national hobby—always looking back over your shoulder. It's nutty as a fruitcake."

"My, you must be debauched completely. Witt and I went to Dublin on our honeymoon, and for me it was coming home. We strolled the first evening along Thomas Street, to the Limelight, just for the show. There was a boy there said to be a wizard with the spoons—"

"And to raise a pint or two—"

"We did, we did that. It's a singin' pub, y'know, and when they sang, oh when those young ballad singers sang"—she closed her eyes and tilted her head back—"*Oh, the trees are grown high, my love, oh, the grass is green, my love, for it's a long and cruel night that I must lie alone—*"

"Alone," Roone said. "They're all alone. Nothing isolates those believers more than their sense of sin. Remember the shelf along the wall, opposite the bar? The lonesome shelf, where a man can stand and rest his pint and keep his back turned to the whole world? For those guys sin is so real it leaves fingerprints."

"Oh, Roone, you see what you want to see. I saw a green country. I could hear the green grass growin'. We found my dad's picture, hanging on the wall of the Green Room, at the Abbey. There he was, alive in that picture, young forever. And the same night, all in one gulp, we saw Yeats's *The Dreaming of the Bones.*"

"What's that got to do with now? It's dead and gone, Betsy."

"Oh no! How can you say dead and gone? The past is alive and right here. It walks alongside you. It's your twin. It's the shadow you can't shake."

"Okay. I surrender. How can you argue with people who like plays called *The Dreaming of the Bones?*"

"Don't you okay me. Just don't dismiss it like that."

He bent toward her. "Lay your pistol down, ma'm. Don't get tetchy. Girls who look like you don't have to bother."

"You pretend you're a deep one, but that's a stupid thing to say."

"Look, if we're going to go, we'd better start."

"Do you expect me to go—with you dressed like that?"

He inspected himself. "What's wrong, boss?"

"Oh, Roone, you're such an artful dodger. You look like Frankenstein's kid brother recovering from trench mouth or athlete's foot."

He grinned. I'm catching on fast, she thought. I had forgotten how young people exchange casual insults.

"You paint a pretty picture of hoof-and-mouth disease, Betsy. So?"

"So I'll get you Witt's razor." Now it was her turn to inspect him. "And a shirt—you're about as big as he is across the chest."

"Ha. Can't be. I'm Hercules. He can't be *God.*"

"And a tie," she said.

"A *tie?* Around my *neck?* You're mighty generous, Pat."

"Anything for a friend, Mike."

He reached across the table and put the tip of his finger under her chin. "I'm no friend, I'm the enemy."

Later, as they walked down the front steps, he glanced down at her and made his pantomime of strumming a guitar. "How Merrily Doth My Lady Jiggle. You walk inside that green dress like you're goin' downtown."

"Stop it, Roone. You embarrass me."

"I think you mean that. It's hard to keep up with you. But if the lady likes poetry—we'll give her poetry."

"But that 'Merrily,'" she said. "It's just a little obscene."

"Relax, Queenie. Between what's bawdy and what's dirty, there's a difference."

"I know," she said. "Price, and who's looking in the window."

He stepped ahead just as they reached his car. As he opened the door, she said, "You can close it. You don't expect me to go to New York in this heap, do you?"

The car was sagging with neglect. Not even a windshield wiper. Rust was everywhere on it, an abstract design of peeling metal.

"I paid a buddy five hard-earned dollars to rent this ramblin' wreck. So don't knock it, Betsy."

"I wouldn't dare. It'd collapse if I touched it. We can go in my car."

"Your green hornet?"

"Buzz, buzz."

"That's the mating call of a honey bee, students," he said cheerfully. "Note that only the female stings."

"Sorry I began," Betsy said. "You're the maddest madman I've ever seen."

"Can I drive your Jag, boss?"

"After we skedaddle out of this neighborhood. With the top down, the neighbors'd give us more attention than a parade." She saw immediately by his special grin that he enjoyed being a conspirator, a magician, a smuggler, anything which baffled or blunted or defied order and convention. This is ridiculous, she thought. I've caught his virus. Why in the world am I playing childish games, hide-and-seek? Each moment changes from solid ground to quicksand, shifting with each step.

She had liked him earlier, only when he had been uncertain, vulnerable. The lady could ride the tiger and show Mason—no, show Roone—who was on top. But maybe that was too harsh. I'm not really the on-top type. Not really. And he had been gentle, clever, amusing, genuine, all of those, with Timmy. For Timmy, an adult man meant being like Witt, a giant on a beanstalk, but Roone had played Jack with the boy so warmly and unself-consciously that she was grateful.

I should remember that to Roone—to give up five dollars for a car, money he could have bought food with—then, my insisting on a shave, shirt, and tie—to him, these must be small surrenders. Most of his jabberwocky must cover up some backstairs pride.

He was busy opening the trunk of the ancient car. The trunk lid had no lock, and swung upward creakily. From inside, over a muddy spare tire, he lifted out a guitar and a folded contraption of canvas and metal tubing.

"What in the world is *that?*" she asked.

"A folding wheelchair. To put into your car."

"Will wonders never cease! You say it so reasonably. A folding wheelchair."

"You get long lines of visitors at the cruise ships. With a wheelchair you can go right to the head of the line." His open triumphant grin. "Great for smugglers."

"Do you want to *wheel* me to New York?"

"Sure I do. In your long green car. With those long green eyes. And that short green dress that says nothin' but tells all."

In her car she felt mastery again. She responded sensuously to good leather, deep carpeting, vigilant rows of toggle switches. She thought of driving as a masculine skill, but with feminine elements, her hair combed by the wind, all speed and grace. I won't be a tomboy—but, man, I can drive. With speed there's only *now*. No past, no pulse tap of memory.

As she shifted gears expertly and accelerated up the elm-lined country road, past her own gaslight lamp, then past the little metal statue of a groom on her nearest neighbor's lawn, past tidiness, snugness, sameness, speeding past just plain middle-age *spread*, her green-silk head scarf whipped back like a cavalry pennant. An onrushing strength ran through her. Today, for once, she thought, I'll be the victor, not the victim.

Halfway between New Haven and Bridgeport, as they approached the first Connecticut Turnpike tollbooth, he raised his voice slightly over the wind's slipstream. "I thought you said I'd drive."

"I've changed my mind. I need the exercise." She steered skillfully into an open lane, downshifted, then braked the convertible smoothly at the tollbooth on Roone's side. When the uniformed toll collector put out his hand, Betsy realized that Roone was the only man she had ever known who had no money. She became embarrassed and protective for him; she had her own thin skin where poverty had sandpapered pride, and she fumbled into her purse quickly to dig out the first folded bill her fingers touched. While she passed the money to Roone she saw the toll collector's eyes flicker appreciatively at the two of them in the car's cockpit, the look of wishful admiration she knew so well and never tired of.

"Real nice day for a ride," the man said. He counted out several dollars in bills and coins.

Roone held out his hand for the change. "Yeah. If the Chinese don't drop a hydrogen bomb on New York."

As the Jaguar sped forward, Roone snapped his fingers. "Cash-and-carry. Your cash, my carry."

"I'm sorry," Betsy said. "I should've remembered you were broke."

"I'm not. I've got two bucks stashed away in my mink-lined jockstrap."

He seemed not at all embarrassed, so she said easily, "Well, that won't pay for the tolls all the way down and back. You'd better keep the change."

"But"—he waved a fistful of dollars—"there're almost twenty bucks here."

"We'll need it. There's a tollbooth around every bend in the road."

"Rich or poor," he said, "it pays to have money."

"Oh, I'm not rich," she began to say, and, when he sniggered, she added, "not really! I've never kept a budget or a checking account balanced—Witt won't even let me sign my own checks, believe it or not—and I'm forever finding only a dime in my purse when I need a quarter for parking."

"Poor Butterfly. Little Orphan Annie. In her green Jag, taking poor Horatio Alger for a healthy country outing."

"Oh Roone, Roone. You're so full of answers, but no questions. Don't you ever say *any*thing simple or straight?"

"I'm not simple, Betts, and I'm not straight. But for you, I'm trying."

She did not answer because they were in the crowded speed zone which passed Bridgeport now. To her, Bridgeport had always been merely a zone of extra care for high-speed driving, a series of banked S-curves and ramps rumbling with intercity trucks. Bridgeport was an industrial city glimpsed off to the right, mostly as a red brick dark-roofed railroad station, which many people still called a train depot; and, to the left, tall chimneys of a power plant puffing plumes of smoke into the offshore breeze across the vitreous blue glaze of Long Island Sound. In all the years she had driven by Bridgeport on this express highway along the shore, the city had always been a crowded blur of brick factories, truck terminals, electric power lines, dun-colored, dreary, a Dublin stripped of gaslight, a river, and charm. She had always sped by as fast as the traffic permitted.

The only time she had ever been in the city had been more than three years ago, when she had driven there with Witt to the County Courthouse where he needed to sign some papers. She had not even bothered to get out of the car, and the only amusing detail she noticed during the tiresome wait was the name of the street: Golden Hill. Of all names, and in all places. At the end of the slope was Main Street, inevitably. But Golden Hill? Surely, there must've been an Irish street-paving contractor to dream up that name. Didn't the Statue of Liberty herself meet us in the harbor and promise us America, from Golden Hill to Main Street?

Southport was only a few miles farther along the Sound, just beyond Fairfield. At this speed she would be passing the Sommers' shore house in a few minutes.

"What's the matter, Betsy?"

She cocked her head toward him without taking her eyes off the road. "What?"

"I said, what's the matter? You look like you're in another world."

"Do I?"

"Playin' on your harp again, Betsy?"

"Oh, don't be so cheeky. It isn't just country Irish to remember things. Even the French do it."

"The French do everything—"

"That line from Baudelaire, something like: I remember as much as if I were a thousand years old." She glanced swiftly at him. "Don't you ever feel that way?"

"No, never. I like to travel light. No memories. Haven't we covered this before?"

"You know," she said, "I think you fake a lot."

"If you tell me what's true, I'll tell you what's fake." When she said nothing, he went on. "To you, true is what you feel."

"Tough guy. You make a simple conversation a contest."

"Sure," he said. "War in heaven. The ovaries against the testicles."

"You're impossible, Roone. Really. A man of unlimited impossibilities."

"But a man, baby. I'll stay that way to my dyin' day. Not a gray flannel huckster who buys cheap and sells dear and stays constipated. David Sommers. His Royal Highness Anthony Hale Douglass. Your husband. New England's men of measured merriment."

"Belittling them doesn't make that true."

"Betsy, ridicule is the only truth left around."

"I'm just the other way. The truth usually makes me sad and sort of misty."

"Well, you said it yourself. There's a blue you and a green you. The green one hears the grass growin'."

"That's when I feel young," she said. "Young and still hopeful."

"But the blue one, Betts? The one that plucks the harp of sorrows?"

"Ah," she said. "We're talking too much. Little boy blues, you blow your horn too hard. Why don't you show off with your guitar, instead?"

"Depends. What do you want me to play?"

"Happy Birthday to You." She gave him a furiously ceramic smile. "Today isn't your birthday at all, is it?"

"Now that you put it that way, no, not exactly."

She copied his tone. " 'If you'll tell me what's true, I'll tell you what's fake.' "

He touched her arm. "It feels like my birthday."

"Don't let failure go to your head."

"Betsy, I mean it. You walked into that joint yesterday, even in that volunteer's uniform, and the temperature changed."

"Yes. Boiling."

"Even now?"

"I'd better warn you—I've got a soul like a samovar. Always boiling."

"Something I said?"

"That. And the unsaid."

"About the blue you."

"That too. And everything else." She threw a stiletto smile at him. "Just when I get myself standing steady and upright, you pull out the rug."

"Betsy, you must look one hell of a lot better downright horizontal than upright vertical."

"There, that's the sort of smart-alec remark I mean. That wolfish idea of—what'd you call it?—burlesque."

"Well," he said, "nothing a big bad wolf likes better'n a good fox. You're no college kid playin' games. Truth or Falsies. I believe in life, liberty, and the happiness of pursuit." He tightened his hand on her arm. "Maybe we should drop the preliminaries."

"No. I've gotten accustomed to lots of small courtesies." She shrugged his hand off. "Make an effort to be civilized. Why don't you play something muscular and full of measured merriment?"

He reached back into the luggage space for his guitar and held it a moment in his lap, picking a string lightly and strumming. Then he began to sing laughingly, *"This world is not my home, Just a poor wayfarin' stranger—"*

She laughed too. "Min was right. You *are* a sketch." She shifted gears. "Hang on. I'm swinging starboard, next exit."

"But the sign says Southport, skipper. We want New York."

She spun into the exit ramp, throwing him against the door. "Listen, tiger," she said, "we go where the lady steers. You're along for the ride."

"You samovaring again, Bettserino?"

"That's right. The worm turns. Synchronize your watch, because this is worm-turning time."

"Little ol' white-picket-fence Southport," he said, as they left the high-way ramp and entered the town. "Now what? I don't get it. What's here?"

"Everything." She slowed the car to an easy crawl. "You can hear the grass grow here, too. When my boy was a baby, we spent our summers here. Here's Pequot Street. All Colonial and Greek-revival Gothic."

"How're they furnished—in early Halloween?"

She hardly heard him. "There's Trinity Episcopal Church. Witt and I were married there."

"I thought you were Catholic." He shook his head. "Faithful Betts. A high-roller with truelove dice."

"Here's where there was a fort—straight ahead."

"A fort? Where?"

"Fort Defense. It's gone now. Mounted a ninety-nine-pounder and kept a night guard."

"Now, how would you know?"

"I walked past the historical marker every day, and read the plaque a hundred times. There're metal plaques all over town."

She took a corner skillfully and pointed toward the end of the elm-shaded street. "See the weather vane on the top of that big house? That's the famous copper sea horse, shaped in the letter S. It's become the Sommers trademark."

"So," said Roone, "that's what Doctor Sommers means when he says he'll be at the beach cottage." They pulled up before the dignified three-story white colonial house. "Some cottage. Tennis court. Greenhouse. Just the basic amenities. I'll bet George Washington slept here."

"The Sommers always have lots of guests, so they keep a place this big. Mrs. Sommers always has a gaggle of diplomats out from the U.N. Or the ladies from L.I.V.E. Or when she's tense about the world's mess, why, she just puts on gloves and garden-clubs herself into tranquility. Don't you just love that doorway—that fanlight?" She gazed at the house. "It has everything—simplicity, delicacy, strength, elegance. I love just *walk*ing through it. And the herb garden that Mother—Mrs. Sommers—planted around the side of the kitchen. Lavender, sweet marjoram, rosemary. Thyme, sage, oregano." She made a lip-smacking sound. "Makes my mouth practically spritz like a fountain, just naming them. And the orchids she grows in the greenhouse—see that little room at the end?— that's a special tropical room she's going to expand just for her prizewinners. When they grew that orchid in Tokyo from a seed two thousand years old, why, she just up and flew to Japan to see it! And study the Japanese abortion laws at the same time."

"She sounds like she was never born, just woven by Betsy Ross. Who made all the dough?"

"DeWitt. My husband. He runs the company."

"Baby, I don't mean *wages*. Somebody started this before him."

"Oh. His grandfather." She sensed Roone was becoming bored. "Well," she said, "here endeth the stroll down ye olde memory lane. Let's go."

"Where's the beach?"

"On the other side. And down there—no, you can't see it through the trees—there's a di*vine* little eight-sided beach house. Remodeled from an old summer gazebo. Timmy used to take his afternoon naps there, all curled up with a tuckered-out corner of his baby-blue blanket." She abruptly remembered her ravaged dream of Roone overwhelming her in the shuttered beach house and laughed lightly to keep herself from feeling the unexpected knot in her throat. "We always mislaid that scrap of blanket."

"I'm that way in my room," he said. "Things get laid, then mislaid."

She eyed him to see if he would cock his mouth in a grin, his way of suggesting bawdy recollections. He knew or guessed so many odd bits and pieces about her. I refuse, she thought, stung, to fit into his two blowhard collegiate categories: I will not be a *thing* that gets laid or mislaid.

How could she explain, even to herself, about her arm flung over her eyes to shut out the shame, in the darkness even *before* Witt had come into the beach house, before the nightmare of Witt turning on the light? Explain anger? The dreaming of the bones? Everyone knew adultery was for adults, and her angers always made her feel helpless as a child. Loneliness, boredom—the words had become ladies' club gags. Most impossible of all to explain even in a dream, her whorish arched posture close to buggery, a pelvic exaggeration of lewd passion when there was none, and only a breathless show of venery would encircle your nightmare companion for the journey, keep you from drowning alone, alone in the deep.

The impulsive pilgrimage to Southport had been a mistake; the sky seemed lower. All she wanted to do now was to kick off her shoes, throw off her green dress, put a stack of folk-song recordings on the hi-fi and sit alone quietly sipping Scotch.

I overdo everything, rub against people like a homeless kitten, just to make sure they'll like me. I need better control, some rudder, some direction. This whole spiderweb of preoccupation with myself, this muted suburban aquatint whimpering alone one minute, rolling like a hoop downhill the next, the cult of clothes, the mirror worship—it's no good. Everyone hungers for beauty and excitement, but Roone's bitter young clowning mockery is hardly bread and wine. And the kiss of death is always smeared with honey. I hope Witt asks me to fly to South America with him. If he does, I'll go. He's as alone as I am and there ought to be the two of us.

Without reasoning, she stepped on the brake so quickly that Roone pitched toward the dashboard. "Hey!" He pushed himself back upright. "What happened, Betts?"

"Nothing." Nothing? Everything has happened. She pressed down the handle of her door and swiveled lithely out of the car. "You wanted to be in the driver's seat," she said. "Here's your chance. Next shift." There was no traffic on the village street, but she closed the door with a careful click.

He did not miss her new undertone. "What's so all of a sudden? I can play with your fancy green wagon? A reward for good behavior?" His head turned with her as she walked around the car. "Good-conduct medals I can get in the army."

She opened the car door on his side. "This is the army, Mr. Jones. Sideways march. Move over."

He lifted his knees over the gearshift and bounced across to the driver's seat. "I smell smoke. You sore about something? Allergic inflammatory reaction?"

"No."

"But yes." He twisted the rearview mirror toward her and pointed at her face in it. "Milady, look yonder at the loveliest mouth in Christendom. Sore as a disappointed mail slot."

"Roone, let's go." All at once his gibberish had become tiring.

"You sure as hell sound like a shaggy on a bash who just got turned off."

"Could we just talk people English instead of drag-style Chinese?"

"Oh? So now madame wants to play cool?"

"Just plain ordinary everyday people English."

"You can't, luv."

"Why not?"

"Let's face the music. You've been packaged. Not the chesty biggada figga, but because you're not plain, ordinary, or everyday. You've got hair blacker than Chinese lacquer and two greenish Persian cat eyes like Volga said, and you walk around aiming that pelvis like a flamethrower." He put an armistice hand on her shoulder. "Smile awhile, and I'll play you my favorite Ferrabosco." He sang lightly, "*So, so leave off this last lamenting kiss . . .*"

"I'm not lamenting. You wanted to drive, didn't you?"

"Ask me no questions, Betts. I tell only lies."

"That's the truth."

"This coupon-clipping potato-chips-and-cheese whip-dip town beginning to get you down?"

"This town keeps me up. Look, music man," she said, "you can put away the guitar. We've had enough gypsy music in high F."

"Mamma mia! All of a sudden! What's gotten into you?" He held up both hands as if to hold back her wrath. "I only asked what, not who."

She dug through her bag for her cigarettes without answering.

"Don't be shy," he said. "You can tell me. Two heads are better than one on the same pillow. I was sure this time we had the real thing—sex."

"Stop it!" she said. "Just turn the car around and drive back to New Haven." Now I sound like an outraged virgin, she thought fiercely. A giddy fool.

He inspected her. "New Haven? Plymouth Rock? Home Sweet Home?"

"You're getting the idea."

"I knew it. I knew it. Something in my coronary arteries could tell, when we turned off the road at Southport. All our lovely loony green began to turn purple as a permanganate Co'Cola douche."

She made a mouth. "Not a straight word. Everything crooked as a corkscrew."

"Well, corkscrew you, too."

"Can't you ever say a single thing just clean?"

His face tightened. He narrowed one eye at her as if sighting along a gun barrel. "Sure I can, memsahib. I've *got* to be in New York, I mean like for real"—he paused, then changed to a forlorn squint, a faithful court jester treacherously stabbed by the Queen—"so you can drop off my bag of bones and hank of hair when we reach the highway. I'll phone Tabac to pick me up."

He was offering her comedy, flattery, a touching helplessness, a line of retreat, a chance to change her mind and yet save face. She saw his surprise when she nodded quickly. "Okay, Roone, do that. Call Tabac's chauffeur service. I'm off duty."

"Matter of fact, Betts, you don't have to drop me. I'll get out by myself."

"Oh," she said. "The blarney. The gay boyish laughter." She pointed to the gearshift. "Home, James."

He bent toward her, bristling now. "Just who the hell do you think you are? A gay girlish Merry Widow slumming around with the ofay swishes and the cats just for laughs?"

"Please," she said, "I've heard it all before."

"I'll just bet you have. When the downtown cat gets to be uptown queen, then comes the height of snobbery. Call girl with an unlisted number."

"I've slapped you once—"

"That was private indoor sport. I thought you needed occupational therapy. Lay off playing games, lady. You're a fast hot filly, Mrs. Sommers, and you ran like hell until you got a rich boy jockey and parlayed him into the winner's circle. But DeWitt's out of the saddle now and you're on a muddy track, right? And you'd rather hang yourself than make a public scandal here on your mother-in-law's Main Street."

She felt a trembling wave, like pain, and held tight enough to tap the tip of her cigarette against her monogrammed case. In a low voice she said, "Let's not fight, Roone, I—really, I can't stand fighting."

"Betsy," he said, "just what can you stand—that isn't wrapped in cellophane with a big bow around it and smells like roses?"

She wanted to light her cigarette, but held back because she was afraid her fingers would shake. This was awful. Thank God there was no traffic. He was right about a public scandal on Main Street. I'd *die*. Everybody in Southport knew the Sommers family. "I'm sorry," she said. "I threw you a curved ball. I apologize. Let's leave bad enough alone."

"Bad?" He taunted her harshly. Don't you mean *naughty?* Little drive in the country air for a pale orphan city boy? An uplifting historical visit to Yankee Squaresville? Guidebook tour of hubby's Colonial Gothic?"

"That's a better style than Late Brutality."

He slapped his open hand on the steering wheel. "Jee-zuzz! Can't you come out from behind those shanty-Irish lace curtains? The Little Miss Biddy married money and now she wants to scratch where it itches."

"Get out!"

"Just listen to that Persian kitten growling."

"I'm not growling. I'm not anything except ashamed. Your jabber-wocky was funny, but now you're talking like a maniac. Please *please* get out."

"Mrs. DeWitt Sommers, if not for the simpleminded fact that I'm going to medical school and have to keep one hundred per cent clean until I graduate in June, I'd kick your cute little ass right out of that expensive seat and give you a free sample of Late Brutality. You've been beggin' for the big O."

She closed her eyes. The dark dream of him of the shuttered summer-house was coming true in open daylight. Why did I turn off the highway and drive into Southport? To play Russian roulette on the Sommers' front lawn? Gamblers always lose. We always find just what we're looking for.

He yanked the car keys out of the ignition and jumped out, slamming the door behind him. She could hear him unlocking the trunk. What for? Then she remembered his folded aluminum wheelchair and almost giggled nervously. It had seemed such a funny circus act only a short while ago. The trunk banged shut and his footsteps came around to her side. A guitar string vibrated mournfully as he lifted the instrument from beside her seat.

"Give my regards to Fort Defense," he said. He mocked her best duchess voice. "It mounts a ninety-nine pounder and keeps a night watch. Come all ye faithful. A big bang for a buck."

She burst into sudden uncontrollable laughter. She couldn't help the way his screwball doubletalk convulsed her. She laughed and laughed, harder and harder, an irrational seizure, until tears ran down her cheeks. My mascara! she thought goofily, then: the hell with it. I wouldn't have missed this Mad Hatter for all the tea in Dublin. Like a girl, she wiped the tears off her cheeks with the back of her hand, and, as she did, she saw him standing beside her with the cluttered look of an old country-tinker cornball, his gypsy guitar in one hand, the lunatic folded wheelchair in the other.

"Lady Godiva," he said, "you're the slickest booby-trapped manhole on

Main Street." He did not raise his voice but she could tell he was burning. "You want to fool the Sommers and make believe you're like ladyfingers, all domesticated and civilized? And still win the Nobel piece prize? Screw 'em all but six, Pat, and save those for pallbearers."

"Now that you've had the last word—" she began to say, but he had turned his back and was walking away.

She made herself pick up the car keys and move awkwardly over into the driver's seat. She straightened the rearview mirror to watch Roone go down the middle of the street. What an angry boy! And yet what mature perception to guess so much about me, so shrewdly. A fight's a fight, and I've had my fair share, but that was a donnybrook, no holds barred, eyegouging total war. What fury there must be bottled up in him! Lord, did he think I'd be a fraternity-house beer bust or a panty-raid pushover? Just because he wasn't breast-fed or toilet-trained or some other God knows what damn-fool slipup, is it my fault? Damn him! I don't have to take his blowhard mouth and gutter jokes and Dr. Jekyll accusations.

She punched in the dashboard cigarette lighter, and while it heated, she watched him trudge toward the corner telephone booth. Slow-footed as the seven-year itch. Charlie Chaplin to the bitter end. Cocky, sure I'm looking after him, expecting me to come waltzing up in high gear, apologetic and in heat.

The lighter popped. She raised its circular glow to her cigarette tip with so unsteady a hand that simply getting a light was a humiliating difficulty.

From the shore where the Sommers' white colonial house stood beneath the golden sea-horse weather vane, the tempting air moved delicately through her open car. The trace of salt brought a rushing flood of haunting recollections: Dingle Bay, Witt fishing, casting with tackle too light to catch the noble mating salmon. The green hills of home, not queer, not quaint, but poor and proud, Mother off to barter some bread in Galway near Spanish Gate. A fear stabbed her. Am I losing my mind? Why does everything remind me of long ago and far away?

She lowered her head. All I really ask, she thought with a flicker of grief lacing her self-abuse, is peace of mind.

□ □ □

Tabac had tied imitation tiger tails to the radio aerial of his old red Cadillac. A magnetic-base plastic statue of the Virgin Mary on the dashboard provided for traffic protection; in the center of the rear-window shelf a flexible toy hula-hula doll shook her breasts and hips and grass skirt as the car vibrated on the road to New York.

They drove down the Connecticut Turnpike, all three in the front seat, drinking beer from pull-tab cans, then throwing the empty cans at passing speed-warning signs. Volga kept the radio on to sing along with the Top Ten Tunes, and as she rubbed against Roone, she sang, "You turn me on, keed," and pulled down his fly zipper.

Tabac jabbed her with his elbow playfully. "Hey, stick to business."

Volga moved her hand skillfully. "Okay. Monkey business. I feel like airline hostess on my weeken layover."

"Nutty," Roone said. "Two nutty fruitcakes, I swear."

In New York, Tabac piloted the old red Caddy off at 49th Street, and parked it in a garage near the cruise-ship piers.

The sun had set; the streetlights measured off the darkness along the East River, and floodlights from the piers shone along the gleaming white hull and decks of a nearby Caribbean liner scheduled for midnight sailing. Before they went to the ship, Tabac counted the packets of drugs Roone gave him, then funneled the capsules into the hollow steel tubing of the wheelchair.

"Bennies and goofballs," Tabac said. "You can make a few bucks in the San Juan market."

"A few?" Volga pulled Roone's elbow. "Listen, lover. He's chitting already."

"Look who says cheat." Tabac showed his teeth. "You. A three-way girl. A girl who does tricks. Fancy French, an I don't mean the language."

"Knock it off," Roone said. "You finished? Let's not spill goofballs going up the gangplank. Make sure those tube tops are screwed on tight."

"Tight," Volga repeated, then cackled.

Roone plopped himself into the wheelchair and twisted his knees inward, sagging arthritically. "Shove off, friends." He pointed a shaky palsied forefinger and croaked weakly, "Westward ho!"

"The big score today," Tabac said, as he pushed Roone forward, "the real *bujo*, it's LSD. Top dolla."

"Nuts," Volga said, "to pay so much jus to dream." She teetered prettily on her spike heels as they crossed the cobblestone streets under the elevated highway.

Tabac jabbed his fist upward. "Bigga wallop, bigga price."

"An experimental drug like LSD," Roone said, over his shoulder, "you think it lays around like cigarette butts? The supply is tighter than a horse's ass in late January."

"Volga," Tabac grumbled. "Animal. *Caray!* See what you teach your studen? Already his price goes up."

Roone snickered. "Supply and demand, Tabac."

"Believe me, I got the demand. But you got the supply in that big hospital."

"I don't hear you talking price," Roone said. "Even the barbiturate stuff I gave you tonight. I'm on percentage. How do I know how much you collect when it gets to San Juan?"

"You think I lie to you?"

"All the time," Roone said pleasantly. Tabac eased the wheelchair over the edge of the curb. Taxis threaded past them filled with women in dressy travel suits and men talking loudly. The outcurving bow of the white cruise ship shone above them like the huge beak of some mythical bird. Several passengers on the ship's deck were throwing colored paper streamers down at the dock.

"Me? Lie?" Tabac muttered. "You don't trust the cut I give you? Cross my heart, you can go to San Juan. Go. Go yourself. You make the collection an then cut with me. It's fair?"

"Oh he's a smart man, that Tabac," Volga said to Roone. "He knows you study doctor." She spat fiercely at Tabac. "How the hell can he go to San Juan?"

Tabac put both hands over his ears. "Big mout! You wanna make a revolution? He gets Easter vacation from school, no? He takes a jet to San Juan. It's like two minutes from here. He's onna island coupla days for collection. An two minutes he's home." He hissed into Roone's ear. "I mean it. In San Juan you collect top dolla."

"It's a deal," Roone said. "If I collect enough I'll buy you both gift certificates for a prefrontal lobotomy."

A mounted policeman trotted by, the horse as smartly groomed and high-stepping as if he were one of the passengers on the Caribbean cruise ship. Tabac dropped his voice. "They got plainclothes Customs agents aroun, so watch you mout, Volga. You hear? When we get to Deck A you follow me till we find a big drunk party. You live it up. Nobody knows who's comin or goin in them big drags. Case the joint. Look in back of the john. Be party people while I find my fren, the night steward."

"Okay," Volga said. She tugged at her girdle. "Let's go-go, amigo. How I look, Roone?"

"Baby, I'm going to fill your lascivious navel with honey and sesame seed and eat you like halvah."

As she started forward, Tabac goosed her. "Jus business! No private customers, hear?"

BOOK III

CARIBBEAN: San Juan

8 A VACANT CHAIR a thousand nautical miles south of New Haven bespoke Mayoso's absence as much as the empty university chair in Dr. Benjamin Sommers' conference room. In San Juan, at La Fortaleza, the chair flanked a chess table in the office of the Governor of Puerto Rico. Unlike the New Haven chair, which had been shaped simply as a seat, the kingly Spanish chair had been constructed as a Gobernador's tribunal where a nobleman sat while others stood. To its legs were fastened metal grips through which poles had once been slid to carry it as a sedan throne on state occasions.

The Governor, Rafael de Jesús Cándido Santos Roque, occasionally used the antique chair as a conversation piece with visitors sent to him by the State Department from what were delicately called the emerging nations. The Governor always pointed out that the chair had begun as a simple monk's *sillón frailero*, but that the embossed leather from Córdoba, the fringed edging fastened to the back posts and seat rails by large ornamental rosette-shaped nails of brass, the Mudéjar inlay, spoke not of contemplation but of conquest.

The Governor's visitors in their floral togas, or cobwebby saris, or finespun goat's hair jellabas, paid knowing attention to what the chair said: The Spain which was then the greatest imperial power of the world outside Asia, and had made the Caribbean a Spanish lake, had buckled to its knees under encrusted pomp and privilege. Spain and Portugal, at about the time the chair had been built, had divided the non-Christian new world between them at Tordesillas with a longitudinal stroke of the Pope's pen. And today, they murmured to one another, look at both those countries. No one mentioned maps divided at Berlin or Yalta or Versailles, but the Governor's visitors always left La Fortaleza thinking: he is one of us, not a big-power man.

The chair had extra-long legs, uncomfortable for the Governor but just right for a man of Mayoso's height. It became Mayoso's chair during the times he came to the Governor's office in La Fortaleza for his weekly chess game.

The chess table had been handed down within the Governor's own family; the arms of Navarra were carved inside foliated scrolls and ivory plaques. No one had ever found what sixteenth-century drollery made the *ebanista* carve three of the table's legs as Franciscan saints, Saint Louis of Brignoles, Saint James of the Marches, and Saint Daniel the Martyr, and then chisel the fourth leg as a voluptuous New World Indian mermaid. The Governor preferred to explain that the mermaid came first, the Inquisition second, and the three saints last.

Governor Santos Roque peered irritably at the grandfather clock. Where was Mayoso? My best chess partner in years. If he's gotten into some Cuban refugee mixup, by God I'll have that mountain lion arrested just to protect him!

The chessmen still occupied the squares they had held when the Governor had checkmated Mayoso at their last game. He had not enjoyed the victory because Mayoso had been lost in thought, brooding vacantly about something unspoken, hardly the blitzkrieg opponent the Governor relished. "Mayoso," he had said, "do me the courtesy of putting up a fight. This is a war game."

"Oh. You playing Mars? Turning off the lights all over Europe?"

"Europe's in good shape, Doctor. But next time, it's us. It's our turn now."

Mayoso's face had bent into his leonine grin. "Who but a Governor named after both Jesus and Candide could say that so casually?"

"It's not casual. I keep reminding myself of Plato's idea that everything arises out of its opposite. So"—the Governor shrugged—"out of war, peace. Out of revolution, society. Out of anarchy, order. And"—he paused deliberately—"out of you, a chess player worth my gunpowder."

Mayoso had raised his massive white lion's head. "You talk a good game. But every other word has an actual fighting sound."

"I hadn't realized. Perhaps because this is an election year."

And now, why was Mayoso so late today? The Governor used the empty time to line up the chessmen for a new game. He handled them carefully; they were objets d'art. Mayoso's grandfather had ordered the pieces from Mexico, and the set had descended to Mayoso's father and then to Mayoso. The white set had been carefully sculptured in a pale pinkish mahogany. Beside the bearded king and pompadoured queen stood two mitered bishops. They, in turn, were flanked not by the usual chess knights, but by handsome angels with outspread wings, and by castles which were miniature El Morros. The pawns who faced the opposing side had gaunt faces, goateed and mustachioed, and wore the peaked metal helmets of conquistadores.

The opposing black set, carved in ebony, was led by a king chiseled as Lucifer grimacing evilly above his pitchfork scepter. The queen was a barebreasted harlot, the bishops intelligent baboons, the knights lost angels with lowered heads, the castles small furnaces of hell. The frontal rank of pawns was a line of Indian faces modeled brutishly, heavy-featured, with matted snaky hair. The Mexican woodcarver, like the

maker of the chess table before him, had created both sides in his own
image of good and evil.

But where, thought the Governor, is Mayoso? Has he forgotten we both
have an appointment with Father Gofredo Möttl? We're to discuss a question which Father Gofredo was unwilling to describe on the telephone.
The Governor guessed the subject was whether or not unwed mothers in
health clinics should be given contraceptive advice.

Last week Mayoso had said he would come to La Fortaleza before the
meeting with the padre so that they could play a slambang time-clocked
chess game. The Governor had hurried through his morning dictation
and correspondence to steal a midday hour for a game which, he had reminded Mayoso, was invented for unemployed rulers and idle refugees.
"When you say that," Mayoso had answered with his Rabelaisian growl,
"smile."

But now the hour was slipping away. Where in blazes was Mayoso?

In old San Juan, the Reverend Father Emil Gottesfried Möttl, O.F.M.,
called Don Gofredo throughout his crowded parish, strode swiftly past
the white marble main altar of the Cathedral of San Juan Bautista. The
long brown folds of his ankle-length Franciscan robe flapped around his
bare ankles; his hurrying sandals clacked echoingly as castanets in the
empty church. His striding pace took him past the walled-in tomb of
Ponce de León in the south transept. The tomb sculpture represented
Spain bent to kiss the hero's casket . . . *Rendered his soul unto God and
his body to the earth in Havana. June 1521. Soldier of Granada. Captain
in Española. Discoverer of Florida. Conqueror and Governor of San Juan
of Borinquen.* A paladin of faith, he thought as he passed. They are no
more. We have leveled the great trees down to a democracy of splinters
and toothpicks.

Father Gofredo schooled himself never to be late for an engagement.
The fact that his appointment was with the Governor of Puerto Rico
made his firm principle neither more nor less important. Render unto
Caesar no more nor less than any other mortal. He did not look at the
nearby graven figure of San Roque represented in the garb of a medieval
pilgrim with a dog by his side, clasping staff, scallopshell and cross. Since
the padre had come here on his first pastoral assignment after exile from
Cuba he had been bemused that the Governor's Christian names, Rafael
de Jesús Cándido, were followed by the family names, Santos Roque,
a theological irony. One of the Governor's many oblique quips was about
his staff and his cross, but no one ever mistook Governor Santos Roque

for a pilgrim plodding through the world like San Roque, with scallop-shell and dog.

When the padre emerged from the deep cool shadow of the cathedral to the head of the worn stone terrace steps, the strong sunlight smote him like a blow. He welcomed it. The discomfort served to remind him that the polychrome interiors of churches, gilded with Peruvian gold leaf and walled with marble to dazzle the masses with the majesty of faith, had become too restful and tranquil. Let us abandon their coolness and comfort and take to the boiling streets, he thought. Only a sternly self-disciplined Church Militant, prepared to suffer, to accept martyrdom if need be, could survive this terrible secular period.

He missed the biting bracing cold of his boyhood home in northern Spain. Here, in Puerto Rico, the seasons were as seductive as Cuba's, honey flowing into honey. Last year he had welcomed the seasonal hurricane warnings as a sign, not of the calendar but as a half promise of a cosmic rain-lashed cleansing.

Since he had come to Puerto Rico, the names of women which the Hurricane Warning Service attached serially to each tempest was another puzzlement to him; Hurricane Agnes, Hurricane Betsy, Hurricane Carmen, and so on down the alphabet. Why not call the storms One, Two, Three, Four? Agh, how these Protestant Yanquis made everything sexual! Cigarettes, cigars, soda water, even men's underwear and shaving soap—all trafficked and huckstered by young females, pagan goddesses peddling eternal youth at bargain-counter prices.

If I permit myself the wrong of annoyance, Father Gofredo told himself, I do so from the depths of humility, a holy error. The day was full of errors. It had begun with irritation: for Bishop Sosa to have stopped me just outside the sacristy after Mass this morning, for him to have said, "Be moderate, padre, when you see the Governor about Mayoso today. He'll recognize you as a deputy only, but even so, he may attribute your words to me. At the moment I prefer to avoid confrontation *cuerpo a cuerpo*. No hand-to-hand combat. This is bigger than his blocking funds for parochial school buses. Displeasure with Doctor Mayoso Martí is our only complaint, for now. Please, no militant *pronunciamientos*. Doctor Mayoso should be handled as a skirmish, not a war. Fire one shot, not a barrage. Be cautious."

Cautious! *Gott mit uns*—and the bishop is cautious! Lord preserve us from a cautious Church in a faithless age! An age debased in even the most minor transactions. Only an hour ago, while walking back from bringing the Eucharist in its golden pyx to a rheumatic housebound *viejecita*, he had stopped on impulse to step on the platform of a sidewalk weighing machine and had paid a penny to find out how much weight he had lost during yesterday's fast. In the flyspecked mirror at the center of the machine's round border of numerals he caught his reflection: a sharp blade of face, long as some bony El Greco saint, a brooding tenderness of brow, and two burning eyes. A tiny ring like that of a sanctus bell tinkled inside the weighing machine; an insolent cardboard tongue poked from a slot at him. He had pulled out the card and had read the obscene printed words: *You are a dreamer of dreams. Your luscious dreams of love will all come true.* Twice his eyes scanned the incredible words. He ripped the cardboard into smaller and smaller pieces, forgetting to note what weight the machine had registered.

A young woman coming up the broad stone cathedral steps toward him began to say, "Padre—"

"Another time, my child," Father Gofredo interrupted. "I'm busy. I'll be late for an appointment."

Her carmine lipstick offended him as much as his discovery of the pink smudges left by the kisses of the faithful on the twisted stone toes of an agonized Christ; almost as offensive as the vulgarities of the weekly petitions to the Holy Mother Mary for faithfulness of a *novio;* for a dying father-in-law to remember to leave his hardware store in the legal possession of his loving son-in-law; and for—these petitions more frequent since Dr. Mayoso Martí had come to San Juan—for the safe protection against another pregnancy. Dr. Mayoso was more subtly dangerous than the wizened crone around the corner who kept a hand-lettered sign in her sidewalk-level window: SPIRITUAL HEALING HERE. BILINGUAL. OCCULT. CARDS. TEA LEAVES. TAROT. PALMS. CAPSILLES ARMENGOT, LOVE PROBLEMS SPECIALIST.

At least, Father Gofredo had thought when he had seen the sign, the old woman doesn't hide under the white coat of science. Venus, venery, venereal; the conjugation of this century's verb, *to love.* If the old woman would only content herself with the first of the three, and Mayoso with the last, I could redirect the middle word away from paganism.

As he crossed the Calle Cristo between waiting taxis to enter the Caleta which ran downhill toward the Governor's residence in La Fortaleza, a laughing group of tourists spilled down the steps of Hotel El Convento. One of the men put two fingers in his mouth and whistled piercingly. "Driver!" he shouted to the nearest taxi. "On your high horse, buddy!"

"Look," Father Gofredo heard one of the tourist women say as he pulled his elbows closer to his waist and skirted the noisy group. "One of those bare-legged priests. Reminds you of Madrid, doesn't it?"

Father Gofredo did not look back as he swung down the cobblestone road. When will I become accustomed to these Norteamericanos, with their undignified women in shorts, and their men who behave like noisy boys just let out of school? They had not the slightest sensitivity that this cobblestone street was laid at a time when their country was a cluster of Pilgrims' cabins in a savage wilderness, a time when civilizing Spanish arms and Spanish ships anchored there at the San Juan Water Gate, sails emblazoned with the yoke-and-arrows of His Most Catholic Majesty and a greater King's cross of the Church Militant. How terrible this descent from imperial glory. To think the world's power was now divided between atheistic Russians who worshiped tractors and spaceships, and materialistic Americans who had brought even to this calm island their infections of obscene films, pots-and-pans culture, and that final destroyer of moral fiber in the tropics, the air conditioner. "The three C's," he had thundered during his television sermon last week, holding up three long sinewy fingers shaking with accusation, "Communism, Concupiscence, and Contraception!"

The uniformed guard at the gate of La Fortaleza saluted him; he accepted a second salute from the Governor's plainclothesman when he entered the tall archway of the government building. The sense of established order and obligatory esteem the salutes conveyed helped make up for the tourists' vulgarity. Even if they did not attend Mass or the sacraments, like the majority of Latin men, at least their mothers had taught them to respect the cloth when they were children. And now his sermons on the weekly televised *Hour of Eternity* proved he was—a young woman parishioner had had to explain the American word to him—a Personality. To avoid becoming an anonymous splinter or toothpick, the divine spark of human worth must today seek salvation along an electronic path, TV. Even though I wear the humble robe of Saint Francis, he thought, the people do not caricature me as *un hombre de faldas,* a man in skirts.

"Ah, Father Möttl," said the Governor's secretary as he swept into the outer office, "we should set our clocks by you."

He recognized the Yanqui "Father Möttl" instead of the Spanish "Don Gofredo," and nodded briskly, not so much to thank her for her praise of his promptness but to acknowledge a fact. "My parents always made punctuality a family virtue," he said, glancing at the double baroque monastery doors which led to the Governor's office. The secretary took his hint and hurried to open them. "If you'll please come in." She held the door politely as he walked past her, smelling for a moment the same strong cosmetic musk which came through the lattice of the confessional each week. Paganism. Dreamers of dreams which will not come true. She closed the door behind him with a deferential softness.

Governor Santos Roque was not leaning back in the massive leather chair behind the paper-covered battleground of the desk. The lofty spacious room was empty. Father Gofredo felt an abrupt twinge of annoyance: I may be cast in the role of only a deputy, a chargé d'affaires, but an appointment is an appointment!

He watched the pendulum oscillating tirelessly inside the venerable grandfather clock which faced him as directly as a stiff wooden Spanish sentry. Each time he was in this office he felt ashamed to admit to himself that he coveted the symbolic grandeur of its heroically proportioned inlaid walnut cabinet and the intricate intaglio of its engraved silver face. The raised numerals were almost lost in the silversmith's portrayal of a maritime nation's guiding sky: planets, stars, phases of the moon and tides, flying angels, feathered Indians of the New World peering through stylized foliage, a border of cabalistic signs of the zodiac; and, finally, minute and hour hands shaped as a small and a large crucifix. An inspired artistry, he thought, astronomy married to faith to bring forth timely order out of cosmic chaos. As he scanned the antique splendors appreciatively, the minute-hand crucifix advanced with a surprisingly vigorous tick to point at three minutes past the hour.

Father Gofredo decided to sit down. He ignored the foam-rubber cushioned visitor's chair beside the desk, choosing instead to cross the room to settle on an uncomfortable highbacked chair. Irritation chafed him. A bad beginning. The day was full of errors. I need to take a firm stand against Mayoso, not a cautious one. He shut his eyes prayerfully. Not my will, but Thine.

A twittering noise in the chandelier overhead made him look upward just as a *reinita*, nesting there, fluttered and chirped past the hundreds of tinkling crystal pendants and swooped from the room out through the open French doors. The birds' nests in the Governor's chandelier were famous, but Father Gofredo did not believe the whisper that the Governor placed unwelcome guests so that the birds could stool upon them. It was not enough that the Governor was Pied Piper for the island, Father Gofredo thought, but he must play Saint Francis of Assisi with the birds, too!

Even the Governor's desk must have been a shrewd choice, partly good taste, but surely a political symbol. It was a solid dark plank, at least three by six feet, set upon lyre-shaped Renaissance trestles which ended in realistically carved lion's-paw feet. The desk told the world of visitors that the Governor was no Americano tool or lackey, boxed in by chrome-plated and cubistic crudity, but a man sensitive to the nuances of his Hispanic heritage, a cultured gentleman. On the wall behind the desk, Governor Santos Roque had framed facsimile passages in goosequill handwriting from Columbus' diary:

The lands under Your Highnesses' sway are richer than those of any Christian power. Hispaniola is a marvel; the mountains and hills, and plains, and fields, and the soil, so beautiful and rich, all accessible and full of trees so lofty they seem to reach the sky. And the nightingale was singing, and other birds of a thousand sorts, there where I was going. I never think of Hispaniola without shedding tears.

The tall Spanish clock ticked again, as loudly and metallically as a pistol being cocked. Father Gofredo looked at it, frowning, then at the double doors. Dr. Mayoso Martí had also been invited to this meeting. Where was Dr. Mayoso Martí?

The Governor, Rafael de Jesús Cándido Santos Roque, advanced vigorously through the French doors on the other side of the room. "Father Möttl," he said as the priest stood up and walked forward quickly to shake hands. "I stepped out into the garden for a moment between appointments." He gestured toward his desk. "I've been rowing hard, just a slave chained to a galley—and I lost track of time."

"*Nada*," Father Gofredo said, suggesting with the one universal Spanish word that they were men who shared an eternal culture, and that a little time more or less was nothing between two gentlemen who were simpático. He warmed at the mention of the garden, to him the most tranquil place of La Fortaleza. A large stone circular table was there, covered by a mosaic inlay of the insigne of Ferdinand and Isabella, with a small fountain spurting gently from the center of the design; the Lamb and Cross insigne was identical with the stained-glass window which threw a prism of colors over the staircase at Bishopric House. A good omen. L'affaire Mayoso may be settled easily, as the Bishop wishes.

"Ah," the Governor said, raising one hand as if asking for more understanding, "since we speak in Spanish, I should address you as Don Gofredo."

"Please." Father Gofredo felt easier and less irritated now. "My entire flock speaks the new hybrid Spanish. Don Gofredo, or Padre, or Father Möttl. I answer to all three now. So please speak whatever comes most naturally."

Naturally, Father Gofredo knew, Governor Santos Roque was a natural politician in the Winston Churchill tradition. Naturally, he was a master of the flank envelopment instead of the head-on assault, all the while stroking a corner of his trimmed mustache as his perceptive courtesies wove patterns within patterns. An accomplished chess player, a weaver of gambits. Although the Governor was of medium height beside a man as tall as Father Gofredo, the upright way he carried himself and his habit of tilting his clever eyes upward to say something smiling made the Governor appear taller. His white linen suit, wrinkled as battle fatigues, was tailored in the current fashion of slimness. Even when Father Gofredo lived in

Cuba, he had heard many contradictory reports about Governor Santos Roque, and, here in Puerto Rico, the padre had discovered everything, praise and blame, worship and anathema, more than half true.

"The least my secretary could have done," the Governor was saying smoothly, "would have been to offer you a cigar." He lifted a silver humidor from the near corner of the desk. "Please," he said as he began to open the humidor, but the padre held up one gothic hand.

"No, *bitte*. Thank you. Thank you very much."

"But these are Conquistadores—native Puerto Rican, a natural leaf wrapper in the old Havana tradition." The Governor held the box forward. "You help our economy. If I recall, you once said you enjoyed them."

"How good of you to remember. But today is different, Governor. Please don't decide I'm fickle. I must explain I have felt the need to impose several small deprivations upon myself—oh, but please! Don't close the box and not smoke on my account."

The Governor set the humidor back on the desk. "I can wait. I'm accustomed to deprivations myself. Not always small." His shrewd eyes glinted. "In this job, they come in all sizes."

A faintly uneasy silence hung between them for a moment.

"I thought Doctor Mayoso would be here to discuss his, ah, questionable practice, Governor."

"Obviously, he's late. After all, the appointment was made a week ago, and his medical work . . ." The Governor's voice trailed off, avoiding just that point. He feinted. "Doctor Mayoso is not like other men, Father."

"I agree. I had heard of him in Cuba. A professional heretic."

"Heretic? No. Unorthodox, perhaps. A conservative nonconformist. A radical traditionalist."

"But those are opposites, Governor."

"Mayoso is just that—a balance of opposites. Faith and reason. Humanism and science. Strong enough to contain weakness. No one simple label will do."

"But in any case, Governor, he is out of step with his time."

"I believe he may be ahead of his time. I'm no Biblical scholar, Father—"

Father Gofredo made a deprecating movement. He had learned that whenever the Governor professed an ignorance he knew the subject very well.

"But wasn't it the prophet Joel who said that our old men dream dreams and our young men shall see visions?"

Father Gofredo was startled. The phrase about dreams on the weighing-machine card! How bizarre!

"And Mayoso is one of the new breed, Father. Old while he is still young."

"Did I just understand you, Governor, to call him a prophet?"

"No, but the dream he dreams is that Hitler and Stalin are not vanished nightmares but still—in effect—alive. He believes they still speak to every man who carries Cain in his heart. His vision is that if men have always stoned one another to death, then others, those who are committed to life, must speak for the new world."

"Has he told you who are these speakers for life?"

"Women."

"*Women?*"

"Yes. Mayoso's vision is to give women power to make decisions about themselves and their children."

"Has he never heard that it was Eve, not Adam, who bit into the forbidden fruit? That only the submission of Mary to God's will made possible a Redeemer for that original transgression?"

"Mayoso would probably call the story of Eve a myth invented by men to justify the bondage of women. As for Mary, I have heard him say that in those places where the people raise highest their worship of Mary the women are most bullied and wretched."

"Astonishing. He must be mad."

"So they said of Columbus"—the Governor pointed toward the Bay of San Juan—"until he dropped anchor in the New World. Mayoso dreams of a new world."

"Most madmen claim to be prophets."

"Mayoso claims nothing. He simply lives each day as he believes, isn't that called bearing witness?"

"Governor, I know he is your friend."

"Perhaps I am *his* friend, Father. He forgives me the innumerable abrasive compromises I have to make every day."

Father Gofredo stroked the rope cincture at his waist. His rigid stance and his silence made it very clear he was unyielding. "Governor, your obvious respect for this man, when it affects public matters, is a stone around your neck. You lead a Catholic country, sir."

"Father—" the Governor spoke with an edge of harshness—"the business of government is essentially disorderly. You say this is a Catholic island. How simple. A firm upright posture. But I have to straddle a seesaw, balancing water on both shoulders. The old religious traditions balanced with new secular expectations. A rising standard of living versus a rising population." He slid on his tortoise-shell half-moon reading glasses and leafed through the papers on his desk until he found one he wanted.

He thrust the letter at Father Gofredo. "Here, read this. Join me on the seesaw."

Father Gofredo's fingers stiffened as he saw the simple letterhead on the sheet: *The White House.*

". . . The President feels human considerations precede all others. To those for whom this reason is not hardheaded enough, he would make two points. First, population limitation has a down factor in lowering the mounting costs of relief and welfare programs, now a major claim on taxes."

While the padre read the letter, Governor Santos Roque hurried to the door and motioned quickly to his administrative assistant. "Jorí," he said in a low quick voice, "I'm getting worried about Mayoso. Some of those Cuban refugees are tough hombres. Look into it right away." He began to shut the door, then had a second thought. "Something urgent might have made him leave the island. Check the airports." He turned back to the room where Father Gofredo was reading:

"Second, an up factor in multiplying the value of foreign aid and investment. As Governor of Puerto Rico you are the bridge between the Americas. No one in the Organization of American States considers you the stereotype propaganda imperialist. Please feel free to discuss this with the Papal Nuncio, perhaps through Bishop Sosa of your own Commonwealth, and give me your views as soon as possible. . . ."

The Governor rocked gently on the balls of his feet, watching Father Gofredo thoughtfully.

Savonarola, the Dominican thunderer, toppled the Medici, he thought. This young Franciscan priest, with his courage and single-mindedness and, mostly, his fervent television sermons, can rock the boat before the next election. He needs to be handled with velvet gloves so I can borrow time for bigger battles. How comfortable for him and Rome to fiddle while South America burns.

When he was younger, the Governor had wanted to be a poet until he discovered that in an economically adolescent country with much pride, many babies, and few resources, like Puerto Rico, a poet could write his dream in the social plumbing and politics which spelled survival of the dream.

Borrowed time were the words the Venezuelan Undersecretary had said on the phone from Miraflores Palace in Caracas last night. *We're counting the hours,* he had said. *A few Army units have gone over to the guerrillas.*

The Fidelista guerrillas had spread underground in eight of the twenty

Venezuelan states. Tommygun units in autos had sprayed bullets across the U.S. Embassy cultural center and the geodetic survey garage. In Maracaibo, the guerrillas had ambushed an Army patrol. Three soldiers killed. Seventeen wounded. In Churuguara they had captured the City Hall for half a day, during which time they made a bonfire of government tax assessments and prison records, held a festival of revolutionary folk songs in the plaza, then vanished as smoothly as fish flickering away under water. *And,* his caller in Caracas had said to Governor Santos Roque on the phone at midnight, *we're in good shape compared with Colombia next door. But we're nevertheless on borrowed time and the Alianza para el Progreso is hardly making progress in the daily beans and bread the people can eat. Can't you sound out Washington on this? Don't they see that South America is the next Asia?*

How much blood interest can we pay on borrowed time, Santos Roque thought. The Vandals are at the gates of Rome.

Father Gofredo handed back the sheet at arm's length. The White House letter must be a sign, he thought triumphantly. And at the very moment the Governor is vulnerable, Bishop Sosa tiptoes and counsels caution! "I appreciate your confidence, Governor," he said.

The Governor lifted his glasses off impatiently. "You're mistaken. My confidence becomes less each day. In you. In Mayoso. If he were here I would show this stick of dynamite to him, too. You both need to raise your eyes and see the world as I do. The Southern Hemisphere is ticking like a bomb."

"Your moral strength in Latin America!" Father Gofredo said messianically. "Your *anima mundi* comes from your leadership of a faithful Catholic country. Mayoso leads only himself and his unfortunate patients. Straight toward hell, I'm afraid. He is an open scandal." Caution had vanished. An elegiac throb had mounted in his voice, the sonorous vibrato he used when he faced the camera on the chapel set in the television studio.

"Ah, now, Father, forgive my taking your words, one might say, *cum grano salis.* You mustn't let yourself rationalize with medieval dialectic. If I recall," he added shrewdly, "you were schooled in Spain, weren't you?"

The padre's jaw clenched. No *cuerpo a cuerpo,* Bishop Sosa had said. No hand-to-hand combat. "Schooled there," Father Gofredo parried, "from the age of twelve, although born"—he hesitated—"elsewhere. Then to Cuba. Exiled by Castro. Back to Spain, then here." He waved one lifted finger in a small negative arc. "Spain is not the medieval nation people say it is. You are much too sophisticated, I'm sure, to believe *la leyenda negra,* the black legend. Spain, the priest-ridden. Spain, the intolerant. Spain, the Inquisition. Spain, the cruel colonizer."

"My family," the Governor said, "came from Navarra. My grandmother was married in black because the people there believed that matrimony begins in mourning and ends in mourning. Her bridal gown was folded away to be used again, as a shroud, when she died."

"A few backward valleys in provincial Navarra—"

"Father, you would be the first to insist all of Spain was our womb, not just some backward provincial valley."

Father Gofredo controlled his voice. "There are so many Spains."

"Yes, but with few rivers. And all the rivers are used to sell dreams down."

"Governor, may I remind you I came here to discuss Doctor Mayoso?"

"And you need to be reminded this island is a Commonwealth of the United States. Fundamentally, a Protestant, pluralistic country."

"Ah, Governor. A republic which refuses to permit minorities or majorities to suppress one another—"

"The Franciscans schooled you well, padre—"

"I only say a simple fact." Father Gofredo ticked off his fingers. "Fact two. This island is essentially Catholic. Fact three, you were born and raised so. Four, even Mayoso was born and raised in the faith—so I use the words open scandal with"—he paused, for some fleeting reason—"ah, with cautious accuracy." The bishop's word, *caution*, still troubled him.

"I believe," Governor Santos Roque said, reaching toward his desk humidor, "I'll indulge myself in a cigar after all. If you don't mind?"

"Please," Father Gofredo said, making a faint bow and inclining his head; he immediately regretted the Germanic tone of his politeness. Yes, he decided while the Governor cut and lighted a cigar, all the stories about him are true. But I will not be blunted nor turned aside. "Governor," he said as the Governor drew on the cigar, "about Mayoso, you do not have to hear each week what I must listen to from the women in my parish—"

"Who was it," the Governor asked, examining his cigar and blowing a stream of smoke upward, "who called women God's second mistake?"

"Ah, Governor," Father Gofredo answered, standing very straight beside the antique Spanish chair, smoothing and resmoothing his cincture with one hand, "now I see why you have a reputation for cynicism."

"Makes man the first mistake, doesn't it?" Governor Santos Roque asked. His eyes began to squint humorously. "Don't the Spanish call Isabella their greatest King?" He swept his hand, holding the cigar, around the spacious room. "Without her, I'd never have this easy, relaxing job."

"I believe in the salubrious effects of ironic humor as well as the next man," Father Gofredo said, "but if I may say so, sir, with no offense intended, this about God's mistakes borders between blasphemy and pulling my leg. I flatter myself that I'm nobody's fool."

"And I hardly flatter you, Father, when I say that I respect your intoxication with theology. I've watched you on television, and your deep sincerity surmounts the glass tube."

Father Gofredo's mouth, but nothing else, smiled. "Governor, I see why your ability to describe the front of a horse and the back of a horse, both with the same words, is legendary."

"Not legendary—exaggerated. If Doctor Mayoso isn't out fishing like a fool, I'm sure he'll come storming in here the way doctors always do, claiming he was held up by an emergency. He's a courageous man, so his not being here must have a reason."

"The reason," Father Gofredo said, "may be that no one wants to discuss with a Chief of State the subject of female butchery. Yes!" he added loudly, deciding—contrary to the bishop's instructions—that the time for caution was gone, *"Ich handele mit Teutonischer Genauigkeit."*

"Father, *Teutonische wäre die falsche Haltung.* Germanic precision may be accurate, yet wrong." The Governor hunched his shoulders and spread his hands. "Doctor Mayoso's typical patient lives with Mediterranean Catholicism, not Teutonic. If you make such a woman confess contraception as a sin, she will not dare to stand up against you. Like all put-upon minorities, she will go underground and try to get la operación. She ignores everything and finds a doctor."

"If you please, Governor! You cannot ignore Doctor Mayoso's open surgical butchery. You cannot ignore the actions of this scientifically trained man, a man with a most historic name symbolizing leadership, one who took refuge here and now abuses your Commonwealth. But for me, my responsibility, the *motives* of my parishioners are as real as their deeds. The Church knows that if it is wrong to *do* something it is wrong to *think* about such a thing. And Mayoso, your prophet of life, has given the thought of ending their fertility to innumerable women."

"My dear padre, women have thought about that idea long before Mayoso. From your television sermons I would have believed you more sophisticated than to propose a devil theory."

"The word devil is not a jest to me. No priest can wait until a wrongful desire or intention becomes a wrongful action. The Church must point to the sinful wish and stamp it for the sin it is before the deed occurs."

"I'm familiar with that concept—"

"But are you familiar with the illicit reasoning which seduces even pious women?"

"I think so, Father. Contraception is a sin and must be confessed. But a woman who has had a tubal ligation no longer has to worry about becoming pregnant. With no contraception, nothing to confess."

"You see the seduction, Governor? It seems so simple. The loss of baptismal grace seems so seductively simple. The women lined up outside the operating room the way they lined up at Auschwitz—"

"Oh, now, Father, let's not get carried away by careless comparisons with the Nazis—"

"The comparisons are closer than you realize, Governor!"

"But Father, Doctor Mayoso is much more meticulous in selecting his patients for the tubal procedure than any surgeon on the island."

"And that completes the myth. Doctor Mayoso Martí. The noble name of Martí. The complete silence from the government which is interpreted as approval—"

"A government elected by the people, Father—"

"And running for re-election this year."

The Governor stubbed his cigar into an ashtray with an expression of courteous patience. I never considered this young priest so formidable, he thought. He wears the toughest armor of all: honesty. He's as unworldly as the patron saint of his order, yet he has the worldly adroitness of a political priest. He knows this election decides who will take the high road and who will take the low. "I ignore nothing," he said. "But I know that after the party's over, a woman wants to feed and educate her kids. Señor husband or boyfriend wants to keep scattering his seed to prove he's a *macho completo*. If he'd have *his* tubes tied off—Mayoso says such a vasectomy is a simple ten-minute office procedure—then the woman would not ask for the abdominal surgery of la operación. She feels she's trapped between the devil and the deep blue sea."

"You cast *me* as the devil now?"

"Who else uses the power of the confessional to force women into becoming exhausted breeders of hungry children?"

"If you please, Governor! If we use medieval words such as *devil*, we speak only of Mayoso. And as we speak, Doctor Mayoso goes free, with unclean hands. A religious population is infected, and he is respected as a humanitarian."

The Governor reached for his silver humidor and raised its cover. "Sure you won't change your mind and have a cigar?"

"Thank you. No."

The Governor helped himself and again made a minor ceremony of lighting it. I wish I knew more, he thought, about the hierarchical subtleties within the church. This suburban pastor of La Virgen de Fátima parish could hardly walk in here without prior consent from his bishop. Is he the bishop's trial balloon? The Church is wise, and must recognize the quality of this man. He slanted a look at the priest. "Father Gofredo, you know Mayoso should be here to iron this out privately. Let me make sure he is here on the spot, tomorrow."

Father Gofredo shook his head. "Tomorrow is impossible."

He recognized his curt tone, but before he could moderate it, the Governor said, "Nothing is impossible, Father. Allow a combat veteran of politics to remind you of that." His voice changed. "And Father," he went on softly, "beware of that old Hispanic failing of being humble on foot and cruel on horseback."

"I owe you an apology, Governor."

"No. We were both spinning our wheels. You owe me nothing."

"I owe you the explanation that I will be gone tomorrow. Tomorrow I am on a chartered flight to Bogotá, to speak before the Sodality Congress of the Lay Apostolate." He spread his hands. "I cannot cancel such a duty. So tomorrow is impossible."

The Governor puffed at his cigar judiciously. "Sit down, please, Father. Your continuing to stand makes me feel the disadvantage of being discourteous."

"Governor, you said Mayoso may be held up by an emergency. If that's true, Mayoso and his surgical clinic have created it."

"Please," the Governor said, "sit down. We can at least begin to discuss this without Doctor Mayoso."

Father Gofredo drew the carved Spanish chair closer to the Renaissance desk and sat down across from the Governor. "No, we cannot," he said bluntly. "If he is not punished, at least he must be forced to stop his preventing the formation of human life, all in the name of medicine."

Like chess players, they exchanged a knowing formal smile. Opening move, the Governor thought. White bishop's pawn is actually a knight, attacking.

BOOK IV
CARIBBEAN: Caracas

9 IN CARACAS, Mayoso had taken a cramped boxy room which grew off the air shaft of the Hotel Miranda. The moment he walked in, the room's coffined closeness and its walls, alive with leprous peeling wallpaper, were disturbingly familiar. Only later did he realize it was like the benign first-stage interrogation rooms which Castro's G-2 had set up inside their tunnel-connected Miramar headquarters. He would have preferred a room which had a second door, or an exit onto the fire escape, but he had accepted this room without a word because the hotel was just off the Plaza O'Leary, in the neighborhood of El Silencio. This old part of central Caracas offered him crowded anonymity, and enough visiting foreigners, interested in its mosaic sidewalks and curlicued lampposts, to provide turista cover if Digepol plainclothesmen spotted him as a newcomer.

Routinely, he had rolled down the shades, run his fingertips beneath the edges of chairs, tables, bedrails, and had unscrewed the plastic mouthpiece of the telephone; all a faintly selfconscious foolish ceremony, but one never could be sure. When fantastic snooping becomes commonplace, he told himself, paranoid fantasies become commonplace. The shadow of a stick looks like a gun. He dropped his medical bag out of sight inside the dilapidated brown-stained armoire and uselessly tried to wind his wristwatch for the third time.

His supper tray was untouched. He had ordered it sent up so that he would not have to leave his room telephone. The air was cool, but his shirt felt sticky across his back. He flipped the switch of the ceiling fan. Nothing happened. He tried rocking the switch back and forth. The fan did not move.

Nothing works, nothing is right. Why the hell did I let Filho persuade me to come to Caracas? My uncomfortable inability to say no to people in trouble, which I fool myself is my medical responsibility always to say yes, but which I know is the way I was brought up and taught and made into a man who too quickly feels the pain of others, the asking ones, the demanding ones, and now I hear myself with surprise saying yes when I should say no.

Even while Filho was trying to persuade me to come to Caracas, he had wisecracked that pity was the fatal disease which had killed even God. Right then, on the spot, why didn't I refuse point-blank? Because he had rolled back the stone and torn off my shroud?

Mayoso hardly noticed he was prowling the length of the room, drumming his fingers along the edge of the chipped hotel bureau as he passed it. Hours ago, like a veteran prisoner, he had paced off the length and width of the room and now reversed his direction automatically after the sixth long-legged step.

Very little reason for alarm, he told himself. The shadow of a stick looks like a gun to a wounded man. You had exaggerated the airport arrival problem. Admit that. Just admit that the airport arrival went exactly opposite of what you had feared. The Customs men were obviously hurrying to get home pronto, before any civil disorder halted the commuter bus service. And had not the talkative Señora Valdez tossed her martini down like a man, thanked you like a lady, and then fallen into the nearest taxi without so much as a backward Andalusian glance? And the Boy Scouts who always come out in uniform to help direct traffic—do they earn some kind of Merit Badge called National Emergency?—even they had equipped themselves with ice cream cones. So admit the distorting element of fear in your mind, my friend. Calm down. Don't let this prison cell of a room start you sweating. Your nerves shoot off your flight-fright adrenalin responses with too tight a hairtrigger, amigo.

But balance the admitted exaggerations of a hurt nervous system against facts. Did you or did you not see Guardia Nacional tanks quietly squatting along the high-speed La Guaira autopista into Caracas? Is it or is it not commonplace for the *cazadores* in their green berets to be bunched along the hillsides, apparently lounging against their jeeps and armored cars, but certainly placed strategically and clearly not practicing their famous parachute jumps? And inside the city limits of Caracas, were all those municipal police prowl cars needed only to stop speeders? Or to stop a coup d'état?

Didn't the street intersections look uneasily empty without the usual gray-shirted whitegloved white-helmeted traffic cops? Their absence is a storm signal, because the threat of street troubles makes the government order them into their barracks to protect them from being shot by rioters who remember years of being shoved around and strongarmed by the gray shirts, the policía municipal. Even when rioters did not bother to remember, they always went after the city cops first on the general principle that few laws or lawmen ever benefited them in lasting ways. There's also the municipales' habit of firing at suspects first and asking questions only afterward. This custom had been unknown to two Peace Corps Americanos not so long ago; they had naïvely passed an airport checkpoint and, when a police car caught them, they had stepped out of their car as ordered, hands up, and had been cut down by gunfire. And thus also to hundreds of students, some of whom were carrying books in both hands at the time.

Aie, my total lack of enthusiasm becomes more total every hour here. Venezuela may have the only freely elected representative government in South America ever to serve out its full term in office, but some guiding intelligence is making doubly and triply sure of that.

Everyone knows about the clandestine arms shipments from Castro to the underground here. Very good arms, sent originally from the States to Batista's military, and later found by the Fidelistas still neatly crated in La Cabaña fortress. Last week the secret agents of Digepol had caught two communist couriers at Maiquetía Airport, the man wearing a vest with many chainstitched money pockets in its lining, the woman girdled in a fake muslin pregnancy corset with similar pockets, the two of them carrying a quarter of a million dollars. Not bolívares. Dollars, cash.

Five assassination attempts on the President, and, even now, he sits in that white pile of Miraflores Palace with his left hand scarred from the burning gasoline used on the last job. Facts, amigo, no?

Admit the subterranean echo effect in the bastille of your imagination; fear exaggerates, but that silent telephone is a fact. Filho has not called. Aie *bendito!* Can it be a whole telephone exchange knocked out? Or worse, the entire Caracas phone system?

Don't go to Caracas. That's what his Americano visitor from Coral Gables had kept insisting two days ago, in San Juan. The visitor had brought to Mayoso's policlínica office the most recent Spanish language copy of *Pekín Informa;* also a copy of the Russian book which took the initials *C.I.A.* for its title: *Caught in the Act.* Mayoso had told his visitor from Coral Gables, who was in the CIA Plans Division, about his meeting on Grand Cayman Island with Filho. He did not reveal Filho's problem with the surgery, but he explained his promise to Filho about going to Caracas.

"*What?*" His visitor had sat up quickly. "Alone?"

"Yes."

"Can't you take a friend? Tranquilino?"

"No."

"I can't imagine why you'd expose yourself to—"

"I'm paying off a mortgage."

"An intellectual form of *macho,* Doctor?"

"Maybe—"

"You're out of your mind to go to Caracas."

"I gave my word," Mayoso had said. "It's medical, totally medical, not political."

"Frankly, I can't follow your reasoning, Doctor. Sounds awfully com-

plicated. The die-on-my-sword type of honor that I thought had ended
with hoopskirts. If you'd, ah, change your mind and join us, maybe we
could offer you some official protection."

"No, I don't want to work for you. I have to be completely free. My
only profession is medicine. I'm willing to read these"—Mayoso had waved
one of his big hands at the books, the copy of *Pekín Informa*—"and tell
you my opinion. But to become an employee, no."

"Listen, Doctor—I don't want you to take offense at what I say—"

"Of course not—you represent la Compañía."

"—but you're not back in the Sierra Maestra as a guerrilla doctor. Not
anymore. That began as idealistic college boy stuff. The Venezuelan-Co-
lombia guerrillas are much more professional. In Colombia, two hundred
thousand casualties. They have Chinese-trained Cuban commissars now.
He's usually the only officer with radio communication knowhow. They're
welding the bandit-style guerrillas into disciplined units. Viet Cong discipline: pay for food and respect the women. Gang chiefs who don't take
Havana orders are betrayed to the police. A sane man like you can't even
imagine the nutsy nonmilitary publicity stunts. The Venezuelan apparat-
chiks hijacked an ocean liner on the high seas. Four people in New York
caught planning to blast the head off the Statue of Liberty. Would you
believe it? Every newspaper in the world would front page the picture. I
can tell you a thing or two that'll nail you down so solid, you'll never go
to Caracas."

"What is this thing or two? Can you say?"

"To you, yes. The information is open in diplomatic circles. Your old
hometown of Havana, Doctor, has a building in the Vedado section with
a sign out in front: ICAP. I believe that's the abbreviation of the Spanish
words for Institute of Friendship Among the People. In this cozy headquarters is the Viet Cong mission and—here's where your own stark-
raving-mad jaunt to Caracas comes in—also sharing the headquarters
space is the Venezuela FALN group. Are you with me so far?"

"So far, sí."

"Now wait—just let me tell you how efficient these guys are. When a
terrorist tried to assassinate Secretary MacNamara in Saigon and got
caught and sentenced to death, the word was radioed halfway around the
world from Saigon to ICAP in that Vedado building. From Havana the
word went pronto to Caracas, and that day an American colonel, a military attaché at the U.S. Embassy, was kidnaped. A hostage for the life of
the terrorist in Saigon. All via ICAP. How's that for coordination?"

"Very skillful," Mayoso had said. "Guerrillas don't waste time writing
memos."

"Doctor, when you said Caracas you said a buzz word. The Viet Cong has closer relationships in Venezuela than in any other country in Central or South America. They're the ones who keep trying to patch up the split between the coexistence Moscow-line members and the kill-America Peking-line guys. Last month your friend Filho caught that Russki commuter special they fly from Havana to Prague, to Moscow, Ulan Bator, then Peking. He left his passport in Prague so that when he came home nothing would show that he went beyond Prague. No visas from Peking. Nothing to show a visit to China. You may have been raised in Havana, Doctor, but I'll bet even you would be surprised to know how many Chinese live in Cuba."

"During my Sierra Maestra days with Fidel," Mayoso had said, "sometimes my sister or my fiancée contacted the Chinese at their place on Zanja Street in Chinatown. We helped infiltrate some of their people as newspaper correspondents working for Hsin Hua because they helped us fight the Batistianos."

"Just for professional interest," his visitor had asked, "do you mind telling me just how you got them into Cuba?"

"Well"—Mayoso made a sound in his throat, a swallowed annoyance—"you know, to most of us in the West, one Chinese looks very much like another. Havana had hundreds of descendants of the coolies who were brought to the Caribbean islands much like the Negro slaves. A native-born Cuban Chinese would give us his passport to turn over to the courier from Peking. The fellow we smuggled in looked just like the native-born picture in the passport to any Batista cop who checked up."

"What happened to the Cuban-born Chinese? The original passport owner?"

"I don't know. I believe the Chinese would ship these poor fellows back to China. At that time we had guerrilla ethics. We only cared about one thing—to bring Batista down."

"Well, Doctor, those were kindergarten days. Now, the Chinese are so well organized that they send people to Egypt, and in Cairo they pick up visas to get to the United Nations in New York. Cozy, because the U.N. Building is off limits to the FBI. In Caracas, they blackmail the Chinese colony with family members in China as hostages. They use the cover of their cultural exchange groups—you know, the Peking Opera Company and all those traveling acrobatic teams—to infiltrate guerrilla experts into Central and South America. When a country like Mexico denies them entry permits, they shift to economic techniques. Buy everything in sight at high prices, and then set up big industrial and commercial trade fairs. Political penetration comes last, usually under cover of the Hsin Hua news agency. My point, Doctor, is that they follow the pilot operation of

your destination, Venezuela. Slogans identical with the slogans painted
on the walls leading up to the Ciudad Universitaria. Popular Front against
Norteamericanos. Stop imperialist exploitation. Sabotage the robbery of
natural resources like Maracaibo oil or Cerro Bolívar iron ore. You know
the rest. Fight hacienda slave conditions for the peasants. Boycott monop-
olistic high prices the Americanos charge even for human necessities—
medicines, drugs."

"The tragedy," Mayoso had said, "is the sliding scale of truth of all that
harangue. From zero in some countries to maybe a hundred per cent in
others."

"Personally, I believe you may be right. But professionally I have
enough problems of my own. In any case, Doctor, Caracas is no place for
a man like you. *Sabe?* You don't work for us, so I have no right to ask questions, but if a woman is involved—*bomba!*"

"I know. Your music is familiar even though the words are new."

"Listen, Doctor, there are Fidelista people right here in Puerto Rico.
Some idealistic students. Others used to be in the old Nationalist Party, the
group that tried to assassinate President Truman at Blair House, remem-
ber? With your name and your prominence, I doubt whether you could go
to the men's room in San Juan without a report getting back to Havana.
This office is probably bugged. On a simple direct trip, like a flight to
Caracas, you couldn't dry-clean your tail even if you landed by parachute.
An FALN radio room in Caracas, in the Urbanización Santa Cecilia, will
get word about you, pronto. I hope you're getting my factual message,
Doctor."

"Sí, sí. You're coming through."

"But," his visitor had said with exasperation, "have I changed your
mind? Have I? You said your only profession is medicine—so why tangle
with professionals in my business? You're very big on this population-
versus-hunger thing. Right? So why don't you settle down and work at it
just here in Puerto Rico? Believe me, Doctor—you go to Caracas, and we
lose one of our best advisers. You have about as much chance of getting
back home as a kamikaze pilot."

Six long strides down the narrow boxy room, then back again. I am not
a kamikaze pilot, but here I am in Caracas. Those intelligence agency
guys—both the overt and the covert types—they breathe only daily secre-
cies, and what began as a job ends as a disease. In the holy name of tough
realism they bribe sadists as allies. Walk with the devil only until you cross
the bridge, they say. But then what? They must sincerely believe that
doom comes tomorrow to convince themselves that what they compromise

with today is vital. And how much they enjoy their electronic peeping Tom toys! The omnipotence of four-year-olds. Nevertheless, my visitor was painfully sincere in his warning. If I could now choose, I would prefer to be back home in my bohío this moment, reading Unamuno or Lorca, or catching up with my back issues of the *New England Journal of Medicine* and *Lancet*, watching that mother-of-pearl zodiacal glow along the horizon as twilight settles in, living as men once lived in peaceful places.

Is it possible that, like Columbus sailing head on into the New World, we have unknowingly rounded an invisible historical corner? That my Old World ethics are as out of date as his heraldic armor or the pendulum clock of Santos Roque or my grandfather's naïve good-against-evil chess set? Even the philosophers no longer search for truth; now they pick over the rubble of Europe bequeathed by Hitler, grubbing for some meaning. Filho knows civilization must remember its yesterdays, but his partisans make a cult of knowing only today; without a continuity, without a meaning to live for, what is there but the sky-diving excitements, the high-horsepowered charades of danger, the daisychain of pointless sexual deaths, the immediate *right now*? Knock off the idols' heads, right now. Yesterday was a fraud, so today is absurd, and the promise of immortality tomorrow broken when we broke open the atom. Cast out of Eden, damned not by that everlasting applebite, but by ourselves. Forever has become much shorter now.

In this G-2 cell of a room, I can glimpse that Filho is confident he can secretly discipline the orgiastic today-right-now of his guerrillas into an obedient march toward his own tomorrow, under avenging flags, drumhead justice. But his followers will become more frenzied after he schools them in chaos. They learn contempt for the old-fashioned bourgeois myth of peasants' revolts—the killing of village masters, then going home to plant the fields. But Filho, the teacher, has not yet learned that when men kill for kicks, and women dress to kill, death becomes a way of life. If all our war games end in radioactive rubblestone and Filho commands his underground to surface and rebuild some kind of civilization, their cave justice will doom him as Vishinsky doomed the Bolshevik veterans in the Nobles' Club courtroom: new executions, new executioners.

Ah, Filho. Dragon's teeth always bite the hand which sowed them.

There was truly no compelling need to keep my promise, to be bound by Old World ethics, to come to help Filho here in Caracas. Unless my beliefs that without compassion there are no ethics, and without ethics no civilized world, unless for me those beliefs are compelling needs.

When I was still home in Puerto Rico, I almost canceled my plane ticket. My visitor had come closer than he realized in persuading me to back out of this Caracas hellbender. Yet I managed to blind myself to danger. How could I have seen there would be so many police, everywhere? City streets, dark as mineshafts about to cave in, a powdery sifting of tension from invisible hairline cracks. Especially when my mind had pictured Filho, my friend of a lifetime, being liquidated *à la cabañita* if I did not help him by some simple surgery for which he is desperate. Especially when my island morning contradicted darkness by its cleansed and spacious air. Who can see dark in daylight?

He sagged heavily and crossed his arms tightly over his chest, thinking: When will I learn that my everyday mind chooses what to see and what not to see? In the cool light of a new day, I fooled myself into coming here.

Ah, how many limitless mornings at home will I need to wash away the prison diarrhea brownness of this room? A room like a cell, confining as a straitjacket. It seems only a moment ago I was able to stretch my arms wide in the doorway of my bohío, free.

A moment ago, dawn was reaching over the mountains, reviving the hillsides. Across the dark green dip of valley a hundred roosters had begun to crow. A hundred dogs had barked back. Two kingbirds had darted past with sharp little cries, plumed arrowheads aimed at dragonflies. A kestrel, one of the smaller island falcons, had plummeted earthward with bombing precision toward some field mouse scampering through the ginger shoots.

Standing in the doorway of his bohío, watching the doll-size capuchin monkey throw bananas at the gaudy macaw, Mayoso had thought: I should shave and dress and pack my bag for the trip to Caracas but I detect a slowing down in myself, an unwillingness to leave this open, boundless morning. Each new day has a special meaning for me after the death-watch years in the Sierra Maestra. And the coffinbox time in Cuban prisons. And those daybreak recreations Sergeant Fulgencio's riflemen invited me to join with my wrists tied behind me. Time, time, only the great bloodwarm gulfstream of time flowing deeply through the ocean bottoms of my brain, kept me alive. I swam freely upstream and down, exploring the centuries in the globe of my head.

A frangipani tree grew beside the doorway, filling the air with a sweet nosegay fragrance. He had eased off one of its ivory blossoms and had thumb-stroked its warm velvety texture, so much like skin, then had held the petals to his face, inhaling the delicate scent. Better to marry than to burn, he had thought, but what woman could share such a life? He dropped the petal on the ground.

Day had begun. He turned back to his room and sat down at a bare unpainted wooden table beneath a window. The open casement was shaded by a flowering tulipán overlooking the sea, the sea of Columbus, the rainbow's route to the spice-and-gold Indies. Europa's dream. Yes, he had thought, the iron chains came later. For Columbus in Valladolid. For others: Devil's Island, Dartmoor, Auschwitz, Vorkuta, Ningsia. For me, Fidel's *cabañita* in Boniato Prison.

Several issues of the *American Journal of Obstetrics and Gynecology* lay on the table with palm leaf bookmarks between the pages. The rough plank shelves of the bookcase beside him were still faintly aromatic with the sweetgrass spiciness released by his crosscutting the satiny blond aceitillo wood. Stacked shoulder to shoulder, the sanity and wit and compass points of the human comedy: Dante, Rubén Darío, Miguel de Unamuno, Gabriela Mistral, Fernando de los Ríos, Jiménez. The linen-covered volume of Thoreau's *Walden* which Dr. Benjamin Nathaniel Sommers had given him years ago in New Haven. Also, among his few luxuries: current magazines of political satire—*Le Canard Enchainé, Private Eye, Simplicissimus,* and *Krokodil.* Alongside them, the digest-size CIA journal, *Intelligence Articles.* On top of the pile was the Spanish-language copy of the *Pekín Informa* his visitor had brought.

Filho's staff is probably reading it right now in Caracas, he had thought. The new simplified Chinese ideographs had been translated into a Spanish banner headline: LATIN AMERICA: NORTH AMERICA'S GRAVE.

The opening paragraph was also in Spanish.

Comrades, Peking may be separated from you by oceans, but our common struggle against North American imperialism unites us. We were once cheated of our silver, like Mexico. Our copper, like Chile. Our oil and iron, like Venezuela. Propaganda agrarian reforms only fool you. The dry land they give you will grow nothing. No bank will lend you credit for tools or machinery. Your wives will have no hospitals, your children will have no schools. Do you believe your ruling oligarchies, with 14 billion dollars in foreign banks, will commit suicide? They live in silks behind a wall of hired police killers armed with American bayonets! Only your revolutionary solidarity with us can tear the American death grip from your throats! The American dogs have been stabbed a thousand times in Vietnam, but they will bleed to death in unmarked graves in Latin America!

What choking rage, Mayoso had thought. From the Opium War onward, from ridding themselves of the white foreign devils and wiping out the warlords, they've tapped the volcano's molten heart. The lava has boiled over the fragile porcelain graces of their Confucian mandarins, and now, with the poppyseed slumber of ancestor worship forbidden, will there be ceremonials of human sacrifice to the volcanic gods?

Before Mayoso on the table lay a thick leather-bound notebook with a deep maroon patina of a generation of handling. His father's initials were tooled in tarnished gold on the cover. The spine was imprinted: *Facultad de Derecho. The Annual Martí Lectureship of the University of Havana. Volume XIX. Lectures of the Law.* The bookplate inside was a burnt-sienna sketch of Don Quixote printed on parchment, designed by his father as a mockheroic comment on his own romanticism.

When Mayoso had lifted it, the thick book had fallen open to the middle pages. From this point onward the pages were blank, unused. Mayoso had decided to use each page to record the lectures he, too, would someday give again at the University of Havana, not in law, to be sure, but in medicine. He had written at least one page a week, like a schedule of lectures, writing in much the same hasty scrollwork script as his father's legal pages, and in much the same oratorical tradition.

His last notes, he saw, compared the birth of hurricanes to the spawning of populations. *The mother of hurricanes is the big-bellied anvil-top cloud, secretly married to the warm tropic sea . . .*

The sun was higher now, tipping the flamboyante blossoms with fire, reaching through the shutters of the tin-roof shack a hundred meters below him, catching the broody hens scratching between the stilts which held up the shack.

In a moment the shutters of the shack would fly open, a ribbon of smoke would curl upward from the breakfast fire crackling between three blackened stones on the *fogón* and his neighbor Placida would call buenos días up the hill and ask if he would like some coffee Americano or Puertorriqueño.

The first year Mayoso had lived on Puerto Rico in his thatched mountain house he had been captured by the slow rhythmic sense of the seasons' rotation, feeling the declining equinox as strongly as when he had first gone north to the United States, to Yale, for his advanced training in gynecologic surgery. The New England elms on the Yale campus and the New Haven Commons touched him with their serene parallel perspectives. At Thanksgiving time, as the first frost glittered whitely, he had read Thoreau in a way he could never have understood back home in the Caribbean. And the pungent sweetness of fresh pressed Connecticut apple cider he could conjure up simply by remembering the road from New Haven to Stepney and Danbury, and Dr. Benjamin Nathaniel Sommers sitting next to him in the Sommers' big car saying, "This is what's missing from your Caribbean paradise. The season of winter."

During Mayoso's first year on the island he had once mentioned to Placida, when she had brought him a neighborly loaf of bread, "The season is almost here for me to harvest the coffee trees. The first berries are bright red."

"Qué no," she had disagreed. "The first picking is always the hard one, Doctor. You know how slow it is? To make sure each berry you pick is a ripe one?"

"That's what I want. Everything slow for a few days. To walk between the trees slowly. To look up toward the cordillera central." He had motioned across all the hills toward the *talas* ploughed into damp red clay above the green cane fields, toward the tobacco *semilleros* laid out like a big design on the high slopes. "I'll pick the berries and make my own café puro."

"Ah, ah, Doctor. You need your hands for surgery, no? And you can buy better coffee cheaper, Americano style, at the new supermercado."

"I am in no hurry," he had said. He had picked the coffee berries slowly, smelling the grass-fire smoke from the valley below, watching the changed autumnal angle of the tree shadows. He had pulped the berries by hand on a board, fermented them in clean glass jars brought home from his policlínica, then he had cleansed and set out the coffee beans to dry for a week in the sun on open screens. He had hulled the beans in a laboratory mortar, then roasted and ground them tenderly. He had brewed his first cup of café puro de Puerto Rico on the spot, and had sat in the open doorway of his thatched bohío at dawn, letting the tonic vapor of his own hillside coffee rise in his nostrils like incense to the domestic gods who guard forgotten household altars. The bread and coffee of his distant Cuban childhood, laughter in his mother's kitchen, his sister playing Chopin on the piano, his father's oratorical voice muffled beyond the double mahogany doors of his library: the lost landscapes of home.

The shutters on the tin-roof shack below him clattered back with the suddenness of musketry. "Buenos días! Americano o Puertorriqueño?"

"Puertorriqueño, gracias, Placida."

Day had begun. He had placed his father's leather-bound notebook back on the table and had begun to pack for his trip to Caracas. He had moved with a deliberate ease; this might make the morning last longer. Shirt, socks—I need very little, he had reassured himself, only enough to get to Caracas and back as quickly as possible. Si Dios quiere. That I should return home safe to pick more coffee berries.

A sound in the doorway. For a moment he had seen only a person's shadow, then, as she stepped forward with a chipped enamel percolator and a dish of fried bananas, he said, "Ah, Placida."

He had lingered, enjoying a gourmet's deliberate tempo by savoring small contrasts in tastes, glimpses of colors, touch and texture. This languor is a symptom, he told himself. No matter how much you delay, the plane will leave for Caracas.

Ché-Ché, the capuchin monkey, gibbered noisily from a hidden perch

among the tree branches. Mayoso gazed through the open window, across
the luxuriant greens, the burning reds where cruz de Malta grew among
the coffee trees, across the great blue vault of sky, caught by a sudden
pulse tap of mortality and wonder.

A fool's errand, he thought angrily as he paced the boxy room in the
Hotel Miranda. Dios mío, that phone call from Filho should have come
hours ago. I gave my word I would come to Caracas. I kept my word.
Y *basta!* Enough! Assume the worst. Assume a big FALN putsch against
the government, a *golpe de estado,* is ready to explode. Begin there. Make
that assumption. Is there still time to do the operation tonight and get
out tomorrow morning?

Mayoso drummed his fingers harder, until he noticed what he was
doing, and stopped. The armored cars, the green berets, the Guardia
Nacional, the gray-shirted municipales, all of them a precautionary military exercise in a shaky country? Or was all hell ready to break loose?

He snapped the wall switch back and forth with rising frustration, but
the ceiling fan ignored him.

The fan had become an opponent, aloof and annoying. Caramba! This
must be an *ataque* of my old prison claustrophobia. What good is my
practice of stoicism if a temporary stress like this gets under my skin?
Damn Filho! I'll give him two more hours to call. Then back to the airport and clear the hell out of here.

He tugged his tie and collar loose while stretching himself on the too-
short bed, bending his knees uncomfortably to fit it, waiting for his silent
partner, the phone, to ring.

10 WHEN THEY APPROACHED the village of Los Teques, near
Caracas, two university students swerved off the Pan-Ameri-
can Highway at Kilometer 21, then drove with their lights
darkened through the back roads away from the paved streets. They
cornered sharply, then steered carefully into an empty stable. While they
were getting out of the car, the shorter one said to the driver, "Remember
to lock all the doors, Luis."

"No. Why act suspicious? If those Digepol bastardos followed us and
search the car, let them find the doors open. Nothing inside except one
geology textbook and my sister's sunglasses."

They had learned guerrilla noise discipline, so they did not speak as they hurried down the unpaved west road toward the edge of the village. A high moon rode between torn clouds, bright at times, then slipping into a pale gauze darkness. As they approached the eight-foot-high walls which encircled an out-of-sight villa, a shadow moved and hissed, "*Alto!*"

They froze instantaneously.

The shadow moved closer. The faint moonlight touched a gun barrel as its bolt clicked.

"Arriba," Luis whispered.

The shadow raised one hand and challenged Luis, spreading five fingers. "Número?"

Luis held up two fingers. Tonight's safe-conduct code was to make a total of seven fingers. The sentry's gun barrel was lowered. "Entrad. Viva nosotros." The shadow melted into the wall again.

The massive double gates were closed. They hung on large iron scrollwork hinges. Luis rapped a spaced tattoo on the metal. A peephole eyed them. Again, the *salvoconducto,* five fingers plus two. The gate opened barely enough for one man to squeeze through at a time. A flashlight shone blindingly in their faces, then went out.

"Follow me to the villa," a voice said. "Don't step sideways. This week we put claymore mines and tanglefoot barbed wire around the outside perimeter. Inside we anchored some zigzag rolls of concertina wire. Alerta! You'll scratch your ass for keeps if you don't watch your step."

Both students stiffened. "You convinced us," Nicolás said.

"Just keep your hand on my shoulder," the voice said. "Let's go. The *viejo* already asked twice where you are. Who says the Spanish have patience? That old dinamitero keeps exploding his temper like his dynamite sticks."

"Well, we're here now," Luis said. "We're here, we're here, hombre. Don't let the old Spaniard scare you. He knows he's a Party legend now, so he allows himself a big head of steam. Vámonos."

"Just don't drop hold of my shoulder at the turns. Don't walk into the wire and then blame me."

"We heard you the first time, compadre. Let's get going."

They formed a single file and snaked cautiously through the minefield and the big expanded coils of barbed wire. When they reached the villa the guide said, "Go on in. I'll go back to the gate."

Inside the dark house, Luis lighted a match, then blew it out as Nicolás dragged an iron cot away from an interior wall. He hefted the floor planks beneath the cot to expose a short makeshift nailed-together wooden ladder which descended into the black tunnel.

With the quickness of men who had been there before, they thumped down the rough planks of the ladder to the tunnel floor. Fifteen feet ahead of them was a steel bulkhead controlled by a wheel, like a submarine. When they turned it, a buzzer sounded softly on the other side of the metal wall. The steel door swung open. A widening fan of light spilled into the tunnel, followed by the smell of stale air, lubricating grease, and musty sweat. They stepped into a long underground corridor lighted by an overhead string of bare electric bulbs. A completely equipped machine shop was laid out along the tunnel: heavy horizontal presses to stamp out gun parts and cartridges, electric welding equipment, modern Swedish boring and milling machines.

In metal bins along the opposite wall were stacks of boxes still bearing the stencil EJÉRCITO DE CUBA: rifles, folding stock guerrilla carbines and their banana clips, flares, grenade launchers, and three types of grenades, fragmentation, white phosphorus, and thermite. Hand-crank gunpowder measuring hoppers were grouped together near an hydraulically operated Wichita reloading and swaging tool. The wall was covered with technical diagrams for the Russian 7.62 RPD heavy machinegun, and Chinese copies of Schmeisser, Swedish K and Russian AK submachineguns. On an alcove desk stood an American radio transmitter, the powerful model called Angry Nine; on its side was the American AID symbol of clasped hands.

A short chunky Spaniard hurried up to them. He was a vigorous man with a fringe of white hair, alert eyes, and the solid hands of an Asturian miner. He kept wiping machine oil off his fingers with the waste rag looped through the belt of his worn corduroy trousers. His bald head was beaded with sweat droplets. With his searching eyes and bald pate and his flattened broken nose, his nickname had inevitably become Picasso.

"You're late," he barked at the two students. "Were you followed?"

"We were stopped by the Federals."

"This isn't a student dormitory—shut that goddam door. Sabéis?"

The younger student, Nicolás, gnawed at his thumb and then spat. "Just a minute, viejo. I get a lousy splinter every time I come down that ladder."

While Luis pushed the metal door shut and locked it the old man said, "Late schedules and thumb suckers—that's how we lost the revolution in Spain. The Fascists had Franco and the Moors, while we had splinter groups and big talk." He turned irritably, and led them past the noisy machinery. None of the machinists looked up. The workers bent over the gun barrels and grenade casings they were making with the concentrated intensity of coin collectors examining fresh proof sets from a mint.

The old Spaniard had a game left leg and clapped the back of his thigh every few steps as if goading on a tired horse. He was angry to be interrupted and angry that Filho should have sent him this Luis and this Nicolás, two university types, for guerrilla indoctrination. One glance at their pressed suits, their white shirts with azabache links in the cuffs and the flawlessly knotted ties, with a fashionable dimple carefully preserved just below the knot—these types were never reliable. Exploitation, strikes, the loss of human dignity, mud hut hunger—all words, nothing more than words, to these bourgeois boys.

"Such types," he had complained to Filho only a week ago. "I'm a dinamitero. Don't make me a revolutionary nursemaid, Filho."

Filho began, as always, by smiling and sliding sideways. "Ah, *viejo*," he had said sympathetically, "your hemorrhoids clutching up on you again? Loosen up, man, loosen up. Without these boys," Filho had said, "we have no protective coloration in the city. Their cover is perfect. They have the clothes, manners, girlfriends, their family cars—"

"They dress like pansies!"

"You're wrong. When you were the miners' Brigade Commander in Oviedo you could have calloused hands and overalls. But now, a shirt and tie are the best uniform for a big-city fifth column. Didn't you ever hear the story of the Englishman urinating openly on a London lamppost? When the bobby came running up, shouting, ready to arrest him, the man drew himself erect and said, 'You can't talk to me like that. I'm a member of the middle classes.'"

"This isn't London," the old Spaniard had muttered. "I remember these types from the *manicomió* days in Spain. Then, later, the Riviera types who wanted to join us in the maquis to capture Lugers, souvenirs from the Nazis, showing off for their girlfriends. After the assassination of Gaitán in Bogotá, even if that was Trujillo's work and not the Party's, we had to organize the streets overnight—"

"You don't have to lecture me," Filho said flatly, no longer smiling. "I remember. I remember."

"But do you remember the thousands of dead? When it was bellyflop in the gutters, snipers on the roofs, do you remember how much help we got from these types? *Los buenos y los bobos.* They all have clean fingernails." He had rubbed his hands together angrily. "The skin on their fingers. They have never handled a tool. They have girls' skin. Some of them refused to kill during *el bogotazo*. 'I can't stand the sight of blood.'" His voice had become prissy and mocking, "'What if I get hit in the stomach?' 'What if the police capture me? How can I hold out during *una flagelación?*' Would you believe such talk? From revolutionary cadres? From Komsomols? Pah! The way these types talk and cry 'madre' when fighting starts in the streets!"

Filho had tapped the old man's knee. "*Viejo*," he said, "I am not train-

ing them just to take over the streets. I am teaching them to take over a
country."

"Filho, we agreed in Havana we cannot make a Marxist-Leninist revolution with boy adventurers—"

"Correct. But you cannot consolidate victory unless you have brains on
your side."

"The peasants have more than brains, Filho. They have balls and they
have guts."

"Guts are for maestro dinamiteros, demolition experts like you."

"Leave me out, comrade!"

"No," Filho said. "You're in, Señor Brigade Commander. When you
left the coal mines of Asturia behind you and walked uphill into the
Moor's machineguns at Badajoz wearing a necklace of dynamite sticks,
you needed guts. When you mined the wall at Toledo. When the Nazis in
Marseilles pulled out your fingernails—"

In a low voice the Spaniard said, "Don't try to start a personal regime, a
personality cult—"

"Then don't try to undermine me. I can match my guts with yours,
viejo."

"Filho, I take orders from the Party, not you. Our strategy is Lin Piao's
Victory of the People's War. We agreed in Havana—"

"We agreed to fight a war of national liberation—"

"Filho, even a national leader is expendable."

"Don't threaten me, viejo. I talked in Peking with Lin Piao. I told him
I agree with five of his Six Principles. To his face I said I disagree with
his principle that local guerrillas should not depend on foreign assistance.
Where the hell do you think we'd be without outside help? From all our
comrades except China. They send Pekín Informa and commissars because they can't spare arms."

"Maybe that's why they're sending Liu Keh-yu here, Filho. To check on
you."

"Liu has no monopoly on revolutionary wisdom, viejo. To be a commissar
is not automatically to become a commander. I'm the one with command
experience."

"Be careful, Filho. We're all expendable."

"Only victory is not! History proves it. When Robespierre ordered the
greatest chemist in Europe, Lavoisier, to the guillotine, he said, 'The Republic has no need of savants.'"

"That was two centuries ago—"

"Exactly!" Filho said. He slashed his hand through the air. "Jets. Computers. We've changed. We need savants. When victory comes, guts and

balls won't run the steel mills and petroleum refineries. We'll need all the brains we have."

"Filho," the old Spaniard said, "even in Peking, they warned me you could talk Venus de Milo off her pedestal and into bed."

The Filho smile. "Not me. She has no arms." He had clapped the old man on the shoulder. "Arms. You and I believe in arms, *viejo!* Now get the hell out of here. Back to work."

In the underground munitions plant, the Spaniard stepped carefully past a welder's sudden shower of sparks and followed a corner into a gallery off the main tunnel. Here the light was dimmer and a half-dozen young men squatted on the floor while a motion picture projector threw pictures on a tacked-up bedsheet; scenes of Viet Cong guerrillas armed with Kalashnikov automatic rifles deploying beside a jungle trail, setting up new Degtyarev light machineguns, then ambushing a file of steel-helmeted enemy soldiers.

The Spaniard jerked his thumb toward the bedsheet screen as they walked past. "A picture's worth a thousand words," he said. "Old Chinese saying, and it's true. In an ambush, men always head for the ditches on the side of the road. So the ditches must be mined in advance. Less heroism for us, but more casualties for them. After the training films these bourgeois kids really listen to what I have to say." He stopped at the far corner beside a workbench and switched on the electric light above stacked bins of boobytrap parts.

"Looks like a hardware store," one of the students said. "Or a pharmacy."

"Exactly," the old Spaniard said. "Only rich countries have a big supply of thermite grenades. Thermite is the rich man's fire maker. For us, we need a hardware store. Here"—he began to explain, and for the first time they saw how true was the legend of his fingers without nails—"this pack of cigarettes—this little box of matches and can of lighter fluid—wads of cotton like this—this combination, after you light the cigarette, it gives you almost four minutes to get away after you rig up a dynamite charge."

"I don't smoke," Nicolás said.

"From now on," the Spaniard said, "you smoke. Also you learn about fertilizer."

"I know all about fertilizer," Nicolás laughed. "That's why I left home to become a geologist."

"Fertilizer," said the old man patiently, "is a gift from the Americanos to the guerrillas of the world. Mao taught us how to make them supply us with weapons in China and Viet Nam. Now the Americanos want to bribe the masses with food so they ship ammonium nitrate fertilizer." His leathery face wrinkled as he chuckled. "Ammonium nitrate also happens to possess the good fortune to be an explosive."

"Qué va?"

"Take my word. It's better than the C-3 plástico, because it doesn't leave an orange stain on your hands for the cops to see. You can drive right up to a bank with it—after all, a farmer, a dozen burlap bags of fertilizer? Ammonium nitrate does not have the *macho* like dynamite, but you screw the enemy with a very big bang."

"It's poetic justice," Luis said.

The Spaniard poked a finger at Nicolás' chest. "Your father owns a farm near San Carlos, no? From now on he'll be ordering truckloads of fertilizer."

"Don't worry, *viejo*. I'll get it."

"Sooner," the Spaniard said, "not later. No delays. No thumb-sucking."

"Enough," the boy said. "You always make a disaster out of little things."

"That's what you're here for," the Spaniard said. "To learn to make a disaster from little ordinary things that any man could carry in his pocket. Now here, you see this little mercury switch? It comes from a washing machine. This switch and a few flashlight batteries can give you one of the best booby traps in the world." He scrutinized one, then the other, carefully weighing them in his mind. "You two must learn while you run. Filho said you were future commanders."

"Filho," Luis said, tapping his forehead, "he uses the psychology of praise."

"Filho," said the old Spaniard, "uses everything. You never know what responsibilities or authority he'll give you. Filho has *macho*. In Bogotá when they knocked off Jorge Eliécer Gaitán on an open street, Filho grabbed history by the short hair. Those *bogotazo* riots gave a swift kick in the ass to the Inter-American Conference. A victory. And who do you suppose was one of our best cadres in the street?" He inspected them contemptuously. "You students don't know history? You can't guess? Go ahead, take a guess."

"No," Nicolás said. "You tell us."

"A young university student from Cuba. Fidel Castro."

"Truly, *viejo*?"

"Cross my heart," the old Spaniard said. "Next to Filho, Fidel." He did not add what he knew but preferred to forget, that in those early days the Party had cooperated with the Batistianos against upstart boys like Fidel.

"*Viejo*," Luis said, more respectful now, "we know you've been around. We're here to learn."

They stood on each side of him, not joking anymore, not even calling him *viejo,* and paying careful attention as he showed them how to rig the battery with the mercury switch. "Just remember," he said, "the fundamental idea of sabotage is exactly this—to make a disaster from little things."

□ □ □

Bottomless oil fields lay below the northern lip of the continent, so it was in the coastal lands of Venezuela the guerrilla attacks began.

Their timing would have been more precise if several novice Party cadres had believed in the tiresome discipline of Norteamericano-style precision, but, despite the amateur irregularities of the paramilitary operation, the sabotage of Yanqui business and the interruption of municipal services were carried out with much style and a degree of skill.

In the public maternity ward of the crowded Caracas municipal hospital where the women lay head to foot, two in a bed, where in the delivery room a baby was born every fifteen minutes, the sound of distant explosions and racing fire trucks was hardly noticed until eight young women visitors to the hospital stood up at a signal. In five well-organized minutes they locked the nurses in a room, took charge of the telephone, stationed one girl with a pistol in the corridor, announced harshly that there must be silence, and unfurled two large sheets of painted slogans which they nailed to the walls. The first sheet carried a large picture of Fidel Castro seen in profile, carefully composed, carefully bearded, carefully Christlike, below which a slogan in red-painted block printing read:
4 OF 5 OF YOUR BABIES WILL DIE IN THEIR FIRST YEAR! FIGHT BACK!
Under a hammer-and-sickle symbol the second sheet read:
ONE MEAL EACH DAY? NO! ONE CHILD EACH YEAR? NO! FIGHT BACK!

In Barinas state, southwest of Caracas, the thirty-inch oil pipeline to El Palito tore open like a great wounded artery. A university student assigned by the PCV ran forward toward the broken pipeline with a torch to set the spraying spurting oil geyser on fire. A shift in the wind turned the oily gush into a cascade of droplets, a dark liquid chiffon veil of death which caught him blindingly in the face, drenching him with oil. He tumbled screaming into a black pool of petroleum, setting it too on fire. For half a minute his screams rose continually higher as his clothing curled and flaked off him like an explosion of flaming paper, then he fell backward into the burning muck with his charred arms outstretched in the wide beneficent embrace of Cristo Redentor on Corcovado.

In Caracas, the seventh-floor ladies' lavatory at the United States Embassy exploded. The Party thereby demonstrated penetration of the innermost sanctum of what the Cuban Prensa Latina broadcasts called Yanqui imperialistic-capitalistic-monopolistic colonialism. Any symbolism of the ladies' lavatory being considered such an imperialistic sanctum escaped the planners of the explosion. Irony and humor were bourgeois residues and contributed nothing to the class war.

The Caracas warehouse of the Yanqui Sears Roebuck and Company suddenly erupted into a white-hot ball of fire boiling upward at great speed. The placement of truly professional incendiary bombs was so skillful that the sheet-metal walls of the burning refrigerators and ovens melted like wax. Because of minor timing differences in the homemade clockworks of the bombs, it was not until five minutes later that the warehouses of Unicar Petroquímica, C.A. and Sommers Internacional Farmacéutica blazed into flames.

A seventeen-year-old Caracas girl took as her signal the sounds of explosion and the leaping glare of redness in the sky over the city.

Her target was the glass-jalousied guard booth under the arched concrete entrance to the Ciudad Universitaria campus. Two of the jalousies had been broken by rocks and someone had already scrawled *Viva Cuba!* at the base of the booth. She rammed her paintbrush into a bucket of red Pittsburgh paint and in broad strokes started to draw a dripping hammer-and-sickle symbol above the letters PCV, *Partido Comunista Venezuela.* Later, just before the police arrested her, she would also print FALN, meaning Armed Forces of National Liberation, which was definitely Castroite but not so definitely Communist. She slapped the paint on the rough wall with a tense muscular ecstasy, uplifted by some intuition of escape from the pettiness of her narrow feudalistic home. Her life had new meaning. The only other time she had felt such a winged lifting of her spirit had been several years earlier, when she was still her mother's unquestioning daughter, a devout believer, and she had knelt with happy tremorousness for her first Communion.

In Pertigalete, to the northeast, six men crept up the back steps of an isolated *casa* at the edge of town, the local bordello. They surprised a young American petroleum company engineer vigorously employed with the most expensive girl in the house. After they had tied the American and the girl to chairs, they shaved the heads of both while promising them no further harm. They spoke very quietly, with exaggerated courtesy, their words thickened slightly by the tight hems of the nylon stockings they wore as masks. The girl could not control the spasms of shivering that swept over her; she bit her mouth and wept silently, submissively. Straining against the ropes, the American insisted on making specific insults and threats of reprisal until one of the polite men pistol-whipped his face with a swift crisscrossing of blows so hard that the American's flesh was opened to the bone. They left him there, and took the girl in her black lace negligee out to the nearest highway. There they stripped her in the glare of a semicircle of auto headlights. As if this were a just punishment for some unnamed crime, the girl did not beg for mercy. They faced her toward town, and, when she did not move, one man slapped her buttock as he would drive a cow. She stumbled away from them, naked and sobbing. Their eyes stared after her through their nylon masks with the harsh righteousness of a duty-bound Inquisition at a hooded, prayerful auto-da-fé.

In Carúpano and Puerto Cabello uniformed members of the Venezuelan Marines joined civilian FALN snipers under the command of uniformed rebel officers and attacked both towns in company strength. They began with rifle fire, grenades, and heavy machineguns against the *puntos fuertes,* the military camps and police stations. Two days later they would continue their fighting with *cañones antitanques* in the smoky haze of rubble and burning buildings as government tanks tried systematically to search them out.

The grimy mercantile streets became transcendent corridors for the exchange of courage, as men sometimes exchange bread. The cobblestones became altars marked by sacrificial blood. The men of both sides crouched sweating behind Coca-Cola signs, tensed to attack, then, as they dashed across the street, were tapped by invisibly lead-pointed omnipotent fingers so suddenly, so much a day of judgment with no appeal, that they went down, dying, slumping forward on their knees as if their rifles were crutches to hold them upright in the attitude of prayer.

Near Cumaná, eleven young men attacked the San José de Aerocur police station. They made the two policemen on duty lie flat on the floor under guard while they systematically collected the revolvers and submachineguns available. Because they felt the two policemen were no more than working-class dupes in the struggle against capitalism, and not personally to blame, they generously and politely allowed both men out of

the building before they expertly placed their dynamite sticks and sent
the police station sky-high in a pillar of smoky fragments.

Far west of Caracas their biggest, most dangerous target was the Yanqui petroleum empire at Lake Maracaibo. Two billion Yanqui dollars had
been invested in this hundred-mile-long lake since the day Los Barrosos
No. 2 had blown the first whale-spout gusher. Now this huge, oily, half-
inland sea rippled across the biggest single Yanqui investment in the
world outside the borders of the United States. Side by side with neighboring European companies, they paid the Venezuelans enough millions
in taxes each day to make the government the richest in South America.
The heart blood of the country was an emulsion of oil and sweat.

Every member of each Lake Maracaibo sabotage team was hand-picked
by the Partido Comunista. Only experienced oil-field roughnecks were
chosen, dinamiteros who could be trusted to hit each target as a job of
hard work, not as a slogan-shouting university-student martyrdom. Many
men wore a circle of dynamite sticks tied end to end, looped over the
neck in a loose necklace. Here was the guerrilla center of the entire Party
operation in Venezuela—the remainder were diversions and demonstrations of Partido Comunista and Castroite size and strength. Other
such demonstrations before world opinion had already been adequately
achieved by the theft of several art treasures from the touring Louvre
show and the daylight kidnaping of a visiting Spanish soccer star. Now
the time had come for major sabotage.

First, the palm-shaded U.S.A. Consulate General building in the town
of Maracaibo was brought under small-arms fire by the students from the
local university. They broke many windows in a dramatically noisy and
gratifying way, hurt no one, occupied the police and newspapermen, and
were therefore kept by the Party out of the way of the grown men who
had more serious targets elsewhere along the quiet night world of the
lake.

Farther along the shore of Lake Maracaibo, as occurred each night, great
stabbing blades of heat lightning forked downward over the Catatumbo
and Zulia River swamps which marked an invisible boundary. The
swamps were the border between twentieth-century men who pumped
petroleum up from the paleolithic bowels of the lake and the Stone Age
Motilone Indians who hunted with six-foot black palm-wood arrows
through the tangled interior as swiftly and silently as eels swimming
through oil. This was terra incognita. Few modern men who penetrated
deep Motilone territory ever returned. So it was here, far from the Army
and the police, where the swamps bordered the lake and a few rickety

palafitos, huts perched on stilts, that the sabotage flotilla made rendezvous.

The low Caribe moon was a theatrically voluptuous tangerine hanging above them, lightly gilding their metal drillers' hats which looked like the helmets of World War I American doughboys. The number-one dynamiter wore his hat tilted, racetrack style, with the edges of the brim curled upward into a metal fedora. Beneath the moon the oil-slick reflections of the lake became a great shining surface, solid-and-rippled-looking as an endless floor of hammered pewter. A forest of steel oil-drilling rigs stood stiffly in strange lunar geometry, rooted rigidly in water, each rig a hundred-foot skeleton whose taproot drilled miles downward toward the liquefied fossil fuel oil.

A complex arterial web of catwalks, pipes, pumping stations, and man-size wheeled control valves linked this steel forest with the bulbous silvery storage tanks along the shore, the refineries at Paraguaná Peninsula, and the fat oceangoing tankers outbound to heat and lubricate half the world.

The small armada of boats was poled quickly and quietly into a tight inward-pointing circle for final instructions, the details of which no one knew until now. The leader stood in the central boat, his legs spread apart, arms folded across his chest, his jaw jutting forward. By his voice of authority, it was clear to the guerrilleros that this *jefe* was from Caracas and that he was not an oil worker like them. It was whispered he was an imported Asturian dinamitero, a hero of the Spanish Civil War, respected in Moscow and Peking, a troubleshooter from Hanoi to Havana.

The *jefe* gave orders, but did not make commands in the curt Army-caste tradition. With each order he explained his reasons, as a guerrilla comrade.

"Remember," the Spanish *jefe* said, "no European-owned installations will be attacked. Mene Grande and Royal Dutch Shell are not our mission, except if their helicopters take off, Cadre 5 will machinegun them down. That must be a certainty. We are zeroed in on Texas, Mobil, Phillips, Sinclair, with the highest importance to the biggest, Creole. Creole Petroleum is controlled by the Yanqui Standard Oil of New Jersey Corporation, against which our comrades in Peru are also fighting. Cadres 1, 2, 3 and 4 will each attack a Creole Petroleum power station. If a comrade is hurt, he must sink or swim. The attack cannot stop even one minute for bandages. *Sabéis?* This must not fail. Tonight we can knock out a half-million barrels-per-day production. But only if each hombre does what he must do." He ran his eyes over them in the encircling silence, then added, "Most of this Yanqui oil goes to Europe for a new bourgeois luxury. Central heating. Also the British utilities. So the world press, not only the Yanqui press, will report everything we do tonight. Tonight, Lake

Maracaibo is a frontline trench in the international class struggle!" He saluted them with a stiffly upraised clenched fist.

Whenever the heat lightning flashed across the overhead sky the soft familiar shadows vanished into a hard-edged chiaroscuro of charcoal black and chalk white, somehow threatening in a nameless way, and, as the boats fanned out toward their targets from which some would not return, a few of the tight-lipped men quickly, secretly, crossed themselves out of habit.

One hour later a rocket flare fired by the leader rode a glowing firework trail upward in the benevolent dark, then burst overhead into a small, brilliant chemical comet. At the signal across the opalescent lake, beneath the low golden moon, one explosive thud began, followed by another, thud upon thud so powerful the air shook, until suddenly the Creole power stations went up in a unified volcanic roar that sent hundreds of white gulls wheeling outward in wide squawking circles of terror across the warm Caribe sky.

11 A NOISELESS RAIN began to fall a few hours after midnight throughout the Caracas valley, sponging out the mountainous bulk of Pico Avila and *teleférico,* glazing with mist the thin line of glare over the Old City where fires ignited by underground squads of dinamiteros reddened the low reflective clouds. Caracas lay at the bottom of a cup of hills, its sleeping houses as sienna-colored and scattered as tea leaves.

A deep well-bottom of nighttime darkness filtered silently through every stone, sifting shadowlessly in every doorway with a hushed expectant nothingness, a suspension of the ancient continent's long-throttled scream of centuries' pain; the dark blood pulsing through the young throat pulled back taut for the stone Aztec knife; the near-naked Indian penitentes hung bleeding, bleeding, crowned with thorns, nails forced into their bleeding flesh during their yearly re-enactment of the Crucifixion; the braided Spanish whips and Portuguese muskets flailing across the bent backs of a submissive shuffling malarial multitude groping through the endless night of life toward the prayed-for eternity of death. The prayer was on every continent the same: in China to Buddha and Confucian ancestors, in India to a pantheon of numberless gods, in Africa to Mohammed, or carved totemic trees; everywhere the same numb hopeless hope: Each day is a dying but do not let us die in an everlasting life. Do not let us live in an everlasting death. In the Latin Americas the prayer was to Christ or the Virgin or Quetzalcoatl or the local saint: Give us this day the bread of hope.

A square-bodied dairy truck whose panels advertised LECHE FRESCA PAS-TEURIZADA backed slowly into the alley behind the Hotel Miranda in the El Silencio district of Caracas. When the truck stopped, a tall shadow detached itself from the deeper darkness of the wall and stepped cautiously up to it. Almost immediately a flash of light struck the man's eyes, then winked out.

"Qué va!" the tall man whispered fiercely as the driver pushed open the door on the passenger side of the truck. "What a time to turn on a light!"

"I had to see you to make sure," the driver said. "Get in, get in. Don't slam the door until we're out on the avenida."

The stacked crates of milk bottles which filled the truck rattled as the driver shifted gears quietly. He started his windshield wipers to clear the mist, even though the rain had stopped, and then drove without headlights through the alley out to the main street. "Now," he said. "Now you can close the door. And lock the door."

Dr. Mayoso Martí kept his head down in the low cab of the truck, bracing himself as they swung around the next corner and stopped beneath the overhanging branches of a chaguaramo tree in front of a *bloque* of low-rent apartment houses. Droplets from the leaves fell on the metal roof of the truck in an uneven nervous tap-tap.

"What's the matter?" Mayoso said. "Why do you stop?"

The driver took off his uniform cap and wiped his forehead. He was breathing heavily. "What a night, what a night," he said. "Rain and fog and not a minute to catch your breath."

"You were late," Mayoso said. "After the first hour I almost decided to go back into the hotel."

"Cool off, hombre," the driver said. "All you had to do was stand there in a dry corner. The rest of us have been running all night like crazy people. Tchah! I was stopped by two security patrols. First the Federals, they at least have some discipline, but the second! Aie, you know our municipales? Brutos. Worse than cops on TV, bang, bang."

"How did they pass you through?"

"I'm really a milk truck driver. I hope you're really the Doctor Mayoso Martí I was ordered to meet. Filho only showed me your picture."

"Yes, I'm Doctor Mayoso," he said. "Here's my passport from Filho." In the cramped space of the cab, he twisted his coat to fumble for a piece of paper in his pocket. He held it toward the driver. "Here. Where's your flashlight?"

"Aie, the little paper. I forgot! That's what I stopped for. I remember, then I forget. I'm going crazy tonight." He tapped his forehead. "I forgot Filho's little passport." He fished a small paper square out of his milkman's uniform shirt pocket and held it in the dim yellow circle of light beside the doctor's piece of paper. Together, touching edges, the pieces made a complete lottery ticket which had been torn irregularly in half. The pieces matched.

"Okay?" Mayoso said out of habit, then caught himself and added, "*Conforme?*"

"*Conforme.* My name is Marro, Doctor."

"Now turn that damn light off, Marro. Let's go. *Cuanto tiempo nos queda? Estoy apurado!*"

They've sent me a milkman instead of a clever man, he thought.

"Filho said you would have a little suitcase with medical instruments," Marro said.

"I have it." Mayoso kicked lightly the small leather doctor's bag lying almost invisible in the shadows at his feet.

"I didn't see it when you got in, Doctor."

"Amigo, I appreciate the revolutionary state of your nerves tonight. But I have less appreciation for an uncomfortable sound I heard when I entered your truck. Like the safety catch of a revolver clicking."

"Mire!" The driver stuck his hand into his pocket. "I forgot to set the trigger back on safety. A bad mistake."

Thus do we make revolutions, Mayoso thought swiftly. From Bolívar and Miranda to O'Higgins and San Martín. There is no one like us in the world for our mystical vision, for our contempt of fear, for bravery before death, for the rhetoric of our passions and our bare-chested courage before cold bayonets, but do not ask us to be on time in attack or cautious about details or practical about a little job like tonight's which has no need, none at all, for style or gestures, no matador's cape-flourishing *revoleras* tonight, por favor. What is it? Why are we so? What is it? We never trust sweat. We believe only in blood. One of our biggest fiestas is the Day of the Dead, and to our children we give dainty replicas of the human skull made of candy. Every one of our most revered heroes died by fire, rope, sword, or bullet. Can it be we are more in love with death than with victory?

"Marro," Mayoso said. "When I was in the Sierra del Cristal, there was a Marro among us. He drove a stolen American sugar company jeep for Raúl Castro."

"I have never been in Cuba, Doctor," said the driver, "but my name is also Marro. The closest I came to Cuba was when we collected almost a million bolívares to send Fidel during *la revuelta*. When Fidel came here to Caracas I saw him close enough to touch him."

"So?"

"Yes. His face, his beard, he looked like Jesus in the schoolbooks. There was much emotion. The tank he rode on was covered with flowers."

Aie, Fidel Castro's face and theatrical guerrilla-leader beard remind him of Jesus. Thus is Marro and thus are Latin revolutionaries.

The headlights of an oncoming car probed down the avenida from a distance, coming fast toward them.

"*Agáchese!*" Marro hissed. "Down! Down!"

Mayoso bent quickly, jackknifing his long legs in the small space, crouching in a dark ball under the dashboard as the car came racing toward them. "Get out of the truck," he ordered the driver. "Take some milk. Quick! Be a milkman!"

Marro reached backward with one hand and pulled a case of milk bottles toward himself. "*Cuidado,*" he said. The oncoming car was very close now, and the doctor could hear the tires squeal as its speed was braked. "I'm going to deliver some milk," Marro said.

"There's a revolver in your pocket," Mayoso growled. "What if they search you?"

"*Mire!*" Marro said. "Here. Here! Take it!"

"Don't give it to *me*. I'm a visitor in the country."

The driver's voice shook. "What shall I do with it?"

"Put it under the seat cushion! Quick!" A pale whiteness filled the upper half of the truck's cab as a searchlight beam was turned on the truck's windshield. "*Vamos!*" Mayoso hissed. "Get out! Open the two doors in back very naturally. Take out more milk. *And close your door!*"

Dr. Mayoso curled himself more tightly into the dark lower half of the driver's compartment as he heard the voices outside begin: the stern official gruffness, then Marro's bewildered innocence with tiny glassy punctuations of the clink of milk bottles as the driver shifted his feet nervously.

This is not necessary, Mayoso thought, pressing his face down into his bent arms. If I had known this stupid risk was attached I would have refused Filho. To be gunned down on a Caracas street would be pointless. When I was young I believed heroics were a part of heroism. Now I know both are useless as death. The Anglo-Saxons are right. Only planning works. Strategy, logistics, tactics. Heroism and heroic improvisations have cut our throats in the Caribbean for four hundred years. Now I crouch like a criminal in a milk truck in Caracas. Fool, fool. If Filho had told me, even without mentioning the rebelión militar he had scheduled for tonight, just a hint that this surgery would not be an ordinary straightforward daytime affair, I would have refused him. I owe him my life, one of those impossible unpayable debts, but I would have refused if I had had even a suspicion of his plans for tonight. Filho's Marxian sense of thesis and antithesis must have been amused by exposing me, an enemy of his Party, to the same risks as a loyal Party member.

He tensed as the two metal doors at the back of the truck suddenly opened. A flashlight wavered dimly and ran over the stacked wooden cases of milk bottles, hardly filtering through to the front space where he became rigid. Not here, he thought. Not here. I survived Batista. I survived Castro. But not to be shot here, curled up in an anonymous ball like an aborted fetus.

"Any extra milk in your truck?" a heavy official voice asked. "I've got an ulcer to worry about."

"Always, señor. Some customer always wants an extra bottle. I can always spare one."

"My partner can use one, too, amigo. He's been on ass-dragging duty more than eighteen hours."

"Two I can spare."

The flashlight went out. The sound of bottles. The double metal doors in the back of the truck slammed shut. The voices, slower and quieter now, but not going away.

Mayoso felt two cold rivulets of sweat run down his sides. Sweat glued his shirt to his back. Breathing had become difficult and he had to open his mouth inside the bend of his elbow to muffle what sounded to him like a hoarse roaring.

This should have been a simple taxi ride with my medical bag to some big noisy office building on the Avenida Bolívar where the police could hardly check the hundreds of people coming and going in the lobby, then the twenty or thirty minutes of surgery with the radio turned up loud to cover any screaming because of the absence of anesthesia. Then back to the airport, then home an hour later in San Juan and up into the cool hills where coffee trees shade the slopes like a benediction. But first, before all this dream of safe return, first it is necessary not to be shot in Caracas.

His aching muscles and squeezed gut knotted painfully as the driver opened the door and slid quickly behind the steering wheel. "Keep down," Marro said between his teeth, keeping his lips from moving. "The agents are watching."

The disembodied reflections in the upper half of the cab vanished as the searchlight was turned off. The big Ford police car revved its engines and began to move. Marro leaned out of his window and waved toward it, friendly but respectful. "Bastards," he spat. "Nefastos!"

"Oh no," Mayoso said, trying painfully to sit up. He began rubbing his stiff elbows. "Gentlemen, that's what they are. In the old days of Pérez Jiménez the bullyboys from the Seguridad Nacional would have emptied this truck, broken every bottle on your head, and then maybe shot you in the street. They would leave your body there. Your wife—who knows? Your new Venezuelan democracy has softened your cops."

"I heard Filho say you were a tough guerrilla surgeon in the *manigua* of Cuba. Nothing soft in those days."

Mayoso said nothing, thinking: my head was soft. Softheaded Mayoso Martí. Softheaded university students. Softheaded New York *Times*. Softheaded almost everybody in Washington.

Mayoso let his breath out and bent over to rub the back of his knees. "My legs are pins and needles." As the driver reached toward the ignition key the doctor said, "Wait, amigo. Don't you think you should deliver some milk in this apartment house?"

"What for? Better vamos. Get over to the autopista. Maybe get lost in El Pulpo."

"No, no. You can't outrun one of those high-speed police cars in this truck. And they will be back."

"How do you know?"

"Believe me, I know."

"Just *sit* here? Caramba! How can you be so sure?"

"My experience warns me, Marro. One learns to make good guesses."

"What can we do?" The driver's voice shook a little.

"You know how to deliver milk. Do it. *Camine, no corra*. Walk, don't run."

At that moment, a pair of headlights swept around the far end of the block of apartments and bored in toward them, slowing down.

"Pronto! Pronto!"

Immediately Marro lifted his delivery rack of bottles and stepped out of his door with familiar competence. By the time the police car came up in slow gear, he was crossing the street toward the opposite side, walking carefully away from his truck. Marro half turned to give the policemen a partial salute, stumbling as he did so. He recovered and continued his easy milk-delivery stride. The patrol car accelerated rapidly and shot around the next corner with squealing tires.

Marro spun around and ran back. He was breathing fast as he jumped up into the truck. Two of the milk bottles cracked as he dropped the delivery rack behind his seat. "Vamos? Rápido?" By now it was clear Mayoso would be giving the orders, even though the driver had been sent by Filho.

"Bueno," Mayoso said. "Now we can make a run for it. Zigzag across the city. Do you know the back alleys?" he asked as the truck began to move.

"Most of them. Cut across el Conde Sur. We're going to the Ciudad Universitaria."

"The University?"

"Yes. The University is immune from search, by law."

"But they can't arrest Filho in any case. He's a congressman."

"Yes, but they can arrest any Party comrade you're going to operate on. And you. What if a wounded comrade died? The papers would have headlines that Filho murdered one of his people by surgery while his comrades were getting killed by the police. That would sit on the stomach like a rock, no? Especially with our excitable students? Or the Fidelistas of the FALN?"

"Filho could explain it somehow. He's número uno."

The driver waved one arm. "Go explain it to the wind. You would be surprised how excitable many of our young activists are. Especially the ones from the soft bourgeois families. They try twice as hard to be tough. You know what I mean?"

Mayoso nodded but did not answer as the metal-bodied milk truck rattled and swayed through the misty darkness. He had assayed political religious fervor in its many forms, the consuming inner fires which wore two masks, the self-deceiving mask of self-sacrifice and the persuasive mask of Party loyalty. He recalled Havana in the old days when everything had been made very simple by the simple hatred of Fulgencio Batista's corrupt regime. The slogan which had held them all together was primitive: *Patria o Muerte!* The enemy of my enemy is my friend. A Popular Front. He and the students from the Havana University had shared their lives like water in the desert. Fidel Castro's rhetoric of *la revuelta* of Havana was their truth and their guiding light was to wipe out hunger, to bring food to *los pobres y los humildes,* for freedom forever. Life each day was shadow. Only their struggle against the Batista regime had substance. The daily jobs of living and studying seemed grubby and small, to be done hastily with the right hand while the left became the partisan's fist, clenched, upraised. The dream of free elections. Work for wages instead of a disguised debt-ridden serfdom on the one-crop *latifundistas'* estates. And a final end to gunbarrel rule by Batista, or Machado's secret police who fed prisoners to the harbor sharks.

Ah, ah. The bitter irony. We all acted, not as actors but only as men raised on the mountain witches' milk of Spanish bravery and the devil's stoneground bread of Spanish style. Ah, style. Style. The flourish of the matador's cape. A ton of dagger-horned death as the bull charges for the kill, but the matador becomes the mystical body of our dreams of glory when he stands slender and shining in his suit of lights, his Toledo blade naked now in the sun, motionless and unmoved in the snorting brute face of doom, matador against bull, man against fate, Prometheus against the gods, immortality against death, our desperate dream to be able to take an ultimate gamble and to carry it off with style.

("Cervantes," my father used to say to me, Mayoso thought in the darkness of the milk truck. "Read Cervantes, my boy. Only he caught the Spanish mystique. Contradictory. Proud. After God granted the Spaniards the three wishes he had promised them, beauty, love, and money, they came back to Him on their knees for a fourth wish. They begged for a stable government. And even God cried out: 'No! That's too much to ask!' ")

Only my father, Mayoso thought as he balanced himself in the dark milk truck, only my father brooding in his study lined with books by Unamuno, Darío, and Blasco Ibáñez, could have foreseen that the same Castro saved from execution by a priest, helped by the American and Mexican administrations as a new fighter for freedom, helped by the world's believers in words like democracia, only my father who had wiped the dust off the history books of the red and the black could have prophesied the greater terrors which would follow. Only my father would have died as he did.

I should have studied more history and less medicine. The faces change each century. The history is the same. The river of time flows back to the past and walking along its banks is the only freedom a man in prison has.

Prison. That's where I must have developed this fantasy habit of escaping in my mind from a rotten *now* to a different *then*, sleepwalking freely through history. Maybe my fantasy is that my scholarly father still lives, still saunters with his Malacca cane along the banks of time, pointing his stick upstream to the past, his monologues still pretending to be conversations.

Ah, Dion, you're in Caracas? Holed up at the Hotel Miranda? Francisco de Miranda. I'm glad his name still lives even if only on a fleabag hotel! What a man! Soldier under George Washington. Miranda tutored Bernardo O'Higgins. He recruited his unemployed Irish veterans of the Napoleonic Wars to fight in Venezuela. And where you are now, in Caracas, he befriended Bolívar. Ah, Bolívar, a revolutionary firebrand somewhat like your pícaro friend Filho. Bolívar was so occupied with the ladies of Caracas that he allowed the Spanish royalists to capture a fortress and then turned Francisco Miranda over to them. In return, Spanish courtesy permitted Bolívar to run off to exile while Miranda was sent to die in a Cádiz dungeon.

*Dungeons, the breeding place of revolutionaries and discoverers. Spain
learned from Italy, which had learned from Rome. The English forgot,
and bred Gandhi and Nehru. The French forgot, and bred Ho Chi Minh
and Vo Nguyen Giap. The Russians and Chinese remember, so they
give their question-askers tombs, not dungeons. My son, don't let Filho
provide you with a restful tomb.*

Filho and I should have studied more history, Mayoso thought in the
jouncing milk truck. How wonderful, in the sense of full of wonder,
for amateurs like us to dream as if for the first time in history of a cleansing revolution of blood. To amateurs like us who followed Castro against
Batista, the dusty sweat of everyday peace has no emotion to compare,
especially when revolutionary life becomes such a therapeutic struggle:
The high-caloric illnesses vanish, the black Sunday suicides stop, insomnia turns into sleep, and the only officially recognized revolutionary neu-
rosis is pity.

Our Spanish-American history is as full of the rhetoric of revolution as
our plazas are filled with prancing bronze equestrian statues of our rough-
shod strongmen. We grow up in school believing the word revolución
and the word democracia are the same. Bedeviled utopians, all of us,
filled with inquisitorial righteousness and penny-catechism answers to
every question. How wonderful was that earlier, innocent time in the
Western world when our young heart-cry of protest made Fidel Castro a
George Washington, a bearded Bolívar, a spiritual descendant of the
José Martí who died for Cuba at Dos Ríos. We who were with Fidel in
the Sierra Maestra mountains could believe we were the heirs of soldiers
who had left bloody footprints in the snow at Valley Forge, in the snow
of the thin-aired Andean cordillera on the way to Chacabuco with San
Martín, in the snow of the high passes of the Pyrenees when our Spanish
cousins fled toward France from Franco's falangistas. In the Sierra Maestra we believed in Castro along with the *Times,* and the Western democ-
racies. Except that when he turned his militia on us, the midnight military
drumhead courts-martial and his secret police, by that time, the correspondents were back in New York exchanging intelligent disillusion-
ments ("the Latin temperament is inherently unstable . . . and they have
no democratic tradition") and the democratic statesmen were in their air-
conditioned cubicles in San Juan, London, Paris and Washington, and
we in Castro's prisons were hanging by our thumbs in the name of the
revuelta we had helped win while the new secret police (bearded, now)
probed us intimately with the slender *picana eléctrica.* Almost every one
of us had been tortured by the Servicio de Inteligencia Militar, the Batista
police, but we had been so young and so full of hate we had survived
in our minds. But now, when Castro's examining magistrates wore mili-

tary insignia, your own insignia of a week ago, and arrested you in the name of your own revolución, used your own old words like *free elections* in a new way to mean Soviet-style, then the pain of the beatings rang hollowly inside the echo chambers of horror within your shattered brain cells. The great stone mountains of boyhood belief slid muddily into the sea, purpose left the world, meaning had no meaning, and you hung with your eyes three maddening inches from a specially blank white-painted wall and you only wanted everything to end then. A part of your thinking brain knew you were being conditioned to want a final release ("When your prosecutor sounds friendly," his cellmate had whispered, "it's not love, it's Pavlov"), conditioned to feel in your bones so nameless a loss that your hundred little guilts spun in circles, faster and faster like floating soap scum in a tub, until your questioners finally pulled the cunning psychological drain-plug and all the fragmentary human guilts clung together before plunging finally into the dark whirlpool of release.

Confession. The open-sky release of confession. The childhood training in confession. *Father, forgive me, for I have sinned.* Confess, bear witness against yourself; order and mercy shall be yours. The release of signing. The release of holding a pen, a real pen, a real civilized *thing* from a forgotten outside real world. The exhausted orgiastic release because by then you were guilty of an omnipresent namelessness beyond reach of groping hands or torn fingernails gouging agonal parallel blood tracks on the white-painted concrete wall. You knew only that you were guilty. Of what, did not matter.

Marro slammed on the brakes of the milk truck. Mayoso awoke from his reverie with a start as the cases of milk slid forward and bumped him. From a side street an armored military car had screeched forward across their route with shot-out empty headlights, two of its six tires so flat they slapped like pistol shots, traveling fast. The hatch cover of the car's gunport was hinged open, its machinegun swinging loosely in a skyward arc. The body of the gunner hung halfway downward out of the hatch with flopping dead arms as the vehicle curved toward them and braked hard to a sliding stop in the middle of the intersection.

Two soldiers in American-design steel helmets, carrying rifles, ran toward them, circling outside the milk truck's headlights, the man on the left holding his rifle horizontally over his head in a signal for them to halt. From the far side of the armored car came a man wearing the green beret of the *cazadores*. He carried a machine pistol and carefully remained on the shadowed side of the car to cover his men.

"Dios mío, Dios mío," the driver whispered to Mayoso. "They have us cornered like rats."

"Valor, hombre," Mayoso said. "Let me do the talking. Listen to what I tell them." Quickly he opened his door and jumped out of the truck with his medical bag in one hand. He hurried into the bright headlighted area in front of the milk truck as the two soldiers circled right and left and the young officer stood still, machine pistol held at the ready.

"Put your goddam hands up," the officer called out. *"Manos arriba!* Up high." He fired a single shot over Mayoso's head. "Up! Pronto!"

Mayoso dropped his medical bag and held up both hands. He heard the lethal little click as the officer chambered another round in his pistol. Mayoso felt every nerve become tight as a trigger. Sweat stung his eyes.

"Sergeant," the officer ordered, "search the big guy. Carlos, you search the driver and the truck." His voice sounded frazzled and dog-tired.

As one of the soldiers moved toward him Mayoso said, "Sergeant, I'm a surgeon. I commandeered this man and his milk truck. The medical switchboard called me to rush to the Salas Emergency Hospital. They need more surgeons."

The sergeant stood to one side of him so that Mayoso remained exposed to fire. "Turn around," the sergeant said. "Move!"

He spun to face directly into the headlights of the milk truck, turning very quickly because their voices had the snarl which comes with killing. The headlights blinded him so that he could not see past them. He blinked to clear the salt sweat from his eyes. What was happening to the driver? As the sergeant expertly frisked him Mayoso said, "My instruments are in the medical bag on the ground, Sergeant. Please tell your commander what is inside the bag. I have to get to the hospital."

With a kick the sergeant shoved the medical bag to one side. He knelt on one knee, opened it, then tilted it sideways to catch a spill of light from the truck's headlights.

"Please don't handle anything inside," Mayoso said. "Some of it is breakable."

"What's the package wrapped in cloth?"

"Sterilized instruments. The small flat package is sterile rubber gloves."

The sergeant stood up. "Lieutenant," he called, "there's a package in this doctor's bag. He says it's doctor's instruments, sterilized."

"Stand back and cover him. I'll see."

He could hear the officer coming toward him from behind, and the hair on his neck stiffened with the sudden recollection of the machine pistol. That single shot had been very nervous. In Havana we would be sprawled on the street now, clawing at the stone, left there as if resting our faces in massive nosebleeds for children to see on their way to school in the morning. His pulsebeats hammered in his head. Now that his eyes had adjusted to the headlight's glare he could see the second soldier motion the driver out of the truck with his hands in the air. A moment later the back doors of the truck rattled open. There was the homely sound of milk crates sliding.

From close behind him the officer said, "Turn around."

He obeyed. With the light from the truck behind him now, he could see that the officer looked very young, with a hairline mustache and blood streaks through the dust on his face.

"Want me to examine your man on top of your car, Lieutenant?"

"No. *Murió*. He's very dead. Where is this package?"

"In my medical bag."

"Show it to me."

"I will have to move to reach it."

"Move. Pick up the bag. Now come this way. No tricks. Open it to the light. Open it wider. Is that the package?"

"Yes."

"Open it."

"That will destroy the sterilization, Lieutenant."

"You can get more at the hospital."

Mayoso untied the top binding of the cloth surgical pack and threw open each of the four overlapping corners. A handful of tightly packed instruments made a small metallic clatter as they fell away from one another. From the military radio in the armored car came a static-filled voice issuing a garble of commands. The lieutenant tilted his head slightly to listen while keeping his eyes on Mayoso.

"All right," the lieutenant said. "You can put them away. You can get more at the hospital." He sounded apologetic now.

"Of course."

He began to rewrap the instruments as the lieutenant called out, "Sergeant?"

"It's a truck full of milk bottles, Lieutenant."

"Then let's go! They just called our unit." To Mayoso he said, "Sorry we held you up, Doctor. Tonight everybody is very suspicious."

"Of course. *Ordenes*. You can only do your duty. What's the news?"

"The *rojecillos* attacked the Retén La Planta two hours ago. Hundreds of prisoners escaped down through the Guaira ravine. We were ordered to cover the Quinta Crespo market area when a police car came up alongside and machinegunned us. They really greased us."

"A police car?"

"The bastards stole three police cars and a dozen submachineguns." The lieutenant wiped his sleeve across his face. "It's crazy, Doctor. Some of the guerrillas are wearing police uniforms."

From the truck the driver called out shakily, "Can I turn off my headlights, Lieutenant?"

"No. Leave them on. If they were off we would have fired at you first. Leave your lights on." To the soldiers moving toward him he barked, "Let's go! The major will think we're dead!" As he followed his men back to the car he called over his shoulder, "If you see me later as a patient, take care of me, Doctor."

Mayoso raised one hand. "Don't worry." He carefully stood exactly where he was while they climbed into their armored car. The dead soldier hanging over the edge of the open machinegun hatch jerked sideways as they started off violently and sped down the avenida.

He picked up his medical bag and walked back to the milk truck slowly, feeling a great weight of fatigue come down upon him. Tremors rippled through his leg muscles and he forced himself not to shiver.

The driver sat behind the steering wheel. His teeth chattered as shaking spasms kept hitting him. "I was sure—I was sure—" he tried to say, but could not finish. A strong goaty smell of sweat filled the driver's cab space.

"Is your gun still under your seat?" Mayoso asked angrily.

The driver opened his lips to speak, but no words came.

"*Carajo!*" Mayoso said. "Your damn cowboy pistol could have gotten us shot on the spot." He covered his hand with his handkerchief and reached under the seat cushion to fish out a small automatic pistol, then wiped it very carefully with his handkerchief. "If you're doing a job as a milkman, be a milkman all the way. Don't try to be a hero with a toy gun." He dropped the pistol out of the window. "Now pull yourself together and let's get the hell away from here."

The driver shakily rammed the milk truck into forward gear, nodding his head to indicate where the armored car had stopped.

"Máquina Yanqui. Did you notice, Doctor? What we could do with even one armored car! We have to lose good men to capture every lousy piece of Yanqui equipment. But Filho says Fidel will send Russian automatic guns sooner or later. Filho says city guerrilla fighting is not like mountain fighting. You need small stuff. Light. Automatic stuff with a high rate of fire."

Mayoso grunted and rubbed his back. "Marro," he said, "just drive. You're talking too much." There was nothing to say to answer the driver. The injustices were so big, so ancient, so terrible, that only the rhetoric of hatred and the evidence of revolutionary blood made sense to this man. Marro knew only this: Cain and Abel. Nothing else.

In Marro's head, and the lieutenant's, there was the distant drumbeat of the swaggering macheteros, the bugle call of liberation from the Ins to the Outs and back again, a long processional: Perón, Batista, Trujillo, Odría, Somoza, Stroessner, Duvalier, Rojas Pinilla, Vargas, Benavides, Terra, Justo, and here in Venezuela, Pérez Jiménez and Gómez. Armies of non-liberation raised by driving the peasants from their huts with blows across the shoulders with the flat side of machete blades, roping the bare-foot *campesinos* together wrist and ankle, and marching them without food or water to the nearest regional general. Who remembered that with them went an officer's note handwritten by candlelight with Iberian flour-ishes while the officer guzzled raw aguardiente: "My General: I send you three hundred volunteers. Return the ropes to me and I will send you three hundred more."

He remembered his grandfather telling him of the revolutionaries' po-lite blackmail of the enforced loan, the *empréstito forzoso*. The military money collector would appear at their house near Santiago de Cuba just before lunch, apologizing profusely to the suddenly frozen lady of the house for the unmannerly guns he wore in two holsters. The platoon of bandoleros assigned the military collector, each man with his sharp, curved *peinilla* persuader in a leather scabbard, would crouch on their haunches before the tall metal-braced double front doors, the recent re-cruits bending forward with the unaccustomed weight of the two car-tridge belts strung across the chest, shadow-faced and motionless beneath their dusty sombreros, only curling their bare toes tightly in the dirt street while they thought of their crops rotting on the ground, their children swollen with hunger.

("Where else," his father had said to him later, much later, while he was still in medical school, "where else—not even in China—do your neigh-bors in the village truly congratulate you when your baby dies and the women praise God for His mercy in sparing the innocent little one from growing up in such a world? Tell me. Where else?")

So, Mayoso thought, from many paths I have now come to this dark avenida in Caracas. So many paths to come here.

One path began in San Juan, a week before Christmas, only a few years ago. He had just begun to scrub for surgery when he heard his nurse running down the hall. She had burst in. "Teléfono! Teléfono!"

He had continued scrubbing his hands with the surgical soap, holding them toward her. "Now? Don't be foolish."

"It's Washington, Doctor! Something about Cuba!"

"Cuba?"

She nodded.

"They said *Cuba?*" He stopped scrubbing.

"I told them you were in surgery. Can you call him out? No. But this is"—she had moved her hand in a helpless little circle—"aie, what is the word—urgent, this is *urgent*, they said. The exchange of medicines for the Bay of Pigs prisoners. This is the American Red Cross calling."

He had dropped the soapy surgical brush and raced to the telephone. The voice had sounded far away in the earpiece, and, without realizing his voice had gone up, he shouted into the phone, "Louder! Louder, please!"

"This is DeWitt Sommers, in Washington. At the Red Cross Disaster Service office."

"DeWitt! My God! How did you find me here?"

"The Cubans told us."

"The *Cubans!*"

"They've been negotiating to release the Bay of Pigs prisoners in return for certain food and drug supplies. I'm representing the pharmaceutical manufacturers—"

"Good, good. How can I help you?"

"I don't know. We're stuck. The Cubans don't trust our inventory, especially proprietary medications. Then they threw out the Alka-Seltzer and aspirin, they rejected our penicillin G and streptomycin—"

"No, no," Mayoso interrupted. "There must be a mistake. They need antibiotics very much."

"That's the point. They're playing this super-ultra-legal. They don't trust our labels. They don't trust our inventories. They don't trust our market valuations."

"Of course. They trust nothing, Witt. What about narcotics?"

"My brother David's been up all night clearing with the U.S. Bureau of Narcotics. We got clearance this morning. Now the Cubans say we're substituting items."

"Are you?"

"Only a drug equal to an equal drug we don't have immediately on hand." Witt's voice sounded weary. "They just don't trust our list."

"Sounds like faking. With Chinese and Russian drugs coming in, they may want other drugs in different units to fit their hospital formularies."

"They asked for ten thousand tons of powdered milk. Now they've changed that—"

"Of course! Listen, Witt, damn few Cubans have experience handling dried milk. They only need to be shown how. Don't let details wear you down. No matter what, get those prisoners out!"

"I've got a list here of mixed-up misunderstandings as long as my arm."

"Negotiate, Witt. Talk, don't stop—those men, I mean, in those prisons—"

"Negotiate is right. Today, Fidel's top adviser said they would trust our drug inventory if you went to Havana—"

"Dios mío! A hostage?"

"No, no, no. As liaison. They guarantee your safe return."

Silence. The overseas phone connection had hummed like a vibrating needle in his brain while he felt something crushing his chest. He had forced himself to breathe while he held the telephone with his two soapy, slippery hands.

"Hello? Hello? Mayoso?"

"I'm here. Who guarantees this safe return? Who told you so exactly where to find me?"

"Some very smooth apple everybody calls Filho. He said you had a gynecology clinic at this number. A gentleman and a scholar."

"Oh. Oh. A gentleman and scholar. Like Trotsky."

"I get the impression he genuinely likes you and respects you."

"He does. I respect him. But we are like cousins on opposite sides, during your Civil War."

"But can you do business with him?"

"If Fidel will give him backing. Filho is Venezuelan, but with a left-handed Cuban Army commission. If Fidel will back him—"

"He did. You, too. Castro spoke of you with great warmth. You were his combat surgeon in the early days, he said. 'Send Mayoso Martí,' he said. 'He has a foot in both our countries. I believe his word.' Can you trust him?"

"No," Mayoso had said slowly.

"Did you say no?"

"That's what I said. Fidel believes what he says when he says it. But tomorrow he can say another thing."

"What about your family in Havana?"

His soapy hands tightened convulsively and the plastic phone began to slide in his fingers. He steadied it and said, "Gone."

"Your *whole* family?"

"Gone. Gone."

Silence, then DeWitt Sommers said, "Who can we get instead of you? I don't have the right or the guts to ask you to go."

"You have the right, Witt. About the guts, don't worry. This is at a diplomatic level, so it's less the guts but more the carefulness about details you need!"

"You're sure I'm not putting your head into a rope?"

"I doubt it, Witt."

"Crazy things happen. You remember how Torre was kidnaped from

Mexico? The kidnap stunts they pulled off in Berlin? Don't say yes too fast. Think it over."

"If I do, I'll say no. I don't volunteer. I'm drafted."

"You'll go?"

"Of course."

"Think it over, Mayoso. Call me back."

"No need. I will go."

Two days later, after Air Force planes had raced him to Washington, then to Miami to check the freighter cargo, he had stepped off a chartered Pan Am DC-3 onto Cuban soil.

As the chartered plane taxied across the concrete runway of Havana's José Martí International Airport, Mayoso recognized the full pressing sensation in his bladder as fear. Only yesterday . . . yesterday? Dios, he thought, three years ago and it seems just like yesterday! On a bright morning he had been extracted miraculously from a maximum-security cell at Boniato Prison and had been delivered like a butcher's burlap sack of bones to this same airport. Filho had half carried and half supported him up the steps of a Cubana Bristol flight to Miami. Filho had been the author of the miracle, and Filho had given him an *abrazo* inside the plane. "Adiós," Filho had said with emotion in his voice. "I won't see you again. Get well. Stop being a brave bull. Get yourself into a hospital and get healthy. And stay healthy."

And now, three years like a day later, just as swiftly and unbelievably and without advance notice, just as three years ago, to be back again at the José Martí Airport with the same tight bladder but a very different passport. A green passport with the word SPECIAL stamped in gold-colored letters under the golden spread-eagle seal of the United States. The passport is not bulletproof, he thought as the plane rolled forward, but it provides a small confidence that They—the capital-T They—the Party They —would avoid shenanigans.

Mayoso saw an enormous airplane at the other side of the field which carried the winged hammer-and-sickle emblem of the Soviet *Aeroflot*. The plane had an extraordinary wingspan and was powered by four turbo-prop engines, each with two counterrotating propellers. This must be the big Tupalov plane, the caviar-and-vodka fringed-silk-lampshades Havana-Moscow flight, one of the last air links to the world outside the island.

His plane turned onto a secondary ramp toward a distant hangar, and a billboard about sixty feet long slid into his view. A fiercely scowling bearded soldier was painted on the sign beside giant lettering: WEL-COME TO COMBAT-READY CUBA—THE ONLY FREE COUN-

TRY OF HISPANIC AMERICA. The European and South American commercial airline hangars around the field were no longer fronted by passenger planes being overhauled. Several squadrons of new MIG-21 fighters and Ilyushin-28 light bombers were deployed among them now.

Mayoso's plane revved up as it changed direction again and taxied toward one of the hangars. Mayoso saw a black Cadillac limousine glide out of the opaque shadow of the building and roll slowly onto the field. A welcoming committee? Three years ago, he thought, they carried me from prison to this airport in a white ambulance. Today I'll return to Havana in a black limousine. I'm here to do a job, and an ordinary working car would be better. This show car is not so good. This kind of reception only means They want something more from me. When the cold vise within his bladder tightened painfully again, he thought: I must learn to control this infantile conditioned reflex. This weakens me. I must learn to react to what is here, not what is past and gone.

I am no longer Captain Mayoso Martí of years ago, commissioned by Castro and standing at attention before a guerrilla court-martial convened without warning at three in the morning, five bearded judges sitting in a shadowed semicircle across the smoky yellow kerosene lamp on an ammunition case. Outside, the guerrilla company slept beside their arms without knowledge that their doctor had been awakened and arrested for refusal to join in the attack to cut the water supply to Guantánamo from the Yateras River pumping station. The vulnerable parts of me were taught instantaneous fear by prison experts, at Boniato and Castillo del Principe, Galera 14. I need to relearn the sensible reactions of civilization, beginning with better sphincter control. Today a long black car with the letters of a military intelligence agency painted on its doors should not automatically mean being gunned down or snatched off the street or sprayed in the face with that cyanide aerosol They had used twice in Munich. Today I carry a special diplomatic passport; accident-and-health insurance, no death benefits in the policy of course, but worthwhile all the same.

The Cadillac parked about one hundred feet away as his plane swung in an arc and braked sharply, then turned off its engines. Mayoso saw a militiaman jump out of the front seat of the black car to open the rear door. Two heavy *barbudos* in olive-green fatigues, wearing cartridge belts and pistol holsters, got out and stood beside the door. *Melones*—Mayoso remembered the fruity opposition name for them: green on the outside, but Red inside. They were also called *caníbales,* but with affectionate and admiring irony while the revolution was still young. Their beards and long hair were insignia of the first revolutionary volunteers, marking them as being among the original three thousand guerrillas who had sworn not to cut their hair or shave until the revolution was won. Now the long hair was longer, he saw, and probably treasured as a military decoration.

The fourth man to step out of the car was Filho. Mayoso stared at him. Filho. Contradictory incredible Filho. A whirling dervish. Charming as a French movie star during an interview or cruel as a Spanish grandee dealing with peons; a fervent Communist pilgrim to Moscow one day, a boozing Caribe pagan in Havana the next. When they had fought together in the mountains against Batista, the peasants had said: Fidel is our heart, Raúl is our hands, because they are Cuban. Then the *guajiros* had tapped their heads and said: but el Ché, the Argentine doctor, and Filho, the Venezuelan lawyer, they are our brains. Young men, but wiser than the elders, as wise as the saints.

Filho was better-looking than men who made careers of being handsome, but he was contemptuous of such narcissism. At public ceremonies he walked with the squared shoulders and gun-barrel spine of a professional military man, yet, among the sugarcane *guajiros,* he went unshaven and uncombed for days, pausing only to eat a handful of olives, some sausage, and to squirt some wine in his mouth from a leather *frasco.* He used his appearance as he used his mind, simply as another weapon in the class struggle. When European or African or Asian cameramen came to Cuba to do picture stories about him, he left the paneled princely house he kept in Miramar and slept on the ground in the cane fields, huddled in a blanket like a mountain guerrilla in a battle zone. These hardy pictures, and muscular shots of him stripped to the waist, swinging a machete during the cane *zafra,* showed the world at a glance Cuba's dependence on its one cash crop of sugar, the iniquity of Americano embargoes against Cuban sugar and, of course, the fervor of an intellectual revolutionary leader accepting common farm-brigade duty on the firing line of agriculture.

He had a Pharaoh's imperial eyes, poached in acid, subtle, worldly, irises black as scarabs. Filho's eyes could convey the flattering handshake of a politician, the command of a general, the laughter of a clown, or the finality of a guillotine.

Usually he wore dark sunglasses, not so much against the glare as against people. Today, Mayoso noted, Filho wore large curving sunglasses, like the French ones used for skiing.

Mayoso slouched in the aisle of the plane, waiting for the metal ladder to be pushed against the fuselage, trying to overcome his trickle of incredulity about being back in Havana. What erratic zigs and zags Filho and I have lived through! Three years ago, when Filho brought me to this airfield in an ambulance and helped me up the metal stairs, I bumped and stumbled like a broken-legged drunk. I was certain I would never be back again. And now, a mere three million years later, here I am, Daniel in the den, armored only by a green-covered gold-eagle passport.

The metal ladder banged loudly into place against the fuselage and the steward pulled back the heavy sliding door.

Filho and one of the *barbudos* left the car and strolled toward the airplane as Mayoso stepped out into the sunshine. As he descended the metal steps his knees seemed ready to tip him over. The men met guardedly at the bottom of the ladder. After a split second of silence, Filho threw his arms around Mayoso in a wide *abrazo*, then leaned back to inspect him.

"Paqueta! Paqueta!" Filho clapped both of Mayoso's shoulders. "It's good to see you back home again."

"This is a pleasant surprise, Filho." Paqueta . . . Mayoso had not heard his revolutionary pseudonym since the days they had fought beside each other in the mountains.

The *barbudo* edged past them and stomped efficiently up into the plane like a customs inspector.

Filho clapped him on both shoulders again. "Let me look at you, Paqueta!" He pulled off his sunglasses and slid them into a shirt pocket. "You must be counting your birthdays backwards! Only one change. The hair. A head of completely white hair on a man your age—very distinguished!" He kept talking. "The ladies at the Casa de España in San Juan must be crazy about you, ah? And the New York ladies feeding the pink flamingos at the Caribe Grand Central, I'll bet they all want to go native with you, pronto, eh? To tell the truth, Paqueta, your being a lotus-eater on a Yanqui island like Puerto Rico has been good for you. You filled out a little since we said adiós here. You look *formidable!* A thousand times better than the last time I saw you!"

How clever, Mayoso thought. He may be talking too much, he may be as jumpy as I am, but he's managed to use my code name from the days of our guerrilla comradeship, to explain away my white hair as a distinction, and to remind me that he was the man to get me out of Cuba. All in less than a minute. That Sorbonne education years ago had not been wasted.

"And you, Filho," Mayoso said, covering his surprise that Filho was enough his own man to ignore the Fidel-style beards and to be clean-shaven, "I can see that life agrees with you."

"The opposite, amigo." Filho laughed. "I agree with life!" He gestured with his fingers to include them both. "You and me, people like us, we burn our lives like candles, no? How many of us are left, who learned to stroll along with death in daily companionship from the age of seventeen? The French say: to each saint his candle." Filho laughed again. He made a clenched-fist salute. "Only one candle to each altar, eh?" He pulled a flat blue star-spangled package of Sputniks from his pocket—"Cigarette? Crimean tobacco, Class A"—and, when Mayoso shook his head, lighted one for himself, holding the long-tubed cardboard mouthpiece with his fingertips, Russian style.

Mayoso examined the bare shoulder tabs of Filho's open-necked fatigues and the beret Filho was wearing. During the revolution, the highest rank set by Castro had been Major. "No promotions? No insignia of rank, Filho?"

"By this time, I don't need any." Filho clapped him on the shoulder again. "Well! It's good to see a civilized man! Often I've wondered about you, hombre. The reports one hears—you do surgery in San Juan, both legal and illegal. Sometimes you evaluate intelligence for the Plans Division of the CIA. Professionally or just as a hobby?"

"Filho, the CIA is the Cigar Institute of America. Like the Cincinnati Reds—a baseball team, nothing political."

Filho looked amused. "But the other reports. You're trusted to collect small fortunes for the Cuban refugees. You serve once a month as a military surgeon out of Miami. You buy guns in Haiti." Then, critically, "Don't you know you can get hurt in all those out-of-the-way places?"

"Filho, don't push. Don't threaten. We're too old to play cat-and-mouse."

"I've always respected your frankness, amigo. I spoke sincerely. Just remember not to let the CIA bait any traps with you as the big cheese, eh?"

What's this all about? Mayoso wondered. Why this little wrestling match of inside information? "And you, Filho? One day I hear you're building guerrilla training schools at Tarara and Minas del Frío for a thousand students. Kids from Caracas and Rio and Bangkok and Algiers—"

"Oh? Your Christians in Action have discovered the obvious so soon? Paqueta, you must have entrée to the E-ring D.I.A. officers at the Pentagon. Do you?"

"Ah, Filho, they've infected you with the prevailing paranoia. All I know is what I read in the papers."

Filho snorted. "Some papers! You must have what the U.N. playboys call cosmic clearance. I've been getting a very good press in China. Do they send you copies of *Hung Chi?*" He wagged his cigarette and answered himself. "No. How could you? That's a Central Committee journal. You must be reading our little singsong paper, *Pekín Informa.* Correct?"

"Yes. You have some good translators. Chinese into Spanish isn't easy. I saw your picture with Chou En-lai at Lop Nor."

"Oh," Filho said, caught, startled. He recovered instantly with a joke.

"What a combination! Mushroom uranium clouds, that gritty Kansu desert weather, jasmine tea and"—his smile widened—"and most lethal of all, that hundred-proof maotai brandy that makes the Russian stuff seem like water. Vodka even the Americanos can drink, but that maotai—!"

Is Filho hinting? Vodka communism versus the maotai brand? "I wondered whether it was you, Filho, or Chou En-lai who came up with that poetic Oriental prediction for nuclear warfare."

"You mean 'The Eastern winds will finally blow harder than the Western winds'? The Chinese deserve the credit. They actually write that way." Suddenly he began to laugh and coughed cigarette smoke. "Paqueta, you would have enjoyed it! Dios mío, the time I asked one of the Peking functionaries to look up the word for love in the Spanish-Chinese dictionary. The definition of *amar* gave an easy example: 'Love. As the Chinese people *love* the Communist Party.' Would you believe it? Even the puritanical Russians thought it was funny."

Now Mayoso was convinced Filho was tunneling toward some point. Sooner or later he would surface. "How do you cover so much territory, Filho? What's your secret?"

With the hand holding the thin Sputnik cigarette, Filho pointed across the airfield at the huge Russian airplane. "That." His other hand made a tight fist, with the tip of his thumb poked out between forefinger and middle finger, the sign language used by Rio streetwalkers. "This size, that's how small the cocktip world is now." He raised his head and shouted up to the airplane, "Corporal!" Without a pause, flexible as a steel spring, he swung back to Mayoso. "You still have luggage on board, no?"

"Yes. They told me to leave it there."

The *barbudo* poked his head through the open door of the plane, "Hola, Comandante?"

"Where the hell's Doctor Mayoso's luggage! What's taking so damn long?"

"Momentito, Comandante. *No me apure.*" The corporal's bearded face ducked back into the plane.

Mayoso smiled. All the revolutionary efficiency had run head-on into momentito, which might mean five minutes or five hours or five days. Or never. "He's searching through my capitalistic pajamas for my counter-revolutionary CIA golf-ball radio transmitter."

"More likely he's trying to liberate some of those stainless steel English razor blades. *Qué machote.*"

"I appreciate such an honor guard, Filho."

Filho pretended to take him seriously. "*Nada.* After all, a Martí has returned to his homeland. Instead of this stupid red-tape delay we should fire a formal gun salute."

"Is that why the cartridge belts? What am I, an invasion?"

"Actually, our men are issued only five rounds each. The rest are blanks."

"Oh? So now you want to diminish the people's firepower?"

Filho lowered his voice, "Forget the wild youthful Cuban revolution that we knew. Let me start you on the right foot. Now, with Russian advisers—"

"That's starting on the left foot—"

"All the old cha-cha-cha Communism is gone, Paqueta. Kids with pistols. Housewives with carbines. Gone. Now everything is Russian efficiency. All the real decisions are made *na verkhu.*"

"What does that mean?"

"At the top. With Russian advisers."

"Aie, Filho. You're between the Russians and the Cubans? You always told me the man in the middle gets ground into sausage."

"Don't worry about me, Paqueta. I'm the meatgrinder, not the meat." He shouted up into the airplane, "Corporal!"

"What's the hurry?" Mayoso said. "This is our first chance to talk. Probably the last."

"Oh no." The puckish look in his eyes, amused at what fools these mortals be, was contradicted by his official serious mouth. "I've arranged to stay with you and the Sommers brothers through all the negotiations."

"But our secretaries and drivers will be routinely assigned from your secret police. Our rooms will be bugged by the DIER."

Filho began to laugh, a trifle nervously at first, then more genuinely. "Christ, how funny! You and me! Di-plo-matic liaison." He stretched the word mockingly. "Only yesterday we were the craziest pair of wild students. Katzenjammer Kids from the funny papers. Remember how we used to fish for sharks off Margarita? Your little invention, to cut the Bickford fuse cords in one-foot lengths so the dynamite and bait package could sink just to shark-feeding level"—he dropped one hand—"*sssss,* then"—he threw both hands up—"cha-*boom!* Scratch one more shark. Those days! Who could ever forget that crazy vacation we took up the Caroní River? You remember the rainy day that half-naked Indian drunk on chicha told us about the diamond *bomba?* Where the river sand was so rich you could rake the gems up from the bottom with your fingers?"

"Loco. Raving loco," Mayoso said. "We had a real roaring Klondike fever. Only two crazy kids would have bought the diving equipment to go prospecting up a jungle river."

The jungle river had been alive with alligators and flesh-eating piranhas, human as well as animal, and the jungle law among prospectors: you keep only what you can defend. The prospectors, a small army, more fierce than any spawned by dragons' teeth, had pitched camp along both sides of the Caroní River. Diamonds were many, but women were few; they were bought and sold and traded in the tent encampments and kept very busy. To steal a woman brought a gun or knife fight. Even worse, however, was theft of a *curiara* diving platform or a diver's helmet. Such robbery guaranteed death. Each night the mob gambled and fought and drank itself into stupor on Indian chicha. The few men who knew how to dive worked in shifts around the clock.

Diamonds were only bright stones. To become money, one had to survive the chicha, the women, the gunfights, the stealing at knife point, then run the gauntlet of Indians along the one hundred fifty mile trip north of Ciudad Bolívar where jewelers' agents from the outside world, from Caracas, paid money for rough diamonds.

He and Filho had enjoyed the Caroní River *bomba* as a colossal collegiate get-rich-quick escapade, until their last night. Filho had been working by waterproof lamps under the water, ankle-deep in the bottom of the river, sifting scoops of sand through a three-level *suruku* mesh filter. He had not seen a face-masked swimmer slither like a water snake behind him. Then everything happened at once. His air hose to the surface was slashed and an arm grappled him across the throat from behind. His diving mask was torn off his face. The diamond filter sack was ripped from his hand.

Mayoso had been up on the surface manning the primitive air pump on the floating *curiara* platform and had not noticed the slack air hose until the popping stream of surfacing air bubbles alerted him. The signal cord floated loosely downstream. He dived overboard without mask or tie line. The waterproof lamp lying on the riverbed had guided him to Filho's limp body. By the time Mayoso had carried Filho up forty feet to the surface his lungs had been bursting. He had surfaced, gasping agonizingly for air, hardly able to keep his grip on Filho. He had dragged Filho onto the mud shore, sinking to his knees, falling, sucking in air through a throat of sandpaper, terrified that he might not be able to resuscitate Filho.

□ □ □

Filho was still talking. He placed one open hand on his chest. "If I had a heart left," he was saying in the bright sunlight of the open airfield, "I'd say it does my heart good to see you, *pescador*. My fellow fisherman. Too bad I can't drop a line with you some night off San Juan Bay."

Mayoso felt his mouth go dry. So They even knew about his midnight fishing. "Filho—" he began to say, then coughed as if he had swallowed a bone.

"We're both good fishermen, Paqueta. We should be in the same boat, no? Look at our situation objectively, without emotion. We've both become halfway men. You're here because you're halfway between the Cubans and the Americans. I'm here halfway between the Cubans and my Ruso comrades." His just-between-us use of the Spanish *Ruso* was a neat touch.

"Ah, ah, ah," Mayoso said. Was Filho surfacing now? I am not slow, but Filho always runs circles around me. What is he saying? Halfway men. What does that mean? He looks and sounds the way I remember him, but he must have changed; now he has so much political power he needs no insignia, no beard. All the real decisions are made *na verkhu*. With power, Filho could not permit himself to play games, pull off practical jokes, and run through his jester's repertoire: the quick-change magician who mystified everyone, now you see it, now you don't, first the tough guerrilla tactician, then the cool logical hairsplitting Sorbonne intellectual, then the haughty playboy from a Venezuelan family so rich that, in a treeless plain, the private road which led to their hacienda was lined with trees for eight miles. Filho's father was of the generation which had amused itself in French nightclubs by dropping diamonds into champagne bottles and letting the first girl who could drink to the bottom keep the gem. Filho's magnificently mustachioed grandfather had been so captured during *la belle époque* by the girls at his favorite Paris bordello ("They could not only can-can," Filho had told Mayoso, "but will-will,") that he had shipped to Caracas the entire establishment: madame, girls, bidets, rugs, tapestries, great feather beds, and a two-year supply of vintage champagne to wet the throat of any guest who might work up a thirst. Perhaps this was why Filho carried power as lightly as a swagger stick; even as a child he could order the llaneros on the hacienda to saddle up and race him to the mountain foothills for a jaguar hunt, or order an overseer to ride all night into Caracas simply to bring back a fresh supply of silk shirts. Filho was in the early Russian tradition of the landed nobleman, the rich intellectual who begins by being offended by the terrible poverty of serfs and ends as a commissar capable of anything in the name of the still voiceless, faceless masses.

How casually Filho had said, *Too bad I can't drop a line with you some night off San Juan Bay.* Is he warning me about night fishing? Or is he hinting at a secret meeting? He has not said one word about the release of prisoners or the shipment of drugs. So They wanted me here for some other purpose. His bladder tightened again.

Then, with the next breath, the separate pieces came together. Filho must have ordered the fine-comb luggage search by the *barbudo* in the plane. His impatience with the corporal was faked, to gain time. Filho knows as well as I do that we have only these few moments in the open airfield to talk freely without DIER surveillance. Behind Filho's liaison cover on this drugs-for-prisoners exchange, he must be training a Russian cadre for future duty in Venezuela or any other Latin American country. Without pulling a trigger, a Russian occupation garrison had taken Cuba, an unsinkable aircraft carrier and submarine base and missile launch pad in the Caribbean. Filho's real power and rank must be with Them. Therefore no Cuban military insignia. Therefore the clean-shaven face. Therefore the show of the Cadillac, symbol of top rank, and the airport guard. *Na verkhu.* But what can They want from me?

"Ah," Mayoso said as Filho touched his elbow to indicate movement toward the car, "do you still play chess with El Ché?"

"Of course. He still talks about your Sitzfleisch opening. You know he directs the Banco Nacional? He says he misses medicine."

"He does? But he's doing surgery."

Filho stared at him. "Qué?"

"Surgery. Brain surgery on a whole country."

Filho pretended to swing a fist toward his jaw and stopped short. "Caramba! You're a fighter. It's good to see an honest man again. But, Paqueta, watch your mouth. Let's have no incidents. Agree?" He dropped the stub of his Russian cigarette and ground it under his shoe.

The bearded corporal came out of the airplane carrying Mayoso's flight bag in one hand and the leather shaving kit in the other. As he came down the steps he said courteously to Mayoso, "Señor, don't worry. I folded all the shirts back again."

"Mil gracias," Mayoso said. "Did you leave me a razor blade?"

"Put the gear in the car trunk," Filho ordered.

He and Filho stepped back from the ladder to allow the corporal to pass them, then strolled several paces behind him toward the long black car. Mayoso saw that the letters DIER on the front door had been painted over the faint remainder of SIM, the designation for Batista's secret police. The militiaman holding the back door and the *barbudo* at the other side both snapped to attention. As he and Filho approached the big car, Mayoso caught sight of the trouser legs of a back-seat passenger in the dim interior, but he could not see the man because the *barbudo's* body blocked the rear window. Suddenly Mayoso's gut tightened painfully. Sweat burst out all over him. He had recognized the *barbudo* standing at attention. He stopped short. Small tremors ran through his arms and shoulders. The *barbudo* was Sergeant Fulgencio, from Boniato Prison.

Filho took an additional step before he halted, turned back, and frowned. "What's the matter? You sick? You're pale."

"That bastard—"

"Who?" Filho grasped his elbow. "You're shaking!"

"Filho, he was the squad leader—"

"Of what?" His fingers tightened on Mayoso's elbow. "Hombre, I just warned you—don't spoil things—"

"The execution squad on the firing range at Boniato."

Filho shook Mayoso's elbow. "Don't be a damn fool! I brought him with me from Caracas. Beards make everybody look alike."

Mayoso wiped his forehead in the bend of his elbow and let all the air out of his rigid chest. "I could have sworn it was Sergeant Fulgencio—"

"He's not. He's a Venezuelan guerrillero in Caracas, part of my body-guard." He shook Mayoso's elbow again. "Can you go ahead, Paqueta?"

"Yes. Goddammit, yes."

"Paqueta, listen to me. Don't lose your nerve. Don't get your old prison sickness. Remember what I said about halfway men. We need all our balance. You want the Bay of Pigs prisoners. We want the drugs. Just keep your nose pointed that way."

Mayoso avoided looking at the *barbudo* as he walked up to the limousine and climbed into the back seat with Filho directly behind him.

The passenger inside was DeWitt Sommers. He put out his hand. "Mayoso—"

"Witt!" They pumped hands. "I'm glad to see you, Witt. After so much time!"

"You don't know how glad I am to see *you!*" DeWitt Sommers leaned past him to speak to Filho. "You gentlemen both looked as if you were having a great little get-together. A real reunion. First time since I've arrived that I've seen you laugh, Comandante. It's very reassuring."

Filho was blunt. "I am not a comandante, Mr. Sommers." He pulled his feet back to let the two *barbudos* clamber in to take the small folding jump seats. Mayoso carefully kept himself from looking at the second man, who so much resembled Sergeant Fulgencio.

Beneath each jump seat, Mayoso saw a submachinegun, not the old clumsy San Cristóbal model he knew so well, but shiny new ones he could not recognize. Probably Czech or Russian, he thought. Level with the guards' knees an automatic magnum shotgun was slung into a special rack. The militiaman in the front seat, beside the driver, held a U.S. M-1 rifle between his knees. Caramba! Mayoso thought. With sufficient armament, how virile we are. The next demonstration of virility will be speed. The driver will no doubt drive like a four-engine bat out of hell.

"Witt," he said, "How's life in Connecticut? I get a letter from your father every so often but not often enough. How's your family?"

"They all want to be remembered to you," Witt said. "I hope we can sit down tonight and have a long talk. Right now we're up to here in details. We've got to hammer out every single item on the exchange agenda."

"How are things going?" Mayoso asked. "Have the prisoners been taken to the ship yet?" He turned to Filho. "I'd like to help with their medical examinations."

"Sorry, Paqueta."

"But it's one reason I came! I *know* those men." The radio voice from Blue Beach, crackling through static: *Are you bastards abandoning us?*

"Thanks, but no, Paqueta. The Cuban Red Cross has enough doctors."

"I thought part of my job—"

"Please tell him, señor," Filho said to DeWitt Sommers, "that his job is exactly this. To sit halfway between us."

"He's right," Witt said. "I know how you feel about seeing those men, but David checked out all of that problem. They've got adequate medical attention as of this morning."

"So far so good," Mayoso said. "They're boarding ship now?"

"Well, not so fast," DeWitt said. "We thought we had a deal when Castro and Donovan agreed that the receipt of twenty per cent of the fifty-three million dollars' worth of drugs and special foods would start their release from prison. That twenty per cent down payment in drugs is here, but now, by God, there's an interruption in the release. Only six hundred and some men have been released, then Fidel stopped it. He's demanding two million nine hundred thousand in cash, not drugs."

"That amount," Filho said quickly, "was agreed to by the Cuban Families Committee for the Liberation of Prisoners of War. The cash was to pay for the release of such prisoners a year ago." He held up his finger, "One year ago. Cash. Before the drugs arrangements. We freed sixty wounded prisoners at that time, but we were never paid as agreed."

"The Red Cross people are in touch with Washington," Witt said. "The Attorney General's burning up the long-distance wires. He's trying to raise the money by tonight."

"I hope so!" Mayoso became angry. "Do you know what the hell it's like to be waiting in Principe Prison to be released? With the ship out there in the harbor? You sleep head to foot in the bullpen cell with lights on all night. You stand in formation in the inner courtyard under the sun. There's only one water spigot in the compound. And you wait. You wait. Even with hepatitis and dysentery. You soil yourself, but you wait." His

mouth tightened. "In Miami, we promised to start the first group of released men back by Christmas."

"Please," DeWitt said, "explain to your old comrade in arms—my school
Spanish isn't idiomatic—that we'd appreciate like hell getting this show
on the road."

"The *show?*" Filho asked. "Is that the same as the British saying: 'Let's
get cracking'?"

"Yes," Mayoso said. "Let's go."

Filho shrugged, conveying noncommittal neutrality, and signaled the
driver to start. The driver nodded, put one hand under his long hair and
pushed it all on top of his head, then fitted on his beret. He started the
engine with a roar. The car rocketed forward, muffler put-putting.

"*Carajo!*" Filho said with disgust. "Tires so hard to get, and that fool
driver leaves five thousand miles of rubber on the concrete. My apologies
for the noise. The car sounds like a truck, doesn't it? Since Wall Street hit
us with the American embargo we can't get mufflers." He leaned back in
his seat and gave himself another Russian cigarette. "I tell myself to see
difficulties in perspective. You mentioned Christmas. During Christmas
week, in 1492, Columbus' flagship, the *Santa Maria,* was pounded to
pieces on a reef not so far from here." He blew smoke through his nostrils.
"There he was, in the middle of noplace. Imagine it. A new world, but
no spare parts. And we think we have troubles."

"Interesting," DeWitt Sommers said politely. "I didn't know your accomplishments included being an historian."

"All Latins are historians, Señor Sommers. We never forget. Dios!
1492. Think of it. The New World, like Sputnik, the first glimpse of outer
space, eh? Spanish armies victorious. The Moors crushed. The Jews driven
out of Spain. Torquemada playing with fire, warming hearts with the
flames of the Inquisition. Spanish strength blind to its weakness. Supreme
imperial power not recognizing a crossroad. Reminds one of the United
States today, eh?" He paused, and when Witt and Mayoso said nothing,
he said quietly to himself, "In 1492 we left home, and we never went
back again."

The car veered suddenly to the right as the driver wheeled sharply
around a column of tanks. Mayoso recognized several Shermans in the
column: holdovers, probably from the Batista regime. He did not recognize the other tanks with their very long gun barrels and unusually low
silhouettes.

Filho nodded toward them, "The Soviets design T-54 tanks with the
enthusiasm the Cubans do women."

"I hear," Mayoso said deliberately, "that their antiaircraft is very good too. Especially the target-seeking surface-to-air missiles around the new submarine base at Bahía Honda."

Filho sounded interested. "You hear so many things. What's *your* secret, Paqueta?"

"Why do you call him Paqueta?" Witt asked.

"Paqueta was a revolutionary undercover name," Mayoso said impatiently. I don't like any of this. Not the verbal jujitsu. Not Filho pretending that nothing has changed. Not this exaggerated courtesy with the car. Not the friendly companionship of the two *barbudos* hung with weapons, sitting knee to knee. "The deal," he repeated harshly. "Let's stick to business. Where do we stand?"

"You sound very Norteamericano," Filho said. "All business."

"Well," DeWitt Sommers said, "the ransom agreement—"

Filho corrected him quickly. "The indemnification agreement—"

"The Donovan-Castro agreement is backed by a fifty-three-million-dollar letter of credit handled through the National Bank of Canada to the National Bank of Cuba. Basically, it's a letter of credit from the Bank of America underwritten by the American Red Cross."

"Any difference," Filho said, "between the value of accepted commodities and the total amount of fifty-three million dollars will be paid in cash. We do not agree on some valuations. So you see, Paqueta, we need your expertise."

Mayoso turned to DeWitt Sommers. "Where's David?"

"He's down at the warehouse checking the cargo from the *African Pilot*. He's been inspecting and resealing the cartons of narcotics with men from the Narcotic Section of the Cuban Ministry of Health. We'll get to see him tonight at dinner, I hope."

Filho said, "Many of the ampoules were listed as fifteen-milligram units in the American export permit. Actually they contain only five, one-third as much."

"Is that so?" Mayoso asked Witt.

Witt looked annoyed, and nodded.

"Were the permits handwritten?" Now, Mayoso thought, I've become a defense attorney.

"No," Witt said. "Typewritten."

"When were these permits written up, Witt? Where was it done?"

"In Miami, yesterday around midnight." Mayoso could feel DeWitt stiffen. "We've conceded the mistake," he said gruffly. "In all that hurry-up, it was accidental."

Mayoso swung back to Filho. "Filho, you don't really believe you're being cheated, do you? It's obviously a mistake."

Filho raised his eyebrows. "A mistake? In narcotics? You, a doctor, say so? To list five milligrams as fifteen? How naïve do you believe we are?"

"Filho, this psychological warfare, it won't work. Some tired stenographer sitting at a typewriter at midnight with dozens of pages could make such a mistake."

"Perhaps. We'll see," Filho said.

Mayoso chuckled. "Filho, you're a maestro. You make it sound like such a big concession."

Filho grinned and shrugged. "Who knows, maybe we'll accept the shipment."

Mayoso could feel the stiffness in DeWitt's arm relax. "And the powdered milk?" DeWitt said quickly, pressing the advantage. "Can't we clear that up, too?"

"Don't push too hard, Mr. Sommers," Filho said. "Your Department of Agriculture cannot use us as a dumping ground for your mountains of surplus powdered milk."

"How much powdered milk can you actually use, Filho?" Mayoso asked.

Filho shrugged, "Ten thousand tons. Maybe twelve thousand tons at the most. But we will not allow a dumping operation—"

DeWitt broke in, "Señor, there's no intention—"

Filho's voice rose. "The technical people say powdered milk does not have a long shelf time. Dump twelve thousand tons on our docks and half will spoil."

Mayoso lifted his hands, fingers outspread, as if holding both men down. "That's reasonable, Witt," he said. "Why not divide the shipments? Bring in maybe four thousand tons for immediate delivery and then stagger the remaining shipments? Spread the total over six months? That'll give the Cubans longer shelf time."

"No problem to that, if the Cubans will trust us to make forward delivery," DeWitt said.

Filho ducked his chin toward his chest while he plucked gently at the tip of his nose with thumb and forefinger. "You should have been a lawyer, Paqueta. When Fidel hears about this, he'll offer you the Ministry of Health. The name Martí in the Cuban government would make every student in South America proud that historical justice was done."

So that's it, Mayoso thought. *When Fidel hears about this. . . .* I'm being wooed. The Russian tactic. Come home, tovarich, buddy, amigo. All is forgiven. He saw the two security guards watching him sideways curiously. "You, Corporal," he said to the *barbudo* on his left, speaking in Spanish, "do you speak English?"

"I do not command that language, señor."

"You play beisbol, Corporal?"

"No." The Corporal shrugged. "But my boys. Crazy for the beisbol. The Nueva York Yanquis."

"Your boys play on teams, Corporal?"

"Sí."

"The Henequeros or the Granjeros?"

"The Granjeros. Once el Máximo Líder came and pitched a game for them. 'A ball is like a grenade,' he said. 'Practice!'" The corporal had begun to sound friendlier. "You have a favorite team to bet on?"

"Sí." Then, for Filho's benefit, Mayoso said, "The Cincinnati Reds."

"Ah. A revolutionary team. They get ration-card privileges to play, no?"

"A few," Mayoso said. He turned to the second guard, "And you? English-speaking?"

"No, señor."

"Is your name Fulgencio?"

"No, señor."

Mayoso raised his hand, bending his fingers to make the shape of a pistol, and aimed his rigid forefinger like a gun barrel between the guard's eyes. He bent his thumb slowly, as if cocking a gun. The guard's eyes became as blank as earthenware. When Mayoso let his hand recoil as he snapped the command *"Fuego!"* the man's eyes blinked. "So," Mayoso said, "you were on one of the prison execution squads."

Filho put a hand on Mayoso's wrist. "Enough, Paqueta."

"Look at the size of his holster," Mayoso said. "It's artillery. He's probably carrying the nearest thing to a hand-held bazooka, a .44 magnum."

"Are you, Corporal?" Filho asked.

"Sí, Comandante."

Filho caught DeWitt's expression. "My men believe in adequate security protection for visitors."

"Thank you," Witt said, "Comandante."

The car stopped at the airport exit to wait for a double file of girls and women who were marching with their arms swinging in ragged military cadence. There were almost a thousand women; the lines stretched back at least a half mile. Each woman wore uniform trousers of blue denim and a checkered shirt. Each wore her hair combed back tightly. As the lengthy formation tramped by, their unit leaders shouted questions and the women chanted the responses.

"Whose daughters are you?" the leaders called.

"Fidel's!"

"Whose granddaughters?"

"Lenin's!"

"What are you?"

"Socialists!"

"What will you be?"

"Communists!"

Then the thousand-voiced shout: *"Cuba Si! Yanqui No!"*

"The battalion of little lost mothers," the corporal said to Mayoso and grinned. "All volunteers." He followed them with his eyes. "Hup, two, three, four! Swing those arms back, señoritas."

"And if they do not volunteer?"

The corporal shrugged. "Naturally, they go to jail. Look at the big blond chassis there." He made biting movements with his teeth. "Agh. Solid as a tank." He pulled a package of Cuban Populares cigarettes from his pocket and offered it to Mayoso. On the package was printed the Picasso Dove of Peace. Mayoso shook his head, "No, gracias."

"It's a big work party of former prostitutes," Filho explained to DeWitt. "Socialist rehabilitation."

"Oh?" Witt's face was blank.

Mayoso looked sideways at Filho. "No more girls around the Terrace Bar at the Nacional? Nobody strolling under the trees along the Prado to meet a friend or two at Sloppy Joe's?"

"There's no law against a little walk. But degeneracy, that's different. We've closed all the shameful bordellos of the old regime. You remember Marx called shame a revolutionary sentiment? Cuban girls no longer have to striptease to earn a shameful living from Yanqui tourists."

"Only Russian and Chinese tourists?" Mayoso asked.

"But nothing wholesale," Filho said. "Not like the jackpot Batista days. Listen, amigo, don't you remember your own revolutionary speeches about Havana, the cesspool of abortions for ladies from everyplace?"

"That's a different subject. That's ladies in trouble."

"What's so different? Something hidden, for sale on back streets—"

"You're talking about criminal abortions done by ignorant *comadres*, Filho. In the Scandinavian countries, in Japan, women are not driven underground just when they are desperate for help."

Filho leaned forward to talk past him, addressing DeWitt Sommers. "You hear, Señor Sommers?"

"Yes," Witt said. "I know it by heart. My father and mother and brother have been fighting that battle for years."

"But the battle we fought on this island was different," Filho said. "You know how Dionisio Mayoso Martí came to his code name of Paqueta?"

"No," Witt said.

"Don't encourage him, Witt," Mayoso said. "My old friend doesn't make conversation, he makes speeches. Give him one ear and he'll talk off the other one."

"Well," Witt said, "we've got a distance to drive. If the Comandante has a story—"

"Not a story," Filho said. "A legend."

"Ah," Mayoso said. "The inflation has begun."

Filho spread his hands outward. "This is only a little history, *compadre.*"

"I know," Mayoso said. "To the victor belongs the rewriting of history." He turned to DeWitt. "You know how your little kids learn hot air about George Washington and the cherry tree? That's how kids here learn about José Martí. Aie, Filho," he said, using Spanish, "*cuando acabará esta campaña?* When will this campaign end?"

"Don't let him change the subject," DeWitt said to Filho. "How did he get the name Paqueta?"

"Paqueta," Filho said, using an unhurried storyteller's voice as if he had nothing else to do, "is the name of an island near Rio. One of those little islands where a caballero takes his girl Saturday evening. A little ride on a boat. Then a little ride in the saddle. The Cariocas call it the Island of Love. So Doctor Dionisio Mayoso Martí became Paqueta when the peasant girls found we had a Havana doctor in our guerrilla forces, a gynecologist."

"It has begun. The facts are different," Mayoso said. "History is being rewritten."

"I stand corrected," Filho said. "It began with that kid who had been raped by a couple of Batista's troopers. She was very upset, that girl."

"Upset," Mayoso said. "She cut both her wrists. Her father carried her up into the hills like a bundle of dead rags."

"So," Filho said, "that's how our friend, the professor from Havana, became known as the man to help a girl in trouble. He went through much searching of soul, the proper young Catholic doctor from Havana. Then decided to be a little lower than the angels, correct, Paqueta?"

"I guided myself by the famous legal case, the trial of Rex versus Doctor Bourne, in London," Mayoso said slowly. "I knew I was dealing with a fundamental principle. I did what my father always did. I looked for precedents. Of course, with our sense of humor, I became the Island of Love. They gave me the code name Paqueta."

"At first Mayoso was angry," Filho said. "His medical honor, his family name. *Escándalo!* It was like calling his mother a whore. But what is one man's voice in a mob? So he became crazy brave. You know when a man wants to prove something and takes chances that are foolish? Not a hero, as all believe, but a brave bull? Listen. The Batistianos cut us off at a sugar mill one night, no warning, just tracer bursts from their machine-gun fire, and this mad doctor picked up a mortar gun barrel—"

"There was no time to assemble the weapon," Mayoso interrupted. "Don't exaggerate."

"He held the mortar barrel against a tree with his bare hands, dropping one round in after another, and he blasted those Batistianos into hell and gone. Did you ever see a man hold a hot mortar barrel in his bare hands? With no baseplate? That little accomplishment began the legend. The *barbudos* continued to use the name Paqueta, but in a different way. Then he became more reasonable about everything."

"All that effort," Mayoso said, "to exchange the Yanqui tourists for Russo tourists? And the Chinese and Albanian tourists?"

"Don't be so smart, Paqueta," Filho said. "The técnicos Soviéticos know their jobs. And the Chinese and Albanians and North Koreans, they keep to themselves. Very correct. It's the Russians who like to put down their briefcases and take off their Hawaii-type shirts and get in the saddle and play Cossack. So for the Cossacks we keep a few of the old places functioning on a public utility basis."

"No wonder your list included so much penicillin," Mayoso said. "No wonder you've lost weight."

Filho slapped his flat stomach with his open hand. "Nighttime maneuvers keep a man in training. Liaison with the Russkis takes stamina. I eat Benzedrine pills like candy. Without enough horsemanship to keep them busy, those girls buck like broncos."

The double file of the women's brigade had cleared the exit to the main road now, and a uniformed woman in the guardhouse began to crank a cable over a pulley. A long section of barbed-wire gate scraped open for the car. Filho sat back, pulled the curved sunglasses from his shirt pocket, and slipped them on his face. The Cadillac heeled over as they curved onto the main road, the driver accelerating with his engine exhaust muffler throbbing like a motorboat at full throttle. He looked up into the rearview mirror to see if his passengers appreciated his style and flourish. He caught Mayoso's eye and winked.

Across the road were three propaganda posters, each the size of a house. Khrushchev beamed at one end. At the other, a grandfatherly Mao Tsetung peered out at his faithful children. The massive picture in the center was copied from the huge bust of José Martí on the Plaza de la Revolución. Red letters, printed with long wavering edges to suggest flames, proclaimed: PATRIA O MUERTÉ—VENCEREMOS!

As the car roared into high speed, the driver turned the dashboard radio up loudly. From it, into the pressing silence among them, poured the *Internationale* in mambo tempo.

Days and nights in Havana spun into a blur. The *African Pilot* was unloaded into a dockside warehouse. The Bay of Pigs prisoners had embarked for the United States, and the American negotiators gave this fact to themselves as their Christmas gift. Mayoso and David agreed that De-Witt would handle the endless formal negotiations with the Ministro de Salud Pública, the Embajador Extraordinario y Plenipotenciario, the Ejecutivo Regional, the Departamento de Relaciones Internacionales, the Agregado a la Misión Permanente de Cuba en las Naciones Unidas, not to mention or ignore or otherwise impute the Subsecretario de Higiene y Epidemiología. Steadily, during each day of negotiation, debate, compromise, whenever there was a pause, Filho had pressed unasked-for favors upon him—a quick run to the *viejo* section of Havana, to the Upmann cigar factory, for a few boxes of Number Ones?

No, thanks.

A quick visit to his childhood home in Vedado? His father's library was still intact, the famous room with the high coffered ceilings, although now, unfortunately, the house is requisitioned by an agency called JUCEPLAN, the Junta Central de Planificación, but if he would like a visit nevertheless—?

Absolutely no, thanks. (My father's library is my father. How could I walk into it, then out again? His voice would be there. *I kiss you goodbye, my son.*)

A quick drive out to the country? To Ciénaga de Zapata, Fidel's favorite hideout, just to say hello for old times' sake?

Not if I can be diplomatically excused. No, thanks.

He awakened at dawn each day, and, each night, late after midnight, dropped exhausted into bed. DeWitt, David, and he were installed in a handsome mansion with marble floors, tapestried walls, and torn window screens; it was reserved for diplomats.

"Like Blair House in Washington, or Rambouillet in France," Filho had said, clearly skipping Moscow and Peking.

Filho installed them at the ménage with a flourish; introduced the three-man guard detail which accompanied them even to the bathroom; unlocked the cabinet of Canadian and Scotch whiskies; demonstrated the fine Phillips high-fidelity shortwave radio-television-phonograph-tape-recorder on which they could watch the leading TV commentator, a Spanish-speaking Chinese, report generous Chinese aid to grateful Egypt while guarding the Egyptian border against Israeli aggression.

Filho ignored the Chinese doing a ballet of body-conditioning calisthenics on the large balcony across the street; made a great to-do because the bathtubs, with Russian orthodoxy, had no plugs; asked genuinely if they wished to have a Christmas tree, Daiquiri cocktails, any particular wine with dinner, or any particular type or shade of girl with this or that talent at bedtime; and managing, throughout the entire display, to persuade DeWitt to drop the word "ransom" and say "indemnification" for the Bay of Pigs prisoners, and to persuade David to add Sabin polio vaccine and Bird inhalators on the next cargo plane from Miami instead of on the *Maximus*, the next freighter.

"Your friend Filho is *muy hombre*," David Sommers had said to Mayoso late one night as their driver raced at fire-engine speed down Avenida Quinta. "Filho is fantastic. His talk, talk, talk. The energy!"

Mayoso had stretched his legs out in the limited back-seat space. Because their driver surely understood English, Mayoso said nothing about Filho's diet of pep pills. "In a war," he said, "a man has energy. To Filho, this is all just waging war by other means."

"War?" David snorted. "You call this clerical fussing a *war?*"

"Sure I do. Each nickel-and-dime clerical error we ran into today was just another nagging detail. But to Filho and his Salud Pública experts, each demand is a skirmish." He sat up straighter. "It's guerrilla tactics, David. They're convinced that Europe and North America are like big complicated vulnerable cities, and that Asia and Africa and South America are like rural guerrillas surrounding the cities. A skirmish here, a skirmish there, never a big confrontation of rural guerrilla power against industrial power. Just hit-and-run tactics. Fight every skirmish like a war." Wearily, he had dropped his head back on the seat. "Remember the Chinese death of a thousand cuts? The Russians call it salami tactics. One thin slice at a time. They've seen the system work. Filho's one of their top theoreticians. He knows a hundred guerrillas can confound a thousand soldiers. That's why Fidel predicted that the Andes will become the guerrilla backbone of South America. And the key to South America is Venezuela. So Venezuela must be first on the list." He waved his hand at the window. "This little island, Cuba? Cuba's only a toehold on South America. But Venezuela, that's the best base on the South American continent."

"DeWitt has an office in Caracas," David said. "You've been there, haven't you?"

"Back in medical school days," Mayoso said, "I used to spend summer vacations at Filho's family hacienda. We even went diamond hunting up the Caroní River one time."

David glanced at Mayoso's lion profile in the flicker of passing streetlights. "Coming back here to Havana starts lots of memories for you, doesn't it?" When Mayoso did not answer, David shifted slightly and asked, "What makes an obviously rich man's son, like Filho, tick? It must be very complicated."

Mayoso closed his eyes, listening to the car barrel along through the beautiful starry night. "No," he said, "other than the childhood part, which is complicated for everybody, it's very simple. Like thousands of wealthy, sensitive, educated Latin boys, Filho—whose real name, by the way, is Pío Hoyo y Suárez de San Andrés Teixeira, if you don't believe me, just ask him—Filho discovered social injustice. In every generation, in every country, boys from comfortable homes, like Fidel in Cuba, or Ho Chi Minh in Vietnam, they go to the university and discover the hunger and poverty of the world. But another thing also happened to Filho. He was hunting on somebody's fazenda in northeastern Brazil, one of those back-country Amazon estates where you can ride for two days to reach the boundary of the property, and he got very badly separated from his host and the other hunters. Completely lost, and when night came, some campesinos, serfs, actually, in Portuguese they're called peons, they gave him lodging. The peons had had twelve children, seven still living, all inside a hut the size of a double bed, bound to the land by a list of debts as long as your arm at the company store. Such a peon is given a piece of dirt in back of his house, the size of your office maybe, to grow a handful of food for all the mouths in that hut. Around there, a baby's funeral costs three cents. In the morning, everybody went without food except the youngest children in order to offer the guest, Filho, breakfast. A gourd of black beans, a spoonful of farina, and a tin cup of watery coffee. Are you listening, David?"

"Yes. Yes."

"While Filho risked offending his host and his host's wife by refusing to take food from children, his host, this ragged bent-over peon of maybe forty years who looked seventy, his host insisted a guest must accept the best a house can offer. During this time the overseer of the ranch drove up in a jeep covered with dust. He was sore as a boil. Have you ever seen the overseer of an Amazon fazenda in northeastern Brazil, David?"

"No. Aren't they the same as all the others?"

"Yes and no. Yes, they have the same love of social distinction, kiss the owner's boots, kick the peon. But no, in Brazil he is different because the cities and the police have been far away for three hundred years, the owner lives in Rio and Paris and inspects the place once a year from the back seat of a moving car. The tired old priest can manage to come by only twice a year on a burro and even then who can pay for a baptism or a burial or a marriage? So the overseer becomes everything. The peasants call him jagunço. Owner. Police. Law. Judge. God almighty, in black high-laced boots, with a Winchester rifle in a leather sling in the jeep, a voice like scraping a spoon over sheet metal, a mouth cut like a wound into his face, and the face—well, David, have you ever seen the fish called piranha?"

"No."

"The fish is only about as long as your foot, but it has a thin mouth filled with razor teeth. The owner of the fazenda sometimes shows the piranha to guests from Rio by driving a pig into the river. In the water the pig snorts and jumps when the first piranha bites it. The red stain in the water is blood. That does it. Hundreds of piranhas surround the pig, the water boils and bubbles and splashes and turns dark red all around that pig as they pull him under. Five minutes later there is the skeleton of the pig, picked clean of flesh by the teeth of the piranhas."

"Good clean fun," David said. "Our hospital emergency room won't seem so rough when I get back to the New Haven jungle."

"Those overseers," Mayoso said, "they have a weekly rise and fall in their sexual craving for cruelty. And that is the overseer who drove up to the peon's hut while Filho was back behind the line of trees to relieve his bowel. The peon took off the torn straw sombrero and said very carefully to the overseer, 'God's morning to you.' The overseer spat into the dust and told the peon that he had come to discuss the theft of a bushel of vegetables from his, the overseer's, kitchen garden. He took his rifle out of the jeep and then tied the peon's wrists crossways. The peon stood there, obeying a lifetime of training in such formalities. When the overseer finished tying the peon's wrists, he made the peon walk ahead of him down the road while he drove his jeep slowly behind. The wife stood frozen and the crying children holding her skirt did not dare move from the door of the hut. The jeep and the peon, who was shuffling barefoot through the dust with his head down, they were out of sight when Filho came back. The wife said nothing. She said nothing until a little later, when Filho was washed and dressed and noticed her face and the children's quiet and asked her. Then her face broke open, like tearing a cloth, and she wept. Her husband would be whipped, she said. It happened to somebody every week when the overseer did not have a girl in his house. You see, any daughter of the peon's the overseer saw could be ordered up to his house and come back ten days later, torn up, to lie in the corner on her poncho until she healed or did not heal. These things were part of the order of life, of course. But the time lost from work meant lost wages and more hunger."

"My God," David had said.

"Not so fast, David. You asked me a question, no?"

"I'm sorry that I did. So Filho saw the life of those peons and—"

"He saw more, David. You see, out of sight around the bend of the road, the overseer had tied a rope from the back of his jeep to the bound wrists of the peon, the way a cowhand ropes a calf. Then he ordered the peon to stand, bound and attached like that, behind the jeep. When the overseer started, the peon had to trot at the end of the rope to keep up as the jeep went forward throwing dust and pebbles up at him from its rear wheels. Then the man had to run as the jeep shifted to higher gear and picked up speed. He ran faster, tied to the jeep, until he made his first sound, a cry, and fell onto his face on the road. The overseer's jeep dragged him up the road for some time, then the overseer stopped and poured a jerry-can of water on the peon to revive him so that the overseer could tell him never to steal vegetables again. Then he turned the jeep around with the peon stretched out on the ground like a thin log, bouncing and bumping, and the overseer dragged the man at the end of the rope back to his hut. While the children and the wife ran out, losing control of their lifetime of silence and daring to scream, the overseer bent over the human rag bundle to cut the ropes off the wrists with his bush knife. That was when Filho went into the hut where he had left his hunting gear and came out with his fine English rifle. The overseer was amazed. It was as if a stone pig had flown in the air from Rio into this jungle, and the piranha broke its teeth on the stone. Filho saw what was left of the face of the peon and he gave the overseer a chance to explain, which the overseer did by throwing his knife very skillfully and at the same time reaching into the jeep for his own weapon. So, at that close range, with that big game rifle, Filho shot him precisely in the face."

"My God."

"Yes. Your God who has been as gentle in these things as all the other vengeful gods worshiped by all the other peoples in the world."

"What happened to Filho?"

"Hoyo y Suárez de San Andrés, you mean. Fine old Spanish names. Filho is a Portuguese name."

"Now let me get this straight—"

"Pío Suárez, as we called him in college at that time, stayed there at that hut. Let me tell you it's not true that Christ stopped at Eboli. He stopped at that hut. The peon developed lockjaw, an overwhelming tetanus infection, and in his fire, his fever, he kept screaming gurgling sounds in his throat because no water or food could enter his locked jaws. I doubt you've ever seen tetanus, David. Have you?"

"We get one or two cases a year. But I've never seen it."

"Imagine tetanus. With no intravenous fluids, no antitoxin, no barbiturates. Nothing. Only that awful clutching of lockjaw teeth, that skull's grin of death. He became opisthotonic, David. An attempt was made to knock out or pull out one of the peon's teeth to make a space to pour in water through a straw, but you know how tetanic muscles go into spasm at the slightest touch? It was impossible. Ten days is a long time, no? What can be done for a man when only his head and his heels touch ground while his back bends upward like a bow to aim the arrow of his soul sky-ward? Of all the terrible inefficient ways to die, tetanus must surely be the most terrible and inefficient. The name of that Brazilian peon was Filho."

"Filho himself told you all this?"

"Oh no," Mayoso said, feeling weary beyond all fatigue, "I was there with him."

□ □ □

Time was a quack, not a healer. Pain still walked with him on every street of Havana. A sign, a doorway, a cafe . . . and there was his father, white-suited, wearing a broad-brimmed Panama hat aslant and carrying a Malacca cane, exclaiming, Hola, Dion!

. . . His mother, small, delicate as lace, meeting him at the dress-maker's shop near the medical school. His sister being fitted for a party dress, bright-eyed and excited. The kiss on both cheeks. Hello Mamá. Hello Liane.

What's the matter, Dion?

Nothing, Mamá.

His sister pouting at him in the mirror. Where's Filho? I thought he was coming to dinner with us?

His mother's pleased smile. Ah, la la, Liane. Not so fast.

His throat had closed. Filho can't come.

Oh those wealthy Venezuelan boys are so fickle. Servants, hand and foot. He may be your friend, Dion, but I think this is very rude of him.

He's never rude, Mamá, Liane had said.

After the fitting, outside the shop, he stopped them at a sidewalk corner where no one could overhear. You both may as well know the truth. Filho's been gone for days. He's dropped out of medical school.

His sister Liane, immediately upset. So suddenly? But why?

Oh Dion, not another one of those Venezuelan political things with his family?

No. A Cuban political thing, Mamá. The Batista police are after him. . . .

. . . His fiancée meeting him at the Little Italian espresso coffee bar near the University Hospital. Dion, amor mío, your people must have some kind of job for me. You can't expect me to stay home doing petit point while you're . . . working.

Each day he recalled his dreamlike image of Havana as an ocean-bottom city, drowned. All voices stilled.

Only work would heal him, so he worked at everything he was given: the finicky details of drug dosage lists, the legalistic gladiatorial matches with Filho. He did his job while the days dissolved from Christmas week all through New Year's to Epiphany.

Filho kept trying to persuade him to stay in Cuba. "Where in the world will you find a place that needs you more than your own home? Even Fidel agrees you should have a top post, the Ministro de Salud Pública."

"Mil gracias. I can't live in a haunted house."

When the drugs-for-prisoners exchange was settled, DeWitt Sommers had offered him a transparently overpaid position with Sommers Pharmaceuticals International. David had asked him gently if he would like to come back into academic medicine and research, perhaps if there was an opening in New Haven?

Mayoso had combed his mane of white hair with his fingers and made evasive remarks about being a barefooted *jíbaro* at heart, a Puerto Rican hill farmer who preferred lazy unemployment under a banana tree. He had allowed them all to drive him out to José Martí Airport with his arms filled, inevitably, with their going-away presents, boxes of cigars.

Filho's bear-hug *abrazo*. "We'll meet again, amigo."

"*Si Dios quiere*. I'm never coming back here again, Filho."

"We'll meet in Paris, who knows? Who cares? New York maybe. I'm very popular at the U.N."

Witt said, "There's no way to thank you enough, Mayoso."

And David. "Will you think about doing research with me? The lab, that's where the answers are."

Answers? To what questions? he had thought. You and I are asking different questions.

When he landed in Miami an hour later he had several regrets: that he had not had the courage to visit his childhood home in Havana; that he still could not see some of his hospitalized friends among the freed Bay of Pigs prisoners; that he missed the friendliness of Witt and David Sommers; that U.S. Customs pleasantly reviewed his declaration of Havana cigars and politely confiscated them; and that he and Filho had chosen to climb the same mountain, but from opposing camps. Filho's prediction was mistaken; they would never meet again.

Mayoso was wrong. They did meet again. Not Paris or New York, but of all places, Owen Roberts Airfield on Grand Cayman Island.

Filho's urgent cable had reached Mayoso in Miami. It had been sent in the open, only its signature, *Paqueta*, a disguise. Mayoso had quickly made what he considered an accident-and-health-insurance phone call to Tranquilino in San Juan, then caught the next available British West Indies Airways plane to the Bahamas.

During the months and years since Havana he had seen Filho only in occasional newspaper pictures in the San Juan *Star*. Filho at a conference at the U.N. raising a toast to the Romanian delegate. With vodka, Mayoso was sure, not maotai. Filho, promoting Habanero cigars at a Mexico City trade fair. Filho stripped to the waist, leading a student volunteer brigade into the cane fields. Filho and Chou En-lai surrounded by Cuban and Chinese advisers, conferring with General Vo Nguyen Giap in Hanoi. A *Pekin Informa* story reported that Filho had proposed to the Chinese the ancient Spanish *degüello* as an addition to their bugle-call commands for troops going into action. *Degüello*. A neck. The long low gravelly bugle note the Spanish had taken from the Moors meant the command: *Cut their throats!* No mercy, no prisoners.

What nimble skill, what punctilio, Mayoso thought, as he sat in the BWIA plane en route to meet Filho at Grand Cayman. How he rides the boiling political surf, always catching the wave of power, always perilously in balance on the knife-edged crest as the water roars across the barrier reefs. The reef is made of living individuals, coral polyps, and, as each generation dies, it forms a layer of minute skeletons on which the new generation builds. The only purpose of the coral polyp, Filho would say from his overriding wave, is to contribute itself to the building of the reef. As with polyps, so with men. The reef must be built at any individual sacrifice, no matter at what cost. The bulwark must be made monolithic, permanent, a rock of ages.

Ah, Filho, Filho, what coldness, Mayoso thought. How warlike with the Chinese, how punctilious with Soviets, how Ulysses-like you sail the tides so narrowly between them. Have you forgotten your university patron saint of so long ago? That crotchety Dietrich von Nieheim, Bishop of Verdun, whose fifteenth-century manuscript you laboriously copied and sent to me from Paris?

When the existence of the Church is threatened, she is released from the commandments of morality. With unity as the end, the use of every means is sanctified, even cunning, treachery, violence, simony, prison, death. For all order is for the sake of the community, and the individual must be sacrificed to the common good.

Mayoso shut his eyes against the light, against the darkness. If only you were as cynical as you pretend, Filho, there would be hope. Your quick intelligence would hack out some answer, some balance with the rest of us. But you have moral convictions, so you want no balance—only total victory.

As the plane touched down, Mayoso warned himself of Filho's sorcerer's ability to waft you magically down one branch of the road while reality goes the other way. But his cable had had a thin undertone of fear. Had Filho discovered that he was not the sorcerer, but the apprentice?

Inside the airfield building, Filho jumped up as soon as he spotted Mayoso. He opened his arms widely, ready to enfold Mayoso in a crushing *abrazo*. A genuine one, not the usual limp-arm ritual.

"Filho," Mayoso said, "your cable sounded like the end of the world."

Filho was bearded now, Mayoso noted. A well-groomed brush, combed and curried, not the explosive rustic bush of Fidel. *We're halfway men,* Filho had said back there in Havana, and his new beard half-Cuban, half-European, proved it.

He was dressed so carefully like a rich Criollo businessman that Mayoso detected an invisible thread of caricature: the cream-colored pongee suit, the white silk shirt with onyx cuff links, the dark knitted silk tie, the black alligator leather shoes. Even his morocco briefcase was expensive.

"Paqueta, I knew you'd come. Good flight from Miami?" Filho asked, shooting a barrage of questions he answered himself. "Good connection? Those British planes! Always on time. Ha! You know the secret of how those British do it? I'll tell you. The way Voltaire said. By shooting an admiral every so often just to remind the others." Filho laughed. "Amazing people. Prescription for the good life, Doctor. British woolens, Russian economics, and Chinese poetry. Ha!"

Mayoso squinted at him through it all. "What's happening, Filho? Why'd you ask me to come to this out-of-the-way island? That cable of yours landed on my doorstep like a gravestone. Why the crack of doom?"

"Not doomsday, Paqueta. Just the day before."

Filho's smile was automatic, but his eyes were half closed, oblique as jalousie blinds through which he could look out at the world, while no one could see in. "Many things are happening, Paqueta."

Mayoso sensed serious irregularities. He looked from Filho to the BOAC plane on the ramp outside, then back again. "You didn't come directly from Caracas via Mexico?" he asked.

"No, no," Filho said. "I avoid Mexico City. That means getting mugged by the Mexican police for the CIA files as one steps off the plane." He shook his head. "Why buy trouble? This meeting of ours has to be completely off the record."

Mayoso growled with disbelief. "Nuts."

"I'm very serious, Paqueta. Are you alone?"

"For two hours. Then a friend from San Juan will arrive to make sure I'm on the return flight."

"You don't trust me?"

"I don't trust your friends."

"Sometimes, neither do I."

"Why are you talking like that, Filho? I haven't seen anybody talk stiff-lipped since I got out of prison."

"I've seen movie shots, close up, of people's lips photographed with a telephoto lens. A good lip reader can decipher four out of five words."

"And next," Mayoso said, "after the folderol of this rendezvous comes what? The hollow-heeled shoes? The microfilm? And the hush-hush password? What kind of loco stunt is this, Filho?"

"No stunt, believe me—"

"Filho, you're too big in the Party to move unnoticed—your cable was sent out in the open—what the hell are you pulling off?"

"I told them I was meeting you, Paqueta." Filho spread his hands in a display of innocence. "Naturally, I told them how much you were trusted in Washington since your big success on the prisoners-for-drugs exchange—" He stopped, watching Mayoso's face. "Now take it easy—"

Mayoso did not speak for a moment, then said harshly, "You. You still trying to recruit me? *Me?*"

"Keep your voice down. Talk naturally, but quiet. Since Havana they believe you're near the top, something like NATO's *cábala* security classification. Paqueta," Filho said, spreading his hands open again, "obviously, I faked it all. I said you might even know about the Pentagon's new guerrilla rifle, the SPIW that fires steel *fléchettes*—"

"Never heard of the damn thing—"

"No matter." Filho lowered his voice. "I tell you, I faked the reason for this meeting, just to see you. Damn it, this is no place to talk." He peered quickly around the waiting room and said, "You never know who's passing through, even on a small island like this. Let's get over to Georgetown."

"Remember, my flight back leaves in two hours," Mayoso warned him.

Two men carrying plastic airline tourist bags strolled by. Filho's eye caught them warily and he said clearly, "Grand Cayman turtle steaks are very popular in my restaurant, señor, but how to get a guaranteed supply? And at what price, eh? You'd think seafood is easy, no? All the best Cuban frog legs are sent to Peking." He paused carefully, then dropped his voice again. "Two hours is plenty of time, Paqueta. Let's get out of here."

In the sputtering little English taxi, Filho offered him a cigar. Filho lighted his own and leaned back casually. "Driver," he said in Spanish, "do you own this taxi?"

The driver turned his head. "Sah? You speakin' t'me?"

"Yes," Filho said in English. "Do you speak Spanish?"

The driver glanced over his shoulder. "Yes sah," he said. "Two words."

He held up two fingers. "*Buenos* and *días*. You gentlemen need somebody who speak Spanish? Iffing so, liddle cinnamon lady hair-presser I acquainted, she speak real good-o."

"No, no," Filho said. "Thank you. Thank you, no. Take us down side streets. Drive slow." He blew out a mouthful of smoke and said nonchalantly to Mayoso, in Spanish, "Everywhere in Latin America, Paqueta, Lenin's two conditions for revolution now exist. Intolerable life for the working classes. Confusion among the ruling classes." He smiled widely, like a salesman carrying free samples.

"Qué va," Mayoso said, and bit into his cigar to keep himself from speaking. Filho had never been able simply to have a conversation; even now he used this smokescreen of diversionary talk. In the center of his whole verbal charade there must be a vital bull's-eye. The slanted tone. The feints, the footwork. Filho would have made a good matador, courageous, fast on his feet, skilled in making the bull believe that the cape was the enemy. Filho had mastered the three great steps of the bullring, *parar, templar, mandar*. First, to stand your ground, even when the bull charges. Second, to control the bull's speed. Third, to force the bull to follow the cape and go where the matador wills it to go. But fortunately, this taxi is no arena and I am no toro.

"Filho," he burst out, "let me ask you a favor."

Filho's cigar stopped in midair. "A favor?"

"Yes. Stop smiling all the time, Filho. You're showing your teeth too damn much. I don't like it. I've developed an incurable case of nervousness—"

"Not you, Paqueta. You're the brave bull."

"Even your handsome English briefcase has a bulge in it that makes me nervous."

"Ha! It's a salami sandwich. I'm like the Party bosses in East Berlin. I carry a briefcase only to conceal my lunch."

"Filho, why the hell are you carrying a weapon in your briefcase?"

Filho shrugged. "A bad habit. Most Venezuelan congressmen pocket a .38 when they put on their pants. You feel undressed in Caracas without something at hand. At the best Caracas restaurants the hatcheck girl always asks for your gun. But what's wrong with my smiling?"

"Filho," Mayoso said, "you remember how your grandfather and my grandfather used to be blackmailed for money contributions by the *empréstito forzoso* bandits? You remember the stories about how the military collector never stopped smiling with his tobacco-stained piranha teeth? Strongarm tactics, but smiling? He always sported big handlebar mustachios, but you're bearded. He always wore ivory-handled Colt pistols at each hip and you carry a small automatic tucked into a briefcase. The collector was very traditional during his visit. The polite oratory, the faultless manners. He always offered the victim an excellent cigar and discussed the weather before coming to the point."

Filho stopped smiling. "I have not come here to be a military collector," he said. "And about the smiling, you're right. It's one of those bad habits a man doesn't know he has."

"You should know you have it," Mayoso said. "The collector had a platoon of shanghaied illiterate peasant soldiers squatting outside, and you have maybe two thousand trained Party activists in Caracas. But the manners are the same. The cigar, the small talk, the friendly-sounding threat"—Mayoso's voice had begun to rise—"even the belief in a strong man on horseback who will right all wrongs. Everything. It's still the same. You're an *empréstito forzoso* bandit with a Sorbonne degree."

Filho jabbed the air with his cigar. "A degree. Education makes all the difference. Do you still believe that the landowners and the bourgeoisie will pay taxes for more schools? You still believe the Church will allow birth control? You trying to convince me you're a fool and an idiot?"

"Filho, please. No fancy capework for the crowd. I'm only an audience of one, stuck in a taxi."

"Paqueta, my most intelligent friend, my Diogenes, you don't believe revolutionary success is on the doorstep? With someone like you I do not exaggerate. Come to Caracas. Give us the acid test. Here, you will say, is Latin American progress at its best. Nothing half so dreadful as Bolivia or Peru or the terrible poverty of the Nordestinos in Brazil. Ah? Not so? Come see the scarecrows and their crowds of rachitic kids living bare-assed and barefooted and hungry under million-dollar autopista bridges. One out of three is completely outside the money economy"—he had leaned across his cigar intensely—"think of it, *one out of three*. Like the Stone Age. In the richest country in South America! Next to this is the biggest multibillion-dollar Yanqui corporation outside the U.S.A. itself, allowed to treat us like the old Indian serfs while the company pumps Lake Maracaibo dry."

"They haven't pumped it dry, Filho. You know that better than I do. And they pay two-thirds out of every dollar back to the country."

Filho leaned forward suddenly and tapped the taxi driver's shoulder. "You see that Carlsberg beer sign up ahead? Stop there."

"That's Pirate's Bar, sah."

"Pirate's prices?"

"Only for off-islanders, sah."

"Well, that's honest."

"Sah," the driver said as he rolled to a stop in front of the tired-looking bar, "them can afford to fly here, them can afford to buy here." He twisted himself to face them in the back seat. "You gentlemen want me to remain waiting in hire for you?"

"Can I afford it?" Filho asked.

The driver looked at Filho's suit and silk shirt and briefcase. "Yes sah." He grinned. "I do believe you can afford to buy this whole taxi, sah."

"Here," Filho said, "have a cigar. Park across the street in the shade, and smoke some really good tobacco with reverence."

Inside the bar, as the waiter filled their glasses at their table, Filho said in Spanish, conversationally, "In Havana, the Coca-Cola is now battery acid and the beer is fermented urine. But this beer, this is very good. And"—he raised a finger oratorically—"made by the only capitalistic Western brewery owned in public trust by a foundation. Ah, those Scandinavians. So civilized. All profits go back to—ah, ah, ah"—he waved a warning to himself with his upright finger in the air before him—"there I go again. More speeches." As the waiter walked away with the empty bottles, Filho snapped his fingers loudly. The waiter turned slowly and looked without expression across the dim room. Filho used one of his smiles and said, "Put a few more bottles on ice."

"Sir," the waiter said slowly, in British English, "if you'll call when you want a bit more. There's no need to snap."

"I am highly sorry," Filho said in English. "I forgot this little rock is a genuine flyspeck in the Queen's overseas island empire. No more snapping. Next time I will most certainly call you, señor."

As the waiter walked away, Mayoso said dryly, "Filho, a genuine worker gave you a useful reminder against starting a new Venezuelan cult of personality. He doesn't know you're Número Uno in Venezuela—"

"True, true," Filho said smoothly. "I accept a social correction from you, a revolutionary comrade."

"Ex-revolutionary. Now just another one of the world's busy gynecologic surgeons."

"Do I detect a note of bourgeois self-contempt? If you were back on our side, you could practice honorably and legitimately in Poland or Yugoslavia or Hungary. No one objects to la operación. Even abortion is more or less legal there."

"Yes. Because the man at the top says so. This year, he says so. Remember when your friend Rakosi made induced abortions a concentration-camp offense in Hungary? He even outlawed the manufacture of contraceptives at the same time."

"Oh," Filho said. "Have your friends, the Sommers, brainwashed you? Even the civilization of France outlaws abortions and contraceptives, which I consider French nicety. Why don't you practice in Japan, Paqueta, where everything anti-population is legal and encouraged?"

"I don't speak the language." Mayoso raised one of his big hands. "And spare me the enthusiasm for Russia."

"Why? The Soviets made abortion legal."

"When you were in Moscow you must have learned Soviet history better than that. In 1920, for political reasons, abortion was legal." He flip-flopped one of his hands. "Then, in 1934, to create manpower for defense, induced abortion was made illegal again. Then, in 1955, legal again."

"Why do you call it induced abortion?"

"Why are you asking all these medical questions?"

"Because I'm interested. And you tell the truth. So, don't be evasive, Paqueta. Why *induced* abortion?"

"The technical word abortion means something different to doctors. By itself, the word medically means any loss of fetus or unborn child."

"A miscarriage?"

"Almost but not quite the same meaning. Induced abortion means to bring about the loss. In medicine we record variations of abortion as induced or spontaneous, therapeutic or criminal."

"Most are induced and criminal?"

"Mostly and sadly, yes. I consider many of them therapeutic."

"How can it be black yet white—criminal, yet therapeutic?"

"Because," Mayoso said, "it is a criminal offense to abort a seduced girl of the pregnancy begun by her seducer." He looked off into space. "A teenage girl is brought into the hospital by her mother. They begin to cry. The girl has been raped. If you talk to the boy, he claims she consented. A big legal difference, no? But I am a doctor, not a lawyer. The girl is pregnant. Whether by rape or consent, what kind of a mother can this child become? But it's a criminal action to remove from her uterus"—he held up the tip of his little finger—"a bit of protoplasm small as an olive pit. A half-spoonful of cells which have not yet become even a fetus."

Filho nodded. "I see."

Mayoso rubbed his forehead wearily. "The ambulance brings in a fifteen-year-old girl, bleeding from the vagina. She is not crying. She says nothing, not even when you examine her. With wide-open eyes she stares at the ceiling. Only later she tells a friendly nurse that her father has forced himself on her for months. It is a serious crime if you say yes to her when she begs you to remove the product of this incestuous union. And when you make ward rounds, there is a young mother, age twenty-three, with four living children out of six pregnancies. And now she has rubella. German measles. It's as likely as not that this new pregnancy of hers will become a baby born blind or deformed, or with a heart malformation so that it doesn't pump very well. Like the young girl, she also begs you for an abortion, not just for herself but for her whole family. But no, that's a criminal act. So she leaves the hospital and buys a permanganate pill, or takes a douche with lye, and the corrosive chemical starts the bleeding. Her husband brings her into the hospital. She is staggering, hemorrhaging down both legs. She needs blood transfusions immediately, but the blood bank is out of her blood type because the thirty ladies who came into the hospital before her have used up all the blood. You telephone everyplace for blood but it's no use because she's dead. You walk down the hall with her husband. What can you say? A neighbor lady comes in the door with his four children who are crying to see their mother. The husband goes down on his knees there in the hall, he holds his arms open for them all, and what can he say? You stand there and you tell yourself: this is upside down. What I did *not* do was criminal. What I should have done would have been illegal but therapeutic."

Filho coughed and took a swallow of beer. As he set the glass down, he said quietly, "So?"

"So?" Mayoso shrugged. "So the second thing you do is you go fishing."

"The second thing? What's the first?"

"The first thing you do is realize how tightly bound are the laws we've made for our women. The eternal triangle. Contraception, sterilization, abortion. Contraception first, because it's the best answer for the most people. But what kind? Where? Why? At what cost? Contraception is not easy for lots of people. And sterilization? That's grabbing a tiger by the tail. Abortion? The word is dirty. It tastes dirty just to say it the way people usually say it. The action is a confession that prevention failed, no? You yourself once said one might as well call a doctor's mother a whore, as to call him an abortionist. So instead of bound feet, we have the bound uterus, and we use our laws like religious whips." Mayoso's lips drew back in a humorless grimace. "So ironic. Japanese doctors can remove the conceptus from the womb as legally and calmly as one of our dentists pulls a tooth."

"So you go fishing. You contemplate what the priests call the *lacrimae rerum.*"

"Latin?"

"Yes," Filho said. "The tears of things. The priests can afford to be resigned. And you go fishing."

"Yes." Mayoso raised his white head and stared across the table directly into Filho's eyes. "Anyway, Filho, why do you keep imagining me in Yugoslavia or Japan? Countries as far away from here as possible. Why?"

Filho had looked at him quickly, then away, then back again. "Because I have to tell you something very confidential about myself. That goes contrary to all my principles."

"Ah. Principles."

"Paqueta—"

"And the confidential confidence. Aie."

"Paqueta, your bitterness should not be for me. For some misguided *milicianos* and the terrible things they did to you, the guilty ones, yes, but I have always been your friend. You had proof of that."

"That's why I'm here, Filho. That debt chokes me. I want to pay back what I owe you—"

"Amigo, nobody pays for a life—"

"No? Didn't you and I help Fidel el Magnifico take a payment of sixty-three million dollars' worth of drugs for one thousand one hundred and twelve lives of the prisoners from the Bay of Pigs?" His voice had gone up harshly despite his iron self-control, and the waiter had turned to glance carefully at them.

"You sound like your refugee friends in Miami, Paqueta. The quarrelsome hidalgos on the Cuban Coordinating Refugee Committee. 'One Spaniard, a speech. Two Spaniards, a debate. Three, Civil war.' Better to forget it."

Mayoso bent across the little table intensely. He was so tall that he eclipsed it, the bottle, the glasses, to approach Filho. "Forget it? *Forget it*? Did you—a man of your intelligence, your sensitivity—forget it? Did you say *forget it*?"

"Amigo, calm yourself. Believe in the proverb: *Es preciso bailar al son que se toca.*"

"No, Filho. The proverb is wrong. It is not necessary to dance to the tune being played. I refuse."

Mayoso's huge hands were clenched into two white-skinned, bony-knuckled fists he placed on the little table like two sledgehammers. "I never sleep any more, Filho. As if everything happened yesterday, I remember every moment, every little detail. You can't imagine what complete nonstop insomnia is like. Medically impossible but spiritually true. My hair is all white. I've tried drugs to sleep. I've tried going night fishing to fill the time. I've tried whiskey. I've tried exhaustion, working on my feet twenty hours at a time until my knees break with exhaustion. I drop. I fall down on the floor wherever I am and when my eyes close the projector in my brain throws pictures up on the screen inside my eyelids."

His two huge fists came together. If his fingers had been open it would have been a gesture of prayer. His jaw muscles tightened spastically, but when he spoke his voice had dropped so low that Filho, two feet away, could hardly hear him.

"I refuse this fate your comrades gave me. One morning I fell asleep on the floor of my little house in the mountains, ten minutes, twenty minutes, the terrible pictures inside my head stopped, and then suddenly I awoke. I had dreamt I was dragged back from the *cabañita* of Boniato to Galera 14 for questioning by Captain Riaga. I dreamt they had untied my arms from the ceiling and my eyes were still open three inches from that white-painted wall—remember that dead blank white wall those Pavlovian Russians said would condition prisoners to feel helpless?—and one of Riaga's men slammed my shoulder with a rifle butt and I fell full-length on the floor. He pinched my nostrils closed and pulled my jaw open, gagging for air, while Captain Riaga stood over me and urinated into my throat. I began spitting and choking. Really choking. Then the Número Uno. Do you know what a metal *picata* in a man's urinary canal does to him when the electric current is turned on? Outside my house it was dawn with the light just coming over the hills like the first day of the world. When they turned the current on the Número Uno I awoke from the dream. I was shaking all over, my whole body gasping for air and choking. I tried to grip the nearest chair for support and my hands snapped the wood like a toothpick. I brought my fists down on the table and smashed it. I was crying, my face was wet. Oh God, *me*, a man who never cries, and there I stood in that little room of my house looking out over the new mountains of a new morning, and I saw the agony of the world spread out before me. Can you even imagine that, Filho?"

For a long moment Filho said nothing, then, finally, "I believe," he said carefully, "that I recall something like it in William James's book on religious experiences." His eyelids dropped like the visor of a helmet, giving him the walled-in look of a victorious general hearing about a corporal's battle wounds.

He is trying to guard his feelings, Mayoso decided angrily. He has taught himself to think only in terms of victory, and never like an imprisoned victim. If a Roman proconsul begins to think like a conquered Jewish carpenter-preacher he becomes a Christian. And that is the end of his power.

"It was like that, Filho. I stood there alone in my house, on top of the mountain. I said to myself: You will not accept this agony. You will roll back the stone and walk among men again. You will not kill, but only because you cannot. You *can not kill*. So you will heal. You know how. That is all you know. Go and do it."

After another moment of silence, Filho said, "A man like you. We should never have lost you to our side."

"Sooner or later, Filho—even if all the tortures had never happened—sooner or later I would have seen the simple difference between Bolívar's revolution and Fidel's new type. I would have seen that you're like Obraztzov's puppets, dancing for Moscow."

Filho waved one hand delicately, pushing aside politics between old friends, trying to keep the tone one of personal concern. "You had your rebirth on top of the mountain, amigo. Now you can sleep again."

"Sometimes. Only sometimes. I still work from dawn to dark."

"So many babies being born?"

"No. Tubal ligations. La operación is much more fashionable with the ladies in Puerto Rico."

"You sound like a surgical machine."

"Don't joke. The biggest export of Puerto Rico is people. The old, old story. Too many people. Too little land."

Filho leaned forward quickly. "Now I recognize the former Paqueta. Land reform is a laugh now. They nibble at the problem by writing land reform into laws, then forgetting the law. You know and I know the descendants of the conquistadores will never give up their land."

"You're one of them. Your mother was Doña Teresa Calixto Cristovão Teixeira Hoyo y Suárez. Your father was one of the richest, descended from a *tesorero propietario* with Bolívar's grandfather. You should know."

"Of course I know! Never give up the land. In the cradle, in school, the tutors, at the dinner table, always, from everybody: never give up the land. That's why only revolution will work. Only revolution will provide land for all. There is no compromise."

"Aie, Filho. Do you really still believe that? That only revolution will provide land for all?"

"Of course. How else can you get enough food to the bottom level of people? And in the United States, sixty million acres are not being farmed!"

"Filho, how long will you fool yourself? Your leaders have always dragged the peasants and their sons into revolution by promising them land reform. After the revolution is won, reform turns into mass execution and deportations of property holders. First, Stalin did it. Then Mao. You think you'll be different? And while you busy the people with half-sawdust bread and bloody circuses your real purpose will not be farms, but steel factories. Weapons. Status. You'll whip the farmers to feed the steelworkers, and tax the workers to buy tools for weapons and jet planes for status."

"Paqueta, from a socially aware man who might someday have been the President of Cuba, that's a reactionary line of reasoning. Are you finished?"

"No. You and I will not be President of anything, Filho. Not someday. Not ever. To think we're leaders is an illusion. We're pushed from behind by our followers. You think I want those adolescent hit-and-run raids on Cuba? Of course not. But when I say, Let's spend all that gun money on helping refugees, I get the answer the Arabs have refined to an art in the Middle East. They tell me, To help refugees resettle in a new life is surrender. Keep them unhappy. Later they'll fight back, better."

"The light of common sense. I'm glad to see it in you."

"And where's your common sense, Filho? Can't you see you're being used as Judas goat? Every revolution eats its young, the intellectuals who began it. You'll be trapped by caste."

"We have no caste. You know that. No class distinctions."

"Filho, don't put yourself to sleep with these lullabies. Whosoever shall know the son shall look up the dossier on the father. The Soviets always describe the man by his father and his grandfather. Stalin never forgot that his best general, Tukhachevsky—the creator of the first modern Red Army, agreed?—came from the aristocracy and was trained as a Czarist Guards officer. Remember the purge trials? Held in the former Nobles' Club? Remember the talk of traitors and dogs? And Tukhachevsky disappearing, probably sent down into the Lubianka execution cellars for his thanks, along with almost half the Red Army officer corps—their families, friends, acquaintances, everybody—remember? And then didn't Khrushchev tell the Twenty-second Party Congress they were all innocent? Am I dreaming out loud, Filho? Or did these things happen?"

"They happened."

"And you, they'll never trust you, Filho. They'll never forget you came from a family of rich landowners. The kind of people who are the most stubborn partners in the triumvirate of Aristocracy, Army, and Church. You taught them the *degüello* bugle call, but it's your own neck you'll have to protect."

"Paqueta, everything you say is in the past. We've learned from our mistakes. The past is all water under the bridge, now."

"Water? When it's your own neck, see if you bleed water."

Filho stroked his beard absentmindedly. "I thought there was hope. I thought you could be persuaded to work with us, not the imperialists. We need you. Badly. Criticize us, but improve us from the inside, damn it, not the outside. Instead of a handful of idle useless women, your medical knowledge can help tens of millions of people. You know as well as I do, right down to your toenails, that the whole southern half of the globe needs more food and more freedom."

"Neither will come without more human control of human fertility."

"Ha! That's *control*, Paqueta."

"By education. Not by decree, like the Russian flip-flop every ten years."

"Every fanatic has his own big solution, Paqueta. Each saint his one candle. The religious say: return to God. The philosophers say: find values. The social economists say: give fathers jobs and the family will be stronger. The psychologists say: your new god is the animal in you, so learn to feed and groom it. A tower of Babel! Now enters the physician to say: it's simple. Control fertility."

"Don't put words in my mouth. Don't make it sound simple. These problems go around the world in a circle, and you have to begin someplace."

"And you want to begin with the Americanos? A psychologically empty country which is not even inhabited by the people who live there?" Filho spread his arms widely. "All those Caribbean islands out there—the Americanos wanted their rum and sugar and spice and profits, and more cotton, so they turned all those islands into a giant funnel for slaves."

"Didn't the Spanish use those islands as a giant funnel for all the gold and silver they could steal from the Indians?"

"I'm glad we agree. The Spanish got their gold, but see them now. The Americans got their slaves, but look at them now." He sighed. "The wrong side, hombre. You picked the wrong side."

"Filho, you conned me into coming a long distance to listen to your salesmanship. I'm stuck for another hour until my return flight. Let's have another beer, and no more harangues."

Filho ignored him. "Wait, Paqueta, just wait until the Americanos discover you cannot buy love with foreign-aid money, and that for every white skin in the world there are twenty not-white. Tsskt! *Degüello*."

"The Americanos play *mea culpa* all the time. They confess their faults—"

"Faults! A blind giant has no faults. He is only suicidally blind. His destruction is inevitable. Paqueta, before it's too late, open your own eyes. Join with the hundreds of millions of have-nots. They'll win because their anger and hunger burn like primitive sexuality. Revolution is their social orgasm. Even if they die themselves. After all, they already consider themselves half dead."

"The whole idea is hatred?"

"There is no more *idea*, Paqueta. Only action. We've changed the rules. Marx mentions that if you want to destroy a man, give him a meaningless job to do. That idea has to be lived, Paqueta, not just inspected like a stamp collection. We won't play a waiting game."

"So," Mayoso said slowly, "South America will become the next China?"

"It's no secret. Fidel tells everybody. A guerrilla army can ignore boundary lines. We can turn the Andes into a new Sierra Maestra. And in the meantime, the faithful will go on breeding like fornicating rabbits. And you? You'll stand there in San Juan, a king of nothing who wants to command the tide of starving babies to stop. Caramba! If I'm Tukhachevsky, you're Don Quixote. Can't you see the failure and the romantic foolishness of your position? Living in a thatched hut on a hill? Fishing with your faithful Sancho Panza? Tilting against Cuban windmills with quarrelsome refugees? Living in a medical no-man's-zone between legal and illegal? Trying to forget that some of your own refugee fighters are former Batistianos, any one of whom might have pulled the trigger on your own family and fiancée?—Ah, to that no answer? Shove the uncomfortable truth down my throat, my *degüello,* but not even a taste for yourself?"

"Aie, Filho. Still the Mephistopheles."

"Ah? And you? Still the Faust?"

"I work," Mayoso said. "I try my best."

"Your best? By charging the working-class Puertorriqueño women the price of a pair of shoes for la operación?"

"I don't like to sterilize women. I very rarely accept anyone with fewer than three children."

"What if her husband dies and she wants to marry again and have a new family?"

"I know, I know," Mayoso said wearily. "I try to talk most women out of it. Sterilization is a one-way street. Contraception is better."

"But you do operate, my noble healer. And the bourgeois ladies from Miami and Rio do not pay peanuts, as if for shoes. Oh no. Not Doctor Robin Hood Mayoso. The Miami and Rio ladies have to pay you what they pay for diamonds."

"Yes." Mayoso's eyes became careful as he looked at Filho. "Yes. They pay not so much as for diamonds, but in that direction."

"Sometimes a lady must come asking for an abortion, no?"

"They do."

"And—?"

Mayoso shrugged. "And I do what she needs. If that is what she really needs."

"You are the judge."

"Sí. That's not always so good, because the transaction is illegal, and a woman ashamed is a woman who lies. The whole thing is as rotten and distorted now as the slave trade a hundred years ago."

"And you require a letter of referral from their own doctors?"

"Yes. Always. The medical standards must be high. My policlínica is not a back-alley taxicab joint, Filho."

"Nothing specific about pregnancy on paper. Just a letter of referral from another doctor."

"Yes."

"You like to have them mention important details in the letter? Whether or not there is high blood pressure or childhood tuberculosis? Diabetes? The Rh factor in the blood? Even something like sensitivity to penicillin?"

"Yes. We're as thorough and careful as we can be. You know so much, Filho, you should do my first-step interviews with patients instead of my nurse."

"I know so much that I know you tell your patients to pay your fees directly to the Cuban Refugee Committee in San Juan. And you live in the hills like a pauper on a refugee dole from the Committee."

"You really took so much trouble to check up on me? Right inside the enemy camp?"

"The Party has some very good people in San Juan. In my briefcase I have a three-page dossier on you. But they neglected to mention you had a nurse."

For the first time, Mayoso began to smile, a big grin spreading over his large face like a field of ice cracking. "Of course I have a nurse. I've been trying to find a psychiatric social worker, too. I told you my standards are high. Lots of women need time for talking. Just saying what's wrong. Saying what they want. You'd be surprised how often a woman's problem is just exhaustion. These we delay, because later, when they decide not to have an abortion, or the sterilization, later on some of them are glad. They were only exhausted."

"Really, Paqueta? You really take time to talk them out of it, and your precious Refugee Committee loses a fee?"

Now Mayoso laughed, but without amusement. "What do you think? You imagined the back seat of a car in some alley? Or a dirty fleabag hotel room? Some old hag sliding a catheter full of soap suds or a plastic knitting needle up the cervical canal, and maybe perforating the wall of the uterus? What the hell do you think I am?"

"I apologize a thousand times."

"You can shove your apologies. Just remember, I'm a doctor. No woman has to whisper with me. I don't put on holier-than-thou and push her out of the office while she's on her knees with an unwanted pregnancy. I take a history. Physical examination. Screening lab tests of blood and urine. I've hired a young doctor to assist me. My nurse is also an anesthetist."

"Anesthesia?"

"Of course. The back-alley butchers wear masks so the woman will never recognize them. It terrifies women. My nurse and I wear surgical masks during surgery, which is scary enough, but at least our patients have seen us before. Most of them understand about germs and care against infection. I even keep careful clinical records."

"I can hardly believe it."

"Why not? I was on the university faculty in Havana before Batista's medical friends railroaded me out. I still keep university professional standards."

"But written records—"

"The patients' names are in code—"

"But records are a rope around your neck if the law ever gets you."

"The law knows where I am. The Governor knows all about me. They don't bother me as long as they know exactly where I am."

Filho rubbed his thumb over his forefingers, the ancient sign of money payment. "You contribute to the police charities, no doubt."

"Not always. Only sometimes. But more than that—I'm a public utility."

"Like a municipal disposal plant, eh?" Filho smiled thinly. "Nobody likes it next door, but everybody wants it."

"If society did not have human pathology in it, Filho, I would not have to do what I consider pathological."

"Just when I begin to admire your courage, Paqueta, you tell me your work is pathological?"

"Of course it's pathological. To abort a physically healthy woman of a normal pregnancy is a confession of failures. Children should be conceived with love and raised the same way."

"You make it sound so simple."

Mayoso shrugged. "It's not complicated. Ninety-nine times out of every hundred times I curette a uterus, I'm a sanitary janitor. I'm cleaning up the last link in a long chain of personal and social pathology, just the way the surgical janitors in wartime combat hospitals clean up the results of crazy wars."

"You mean it?"

Mayoso shrugged again. "It's my work. I can make speeches about it the way you make speeches about your work."

"You should be in the Party, Paqueta. Every university student in Latin America would listen to you."

"Why discuss it, Filho? We've finished all that talk. You should think of me as an enemy."

"I, personally, refuse to. To me, Paqueta, you would be a great asset to the Party—a tremendous asset, that I will admit—so to me you are no enemy. To me, personally, you are a friend."

"How can you speak *personally*? You have no personal life. You're one of the top men of the Party apparatus."

Filho spread his hands and crouched slightly. "Shoot me. I insist on being personal."

"They will. For having a personal wish to a personal life, they'll shoot you. After a variety of preparations to help you make a voluntary confession."

Filho drummed his fingers on the table and gazed into space. Once or twice he began to speak, then stopped. Suddenly he said in a rush, "Would you walk two steps out of your way to save me, Paqueta? *Contesta sí o no.*"

Their eyes met and locked. Filho's face had become expressionless, and he kept himself sitting very still. From outside came the sound of an airplane circling overhead before landing. Their eyes held, a world swung silently between them as each searched the other for some trustful compass bearing.

"Filho," Mayoso said, "I know you did not send me that urgent cable for nothing."

"True, Paqueta." He nodded—sadly, Mayoso thought. "Yes, that's true."

"And all this talk of yours, Filho. My politics. My medical methods. Not just talk, ah?"

"Of course. I needed certain information. I need to be able to trust you."

"And for someone like you to remind me of what I owe you—such a vulgarity could never be easy for you."

Filho said nothing. His face had become blank, stony.

"Even the arrangements to fly to this island," Mayoso said. "That must have been hard for somebody as well known as you."

"That was the easiest part. Many Cuban planes stop here."

At first they did not hear the waiter saying, as he unexpectedly stood over them, "Will there be another drink, sirs?"

Filho snapped his head upward angrily at the interruption. "No. No more. Nothing." Then his eyes focused on the waiter. His smile came back and his voice changed. "Thank you, but no. No, thank you."

The waiter nodded and walked off.

Mayoso leaned forward and kept his voice controlled and low. "Filho, whatever it is, whatever they've told you to tell me, whatever bribes they offer, even if they pretend my father is still alive and they offer life, no matter what, Filho, I will not go back."

"This has nothing to do with the Party."

"Impossible. You are the Party. The Party is you."

"In that sense, I agree. I mean, this is nothing political for you."

"Impossible. Why else would you cable me to come, and then talk to me like this?"

"Because I need you as a doctor."

Mayoso's big face changed subtly. He leaned back and rested his long arms across his chest and said nothing.

Filho scratched his chin with his thumbnail and said, "It's the oldest story in the world to you. A middle-aged man knocks up a young girl—"

"How young?"

"Who knows? A girl can lie so easily. Maybe seventeen. She says twenty-two. The trouble is the middle-aged man is a national leader, a Party leader. He has a long record of a no-nonsense policy that every activist is a soldier in the class war."

"I read the May Day speech you gave in Tien An Men Square. Peking must have applauded the Party gospel according to Saint Filho. 'To live a personal pleasure-seeking life is like a sentry in war going home for a cup of coffee.'"

"Now I'm stuck with my own speeches."

"So serious?"

"Yes," Filho said. "You remember the explosion in London about the Cabinet Minister and the call girl? It's something like that."

"You might even get an invitation to Moscow? Some fake reason—a conference on *glavni vrag*, the main enemy. The big Latin-style bear hug at Sheremetyevo Airport. A samovar of tea at Dom Priemov. And then you disappear. Siberia, if you're lucky. Lubianka Prison if you're not."

"Don't be ridiculous."

"I'm not, Filho. Cruel, yes. Ridiculous, no."

"I always thought you were the one man not capable of cruelty."

"Everyone is cruel."

"Not you, Paqueta. When you fight next to a man in the mountains, in the heat, in the blood, you can tell. In two years one sees everything. A man who crawls two hundred yards under machinegun fire to drag back a wounded boy. A big man with hands like a woman with the bandages, the splints, the plaster casts. I used to lie there on the wet mountain ground and watch you moving around at night to check the wounded. This is what civilization is about, I used to think. When I lived in France I believed that crap about how a country eats and makes love is civilization. It's not. Civilization is a boundary everybody agrees to. Pizarro drew a line in the ground with the point of his sword and said, This far. No farther. You are the only one who can be trusted to draw a line and stand by it. Beyond that line, *empezó la barbarie*. Barbarism has begun."

Mayoso turned his glass in his hand, looking into its depths, then said without looking up, "We have all changed. Everyone is cruel."

"Not you."

"I am now."

"Don't cat-and-mouse me to death, Paqueta."

Mayoso looked up. "I won't. You've been hanging by your thumbs staring at a white wall long before today."

Little beads of sweat shone on Filho's forehead. "What the hell does that mean?"

"I'm just remembering your speeches about the rich hidalgos and estancieros and how they used their peon women. Even your own father. And how prostitution was the product of a rotting capitalism."

"This girl is not a prostitute."

"*Dispénsame.* You did say a call girl."

"I said that of the London girl, not about this girl. This girl in Caracas does not sell anything."

"A working girl?"

"Yes. Refreshing as a *cafezinho.*"

"Are you saying you're in love with her?"

"Out of the question, it was an accident."

"Then that's worse. Then you're exploiting a poor working girl all alone in the big city. Be yourself. Be a rich Criollo. Can't you pay her off?"

"You don't know her. Strange and wonderful. An enchanting tiger cub. A sophisticated primitive. Everything with the whole heart. She would throw the money in my face. You can't believe what she might do if she even imagined I'm insulting her."

"She would talk? To the newspapers? To her priest?"

"Well, she's more or less Catholic. You know how religion goes in the islands."

"She goes to confession?"

"Not in Venezuela. Not while I've known her."

"Oh. She's not a Caraqueña?"

"No. She's not really anything except a Caribe islander who speaks the patois of three languages and some Papiamento dialect. Father was Haitian French. Mother Puerto Rican. She went to school in San Juan. I met her in Mexico City."

"At a bar, like a sailor? *Elle avait deux p'tits boutons?* And she looked so clean."

"This vulgarity of yours is very distasteful. I never heard it from you before."

"I've already explained. It's cruelty."

"To me? To *me*? Of all people. Why?"

"I have very few opportunities to be cruel. This is a good one. I owe you too much, Filho."

"Don't hold that against me, Paqueta. You saved me from drowning." His crooked smile. "I forgave *you*."

"That was different. We were kids. One quick dive underwater. But you must have risked your head every day for months to get me out of Fidel's hellbox."

"If you could convince yourself I got you out for self-serving political reasons, you wouldn't mind, eh, Paqueta?"

"No. But that you gambled your own life generously—"

"Forget it, Paqueta. Only remember that pity was the fatal disease that killed even God."

"Aren't you asking me to pity this girl?"

"No. I remind you what you told me right here, amigo. You have a strong emotion for ethics, no? You drink beer, not hemlock, but you still owe a cock to Aesculapius."

"Filho, don't try to use my own decencies against me. Don't try psychological blackmail with my debt to you, and my medicine. You can find a dozen doctors in Caracas who can do this job for you."

"And every one of them could talk. This has to be foolproof. Top secret. Absolute security."

"Can't be done, Filho. Your lieutenants will know."

"They know now. But two or three men, by themselves, my immediate aides, they can be controlled."

"This girl—what's her name—?"

"Cristina." The corner of Filho's mouth twitched.

"That's all? Just Cristina?"

"That's all for now."

"All right. Cristina. Is she willing?"

"For what, an abortion?"

"Yes. If she's religious she may believe it is like murder."

"Well, she doesn't actually welcome the idea."

"The Venezuelan prison penalties for an unwilling abortion are double the regular penalties, Filho."

"Actually? That's a legal fact?"

"Yes. The laws come down from your father's time, when brothers told their sisters what to do, and fathers told their daughters. The hidalgos and hacendados would order the foreman to send the most recently pregnant peasant girl into town in the back of a wagon, no matter if she was unwilling."

"I'm not sending Cristina anyplace in the back of a wagon."

"Send her back to Mexico City where you found her."

"Believe it or not, I found her at work, at a trade fair in Mexico City. She was in a booth selling competitive Puerto Rican cigars."

"Does she carry a rose in her teeth? That dog-eared old Carmen myth?"

"Ah, stop. Stop."

"What I say disgusts you."

"Yes, Paqueta. It does. I hate to say it, but it does. You're too big a man, you have too much intellect and too noble a name, for petty sarcasms. There's no Carmen, no rose, no balcony. Just one of those very worried young ladies you boast you never kick out while they're on their knees."

Mayoso leaned forward. "You know, Filho, the whole story sounds invented to me. Why are you or the Party really trying to bring me to Caracas?"

Filho answered bitterly. "The Party? Caracas? You're paranoid."

"That's an insult, not an answer."

"Paqueta," Filho said, "we're fighting a war in Venezuela. Fidel and Ché moved us up on the timetable, ahead of Colombia or Peru. We don't need people like you hanging around. I'm a general. If I don't win, I lose very badly. Believe me, you're the last man the Party wants to see in Caracas. *Qué sencillo!*"

"Time is short," Mayoso said. "Let's finish quickly. I didn't come to play dialectical chess games."

"This is no game, believe me."

Mayoso leaned back, watching him. This was a different Filho, afraid of dying, feeling like a victim for the first time in his life. "The Party knows you're here today," Mayoso said flatly, not as a question.

"Of course," Filho said. "I'm supposed to be trying to convert you. I told you that. We're very badly short of doctors. I told them you were still vulnerable."

"I'm not. You, nobody, can give me the *palotazo.*"

Filho shook his head. "I know." The *palotazo* was a killing sideways blow delivered with the flat of the horn by an enraged bull, and Filho sounded genuine. "I have no harm in me for you, Paqueta."

"But if the Party said: Do him harm. Show no bourgeois sentiment. This is war. Then you would become harmful, Filho."

"Maybe."

"Not maybe. Generals are more obedient than privates."

"I would protest. I've earned the right to be heard at the top. Both Fidel and Ché listen to me."

"Ah, first the protest. *Na verkhu.* The *alfabetizado* of destroying former comrades. First the reluctance. Then the stern duty. And then the harm."

Filho raised his head. "I swear on the childhood we shared," he said in a low voice, "I am not here for the Party." He touched his lips with his tongue. "If the Party knew the real reason I'm here, I would be—I don't know—disciplined."

"Hah. Over a girl?"

"It is not the girl. It's the hierarchy of the revolutionary situation. What if a cardinal in Rome had trouble with a girl?"

"Filho, Filho. You know how funny you sound? Let me offer you sanctuary in the United States."

"You are more cruel."

"Admit it yourself. First, a guerrilla general. Now a cardinal in the church of Moscow . . . or is it Peking?"

Filho bent over and fumbled with his briefcase. "Let me show you something. It's a little book I pay to have printed in the tens of thousands of copies in every language, including the Quechua dialect." He straightened and handed Mayoso a small crudely bound booklet on whose torn cover was printed an upraised clenched fist, under a Picasso Dove of Peace. "It's half a training manual for our guerrilla school in Minas del Frío and half Bible," Filho said. "We live by it."

Mayoso read the title page. *Guerra de Guerrillas,* by Ernesto Ché Guevara Serna. "Hammock reading?" he asked. "Bedtime stories?"

"Now you're the one who sounds funny. Open it to the place where the page is turned down."

Mayoso opened the book to the marked page and read: "The will to win obliges the guerrillero to forget romantic and sportsmanlike concepts. To attain the stature of a true crusader, the guerrillero must display impeccable moral conduct and strict self-control. He must be an ascetic, perfectly disciplined. Absolute secrecy is crucial. Trust no one beyond the nucleus, especially not women. The enemy will undoubtedly try to use women for espionage. Anyone who repeatedly defies the order of his superior and makes contact with women must be expelled immediately for violation of revolutionary discipline." Mayoso raised his head. "Coming from those bearded celibate monks in Havana," he said, "makes this a jokebook."

"Amigo," Filho said, "because of this jokebook men die or go to prison every day. Ask in Peking, or Hanoi, or Saigon, or Leopoldville, or Bogotá, or Santo Domingo. Ask them if they are laughing. Next to Mao Tsetung's *Tactics of Guerrilla Fighters* this book is the truly revealed Bible. I told you, my men live and die by it."

"You really think the Party would discipline *you?*"

"Why not?"

"You're a hero. A genuine—"

"A hero?" Filho interrupted. "Major Pena—you remember Felix?—wasn't he a hero?"

"No doubt of it. A real *barba* from the hills."

"They found his car at Camp Columbia. He was lying across the front seat with a bullet through his heart."

"Suicide?"

Filho spread his hands. "What else could it be? You remember Doctor Carlos Peña Jústiz?"

"The lawyer who saved us in 1953 after the Moncada Barracks?"

"Sí, sí. The man who saved Fidel from death. The one who went with the Archbishop Pérez Serantes to intervene with Batista to spare Fidel's life. A hero, you would say?"

Mayoso said nothing. I prefer not to remember, he thought, but I remember. Then, the revolution was genuine. What we believed in and suffered for was genuine.

"Well," Filho said, "Doctor Peña Jústiz has been sent to prison as a counterrevolutionary. I doubt he's alive. And the archbishop? You remember how he greeted the victorious Fidel, the man he had saved, the night we entered Havana? You remember that greeting, those open arms, on the platform in Céspedes Park?"

"Gone?" Mayoso asked. "I heard he was shipped into exile with that shipload of priests and nuns on the *Covadonga,* to Madrid."

"Heroes," Filho said. "Who was our biggest hero? Think a minute. Who was the biggest solid genuine hero of all?"

Mayoso said nothing.

"Camilo Cienfuegos," Filho said. "Camilo was one of the really great ones, no? Fidel didn't make him Chief of Staff for telling jokes."

"Sí," Mayoso said, "Camilo was a real one."

"And where is Camilo?" Filho asked softly. "After twenty thousand heroic dead, after the Batista police, after the Sierra Maestra, where is Camilo?" He leaned forward tensely. "On a routine flight, in a twin-engine Cessna, on a clear day, from Camagüey to Havana, he disappeared. Like that, gone. No trace of the plane was ever found. Nothing. Fidel enshrined him as one of the fallen heroes." Filho clasped his fingers together. His hands were not shaking, but he kept them held tightly against himself. "I don't want to be enshrined as a fallen hero."

Filho closed his eyes, pale and silent. His head bent forward slightly, a gesture so unlike his violin-string tautness, so much a kind of surrender, that in a single moment Mayoso believed him and pitied him.

12 CIUDAD UNIVERSITARIA—University City—sprawled across an elevated plateau in the Caracas hills. Sports stadium, dormitories, classrooms, laboratories, libraries; a geometric convocation of radiant white sugar cubes among which giant slab-walled dominoes shot up, glossily thousand-eyed under cantilevered concrete solar eyebrows. Here was where Marro had been ordered to deliver Mayoso in the milk truck.

Modernistic bands of color were bound horizontally around University Hospital like giant bandages alternating in widths of arterial red and venous blue; four hundred years of church polychrome and gold promises of afterlife became here a red white and blue temple. From elevations, vaguely Grecian statues with heroic muscles and streaming cement hair gazed with classic indifference upon the hope of the nation, the students.

Among the arch-shaded walkways and the gentle greenery of young bamboo plants, among the patios walled in by Villanueva's abstract mural colorblazes and majolica façades, some students had mounted commemorative plaques to their friends who had been killed. Slogans were daubed the full length of the esplanade from the Paseo de los Illustres to the main campus gate behind the sidewalk vendors of *perros calientes* and the wheeled music-box *carretas* which sold flavored shaved-ice rasperdos. *Libertad!* was scrawled beside *Fuera la Policía!* and the Esso petrol slogan, *Ponga un Tigre en su Tanque.*

Bravery, honesty, rhetoric, the never-completed dream of the young to sweep aside all the world's *mierda,* including their fathers' success shams and their mothers' vacuous between-sheets compromises. Here the sons and daughters of bankbookish well-to-do families lifted up their voices fiercely about the peasants' and workers' hunger and hopelessness but mutely camouflaged the ambush of their own hungers and hopes: the throat bites of spring, the erectile thrust of manhood; the womanly wish to create, to avoid becoming not-a-woman, to love and be loved.

Some wore the sweatshirt armor of total guru indifference; to feel anything—indignation, affection, *anything*—was to discard their brittle armor before a head-frugging poon-scomping nothing world.

The primal human need to belong was acceptable only in the group cohesion of hatred for the dollar-worshiping computer-directed Yanquis. The United States was without doubt a castrator of Latin men by refusing to teach them to become bosses who could control the multiple levers of modern technology. Even the newsboys who never read the papers they stacked on their heads felt insulted by history. Had not the United States sent five armed Marine interventions into the Caribbean? Recruited assassin Batistianos? Given the Legion of Merit to the dictator Pérez Jiménez with words of praise from el Presidente Eisenhower?

Some of the students carried few books. They were men in their thirties, passionately and calmly on the left of the left, professional revolutionaries, officers in the powerful student federation, men who enrolled for classes repeatedly but never graduated. They had nicknamed the School of Economics Stalingrado. Those who were public Communists or members of the known terrorist apparatus could not openly leave the campus. That would risk arrest. They were immune on the campus, for the University could not be entered officially nor searched by the police. Like medieval churches, this was a solid refuge won bloodily from tyrants. The fortress of the University, the dormitory arsenals and caches of weapons, could not be pierced.

□ □ □

Marro parked his milk truck directly opposite one of the side *puertas* to the University campus. He jerked his head from side to side to make sure both ends of the street were clear of police cars, then said to Mayoso, "We're late, but we're here. Let's go."

They ran together along the screening hedge until they reached a stone archway, then Marro motioned for Mayoso to follow him along the parking lot which angled off beyond the Estadio Olímpico. Mayoso recognized the bulky gray outline of the Aula Magna among the nearby group of University buildings and the tall red-white-and-blue-striped hospital.

Without looking back, the milkman ducked into the modernistic terra cotta entrance of a dormitory and led Mayoso, leaping two steps at a time, up to the second floor. The fatigue must be catching up with me, Mayoso thought; this medical bag is heavy as lead.

Marro stopped in front of one of the solid wooden doors and knocked, one-two, one-two. Mayoso could hear telephones ringing inside the room.

The door was held ajar on a chain lock. "Hola, Marro!" A student threw it wide open. "Come in! We were beginning to worry."

"Qué va, Luis? Why worry? Did I ever miss a delivery?"

As Luis locked the door behind them, Mayoso saw two men bent over separate telephones which rang the moment the receiver was replaced. One of the men was Filho. He was facing the other way, crouched, a telephone pressed against one ear, a hand soundproofing the other, talking in short coded phrases. Overflowing ashtrays smoldered beside the telephones, knotted streamers of smoke swirling upward thickly.

The second student, who was handling the telephone beside Filho, hung up and said, "You got here, eh, Marro?"

"A miracle, Nicolás. *No quedó no el gato.* Not even a cat was alive."

The telephone rang in front of Nicolás and he grabbed it up immediately. He had the curt sound of a combat artillery observer delivering map coordinates, Mayoso decided. Clearly this was a paramilitary command post. Now, Mayoso thought, the shadow of a gun is truly a gun. The sooner the surgery is finished, the sooner I'll get out of all this and back to the airport.

Filho slammed down his telephone and swung around. His face lighted. "Caramba! You're here at last!" His phone rang again. "Luis, take it." He came forward and shook hands with Mayoso, then with the milkman. "Trouble crossing town, Marro?"

"We were stopped twice," Marro said. "We're lucky to be here. How does it go?"

"It goes," Filho said. "Every objective has been hit hard, yet very few casualties. I hope the stupid army gets jittery enough to try setting up a military junta." He rubbed the back of his hand against his beard. "What a night, what a night. The dark night of the soul."

Mayoso spoke for the first time. "You can say that again."

Filho clapped him on the shoulder. He was being vigorous, mighty in battle, a winning guerrillero. "Reminds you of the old days, eh, Paqueta?"

"Yes. Very much so." To hell with you, Filho, he thought. You've double-crossed me, you bastard. From now on *sálvese quién pueda.* Each man for himself.

"You feel young again, Paqueta? Viva la revuelta! Viva el bravo pueblo! Viva right now!"

Mayoso exploded. "Viva your grandmother and your *madrina!*" Then, speaking angrily in French, he added, "Name of a name, there was no goddam need to schedule my coming to Caracas at such a time."

In French, Filho answered. "It seemed like a wonderful idea, and I never expected you to get involved. I'm truly, truly sorry you were subjected to so much danger. A thousand apologies."

"I know your sorrow. You'll pay for the candles at my funeral with Party funds." The thick smoke scratched in his throat.

"I'm in a war," Filho said. "As you see."

"You asked for a surgeon, not an infantryman. I am not a revolutionary statistic. I'm ready to turn around and go back to San Juan."

"You can't. All outbound flights will be canceled any hour."

"You must have expected that to happen."

"I did. To tell the simple honest truth, I did."

"This simple honest truth of yours is refreshing, Filho. Especially after so much dishonest truth."

Filho took his arm and spoke in Spanish, "Paqueta, you're hot, you're tired—you need some soap and water—"

A telephone rang and one of the young men said, "Filho—"

Filho waved his hand impatiently, "Momentito—"

Marro, who had been standing silently, said, "Filho, *estoy apurado*. My wife and kids will begin to ask questions—"

"I know you're in a hurry," Filho said. "You did a good job."

"No," Marro said. "The doctor did it. He got us through. He spoke with much control when every word counted."

"You are now off duty," Filho said. "Get your truck away from this University neighborhood. After their breakfast, the detectives will be watching campus exits like buzzards." To Mayoso he explained, "The University is immune from police search. So plainclothesmen watch the exits from unmarked civilian cars."

"I know." Mayoso held out his hand to the driver. "Adiós, Marro."

Marro shook his hand. "If you get me as a patient, take good care, ah?"

That's what the young lieutenant with the instantaneous death-making machine pistol had said, Mayoso thought. All these boys on both sides want the red badge of courage, but the hard slap in the face, the real possibility of the final wound of death, hits them unbelievably.

Marro straightened to attention and saluted Filho, who returned it casually. "*A sus órdenes*," Marro said, and went out quickly without any civilian goodbyes to the two students at the telephones. The phones had stopped and both young men had lighted fresh cigarettes. "What did Professor Nazario have scheduled for today's seminar?" Luis asked.

"A review of the pre-Cambrian crystalline rocks of the Brazilian Shield," Nicolás said. "And the geosynclinal Chaco Boreal with outliers of early Paleozoic carbonate sediments. We keep going into deeper formations for oil every year." The telephone beside him rang and he reached for it. He listened, then said, in a voice like Filho's, "Hold your position. Station snipers on the roofs to keep the police under fire. We'll get more ammo and *fósforo blanco* grenades to you."

Rooftop snipers, Mayoso thought, white phosphorus grenades. Those hombres know street tactics.

"Come on," Filho said to Mayoso quietly. "I'll get you a clean towel. Leave your medical bag here." He looked back reflexively as another telephone rang. "That story of Tolstoy's," he said. "Kutuzov outside Moscow. That's how I feel now. Once your forces are committed . . ." He stopped, lost in some solo argument with himself, then repeated, "Come on."

Mayoso followed him into a modern bathroom. Filho waved one hand. "Hot water. Plenty." He pushed open the sliding mirrored door of a built-in medicine cabinet. "Razor and shaving soap right here."

Mayoso surveyed the woman's things on the shelves of the cabinet— several lipstick tubes, jars, two small bottles of perfume, a rounded hair-brush, a plastic cup of hairpins. Filho followed his glance and said, "Cristina's. She hardly uses this junk."

"She's *here?* At a guerrilla command post?"

Filho kicked the bathroom door shut with one foot. "Of course. It's the safest place in town."

"Also you can keep an eye on her."

"A good thing. She's behaving in a very funny way." Filho sat down on the commode, but immediately jumped up. "What the hell am I doing? You probably have to urinate."

"I do," Mayoso said. "But it can wait a minute."

"*Qué bravo.* Such control."

"Forget my control. How's her control, this Cristina? What did you mean, *funny?*"

Filho spread his hands. "She hardly says a word."

"Usually she's a talker?"

"Pleasantly so. An enjoyer of life." His lips hardened. "It's odd. A bright girl has turned into a mummy."

"So much changed?"

"Well, all of a sudden, no makeup. Not even lipstick. Usually she combs her hair like any attractive young woman. A few times a day. Now she forgets to. To cheer her up I bought her a present, something she saw, to go with a white dress. An elegant black vicuña shawl, the silky kind you can pull through a wedding ring." Filho paused and scratched his bearded chin.

"And—?" Mayoso prompted him. He could see that Filho was not aware of his marital description of a ring.

"And she took the shawl. Not a word of thanks, nothing. Folded it lengthwise and wears it over her head like an old woman in mourning."

"No talk of suicide?"

"Oh no. No." Filho seemed genuinely startled by the question. "Nothing like that. And she is too deep for the usual dramatic gestures—you know, the cut wrists. Drinking iodine. She reminds me of the Indian women in mountain villages. *Macacoa.* That stoic silence."

For a moment they did not speak. Both knew a great deal about the stoic silence, but only Mayoso thought of the Indian women as individuals. To Filho they were a faceless suppressed exploited mass. To his grandfathers they had been a faceless mass to be suppressed and exploited.

Filho wanted them bound together, as guerrilleros. His grandfathers had also wanted them bound together, as serfs.

From the other room came the sound of the two students talking. The telephones rang, stopped, rang again. Filho nodded toward the door. "Geology students. Very precise. Unemotional. Later they will run the petroleum industry for us. That's why I picked them. You probably think they're a little crazy."

"I do," Mayoso said. "Those telephones keep reporting men with their guts blown open, and they talk about prehistoric mud."

"They take a long view," Filho said. "In medicine you take the short view."

"Very short, such as immediately. I'll wash up and be out in a minute."

"Don't you want a bath and a shave first?"

"No. Not if she's been up all night wearing a black shawl and waiting for me like waiting for an executioner."

Filho looked at him without speaking. For a moment their eyes met, and Filho shook his head a little, soundlessly. Then he said quietly, "I know you came only to pay back a debt. But a girl like Cristina, I mean a really good person like her—she needs somebody like you. I don't want any harm to come to her."

"You also don't want any harm to come to you."

"I told you before, Paqueta, I'm in a lifetime war. And now I'm winning."

"And I'm in a bathroom," Mayoso said gruffly, "and now I'm bursting." As Filho opened the door to leave, Mayoso said, "Leave my medical bag where it is. I just want to talk with her at first."

After he used the commode he tried to flush the water, but the plumbing did not work. He tried the faucet and got a trickle. While he washed, a faintly reminiscent fragrance touched him. Cristina's cosmetics in the open medicine cabinet. Face powder, Coty. This Cristina is no barefoot beachcomber. Certainly not one of those poor little Juanita Bimbos who drown their hair in *bejuco* and use heavy pink face powder from Madrid boxes printed with a simpering 1928 picture of a boyishly bobbed blonde. The faintly suggestive scent was stronger now. It came from a graceful bottle of eau de cologne labeled *Frangipani*. Of course! The tree which shaded the doorway of his bohío. He had crushed one of its blossoms in his hand only a moment ago, at dawn.

He caught sight of himself in the mirror. For a moment he saw himself as someone else. Two dark monocles of fatigue ringed his eyes. A sandpaper stubble. A dueling stare of suppressed anger. A wilted shirt collar and suit. Wrinkled as pajamas. A scarecrow. You'll frighten her to death, he thought, unexpectedly remembering her black shawl, then bent over the bowl to finish washing quickly.

The girl stood up as Filho opened the door and motioned politely for Mayoso to precede him into the room. She had been sitting on a straight-backed wooden chair near the window, watching the slow grayness of morning filter into the dissolving darkness. On the wall hung two framed pictures, an impassive tartar-eyed Lenin and a chipmunk-cheeked laughing Castro. Opposite them was a print of Meissonier's *The Barricade.* "Cristina," Filho said very heartily and formally, "this is Doctor Dionisio Mayoso Martí."

She did not move from the window as they sized up one another, he with a watchful quietness, she with the coiled immobile wariness of a kitten cornered by a dog. The black shawl had slid backward on her draggled black hair to become a loosely bulked collar which made her face a small, pale oval. Her eyes were so surprisingly large-pupiled, two polished black stones, they seemed momentarily unreal. She wore a simple sleeveless black dress, and, later, he saw she was barefoot. Aside from the startling drama of black hair and such eyes, she looked as unpretty as one of the young nuns who can teach only crocheting and needlework.

He saw her eyes move in her impassive face, over his uncombed hair, over his stubble beard, his wrinkled clothes. Filho must have seen the glance of inventory because he began immediately to talk while smiling as he always did when he was uncomfortable.

"Are you hungry, Cristina? No? Really not? You, Paqueta?" Then, turning back to the silent girl, "The doctor has been traveling steadily. San Juan to Caracas, across town under fire. And he was up all night without even a chance to shave or change clothes." Then back to Mayoso. "You must be starving. Now that most of our telephone reports are in, one of the students will bring you some breakfast. Café Puertorriqueño, I assume?" Then back to Cristina. "Remember our first week in Zihuatanejo? Remember that wonderful lazy week, Cristina?"

The large wounded eyes left the doctor and moved to Filho.

"Remember?" Filho repeated.

"All I remember," she said tonelessly, "is the little Indian boy who slept in the street outside the hotel and brought flowers for me each day. I remember him. The man at the hotel desk said the boy was hit by a car the day before we left, and I didn't have the time to bring him flowers or food at the hospital. I asked him once why he brought me flowers. He said he wanted me to be his mother. I asked him: where is your mother? In heaven, he said. He remembered many children, all brothers and sisters, all living in one room, always hungry, and the mother dying, then something with the father, he didn't know what, and then all the children just walking down the road going away to someplace, and then being alone and learning to live like a small animal, always hunting for food, sleeping on the ground. Good, bad, rain, shine, everything was the same to him. You could count his ribs from across the street. I won't be any trouble to you, he said. I'll sleep outside. The school is not so necessary, he said, but the mother is necessary."

Filho glanced swiftly at Mayoso, but the doctor was watching Cristina, listening carefully and nodding slowly. "Yes, señorita," he said, "to remember that is like remembering other sad things from long ago. So much to remember makes you want to weep."

She stared at him, then took an inward sobbing breath, with the back of her hand held up against her mouth, and sat down brokenly, doubled over in pain, her head bent downward into her arms.

Mayoso looked at Filho, whose face had become drawn, and motioned him toward the door. Filho went quickly out with the tiptoeing care one uses in the rooms of the sick or dying.

Mayoso waited until the door closed, then crossed the room and scraped another chair up to face Cristina. She kept her head buried in her folded arms on her knees.

He slumped in the chair, footsore and weary. For the first time in many hours he was off his feet, and he could feel the aching muscles in his legs, his back, his shoulder blades, his neck. He glanced down at the weeping girl who needed so much to weep. From inside one of her clenched fists hung a delicate gold chain with a little crucifix.

More or less Catholic. Isn't that what Filho had said? *Everything with the whole heart.*

A probing touch of sun, the new day. The uppermost valley was brightening where the sun barely touched Pico Ávila; the lower city was pooled in dwindling darkness. Over the entire length of the hugely fertile unkempt riotous garden that was Latin America the sun was rising: from Tierra del Fuego's lethal millrace of tides to the dusty awakening Mexican villages of Chihuahua; a sunshaft vaulting over the treeless llanos held by Filho's family, lands so endless that a barking dog on their hacienda could not be heard at the next and the cocks crowed only once because there was no answer; sun glinting off the Andean ice peaks above the remote Indians of the high valleys who even now spoke the Spanish of Cervantes. Mayoso squinted, imagining the sun dazzling the ocean spaces below his bohío, spanning out to infinity. With his knuckles he rubbed his eyes blearily. Hot coffee, shelves of friendly books, Nefertiti trailing her featherduster in the yard. So near, so far.

The early morning light hung stilly above Caracas like a suspension of milky glass. A single white gull sailed weightlessly on an invisible thermal updraft; legendary messenger, he thought, to all those ancient mythical gods of the great slumbering continent.

This girl's ancient gods, unyielding to her crucifix. Just beneath the gold-leaf veneer of formal Catholicism, there ran an underground stream of pagan cults. From the candomblé of Brazil to the *espiritistas* of Puerto Rico and the voodoo of Haiti, as different from Spanish Catholicism as the stone jaguar gods were different from wooden Christ figures and ceramic madonnas.

I know them well, these Latin ladies who face twentieth-century mirrors but live inside nineteenth-century heads, with eighteenth-century men who have seventeenth-century sexual codes based on sixteenth-century Indian and Negro slave women baptized more or less in fifteenth-century religion. In taking a medical history one needs to listen not only to their words but also to which century spoke. Three statements in a row may come from three different centuries.

The mind and body of Cristina will react to an abortion, he thought, with pulse and respiration and pain responses determined by inwoven old wives' tales very different from her outward world of Coty face powder, Frangipani perfume, and vicuña elegancia. Her wish to be Lilith in the Garden meant biting the fruit of knowledge which has turned her not into Mary but into Eve. If there were no hells, who would conjure paradise?

He looked down at Cristina's tangle of black hair and her smallboned shaking body. Her clinical depression, her posture of Pietà, the exhausted weeping of an ashamed child—she's back to what she learned as a convent girl. Black shawl, black dress, the tiny gold cross, all a surface of what Filho had called more or less Catholic. He had said she was from a mixed family—Spanish and Haitian French, but schooled in Puerto Rico. A sophisticated primitive, which complicates her prognosis.

How many times I've seen women walk this long lonesome road, weeping for blurred reasons they hardly know themselves, weeping as they walk with a stoic courage no man knows: and as they weep they feel again what the young girl feels toward her brother, her mother, her father, what the growing girl feels for the dancing circle of boys, then the hoped-for dreamt-for man who would caballero the journey and partner the bed; then weeping mostly for the unknown growing fetus attached inside, fruit twigged to a tree, which, if one tore off the placental stem, invoked the enraged atavistic terror of centuries back to the cavedweller's womb of time before there was time. Even prehistoric men sensed that he who darkened the light was endangering survival and must be struck down.

Aie, if only I were capable of doing a quick one-two-three job of uterine surgery, professionally regarding the patient only as a large mammal carrying a small apple-sized muscular vessel from which I must surgically scrape a thimbleful of protoplasm. How much simpler everything would become if I considered only the mechanics of technique, and this crushing sense of commitment to the impossible would lift from my back. I'm stooped as any Negro slave who planted cotton or any Indian serf sweating underground in the airless silver mines, and, like this girl, grown from the same root-branching soil of centuries. Never eat the first fruit from the tree, the campesinos said. The soil was nourished in too much blood.

Cristina had stopped sobbing and shivering, but kept her head down in her arms, breathing audibly through her mouth, like a distance swimmer cast up on shore. He held back the impulse to touch her shoulder in sympathy because he knew the desperation of the dying, the drowning, the deeply fearful, and how quickly they could weave a cocoon of omnipotence around the doctor, dooming themselves to disappointment and him to a crumbling clay pedestal.

"Cristina," he said quietly.

With that she slumped forward to her knees at the side of his chair. She kept her eyes closed, her eyelashes spiky with tears, her head bent submissively, her fingers locked together before her with the tiny gold cross dangling beneath her rigid handclasp.

"Forgive me, forgive me," she whispered.

"There is nothing for me to forgive. Here, sit up on the chair—"

"*Mère du Christ, priez pour moi . . .*"

"Cristina," he said, "there is no need for the litany. I need to ask you only a few questions."

"Are you really a doctor?"

"Yes."

"I was so afraid. And when you came in, maybe somebody Filho ordered in from one of his cadres—"

"Cristina, I only look like this because of what Filho explained to you. Do you believe that?"

"Yes. You sound like a doctor . . . but he calls you by such a strange name."

"A nickname from years ago."

"Oh."

"Wouldn't you prefer to sit back up on the chair?"

"No, no. Please. I feel better this way."

"On your knees?"

"Yes."

"But I am your doctor, not your confessor."

"I know. But when I was a child—"

"In Mexico?"

"No. Haiti. Our little church, it had a dirt floor, it did not have a confessional. The priest, he came only one time a month, and we all had to take turns going up to him one at a time, kneeling on the dirt floor even with a clean dress."

"And this, now, is like that?"

"Something like that. Let me stay here."

"Do you understand clearly that I am a doctor?"

"Yes. I believe. Even if you are not, I believe you."

"Then you do not believe me. Then you are still afraid."

Silence. Her neck bent lower.

"Cristina," he said, "I am a medical graduate of the University of Havana. I took extra years of postgraduate training in obstetrics and gynecology at Yale University. Do you know about it?"

She nodded.

"But my career was broken in Cuba. I knew Filho from the old guerrilla days in the mountains. I live in San Juan now. I flew here yesterday only as a favor to an old comrade. *Sabe?* Filho wanted somebody from outside Venezuela. He also wanted an experienced doctor for you."

Silence. The silence in the room, her crushed stoic immobility, what must be happening in her head—it all had the quality of a banging door.

"I hope you believe me."

"I want to," she said, and he saw tears run from her closed eyelids down her face. Clearly, she did not believe him.

She may be near the edge, he thought, weaving sleepily back and forth across the dazed line between what is real outside and what is real only inside. Perhaps a crude mental-status examination should come first.

"Cristina," he said. "What is your full baptismal name?"

"Cristina María de la Concepción Bretand Pagán." She gave her last name the Spanish pronunciation, pah-*gahn*.

"And my name? Do you remember my name?"

She shook her head.

"Doctor Mayoso." All the rest is my mother's Latin lace trimming or my father's ironic sense of humor, he almost added.

"Doctor Mayoso," she repeated.

"Some simple questions, Cristina. What season is this?"

"The flowering season."

"And your birth date?"

"November twenty-third."

"Twenty-three and twenty-three. How much is that?"

"Forty-six."

"You've heard the saying: A rolling stone gathers no moss. What does that mean to you?"

"Oh," she said, "that could mean many things."

"What does it make you think of?"

"Oh"—she waved one hand vaguely—"it makes me think of sad songs."

"Sad songs?"

"Yes. Like *Lamento Borinqueño.*"

"What part of the song?"

She hummed to herself, like a child at bedtime. He waited, but she said nothing. Finally, he asked again, "What part of *Lamento* is that?"

"*Que será de Borinquen mi Dios querido, que será de mis hijos de mi hogar? . . . Ahora que tu te mueres con tus pesares déjame que te cante yo también, yo también.*" What will become of my children, beloved God, what will become of my children and my home? . . . Now that you are dying of your sorrows let me also sing to you.

"That is what the saying means to you, Cristina?"

"Well, a rolling stone has no home, no family, no friends to turn to in trouble, no chance for roots where it stands. No moss grows on it."

"The saying, to you, is sad?"

She nodded. "Yes. Very. Why do you ask such things?" She glanced at him shrewdly. "The doctor for the tobacco company near Ciales, when I went to work, he only asked medical questions."

"These are medical of a different kind. What was your work?"

"Well, first, just to inspect the tobacco and put each leaf in the right box. We had many different quality boxes."

He nodded. He had seen the girls standing in long lines, each girl with her own tubular fluorescent inspection light and tobacco-leaf sorting bins. "It's a long way from Ciales in Puerto Rico," he said, "to Caracas in Venezuela."

"Oh," she said, speaking a little more freely now, "our plant had a steel band and a mariachi band. You know, wearing shirts with the name of the company on the back, and I won the contest for the calypso girl. We traveled all over Puerto Rico and St. Thomas and St. Croix. We called ourselves The Islanders. We did everything calypso. *Aguinaldos. Cantos.* They taught me some music. After that they found out I could speak three languages, not so very good, but good enough—you know, good morning, buenos días, bonjour, like the airplane stewardesses—so when buyers came to the factory I could leave the inspection line and show them around. Then we went to Mexico City, it was a big trade fair, and the company wanted to show we could make cigars as good as the Ha-

vanas, so we had a big booth, and the band went, and I went, and I met
Filho there. Is all this of medical necessity?"

"We're just talking," he said.

"I don't mean to criticize you. Anything, just ask me anything, no matter what, I'll tell you if you need to know."

How frightened she is, he thought, Ophelia at the riverbank with rosemary for remembrance. Everything is a blur, the landmarks are lost in fog, you steer by calling out across the gray waters and then strain to hear an echo. "Gracias, señorita," he said. "We're just talking. Tell me, how old are you?"

"Twenty."

"Your family?"

"My father died when I was eleven, after we moved to Puerto Rico from Haiti. He was shot during an Independista demonstration. He is buried there in that small cemetery by the shore." She swallowed, weeping again. "If he were alive now, I would not be here, like this. He would come for me even if he had to swim all the way."

"Your family was only your father?"

"I had two sisters. Both died when they were babies. My mother lived in La Perla. If she were alive now she would try to beat me."

"Because you are not married?"

"No. Because I left a good company job. And pregnant. And because I do not blackmail Filho to pay."

"Did she ever have an abortion?"

"Never."

"You know that?"

"Yes. I heard her talk to the neighbors. She said it is murder in the eyes of God."

"Oh? Did she ever have a child outside of marriage?"

"Two. After my father died. Both girls. Both died."

"From what?"

"The diarrhea."

"Your mother carried them through nine months' pregnancy?"

"Yes."

"Do you look like your mother?"

"Only the hair and the eyes. She told me I looked like my father. He was French."

"If you are pregnant now—"

"I am." She lowered her clasped hands over her abdomen. "I know I am."

"Did you have a pregnancy test?"

"What is that?"

"A test to see why your last monthly period stopped. If the absence was due to pregnancy."

"Why else?"

"In medicine, we know of a half-dozen other reasons."

She smiled very faintly, crookedly, and a tiny muscle beside her mouth twitched. "I don't need tests. I'm pregnant."

"Well, we'll see. If you could carry this pregnancy nine healthy months, in San Juan, could you find someone to take you in?"

"Yes. In La Perla. But it would be a misery." She dropped her voice so low that he had to lean forward to hear her. "And Filho said no when I mentioned maybe I should go back to San Juan to have the baby."

"Oh? Filho does not want a child?"

"Yes. But not now, not at this time, like this."

"You could go to Rio where they are more tolerant."

"Filho does not worry about tolerance. He fears his own intellectual students and activist cadres. Mostly I think he fears the Soviets. They are very strict about a man's private life. Especially if the woman is outside of the Party. They would never trust him with a top command again."

"How do you know?"

"On his last visit to Moscow, Mikyarkhin told Filho that Filho's Latin jokes about señoritas sounded like a bourgeois who followed his two *cojones* instead of his revolutionary mission. Filho sounded afraid when he told me about it. He tried to make a joke with Mikyarkhin by saying his father had borrowed the family crest from the old Medicis. You know, three balls. But Filho sounded worried."

"He told you this himself?"

"Yes. Maybe, also, my knowing so much is why he does not want me to leave Caracas with his child."

"Is it his child?"

"You do not know me. If I am with a man, I am with him. I don't like to dance on two-way streets."

"And would you like to leave Caracas?"

"Yes. Very much. I dream of the little islands. Here in this deep Caracas valley I feel I am in a coffin. Filho is a different man now. His work is twice as much because he feels he is winning. Our time in Mexico City and that week incognito at Zihuatanejo, all that sweet *novio* talk he just remembers in front of you to make me soft, to make me do something. He told me to get rid of this baby the way he tells his cadres to blow up a pipeline." She snapped her fingers. "Go. Do it. Like that."

He nodded. Ninety-nine of every hundred women he had seen accepted without question that this was entirely their own problem. ("I'd rather die than crawl back to him for help." He had heard that so many times. In some quiet moment I'll have to figure out why, he thought.) "Do I understand you, Cristina? You want to keep this baby?"

She stared straight ahead. Her face closed again, brooding. They were back at the beginning.

"Cristina," he said. "Will it be better to sit in the chair? I think you understand you are here in Caracas now, not on the dirt floor of a country church in Haiti."

"Yes," she said. "Now I feel back to myself." She began to rise but stumbled and would have fallen if he had not caught her arm. "My knees," she said. "They feel broken. All over, I feel broken all over." She held his arm tightly.

"You're all right? You can stand?"

"Yes."

He lowered his supporting arm slowly.

"You're strong," she said.

He shrugged. "Most people say big. Do you want to sit down? Or are you more comfortable standing?"

"Standing. Look, the sun is coming up." From the window she glanced over her shoulder at him briefly. "Last night, all night, I thought that by this time I would be dead."

He waited, but she said nothing more, so he added, "And then I came in looking like some kind of bum."

Looking out the window, at the sun, at the flaming flamboyante, she said, "I wanted to die before you could touch me. Then you said something very quiet about sadness and I could not hold it back. After so many days of discussion with Filho and so much being alone—I never let Filho see me cry. *Esa calma mía.* I forgot how to cry except sometimes after I would lie awake all night staring at the ceiling, and when the light would begin to come into the bedroom my eyes would be burning dry but I could feel a wetness on my face." She moved back from the window to look at him. "You sound like who you are, Doctor Mayoso, not one of Filho's cadres."

"Forget Filho. As a physician my only responsibility is to you."

"But Filho pays you."

"Not me, señorita. He pays the Cuban Refugee Committee in Miami."

Her eyes tightened. "Filho? How can he pay *them*? You know how much he speaks French? He calls them *meurtriers*. He hates them. They are the enemy of Castro and all the Fidelistas."

"So am I."

"You are not a Party member?" She was amazed.

"No."

"Not even a Fidelista? A Popular Fronter?"

"No."

"But you fought in the mountains in Cuba?"

"Yes. That was when the whole world believed Fidel's talk about free elections, no Batista SIM police, a new world. At first we saw only the improvement in life at the bottom. But later we saw Moscow and a new secret police and all the rest."

"I see. I see." She looked at him hard, then repeated, "I see. He is a very complicated man, Filho, and he must have some reason to trust you."

"He knows I am silent. He knows I know my medical work exactly. He knows that I would not be alive today without his help. He also knows he can believe what I say. We both grew up in families that believed in the old honor. *Qué honra para la familia.*"

He could see something quite subtle change in her face. The nunlike pallor was gone, the bent posture, the choked voice of a dirgelike pavane for a dead princess. She looked fifteen now, barefoot and innocent in her sleeveless black dress, her lips the color of lips, the unusual sloe-colored eyes catching the window light and made startling by her dark ivory skin and deep black hair. Mayoso began to see what Filho had seen, that mixture in her of the Caribe islands which Filho had called *cafezinho,* which, they said, had more delicacy than a porcelain heirloom, more warmth than a bride's pillow.

Through the window beside her he could see the morning light, higher now, with the nearby mountains humped upward into a cluster of cotton-flower clouds. Down the valley, over the edge of Caracas, hung a wall of smoke above the area which had burned so fiercely only a few hours ago. A pillar of fire by night, he thought, a cloud of smoke by day.

"Doctor Mayoso," she said suddenly. "I would like to ask you something, too."

"Of course." If she were gaining a little confidence in him, he would gain a little in her.

"An operation like this—" she began, then stopped.

"Does it hurt? Is that what you want to say?"

"No. I expect it to hurt."

"In my clinic, my patients get anesthesia. But that means having a trained person to help. Here, by myself"—he spread his hands—"it is not the same."

"Could I drink some whiskey?"

"No. An empty stomach is best. If your stomach should start to heave, it is better not to have anything inside which could go down into the lungs." He paused, then asked, "Do you know what this kind of medical procedure does?"

"Yes," she said. "You take out the womb."

"No," he said. "Nothing like that. Nothing like that."

"Truly?"

"Truly nothing like that. When a dentist fixes a cavity in one tooth he does not need to take out every tooth. It is more like that."

"Then what do you do?"

"Did you ever hear of dilatation and curettage? Doctors call it by the letters, D and C."

"No. Curettage is a French word, I know. It means scraping."

"Well, that's the idea. The womb is about the size of a pear. Where the stem of a pear would be, there is the opening to the birth canal."

"Aie. How could a baby move through such smallness?"

"After nine months of normal pregnancy, there is a very slow and gradual stretching."

"But with me? I have only one month."

"Yes. That's why the word dilatation. The small space of the canal is gradually dilated with thin, then thicker, sterilized metal instruments."

"That hurts."

"No. There is almost no feeling in the opening part of the womb called the cervix."

"How can that be? A woman has very sensitive nerves there."

"It's like going into a house. The room can be full of sensitive electric wires, but the front door is nothing but solid wood."

"Truly? You don't say this just to make me more calm?"

"You are not calm?"

"My heart is going so fast."

"In a few minutes I will examine you, Cristina. But first I want you to understand your body, and what you have to do, and what I do."

"Yes. Then it will be easier for everybody. This talking helps, but it is impossible for me to be calm."

"Of course. It is natural. I only want you to know very clearly what this medical procedure is and what it is not. It is only to scrape out gently the inside of the womb, like a spoon scraping out a food bowl."

"Aie, *bendito*. Some food bowl."

"The procedure does not take out the womb, you understand?"

"Yes."

"You truly understand?"

"Yes. You just said it. Like a spoon, that's all."

"Yes. You still have the womb. You can still be a mother again. The inside will be healed in a month or six weeks."

"Will it change my nature as a woman?"

He spoke very carefully. "The actual scraping will do nothing except be like a spoon. But if you believe that surgical spoon is an instrument of murder—"

"Of course. It kills a child."

"Cristina," he said. "For thousands of years men have disagreed about what is removed. From a medical point of view of a child that you think of as a baby, with a face and body like a very small infant, there is nothing like that for the first few months."

"I know, Doctor. It is called quickening."

"That's more or less the biological part."

"Then why is it said that a life is destroyed?"

"Because the female ovum is the size of a pinpoint and the male sperm is much smaller than that. When the two join, they become one, then two. The two becomes four, then eight, then sixteen, and so on. What began as a pinpoint becomes a combination of microscopic cells which keep growing. At first, with your bare eye, the growth looks like a soft cherry. It does not look anything like the human being which develops later, but it is the beginning form of life."

"*Qué más?* It's so complicated."

"Let *me* think about that part. I only want you to understand very clearly what this is all about. I will do nothing if that is what you wish."

Her eyes went over his face very carefully, trying to decide the most ancient human question: to trust or not to trust.

"Truly?" she asked. "If I say to do nothing, you do nothing?"

"I am your doctor, not Filho's employee."

"I am beginning to believe you, Doctor. But Filho is still a serious problem. He is not an ordinary person with his *novia* pregnant before the wedding."

"But if you decide to say no, señorita, it will be no."

"And you will lose your fee?"

"I lose nothing. The Refugee Committee bank account will be less for a day or two. It is nothing. You need to think only about what you decide, nothing else."

"I trust you. Now I believe you."

"Señorita, there is nothing to believe or not to believe. If you say no, we will both walk out of that door and tell Filho we are starving and go have breakfast."

"I can't eat. My stomach is like a stone in my throat."

"I understand."

She lowered her voice to a whisper. "But what would we tell Filho? He will not let me just walk away, anywhere I want to go."

"You think he would harm you?"

"Not personally. Personally, he likes me very much. But impersonally he keeps saying he is in a war, and in a war he expects anybody, including himself, to become a casualty. So could you. He would genuinely regret it, but he would do it if he thought it would help win his war."

"I know," Mayoso said. "He is the descendant of the High Inquisitors who could kneel beside a heretic and pray for his immortal soul before they put a torch to him."

"Ah. So. You hate Filho."

"No. Something much more difficult. I understand him."

"But you would double-cross him?"

"I told you before, Cristina. In the beliefs of medicine, I can be only your doctor, not his employee. I can do only what you and I decide after my physical examination."

"No more questions?"

"Just one. The one you never answered."

"About whether I want this child?"

"Do you?"

"I want a child. But a child should be wanted, and I do not want a child from Filho."

"You just decided?"

"No. I decided when Filho said: Get rid of it. Like ordering a mecánico: Fix it. I thought: *Y basta!* That's enough! That's why I agreed to be here and wait for you. Now I'm glad I did."

"You're young," he said. "You're only at the beginning."

Her small crooked smile came back and again the tiny muscle in the corner of her mouth twitched. "The beginning?" she repeated. "Who would believe it? I was sure it was the end."

He stood up and pushed aside the hard wooden chair. "I'll get my medical bag and come right back."

In the outer room the telephones were silent, the two geology students were gone, and a ground fog of smoke had settled along the floor. Filho was sprawled in a corner with his collar open, his head sideways, sleeping exhaustedly. When Mayoso picked up his bag Filho awoke with a start, alert immediately. He rubbed his forehead.

"A head full of rocks. Got any aspirin in that bag, Paqueta?"

"Yes."

As he began moving the clutter of instruments in the bag, Filho asked, "How is she?"

"I'm going to do a physical examination now."

"Only now?"

"I take a very thorough history."

Filho put on his smile. "People lie to you, ah?"

"Not always. But often."

"I didn't want to interrupt you."

"Here. Here's aspirin." He tossed the package across the space between them. Filho caught it. Sleepy or not, Mayoso noticed, his coordination is very good.

"What are you doing?" Filho asked. "Putting those instruments on the floor!"

"The sterilized wrapping was opened by a soldier last night. We'll have to sterilize them again if I need them."

Filho's eyes changed. "What do you mean, *if* you need them? You need them."

"Are you sure she's pregnant?"

"Of course. She missed her time. She told me her nature is like a clock, every twenty-eight days. So she missed, so she's pregnant."

"Did you arrange a pregnancy test?"

"What for? Why run the risk?"

Mayoso snapped the two upper halves of his bag shut. "She's probably pregnant, but no doctor is ever sure about that until he makes sure."

"Other things can happen?"

"Yes."

Filho stood up. "Paqueta, this is one of those times. Every word you say counts. You talked to her a long time. And very quietly."

"Would a lecture on gynecology convince you?"

The smile. "No. I know how complicated it can be. But a short, simple explanation of how a girl can miss a regular period for more than a regular reason."

Mayoso put his medical bag down. More than anything he wanted to stretch out and sleep for a week. This quietness of Filho's was the hair-balance quiet of a man very high on a drug kick, so high he had leveled off by holding himself carefully, omnipotently, in control. Any moment this could change. "Filho," he said. "Some women are born with an abnormality of structure."

Filho waved one hand, dismissing it. "What else?"

"Diabetes."

"So?"

"Malnutrition. Tuberculosis. Mumps. Influenza. Syphilis."

"Are you serious?"

"I'm just beginning. There are hormone reasons, sometimes."

"Which one? I know there are more than one."

"Any one. Thyroid. Ovary. Pituitary. Adrenal."

"So many diagnostic possibilities?"

"I'm only halfway down the list."

Filho held up one hand. "Enough. But I know she is pregnant. I have an infallible intuition."

"I envy you. I have only some training in differential diagnosis."

Filho really smiled now. "Touché, Paqueta. You must be starved, *compadre*. I told them to wait so your breakfast would be hot. She cannot eat now, can she?"

"No, not yet. And I can wait. The examination does not take so long."

"With her, you never know. She is very modest in some ways."

"If you want, I'll give you the rubber gloves. You do it."

"I apologize, amigo. I keep forgetting you are twice as tired as I am. Really. I apologize."

Mayoso recognized that this moment was the time. "Filho. We have to agree on something. With your cadres you have to be the *jefe máximo*. But in something like this you will have to change. You can't command human biology."

"Paqueta, don't be such a stuffed shirt. In one word: In your field, you give the orders."

"Exactly."

"I've apologized already. You still sound angry."

"Not with you alone. When I think that a thousand-bed University hospital, the biggest in South America, stands less than a mile from here, and all *this*"—Mayoso held his bag up—"is supposed to do what should be done in that hospital, with anesthesia, with antisepsis, with facilities for laboratory tests and blood transfusions—"

"Blood?"

"Yes. Hemorrhage is one of the most common complications."

"Avoid it, Paqueta. No matter what, avoid it. Hemorrhage is out of the question."

"I'll give you a written guarantee, Filho."

"You're right to be angry. In my work or your work, amateurs should not interfere with professionals."

"Exactly."

"I'm glad to hear you sound so—what shall I call it?—so military. Good men talk like that. So, you'll call me when you are ready?"

"Yes." Mayoso went into Cristina's room and shut the door behind him.

Cristina had not moved from the window. As if she were in solitary confinement, he thought. The civilized French idea that each has his own taste needs updating: each has his own prison.

Cristina turned from the window, glanced downward at his bag. "*Mire.* There's smoke over the city. Some big fires must have been started last night. The city and the hills in the smoky light, they remind me of a painting of a Spanish city. Toledo, I think."

"View of Toledo?"

"Yes. *View of Toledo.* By El Greco, no? You look surprised."

"A little. When a young lady works in a tobacco plant she has no chance to see such a picture. Not even when she goes to an Americano type of high school in Puerto Rico."

"But when she lives with Filho there is much chance. In cardboard folders he has whole collections. El Greco. Picasso. Diego Rivera. Tamayo."

He grinned a little. "To live with Filho is an education."

"A walking university. More than paintings." She made a circular gesture. "Everything."

"But every subject has a political handle?"

"Yes. Because to him everything is political. But at least he sees everything big. History. Geography. He calls it geopolitics. He sees everything big. What he gave me—copies of paintings, operas on records, books and books in three languages, the talks half the night with his student cadres until the head sits on the neck like a broken piano. Would you believe it —he even studies now how to read and speak Chinese. He is a phenomenon."

"In all ways?"

"Not in all ways, but in most."

"You love him?"

"*Vaya . . .* who knows what love is? Not a hand in a long white glove, like those Spanish cinemas. Not the biting and cheating I see in the French cinema. For Filho I have more respect than for anybody I ever met. That is love, no?"

"Well, a part of it."

"A part of it? What is more, Doctor?"

"To answer that is a long story."

"And we have some short work to do. I know, I know. And I keep talking in the opposite direction."

He put his medical bag down and said, "Cristina, have you ever had a medical examination of the female parts?"

She shook her head. He was learning that she had a range of responses. She could move in a moment from a charade of sophistication to the reality of fright, hardly able to speak except by gesture.

"Do you want me to explain it to you?"

She shook her head again. Then she said, "No. The sooner you finish —I mean, we finish—the better."

"Certainly. But there may be a few more questions."

"Will the examination hurt?"

"One or two tender spots, maybe, but no big pain. And please don't worry about modesty. A doctor has no more erotic feeling about this than a mechanic checking an auto engine."

"It's so funny," she said. "I always had a dream of how this kind of pregnancy examination would be. First a slow lunch with a handsome rich husband. Then I would walk into your beautiful air-conditioned office—the Señora Snob Granfino, you know?—and I would drop off my white cashmere coat while the nice nurse did something medical but comfortable. On the walls there would be some fine Italian paintings of the Renaissance, with healthy little fat cherubs"—she waved her hand at the room, and, for the second time, he saw the framed prints of Meissonier's *The Barricade* and the official *jefe máximo* pictures of Lenin and Fidel Castro—"not these. Dios, why does life do this to us?"

She was very serious and he did not smile about her capital-L pronunciation of life.

"Maybe life is us," he said. "We ourselves do the doing."

Her long porcelain eyes with their pupils dark as agates, met his. With the unwinking swiftness of a camera click, she focused on him as a person. "You're tired, Doctor Mayoso. You are far from home in a bad situation with no sleep, no food, nothing."

"Nothing serious, señorita."

"Sometimes you call me Cristina, and that makes me feel like a young girl. Sometimes you call me señorita."

"Which do you prefer?"

"I don't know. Sometimes I prefer the one, sometimes the other. Maybe that's why you say both?"

"Maybe."

"Maybe I should stop so much talk, talk, talk."

"No. No."

"You sound like yes, yes." She smiled, not the crooked sideways smile she had had at dawn with the buried small muscle twitch, but her first real step back in the world. She slid the black shawl off her shoulders and dropped it on the chair beside her. "So, Doctor, now we inspect the engine?"

Twenty minutes later he stripped off his rubber gloves and stood up. "You can get up now. And get dressed."

Now that the examination was finished something changed; now she was a woman in a room reaching for a neatly folded dress. He turned his back and walked to look out at the landscape which had become so remarkably familiar. Students carrying books were scattered between the neighboring buildings; they had the quick intelligent look of university students who had schedules, classes, goals. They reminded him of his days at the University of Havana when the enemy was simple, the methods exciting, and utopia within reach. And yet, he thought, the students who want only the comfortable chair, the comfortable money, the papa and mama comfort, those students are already cautious middle-aged do-nothings. When they reach actual middle age, they'll become frantic searchers for a purpose, for a meaning, for some Holy Grail worth living effort. How many women will search from bed to bed and sooner or later come to see me? Not as the working-class women come to me, their faces exhausted, beaten—but see me as they would see a shoemaker with the heel broken off one of their party shoes the night of a big dance. Fix it. Get rid of it. And the complicated hidden angers of my medical colleagues who become judgmental moralists and say, "She had her fun. Now let her pay for it." Ah, those pleasant simplifications of guilt and innocence, crime and punishment.

"Doctor Mayoso," she said behind him. "Doctor Mayoso."

He turned abruptly. "Have you been standing there, waiting?"

She nodded. "You didn't hear me at first, so I waited. You looked far away."

"Talking to myself?"

"In a way. I didn't want to interrupt you."

"Don't let me frighten you, Christina. I am alone so much I pick up the monologue habits of lonely people."

"I'm not afraid, Doctor. Does the surgery part come now?"

"No. Not now. Not later. You are not pregnant."

She stared at him. "But how can that be?"

"It can be. It is not unusual."

"But I never missed my monthly time before. And another was due this week and it has not come."

"I know. I know, I understand all that."

"Are you *sure*? How can you be so positively sure?"

"I am not one hundred per cent certain. Only ninety-nine per cent. Your body shows none of the changes of early pregnancy."

"But the belly does not get big until later."

He could see she did not believe him. "Cristina, in a healthy young woman with regular menstrual periods, pregnancy is the most common reason for periods to stop. But there are other reasons."

"You could tell such an important thing from that examination?"

"Yes. There are no changes in the breast or nipples. The pink lining of the vagina has not the darker appearance of pregnancy. The neck of the womb does not feel as soft and as flexible as your bottom lip—it feels as half-stiff as the cartilage of your ear. The uterus is as small and as firm as a new pear, not bigger and spongy. You remember I felt each side, to the right and the left."

"That was tender."

"Yes, I know."

"How could a man know?"

"Because to examine the right and the left testicle is as tender as to examine the right and left ovary. And you do not have a pregnancy in the tube from the ovary to the womb."

"You're so sure? I knew a lady in San Juan who had a pregnancy in this tube. She never knew it until it broke open and she nearly died on the way to the hospital."

"You do not have it. A pregnancy in the tube at this time, about six weeks along, would feel like a soft, spongy plum to my fingers and like the pain of appendicitis to you."

She put both her hands up to her face. "I'm not pregnant. Dios mío! I can hardly believe it. You're *sure?*"

"Yes."

"I mean, I mean, you have been so nice, you have explained so much to me to make me feel better, are you just trying to make me feel better?"

"No. I am ninety-nine per cent sure."

"That's a very high percentage."

"Nothing in medicine is a hundred per cent, Cristina."

"You. You are a hundred per cent."

"Not if I go without some food all this morning."

"Aie, *bendito*. What will we tell Filho? If we tell him this he will make me stay in Caracas."

"You don't want to stay here?"

"No. Not anymore. No, I feel ten years older than when I came. I feel as if more has happened to me than in my whole life, and now I only want a little peacefulness. I don't want him to touch me. He said to me: Get rid of it. I wish I could say to him: Get rid of yourself, Filho."

"That's not so easy with Filho."

"I know. He can be very military. But what can we tell him?"

"I can tell him something, but I must be sure you do not keep changing whichever way the wind blows."

She crossed herself nervously. "I swear it. If you go away without me I will be like a dog in a big estancia, free to run but always there is a fence around it. You know what I mean?"

He looked at her carefully, measuring her and the idea. Filho was Communist in his world, but very Spanish about a woman. For another to interfere could set in motion a sequence as formal and unwritten and deadly as the old back-country feuds.

"For me to do this," he said, "that would be very serious. I would have to depend upon you very much."

"I know," she said, "you think I will lose my nerve."

"Not at all," he lied.

"You don't know me. I have the most courage when the sky comes down. If you tell me what I should do, and I can do it, then I will really do it. Cross my heart."

"There is nothing for you to do. Just put that black shawl over your head like a mourner in church. Be as you were. Say nothing or only one word. The door will be open so you can hear what I say. Do you hear?"

"Yes, yes."

"You don't look it."

"I hear you. I hear every word. Only suddenly I am frightened. It's hard to breathe. What if something goes wrong? I don't know what he would do to us."

"Better, then, not to try?"

"Oh no!" She put her hand on his arm. "Oh *no*. We have to try."

"Then put on the black shawl." As he began to turn away from her she grasped his hand in both of hers and raised it to her lips. Her fingers were cold as metal.

Filho was talking into one of the telephones when Mayoso came in. He left the connecting doors between the rooms open and took the chair Filho gestured at and sat down. Filho did not take his cigarillo out of his mouth and it bobbed up and down as he talked. "Tell them this," he was saying, sounding very strong and firm despite the deep fatigue lines in his face, "just tell them that any Americano representative will get a hot reception that will make the one we gave Nixon look like a tea party. After the success of last night, they know we are not boasting . . . yes . . . yes . . . I will review it with the Central Committee. . . . Sí . . . sí . . . *El viejo* . . . and the Chinese will be here . . . adiós."

"Well, Paqueta," he said as he put down the phone, shifting with executive ease from one problem to another, "you looked so weary before that I thought you had gone to sleep in the bedroom."

"I don't need a bedroom, Filho. I need an operating room."

Filho took the cigarillo out of his mouth. "I thought you came prepared for less than hospital surroundings."

"I did. But do you know what ectopic pregnancy is?"

"You mean something that is not natural?"

"Yes. When the human ovum is fertilized in the Fallopian tube—"

"That I know, the tubes—"

"And when the ovum settles in a narrow tube to grow, instead of in the uterus, sooner or later the growing ovum must come out or the tube will burst."

"So take it out."

"That's an operation. Through the abdomen. That means having instruments and anesthetic. A blood bank with matching blood."

"And if this is not done?"

"The tube breaks open with great pain. All the bleeding is inside the abdomen. With hemorrhage comes shock. Then surgery must come immediately before the shock is irreversible."

"What does that mean? Death?"

"Yes."

Filho stubbed out his cigarillo in the crowded ashtray. "Did you explain any of this to her?"

"Yes."

"Why?"

"For two reasons. Professional and moral."

"Spare me the moral, Paqueta. Just the professional."

"Girls like Christina can almost put themselves into shock out of fear alone."

"But if a girl cannot understand a medical explanation—"

"No matter, Filho. They know a doctor who takes the time to explain must be thinking of them. And they feel better. The heart rate becomes steady. The pulse slows down. The breathing becomes normal. It's like a transfusion of confidence."

"I never knew this. Interesting. And the moral reason?"

"Are you having a student debate with me?"

"No. You demonstrated to me once not to do that. I don't have the energy left for twice. I only ask the moral reason you made a girl your *confidente*."

"Because it's her life."

"Oh? You will say my perspective is distorted. I lost many men last night."

"She's not one of your cadres, she's not a soldier in the class war. She's a girl on the border of great pain, a ruptured tube, and all the rest."

"Paqueta, you know I am not an unfeeling person, but I have no facilities for surgical emergencies. And the need for secrecy is now a hundred times greater. I have important people coming here today." He rammed another cigarillo between his teeth. When he held the lighted match to it, Mayoso saw that his fingers shook. He took a few steps across the room and bent sideways to peer through the connecting door into the next room.

He came back and dropped into the chair beside the doctor. "She looks like a ghost," he said.

"Yes, she does." Mayoso stood up and put out his hand. "So, Filho. Adiós."

Filho stared upward at him. "What the hell do you mean? You can't just walk out!"

"I'll spend a day or two at the hotel until the airport opens. This is an expensive delay you never mentioned."

"Please, don't pick now to be angry. You probably feel you've balanced accounts with me, no?"

"More than balanced, Filho. I could have been gunned down in the streets last night. You *pícaro*. You manipulator."

Filho jumped up beside him. "Paqueta, I don't blame you for being sore. But be reasonable. You know I am an acrobat with no safety net. One wrong step and I'm kaput. How could I tell you of such a big paramilitary plan? Don't pay me back by leaving me with such a seriously sick girl."

"You have an excellent hospital right around the corner."

"Impossible. We discussed all that before. People in pain talk. People in anesthesia talk. Do you realize the disaster if she dies?" Then he repeated, "A disaster."

"You're a big shot in this country. Fix it."

"Ah, stop. Don't be so sore about last night. You're alive. You only have to lift a hand."

"Which hand?"

"Any hand. She needs a clinic. You have one in San Juan. Take her out of the country with you."

"And if she ruptures in the taxi? Or at the airport?"

"You have your doctor's bag. Give her a shot. Some kind of sedative."

"But I would have to be with her every minute," Mayoso said.

"Of course. Don't worry. Not too long. A few hours more or less."

"You mean stay here tonight, Filho?"

"No, no. Of course not." He tilted his wrist and tapped the face of his watch. "Time. Time. I have to get moving. Some important comrades are coming this afternoon. I don't want you or Cristina here. Both of you must get out of here." He snapped his fingers. "I've got it. Paqueta, amigo, it's so simple." He smiled widely, the chess master who had a winning gambit. "She stays with you at the hotel. If something happens, she's your girl. It's so simple. She's from San Juan, just like you. And if nothing happens she'll be in your clinic tomorrow afternoon. Now, isn't that simple?"

"All except the payment, Filho."

"You squeezed me the first time, Paqueta." His eyes narrowed. "Imagine, just imagine, if my people learn that Party funds help pay for your crazy refugee arms purchases." He shook his head tensely. Almost a shiver, Mayoso decided. "To make that payment in Miami was not simple."

"That payment was for surgery, Filho. This new risk is much bigger."

"But you never did the surgery, Paqueta. To charge would be unethical."

"True." You *pícaro*, he thought. You conquistador.

"So make it a payment for this, no?"

"If I do, it's only because I'm here already."

Filho clapped him on the shoulder. "I knew a man like you would say yes."

"I haven't said yes yet."

"A shave, a shower, a hot breakfast. You'll feel better. I'll pay you an extra three hundred B's."

"What good will three hundred bolívares do me if something goes wrong?"

"Nothing will go wrong. I'll explain the whole thing to Cristina. She's sensible and she'll understand she needs, as you say, a hospital room, not a bedroom."

"Filho," Mayoso said, "it is no wonder your men follow you. You could talk the statue of Simon Bolívar off his bronze horse."

"I know," Filho said with some modesty.

A Mercedes sedan stood in the Residencia parking lot, and, as they walked toward it the student said apologetically, "It's my father's car. It's a good cover for you. I was lucky to get it on such short notice, but Filho wanted it so because of the police roadblocks." He held open the back door for Cristina and Dr. Mayoso, and took her elbow while saying politely, "Allow me to assist you."

"Gracias. There is no need."

The student smiled. "Filho's orders, señorita. He said you were primera clase, *entrega inmediata, perecedero, fragil, cuidado.*" First class mail, special delivery, perishable, fragile, handle with care. As he slid behind the wheel, he looked up into the driver's mirror to talk to their reflection. "Naturally, I do not know the circumstances. I am only your contact from here to the hotel. But if that is what he said."

"We appreciate Filho's concern," Mayoso said. "We've hardly seen him since this morning. We were occupied all last night and all day today."

"So were we all," the student said. "It was a fantastic success. A thing of military beauty." He began to put the car key into the ignition, but stopped when Cristina said, "Momentito. Our baggage."

"Don't worry, señorita. Everything has been arranged with military efficiency. My sister got your key and packed everything while I went to the doctor's hotel to do the same for him."

"You checked me out of Hotel Miranda?" Mayoso asked. Filho must have had a considerable anxiety to get the girl gone. The glib phrase about special delivery, handle with care, was no accidental choice of words.

"Sí. Filho gave very exact instructions. For a Latin he has a great precision," he added admiringly. "That is why I wear this wristwatch, just like his. A Swiss Military watch! With a twenty-four-hour dial. I brought your *equipaje* to the new hotel. Filho said you both should have the cover of rich turistas. It will be easy because the hotel is full of people who came from the airport when all flights were canceled."

He thinks we're Party couriers, Mayoso realized, and he is enjoying every minute of what he considers to be revolutionary espionage. "Will the airport open tomorrow?" he asked.

"Tomorrow, yes. Through my cousin at the airline I was able to get you two seats on the first afternoon flight. The tickets are in your baggage."

"An afternoon flight? Nothing earlier?" A trick? Delay by Filho? Anything was possible. Although Filho's relief ten minutes ago when he had said goodbye to Cristina had been such an obvious flag-waving thank-God-you're-going that he could hardly have faked. For a quick revealing moment that was part comic, part sentimental, he was not the *jefe máximo* of *la revuelta*, but only another lover boy caught with his glans down.

The student twisted in the front seat to speak directly to him. Clearly, he was insulted. His honor was suddenly at stake. "Believe me, Doctor, to get tickets even for an afternoon departure was an accomplishment of size. The turistas are offering my cousin up to three hundred B's under the counter. The afternoon radio news comes in a moment. You can hear for yourself."

"My apology," Mayoso said. "I only expressed a hope for an earlier departure time. You achieved Filho's instructions with"—his brain spun for what he knew must be the right word—"with military efficiency."

The boy's frown smoothed. "*Nada*. When I bring you to the new hotel in this car, your cover as rich turistas will be complete." He glanced at Cristina. "You are not content, señorita? You are so quiet."

She looked pale, without lipstick; oval cameos of fatigue were embossed beneath her eyes. She had parted her black hair in the center, letting it hang loosely, and in her black sleeveless dress and black flat-heeled shoes she looked like a convent girl on her way to have her tonsils removed. "I am content," she said. "I have the feeling I slept only a few minutes this morning, but now I see I slept until afternoon because you accomplished so much." Her knee touched the doctor's as she added, "And with such military efficiency."

"*Nada*, señorita. After last night, the world knows the Party can bury the Yanqui lies about the lazy Latin *mañana*. We can be efficient. Our cadres are the most disciplined in South America."

As the car started forward Mayoso said, "What were the casualties last night?"

"Not many for operations of such a size. We can just catch the afternoon radio news if the señorita will not be troubled."

"No trouble," Cristina said. In her most characteristic gesture, she folded her hands in her lap. She possesses a deep undemanding private silence, Mayoso thought. Suddenly he remembered a young girl he had seen in a country village church in Cuba. Beneath a primitive altar lighted by a few poor candles a carved wooden Christ lay supine. His bones and corded muscles were carved in detailed realistic agony, and under the crown of thorns on His brow worshipers had left dark smears of their own blood. The young girl must have been praying alone, on her knees in the dim little church, but when Mayoso saw her she had fallen sideways against the Christ figure with her cheek pressed against the clotted blood stains on His face, and she was torn by sobs. As he came closer, Mayoso saw that she was perhaps fourteen and her belly bulged with an unborn child. He stood beside her, deeply moved. Even in hospitals, he had rarely seen such profound and bottomless grief. Finally he touched her shoulder and said, "Child, I'm a doctor. Can I help you?" In the candle-lit dimness her great dark eyes rolled toward him unseeingly. "The world is so terrible . . ." she whispered in agony. For a moment she clasped her fingers together in a nameless shuddering pain, then dropped her hands with complete resignation.

The auto radio came to life playing military music. As they turned into Guzmán Blanco Avenue, a long convoy of jeeps and military trucks came toward them. In El Pinar Park, on both sides of the wide road, several companies of paratroopers were assembled under the trees.

On the radio, the brassy music stopped and the radio announcer began to speak, but the roar of the passing military convoy drowned out the voice. The student turned up the volume control, but only occasional words came through.

Mayoso watched the trucks which passed them. Discipline was tight, clearly, with definite speeds and distances between vehicles, and communications jeeps spaced at intervals with their tall thin aerials whipping in the breeze.

"Please," the student said loudly over the noise, "if we close all the windows we can hear the radio." He glanced up at his rearview mirror, and they both nodded.

Now, with the windows closed, the radio became intelligible. ". . . the attack upon the petroleum industry was concentrated against the Lake Maracaibo installations of Creole Petroleum, a U.S.A.-owned company. Four transformer stations were destroyed. The management estimates that forty per cent of their crude oil production has been knocked out. The management has issued this statement: 'The sabotage of Creole Petroleum facilities is more an attack upon our workers and the people of this country than it is upon our company. Our record of voluntarily sponsoring modern employment practices, housing, schools, hospitals, and the promotion of Venezuelans to responsible positions is clear for all to see. Those who attacked—"

The announcer paused, then said, "One moment, please—we interrupt for a special announcement."

"Caramba!" the student said. "You can tell we really hit them where it hurts."

A new announcer came on the air. "Please stand by. In a moment we take you directly to Miraflores Palace. . . . His Excellency, the President of the Republic."

A silence, then the President's voice boomed from the loudspeaker.

"My fellow citizens. The Republic is in mortal danger. As you know, after generations of dictators our people are deeply committed to constitutional guarantees of life, liberty, and the due process of law. Among all the nations of the Americas, we are among the few which have not fought Castroism and Communism with the dictatorial methods of Castro and the Communists. However, our constitutional guarantees of freedom have been used as a protection by both our internal and external enemies. The sabotage of our country's economic life and the planned murders of dozens of policemen have been handled as severe civil disorders, but constitutional law has remained intact. The press has remained free. Political meetings, including Communist Party meetings, were held freely. No home could be entered without a legal search warrant. There were no secret arrests, no torture, no counter-terror. Last night, using these freedoms, the Communists and their Castroite supporters deliberately tried to demonstrate a military power to kill, kidnap, steal, burn or destroy at will.

"A three-ton supply of rifles, machineguns and ammunition has been discovered cached under the sand at a beach on the Falcón Peninsula. Many of the weapons bear the markings of the Cuban Army. Even worse—" the President's voice stopped, then began again with a growl—"the pride of Venezuela's national development, the General Rafael

Urdaneta Bridge across Lake Maracaibo, the longest concrete bridge in the world, the symbol and life-blood link between the industry of Maracaibo and the agricultural district of Venezuela built at a cost of more than three hundred million bolívares—explosive charges have just blown a gap which demonstrates these terrorists want to sink their teeth into your throat and mine.

"For all these reasons, your elected representatives have granted my urgent request to mobilize the reserves of the armed forces and to suspend for thirty days certain constitutional liberties. I urge you not to interpret these steps as dictatorial martial law against a liberal minority. This is self-protection, by the open legal methods of a republic, against guerrilla attacks financed and supported singly or in combination by Havana, Moscow and Peking.

"They hope to demonstrate to the world that constitutional democracy is weak. They hope to convince our military high command that only a military coup by an iron-fisted junta can run the country under martial law. After that, in the name of a liberal struggle, they hope to create a Popular Front to tear down the military and seize power in the Castro pattern. None of these events will occur.

"I have just signed a State of Siege order which declares illegal the PCV, the Venezuelan Communist Party, and the FALN, and the Movement of the Revolutionary Right. I have signed an order to suspend constitutional immunity from arrest of the twenty-three Congressmen of these parties. There is evidence these men include the secret high command of underground saboteurs of our country. Units of our regular and newly mobilized reserve forces are taking up strategic positions as I speak. All are loyal to your elected government. There is no coup. No putsch. No military junta. The underground will be crushed. These martial laws are strong but temporary measures for thirty days only. Circumstances may force us to break tradition and to penetrate the University. Law and order must be restored. Law and order will remain. Long live the Republic!"

The student shut the radio off with a quick movement. "An act of desperation," he said. "They're on the run."

"But Filho has just lost his immunity from arrest," Mayoso said. "Now he'll be on the run."

"Filho expected the whole thing," the student said over his shoulder. "He made complete plans to go underground. Who knows? He could be halfway to Cuba right now." He shook his head admiringly. "That Filho. A genius."

Mayoso and Cristina did not risk even glancing at one another. All their cleverness had simply saved him the time and bother of kicking them out.

The wide green-leaved crowns of the bucares hovered over the oval pools of shade they cast at spaced intervals along the side of Autopista del Este. Ahead, high in the hills above the Caracas valley, the new hotel glittered whitely in the sun, a fanciful sepulcher. They sat back in silence as the car broke away from the dust of the passing convoy and turned upward past banks of wild orchids toward a different world.

13 Two VISITORS at Filho's University headquarters watched Filho pace back and forth: the Spanish dinamitero and a Chinese officer wearing civilian clothes. The Spaniard was called Picasso by the students, not as a code name but because he resembled the painter and disliked student humor. The Chinese officer was Liu Keh-yu; his current *apparatchik* code name was Pao-Yu. Both men were dressed almost alike: dark canvas rubber-soled shoes, wide-bottomed khaki-colored chino trousers and two-pocket semimilitary shirts worn buttoned at the neck without a tie, the style Stalin had begun and Mao cultivated. When they were not speaking, both kept their mouths thin-lipped, compressed with metallic skepticism. The Chinese officer wore two wristwatches, just as Fidel Castro did. The steel civilian watch on the outer surface of Liu's wrist gave Havana time; the radium-dial military watch, which he wore facing inward, was set at Peking time.

From the next room, the sound of ringing telephones mingled with the military music from a portable radio.

Filho flung open the door between the two rooms. "Shut off that goddam radio," he said to the geology student at the nearest telephone.

Nicolás swung around, amazed. "But didn't you tell me to leave it on? For bulletins?"

Filho rubbed his forehead. "Of course." He did not like the smiling undertaker look on Liu's face; each small irritation exasperated him.

The student tapped the black-faced watch on his wrist. "Our transmitter at Los Teques is scheduled to break in on the local wavelength at 1730 hours."

Filho straightened. "Phone them right now," he said commandingly. "Tell them all public radio announcements must be from a mobile truck. A mobile truck that keeps moving. No siestas! The Guardia Nacional has electronic triangulating equipment. They'll pinpoint Los Teques. We can't risk losing our munitions factory for a transmitter."

"Yes sir."

Filho shut the door and turned back. The Spaniard Picasso and Liu Keh-yu had not said a word; they watched him as silently as the heroic picture of Lenin on the wall. Only the bearded portrait of Castro beamed broadly in the room.

"Well, Filho?" the Spaniard asked. "You don't have much time to decide."

"There's time," Filho said irritably. "I don't want to commit our main force before tonight. There's time."

"I agree with Picasso," Liu said. His code name, Pao-Yu, had been borrowed from the classic Dream of the Red Chamber as both an irony and an Oriental subtlety-within-a-subtlety, because in the book Pao-Yu was a Taoist saint. Liu Keh-yu was not, as he had discovered during the Heroic War in Korea. In another dynasty he might have been a jade sculptor or a poetic Confucian official. Today he was like many intellectual men, totally preoccupied with the most intoxicating research questions: Who has how much power? On the three-dimensional international chessboard, could operational systems analysis and multi-vector game theory predict the shift in power balance from Soviet Asia to Chinese Asia? When human masses are energized toward far-off goals, do the thermodynamic laws about mass and energy still work?

Of the four Peking intelligence agencies, Liu Keh-yu was a member of two: the Teh Wu operations branch of the Hai Wai Tiao Cha Pu overseas espionage division, and the much more powerful Kungh Siung Hutung apparat whose authority was feared because it checked internally on the Party's own officials. During the Korean War he had been lifted out of the English Language department of the Anti-Japanese University in Yenan and commissioned in the Public Security Forces; but later, during the Hundred Flowers period of open criticism, he sensed that speaking English had become a badge of two frequently confessed Party sins, professionalism and bourgeois tendencies. He had joined the hard-line purge group and had admitted that his father and brothers, although not counterrevolutionary, were foreign-speaking bad elements. When they disappeared into a Ningsia prison camp for patriotic labor and rehabilitation, Liu Keh-yu's application for the overseas espionage division was approved.

After several successful tours of duty in Africa, Liu was stationed in Mexico City. Now he traveled as a Latin-American correspondent on the staff of Hsin Hua, the Chinese news agency. His Spanish, like his Russian, English and French, had only a tongue-tip accent on the sibilants, the disarming sound of a child with a slight speech impediment.

"There's time," Filho repeated. "The Caracas police will not invade the

University. The special police on the University payroll would block them."

Picasso bent forward to speak, but, when Liu Keh-yu glanced without expression at him, he immediately slumped back in his chair to let the Chinese say quietly to Filho, "But what if the Caracas police ask the *cazadores* to blast their way in here?"

"They won't. They wouldn't dare. All over Latin America millions of people—and they include every class, including the oligarchy—they would rather see an earthquake than to give up the universities' privilege of asylum and refuge. Their forefathers died generation after generation to win the sanctuary of universities from the Spanish."

"But what if the Caracas police do? There's always a first time for everything."

"He's right, Filho," the Spaniard said. "Last year Franco sent police into the University of Madrid for the first time."

Filho shook his head. "It can't happen here. Under Franco yes, but definitely impossible here under a democratic regime. Even during the dictatorship of Contreras and Angarita, even Jiménez, nobody—not even the Patriotic Military Union—dared to enter the sanctum sanctorum of the University."

"But what if they do?" Liu asked softly. "Is not the essence of our revolutionary tactics to make the impossible become possible? Have you even considered the possibility that the Federals may ignore the impossible and enter the University this afternoon?"

"Of course I have. I know you're supposed to be a Latin American expert, Liu, but you can't know every detail. Forty years ago, when the people were so weak they called Gómez the Well-Deserving, the Restorer, the Hero of Peace and Work—that was the last time a dictator, an illiterate man with complete power, that was the last time anyone dared to attack the University. In 1928, Gómez was the last to break a student strike by arresting the students and shipping them off to hard labor and slow death."

Picasso's eyes slid to Liu, as if for permission to speak. Then he said, "Is that your memory, or is that a fact?"

Filho made two fists and, holding them up at his belt line, bumped them together as he controlled his voice. "Don't peck at me, *viejo.* You want facts? My oldest brother is buried with maybe a half-dozen other students in some jungle road ditch. They never told our family where."

Liu Keh-yu half shut his eyes and lowered his chin toward his chest. No one spoke during his immobile contemplation. He was thinking that a Westerner like Filho sounded as if 1928 was long ago, instead of only yesterday. What can they know of time, he thought. We invented astronomically accurate clocks a thousand years ago when they still wore the stinking skins of animals. When their brutish tribal chiefs pushed down any coarse wench, our polished emperors moved night by night, in an ascending ceremonious order of concubines and outer-palace wives until finally, precisely on the night of the full moon, to the dignified bed of the queen consort. We have four thousand years of civilization, and they are a passing barbaric accident of history.

In the next room the sound of military music stopped and a radio announcement began. A moment later Nicolás rapped on the door and opened it excitedly. "A bulletin! All air flights have been grounded! Commercial and private planes. Cargo. Everything." He grinned. "Maiquetía Airport is ceiling zero-zero."

Liu Keh-yu nodded benignly. Nicolás stopped grinning and closed the door.

"You see?" Filho said. "Closed down more completely than if we had dynamited the control tower." He swung to the Spaniard. "Which is what you wanted yesterday, no?" He paused, and when the Spaniard said nothing, Filho repeated, "Yesterday you wanted to blow up the control tower, didn't you?"

"I was wrong," the old Spaniard said. "I salute you."

"Fear," Filho said. "Better than dynamite. If you use fear precisely it's better than bombs."

Liu slid his fingers together, then apart. "But fear is not always enough, Filho. You like to look at history? You mentioned 1928. In 1927, Chiang Kai-shek wiped out our Party cadres in Shanghai and Hankow. He created your instrument of fear. Chiang Kai-shek built an army of a million men and drowned us in firepower in five campaigns. More fear, but still not terror. Our Long March was the longest retreat in history. A handful fighting a rearguard action all the way to Yenan. Terror might have destroyed our cadres, but fear only strengthened them. With small injections of fear, like inoculating children, society develops an immunity."

"Are you saying that terror," Filho demanded, "should be used like an overwhelming infection?" He had a fencer's stance now, ready to thrust and parry.

"Yes. Fear is a little inflammation here and there, like boils. Terror is a massive infection all through the body like bubonic plague."

"Ah." Filho aimed his riposte. "That destroys your argument. Epidemics backfire. Epidemics kill the people who begin them."

"Not when used with skill."

Filho shook his head. "No. Massive terror is too much like using gas warfare. The wind shifts and your own men get caught by your own weapon. Small local fears is a better tactic."

"History contradicts you, Filho." Liu Keh-yu spoke calmly, as if to a War College seminar. "Terror consolidated the French Revolution in Europe. In China, after the Long March to Yenan, the fear of some members of the Politburo made them say: Go slow. Take a soft line. But Mao told them it is impossible to win a revolution by going softly, gradually, carefully, considerately, respectfully, politely, pleasantly and modestly. The hard line won."

"The Party has dropped terror as an instrument in the Soviet Union."

Liu tapped his forehead. "Think. Think what a fatal mistake that is! You don't believe me, Filho? Look at their cancer symptoms. Look at the Soviet arts. You agree that the arts of a country are the unspoken dreams of the people?"

"More or less. Even when they lie, artists tell the truth."

"How the Russians drool over their ballet companies, the nineteenth-century hothouses designed to breed graceful girl toys for decadent aristocrats. Their paintings? Postcard tractors. Or icons of Lenin as a god, not a human genius. Their poetry? Corrupt Western jabber through a mouthful of borscht and hot potatoes. Their amusements? Playing golf at the Club Diplomatique in Bucharest."

"But China is a member of the same golf club."

"We need the communication channel to Westerners, but the new homo Sovieticus *enjoys* the game. They have forgotten the passion of their own revolutionary history. Why do you shake your head, Filho? During their revolution Antonov took your position. He chose fear. The mine owners in the Ukraine were capitalistic savages, so he put them into prison to frighten them. This only unified them." Liu nodded at the eagle-eyed godhead portrait of Lenin on the wall. "Lenin understood terror. He understood it from his boyhood, when the Czar executed his brother Alexander. His intelligence was to grasp that history's leftovers make tomorrow's meals. He remembered the mistake of the French Commune. When they rose up they humanely arrested only four hundred of the bourgeoisie and aristocracy. When counterrevolution crushed these humane Communards, the gendarmes and army took all those humane men in batches of six until they had executed twenty thousand. Lenin remembered that this reactionary terror succeeded. Why else do you think he took on top of all his other jobs the post of Commissar of the Cheka? With the secret police he controlled terror. He could avoid Antonov's mistake. Lenin understood everything"—Liu pointed his fist and outstretched index finger at Filho, like a pistol—"and he knew the difference between terror and fear is the difference between a bonfire and a matchstick."

"We've gone beyond fear," Filho said. He was beginning to sound defensive. "The most precise weapon is assassination. Maximum effect at minimum cost. You have to admit the attempt to assassinate the President was the correct tactical choice."

"But the remote radio control of your bomb malfunctioned," Liu said. "He lived."

"Agh," the Spaniard said. "My apparatus functioned. The failure was a human one. Filho's man pressed the control switch two seconds late."

"The Hegelian thesis," Liu said as he slid his fingers into a locked position, then separated them, "is that law and morality are indispensable requisites to freedom. Society and the State are the conditions in which freedom is realized."

"Who the hell is talking about freedom?" Filho said. "What we want for our peasants and workers is not some petty bourgeois freedom they can't eat, but the liberty to live."

For the first time, Liu let a little smile touch his face as if he had knotted upward each end of the thin string of his mouth. "Exactly. Liberty, not freedom. Your fear tactics have no muscle, Filho. They extend from a milky liberalism. The tactics for liberty are more modern."

Filho stared at him. Liu's fingers stopped their sliding, locking and unlocking. "Terror," he said.

"This is no time to play games—" Filho began to say.

"Of course," Liu said. "Stay in the game, only change the rules. I am quoting you, Filho."

"But we've caused terror—"

"Only in the diluted European sense, Filho. For real terror, you must study our tactics in Africa and Asia. Look at the work of Liao Cheng-chi since he became First Secretary of our Overseas Operations Department. He established the Afro-Asian Solidarity Committee, our Cuba in Africa, and terrorized the Europeans by a total absence of pity."

"Please," Filho said angrily. "Running a handful of back-alley agents out of some Chinese embassy in Cairo or Conakry is a thousand times easier than my mission here."

"Fear is gradualism," Liu said. "Fear is Zhukov telling us in Moscow that we are dogmatists and sectarian. That we must accept bourgeois nationalism as a progressive step." His voice rose. "We reject this Moscow gradualism, just as we reject being surrounded by white power enclaves from Kazakhstan to Vietnam. When Mao wrote that war is the highest form of struggle, he meant wars fought with blood, to win. Nothing gradual. Fear only temporizes, as we learned in Vietnam against the French. Fear delays. Terror wins."

"Comrade," Filho said carefully, "I object to your taking an academic critical line at a time like this—"

Liu spread his hands, "But you yourself said that everything goes on schedule. There is no hurry to leave, you yourself said." He raised a finger. "Only one thing stands in the way of the tactical use of terror—your white-skinned European mentality. You are still your aristocratic grand-father, like the Australian aborigines who believe time is only now and they are their own ancestors."

Filho shook his head. "No," he said, "you don't impress me with double-talk. In Peking, in Cairo, in Conakry, you can impress your embassy comrades. You can set up solidarity movements, student friendship ex-changes, women's cultural conferences and infiltrate the trade unions and professional guilds. Basically, you're a night worker, a corkscrew brain-washer. You think I haven't considered ten times before now every-thing you've said? This is different. I'm a field commander in the middle of battle, and I'm winning."

"The battle, yes. But not the war, Filho."

"Don't be so pessimistic. You remember when Ho sat there in Hanoi during the worst of the bombing, sipping at his glass of beer, stroking his white beard, and saying that a revolutionary who is not optimistic is not a revolutionary?" Filho tapped himself on the chest. "I am more than optimistic. You are the pessimist."

"Of course I am, Filho. When I see even your labor unions dancing cheek to cheek with the American AFL-CIO?"

"Not so fast. Just the opposite! The Confederation of Christian Trade Unions has demanded immediate social revolution, using force if neces-sary."

"Latin rhetoric. I'm still pessimistic."

"You admit it?" Filho swiveled to the Spaniard. "You heard him. He admits he is a pessimist."

"He can afford it," the Spaniard said cautiously.

"You neglected to make a solid agitprop foundation for a general strike, Filho—"

"That's a later weapon—"

"No. No, Filho. Don't let your timing be two seconds off again. You need a general strike to choke this government to its knees, and you need public examples of terror to kill it."

Filho spread his hands apart and chopped small slices in the air as he made each point. "Let's be specific, not philosophical. We've gunned down cops in the middle of town. Ten of our boys boarded the train to Maracaibo as passengers and then shot every Guardia Nacional in every railroad car. When we captured the sentries on the General Urdaneta Bridge we tied them with detonating cord around our dynamite charges."

"That was technical necessity, not planning," the Spaniard said. "We had too little explosive, even for a simple demolition of one span. We had to tamp down the small amount of dynamite we had with the sentries' bodies to keep the force of the blast going in on the bridge, instead of losing it out into the air. Technically, sandbags would have been better."

Liu Keh-yu shook his head. "A pinprick demonstration. Too small. Terror as a tactical element has to be big. Everywhere. Omnipotent. The people must see their own rich parasite class suffer alongside the foreign imperialists. Elegant restaurants, tennis clubs, hotel lobbies, expensive crowded places. You have to spread a big net, very big, not a few little fishhooks here and there."

The door to the room was thrown open. Nicolás stood there, shouting, "Listen! Listen!" Luis came up behind him spooling out an electrical extension cord, holding a portable radio so they could hear the announcement:

". . . I have just signed an order which declares illegal the PCV, the Venezuelan Communist Party, and the FALN, the Movement of the Revolutionary Right. I have signed an order to suspend constitutional immunity from arrest of the twenty-three congressmen of these parties. There is evidence these men include the secret high command of underground saboteurs of our country. Units of our regular and newly mobilized reserve forces are taking up strategic positions as I speak. All are loyal to your elected government—"

Nicolás gestured to Filho, his eyes shining with admiration, "At last! They're running dogs. We're winning!"

"—There is no coup," the President's voice continued. "No putsch. No military junta. The underground will be crushed. These martial laws are strong but temporary measures for thirty days only. Circumstances may force us to break tradition and to penetrate the University. Law and order must be restored. Law and order will remain. Long live the Republic!"

The radio began to play the national anthem. The room was silent. Luis lowered the volume and took the radio back to his desk in the other room.

Filho motioned for Luis to close the door, then he leaned against it as if shouldering a great weight.

"He believes he can hold out," the Spaniard said. "You can tell in his voice." He stood up. "Well, Congressman, your immunity is shot. Your sanctuary shot. If they catch you, you'll be shot."

Liu also stood up. He held his arms with military stiffness to his sides, almost at attention. "So," he said to Filho, "you agree you cannot cure cancer gradually with aspirin? Only immediate surgery will cut it out." When Filho did not answer, Liu added, "So there arises the immediate necessity for a general strike." Filho busied himself with fishing out his blue pack of Sputniks. Before he could tap a cigarette from it, Liu held out his own flat tin of Chinese cigarettes. "Real tobacco," he said. "Not Russian ersatz."

Filho threw the Sputnik down and took Liu's cigarette. Liu offered one courteously to the Spaniard, as if passing a ceremonial peace pipe among hostile chieftains, then lighted one himself. As their smoke mingled, Liu repeated, "A general strike."

Filho looked at him directly. As their eyes clashed, Filho dropped his. He made an effort to speak. "Yes," he said. "They'll learn a lesson. We can fight fire with fire."

14 THE YOUNG DRIVER of the Mercedes nodded at the terra cotta bulk of Hotel Laputa as they climbed the hill toward it. "Filho said you will be more safe here. Just remember always to act like rich turistas. When you claim your baggage, make a big fuss."

Mayoso frowned as he looked at the hotel. Isolation up on the mountain made it safer, maybe, no better than maybe, but also more dangerous because it was the end of the road. If the Digepol locates us, there is no place to go from here. No exit.

The Hotel Laputa was what travel folders called *le dernier cri*, not unlike the flying island of the same name in *Gulliver's Travels*. It had a Spanish Colonial weddingcake façade, all majolica, red tile, arcaded mosaic walls bearing Spanish escutcheons, and a colonnaded lobby remodeled into a glasswalled honeycomb. Now the hive was a hornet's nest of travelers, luggage, talk, confusion. Well-dressed men and women buzzed in knots, spilling out of the lobby, swarming from the terrace to the patio, to the lounge, clustering under the candy-striped awning of the poolside bar.

In the lobby, bellhops and porters were in a frenzy, redfaced and sweating, waving their arms and shrugging helplessly as dozens of stranded air passengers droned around them with demands, bribes, threats. The facts of life in the jet age world had suddenly become fantasy. Women hovered everywhere, sliding their bracelets back and forth nervously, chattering *plática* like castanets, sprawling with exhausted nylon annoyance on the foam-rubber chairs. Some of the younger ones enjoyed the disorder and spontaneity, as if Caracas had turned into a drama *de tramoya*. Everyone knew a man with money could buy his way into or out of anything.

It was only a matter of putting up with annoyances for a day or two. Appointments at the beauty salon would become crowded.

Cristina was almost knocked off her feet. "Hold on to my coat," Mayoso said. He shouldered ahead of her, big but not pushing, always courteous, inching his way forward.

The room clerks and assistant managers held the bridgehead by emptily writing down names, repeating over and over, "We are full up, señor. If you and the señora would be willing to take another hotel in town—ah, well then, señor, perhaps if you leave your name or your card—ah, well then, señor, our bar is a possible refreshment—sí, sí, señor, if any space should open—"

"This is impossible," Mayoso said to Cristina. "We'll take a taxi and go back into town."

She gaped up at him, astonished. "Go back? People are being shot down in the streets."

"We'll stay off the streets. Lie low, someplace out of the way." He spotted two soldiers with Sten guns at the terrace entrance. Blue uniforms, black boots, flame shoulder patches. Special bodyguards?

"But in a small place the manager notices you quicker and calls the police quicker. Filho said the Digepol has plainclothesmen everywhere." She shivered slightly. "When I was a little kid we lived in Haiti. You know Duvalier's *Tonton Macoute*? I have a great fear of secret police."

"We'll find a place in La Guaira near the airport. Foreign passports are very ordinary things around there."

"We can't," she said. "Our baggage was brought here. Remember what the student said?"

"I have my medical bag," Mayoso said. "I won't mind losing my other one."

"I will," she said simply. "Every stitch I own in the world is in my two valises."

He looked down at her face. The tiny upslope of her eyes above the chiseled planes of Indio cheekbones gave her face an impassive cast, heightened now by the framing circlet into which she had bound her long hair. With her fashionable clothes, her warm skin-scented trace of frangipani, her mask of self-containment, she had the poise of a sophisticated young woman. The phenomenal survivor strength of the female of the species, he thought. It was as if the chalk-faced sacrificial convent girl had never existed. "But you say every stitch so casually. Your home is in two valises?"

Her direct eyes came up quickly, but her face remained stoic. "What can I do? I have to stay here no matter what."

"We can sit here in the lobby all night. Watch the performance."

She scanned the lobby. "Standing room only."

"After these last few days, and this morning, how are you feeling?"

She moved her head in an unsure circle. "Upside down. Everything has changed so fast. I was dead. Now I'm alive."

"But upside down?"

"Yes. I liked Filho very much. Then I hated him. Now I am only a little afraid of him. And maybe I feel a little sad."

"We thought we were fooling him. And all the time he must have been planning to throw everybody around him overboard before the Digepol could arrest him."

"I heard him talk about his risks last week," she said. "He was saying that his term as a congressman, his immunity to arrest, it would end sooner or later. He said arrest would mean his trial in a military court." She shook her head slowly. "A brave man." When he did not answer she asked, "Don't you think so?"

"It means so much to you?"

"Yes." She touched his arm. "Please don't laugh at me. I thought about him, and about everything, all the time that student drove the car and trucks were going by and the President announced the arrests. If they arrest him they will use the old trick of shooting him and saying he was trying to escape."

She has already executed him in her mind, Mayoso thought. Soon she will raise a statue in honor of his memory. She has the fatalism of centuries; death is part of life, to be entered like a doorway. Death will free you from this life—who had said that? Who had had such a confidence in death?

"You are so quiet all of a sudden, Doctor."

"Well," he said, "in all this noise there's not much inspiration to talk about bravery."

"But the noise is like a wall around us. We are alone. You think you will hurt my feelings if you say Filho has no bravery?"

"No. I think I will hurt my own if I say he has. Bravery in front of a firing squad is not so difficult. Not easy, but not difficult when your Latin upbringing and the Spanish mystique have taught you how to behave. Everybody—even your killers know how they must behave. It is like our favorite drama, the bullfight, no? Each has memorized his part and the bravery is only in taking the first step. The first step is the difficult one. After that, from the first step out of your cell to the final halt before the firing squad it is like the law of gravity, without free will."

"You sound as if you really know."

"I do."

"You were a prison doctor?"

"No. A prison prisoner. At Boniato. There was one week when I died each day. You didn't know I was immortal, did you?"

"Each day?"

"Each morning, before dawn, they came. You try to stand up as they say, 'Valor, hombre. Empty your bladder here, *hijo.*' "

"Oh no—"

"Sí, sí. To soil yourself later, at such a time, destroys a man's dignity, no? You couldn't walk very well because of certain injuries, so they helped you. Especially to take the first step. They tied your hands behind your back and threw you into a jeep and drove you to the Campo de Tiro firing range. There was an open trench there, full of bodies. They cut the ropes off your wrists and offer you a blindfold. No. You've been blind so long—why wear a blindfold now? You face a firing squad of militiamen. The priest rings a little Sanctus bell and says a few words—*Te igitur clementissime Pater*—while the squad lines up. He is young, once a country boy like the militiamen, scared and sweaty and being courageous because his faith holds him together. 'Pax *tecum*, my son,' he says. 'Death will free you from this life.' Because you refuse the blindfold, the squad leader shows his boys he's a good guy by giving you one cigarette to smoke. He lights it for you, being muy Español, and explains apologetically your sentence includes the dishonor of not being allowed to face the firing squad.

"In the distance, where the line of trees begins, you see barefooted farm boys straddling the lower branches to watch your execution. A long black car pulls up under the trees and two men in uniform and a lady wearing a yellow dress step out to see better. The human comedy is them, not you, because you know you are alive, you feel the morning-mouth cigarette taste. One of the militiamen is gulping water or coffee from his canteen, the light is lifting so there is a sound of birds. How can you be dead? Read Jeremiah, you tell the priest. He shakes his head, almost asleep on his feet. He's trying to hold the ragged edges of his sanity together like a broken dish. He's been rowing his passengers to the grave back and forth across this dead river since after midnight, when the morning executions begin."

"Oh, Doctor Mayoso—I mean—how can you stand here—I mean don't you think you should stop?" Cristina's voice broke. "Your hands are shaking."

Mayoso pushed his fists into his pockets. "Jeremiah," he said, talking to himself now because he had never said all this to himself before and now that he had begun, if he did not say it now, he might never get it out. "The priest seems at the end of his rope, so you tell him the words from Jeremiah as sympathetically as you can. The way you protect a child from a nightmare. *My grief is beyond my healing, my heart is sick within me, . . . Summer is ended, and we are not saved. . . . Is there no balm in Gilead; is there no physician there?*

"The young country priest stares at you and for the first time his hold on himself breaks. He weeps. You finish your cigarette with one of those long drags that make you dizzy and you cough, which somehow makes one of the men in the firing squad cough too. The soldier bends over, coughing, breaking the smooth military tempo of impersonal killing—coughing, you see?—and the sergeant becomes sore as hell. He needs to wipe out that cough. That pinhole leak of human feeling. If that pinhole opens up, human horror will gush out and drench the revolution. He throws the blindfold down on the ground. You have caused a crack in military discipline, conduct unbecoming et cetera, so your crime has a punishment. He orders you to face the squad and shout the commands for your own execution. Your voice tries to come from somebody else. Nothing is real. You cannot even whisper. Sergeant Fulgencio slaps you. 'Say *aim!*' he commands. How can you speak? '*Aim!*' he shouts at you. '*Say* it, you goddam coward.' He slams you in the face. '*Say it!*' You can see and hear and you can taste blood in your mouth, you know you're alive, immortal, it's all so clear, there you are, all of you, so you raise yourself as much as you can and say: *Aim.* You feel a great dignity. Your father said I kiss you goodbye my son, and your voice chokes on *Fire.* And then, silence."

She was staring at him as if they were alone, not in a swarming lobby. In a low voice she said, "And the squad fired—over your head?"

"Never. They never fired. One time Sergeant Fulgencio was away. That one morning a young corporal was in charge of the squad. First he was very tough. 'A noble name like Martí is no protection,' he said. Then he vomited."

"And they did that to you each day for a week?"

"Not day. Just about dawn. There is a difference. Once they made an exception. They held up the execution of Despaigne until the light of day for the convenience of the television cameramen."

"You think about this all the time?"

"Almost never. But the burning and killing last night, and the student, our driver, so intelligent, so angry, so foolish. And you talking of Filho trying to escape. Executions. Bravery. To kill, for what? Brave, for what? It was like hearing music you remember, but you don't recall the words. The words of religious fanatics—Communism's a religion, you know—the words always become mystic ritual to the insiders. Say 'worker' to an ordinary person—it's a word. Say 'worker' to a Communist and a whole brain lights up. Say 'revisionist' or 'personality cult' and the air crackles with tension."

"Oh," she said, "how much grief I've seen from words."

"For a physician, no grief should be beyond healing. Medicine always assumes a purpose. Every effect has its cause. Dying is so important, there should be a reason."

"I never thought of it that way."

"It is worth thinking about. The century grows darker, no? We need to invent a new kind of bravery."

"Is that possible?"

He smiled in pain. "No, probably not. But I think we must always believe it is possible." Cristina stared at his distorted smile and felt an unexpected piercing heaviness inside her. A stiletto of understanding as she realized what a mask of anguish he wore. He suffers, she thought with amazement. This big strong tower of a man *suffers* like the small and the weak. What honor! In the jungle, a lion who lies down with the lamb. His strength is his weakness.

"I feel I've known you a long time," she said very simply.

His unguarded face changed. The latent knotted lines around his eyes and mouth eased. "In times like this—" he began to say just as a tow-headed American, almost as tall as he was, came up to thump him on the shoulder. "Mayoso! Of all the pleasant surprises!"

Mayoso was startled into silence, then amazed. "Witt! *Mira! Aie Dios mío!* Witt Sommers! *Qué milagro!*"

"Caracas! Now who on earth would dream Mayoso Martí would be in Caracas!"

"That's easy. A Caribbean fish like me swims everyplace. But you, you gringo! The last time I saw you was in Havana!"

"By God, a hundred years ago, wasn't it? How's your friend, the Comandante What's-his-name? That smooth operator."

"And Betsy," Mayoso said, ignoring the question about Filho. "This beautiful lady with you is Betsy!"

"Mayoso el Magnífico," Betsy said. "It's been a long long time. How *are* you?"

Mayoso opened his arms widely to fold her into a bear hug. "Betsy, Betsy, Betsy. You and Witt must live charmed lives." He held her at arm's length. "You look more beautiful than the day you were married."

She measured him instantly, her eyes lighting up with the momentary all-seeing blaze of flashbulbs. "You look different—"

"My hair—"

"Maybe that's it." She swiveled to Witt. "But he still looks like Moses, doesn't he?"

"Betts," Witt said, "this is hardly the Promised Land."

"Betsy," Mayoso said, "that slight touch of Irish brogue you had—I don't hear it now. Where are those green Tara harpstrings?"

"Oh, it comes and it goes."

"Sure," Witt said with a vaudeville Irish accent, "the ould sod still grows full green when the whiskey's passed around—"

"Now, Witt—you know I don't drink anymore—"

"You don't drink any less."

Betsy rolled her eyes upward. "Heaven protect me from my friends and Protestant infidels! Today I'm a back-seat driver, so I'm not drinking." Then, as they all laughed, she changed the subject by stepping back to look past Mayoso at Cristina.

Mayoso turned. "Cristina," he said, "let me introduce some very dear longtime friends. Mrs. Betsy Sommers and Mr. DeWitt Sommers. This is—"

DeWitt had already begun to say politely, "Señora Mayoso Martí."

"No," Cristina said with considerable formality. "Señorita Cristina María de la Concepción Bretand Pagán."

"What a nice name," Betsy said. "It scans like poetry."

Cristina shrugged. "Pagán is like Smith in your country. You know something? I feel I know you, you look familiar. Did I see your picture in a magazine?"

Witt said, "Her picture gets around. The FBI and Dior have her on their list of the ten most-wanted best-dressed women. It's the only police photo they print in color."

When Betsy saw the look on Cristina's face she touched the girl's arm briefly. "Don't let my husband's sense of humor bother you, señorita."

Cristina began a slow tentative smile. "A joke, no? A compliment, I think, because you have the black hair and the green eyes?" To Mayoso she said in Spanish, "Yanqui humor. It's hard to understand sometimes. This always joking."

"What's news of home?" Mayoso asked Witt. Before Witt could answer, Mayoso clapped an open hand against one side of his chest. "The letter! The letter to New Haven! I never mailed the letter!" He pulled the airmail envelope out of his inner pocket and tapped himself on the forehead with it. "What's happening to my brains? I wrote to David in the airplane and forgot to mail it."

"David's fine," Betsy said. "I saw him at the hospital just the other day. He's busy, busy, busy."

"All the Sommers," Mayoso said. "The whole Sommers family has always been busy, busy, busy. Your father is well, Witt?"

"Sassy as a kid. But as absentminded as you. He missed you at the annual meeting of all his former chief residents."

"I was sorry to miss seeing him," Mayoso said. "I was busy, busy, busy."

Betsy glanced lightly at Cristina, then back to Mayoso. "Lucky you."

"I saw Mother in Washington," Witt said. "A meeting with Santos Roque at Blair House. She sounded awfully anxious to have you there."

"I got her letter," Mayoso said. "Very impressive, her title under the seal of the United Nations. I'm certain she will be the first woman President of the United States."

"Friends, Romans, countrymen," Betsy said. "Do we have to say all these nice things standing up? Since we're all staying here why don't you come up to our place for a dollop of a drink?"

"We're not actually staying here," Mayoso said. "We were just waiting for the luggage to be delivered." He looked around the lobby. Outside, an airline limousine was just discharging another load of passengers. "As you see," he said.

Betsy put her hand on his elbow. "In this mob," she said, "you can't subject this lovely child to the lobby ladies' room." She tilted her head slightly toward Cristina. "I wish you'd say yes, my dear."

"You are very kind," Cristina said. "But you are on a holiday—"

"Not at all," Witt interrupted. "One of the places the FALN burned down was our warehouse here. We scrambled into our plane and flew here, pronto."

"Oh?" Mayoso said, then added slowly, "You came here in your own airplane?"

"Not mine," Witt said. "It belongs to the company."

"And you have space here at this hotel?"

Betsy laughed. "Space? It's a Grand Central! Westward Ho House!"

"I could see what was happening here," Witt explained, "so I phoned Jorge Fiona at his home in Mexico City. He and I belong to the same mosquito-swatting jungle-juice fishing club, the Club de Pesca on the Sarapiqua—you've been there, haven't you?—and he's executive vice president of this hotel company—"

"And now," Betsy said, "*voilà!* We have the whole presidential suite on the top floor." She swung to Witt. "I've got a marvelous idea. Didn't Jorge say on the phone we had so many bathrooms and bedrooms he might fly down for a big party? Why can't Cristina and Mayoso find room at the inn with us?"

"You're right." Witt shook Mayoso's arm. "Don't look like that. Cheer up. She's absolutely delightfully positively right."

"Witt, you are very kind, amigo, but you can hardly be serious."

"Matter of fact, I am. The only time you'll find me more serious will be tomorrow, when I get the bill."

"Witt," Mayoso said carefully. "While we're talking about serious things.

Cristina and I have a serious need to leave this country, but the airports are closed to commercial flights. Could you also provide a serious plane ride back to San Juan for Cristina and me?"

"Why not?" Witt said casually. He looked from Mayoso to Cristina. "What's the matter?" he asked. "You both look flabbergasted."

"We are grateful to accept your extraordinary hospitality, Witt."

Witt saw Betsy frowning a little, puzzled, and shook his head slightly to indicate she should not ask questions.

"Please." Cristina was unbelieving. Quickly, in Spanish, she asked Mayoso, "We are staying in the presidential suite? And flying in a private plane back to San Juan? How can that be?"

"It can be," Mayoso said in English.

"Marvelous!" Betsy said. "Now we can have a party."

Mayoso's voice became more brisk. "Cristina, you and I will not leave the lobby together. You will please go upstairs with my friends and I will take my time here to mail this letter to David Sommers and collect our luggage." He bent toward her. "You see? I told you everything would be all right."

"I knew," she said, "that if I prayed with a full heart—"

"That's what did it," he said, and suddenly tilted his lion's head backward and laughed out loud.

Mayoso watched Betsy and Witt and Cristina thread their way through the crowded lobby to the elevators. He wanted to see them get on an empty elevator, an elevator with no one else, so that he could reassure himself that the Venezuelan Digepol plainclothesmen were not following Cristina. When a half-dozen people got on the elevator he felt annoyed with himself because he had not asked Witt to take the simple precaution of getting off halfway up to change to another elevator.

And even if Digepol should arrest Cristina, he asked himself, how bad could that be?

Very bad, he told himself.

How bad is very bad?

Well, very bad was to be held incommunicado under temporary martial law. To be questioned. The lights, the chair, the seesaw of anger and boredom, the apparatus of hunter feeling victimized by his prey. A girl like Cristina, as simple as rain from heaven, would talk right here at the hotel if she was questioned skillfully. If unskillfully, a girl like this one is capable of persuading herself to walk off a balcony because to die is simply to walk through a doorway. She is one of the millions who believe their greeting: *Que estés con Dios, siempre.* His heavenly eye is on the sparrow, they learn that as tots; we are all only birds of passage.

And what if Filho's people learn of this and decide to liquidate the possibility she should talk? In all this hotel confusion, any one of Filho's young gunmen could slip in and out. *Just pretend you're a rich turista*, the student in the Mercedes had said.

And you, my friend, he thought. If Digepol asked you a few questions, just how, exactly, would you explain yourself? A dirty abortionist, working for exorbitant fees? Boyhood friend of a terrorist commander? Explain the memory of the drowning struggle underwater at the diamond *bomba* on the Caroní River? Explain about the man who fought beside you in the Sierra Maestra against Batista? The man who carried you like a broken-boned child out of a prison punishment cell into an ambulance and out to an airfield? The man who sat opposite you in a jerry bar on Grand Cayman Island with a fanatic's unquestioning belief that he would lead millions of peasants out of serfdom, and all the while death's pale shroud of contradiction, the fear of execution by a revolutionary tribunal, clamped upon his face?

Filho's voice: *Pity. The fatal mistake that destroyed even God.*

How pleasant, he thought, to be a fanatic, a true believer like Filho, a comrade of other true believers descended from furious utopians dazzled by great visions, as blind to pain or individual torture as the ancient Aztec priests. *Mierda.*

He was startled as a woman exclaimed beside him, "Doctor Mayoso!"

He froze, then with relief saw who she was. "Ah, Señora Valdez," he murmured politely.

"I recognized you!" she said. "I knew it was you, even from the other side of the lobby. You stick out in a crowd, you know. Didn't I tell you on the plane that it was better to stay at a hotel?"

"Yes," he said. "More privacy."

"If the terrorists drop a bomb here right now, goodbye hoi polloi." She lowered her voice. "What a laugh that is. A whole world of people who drink instant coffee is jampacked here. Sardine society. I've seen more people in this lobby, old friends, relatives, people I haven't seen in years —and you thought I was foolish when I said the airport might close down!"

"I was foolish. You were right."

Her eyes, heavy-lidded with mink false eyelashes, swept over his face suspiciously. She decided he was complimenting her and leaned toward him to whisper, "Have they given you a room? If not—"

"I have one, gracias."

"Seriously?"

"Very. The presidential suite."

"*El* Presidente?" She put her hand on his arm as if to steady herself while she leaned back, laughing. "Oh, oh. Everything about you is big. This big comic exaggeration you have—who would believe it?"

He held up the airmail letter to David Sommers, "If you'll excuse me, señora," he said very politely, "I am in search of a stamp."

She stared at the letter. "The envelope says Iberia. Isn't that the same letter you had on the airplane?"

"As a matter of fact it is."

"What do you do," she asked, "carry it as a prop?"

"If I tried to explain," he said, "you'd be uncharitable."

She glinted through the foliage of her lashes into his eyes. "I'm sure I wouldn't," she said, "but try me. If I could, I'd ask you to buy me a drink at the terrace bar, but I can't move from this spot."

"I thought you were with friends."

"Only in a manner of speaking. A planeload of priests on their way to a religious meeting in Bogotá was just dropped off here, and in the middle of them I find Father Gofredo! Can you imagine? Like a messenger from heaven! He vowed to meet me at this spot in ten minutes, and when he makes a vow, you can count on it." She smiled brilliantly at a woman who was pushing delicately past them while trying to follow on the heels of a man who was butting a path through the crowd. "Elena! Stuck here too!"

The woman raised one hand to her mouth and said in a giggling stage whisper, "Like all those jokes about being marooned on a desert island with a sailor, no?" She rolled her eyes toward the man she was following. "Maravilloso! I've got to run."

Just beyond her, Mayoso saw Father Gofredo Möttl working his way toward them. Above his stiff collar, his thin face looked tired and he was frowning. "Ah señora, señora. It's infuriating," Father Gofredo said loudly as he came toward her. "I always thought British West Indies Airways flew a precise efficient experienced airline. I was certain I could find two seats." He shrugged irritably. "But now they say they can promise us nothing. Nothing. Absolutely nothing. Not two seats. Not *one* seat. Nothing. They don't even know whether they are flying or not."

"So," she said, "we're marooned." She shrugged, then said, "Father Gofredo, do you have the acquaintance of Doctor Mayoso Martí?"

Father Gofredo's frown deepened. "Mayoso?"

"I've seen you on the television, Father, with much admiration," Mayoso said as he put out his hand.

Father Gofredo ignored it. He raised his head stiffly. His face had become gaunt, a cutting blade. "And I, Doctor," he said with tight-lipped formality, "have just the opposite feeling from what I have seen of your doings in San Juan."

"Oh?" Mayoso said carefully.

"Not admiration, Doctor. Horror."

"Father—" Señora Valdez said, then stopped.

"Maybe," Mayoso said, and waved his hand at the disordered lobby, "all this has made everything seem very, ah, abrasive to you."

"Nothing of the kind. I don't permit myself to make large judgments during small irritations. I never speak except after the most careful deliberations. I took the trouble to arrange a meeting between us at La Fortaleza, through Governor Santos Roque's office. You agreed to the appointment, but you did not even trouble yourself to come."

"Qué no!" Mayoso said. "Of course, you're right. I completely forgot."

"That kind of forgetting is not merely administrative rudeness, Doctor—"

"I must apologize, Father. Things crowd in on me and I forget."

"Vacations in Caracas do not just crowd in. They are planned in advance. How could you have accepted an appointment to discuss such vital matters—"

"You would have to understand how I live from day to day—"

"Doctor, how you live is your own business. But when it concerns my parishioners in matters of life and death—and life and death is no careless exaggeration, believe me!—then what you do becomes my concern."

Señora Valdez broke in. "Doctor Mayoso Martí's family were very good friends of my family in Havana—"

"Señora," Father Gofredo said, "I recognized the name. Who does not know of them?" He swung back to Mayoso. "In such a family you have all the greater burden—yes, and the greater privilege—to provide a model of decency and leadership."

"Are you talking about my patients who required la operación?"

"Required?" Father Gofredo's voice had dropped and then rose again. "*Required?*"

"Now just a minute, Father. Medical opinion—"

Father Gofredo threw up one hand. "Stop! Rationalizations are only respectable lies! How does a man of your background and breeding even *dare* to set himself against centuries of moral law? Have you no thought for your immortal soul and the eternities of Hell—"

"Believe me, Puerto Rico gets hot enough—"

"You are so crass as to joke? To make sport of the possibility of excommunication? You would be cut off, Doctor, not allowed to receive the sacraments, and ordered to attend Sunday Mass in the rear seats reserved for lepers and lunatics."

"The lunatic Hitler, the leper Mussolini—were they ever excommunicated? Father, think twice before you say crass to others."

"Your dear parents in Heaven—what can they think of a prodigal son who destroys women? The shock. The sorrow. To fall from grace—a grieving and a weeping for eternity." With effort he lowered his voice. "Your parents then, the holiness of motherhood. When the wounded heart of Mary looks down on your infidelity to your Church and your profession she must relive the agony of Gethsemane!"

"Do you know how threatening you sound?"

"Who will warn you if I do not? You should fall on your knees for cleansing prayer, then throw yourself into the maternal arms of Mary to beg forgiveness. No Satan can seduce you from our Holy Mother."

"Any man," Mayoso said very softly, trying to hold back his anger, "who can set up a court of Inquisition in a hotel lobby and make himself judge, jury, prosecutor—"

"Please! Please!" Señora Valdez held up to them both her tightly clasped hands. She had a cracked obsessive moment of wanting to blurt out that Mayoso had refused her la operación. "I beg you to stop this terrible talk."

"It can stop," Father Gofredo said firmly, "but only when this man stops his massacre of the innocents."

"That's a terrible accusation, Father."

"It's more terrible an act, señora. Don't try to defend him."

"I'm sorry you feel so strongly," Mayoso said, "but I will not tolerate such language. My hands are clean."

Father Gofredo snapped his head upward. "No. Your hands are bloody. You cannot claim you are criminal out of ignorance. And a Martí cannot claim the ordinary feelings of ordinary people. If you cannot be the good Catholic you must have been raised to be—but no, even the pagan Greek oath of Hippocrates which you took in medical school has been violated by you."

"Father, your cloth protects—"

"Nothing protects me but my faith! But you—nothing protects *you*. If divine wrath means nothing to you, then Caesar's anger will. You can feel Hell on earth as well as through eternity. If you will not render unto God then remember that even the civil laws of the state do not protect you. Medical societies can censure doctors. States can withdraw a doctor's license to practice. Hospitals can close their doors to you. You can be cast out like a leper."

"Ah," Mayoso said with great quietness, "I knew we would come finally to punishment and the laws of the state—"

"Only with great reluctance. Forgiveness is always possible. Legal actions need not be."

"What of the laws of slander?" Mayoso gestured toward Señora Valdez. "I have a witness."

Her mouth opened, but she could not speak.

"You cannot bring me to trial in an American civil court, Doctor. That's a special heinous offense, absolutely forbidden in our Church, punished by automatic excommunication."

"Padre," Mayoso said, "we're in different centuries."

"You are, Doctor. You're a temporary man. But I speak for the eternal."

"Not only is God displeased, Father, but you are, too?"

"Sacrilege and sarcasm are the refuge of the damned."

"Very un-Christian, Father." Mayoso bowed slightly to Señora Valdez. *"Encantado, señora."*

"I'm so sorry—"

Mayoso's face broke into a one-sided smile. "Father," he said, "I forgive you. Make a good act of contrition."

Father Gofredo was genuinely shocked. Señora Valdez lowered her lashes to shut out Mayoso leaving, shouldering his way. She had never seen two men, both of whom she respected, confront each other like these two. A slap, a knife, even a gun—these were understandable ways for a man to uphold his honor and dignity, but such a ferocity of intellect against intellect? A padre and a physician? Me, she thought with horror, a witness—a tremor rippled through her veins. I have one week of freedom out of the whole year and Caracas was supposed to be such a holiday. For a moment she saw herself in her hotel bed with Mayoso, his largeness filling her, the forbidden words of abandonment. She kept her eyes closed, feeling little warming shivers—and a new wave of self-pitying anger washed over her. Intellectual men, she thought furiously, more ready to fight for ideas than for a woman. A woman needs every minute of happiness she can steal from her daily world.

In the elevator, as they went upstairs, Father Gofredo was very pale. "I have no hatred in my heart for anyone," he said in a tight low voice, almost a whisper. "Mayoso can be saved only by love."

She eyed him with disdain across the few inches of space which carefully separated them, then as the elevator stopped to let them off at their floor, she said sarcastically, "Love?" What Mayoso needs, she thought, is a few nights with a woman who understands him. A woman or a whipping, the only two feelings men understand. She glanced guiltily at the priest to see if he had read her mind.

"Excuse me, padre," she blurted, "my head's splitting." She beat a headlong retreat toward her room.

Father Gofredo watched her soundless flight down the carpeted hallway, vaguely disappointed at losing someone with whom he could expand the spiritual worth of forgiving Mayoso. The Church has never failed to open her arms, never closed off a return to grace. He wanted to repair a damage he regretted, restore his own self-respect, perhaps hint at error, *vanitas*, admit he had been unsettled when confronted by Mayoso so unexpectedly. The acoustically hushed corridor lengthened before him, dim, spaced by deadpan slabs of doorways, a perspective of catacombs.

□ □ □

Betsy swung open the broad hotel door with a flourish. "Come in, come in, come in!" she said gaily. "My, you make a doorful! Is that *all* the luggage you and Cristina have? Through darkest Caracas, with only bikini and toothbrush?"

"Yes," Mayoso said, "this is all. And I had one hell of a time finding it, too." He set the luggage down. "What a madhouse downstairs."

She closed the door behind him. "I wondered what was taking so long."

"In the lobby, I ran into Ignatius Loyola and Lucrezia Borgia."

"Great! Why didn't you invite them up to our party? Come as you are. I'll be Mary Magdalene." She waved her hand at the telephone. "I'm on the phone with el Señor Capitán of Room Service right now. What do you prescribe for tropical travelitis, Doctor? Scotch? Bourbon? Cuba Libre? Gin-*con*-gin? Name your favorite truth serum. What do you prefer, amigo?"

"Right now I'm the walking wounded. All I can taste is blood."

"Doctors drink it straight, I know, like zombies. If you tell me what type I'll order a bottle for you from the blood bank." He watched her cross the enormous light-drenched living room with her quick whippet stride. She sank onto the couch with a graceful half turn, like a skillful actress, and picked up the phone. "Señor," she said, "the bar you set up is magnificent, but I need more ice."

She was so much like what he remembered long ago in Havana that the in-between years dissolved. Now, as then, he saw her too-alert responsiveness, her winsome tilted chin, vulnerable as a child's, the slender flicker of legs as skittish as a delicately-boned colt, the startling contradictions between her careful genteel propriety and the carefree leprechaun ready to run barefoot, capering blithely from glee to vulgarity and back again. Even her unusual voice was the same: the throaty glottal slur, the on-again off-again dabs and smidgens of Irish lilt from her Dublin childhood, the breathless hurrying to finish before you interrupted her, the smoky languor that hinted an invitation for your interruption anytime, anyplace.

When she had been his patient in Havana she had been so playful and *toujours gaie* through all the infertility studies that he had been exasperated. She should have become annoyed and tired of the endless tests and probings. No one in his experience had ever pitter-pattered so good-naturedly between basal body temperature records taken by rectal readings at waking time each morning and serial vaginal smears and endometrial biopsy and tubal insufflation and all the rest, pirouetting from one to the next as première danseuse, with him as a ballet partner. He was very conscious of dignity in those youthful days, a wearer of spotless white clinical coats, pressed and starched without a crease, and a believer that medicine was a science.

But, during an unexpected visit to her hospital room one evening, he found her weeping, shattered, alone amid the alien corn of Havana, his fertility clinic, the priapic stainless-steel intimacies of clinical penetrations, the glass pipette violations. He discovered how thin and brittle were her alternating masquerades of being either a simple Connemara colleen or a sleek big-city jet-set type. As he sat beside her in the hospital in Havana he had sensed how close to the surface ran her underground stream of tears.

To lie alone in a room—any room, but especially an aseptic hospital room—was her greatest terror. To be wanted, to talk and talk, was the reassurance she needed to inhale like air. To be, she had to be wanted, and being wanted by men was a response she had learned to diabolize with a single reckless gesture, a quick-turned Irishy phrase, a sideways demure look, a half-cocked eyebrow, a slow leaning back and crossing of finely shaped legs, and, most effective, a subtle pretense of esteem and unexpected touching flashes of candor. Being picturesque came easily to her; she practiced the fine points of what she called being attractive continually and seriously. Inevitably, from sixteen onward, she had been a fashion model at Marshall Field's in Chicago during the years before Witt married her, and everything about her showed the standardized public gloss: the higher-than-high heels which gave her quick tiptoeing swaying stride a pleasantly contradictory, delicately wanton strut; the standing posture with one knee slightly bent and hips turned obliquely for the slimmest angle, the shoulders squared bravely back, breasts high; the black helmet of perfect hair parted precisely in the center and used as artistically as a matador swung a cape. Her hair fell to her shoulders in a long easy wave, unusually black and mobile, swinging with a demoralizing grace as she walked, slipping forward to one side as she tilted her head, spinning outward gauzily and falling back as she glanced sideways one of her rapid, green-eyed, searching looks.

She desperately wanted to be a girl, not a woman. He guessed this by her hair, not her face. Her face was a woman's: flawless when she finished under the implacable lights above her mirror, warmly flushed beneath the brushed-on silkiness, a fine small nose modeled with just a delicate flare of nostrils. So, he remembered thinking, the face of an uncommonly pretty, wealthy woman, not a girl. Woman and girl, which was Betsy? Not until later did he realize there was no mystery. She had as many selves as a talented child performer with a trunkful of grown-up costumes.

After listening to her all that night in the Havana clinic, he could not chalk her off as the uncomplicated girl-toy figure she pretended she was, even to herself. Before her hospital stay ended, he recognized her catechismal sense of sin covered by a silken sensuality. He had had to force himself to think of her in clinical terms.

When he had palpated her abdomen and she had said, "Your hands are *warm*. Don't doctors' union rules call for *freezing* hands?" he had simply looked at the opposite wall and concentrated on the information he needed.

When she lay flat on her back, straddling the gynecological stirrups, knees parted and draped, her perineum lighted nakedly for anatomic clarity, her lotus sex was pinkly membranous as parted lips. An assisting nurse stood beside him as he inserted a smaller-size speculum. Betsy had startled him by asking, "Cobwebs?"

Both he and the nurse had stared dumbly at her—what kind of vulgar Norteamericano remark was this?—until she pointed straight up at where a spidery veil floated lightly from the ceiling. As he grunted and lowered his head to insert the slender tube for a Pap spread sample, she had laughed, mocking them very faintly, and said, "No cobwebs in *that* department!" You teasing Lorelei, he had thought with a spasm of irritation.

He had been late for his daily lunch date with his fiancée. Hurriedly, he dropped the Pap slides into the lab container, and yanked off his rubber gloves so rapidly that one tore. At lunch he hardly touched his food. When his fiancée spoke to him, he answered off-handedly, without looking at her, feeling an intangible and dishonorable deceit. His upbringing had not prepared him for this. It was confusing; who was to blame? Betsy, pretending to be artless, yet always attractive? He himself, camouflaging his ambivalent feelings with a young man's mock pompousness? He loved his fiancée. She was as dark-haired, as small-featured and pretty as Betsy, but as different as an intelligently ordered life differs from a bacchanalia.

Betsy became exaggeratedly casual and cooperative, and the longer she remained in the clinic at Havana, the more he felt there was a silent duel between them. If he accepted her choice of weapons, and reached toward her, she would dodge, and laugh throatily with surprise and contempt as he sprawled on his broken ethics. He had to reason out—disliking his theologic need to reason at all—that he was twice as much mountain for her to climb because he was off limits, fenced by professional bounds. He saw that whatever was forbidden fascinated her.

She had a way of cradling her chin, listening to him as if he were some bronze god, the university clinic a temple, she the humble adoring novi-tiate whose hair only happened to splash down one uncovered shoulder while she kept the green blades of her eyes resting lightly and unyielding on his. The television-commercial obviousness of the performance an-noyed him. She had been given beauty by the gods, a nimble knack to make and unmake men, and should never push herself as consumer goods.

He warned himself not to lose his head. Understand that her unspoken *I'm-selling-who's buying* was the frantic reaching-out of a girl who had the devil to pay and herself to punish for being childless. Science, the Sommers' god of power, was powerless to help her. Medical explanations that a chemical something in her vaginal fluid was lethal for her husband's sperm was a mystery to her. The out-of-reach invisibility of the chemical something was like a spell; cursed, fated. So reasoning did not reach her, and he sensed that she felt sentenced to be manhandled, to be wound up with a strange concealed key, to revolve in a doll's sterile carnal show. When he managed to think this way, he was able to remind himself that Witt was his friend, that his fiancée would be hurt—all the while uncom-fortable that the real reason he did not join her in bed was that such an *en passant* encounter would be as much a barbarism as molesting a child.

Once, as the struggle tightened, during her final physical examination before she was to be discharged from the hospital, he came close to for-getting his tortuous restraints and rationalizations, and simply taking her as she was.

Examining her breasts as she lay flat with her arms crooked above her head was simple and quick—she was as small as a young girl and the tissue spread easily over the unyielding chest wall—but when she sat up and leaned forward for the second part of the breast palpation he felt a subtle tremor run through her. Her nipples rose, delicate distensions so hungering that his medical automatism of a thousand such examinations vanished in-stantly. Betsy's mammary tissue, gone; instead she now lifted two up-swelling sensuous pyramids heaped with promises to come. Her legs slid beneath the waist-high clinical drape, rustling as her knees stirred slightly. She leaned back with a soft yielding sigh. He caught his breath, ready to ignore all his careful reasoning, forget all the years of training, codes, beliefs. The moment hung suspended. Then, just as she began to lift her hands to cover his, the nurse came briskly through the double-hinged swing door with two sterile cloth-wrapped basins.

He began to percuss the posterior bases of her lungs. "Deep breath in," he commanded tonelessly as the nurse put the basins on a metal stand.

"That's it, hold it. Breath out, please."

The nurse bustled off. His swift stud erection had become slack; the sea surge of abandonment which had swept over him washed away. The next tide swamped him with a useless anger: against himself, his clumsy hesitation when lifewarmth demanded yes or no; against the crack across the mirror of his professional self-respect; against the petrolatum-rubber-gloved-floorwax-smelling room which had deformed a moment's thee-and-me joining into a vulgar sophomoric fumble.

Betsy drew both her cloth-covered knees up and lowered her head to rest on them. She seemed curled and orphaned, small, alone. Into the sheet, muffled, she asked, "You angry?"

"No." He kept himself from touching her bent shoulders. "I'm only apologetic," he said stiffly. "Gynecologists are trained for years to know better."

She straightened quickly to face him. "It was my fault. It's me. You're not the answer, are you?"

"I don't like to admit it but I'm not."

"Well," she said, with an undertone of self-punishment, "it's too late for a nunnery and too soon for a whorehouse." Then, accusingly, "If you're so smart, what *is* the answer?"

"Other than everything we've already talked about, I don't know."

"Hell of a thing for a doctor to say. Just screwing around, that wouldn't work for me, would it?"

"Lots of people try it—"

"Does it work?"

"For some."

"And for the rest—it's only another rusty turn of the screw?"

"If you're going to talk hardware, Betsy, for you, casual screwing would be mostly nuts and bolts. For you, the real answer is love."

"That's no answer," Betsy had said there in Havana. "That's the question."

Betsy covered the hotel phone with her hand. "Sorry about taking so long, but if there's one thing I've learned from Marjorie Sommers, it's that gracious living takes beaucoup de persuasion." She pointed with the phone. "Your luggage goes thataway, luv. I think you'll find this better than camping out."

As Mayoso trudged out of the room with the luggage, he heard her slightly husky voice saying persuasively into the telephone, "And, señor, we will need some musicians. No, no, *not* physicians. *Musicians.* Four or five. . . . Oh, yes, expenses, of course. You'll earn my gratitude *and* a contribution from my husband to your favorite welfare fund. . . . Oh? The welfare of your wife and kids, sí? I don't care if you have to steal the músicos from the bar. . . . Sí, sí, the presidential suite on the top floor."

The bedroom he walked into was almost as large as the living room; one entire wall made of glass could be rolled aside to open on an outside balcony. The slanting afternoon sun, seen from this height, with only distant clouds and endless sky beyond the balcony rail, made the room appear lighter than air, buoyant. The hush of its carpeting and acoustical ceiling, the deep chairs, the raw-silk wall covering and watery gleam of long mirrors—all very different from the noisy jostling hotel lobby. The only sound was of a shower splashing vigorously in the bathroom. Cristina has much from Filho to scrub off, Mayoso thought as he set the luggage down at the foot of a king-size bed. I like her looks, her unpretending honesty, her uncomplicated warmheartedness, her complete lack of coy affectation. That she should get out of here without complications. That my jumpiness is only the shadow of a stick.

As he straightened he saw the man in the mirror on the opposite wall also straighten. He looked at himself as if he were a sea creature trapped in amber, brought up unexpectedly from the depths to be examined by sky light. Nothing in the glass pleased him. His big frame seemed hulking, crouched primitively, alert for attack. Under his whitecotton bramblebush eyebrows the eye sockets were shadowed, the defiant mane of hair tangled and untamed. Moses. Betsy just pictured me as him, downstairs. Aie! If so, only after forty years of wandering through the wilderness. God's angry man.

No. Father Gofredo is God's angry man. I am only a matter-of-fact man and that is more difficult. My bookish friend Dante wrote it very well: *In the middle of the journey of our life, I came to myself in a dark wood where the straight way was lost.*

Father Gofredo has faith; I have doubts, the straight way lost. Father Gofredo never questions his own strength, but I question mine all the time. Great currents run under his world while I live in a thatched bohío on an island, myself an island. No one can drink in the light of day unless he has been through the darkness of the many darknesses. So, I cannot let an ecclesiastical confrontation, an accidental ecclesiastical confrontation on a miniature stage crowded with players, all sound and fury, open a vein of doubt in me. He stoops to conquer, not to understand, arrogant as a medieval prince of the church, while I can only feel humility and understanding of what he will never know: that I am not the dark side of the moon, he the light, but actually we share the same earth and suffer for all the suffering. We are brothers in ways far deeper than his ritualistic conception.

Filho is more his enemy than I am, but, in his own way, Filho too wants to lift the stone of suffering from the backs of millions. Filho, too, has the princely arrogance, the absence of doubt, the sustaining membership of a

world community. Between them, they mark the century: entrance and
exit wounds.

He took his eyes from the dissecting lens of the naked glass, walked
soundlessly across the room and slid open the transparent wall which led
to the balcony. As he stepped out, he heard a sound and turned to see
Betsy standing thirty feet away on the long strip of balcony at the point
where it encircled the rounded corner of their penthouse suite. She was
leaning forward with both her elbows on the rail, smoking a cigarette with
an islamic calm. As he walked toward her she threw him one of her green
sideways glances and made a sweeping motion toward the sky, the leafy
perspective of diminishing hills which led to the city below them.

"Welcome to Cloud Nine," she said.

He followed her glance downward to the flat hotel play area, smooth as
the landing deck of an aircraft carrier, with a grassy prow jutting forward
under a rim of spaced flagpoles flying the colors of twenty-one countries.
The aquamarine water in the curved swimming pool was so clear that he
could read the name of the hotel, spelled in tile on its bottom. The putting
green on the lower slope was an empty velvety space: no one was bothering to practice golf today. Chaises longues and deck chairs had been set
out under tilted umbrellas and fringed-canvas blue-and-white canopies. A
group of guests milling around the bar end of the pool looked like a stagey
birthday party for grown-ups.

"My English," Mayoso said to Betsy, "is not quite up to Cloud Nine.
What is it?"

"Oh," she said, "just an expression. A bon mot. It means way out in
space. Shangri-la—out of touch."

He pointed down the length of the valley at the thin gauzy streamers
of smoke wavering upward above Caracas. "See that?" he asked. "We're
still close to earth. Maybe right on the doorstep." Dante, he thought, you
wrote better than you knew.

"You mean all that revolutionary running around? It can't be very bad
because Witt is down there right now. I'm sure he's arguing with somebody to make sure he can file a flight plan for our takeoff tomorrow."

Mayoso scowled. "Witt went into Caracas? But I saw him come upstairs with you and Cristina."

"He did. But you know Witt—extrasensory perception. I think he got
some sort of message from you that you'd be perfectly happy to vamos
out of here pronto."

"But I would never want him to go into the city today—"

"Witt always sounds casual. You know, one of those snap-the-finger
problem solvers—'the impossible takes a little longer.' This morning he
decided to rebuild his warehouse, fireproof this time, and this afternoon

he got right on *your* problem. He called our pilot and co-pilot at Maiquetía. When they told him the airport was no-kidding closed down he said he'd come right along and see about opening it up." She paused. "Why are you shaking that shaggy head?"

"I'm amazed," he said. "Every day something else amazes me."

"Sounds like eternal youth," Betsy said. "What else is on your amazement menu for today?"

"Well," he said. "The hors d'oeuvre. That's being alive after a night when I was not so sure. The soup"—he shrugged—"I can't explain now, but the trick is to get out of the soup." He tapped his forehead with his knuckles. "Knock on wood. The entrée is to be in this presidential suite with you and Witt. A Cloud Nine lady. A problem-solver man who does not doubt that his personal visit to a few military authorities will open the airport and the sky to him."

"And dessert," Betsy said, smiling widely with her bright red lips and perfect teeth, "that's my party tonight."

"Yes," he said. "For coffee, I will sing *Ojos Verdes*. I haven't sung in years, but tonight I think I will sing. And the brandy," he said and reached out and touched her at the top of her dark head, "that's you."

"What's *Ojos Verdes* mean?"

"Green Eyes."

"Coming from you," she said, "that calls for a drink."

"First," he said, "I have to tell you how good it is to see you again. I remember how you looked the day you were married. In that lovely big house the Sommers have in Southport—"

"Ho. What I'll never forget is that lovely big staircase. I tripped on my long lovely train and almost broke my long lovely neck."

"No problem," he said. "The Sommers are royalty. All the king's horses and all the king's men would have put you back together again."

"A few of the king's men had already tried that and decided it couldn't be done."

"What's your secret, Betsy? All brides are beautiful but how can you be twice as much so—how long is it?—thirteen years later?"

She shrugged prettily. "Thirteen's just a lucky number, I guess. Could an old friend ask you for a crumb? Drop the cheerful medical house-call tone, will you? Dishonesty doesn't become a big doorful of a man like you."

"I was just remembering that time we talked in Havana, Betsy—"

"What goddam babes lost in the woods we were."

"Later, the woods became mountains."

"What an aching time that was. You were keeping company with a revolution, and a nice formal fiancée, weren't you?"

"Yes."

"Somehow I don't remember you as a sinner, but as a tempted saint."

"Betsy, Betsy. I marvel at your acrobatics. You're the only one I know who can spin out a cobweb of words so that every nosedive turns into a trapeze."

"Every acrobat swings over a safety net. For me, it's words."

"You think so?"

"I don't think anymore. I try to go by feelings."

"Does it work?"

"Yes and no. In the elevator coming upstairs, I felt envious as hell of your girl, Cristina."

He chose to misunderstand her. "All Cristina's worldly goods fit into two valises, Betsy."

"But she's young. And I saw her there in the lobby with you standing beside her like some great tree casting shade."

"This particular tree was mostly casting doubts about where in the world to sleep tonight. And presto, there you were."

"Where am I? In the wrong bed."

"Betsy, I apologized in Havana. As you point out so delicately, I was a damn fool. I was logical when I should have been biological."

"Now there," she said, and pointed a finger straight at his chest, "that really calls for a drink, amigo."

"Betsy—forgive me, but after all I've known you and Witt since—well, you might say since you were both kids—you sound unhappier than ever."

"Who isn't?"

"Now what kind of talk is that?"

"Panic in the streets! Just when I think you've got real bottom, you turn into a cornball optimist, Doctor Mayoso of the history book Martís."

"Bottom? What's that?"

"Medical student slang. Savvy. Style. Cool."

"Ah. You've enrolled in med school?"

"No, but some of my best friends are."

"Aren't they taught to be optimistic?"

"If they are, it doesn't show. When's the last time you saw optimism?"

"Cristina. Right now she's standing in the shower, all that warm water streaming over her like a mother's never-ending love, and believing she can fly like a bird back home tomorrow."

"Cristina is a creature of nature," Betsy said. "They don't make 'em anymore. Name two more."

He put his finger on her head and bent forward slightly. "Little Miss Betsy," he said, "I'm your guest. Didn't your mother teach you you're not allowed to be rude to a poor helpless guest?"

"Oh, I'm sorry. It's my turn to apologize."

"I was not so serious."

"My mother always used to say things like that Spanish slogan for hospitality you told me in Havana—"

"*Mi casa es su casa.*"

"My house is your house. Isn't that what it means?"

"Yes. Your mother had the idea."

"We were always coming and going in our house in California. Oh, it was a turnstile, believe me! Round and round, all that talk, talk, talk. And that hilarious chaos, Shakespeare and watercress sandwiches, with the teapot forever being carried to the well. All that reminded me of California." She waved her arm at the hills across from the hotel where the slopes ran down in leafy green V's at the far end of which, in diminished perspective, stood the sand-colored buildings of Caracas as narrow and upended as oblong toy boxes.

The hill opposite the hotel was terraced by houses, some of the newer ones cantilevered on oblique girders stuffed into concrete footings; this gave them a perched bony-legged look of airy suspension. Great reddish-brown earthen scars pockmarked the hills where the bulldozers and cranes had gouged away roads and driveways.

As she motioned she said, "That blue pool down there and that green hotel lawn turning brownish from not enough water and those red tile roofs and the Mediterranean style of architecture—it all looks like California, doesn't it? And a funny thing, standing here a minute ago, when you mentioned a mother's never-ending love, and looking down at the swimming pool—you know how you get a sudden memory? I suddenly remembered California—my mother in a bathing suit sitting in the shade at the edge of the water, combing her long finespun black hair. The black Spanish midnight was in the hair of the whole MacDiarmada brood—mother was born Mary Elenor MacDiarmada—descended from a survivor of the smashed Spanish Armada. Where was I? California? Across the street a hotel orchestra was playing for a tea dance, 'Stormy Weather': *Can't go on, everything I have is gone, stormy-y-y wea-ther* . . . I knew I would never be able to go to a hotel like that, even to dance, but it didn't matter because I was walking toward the most beautiful mother in the world, loving her and the way she tilted her small shining head toward the side she was combing with long strokes like a mermaid. And Mother pretending to be stern with me: 'Betsy Mary, you're not some kind of a *fish,* girl, to be swimmin' right after havin' milk and three sandwiches and riskin' maybe a swimmer's cramp. Swimmin's grand on a hot day, but let's not be debauched en*tire*ly, child! What if I lost my one slip of a girl? My own life would surely go. Come on, now, rest time. I'll make you a lap where you can put your nead down.'"

"Sometimes I think that's what all of us are looking for."

"A safe place to put your head down?"

"In a way, yes."

"Now there," she said with a harsh self-protectiveness, "that's a sentiment that really calls for a drink. Flush out our pipes."

"I believe," he said, "you say in English: 'I'll buy that,' no?"

As they stepped back into the living room Mayoso noticed vases of fresh flowers around the room; a small bar had been rolled into one corner. A circle of bottles and glasses fenced in a silver bucket.

"Only the Sommers," he said, "know how to do this. Move into a hotel room. In twenty minutes the interior decoration is improved."

"I think the phony make-believe native Caribe pictures are awful. I told the manager I wanted them changed. Like *now*. The manager has some nice Dufys he'll loan me."

"All that leaves is the sick-looking rubber plant in the corner."

"Doctor, your diagnosis is right, but that one poor thing stays. A rubber-plant pot is the only place a girl can dump her drink when some gay dog in a hurry keeps pushing straight Scotch at her."

"You just made that up."

"Oh no. I *know*. A rubber plant in a hotel is a working girl's best friend. The plant gets potted while the girl stays sober."

"Okay, Betsy. The pot stays. The pictures go. Presto. You're magical."

"It's really very simple. Flattery and money will get you everything."

"You're too young to be so cynical."

She shook her head. "Uh-uh. I'm too old to be stupid and I've been too poor not to know that money talks. Talks? Hell, it *sings*. It laughs. It turns your idiot vices into idiosyncrasies." She pointed out the open door toward the valley where the city's smoky streamers curled lightly upward. "You thought I was a little stupid a minute ago. That I didn't know what revolutions were."

He was caught off guard. "No—no—"

"Well, we Irish are always for the underdog, y'know. We love wakes, weddings and wars. We're raised on 'em. With our milk and porridge we're fed revolutionary stories." Her voice rose as she declaimed loudly, *"Poblacht Na H Eiann! In the name of God and the dead generations . . . through her secret revolutionary organizations . . . supported by her exiled children in America . . . we hereby proclaim the Irish Republic. . . !* The declaration of independence from the British," she said, "and one of the seven signers was a MacDiarmada. My own uncle, my father's oldest brother, was wounded during the Easter Week troubles.

Condemned to death at Kilmainham. In the prison chapel, an hour before his time, he was propped up in his stretcher to marry my aunt Evie. Then the litter-bearers carried him out and propped him up again in the execution yard where a dozen of his friends had died before him. So don't try to revolt me with revolutions, amigo."

"Betsy," he said, "would you just be a good-natured ordinary illiterate girl and mix a weary foot soldier a magic potion of something and water?"

"Scotch. Turns it into holier-than-thou water."

He nodded, then said almost to himself, "My holy friend Loyola, in the lobby, called me a temporary man."

"Sounds threatening. Assassination?"

"No. Probably something bracing, like boiling pitch in purgatory. At this particular moment of this particular day I cannot make a smile about revolutions."

"Ha," she said as she went to work behind the small portable bar. "Just because you're twice as big as a barn door you can't scare me. We both come from the same race of madmen. The Celts and the Iberians, remember? The Celtic fires burn with as deep a passion for martyrdom as the Spanish."

"I thought about that last night. Believe me, the Spanish hold the original patent."

She finished making her own drink, at least two ounces straight, he noticed, and brought him his. She sat down in a chair opposite him in her graceful, faintly artificial way, and raised her glass to him. "Salud. *Pesetas y amor.*"

"*Y tiempo.*"

She flashed him a grin to show she knew about the testicles called for in the remainder of the toast, an attempt to be biologically complete in a commonsense way. "Ah," she said, taking a long swallow, "that lubricates all the little places after a long day's journey. Flushes out the pipes of Pan."

She set her glass down on the free-form Noguchi coffee table before her. "You won't give the Irish their historical priority for the invention of passionate martyrdom? You've never heard of Brian's Irishmen, fighting the invading Danes near Clontarf on Good Friday, singing as they charged into Danish chain-mail armor? *Singing.* Going into battle against armor singing and wearing light linen tunics? Don't you remember that we were the people that God made mad? All our wars are merry and all our songs are sad."

"You don't sound sad to me."

"Of course. I'm merry. I'm at war."

"At war?"

"With myself. Who hath greater combat?"

"Betsy," he said. "Let me warn you—"

She interrupted him by wagging a finger at him. "Warn me no warnings, amigo. Drink up." She lifted her own glass to her mouth and tilted it so sharply that the ice cubes rattled down against her nose. Into the glass, sounding muddled, she said, "You're such a good listener—"

"What did you say?"

She lowered her glass. "You're such a good listener—I mean, you really *listen*. I could talk to you for hours, the way I did years ago in Havana. Women may like their lovers, but they love their listeners. Wasn't it Boccaccio, during the plague in Florence, where they all moved out to the country and sat around telling those marvelous vulgar stories for days?" She wagged her finger at him again. "You don't have to look so, so *quizzical*. With us, it's more than the Español courtesy of my house is your house. Most of us, y'know, we were always what Papa called so potato-famine-poor there wasn't much in the way of houses, and not even the bloody English could put a tax on *talk*."

He saluted her with his glass. "Your talk is my talk," he said. "There's plague down there in the city. I'm a temporary man and you manage to be permanently delightful, so let's sit here upon the ground and speak of the death of kings."

"Okay." She wiggled her feet out of her high-heeled shoes and tucked her legs under her. "Go down, Moses. Speak."

"After you, señora."

"Have you ever had the feeling," she asked him, "that you're not quite sure where memory leaves off and imagination begins?"

"With your imagination, Betsy, what the hell's the difference?"

"Oh," she said, "you're sweet to make it sound like a gift from some birthday fairy, but it can be a torture"—instead of a statement, her voice made it an intimate confession, a question—"y'know?" One of those swing-high, swing-low-sweet-chariot things, y'know?" She slid to her feet holding her empty glass in one hand and held out the other for his. "Let me freshen that with a wee drop. Won't alcohol sterilize all these plague germs, Doctor Boccaccio?"

"Thanks, but—how do you say it?—I'll just nurse this one along. I'm flying on one wing. I was up all last night."

"Lucky you," she said as she padded back to the bar in her stocking feet. "*Pesetas y amor*." He saw that she assumed he referred to Cristina. She motioned with her head toward the door leading to the far bedroom. "The minute I laid eyes on Cristina—no lipstick, no fake chichi—just that long loose hair swept up on top and that jeune-fille madonna look—I knew right off I'd seen her someplace before."

He sat up straighter and tried to sound casual. "Oh? Where?"

She finished pouring without bothering to put ice in her glass. "In one of those big coffee-table art books. A Christmas edition of the famous paintings of the Madonna. A Velasquez girl."

He leaned back and sipped his drink. "That's very nice. A bit exaggerated, but very nice."

She grinned across the rim of her glass, the imp again. "Well, I can't help it. That's how I am. Exaggerated but very nice."

"Betsy," he said, "I know how much you like to wear different costumes and play different parts—"

"Oh, I do. Oh I *do!* I love bells on my fingers and rings on my toes—"

"But what's all this Irish talk about?"

She waved her arm toward the valley of Caracas. "Plague has broken out in the city and I'm the Irish Boccaccio. Will somebody strike up Florentine music, please? A few lutes and a viola d'amore." She pointed to him. "You think I'm stark raving, don't you? You're as chickeny as Witt. Counting my drinks."

"No, I haven't."

"I always take two. They're small. Deliver me from temptation."

"If you weren't so pretty, who would put up with you?"

She dropped one eyelid. "Our old family doctor has presbyopia and forgot his glasses." She ran a fingertip under both her eyes. "Here. And here. Pretty baggy. Pretty saggy. Who was that crazy poet who wrote that the ghosts of beautiful women fly backwards so that no man can see the markings of worms on their faces? And the only way to lay a ghost is"— she raised her glass—"with holy water, fasting, and prayer."

He couldn't help laughing. "A pixie, yes. A ghost, no."

"Of course I am," she said. "You can see right through me, can't you? You see a pretty woman who's getting older—the oldest corniest story in the world—but when that ol' black magic in the mirror hits you in the eye, you *per*sonally—there's nothing statistical about it. When you've got too much time on your hands, you get too much of yourself on your mind. You wonder who you really are, and where you come from. I've made a brown study of it, so you can quote me."

"Oh," he said, "and that's where the Irish comes in?"

"Yes," she said, "charging into battle against armor, singing. And wearing light linen tunics. I just love that legend. Wearing linen into battle like divine lunatics. How I remember," she said without pausing, "my mother wearing a muscade-yellow Carbery homespun tweed coat and a sweet-and-twenty-style expensive Grafton Street cloche hat for the fantastic voyage that brought us to New York."

"And you? In a light linen tunic?"

"Oh what a day that was! Mother and Papa and me standing there on the deck, me just a toothpick of a kid and feeling like Columbus discovering the New World while the Statue of Liberty slid by and Papa covering up his feelings by joking—maybe because he couldn't get a drink at the moment!—and his standing there on the deck declaiming: 'Bring me your poo-hoor, your huddled masses, lift your lamp beside the golden door,' and telling some nearby passengers who were caught by his Yankee-Doodle-Dandy blarney that he preferred the smaller statue of Liberty which stood on the Seine. Less *showy!* When Mother whispered to him to stop his blathering, he'd never laid eyes on Paris, he held his hat over his heart and said, 'Bit of Thespian expression never hurts! Just good box office! What'd you expect at a time of glory like today, woman—*silence?*' I still have a picture of us in my bedroom, back home.

"Oh, that was the beginning of the sun-drenched years with Papa, that ocean trip. The magic carpet from acting in Dublin's Abbey Theatre to the strange new world of motion pictures in California. Some film about the Irish revolution had been very successful, then a play by Sean O'Casey had been very successful, and Papa was sure as God made little apples that he'd also soon be very successful. He could do everything. A music-hall country jiggity-jig, sure-an'-begorra style, spittin' on his hand and wipin' it on his trouser leg before shaking hands hello. He could make you feel the quiet fearful fury of a Sinn Fein Volunteer caught by Black and Tan gunfire pouring down Sackville Street at the General Post Office steps on that terrible Easter morning."

She paused, then snapped her fingers. "Just like that, the memory—I saw those red tile roofs out there and a rush of memory caught my heart.

"Those years that Papa was successful in California, now those years seem to be the golden ones. Our small stucco house off Wilshire Boulevard with the curled red-tile Mediterranean roof. Everything so unlike Dublin. Mother with a daily to come to do the cleaning, and myself dressed spotlessly by Mother for our daily walk to the North Rodeo grammar school. Ah, those open *generous* archways of that school—you know that early Spanish California monastery style?—every entrance looked dazzling and playful and free to me. It's crazy, isn't it, how long ago it was and here and now it seems, the sunlit strolling players of my childhood. Those surely were the grand days, the house always filled with actors and picture people, the talking, oh the grand talking as gay and irrelevant and free-wandering as a tinker's painted wagon, and those epic noisy tribal arguments with all the fake thunder of summer storms! Mother now the woman of the house, her own sunshiny house in America. Mother flushed with the pink pearl glow of pleasure as the men lifted me off my feet and raised me high. 'And who may this little charmer be? How

old are you this week? I'll need to know 'cause I've got a young son who
ought to promise to marry you. If you'll have the beggar.' The men always
lifted me and stroked my hair and hugged me like some lifesize doll. I
was forever being embraced fondly and being pulled onto some affectionate man's lap. You know, amigo, I wonder sometimes now if maybe I
grew to breathe their admiration as needfully as air.

"'Draw up now and take some tea,' Mother would say if some Dublin
actors were visiting us, especially if they had said to her in old-country
style as she had greeted them at the door, 'God save all here.' Ah, all the
world was a stage, then, and Papa was the prince of players."

Betsy stopped, and, after a minute Mayoso thought she wanted to say
nothing more. Then, with her voice changed, she said, "So one day we
rode high, Papa buying expensive suits and bringing California flowers
home—'Just for the table, now, so don't get excited, they cost less'n pint
of stout at Neary's'—and then came the terrible day when everything
changed. The powers on high at the studio reviewed Papa's lovely contract and dropped his option. D'you remember the Depression in the
thirties? The soup kitchens and breadlines? Papa staggered home clutching his dismissal notice like a dagger to his chest, and looped as a hoop.
'Terrible, terrible,' he kept mumbling to Mother. 'Darker'n eclipse o' the
sun.'

"'We've been poor as breadcrumbs in Dublin,' I remember Mother saying to Papa in the kitchen, 'and I'm not one afraid to be poor again, so
there's no need to use pot whisky to stiffen up your spine.' She tried to
talk him back to his feet. 'There's nothing at the bottom of the bottle but
trouble,' she kept telling him. 'Maybe these moving-picture people will
call you back here someday, and maybe they won't. We'll manage elsewhere without 'em. Chin up, man. Don't let 'em rain on your parade.'

"But the rains did come. A cloudburst of alcohol. A rain of whiskey.
And just as Mother had once strode forth for her man at Neary's Pub—
Lord, how embarrassed and angry she was when she took to the warpath
—now she made the trek through those long dreary desert blocks of Los
Angeles to the Retake Room—that was the place near M-G-M where the
studio people went because their commissary didn't serve liquor—and
that's where her prince of players said he surely took his swimmin' lessons,
divin' to the bottom of the bottle. Now maybe you don't believe in prayer,
but Mother prayed on her knees, leaning her forehead down against the
side of the bed, and wouldn't you know that four months later an offer
came to Papa from a repertory theater in Chicago? It came, oh it came
like the opening of a door! The offer wasn't just an acting *job*, Papa said.
It was a repertory position. The good-luck farewell parties began, and I
guess all that boozy fellowship helped Papa borrow money for our tickets

on the Twentieth Century Limited. Papa would take no other train for his arrival in Chicago. It was the Statue of Liberty act all over again, but now Chicago. 'I'd walk there,' Mother said, 'if my own two legs could save the outrageous cost of such a puffed-up arrival.'

"'*Walk?*' Papa put one hand over his heart. 'On the two prettiest shin-bones a man could ever watch go by? Why, they carry the future o' the world! Oh, you'll walk to Chicago, sure thing. But only from the train stop!' Oh my, how Papa became eloquent again! Politics, speeches, slogans of the downtrodden. 'Through ages thou hast slept in chains and night. Arise now, man, and vindicate the right!' Really, you can't imagine. The eclipse had ended. With all his great ham oratory he half convinced himself. The sun was high in the sky again, and he carried his most important luggage in his pocket, corked."

She sighed deeply. "Within two weeks we were in Chicago. We moved into a long funereal apartment—the kind with a turdy chainpull water closet, it was on the South Side, called a railroad flat, all very different from the little stucco house with the curled red-tile roof. I went to St. Anselm's parochial school and then to St. Cyril's High School. The generous open archways were gone"—she caught her breath with pain. "In two years more, Mother was dead."

She raised the back of her hand to her eyes, "Oh God," she said, sounding choked, then stopped and shook her forehead slightly against her hand. Then, as she always did when she was deeply moved, she reached for comic relief. "Why do they make tears so damn *salty!*"

"We all come from the ocean," he said, then realized how stupid and meaningless that must sound to her. As the arrested quiet expanded, he remembered the medical lecture he had written in his leather notebook only a few days back. Oceans. Hurricanes. Our guts contain hurricanes. Those lecture notes, only a few days ago? Where had the time gone? Just as Betsy had put it: how long ago it was and here and now it seems. And in a secret burial place within his ear, his father's voice saying through a telephone: *I kiss you goodbye, my son.*

She took a quick swallow, wiggling the melting cubes inside her glass with her tongue. Who had said something to me about the salt ocean? David? Witt, years ago, fishing for salmon at Dingle Bay, that blind biological thrashing of brave salmon, mating biblically two by two, fighting upstream to spawn and die exhausted. Oh Witt. It was lovers' breath fogging a mirror. Meeting, not mating. Then gone.

She slid down in the deep chair with both legs stretched out straight before her and her head lying back. "Oh my," she sighed and closed her eyes. "It's so nice to talk to a reasonable intelligent man who *listens* without all the usual hanky-panky or jujitsu or karate or whatever they call this new no-holds-barred game that people play." She opened her green eyes suddenly for one of her spearing looks. "You aren't just playing for time until you can lay me, are you?"

"As a matter of fact," he said, "I'm not."

"When I drink this much I become very direct."

"Me, too."

"You're not being pompous and very clinical?"

"No," he said. "I'm not on the job this particular minute."

"Where are you this particular minute?"

"Well," he said, "coasting."

"That's not like you. Witt says you never lower your guard."

"Ridiculous," he said. "I'm enjoying every minute of it."

"You sound oh-me oh-my."

"As a matter of fact, I am."

"I didn't mean to bore you with that whole gush of mine. I should just give my name, rank, and horsepower, then shut up. It's just that I was standing on the balcony thinking about it when you came up."

"You didn't bore me."

"I don't often talk such a gushy streak, but when I get started—! Papa used to say if I'd been born a boy I'd have grown to be a spoilt priest."

"My mother," he said, "wanted me to become a priest but my father was one of those burning men and he made sure I went the other way."

"It's nice," she said, "just talking back and forth like this. Most men never talk to me. They sort of spar around, as if I'd challenged them to a fight or something. And women dislike me at first sight. So it gets lonesome."

"But not now. Here we are. Lots of time. We're not going anyplace."

"Aren't we flying to Puerto Rico tomorrow?"

"No," he said. "Witt and his pilot won't get military clearance at the airport for their flight plan. They'll get a polite run-around—"

"Witt never takes no for an answer."

"He will, this time," Mayoso said. "I don't think you and Witt know how bloody serious all this revolutionary business is. There are men out there this minute who could stop Witt at some street corner just to commandeer his car for a getaway. And if he didn't take no for an answer he would have all of two seconds to be the incredulous American citizen before they shot him down."

"He said he smelled trouble around you. He wants to get you out of the country as fast as possible."

"Damn those people who trapped me in the lobby. If I had gotten here sooner I could have stopped him. Too many people who've helped me have been punished for it."

"That's a daffy thing to say. You always help others."

"That's different. I'm a professional. Amateurs get hurt."

"In this room it all seems a speck unreal, señor."

"I know. I used to live in rooms like this myself until I found out that the foundation is built of paper and the basement is full of matches."

"Is that why your eyes keep moving?" she asked.

"Moving?"

"Yes," she said, "you look so—so, I don't know—so *watch*ful. In the lobby, you kept scanning the people, the elevators, the entrance—"

"Really?"

She nodded. "Only your best friend would tell you. You probably think you have a poker face."

"I do."

"You don't. You look watchful, like radar. Like a sentry. Or are you some kind of escaped convict?"

"Radar, yes. Convict, no. Not yet."

"In Havana," she said, "you were such a nicely tanned suave intelligent handsome—"

"Stop. One more word and I'll burst into *Bésame Mucho*."

"Really. I mean it. You were very different."

"I know. My hair was black."

"No. It's more than that. The way Marjorie Sommers looks. Ownership. You owned the joint, then. Now, you give an impression of alertness, y'know? As if you expect somebody unpleasant to come around the corner any minute. In Havana you were very different."

"In Havana I was stupid. We agreed on that, no?"

She misunderstood him. "So was I. I tried to call you, like Room Service. I didn't understand your kind of pride."

"Well, that was complicated. Witt. The Sommers family. My fiancée. The medical years of habit, no nonsense with no exceptions."

"I know."

"And the political things were beginning. How did you call it? Keeping company with a revolution? I was starting to learn the basic fact of life in most places. Terror."

She stared at him. "Did you say terror?"

"Yes."

"*Terror?*"

"Yes. In Havana, history meant nothing. All the skirmishes and battles of the great religious war we've been fighting since 1914 were only things in schoolbooks. When the Germans invaded Belgium in 1914 we all ran out of the overstuffed living rooms of our lives down into the dark cellar and we've never come back upstairs."

"I'm not sure I know what you're talking about."

"It's simple," he said, and stood up. He motioned for her to follow him and walked back out to the balcony. The low horizontal sun had thrown into shadow the valley leading toward the city. Three single-seater jet fighters, high enough to catch the last of the sun, gleamed metallically as silver arrowheads as they dove from their height into the smoky haze above Caracas.

"Here we are," Mayoso said, "on Mount Sinai. Across the road are the red rooftops of the happy part of your childhood. The green hills on this side are like the hills of Cuba I used to climb with Filho when we were boys."

"Filho? Who's he?"

He began to say *a friend,* but he heard himself saying, "A man of the times. He doesn't think of terror as personal unhappiness, the way bourgeois sentimentalists like you and me think. You remember your uncle executed in 1916. Witt must remember Korea every time he combs his hair to cover that scar on his scalp." Then, as her eyes widened slightly, he added, "Yes. Of course I know what happened to him—"

"And to you, with your hair all white?"

"Yes, I make the mistake of becoming personal. We're as childish as the lady four hundred miles from a hurricane who complains that rain has spoiled her picnic. Filho doesn't think of local personal rain or picnics. He overviews the world. He thinks of great weather systems, the forces that turn the sun and water of life into hurricanes of death." Or, he wondered, maybe I am the one who thinks that way, not Filho.

As the valley shadows darkened from gray-blue smokiness into a deep translucent purple, the lights of the city below them wavered and flickered like innumerable messages sent by blinkers. "The terror down there," he said, "it isn't personal anymore. Muscle-bound cities. Hit the few vital centers and they're paralyzed. The brain, where the inside apparatus of government sits. The eyes and ears—the television and radio stations which are the only way most of us can see or hear the world. And a throat—'Cut the city's windpipe' is the phrase they like in their orders for battle—that's done by scattered acts of brutality. These the leaders regret, because they are sensitive fastidious men, but they are trained to think like surgeons. Cut out the tumor at any cost. And terror, real terror, freezes opposition."

"I don't like the way you sound. You sound as if you know too much about it."

"We all know too much about it. Maybe that's why we pretend so hard we don't."

She looked down at the swimming-pool terrace below them. Concealed lights had been turned on everywhere, catching the parade of national flags whipping in the breeze, silky and unsubstantial as medieval pennants. Women in bright Caribbean colors wandered with their escorts in evening clothes between mushrooms of shadow and grassy lagoons of light. Underwater illumination made the pool a sapphire pond. A single swimmer stood on the elevated pulpit of the high diving board gleaming with statuesque wetness as he raised himself on his toes then ran lightly down the board—Betsy and Mayoso could hear the solid *thunk* as he high-stepped skillfully in a final springboard leap, soaring outward with his body arched and arms outflung, a winged Icarus silhouette, and then, at the peak of his arc, bent and slid downward into the cleanly parting surface of the pool, followed by a snaky train of bubbly turbulence streaming backward underwater until he surfaced.

Betsy grasped the railing with both hands, leaning over it, and, just as the diver surfaced, she called out, "Bravo!"

She swung toward Mayoso with shining eyes. "Did you see that form? Tarzan doing a ballet."

Mayoso said nothing, surprised that her abrupt changeability should still surprise him. He had just been telling her what he had carefully avoided thinking about in the privacy of his own mind. To speak with such an open offering of his thoughts was, for him, as intimate and trusting as the embrace of love. But she had changed costume again. She gave one of her throaty little laughs and said, as the muscular diver pulled himself up the poolside ladder, "He looks delicious enough to eat."

"Call Room Service. They'll send him right up."

She put a quick slender hand on his arm, "Oh, I've offended you—"

"Of course not."

"You were talking about terror and I didn't think I could stand it another minute. I can't stand grimness or pain. When I was younger I used to turn the other cheek. Now I turn my back."

She turned to the rail and stared down at the diver who was mounting the chromium ladder of the high diving board again. Without looking at Mayoso she said, "Men don't understand a thing like that. They can understand if a woman takes a pill to sleep, but not if she takes a man." She kept her eye on the diver's gleaming wetness.

"Betsy," he said, "what's happened to you?"

"Oh, please—I can't stand it when you sound professionally kind and understanding. Women like quiet men—they think they're listening. I'd rather have you the way you were a moment ago, quiet and angry."

"Because you're angry?"

"Yes. The least crumb of kindness disarms me. I turn into a naked orphan child, all melted because someone gives her a few warm clothes to wear. I'd rather stay armed and adult."

"At adultery."

She froze, as if deafened by an explosion, then confronted him. Her unusual eyes zeroed on him, aiming pulsed green flares like Roman candles. "You had to slug me, didn't you? Sooner or later, I knew you would. You can't scare me by sounding pompous. You had common bucking-bronco crotch fever that time in Havana and you've never forgiven yourself."

"Betsy," he said, "you're wrong. Now that you make me think about it, it's you I don't forgive."

"Because I was Witt's wife, his property, and men have to stick together to keep the real estate values up?"

"Maybe some of that. Maybe. But you said it yourself. You treated me like Room Service. You didn't really know me, or want *me*, but only a sleeping pill for some forgetfulness."

Her lips parted to say something but she stopped, then said, "To forget what?"

"All the things you're angry about."

"Such as?"

He said civilly, "I don't know. If I knew that, I would really know you."

"And not even I really know me," she said with a faint tremor of uncertainty which contradicted her light tone. She put both hands to her face, the shameful reflex of a child, and made a soundless O with her puckered lips. "Awful," she said. "Here we are on Mount Sinai while Witt's down there in the City of Man."

She swerved away from him on her slim feet and hurried to the telephone. She had become the guilty but considerate wife. "I'll call Witt at the airport right away," she said as she dialed the hotel switchboard operator. "Hello? Operator? Will you please ring Maiquetía Airport for me right away?" Her face changed as she looked at him across the room. "No outgoing calls, she says."

Mayoso walked toward her. "Here, let me have the telephone." She handed it to him. "Operator," he began, then spoke in Spanish. "This is very urgent. We must reach one of your guests who is at the airport."

"Señor," the operator's voice said, "this switchboard is falling to pieces. You cannot imagine! Everybody is calling the airport. If you'll take your turn, please give me your name and room number."

Just as he began to do so, he changed his mind. He did not want to leave his name and room number. "Many thanks," he said, and hung up. They looked at one another in silence as he shrugged.

Slowly she wavered and drifted across the noiseless rug to the bar.

"When frustration is inevitable," she said to herself, "relax and enjoy it." She wheeled impetuously and brightened, a dutiful hostess cheering up a guest. "Don't worry about Witt. Witt's a bit of all right. When he aims at something, he hits the bull's eye." As their eyes met and held, she added gently, "Except that one thing, of course."

"I know."

"Remember that story in school about the Spartan boy who carried a wolf cub inside his shirt and never complained while it bit him? That's how Witt carries what you explained to us that time in Havana."

"But," he said cautiously, "I thought he understood the important medical details. It's a medical problem, not a personal criticism."

"No matter how gently you explain it, can a man understand a sock in the jaw?"

"But I thought Witt understood that your not being able to have his child was not anyone's fault. There have been other cases reported where a woman produced something inside—just what, nobody's sure—that destroyed sperm. It wasn't his fault and it wasn't yours."

"I remember. God, do I! One couple in ten or twenty, you said."

"And I've seen the problem solved. Hormones, diet, avoiding fatigue, just commonsense general health measures—any one or a combination could change the picture for you." Her forked lightning gone, the electric air less charged, now that they stood on clinical ground.

She beelined behind the bar and poured herself another drink. When she raised her head and saw that he was contemplating her she said, "Well, nothing has changed."

"How about artificial insemination?"

"Witt gets furious at the idea. You know that go-away withdrawn manner of his? I've tried talking to him. So's David. Witt was dead set against adoption until I just went underground and did it anyway." She raised her chin. "I've been very bad for Witt. All his mother's predictions have come true. The lace-curtain Irish girl from Chicago never quite made the first team. On Main Street, U.S.A., I can knock a man dead at twenty paces. But in Marjorie Sommers' special blue-chip New England world I'm just twenty miles of unpaved road. Nothing"—she stopped and grinned mockingly—"nothing distingué, recherché, savoir faire or debonaire."

"I like Marjorie Sommers. She's a woman who lives in a doing world."

"Oh, hers is certainly a doing world."

"Now, Betsy, don't scratch. It would be so easy for her to live in her greenhouse and raise orchids. I like Marjorie Sommers very much."

"And me? Don't you like me very much?"

"If I'm her friend, do I become your enemy?"

"Anything I say will be held against me."

"Are you being seductive in reverse gear?"

"With you? Never. Only one ticket to a customer. Anyway, my li'l ol' engine doesn't *have* a reverse gear."

"Then you need retooling, señora. Every lady needs a reverse gear."

"I'm no lady. I'm a wife."

"You're both. The girl who almost broke her long lovely neck on those stairs was very much a lady."

"Amigo," she said, "you and David are the only men I know who don't dish out nonsense. So do me a favor and don't start now."

"I mean it, Betsy."

"Oh," she said, "those lovely Latin loose-lipped lies. Tell me the truth, do men really become impotent just from feeling angry or scared? Could that kill cock robin?"

"Yes," he said.

"I've heard it, but I never believed it. I thought the tilt of the kilt was automatic, like the erection in animals."

"Well," he said, "that animal he-goat stuff is a female myth. I'll tell you a secret, Betsy—men can be sensitive, just like women. Witt needs all the help you can give him."

"But he's not easy to help. The harder I try, the angrier he becomes that I should try so hard." She wore the contradictory self-protective ceramic smile of the wounded, who must, like Orientals, save face at any cost. "Saints preserve this sinner," she said debonairly, as if telling an anecdote, "but I've cried me a river."

At once he recognized she was making a mute votive offering of her most hidden intimacy, her unshed tears, more secret for her than the simple trombone-slide of sex. She was begging what women had always begged from totems and saintly Liberatas, from the incense-shrouded oracles and sibyls, from the garbed priests and alchemists and learned doctors—the how and why and where-to of the womb's delicate manufacture. She was willing to forgive his failure to help her in Havana if only he could succeed now with some prophetic word or ritual act, some symbolic formula or repentance or scribbled cabalistic prescription.

How we must delude ourselves, he thought, in these elevated platforms of penthouse presidential suites, when actually we are down there in the valley, on our hands and knees. Who among us does not wish for magic, the healing water of some wishing well? And hell has no fury like a woman who finds no water in the well.

His fatigue had sponged up the Scotch and he woozily recognized the beginning of his old prison trick, the escape through the hatchdoor of his mind onto an imaginary shoal where he could crouch wrapped in an animal lassitude like an Indio blanket.

Snap out of it, he commanded himself contemptuously. One eyedropperful of whiskey, and you see all-wisely?

He discovered himself on his feet, holding his glass. Logic logic logic required that he walk ponderously to the bar and mix himself the size drink this kind of naked talk required under such noncompos pixilated *revuelta* circumstances. As he made his way back and dropped his big frame heavily into his seat, she threw out one of her theatrical silvery laughs, like a scatter of coins. "Me oh my! I've never seen you like this. So very *talk*ative."

He swallowed some of his amber medication, thinking: She and I live on different planets, sending signals by mirror flashes. On my planet some distinctly unwelcome things may happen by midnight. Her planet is all interior, a chamber of echoes. He brushed her mocking comment aside by flicking his fingers in the air lightly, then asked her bluntly, "Have you been doing a great deal of lying lately?"

She let her eyes close, tilting her head back slightly and seeing the medical student, Roone, in the car beside her. Little Boy Blues, come blow your horn. You arrogant, lean, provocative, bewitching *bastard*. She raised her eyelids with effort and, when she saw the brooding compassion in Mayoso's face as he considered her, she was pierced with gratitude. She wanted to blurt out everything, but all she could say was "Yes. Some lying. But only to myself." Then the automatic panel of her reflex protectiveness slid like a wall between them. She stretched out her legs prettily for her elegant fetish shoes. "Duty calls. Everybody up." She busied herself with wiggling her toes into place and stroking a wrinkle out of her stocking. "On your feet, men. There's my party to organize." She stood up, not with her usual provocative forward thrust of breasts, but simply standing there a moment before becoming efficient. "I knew I'd be sorry when the Scotch wore off."

"Betsy, forget it. It's as if you never said a word."

She shook her head. "That's not true. I keep forgetting that whom the gods would destroy, they first make sincere."

□ □ □

In his room, Father Gofredo paced back and forth uncomfortably. Mayoso's barbed defiance in the lobby. How distasteful. Such blunt argumentation, like an exchange of cudgel blows. Why did I allow myself to be ambushed into this nameless feeling? This thumping in the chest, this dry mouth. Anger? No, of course not. Pity for a lost man, a soul in torment. He tugged at his sweat-soaked collar.

After so many years, how unpleasant to wear a fitted clergyman's suit instead of a loose robe, to wear shoes and socks instead of sandals, to tread on the lascivious softness of the carpeting instead of on bare monastery floors, to be in a hedonistic hostelry such as this without advance permission from the bishop, to be away from the ordered pattern of offering Mass, hearing confessions, the baptisms and funerals, the antiphonal rhythm of devotions, Angelus and Vespers. He felt the nausea of his distaste rise.

Fretting and bedeviled, he pulled off his reverse collar and his black coat and threw them on the nearest chair.

This pagan pool of Narcissus, he thought. This room, this wall of mirror large enough for a dozen men, a bed at least six cots wide, with no crucifix above it, the uproar of jungle colors from the wall, the outlandish lampshade, the voluptuous furniture.

Outside. An airplane approaching, roaring almost overhead. Thank God! Airline service restored. He hurried out onto the balcony, then stared upward numbly as the plane flashed by. It was not a big passenger transport, but a small missile-pointed military jet.

Directly below him, on the edge of the manicured hotel lawn, he watched the Yanqui host of a gay poolside party leave an umbrella-shaded table on the flagstone terrace and walk unsteadily toward the color-hung crescent of brave flagpoles. The Yanqui cupped his hands and called to a waiter who was crossing the grass with a tray of pisco sours from the bar.

"Hey, caballero!" the Yanqui host shouted, waving his arm vaguely toward the red glow across the Caracas valley below them, "What's all the big fireworks celebration downtown?"

"A few university students, señor," the waiter said as he came toward the hotel guest. "Some kind of politics. We have more people than food. As always." He shrugged. "*Nada.* It is nothing."

A lady wearing only a wet white silk bikini and a startlingly large aza-bache ring reached over the waiter's shoulder and lifted a glass off his tray while calling out, "At last! Joy juice for the kiddies! Come and get it."

The waiter began to turn politely toward her with his tray, until the absence of her clothing struck him. He turned back to the host immediately, offering him the tray, and said politely in accented English, "Please take, señor. Have fun."

Fun, Father Gofredo thought. He bristled with annoyance. The new conquistadors were still seducing the natives. The pagan god was now called Fun. Some of my younger parishioners talked like *piti-yanquis.* *Have fun,* they said, instead of *adiós,* goodbye, go with God, or even *hasta luego.* The new eleventh commandment, *Have fun.* Then make an appointment with Doctor Mayoso. A dilatation here, a curettage there, one, two, good as new, and go back again to *Have fun*.

My next television sermon, he thought as he turned to go back into the noisy bombardment of color in his room. Just then he spotted three unusual young people at the farthest end of the terrace, beyond the umbrellas and aluminum chairs, in the corner where the grass ended in rows of paving blocks running up to the white flat-roofed cabañas. Two young men in white suits were carrying what appeared to be, from this distance, a large square-sided log. Astride it, a third young man dressed in black rode it like a clown on a wooden horse. No one at the busy party on the terrace noticed them. Something about the movements of the young men, a kind of toy-soldier stiffness, held Father Gofredo on the balcony another moment. As if everything had been smoothly rehearsed, the log was set down in the corner. Father Gofredo watched them open the lid. The large log was actually a box. The rider dressed in black lifted out a flagpole with a printed banner and planted it into the grass with a hard spearlike thrust. The other two young men lifted out colored plastic bottles of fluid which they began to pour comically over the flag carrier.

The red flag fluttered open. On it was sewn the unmistakable profile of Lenin over PCV and PATRIA O MUERTE. Just as Father Gofredo read the words and recognized that the box was a coffin, the young man in black finished planting the banner and calmly flipped a cigarette lighter into flame. He touched his chest with it, and fire flickered upward toward his shoulders. The people on the terrace froze. A woman screamed like a frantic wounded animal. The two other young men raced behind the cabañas and disappeared as a stunned anguish, a convulsive exhalation, ran through the watchers. The breeze which fluttered the PVC banner gruesomely fanned the human candle.

The boy was completely ablaze now. Even his hair was burning, his charred clothes scaling off into ash flecks while he bent forward in slow motion, a melting wax mummy bowing grotesquely to the world inside a macabre enclosure of fire.

Father Gofredo felt a sickening heat sweep upward within him as the cremated boy collapsed in a ball of yellow flame. He wrenched himself away, weak with horror, and staggered into his room. This could not be! This could not be! This shuddering nightmare of inferno could not be! Then why were people screaming and shouting outside? Oh God, what agony of spirit could lead a young man to such a terrible act? To be a martyr in Christ's name, that could be understood—but to sacrifice one's soul in burnt offering for a political cause was monstrous suicidal blasphemy.

He stared into a bottomless pit. To worship an idea as this student did, or to put science in the place of faith as Mayoso does, means the destruction of the Church's eternal rock and the idolatry of the mushroom-shaped cloud; how many millions are hellbent with open-eyed blindness toward that infernal apocalypse? The vision shattered him. His temples were drumming feverishly now, his headache tightening into two metallic knots. He stumbled on the wide desert of carpet, then went down on his knees.

"Our Father," he prayed, "forgive me for losing sight of Thy healing love. Let me dedicate myself totally to the mystery of man's passion and redemption. Let me empty myself so that I may be filled with Thy Holy Spirit. Give me the strength and the willing heart to exhaust myself in whatever task I am given. Let me understand the spiritual pain which drives a student to such betrayal of Thy healing love and the bitter loneliness of a godless physician who was once in the community of the faithful and has now fallen away from the use of the sacraments and from the faith itself. Accept my Sacramental Penance and let me once more be refreshed in the Word of God of the double table of Sacred Scripture and the Eucharist. Let me never forget in my performance of my office that I am never alone but strengthened always by Thy power. Cause charity to grow within me for we are all strangers in the world. Let me remember as a priest that I am a brother among brothers with all those who have been reborn at the baptismal font. I live by Thy words: *Take courage, I have overcome the world.*"

He held the knuckles of his clasped hands against his lips. Strength. God give me strength. If only this were noontime of a Friday! In every Franciscan monastery in the world the strengthening Rule would be read: *No man putting his hand to the plow and looking back is fit for the kingdom of God.*

Up from the valley, the thudding of giant drums. Somewhere in the city artillery fire had begun.

□ □ □

Mayoso stood soaking himself under the bracing downpour of a cold shower. At the end of the shower-curtain rod Cristina had hung two pairs of washed stockings. The girl had not wasted a minute settling down to domesticity, he thought. She must have either a good deal of strength or a shrewd simplicity to have recovered so fast from the last few days. Or all three, the simplicity and the strength and the shrewdness. The poor can't indulge in the usual escapes. They bite down and survive, or exit by going completely loco. Cristina would be one of the survivors. For now, live. Hell is crowded and heaven will wait.

When he had left Betsy, he walked into the bedroom expecting to find Cristina fussing with luggage or clothing. He had been surprised to find her sleeping deeply, face down as if drowned, sprawled across the waist of the big double bed. She was wearing a wide-sleeved white nylon kimono which accentuated her tan skin and black hair. For the first time he noticed she had lovely legs, a straight back tapering smoothly into hips as firmly rounded as mandolins.

Ah, hombre, your musical ability to recognize fine stringed instruments remains intact? Beside her the bedside radio was playing a Viennese waltz.

He saw that she had brushed her damp hair back into a chignon held together by an elastic band at the nape of her neck. How familiar she looks, Mayoso thought. Filho was clever to have recognized how much more she had than prettiness. Intellectuals always admire direct feelings and uncomplicated courage.

Suddenly the radio crackled as a voice broke in on the same wavelength: "Citizens and workers of Venezuela! This is your Freedom Radio. The corrupt government of imperialists who live in luxury on your work for Yanqui profits is now dying—"

Mayoso stared at the radio. Filho's voice? A recording? Now what? Cristina stirred but did not awaken.

The waltz played on mindlessly. Mayoso tried to listen for nuances in the stern radio voice typical of Filho, but the poor transmission of what must be a tape recording made it hard to decide. The ongoing music jammed careful listening.

"Join together to throw off their crushing weight from our backs! Workers, patriots! Wherever you are, whatever you are doing, stop! Fold your arms! Pick up no weapons but put down your tools! We proclaim a general strike to begin immediately! I repeat, a general strike begins immediately. If you stand firm, if you do not knuckle under, if you do not break, no harm will come to you. Your fighting comrades salute you! *Patria o Muerte!*"

Mayoso stood still, hardly hearing the light waltz which had strangely continued without pause. So Filho had called a general strike. The rhetoric of promise, threat, and glory. But why so suddenly? Was this cleverness, or was it desperation? Why no handbills, posters, streetcorner agitprop, popular front appeals—all the usual careful advance preparations? We could be marooned here for days or weeks, he thought, and almost groaned. A general strike!

Betsy's joke about Boccaccio and his sybaritic friends marooned outside Florence during an epidemic might not be so farfetched after all. He glanced down at Cristina. Each day doubles our danger, particularly in this hotel; its isolated location and numbered occupants made it a luxurious prison. Whether it's Digepol plainclothesmen or Filho's activists, we're hung up here on neat convenient pegs.

Cristina looked very much like his fiancée in Havana. Not as tall but with the same long black hair, the same serious dark eyes that smiled with quick responsiveness, the same importance given to robust direct-ness. The last time he had seen his fiancée María was after one of Batista's SIM cars had delivered her to her parents' home in Vedado. She had been caught carrying several automatics while on the bus to Santiago de Cuba. Mayoso and her father and her brothers had spent three months and twenty thousand dollars to get her back, and, when Mayoso got the tele-phone call from her father, the old man had barely managed to say, "Bring your medical bag. I'm afraid she's dying."

María was still alive when Mayoso came into her bedroom, her fore-head shining with the holy oil of Extreme Unction. Her mother was on her knees beside the bed, her shoulders shaking convulsively as she prayed with the priest. María had been completely unable to speak because her jaw was broken but her crystalline eyes had moved with something of her darting intelligence. He did what he could while he waited for an ambulance to carry her to the university hospital. That night she died, her fevered eyes alive until the end. After that nothing was ever the same.

□ □ □

At Maiquetía Airport, Witt, his pilot, and co-pilot stood in the shadow of the wing of Witt's company plane. Someone had set fire to a store of kerosene drums at the opposite side of the airport and, when the wind shifted, an acrid dirty smoke swirled past them.

The pilot pushed his uniform cap back on his head and said, "You want my honest opinion, Mr. Sommers? They've got us by the short hair. I've seen some banana republic bust-ups, where the palace guard and the poli-ticians play musical chairs, but this looks like the real thing." He coughed. "Agh. That smoke sure stinks." The co-pilot nodded. His face was sweat-streaked and, because he was in shirtsleeves, Witt could see two dark wet patches under his armpits. "I tried everything, Mr. Sommers. I told 'em we only touched down for ramp and flightline service, that we're in transit. I told 'em I'd file any flight plan they wanted just so they'd clear us for takeoff tomorrow. I even tried a little polite bribery. Offered 'em double the gallon price to refuel us."

Witt frowned. "That didn't work?"

"No sir. The foreman told me there were too many kids playing with matches around here."

Witt stared at the ground between his feet. Mayoso was the problem. Betsy and I, he thought, we can manage indefinitely holed up in that hotel penthouse. They give me a telephone line and I can stay in business. But I don't like the way Mayoso looks. I don't like the self-restrained way he talks. He didn't come to Caracas just to spend an offhand weekend in the hay with his pretty girlfriend. Cristina had been so obviously frightened in the hotel lobby, a gray pallor stamped on her face. Like all decent people Mayoso managed to be a bit of a nuisance and, Witt thought, he deserves every chance to go right on being one. Governments should learn what all women know: a good man is hard to find. He raised his head and slowly inspected the plane. Its fuselage and wings were usually a high-gloss white; the only color glinted from the golden sea horse painted on the tail in the shape of the letter S. Now a veil of gray-and-black-streaked soot lay over everything.

Witt was convinced that the pilot was not exaggerating so that he and the co-pilot could have a comfortable shackup for a few days. Like many executives, he was alert to staff members who tried to manipulate his decisions by carefully put half-truths, but his trip across Caracas and down the mountain road to the airport had proved this was no powder-puff revolt. The police in Caracas had stopped his taxi several times. At the junction of Avenida Sucre and the entrada autopista, the Guardia Nacional had set up roadblocks at all entrances and exits. He had decided that the government was very serious about closing the airport when his taxi had been flagged down near the Administration Building by a platoon of green-beret *cazadores*. He had seized the initiative. He jumped out of the taxi before it stopped, and strode toward the sergeant. "If you please," he had said forcefully in Spanish. "I'm in a hurry, gentlemen."

Several of the soldiers laughed and Witt heard one say to the other, "Un bravo. He's in a hurry."

"American?" the sergeant asked.

Witt shifted to new tactics. "I apologize for my accent," he said. "I apologize for being a neocolonial imperialistic bloodsucking capitalist"— by now most of the soldiers had recognized the time-honored combination of sardonic bombast and irony—"but I have an airplane sitting on the ground that has to be checked out."

"Nobody flies," the sergeant said. "Even the birds walk today."

Witt took his cigarette case out of his pocket and snapped it open. He gave himself the first one with patient dignity to make it clear he was not toadying to anyone. He emphasized the point by offering the second one through the open window to the taxi driver, then to the sergeant, and then he passed the case among the men. When the last man handed the case back, the paratrooper said, "You must be filthy rich."

"Aie, *hijo*. I've already confessed that," Witt said. "What else is new?"

"Listen," the sergeant said, sounding friendlier as he took a long drag on the cigarette. "You can get your ass shot off running around loose like this. Be smart, go home." He waved the cigarette smoke from his face. "Where do you live?"

"In the States."

The sergeant coughed. "*Coño.* That's a good one. You remind me of the captain I trained under at Fort Bragg. Where are you in Caracas? Tell the truth, because we can check in a minute on our jeep radio."

"That's great," Witt said. "You can call the Hotel Laputa for me. Tell my wife not to worry."

"What's your name?"

"Just ask for Mrs. DeWitt Sommers."

Shrewdly, the sergeant asked, "Room number?"

Witt shrugged. "I don't know."

"You pay the price at Laputa and you don't even know your room number?"

"We don't have a number. We're in the presidential suite."

The sergeant coughed again and inspected the tip of his cigarette. "Listen, Mr. Sommers," he said finally. "If we let you in to check your airplane, you are forbidden to take off. You have to come out this road again. In the meantime my radio man will check the hotel. If you're lying, we'll come in to pick you up. Is this understandable?"

Witt nodded. "It's a deal." He rode off in the taxi before the sergeant could change his mind.

Now, standing in the shadow of the plane's wing, Witt said, "Let's change tactics. Is there any food on the plane?"

"Yes sir," the co-pilot said. "There's some stuff in the ice chest and a big Thermos of coffee." He scratched his chin, "And of course that snug built-in bar ain't exactly empty."

"Maybe," the pilot said, "we can refuel with Haig and Haig, Mr. Sommers."

"You can wash your feet in the stuff," Witt said, "or rub it into your scalp. But I'm going to get us out of here, so you have to be ready to take off for San Juan on zero notice. The drinks are on me when we get there." He looked from one to the other. They nodded. "Don't leave the plane, except one at a time. I mean, one man sleeps inside while the other keeps watch out here. Four hours on, four off." Again, he looked from one to the other. They both had had military service and knew what was expected in a tight crunch. "I'll get over to the Administration Building," Witt said. "I don't know how, but we'll fly out of here tomorrow."

A masterstroke hunch as he walked away from the airplane. He turned on his heel to go into the office of the company which serviced private airplanes like his. The girl behind the counter was chattering at machinegun speed into the telephone, but broke off when he walked up to her. "Yesss?" she said, using English.

"Señorita," he said, choosing to use Spanish, "I need to place a telephone call."

"But that is impossible, señor. The telephone situation is very bad."

"I know. Everything is very bad. The only thing that is good is the business we bring into this company every month."

"Ah," she said. A man's voice crackled in the receiver she was holding and she ducked her head to spit "Momentito!" into the phone. She had her face under control when she raised it. "Señor?"

"I have to call Miraflores Palace immediately," Witt said. Her mouth fell open and her eyes changed. "Also," Witt said, "I want you to get me the international operator to place a call, person to person, to San Juan. The man I want is Governor Santos Roque." He paused as she hung up on her own call silently. "Señorita, I beg your pardon for troubling you this way, but is there a more private place where I can take these calls?"

She touched her lip lightly with her tongue and said softly, "Yes, señor. In the manager's office. If you will be so kind." She motioned her head toward the glassed-in space at the far end of the ready room.

"Thank you, señorita." As he walked toward the little office, he heard the sirens of fire engines rising and falling, the distant wailing of a hurt city.

□ □ □

The lobby of the Hotel Laputa had become a madhouse. The porters and desk clerks had disappeared and, as Betsy got out of the elevator, she saw the hotel manager and assistant anchored as heroically behind the counter as Horatio at the bridge. The voices in the lobby had a swarming waspish hum; rackety, startling but somehow exhilarating. All our wars are merry, she thought, and the impossible just takes a bit longer.

She wobbled slightly on her high heels. Oh-oh. I've had a wee drop beyond discretion. If Witt were here he'd be annoyed, and I would be annoyed because he was. Do anything you like in public so long as you keep moving. Otherwise do it privately.

She saw a deeply tanned man wearing a light silk suit and sunglasses despite the green gloom of the lobby and she could sense that behind the opaque circles his eyes were running over her like hands. Now that, she thought, is something I could use in private, especially if *he* kept moving. You can get pregnant just the way these men dance. He'd make a divine guest for tonight's dinner party, she thought as the man began to smile knowingly, a slow toothy invitation. Her heart started to pound like a girl's. She turned and fled.

The dinner party. If you want results, Witt always said, go straight to the top. But when she looked at the manager behind the desk she voted against the top. He looks like the embalmed founder of an underground school for morticians, she decided, so she spent the next half hour battling through crowds of people and hurrying down dead-end corridors until she pushed open the two swinging doors which led to the main hotel kitchen.

It was the size of a small gymnasium made of stainless steel and, in the far corner, under a long rack of shining pots and pans, about a dozen junior and senior cooks wearing white aprons were clustered about a portable radio. They were listening very hard, and ignored her. In an open doorway near her stood a short fat man wearing a master chef's tall white hat; he was lifting food off a rolling chromium cart beside him. As Betsy walked toward him she saw that he was giving boxes and bags of food to a woman and a small crowd of ragged children. Whenever one of the children dropped a package and reached for it, another would stamp on his hand and grab it away. The woman kept turning to scream at them, and, when she did, Betsy saw an infant slung like a knapsack in a black shawl on her back. The baby was asleep, his head lolling backward and rolling slightly, each sudden swing launching a cluster of flies off the dribble of dried spittle on his chin.

For a moment Betsy remembered the gray starving back alleys of Dublin, with only the accident that she was her mother's one live birth to keep her from living half starved in such a pack of children.

She stood there nervously fingering her single strand of pearls, feeling pity for the kids' hunger and their reaching hands and distaste at being reminded that this luxurious hotel, with its famous lobby decor, was decorated so differently here downstairs in back. Thank goodness I had a drop or two to keep my chin up, kiddo. I've spent my life running away from knowing this can happen, and now all I need to do is order a lovely dinner party.

As the chef turned to pick up a carton of ground meat his eyebrows went up, giving him the expression of a startled Santa Claus. "Ah! Señora! *Qué hubo?*" Continuing in Spanish, he added, "Bless your employment agency!"

Betsy gave him the smile she reserved for state occasions. "I'm awfully sorry," she said. "*Como está usted?* That's about all I know in Spanish." She became helpless, undefended, a lady in need of a strong protector.

"No Spanish?" He looked incredulous. "*No habla español?*"

She brightened her smile. "Only a little Texican. Or Franglais. I'm awfully retarded about languages." Her voice made it more than an embarrassing confession, an intimacy.

He softened. "It's alla right," the chef said gallantly. "I spik all language. Your agency gives me two, four, how many cooks?"

"I'm a guest in the hotel," Betsy said. "I want to arrange a very important dinner party."

The chef stared at her with operatic intensity. "Señora? A dinn' party—?"

"Oh, nothing big or fancy. Just four of us and some food for the musicians."

"*Musicians!*" The chef exploded and threw the food onto the cart with fury. The peasant woman pestered him; he did not listen.

Betsy was charmed. She had heard that great chefs were as temperamental as symphony conductors. In the end, he would come around and the food would be marvelous.

"Señora," the chef said loudly, "don't you have eyes? You can't see? The hotel has no waiters, no cooks, no nothing! Tonight each guest gets a *pique-nique* plate. *Ecco.*" He measured off the last joint of his little finger. "This much."

Just beyond the doorway the children were jumping up and down and shouting at the chef to hand out more. The woman was busy tying her ankle-length black skirt under a waistband to make a carrying apron. The chef followed Betsy's eyes. "Poor people. Mostly we have ten times so many. Only tonigh' nobody can go by the soldiers."

"Soldiers? To stop starving people?"

"No. To stop the *revuelta.*" He completely ignored the shouting children and made a circle with his forefinger. "All around the hotel, soldiers. Nobody come, nobody go. Maybe they want somebody in the hotel."

The woman outside the door stretched out her hand to the chef and pleaded in a low toneless voice. The chef shook his head, talking fast in Spanish. "*Mas vale pájaro en mano que ciento volando! No!*" Betsy recognized only his last word.

"Maestro," Betsy said. "Don't close the door. What does she want?"

"She crazy. Wants a whole ham."

"Give it to her. I'll pay for it."

"Money is no good, señora. I need food to feed people." His eyes met hers. "I know how you feel. That's why I give them the stale stuff."

With a quick impatient gesture Betsy fumbled with the clasp of her necklace and then held out the strand of pearls to the woman at the doorstep. The woman squinted at Betsy, bewildered, then her eyes hardened. She stared with such feral hatred that Betsy shrank back. The older children began leaping and waving their skinny arms and shrieking. "Señora! Señora!" The chef shouted, then pushed the door closed. He locked it and turned to face her.

"They don' unnerstan' you want to help. Always, they give up the pride for somethin'. Pride for food. For medicine. Nothin' free, ah? Pride is ver' high price, no? A poor woman like that, she would be arrest for havin' such pearls." He fumbled in his apron pocket until he found a toothpick and began to use it expertly as he watched Betsy put her necklace back around her neck. "It's not to worry, señora. T'ousan', ten t'ousan' like her in Caracas. Hungry people everywhere."

"I know." She turned to go. Her stomach hurt with pity and confusion. It was Mayoso's fault. He had lifted off the colorful silks of the famous hotel. Like blood under skin, anarchy and hungry squalor ran just beneath the surface. Damn him. Now I feel all shaggy. My mellow wee willie winkie whiskey edge worn off.

He shrugged. "Maybe I can fix you up a little somethin'. Nothin' fancy. Artichoke rarebit with some biff, ches'nuts? You like mushroom? Kumquat wine jelly salad? Coffee? Sneak it up the service elevator."

"You're awfully nice," she said, "but it would stick in my throat."

He put his hands on his hips, hunching slightly, then threw his arms out wide, helpless. "Señora," he said, "deat', taxes anna poor. Always they are with us. Don' look. Don' see it."

"Oh, please. Don't say that. I know what poor means, and I hate to think like that."

"Señora, I was poor too. One meal a day." He held up a forefinger. "One, anna one with no bread. So I know."

"Then why do you say things like that?"

He put his hands together, as if praying, and shook them at her. "Even the Bible says so."

"Then why give that woman food?"

"She's a widow of one of our kitchen help."

"Maestro, I like to hope for more from the future."

"Señora," he said, "I like to help you. For you party, you demand champagne?"

"Maestro, I demand nothing. But to relax, I mean *work* at it, champagne would be very nice."

"Regret. I have none. No truck delivery for two day. But a few magnums I have of *vin mousseux*. Sekt, you know?"

"Some Sekt is from the Champagne district—"

"Ah, a señora not scare by fancy labels? The German salesman who sold me one trial case of Sekt, he swears it is Champagne district. But if the señora is willing to take a chance—"

Betsy raised her chin. "Maestro, I have an idea. Why can't I bring the people to the food? Down here?"

"Here? In the kitchen?"

"Of course. Be my guest. A kitchen is always the best place to eat"— she imitated him—"no? Self-serve. Buffet style. A few magnums of Sekt. *Voilà*. A party."

"It's craze," he said. "A *bachata*."

"But you're smiling."

"I like the idea." With a flourish he threw his toothpick into the waste-basket beside his desk. "I do it! What time?"

"What time do you finish slicing the *pique-nique* for the *haut monde* mob?"

"Nine, with help. That *tumulto*. With no help, maybe nine-dirty."

"Great," she said and put out her hand. "It's a deal, Maestro."

As he shook her hand, the chef said with profound sincerity, "You' husban', he mus' be a lucky man."

□ □ □

Under the waterfall noise of the shower Mayoso was not sure of what he heard until there was a second scream. He shut the water off with one hand and rammed back the shower curtain with the other as Cristina cried out again. He yanked open the bathroom door and ran into the bedroom.

She was sitting up in bed gazing into space with blank unseeing hypnotic eyes. When he grabbed her shoulders, she turned her head slightly, like a sleepwalker, but the dark pools of her enlarged pupils pierced through him. He was and was not there.

"Cristina," he said, and shook her gently. *Qué más*? Somnambulism?

"Dios mío," she murmured, still in some far-off trance, and pointed at the empty wall on the other side of the room.

"What do you see there?" he whispered.

"How terrible," she said. Then shook her head. "How terrible. How terrible." Tears shone in her eyes.

"What do you see there, Cristina?"

She shook her head and crossed her arms over her breasts. In a hushed voice she breathed confidentially, "Oh, how people suffer. Madre santísima!"

"Cristina," he said. "Do you know who's talking to you?"

She nodded, still looking through him blankly with an eerie hallucinatory vividness.

"Where are you? What do you see there?" She raised one arm limply, her hand trembling as she pointed at the wall. Her mouth formed a word but she said nothing.

"What do you see?"

"Filho." Her voice was hushed. "They're going to do something to Filho." Using both hands she pushed herself backward slightly, beginning to cower. "Ohhh," she breathed.

"Do you know who I am?" he asked.

She nodded but did not answer.

"Who am I?"

"Filho's friend. The kind man." A watchful animal wariness muffled her.

"What's my name?"

"Mayoso."

He looked into her eyes. She was seeing and unseeing at the same time. He moved his hand before her face but her expression remained unchanging. He touched her face with his fingertips carefully. "Do you know where you are?"

"In the hotel. With the Americans."

"Do you feel safe?"

She shook her head.

"Do you want me to wake you up?"

She shook her head again, shrouded in a closed inscrutable brooding.

"Do you want to go to sleep?"

"Yes." Slowly she lowered herself to lie curled on the bed. He stood there watching until her breathing became regular, then realized he was dripping wet and went back quickly to finish his shower. Had she been taking drugs? he wondered. He had seen such dreamlike oracular behavior only several times before in children muttering nightmarishly during high fevers or with the occasional use of intravenous sodium amytal for psychiatric interviews, but Cristina had been so strangely lost within herself and yet aware of where she was at the same time. I suppose we always tell ourselves the truth in sleep and only lie when we wake up. The truth can hardly make us free, because so often it's intolerable.

While he was shaving, he heard sounds from the bedroom, luggage being opened and snapped shut. He rinsed his face quickly, dried it, wrapped a long towel around his middle, and walked into the room.

Cristina was bending over an open valise rummaging for something and she looked up as the door from the bathroom opened. For a moment they looked questioningly at one another, aware that they were like husband and wife getting ready for a party, and yet at arm's length. The wingslants of her eyes lifted; she shared her private inward laughter with him.

"I packed so fast," she said with mock helplessness, "and now I can't find a thing." She straightened as he walked across the room to pick up his valise.

"Maybe Betsy will make this a come-as-you-are party," he said.

"You could be from Tahiti."

"Betsy's natural but she's not primitive." He watched her. She was completely different from the haunted dreamer of a short while ago. "And I still have one clean shirt. See? I'll go down with all flags flying. *Le bourgeois gentilhomme.*"

"What do you mean 'go down'? To die?"

"Nothing. It's just an expression." He pulled an undershirt and socks from his valise and said casually, "Why do you ask?"

"I don't know. I had such a strange dream."

"About what?"

"I don't know. I never remember my dreams." She put one hand on her chest. "But my heart is beating so fast."

"Your heart? Do you take pills for something?"

"Oh no. I'm never sick. I swim like a fish and eat like a horse."

"Good. Betsy likes hungry guests."

"Your American friends are very nice for such rich people."

"Don't you think rich people are nice?"

She shrugged. "Mostly not. The men are very haughty. They treat girls like Kleenex. The women dress too much and treat their maids something terrible."

"Do you know many people who are rich?"

"Only a few. At parties. Things like that. It's like they say. The rich don't bother to be nicer."

"Some of my best friends are rich."

"I don't care if you make fun of me, Mayoso. It's true, isn't it?"

"About eighty-five per cent true."

"These days, that's very true."

He laughed. "The Sommers are not vulgar rich. They are quiet rich. Do-good rich. Live-quietly rich."

"Ah. But the way she dresses—"

"Betsy Sommers was a fashion model many years ago. As a girl. Nothing glamorous. Very little money."

"She does this high dressing up now, why? From boredom?"

"I suppose so. She shines with a beautiful light, no? She's hard to hide under a bushel."

Cristina nodded. "I'm only pretty. She's beautiful. How can a person have such dark black hair and such light green eyes? Rich men marry them, don't they?"

"Not usually. Not the quiet do-good rich."

"Why not? Everybody wants beauty."

"But not married to it. It's a strain."

"I know now," Cristina said, "where I saw her picture. In a magazine in the beauty salon. *Harper's.*"

"Impossible. *Harper's* is not that kind of magazine. No fashion pictures."

"I saw it." With one finger she made a quick sign of the cross over her heart. "Believe me. A whole page, color. She wore a green suede coat, a green suede jockey cap, and she stood beside a long low green British car. It was one of those color pages that make you stop to look twice. And the name of the magazine was *Harper's.*"

"You must mean *Harper's Bazaar.*"

"That's what I said."

"Okay," he said in English. "That's what you said."

"You know, you're nice. I've heard people say that when a big man is gentle, he's twice as much so."

"Just try telling that to Father Gofredo."

"In San Juan? The television padre?"

He nodded. "The hi-fi voice of the Lord. Deus ex machina. I ran into him in the lobby. He wants to burn me at the stake."

"He's strong, that padre. A protagonista. How can he know what it's like for people to be weak?"

"I think he's going to make trouble when I get"—he corrected himself—"we get back to San Juan. If we get back."

His seismic inner ear had just detected the faraway thump of remembered kettledrums. A rapidfire sticksnapping tattoo followed, then the distant vibrations, repeated.

She put her thin tanned hands up to her mouth. From behind her fingers she said, "What do you mean, *if* we get back?"

"Filho has called a general strike."

"You're sure? Last week I heard him say it would never work here in Caracas. Too many people would turn their backs on the idea and keep the city going."

"But thousands will obey him. You only need a few in a modern city. Food handlers, shippers, transportation workers. The radio and television communications people." He shook his head, "We won't get out of here with one quick jump, *guapita*."

"Nothing frightens me anymore." She waved her hand in circles. "Look at where we are. If you told me this yesterday I would say you are loco. If you told me this morning we would be here like this, with you wearing a towel—" She shrugged and made a little final circle with her finger by her temple. "So when we come to tomorrow we will see."

"We'll know better as soon as Witt comes back from the airport. If he gets back."

She raised her eyes to the ceiling. "If! If! Again he says if. Such a big man with such small faith."

"You think it's easy to get down from this mountain? You saw what it was like when we drove up. And then through the city? Roadblocks and checkpoints. And then down an autopista filled with soldiers? To an airport sealed off by the military? And then to get all the way back here?"

"I can see," she said, "that you are a born optimist. Me, I'm a pessimist, so everything good surprises me. So tonight I think I'll celebrate everything and drink too much. Will I embarrass you with that knockout Señora Sommers?"

"No. She takes baths in the stuff."

"Really?" She pointed at him. "You. You're making fun of me again." She put both hands over her stomach and pretended to droop. "You shouldn't make fun of a girl who is starving."

"Don't worry. We'll eat soon. Would you rather get dressed here or in the bathroom?"

"It's up to you."

"No. Up to you. Ladies need more elbow room."

"To be modest is so foolish. After that examination this morning."

"This morning I was your doctor."

"Not now?"

"Not now. That's finished. Now we're two shipwrecked fishermen in the same lifeboat, Cristina. Let the Sommers think we're lovers. It's no time for usual modesties. If this doesn't bother you, it doesn't bother me."

She shrugged and turned her back and began to dress. An evocative warmflower scent of frangipani drifted from her, as if he had just tugged off a blossom from his doorway tree and today was simply another bright day before tomorrow.

Tomorrow? That tomorrow should come, for this is not my bohío door-way, Witt is not yet back, and meanwhile we have the eternity of this night to outlast.

□ □ □

Round and round she danced, twirling as she went, balancing the empty champagne bottle on her head with one rose stemmed into it, an-other flower in her hair, round and round, barefoot and balanced and smiling privately to herself in a spinning tipsy dream. "Olé Cristina!" Mayoso applauded.

They all clapped their hands in rhythm, singing along with the small orchestra in the room behind. The musicians could see her clearly through the wide double doors which opened on the large tiled terrace, and they stomped in tempo as she whirled from the dark outer edge of the terrace through the oblong spill of light and wheeled back into darkness. *"Ojos verdes,"* sang the leader passionately, *"y tu tienes ojos verdes que yo nunca olvidare. . . ."* He and his four caballeros had been given three magnums of Sekt, the German champagne, by Betsy. The royal gesture was muy simpático. After all, the work of making nonstop mariachi music can raise a thirst, and all three bottles had been emptied with manly dis-patch. The musicians were now prepared to swear that night was day, love eternal, and to play "Green Eyes" continuously, intermittently, any-where, upstairs or downstairs or in my lady's chamber. Cristina might be the dancer, but their music was an open gallant courtship of Betsy.

"Don't you want to stop for a rest?" Mayoso called out as Cristina spun on one toe past him. His voice was edgy. The gunfire in the valley had paused. But for how long?

"Marvelous! Marvelous!" Betsy cried, clapping her hands with the beat of the music. "How does she do it?"

"She'd better stop," Witt said, "before she conks out."

"Ah," Betsy said, "but what a way to glow." Just then the rose fell out of the bottle.

"Stop!" Witt called out. "La vie en rose is down, down, down." He stepped forward and the music stopped. "Next turn. Those are your own rules."

"I don't want to stop," Cristina said, breathing heavily, open-mouthed, swaying with her eyes closed. "Don't stop me. Don't throw me out of heaven."

"Come back to earth," Mayoso said. "Just for a minute."

"There is no earth," Cristina said dreamily. *"Nada."*

"Then how do you know this is heaven?" Witt asked.

"Because," Cristina said, "last night I was dead."

The penthouse balcony on which they stood was hung with trailing green plants so that the air brushed them with jasmine or oleander in each breeze, and, standing on their cantilevered platform outthrust from the topmost floor, they hovered in flight high over the mushrooming umbrellas of the patio below, over the watery turquoise glitter of the free-form swimming pool and the manicured putting green on the lower slope. In the spaceless nighttime distances around their mountaintop terrace they were suspended timelessly, lost anonymously between the soft tropical scatter of stars and the earthy tumble of city lights. Military convoy head-lights streamed in parallels down through the Caracas valley. They were airborne, Olympian, above the soundless metronome of battle makeready in the encircling hoop of hills.

Cristina lifted the empty champagne bottle off her head and ceremo-niously offered it to Witt. He picked up the dropped red rose and shut one eye as he aimed its stem at the bottle opening. "Fuzzy, fuzzy. I see two bottles." He turned to ask Mayoso, "Where did little María de la Con-cepción ever learn that only illusions are real?" But Mayoso had gone into the living room with Betsy to pass some chilled champagne among the perspiring musicians. Witt lifted the rose-crowned bottle carefully to his head. "How the devil do you balance this while you spin so fast?"

"Oh," Cristina said, "when you grow up in Haiti scratching dirt and barefoot, carry every drop of water from a pump, you learn to balance anything up to piano size on your head."

"I thought you grew up in Puerto Rico."

"Name an island," she said, "and I grew up on it. I can even talk papiamento. Tonight I can talky-talk *any* language."

"The gift of tongues?"

"You know something? You ask a lot of questions."

"That's how I earn a living, Cristina. I'm paid to keep asking."

"Now let somebody else ask you, okay? Deduct it from your pay."

"Okay."

"You were gone a long time today. How did you get through all the soldiers and back to the hotel?"

"If I told you, you'd never believe it."

She threw back her head and laughed. "Oh, I can believe anything after these few days. Anything! Anything at all. Tell me that moon out there is made of mangoes. I believe it. Now one more, okay?"

"Okay."

She looked over her shoulder to make sure no one was close enough to hear her, then asked, "We can truly fly to San Juan in your plane to-morrow? The airport allows?"

"I don't know," Witt said. "I'm expecting a telephone call sometime tonight."

"A definite yes or no?"

"A definite maybe. I'm afraid that's the best we can hope for."

She crossed her arms to cradle her elbows in cupped hands. "I'm sorry I asked you," she said. "Now I'm worried again. I hoped the champagne would drown it—"

"I did the best I could."

"Oh, please," she said quickly. "You have been so generous to us. Please, I'm not complaining."

"I am," Witt said. "I intend to file a bloody strong protest at the Embassy."

"That's a Yanqui joke, no?"

"No," Witt said. "Just a poor try."

"The nice thing about you, you like Mayoso very much."

"Well," Witt said, "he's worth it. Just when I begin to think he behaves like a damn fool, I realize he's doing something very unusual. He does what he can about things worth doing. Even with the risks."

"How terrible," she said with her voice catching, "if he is killed."

"Is it as bad as that?"

"If I told you, *you* wouldn't believe it."

"I'd believe it. After all, you've known him quite a while, I'm sure."

She hesitated, then said, "Long enough."

"My brother thinks it's an awful waste of ability—the way Mayoso beats his brains out on refugee bickering and politics instead of sticking to medicine."

"Oh," she said, "many Latin doctors go into politics. Look at Argentina, Santo Domingo. Even Venezuela years ago. The doctors are the only men the hotheads on both sides will trust. It's a great honor. Mayoso follows a noble tradition. What he says or does, it affects millions of people, not just one at a time."

"I'm not criticizing Mayoso. Don't think that for one minute. My brother David is one of the new academic doctors—you know, the great god Research will save the world. He's very good with his individual patients, but his heart belongs to all those shiny test tubes."

"He does not like Mayoso?"

"David likes Mayoso. He respects him. But he considers politics a waste of time. My mother is the politician. A magazine story about my mother said she was never married, but only signed an alliance. She admires

Mayoso because he does what she believes people with brains from established families should do."

"Politics?"

"Not exactly. Take responsibility for how things are, is what she says."

"Noblesse oblige?"

"Not really. She welcomes anybody with brains and guts. It's just that she's found the descendants of the old families can afford to take the time to take responsibility, and most of them aren't doing it." He paused, then said, "Great party talk. I don't mean to spoil the party."

"Oh," she said, "please. I like to hear about Mayoso from his friends. He always seems so—how do you say the word, lonesome? Not lonesome —no. Alone. So alone. He takes chances alone. He could be hurt or disappear, and no one would know."

He nodded. "He never dealt with the old Batista crowd, and now he's fed up with the refugee hotheads." He looked at her in the transparent darkness. "I don't mean to ask what I shouldn't—but is he trapped by his own hard-line guys? The ones who make gunboat raids? The hawks who'll accuse him of appeasement if he stops pouring every dime he earns into anti-Castro raids?"

"I don't know. Everything begins with idealists and ends with fanatics. A good man like him is trapped mostly by himself."

"You understand him very well."

"I learn more all the time. Oh, I had such a mixed-up loco education. In San Juan, after school hours, my mother made me go to Baldorioty High School for extra English lessons. But my school was also to work with my mother in a backroom cigar shop. I learned so much from our reader."

"Your reader?"

"One of the cigar makers always reads out loud for everybody, because the work is monotonous. You sort and sort the tobacco. Many grades. Wrapper, filler, you slice out the center stem, *tsst*, trim the leaf, *tsst*, lay it out, fill it, roll it, band it, box it. So it helps when the reader reads something good. Lorca, he was my favorite. Can you imagine Franco's men executing such a poet? Chekhov I liked better than Tolstoy. Also, *Les Misérables*. Also, Dickens. Some of those old stories were very real to us, because in our corner of the world we are still partly in that nineteenth century. I think so, do you? Sometimes I would cry. Like peeling onions."

"A girl like you? I can't imagine it."

"Oh, you'd be surprised how easy! Mayoso made me want to cry this afternoon."

"Mayoso? Not Mayoso."

"Did he ever tell you how they took him out for execution every morning for a week?"

"A *week*? Every morning?"

She nodded.

"My God," Witt said, "how did he keep himself from going mad?"

"He said we need to invent a new kind of bravery. Maybe that is what your mother also means by responsibility, no?"

"Cristina, I can see why you're Mayoso's girl. For a babe in arms you're plenty savvy."

"Not me. I was just always hungry, and you learn fast like that, no? When you are twelve, already you are a little old lady. You know if you pray enough and wait long enough, you get everything you want—too late."

"Here they come," Witt said. His voice dropped. "Don't mention I'm waiting for a phone call. I don't want to worry Betsy."

"You behave yourself, DeWitt," Betsy's voice said, coming closer. "And stop making passes at other people's lasses. I think the musicians want to go home, dear. Time to pay the piper. You'll need a bucket of bolívares."

"I'll sign a chit," Witt said. "The front desk will cash it for them." As he walked into the apartment he threw over his shoulder, "And if *el líder* of the band keeps looking at you like that, I'll challenge him to a duel."

"I never saw anything like it," Betsy said to Christina. "I mean, how do you keep the bottle from falling off your head?"

"Oh, that's nothing. You should see when the bottle is full and the head is empty!" She jumped slightly at the nearby metallic clatter of a machine pistol. Silence. Another rattling burst of gunfire further away, then silence again. Mayoso came out on the balcony to join them.

"Trigger happy," Mayoso said. "They even celebrate Christmas with blockbusters and *triquitraques*. It's illegal, so of course the fireworks are sold on every streetcorner before Christmas. An anarchist in every soul."

Betsy and Cristina were motionless on each side of him, staring into the oppressive darkness. Everything about them contradicted the gunfire: the loud laughing and talk of the musicians as they packed their instruments in the living room; and their casual make-believe *liqui-liqui* tunics with the hotel's palm-tree symbol embroidered below the shoulder; the mesmeric plum-colored jasmine-scented air; Betsy's green sheath and high-piled hair caught in a circlet of green jewels; Cristina's bare feet and the suggestion of tawny nudity vivid through her yellow lacework dress.

The gunfire diminished by steps, dissolved in darkness; its absence left them tensed as eavesdroppers.

"Oh Lord," Betsy said finally. "The silence keeps making me jumpy."

"The guns don't bother me so much," Cristina said in a low voice as if talking to herself. "It's all those soldiers you can't see, all in a circle around the hotel." She tilted her head upward. "Listen." They heard the distant thrumming of airplanes approaching invisibly overhead.

"One hell of a party," Witt said as he walked back onto the terrace to join them. He cocked one ear sideways. "Airplanes? Sounds like a squadron of fighter planes. I wonder what's happening."

"I think," Mayoso said slowly, "what began as a raid has turned into a do-or-die offensive."

"But who?" Betsy asked angrily. "Against what? What's it all about?"

"New elections are coming up," Mayoso said. "The FALN and Communists want to bring the government to its knees before election time. They don't want the President to have the first freely elected government to serve a complete term and then turn the power over to a new free government. Every Latin politician promises not to perpetuate himself in power, but the President is keeping his promises. He's stepping down, and that's revolutionary." The airplanes were directly overhead now and he had to raise his voice. "First the general strike. Now all this. It shows the underground must have decided to slug it out."

Filho, he thought. Do you still think you give orders to a hurricane? Tonight we'll see. You can't spend years teaching the hungry and humiliated a catechism of injustice, to burn down the world—not without being trapped in your own firestorm. Sow the wind, reap the whirlwind. You play Russian roulette. The Church plays Vatican roulette. We others take our chances.

From the long reaches of the night came the snarl of a squadron diving into strafing runs, then the stammering rattle of airborne cannons. They must have observers up on Mount Ávila and in Cagigal Observatory, with detailed grid maps and artillery coordinates of the whole city, Mayoso thought. And the dome of the Capitol, with its sheath of gold, would give an easy measuring point for gun directors, even at night. Filho might be able to put enough firepower into the streets to attack the Círculo Militar, not because it was worth anything tactically, but only because the ten-million-dollar marble playhouse built for his officers by Pérez Jiménez stuck in everybody's throat.

Like a devil's festival of lights, illumination shells burst into chalky chemical suns which drifted downward lazily on trailing smokestems. Parachutes of color signal flares blossomed brilliantly. The sky seemed hung with holiday chandeliers.

How we stand here, Mayoso thought. Filho has gone mad, like Nero, and we're the Roman circus. Every police station must be a fortress, the communications centers and main government buildings choked with the smoke of overturned and burning cars and gasoline-drenched tires, telephone lines cut and looped along rubble and splintered glass, garbage cans lying everywhere in their own reeking litter.

A ragged fringe of artillery flashes stabbed upward over the darkness. After an eerie silence, the sound came finally to them as a hammering *thud thud thud* of high explosives. The fighter planes must have circled out over the sea because everything became noiseless except for a remote quiver in the echoing air. For a moment the following silence ticked with quiet heartbeats, like one's own pulse tapping intimately within an eardrum, saturated mutely with more than a million people crouched behind closed shutters, locked doors, barred cellars, in tin shacks, under bridges. The lunatic humanoid sound of sirens screaming drifted up the valley, rising and falling; the city was stretched on the rack of night.

Mayoso grasped the terrace rail tightly. Cristina put her hand on his arm. She felt the tremor in his muscles. As if he were answering something she had asked, he said, "The more they kill, the more blood each side claims as martyrs. Aie, they make death the only cause to give life some meaning."

If there could be only wounds instead of death, he thought, an arrangement to hurt instead of kill, the whole crazy game might stop. This mutual intertwined death, both the drowning and the rescuer going under together. What will we find in a burial embrace and our return as molecules to the sea?

Beside him, he heard Betsy say to Witt, "Are we safe here?"

"More than anyplace else."

Mayoso felt Cristina's hand tighten. He put his own hand over hers: her fingers were chilled. They dug into his skin as the telephone rang startlingly behind them.

"The telephone!" she said, as if only she had heard it.

He looked down at her. "Expecting a call?"

Cristina's eyes followed Witt as he went indoors to answer the phone. "Telephones. . . ." she said vaguely.

"Nervous in the service," Betsy said. "All of us. But you heard what Witt said. We're safer here than anyplace else, Cristina."

"That just makes me feel like a coward. Don't ask me why, but that's how I feel."

"The party's over," Betsy said. "It may have started with a whimper, but it sure ended with a bang. I'm exhausted."

"How you persuaded the chef to feed us," Mayoso said, reaching for neutral ground, "I will never know."

"For once in my life," Betsy said, "I was honest. Wasn't he a dear? I didn't fool around or fake around. Men are always so impressed by a little honesty in a woman." She raised her hand and waved her fingers gently. "Goodnight, children. A flight of angels sing thee to thy rest."

As she walked with her own special sway off the terrace, Cristina whispered to Mayoso, "In my whole life, I never heard anyone talk like her."

"Nobody does. They custom-built only one, and that was it."

"One minute she talks like anybody, the next minute she sounds like an actress making fun of herself. I don't understand her."

"Don't try. Betsy's not for understanding. She's like rain or wind. You don't understand her. You just experience her."

At the perimeter of the hotel terrace, beyond the semicircle of flags, many motors started up at the same time as if at a signal. The engines were revved up and down nervously. A two-eyed chain of Jeep headlights, each illuminating the vehicle in front of it, all came to life as the convoy began rolling on the road which curved around the rim of the hotel and dipped toward the valley.

"Will Filho win?" asked Cristina quietly.

"I don't know. Only if the people back him up against the police and the army."

"He kept saying it was a people's war."

"If it is, he'll win. But I don't know," Mayoso said. "He's fighting a President who's honest and smart. In '28 when Filho's brother was killed in student fighting, the President was a student fighting in the streets, too. He spent time in a Gómez dungeon, in leg irons. He helped organize a worker and peasant bloc. He lived in exile in Puerto Rico. When he came back here as President he kept his promises about land reform, free elections and things everybody could understand, even small things like government redemption of pawned sewing machines. Maybe the people will stay with him and refuse to help Filho. Filho's men are like fish—without the people, they have no ocean to swim away and hide in."

Witt's voice came from the terrace door. "Goodnight, you two. I'm going to hit the sack."

"The telephone?" Cristina asked huskily.

"Oh, that was the chef calling me up to say thanks for the little envelope I left in his apron pocket. And he gave me a bulletin. The radio reported another United States Embassy military attaché has been kidnaped." When no one spoke, Witt tried saying more cheerfully, "Wasn't that the damnedest dinner party you ever went to? Self-service in a hotel kitchen."

"A miracle," Cristina said. "I never enjoyed food so much in all my life. You and Betsy are miracle workers."

"Look who's talking." Witt put his hand on top of his head. "Full bottle, empty head. That's our secret."

"Thanks," Mayoso said. He hesitated. "For everything."

"Not so fast. Let's wait until we touch down in San Juan before we hand out the medals, okay? Goodnight."

"Goodnight," they said together.

Sirens again, far away this time, a fatigued lament.

Mayoso put his hand under Cristina's chin and raised her face so that she was looking directly up at him. "What's all this about the telephone?" To his surprise he saw her smile privately in the moonlight.

"You told me the truth. I'm glad you're not the doctor anymore."

"Listen, Cristina, you should explain about the telephone."

"You think I'm waiting for a phone call from Filho?"

"Of course not."

"Then why do you sound like that?"

"Because I don't appreciate secrets at such a time. I told you before, we're in the same lifeboat."

She lifted her chin off his fingers and turned her head away. "I had such a loco dream about you. I dreamt I saw you with nothing on, dripping wet, and you know"—she swung back to face him—"when I woke up there was a big wet patch on the rug next to me. Very spooky."

"Don't change the subject, Cristina. The telephone. Every hour counts. The party is over. The police will go through the hotel tomorrow, person by person, and you and I are personae non gratae to both sides in this mess. So just explain the telephone."

"Don't sound so angry."

"I'm not angry. I just want to come out of this alive, don't you?"

"Witt is expecting the telephone. He told me he made some overseas calls."

"That's all he said? Just some overseas calls?"

"Yes. You know how he talks. He said the best we can hope for is a definite maybe."

He took a breath and let it out slowly. "That sounds like Witt."

Mayoso faced outward in the darkness, looking beyond the watery gleam of moonlight on the nearby hills, contemplating the smoky red crucible in the valley. Patches of clouds over the city shone on their bottom surfaces with pale reflections of burning buildings. Scattered gunfire, far enough away to sound like the popping of toy corks, reached them in short bursts. How often young men with rifles had crept along the streets down there, hugging the walls and frightened about being brave enough because they were too proud to learn the technology of street warfare, hanging their banners from the fancy scrollwork of Andalusian-style lampposts, searching for something in themselves that they thought they would find in a new classless world. How could they believe otherwise? he thought. Thieves take on authority when judges steal themselves.

Cristina touched his arm lightly. "What can we do now?"

"Nothing."

"But that's the hardest thing in the world."

He looked down at her. "Go to bed. I'll sleep on the bedroom sofa."

"No," she said. "You'll never fit. I will."

A great invisible drill came boring through the night. Bombers! Mayoso searched the sky. "Twin-engine bombers!" he said. "Dios! Do they have to use bombers?" New flares rocketed outward and burst whitely above the city. "If this keeps up—" he began to say to her, but stopped, surprised. Cristina had gone away soundlessly, silent on her bare feet.

He turned back and again grasped the terrace railing, tugging it helplessly as a jammed unsteering rudder.

The fighting in the city must have become very stubborn. He dammed back the tide of fatigue which made his head feel heavy and tilted. He could hardly distinguish the many different calibers, firing randomly. For some time there must have been strong positions and barricades, each side bringing up reserves and heavier weapons. He stood hypnotized, his bones aching to sleep, unable to break away from where he stood helpless above the battle. At a god's height, he stood at the volcano's head. This should be a night without a moon, he thought, not this clear oracular whiteness bright as daylight. A sharp insomniac clarity magnified everything; each gunflash summoned up a laceration of the dark deep-bosomed earth.

Something had changed violently since he had seen Filho. Something, somewhere, was so wrong and unplanned by Filho that the city's jaws would close in on them all, slowly and surely as a nightmare in which the walls of a room close inward relentlessly as a vise.

Filho knew better than to try to exchange manpower for firepower, even in street fighting. Militarily, was he counting on the mountain terrain? Politically, on a popular uprising? A charismatic leader might succeed against impossible odds as Fidel had done. Or was this night of fire the result of trapped rage, the fury that tears up good tactics to send massed men up against the muzzles of better-trained professionals, as Stalin had demanded during that first summer of the Nazi assault? That crazy eighteenth-century courage of Stalin's infantrymen running elbow to elbow, cheering, singing, roaring Russian *urrah!*, storming the Waffen SS with useless bayonets point blank into overlapping machinegun fire, scythed down in windrows at Rostov; the saber-swinging stirrup-to-stirrup Mongolian cavalry charge mowed down at Musino. A mad brotherhood of bravery, men to move mountains, the unfree Marxist grandsons of serfs, squandered as sacrificially into moloch machines as Marx's fatted factory owners had once consumed masses of child-worker sacrifices. Marx's fol-

lowers had secretly torpedoed the Treaty of Versailles and helped rebuild
the Wehrmacht in Russia during the decade 1923 to 1933. Hitler's men
had returned to Russia to thank the followers of the followers.

And now, in Caracas, the Marxist followers had become students. The
clever Tukhachevsky had become Filho. The tough brave hardship-
enduring Russian infantryman's Red Star had become the badge of
Chinese infantrymen and Latin American schoolboys. They hated the
factory owners' clumsy gods and fought to build more efficient modern
gods; assembly-lined, computer-linked, rehabilitative labor chosen by secret police. Everywhere, the unfree grandsons of serfs fought old slavery
with new slaveries. Mayoso's mind spun outward, widening, gulping disconnected ideas into a single vortex.

Just as there had been Roman proconsuls, Venetian envoys, Spanish
gobernadores, Vatican nuncios, French chargé's d'affaires, German
Gauleiters, British ministers, American advisers, so, also, Filho must have
Russian or Chinese commissars. Filho's counselors, like all such men,
would coolly use a local revolt in Caracas as one square of a global chessboard. This Caracas uprising, by itself, by modern standards of efficient
mass destruction, this is a tinpot skirmish. But it was so clearly a pilot
test for more to follow: Bogotá, La Paz, Rio, Buenos Aires, Santiago. Mayoso
had a vision of smoke rising from the altars of burning treaties, new
stainless-steel gods demanding human sacrifice. The veins of nations would
hemorrhage down the gutters of the continent.

Mammoth anvil thuds began to detonate in Caracas under umbilical
chemical flares. A blasting clobber of bomb concussions drubbed the tight
drumskin sky. Tambourine rattlebone clatter of machineguns, caroming
from hill to hill. Canvas-ripping ricocheting automatic fire. The *crump-
crump-crump* of mortars. A rising gauze of smoke drifted in the moon-
white, shifting in hazy layers, making strange rippling shimmers. A
nightmare mirage dazed him; his skull cracked with firelit apocalyptic
delusions.

Not Caracas below him, but all Latin America would be the second
front. The heartland of battle had moved from Europe's crowded
slaughter-house to the vast abattoirs of Asia. In his mirage, green bamboo
shoots sloped between mass graves, riceplants rooted in bloodponds. Vul-
ture-fed Asia, nirvana-seeking, Asia's beggar-bowl mobs disemboweled by
hunger. Fly-heaped, fecund and swarming and famished as Latin America, a convulsive tidal wave from the China Sea to the Caribbean. Who
but madmen in that oceanic humanity wanted a sooty incinerator death?
Yet, fatherlands would train youth militias, motherlands would be mobilized, *urra'd banzaied,* lives hacked down in new technical dyings with

the one universal timeless word: mamma, mamita, mère, Mary, the only outcry for love men still believed was stronger than death.

He stood paralyzed, tensing his eyelids to keep them open. His motionless grip on the terrace rail had been so powerful that he had to make an effort to open his fingers, spent and worn as if he had been in combat himself.

The telephone. It rang with shrill continuous insistence. He heard Witt's voice talking, protesting, rising; a moment later Witt, wearing pajamas and slippers, hurried out to the terrace.

"Mayoso! It's San Juan! They're talking Spanish too fast for me."

Without a word Mayoso followed him into the living room and picked up the telephone. "This is Doctor Mayoso Martí. Who is this, please?"

"This is the night operator at La Fortaleza, San Juan. Governor Santos Roque is returning a call from Señor DeWitt Sommers."

"Is he on the line?"

"No, señor. The Governor is asleep. We tried for hours to reach you. The message is that he has succeeded in the request of Señor DeWitt Sommers with the Venezuelan government."

"Just a moment." He put his hand over the mouth of the phone and said quickly to Witt, "Did you telephone Governor Santos Roque to make some kind of request of the Venezuelan government?"

"Yes," Witt said tensely. "I want them to let us out of here. I mean *get* us out of here."

"Smart move, Witt."

"I didn't tell you because I was afraid it wouldn't work. What do they say?"

"The phone connection is rotten. It must be rung through a patched-up line here in Caracas." He paused, then said, "Oh Christ. A woman's voice. It could be a fake." He and Witt stared at one another.

Slowly Witt said, "I have to ask you. Which side are you on?"

"Each side thinks I'm an enemy."

Witt clenched his teeth. "Great."

"I'll try to make sure of this," Mayoso said. In Spanish he told the operator, "If you are in La Fortaleza you can ring the Governor's telephone."

"Oh no, señor."

"I must talk to the Governor personally."

"Señor, I told you. The Governor is sleeping."

"I take the responsibility. Ring his telephone."

Her voice faltered. "Señor, I cannot do that."

"You have no decision to make. I will explain it to the Governor. Now, ring his telephone."

She said nothing but, when he heard a new buzzing sound over the wire, he looked up at Witt. "Now we'll see if this is fake or not."

He raised his voice. "Hello? Hello? Santos Roque?"

"Mayoso?" The voice faded and became a blurred gibberish.

"Hello! Hello!" He was shouting now.

Unexpectedly, the Governor's voice boomed in his ear. "I can't hear you!"

"Others may be on this line!" Mayoso shouted. "Speak English!"

"Of course! I speak French to women, German to the Chamber of Commerce, and Spanish to God. How the hell are you?"

Relief swept over Mayoso. "It's Santos Roque, nobody else," he said to Witt.

"I talked to an aide-de-camp at Miraflores Palace a few hours ago," Santos Roque's voice went on efficiently. "He promised to send an army car to get you all out of there."

"A thousand thanks, Governor. I can never repay you."

"By God, you can."

"How?"

"I'll tell you when I see you. I'm having my own troubles here and I need your help. I'm counting on the Venezuelans to get you out of there tomorrow morning. How do things look?"

"Very bad."

Silence, then: "I'm glad we talked. When you land in San Juan tomorrow, call me pronto, ah?"

The phone clicked and the line was dead. Mayoso put down the receiver very tenderly, as if it were glass and any arrangements made on it could be shattered by a careless blow.

"My God," Witt said, "don't just stand there! What did he say?"

"The Venezuelans will send an army car for us in the morning."

Incredibly, he watched as Witt threw his head back and whooped with relief. From opposite sides of the living room, Betsy and Cristina came running in.

"What's going on?" Betsy asked, turning her head rapidly from Witt to Mayoso and back again. "What are you two cooking up now?" The floor-length green Chinese silk robe she wore would have made her questions sound imperious if she had not been comically toweling off the last smudges of her cold cream. Cristina was silent and pale. She had loosened her hair and stood tugging the belt of her white kimono. Again she seemed the frightened girl Mayoso remembered.

"That Santos Roque! Would you believe it? What a man!" Witt marched up and down excitedly, explaining what had happened.

"How marvelous!" Betsy flung the towel over her wrist, like a waiter.

"This calls for a celebration. There's still a magnum of bubble *wasser* in the refrigerator." Over her shoulder, as she hurried to the shiny kitchen of the suite, she called back, "Grab your own glasses! The ones with the lipstick are for the girls."

Cristina had not moved as Witt hurried around the room turning on lamps. Mayoso asked her in rapid Spanish, "What's the matter, little one?"

"I don't know."

"Too many miracles for one day?"

"I think so." She was worried. "This telephone call. Can I ask you something?"

"Of course."

"You knew exactly who you talked to? No mistakes?"

He nodded. "I was careful about that. Don't worry about mistakes."

She walked toward him haltingly, her face beginning to change. When he put his arms around her she leaned against him and began to cry.

"Now now now," Betsy said as she came back carrying the big bottle of champagne, "this is no time for that. My Lord, I was so sleepy a minute ago, and now I'm bright as a soldier's button."

"Take it easy," Witt said. He took the bottle from Betsy and began peeling the foil off the cork.

"What's wrong?" Betsy said to Mayoso. "Can I do something to help Cristina?"

Cristina shook her head.

"She'll be all right," Mayoso said. "Too much all bottled up—" he began to say, but just then the cork popped with a loud bang and a small shower of champagne sprayed out over them. For no reason at all it seemed very funny. They all began to roar with laughter while Witt filled their glasses.

Betsy proposed a toast. "To tomorrow."

"No," Witt said, "to the Venezuelan Army's rescue car."

"No no no," Mayoso said. "To DeWitt Sommers."

Cristina raised her head. Her eyes had a sheen of tears, but she was smiling. She lifted her glass and said, "To being alive."

They all downed their champagne and Witt began refilling the glasses.

An hour later, in their bedroom, Betsy slowly asked Witt, "Is something wrong? I'm beginning to feel there's something very wrong."

"Forget it, Betts. Everything's all right now."

"Are those two in some kind of real bad trouble?"

"No. Not that I know of."

"Witt, even your best friend won't tell you. You lie so *bad*ly. Mayoso keeps staring out into space, and Cristina—she's wound up like a clock. And that strange toast of hers, 'to being alive.' Didn't that seem strange to you?"

"No," he lied. "Seemed like the most natural thing in the world."

When Mayoso finished putting on his pajamas and came out of the bathroom, the bedroom seemed opaque at first. Then, as his eyes adjusted themselves, he saw Cristina outside on the balcony. He walked across the room in his bare feet, saying "Cristina" quietly so that he would not startle her. She turned, but she said nothing. As he walked out on the pale cool tiles of the balcony he could see an iridescent glow in the valley. There was no gunfire. A light wind had risen, and, below their balcony, palm fronds scraped together dryly. A small sweet moon hung innocently over the hills. When Cristina moved her head, her dark hair swung lightly as a veil.

"I'm sorry I cried," she said sleepily. "I'm really happier than I've been in my whole life. Please," she added quickly, "don't think it's just the champagne talking. I'm not so good about explaining how I feel."

"You don't have to explain," he said gently.

"Before," she said, "I was so tired I was ready to fall down. You were the one who was wide-awake."

"Well, as Betsy said, tomorrow's another day." Tomorrow. Aie.

"I saw how you looked as you watched the battle in the valley. Like me, bad dreams."

"Yes."

"I understand you much better now."

"Tomorrow," he said, "we'll be back in San Juan. All this will seem like a bad dream."

"Oh, please," she said impatiently. "Don't comfort me like a child."

"I'm not. I'm talking to myself. I'm just being hopeful."

"I know you think of me as a child."

In the darkness he smiled. "Was that a child? The one in the yellow dress, dancing barefooted with a bottle on her head?"

"Don't try to make me feel better with nonsense. You said yourself you're not the doctor anymore. Just somebody in the same shipwreck, the same lifeboat." She leaned toward him. "Don't try to fool me. You're as worried as I am. You have to be strong all the time because you are a Martí. You're somebody other people depend on, but down inside you have a weakness that changes you from a leader back into someone ordinary. I could see it on your face all night. You don't want people to die."

He said nothing. This obscure anger, where did it come from? With her dark hair down, washed in this light, anger was all wrong. Her toast to life had been better.

"I understand you," she said. "Better than you know. In a lifeboat you get to know somebody very fast. You understand what I mean?"

"Yes. I understand you better than you know."

"Aie. You make jokes like your American friends."

"Well," he said, "since that telephone call I'm feeling much more cheerful about things." Tomorrow and tomorrow.

"You should have more dignity," she said very seriously. "Now I see that someday you could be the President of your country."

"That," he said, "is one cup I'll let pass me by."

"Can you guess," she asked him, in a different tone, "you are the first man I know who is gentle? I keep asking myself: Is it because people are like this in lifeboats, or is it because that is how you are?"

"Half and half," he said. "Fifty-fifty."

"Oh," she said irritably, "stop being so cheerful. You're almost as bad as your friend Betsy, when you talk that funny way."

He reached out and put his fingers around her arm. "You," he said, "the young one, the pretty one, who makes toasts to life. You should have more charity for fools."

She took a step toward him and slid her arms around his waist, then ran her hands up under his pajama jacket. A tuned wire hummed between them. In the clear slant of moonlight her face looked up calmly, with her still serious directness, as he put his hands on her slight shoulders.

"That's better," she said softly. Unguarded, whispering to herself, she said, "No one can live alone, not even you." She murmured *Mmmmm* and caught his bottom lip between her teeth.

"You," he tried to say happily, "you'll pay for that."

At first they might have been familiar as friends sharing bread, unhurried affectionate lovers, the rounded reckless thrust, breast and thigh, his stroking her long living hair, letting it spill through his fingers, touching her cheek, tracing the lovely yielding curve of her small-boned back, until everything became breathless, immediate, as he kissed her so strongly their teeth clashed, her lips opening, tongue darting, the warmth of her mouth running through him like the mingling of blood as she arched up against him, knees parted widely now, pressing searchingly.

All his harsh armor fell away from him as they moved into the room. There was life again, a living space between dark and dark. Her silken breasts and belly burned against him as they joined, no longer starving, shutting out everything joyfully, celebrants together.

An hourglass of time, sifting, a thread of measured sandgrains, sifting into a heap without sound. The night unraveled, all moorings gone.

Across the void, from some outer boundary almost beyond hearing, gunfire spanned the valley—evenly spaced throbs, as the abraded heart of the city sent its pulsebeats through their arteries.

Cristina stretched her body lazily along his, then trailed a fingertip across his face. "Worried," she said. "I feel it."

"Sí."

"The city? The fighting?"

"That. And everything." Tomorrow . . .

She curled closer against him. "But we're up here, alive. I feel twice as alive."

"And I feel you."

He eased himself toward her and brushed back the damp hair at her temples. He passed his hand over her, lingeringly. The tender abandoned mortal rediscovery of all, the opposite of nothing, all, the moonpolished slope of her shoulder, the undulant ingoing of her waist, the supple out-swelling hip, the wellmade roundness of belly—"Ah, stop, stop," she whispered—the dallying languor of thighs.

"*Diablito*," she murmured against his ear.

"Me?" He laughed deep in his chest. "An innocent bystander."

She raised herself on her elbow and grasped a handful of his hair to pull him closer, then kissed his cheeks, his eyelids, the pillar of his neck with her warm dry lips. "My innocent bystander." She stirred so that his hand possessed the hollow between her legs. "You feel it?"

"This?"

"That. Can't you tell?"

"What?"

"I can tell. I began, inside, a new life."

His deep bass laugh again. "By yourself? *No hay hijo sin padre*. No son without a father."

She bunched another handful of his hair and rocked his head toward her so that his lips slid past hers. "And if a daughter? Ah?"

"Wonderful! A beautiful frangipani-blossom daughter."

"*Qué va?* This child can't be a frail flower."

He explained to her about the frangipani, the tree beside the doorway of his bohío, the velvety blossom which had left an essence scenting his hand for hours. She rested her head against him while he told her how he lived, the warring refugee groups, his public medical practice, his private club of friends stacked on his plank library shelves. He sketched with gestures his window overlooking the world, his desk's anarchy of notes, his mythmaking scrawl of future lectures penned in his father's leather-bound notebook, the heady chicory aroma of coffee beans drying under the sun in his front yard while Nefertiti strutted and the little capuchin monkey, Ché-Ché, dangled from a branch with one small paw while the other scratched his bald monk's pate.

She hovered above him in the dark, her chin touching his as she spoke. "I'll help you pick the coffee beans. That's slow work."

"We're in no hurry, Cristina. Here, we're forced to hurry. But back home, no."

"A man your size. You need more than coffee for breakfast. Just wait till you see what I make for you."

"*Coño*. I'll gain too much weight."

"Impossible."

"You want to domesticate me?"

"No. Impossible also. Will you be ashamed if I live with you?"

"You and me and the small blossom—the three of us? I'll be proud."

"Aie," she whispered huskily, "don't talk like that. You make me want to cry."

"Why?"

"You give me back my self-respect."

"Also," he said, "a new life." He outlined with his fingertip the tender wingslant plane above her cheekbone. "From a mother with beautiful eyes."

He kissed her, beginning as a caress, but responding to her skin's warmth, the whorl of her quick cunning tongue, her elbow locked under his neck, her flanks spreading to grip him, alive, twice as alive while the heartbeat of anonymous dyings pulsed beneath them, her rising voluptuously, opening, his welding their mounting urgency so tightly they were no longer two but one, a shared giving and taking, without barriers, one, two mingled halves of one, one total joining, timeless, infinite beyond time's galaxies, the ice age glaciers, the inchoate saltsoaked waters.

She lifted exultantly, exhaling a fathomless shudder of completion as the long wave swept her breathless and panting onto the night's shore, then let herself fall back into the black spray of her hair.

When he began to withdraw, she pressed him back to her. "Don't go. Stay."

He kissed her throat.

She threw her arms out widely, then curved them back to circle him again. "Never," she said. "Never in my whole life. How can I be so happy? Ah? *Qué como fué?*"

He put his mouth over hers, but she rocked her head sideways. "Aie, you made twins that time."

"You can tell?"

She stuck out her tongue and lapped the tip of his nose. "Sí," she said. "That's my diagnosis, Doctor." She took a deep breath. "How wonderful.

No trying. No pretending." She rubbed her knuckles softly across his ear. "Like friends, ah? The more you give, the more you get."

"Sí."

"My diagnosis—" She hesitated; a tremor had come into her voice.

"I hope it comes true." He held her face between his hands. "I hope it does."

Outside, airplanes orbited past their highland, dropping parachute candles which sent bleared probes of flarelight streaking across the wall. Massive smashing explosions followed, tearing apart the air so violently that their sliding glass balcony door shivered metallically. She clasped him with all her strength.

"My oh my," Betsy said as she dropped her head back against the car seat with annoyance. "Will I ever be glad to vamos out of this place!"

She and Witt, Cristina and Mayoso, were crowded into an Army olive-drab sedan and they had just been halted at the third checkpoint on their way to Maiquetía Airport. Their tension about leaving had made each step of the departure amazingly slow and inefficient. Without hotel porters, who were on strike, Witt and Mayoso had had to make several trips to bring all their luggage down to the lobby. As the small crowd in the lobby looked on curiously, they had arranged and rearranged the luggage in the Army car until they could manage to fit driver, passengers, and valises into the limited space.

Their first checkpoint had been the driveway leading out of the hotel. Two soldiers guarded them while the soldier who was their driver got out of the sedan to show his identification and written orders to an officer. They realized how strict the security precautions were when the officer made each of them get out of the car for individual matching against their official descriptions.

In the city, armed Jeeps and tanks and truck troop carriers prowled the streets. Alternate streetcorners had sandbagged machinegun positions and as their driver took detours through side streets, the litter of skilled resistance was everywhere. Paving stones had been torn up and made into barricades several feet thick; only tanks or artillery could overrun them. Side streets had been blocked off by overturned cars and, from the burned-out holes around them, Mayoso could see that mines must have been scattered to make any quick rush by infantry impossible. Stone balconies and stucco walls along the route were pocked and scarred with what must have been a series of close fire fights. Here and there were broken bottles and flame-blackened walls where Molotov cocktails had been used against tanks. In one alley, Mayoso smelled the chemical stink left behind by white phosphorus grenades. Many of the balconies, he noticed, were strangely lined with white sandbags—pillowcases, he decided —which meant a widespread use of snipers against the Army. Snipers meant a stubborn struggle, the worst kind of city warfare, street by street, house to house, fighting from one doorway to the next. From all sides he could hear isolated shots and the ripping sound of machine pistol bursts. Mopping-up operations? Rooftop snipers? Or is this just a temporary lull before heavier weapons move in?

Now, at the third checkpoint, they sat and watched while a sweat-stained officer checked the driver's papers line by line. At the end of the block a big city bus had been turned on its side and set afire. Black smoke billowed hugely from it, and, when the wind shifted, enough reached them to make their eyes sting.

"Good Lord," Betsy said, "if we're asked one more time to get out for inspection—"

"We'll do it," Witt said. "Just don't give anybody any back talk."

Mayoso was sitting in the front seat beside the driver. The other three were in back. He glanced over his shoulder at both women. Cristina was expressionless; she knew all about officers and officials who took their time deciding who should pass and who should not. Betsy looked trim and sleek, as always, as if the world were a setting through which she could stroll to downstage center dressed like a cover girl on her way to the Colony for lunch. To her, Mayoso thought, the cities of the world must be a blurred chain of luxury hotels, air-conditioned cars, airports, and the problems in all these places were simply those of finding the best restaurants, persuading the chambermaid to do a reasonable job of keeping the hotel suite in order, and flattering the beauty-shop operator into rising above his limited talents. Everything else must seem a shade fuzzy and out of focus and, quite reasonably, too complicated to understand. If anything, local poverty and street fighting might be faintly picturesque, especially when surrounded by flamboyantly green and red tropical flowers and colonial Spanish lampposts. Betsy would remember Caracas only as the place she had so cleverly arranged a buffet supper in the hotel kitchen, and a penthouse suite with dark-eyed musicians singing *Ojos Verdes*.

When the officer came over to their car Betsy rolled down the window beside her and gave him her smile. "Please, Colonel, do we have to get out again and stand at attention?"

The officer did not answer until he had scanned them slowly, then said to her in Spanish, *"No me puedo defender bien con el idioma."*

Mayoso translated. "He says he does not defend himself in your language very well."

"We still have the snipers on the road," the officer said to Mayoso. "All around. On the roofs. The street is too dangerous." The officer motioned for the driver to get out of the car. They walked a short distance away while the officer explained something very seriously.

"I do hope we don't have to get out again," Betsy said. She stage-whispered to Cristina behind her hand, "If I'd known we'd be doing this much exercise I wouldn't have worn a girdle."

Their driver came back scowling and slid behind the wheel. He folded his papers and put them carefully into the pocket of his uniform shirt and turned to Mayoso on the front seat beside him. "This officer thinks we should back up on Avenida Sucre and take the extra time to go around through Real los Flores. To try to make a run past that burning bus is too dangerous. If we get stopped by a flat tire, the snipers might try picking us off. They think civilians in an Army car must be informers."

Mayoso nodded. "I think you should do what he says. Better to lose a little time than take unnecessary risks. Is this a staff command car?"

"Yes," the driver said unhappily. "They always try to knock off people in staff cars." With an overstrung tension he jammed the car into reverse gear and the sedan shot backward to the streetcorner, screeched to halt, then heeled over as he rammed it around the corner in forward gear. Just as he began to accelerate, a large flaming timber came tumbling end over end like a giant pinwheel and fell heavily into the middle of the street. The driver slammed on his brakes so hard the car skidded sideways into a gutter.

From somewhere ahead of them came the crunching sound of grenades exploding and, in a moment, a heavy chemical smog began drifting toward them, curling upward. From a doorway a short distance ahead, a young child screamed and ran into the street. She was clawing at her face and her dress was half burned off. In the same moment, Mayoso spotted three older children lying on their stomachs in the entryway of an apartment house across the street. They called out to the child, who was about three. As she turned toward their voices he realized she had been blinded.

Behind him, Cristina said, "Dios mío! Look at that little kid!"

The car had stalled. The driver pumped the gas pedal, swearing furiously, turning the ignition key indignantly. Nothing happened. He cursed it and trampled the pedal repeatedly, flooding the engine again.

The child wavered across the street as the older children called to her. Then, as she reached the curbstone unseeingly, she stumbled and fell prone to the sidewalk. Mayoso grabbed the door handle and said to the driver, "Just sit tight. I'm going for that child. Just start your engine." Down the street another phosphorus grenade went off and a fresh wave

of smoke swirled into the air. The driver was shaking now and still pumping gas.

Witt reached over from the back seat and grabbed the driver's shoulder.
"Stop it!"

"Witt," Mayoso threw over his shoulder as he got out, "climb over into
the front seat. Get this car started while I get that kid. We can get her to
an aid station." He did not see Cristina opening the opposite back door.

A spray of bullets hit the building beside them and several ricocheted
with sharp *pings* off their metal roof. Mayoso ducked, then, as he straightened, he was amazed to see Cristina running ahead of him. "Cristina!"
he shouted.

"Stay back!" she screamed. *"Stay back!* They need you." She picked up
the child as he began to race toward her, then something invisible gave
her a hard push. She took one or two steps forward and dropped the child,
going downward on her knees as if picking flowers from the pavement.
The children lying in the entryway of the apartment house were all
screaming as he reached her. He heard none of the bullets splatter against
the walls. He smelled no smoke. He knew only a moment ago she was
alive and running and now she was doubled over. As he picked her up,
someone came up beside him and grabbed the child from the sidewalk.

When he and Witt reached the car, its engine was turning over. The
driver shakily helped Witt into the front seat with the child while Betsy
jumped out of the car, a face like chalk, and helped Mayoso stretch
Cristina across the rear seat. Cristina's entire back was streaming blood.
Betsy and he squeezed into the car and slammed the doors as the car began
to move. Mayoso turned Cristina over so that she could lie face downward and no bleeding into the windpipe would choke her. Her mouth
kept trembling as if she were trying to speak, but only an agonizing animal sound came out. Beside him, Betsy was whispering, "Hail Mary full of
grace . . ." and he heard Witt giving the driver directions as the car
picked up speed.

Mayoso ripped open the back of Cristina's dress to stop the bleeding,
but from shoulder to shoulder her raw torn flesh was too widely butchered.
She raised her head slightly from the edge of the seat, flexing her knees
in pain, then sighed in a long exhalation and became limp.

Mayoso stared at her, stunned by lightning, unable to believe she was
dead. There was no need for her to die. She had her whole life before her!
A moment ago she had had her whole life ahead and now she was one
more on the pile of blood-drenched skulls which never stopped growing.
There was no reason. No life could be taken so suddenly, so indifferently.

A horn of agony gored him between the eyes. Dead! Cristina should
not be dead! When would it end—this human sacrifice to fanatic gods?

Let them kill their gods before one more such meaningless death! He raised his head with a wild ancient anguish. *Let them first kill God!* Like rapping his blood-smeared knuckles on a soundless coffin, raging, infuriated, he shook his helpless fists toward a merciless counterfeit sky.

BOOK V
CARIBBEAN: San Juan

15

THE SUN STOOD STILL.

One moment it was winter, the Northern Hemisphere tilted toward gray ice, cold bitter twilight plunged into freezing night. Then, slowly, the sun's magnetic grasp slanted the planet toward spring. Directly over the earth's midline, the sun reached the celestial equator, its astronomic tug tilting the hemisphere toward the moment of vertical sunlight at noon, day and night precisely equal, the solar pause for the split second of vernal equinox. The day the sun stood still began the year; no one cared about the calendar's first few winter pages. Life quickened with springlight.

A coral arm casually embraced the shoulders of continents, the long elbow of Leeward and Windward islands curving from the Venezuelan Basin toward the Greater Antilles. Underwater, a druidical Stonehenge of drowned mountains loomed up from the seismic Mona Deep of the bottomless Puerto Rican Trench.

Ocean tides crested higher from the Golfo Triste near Caracas along the Antillean island chain, churning whitely against reefs, greening the shoals. Warm incubating wavelets trembled beneath the trade winds, directionless, a random meeting of compass points, lifting over the submerged Aves Ridge, running more strongly through the passage between La Fortaleza and Isla de Cabras into the Bay of San Juan.

In San Juan, the hurricane-hunter squadron of Air Force planes sat on the ground. This was not the season for hurricanes.

But a blackening copper sky, dark as ancient coins, glinted dully over San Juan. Far out at sea, away from the busy tanker lanes from the Maracaibo and Aruba refineries to the new Puerto Rican petrochemical plants near Bayamón, a faint rumble began: the ominous sound of mammoth cargoes of rock, shifting.

In San Juan, the barometric needles moved a trace. The wind was rising. In the old section, San Juan Antiguo, small dervishes of dust twirled and spiraled along the blue cobblestone gutters of Calle Cristo. Rusty television aerials shivered and rattled. A few corrugated tin roofs on squatters' shacks shook loose in El Fanguito and clattered into the oily tides of Martín Peña Channel.

In the belltower of Father Gofredo Möttl's church, La Virgen de Fátima, the rope pull-cords began tapping the metal lips of the bells and, once or twice during sudden gusts, the brass clappers within the bells swung slowly back and forth in a private unheard tolling.

Father Möttl would remember the day as having been set apart by bells, an entrance of the Angelus, a departure of Vespers.

An hour or two after the morning Angelus, he climbed the stairs to his room on the second floor of the rectory. He went directly to his writing table to begin a draft of his sermon for this week's *Hour of Eternity* television program. The parochial school notepad on which he wrote was in his desk, and, when he pulled open the shallow drawer he saw with distaste the small carton which lay beside the paper. On its cover was the colorful figure of a harem girl in transparent silk lolling on seraglio pillows. One of his parishioners, a pharmacist, had brought the carton to him because the name FATIMA was printed on it. This insulting obscenity degraded the name of his own church, La Virgen de Fátima; all the more offensive because the package had actually been printed here on the island by the Sommers Pharmaceutical Company. When his parishioner had opened the flat cardboard carton and had unrolled one of the condoms from it, Father Gofredo Möttl had stared down at the repugnant latex sheath in outrage.

"How commonplace is this—thing?"

"Padre," the pharmacist said, "these *gomas* are everywhere. Like bird droppings. My uncle in Chile told me the padres there close their eyes to these things."

"Impossible!"

"Padre, I don't mean to judge in matters of faith or morals, but in Chile they say this is better than their thousands of criminal abortions. I brought it to you only because their use of the name Fatima is insulting to our Church."

Now, Father Gofredo avoided touching the brazen package as he lifted the notepad he needed out of the drawer. To what length barbarians go! Of all the names for their salacious product! To have vilified the name of a church, the name of Mary, the miracle of Fátima. Pointless, purposeless profanity. *Eine Krankheit.*

He loosed the edge of his scapular collar and massaged the back of his neck. His muscles had stiffened as if he were about to raise his arms either in prayer or to strike a killing blow. Easter will come soon, he told himself comfortingly, and this may be the darkest hour before the dawn. So, not in bitterness must this week's television sermon be written. No blows struck. Even if the insult were forgiven, the *gomas* are unnatural barriers to God's will. Bishop Sosa should speak to the Governor about these Yanqui despoilers. The people must be told this, not in anger but with a logic built stone on stone until the jointed arch of its proof and argument point upward like a spire. In his deliberate half-cursive monastic calligraphy he began to write his sermon: "Oh my brethren, a peril walks among us in the name of science!"

In the name of science. Doctor Mayoso, there in the lobby of the Hotel Laputa, saying: My hands are clean.

Father Gofredo's pencil stopped. In the name of science. *Scientiae Medicinali Artique Salutari.* Latin Spain. Latin Spain, conqueror of Moors and Moorish harems, Isabella's Spain where the mendicant Order of Franciscans had shamed affluent churchmen, where militant Jesuits had driven out concubinage and corruption, and the Inquisition of the Holy Office had cleansed heresy from the lecherous bosom of the body politic.

He took a deep breath and began to write again: "Where the State and its leaders permit evil, evil will flourish . . ."

Above the living quarters of Governor Santos Roque in La Fortaleza, the flags of the United States and Puerto Rico danced a tethered airy ballet side by side. On the Governor's tall antique clock the crucifix-shaped hands coolly pointed toward unhurried *anno Domini* time, while the Governor's staff sweated impatiently. Santos Roque hovered hour by hour above his clamoring telephones, swiveling from one to the other as his switchboard jangled with calls from Caracas, Washington, Mexico City; from the Swiss Legation in Havana, the Papal Nuncio in Santo Domingo, Alianza officials in Brasilia. Local island politics were set aside for the moment; the primary elections soon, the final elections in November. He bowed his head when he learned how Mayoso had returned to San Juan and he accepted Mayoso's absence. Chess games must wait; the chessboard was on fire.

At Camp Crozier, the Peace Corps training center, a visiting Italian agronomist said the wind was very much like the Mediterranean sirocco. A member of the Israeli technical mission told his chief, General Moshe Edin, that the air had the nervous sultriness of a khamsin.

Everywhere, palm trees bent back their long fronds like fringed whips, flicking back and forth, expectantly.

At Ramey Air Force Base, in the Roosevelt Roads staging area, across the Marine Base on Vieques Island, staff officers checked wind gauges and rescheduled aerial operations such as paratrooper jumps and smoke-screen demonstrations. Where the hell did these unseasonal crossbeam winds come from? The hurricane hunters squinted up at the far-off thunderheads and telephoned the weather boys in Miami.

Along the sleek brushed shores of Condado Beach a mounted policeman on routine patrol wheeled his chestnut *paso fino* so that the gritty
windthrown beach sand would spray his back instead of stinging his face.
Outside the tall air-conditioned oceanside hotels, multistriped towels ballooned with each airpuff and rippled snakily out of control of the uniformed cabaña attendants. In the narrow segments of public beach
between the raked stretches of private hotel property, the weavers of
palm-leaf hats lowered their heads against the sand flurries, then plaited
wider-brimmed headgear not for sale but for themselves. The pushcart
vendors of ice-cream sticks and *bacalaitos* fritters folded their large orange
umbrellas and patiently rumbled away.

Inland, the wind skipped like a small boy with a stick across Experimental Farm Number One of the Sommers Pharmaceutical Company,
slapping down the green shoots of carefully nurtured dioscorea seedlings
toward their hydroponic seedbeds.

Witt Sommers walked between the narrow concrete hydroponic
trenches, inspecting the dioscorea rootlets disturbed by the wind. His
idea was to create here a botanical farm, but without a farm's wasteful
inefficiency; a botanical farm organized in assembly-line sequence to make
contraceptive drugs. From the mixing shed at one end came the nutrient
chemicals which trickled through the gutters to bathe and feed the growing seedlings. Space, plant height, moisture, acid-alkaline balance, harvest-
ing technique; each detail was being studied to find a combination by
which high-yield dioscorea could be transplanted to soil, then harvested
with maximum efficiency. Their scooploaded roots would be chopped into
a soggy pulp: from this dioscorea mash skillful chemistry would extract
diosgenin, and Sommers Pharmaceuticals controlled patents on converting
diosgenin into valuable cortical steroids. Among these steroids, those
which went into the oral contraceptive pills were now in world demand.

Witt fretted as watchfully over the dioscorea seedlings as a nurse caring for premature infants. He was risking over two million in pilot-plant
experimentation alone. The gamble might pay off. If his experimental
hydroponics farm could triple steroid production at one-third the cost, the
Mexican monopoly on the world supply of dioscorea root would be broken
overnight. Additional farms could be built in subtropical countries, such
as Israel, which had skillful organic chemists. Sommers Pharmaceuticals'
foreign exchange balance and cash flow would quadruple in the next fiscal
year. Rocketing earnings per share meant little more than paper gains

to Benjamin Sommers and the new trustees who held Marjorie Sommers' stock. To Witt, however, profits pouring through the window only to sluice right out the door in taxes—and, later, the steep estate taxes—meant an opportunity to convince his father and mother to vote their controlling interest in favor of his next big corporate move: to reincorporate in Delaware and plunge into the Wall Street world of offering shares for public ownership. That would be a victory. I've been feeling somehow defeated, he thought. I need a victory.

Witt called the foreman over. "How can we protect these seedlings?"

"Maybe stretch some Saran mesh over them."

"You mean the way they grow tobacco under screens up in Connecticut?"

"Shade, sí."

"If this wind keeps blowing—" Witt said and frowned again. Sweat, dollars, research brains, he thought. I pour my guts into contraceptive chemicals. And Betsy is sterile.

An aerial engine clatter made him look up. It came from the blue-and-white Sikorsky helicopter from the Water Resources Agency in which Governor Santos Roque ferried visiting big shots around the island. These visitors must be the Israeli technical mission under that general I met in Washington.

He straightened his shoulders and strode toward the open field where the helicopter would land, feeling better immediately. The world of doing and deciding was back; he slammed shut the secret trapdoor to the basement of his mind and shut away, even from himself, the never-ending spigot drip of bitter anguish.

☐ ☐ ☐

During the week which followed the street warfare in Caracas, Mayoso buried Cristina's body in the Old Cemetery by San Juan's north seawall where the white foam-topped combers rolled in from everywhere, endlessly; surely washing away, the custodian assured him, all the sins of this life. Mayoso stood beside the grave, massive and silent as an uprooted tree.

The custodian, a gnarled coconut husk of an old man with a gray scrabble of unshaven beard who politely held his straw hat in his hand, was pleased to have so quiet a captive audience. "Be glad, señor," he said. "The sea is eternity, and eternity is the soul, no? So this resting place beside the sea is the finest offering you can give. You're lucky Easter is so near. The risen Christ will remind you death is swallowed up in victory." He held out to Mayoso both his veined hands, worn parchment skin stretched over chicken bones. *"Mire.* Each day you and I die to some small amount, no?" His voice quavered. "But the soul in these two hands is stronger than death."

Mayoso shuffled slowly down the narrow grassy lanes. He was a wounded lion; foot-dragging, half-closed injured tawny eyes oblique beneath shaggy brows, his uncut leonine white mane bowed above heavy-muscled shoulders.

Old gravetender, he thought, I can't bandage myself with your belief in glory everlasting, but I might buy you a therapeutic shot of rum and we can drop your word *soul.* Exchange it for the life molecules mingled when a man and a woman truly become part of one another and your slave-myth of immortality would become a newer truth worth a new toast: our children.

But mine died with Cristina. *A daughter,* she had said, smiling in the dark. *What if it's a daughter?"*

Three more deaths to mourn, including my own.

The walled-in cemetery square was awash with murmurous ocean sounds, and, as if he held a nautilus shell of memory to his ear, he heard an intermingled hum of voices, all his lost ones: his fiancée, his family, his friends gunned down at Blue Beach, Cristina. Only you, he told himself, only you always managed to walk away from each disaster alive. That is not a healthy way to view your life, but there it is, the plain fact that they are gone and you are here.

To each side of him, bereaved marble Madonnas grieved with bent heads, separated by funerary urns, sepulchral tablets, polished scrollwork tombstones and sad-eyed seraphs with folded wings. Near the archway of the entrance to the cemetery, an entire family, a kneeling mother and her children, were carved life-size to mourn together forever. A stone world of the dead, as contradictory as the stone world of the living. Lavish monuments to life eternal, yet sculptured resignation. Flamboyant expensive showiness, languid plastic-flower horrors, and yet a suffering too deep and lasting for words.

Through the frame of the arched entryway he could see, across the street, the vertical rock wall of the ancient fortress with painted symbols from another world: the letter Z for the TV hero, Zorro; Valentine hearts, each with a pair of initials; words of contempt for the act of sex, some sloshed over with whitewash; political posters for Santos Roque, the man who had brought bread, work, and schools to the island; placards for the Statehood Party, promises that Puerto Rico would be equal-shouldered to any other state in the U.S.A.; and the Independista Party which promised to give the island dignidad nacional, nationhood and manhood.

At the archway Mayoso glanced back. The old custodian was hunched on his knees beside Cristina's grave, tremorously measuring the space where her stone would be set. Like the devout artist Fra Angelico who used to paint celestial glory on his knees.

Mayoso turned heavily and went out.

His friend Tranquilino had sent him one of the maestro stonecutters in San Juan. For the *escultor* Mayoso had sketched what the gravestone should be: the upright figure of a girl with a waist-length cascade of hair, her hands just beginning to rise from her sides with expectation, a girl who gazed levelly across the waters with faintly wingslanted eyes. "Doctor," the stonecutter had said, "you want to breathe life into stone? To me, the sadness of my work is knowing that cannot be done."

Mayoso climbed the hill from the cemetery to the neighboring slope of La Perla, the huddle of shacks where Cristina had once lived with her mother. Little girls with braided pigtails, wearing homemade school uniforms, scooted past him on their way home from Abraham Lincoln School. Their older sisters from the neighboring Baldorioty High School cooed in clusters like pouter pigeons, tiny bells on their shoelaces tinkling while they giggled and screeched across the street, as once Cristina must have done. Which one of them, he mused, might grow up to be another Cristina María de la Concepción Bretand Pagán?

At their spacious Condado Beach house, Betsy and Witt circled warily around Mayoso in a generous pretense of normalcy. Betsy was up and at the day each morning, as she never was back home in New Haven; she was determined to keep her husband and her guest company at breakfast. A messenger came daily from the airport with a buckled leather briefcase of memoranda flown down from New Haven in a company plane that morning, family mail, copies of the Washington *Post,* the New York *Times,* and, now that Witt was parleying with General Moshe Edin, the English language Jerusalem *Post.*

Witt spotted newspaper reports filed from Bogotá that Major Pío Hoyo y Suarez de San Andrés Teixeira, alias Filho, was said to have escaped from Venezuela over a back-country single-track smuggler's railroad into Colombia. Witt went on squeezing lime juice over his breakfast papaya without mentioning what he had read. Another dispatch reported that Filho was in Havana. He had been seen cheerfully umpiring a *beisbol* game during the three fearsome innings Fidel Castro had pitched. Witt folded the paper and shovelled it out of sight under the manila folders in his briefcase. The company car tooted its horn twice outside and Witt kissed Betsy above her barely lowered teacup as fleetingly as a commuter hurrying to catch his train. To Mayoso he called, with slightly excessive cheerfulness, "See you later," and left. He worked each day at the local office of his company or crisscrossed the island in the Water Resources Agency Sikorsky helicopter, searching for rare patches of level acreage suitable for growing his precious dioscorea botanical plants. He usually invited one of the agronomists of the Israeli technical mission, or General Edin himself, to come along.

At the breakfast table, Betsy dawdled over a fresh cup of tea. Occasionally, she read aloud from newspapers to Mayoso, like an astronaut cheerfully sharing from a space satellite the strange doings of earthlings. The headlines she skipped went as unnoticed by Mayoso as Witt's censorship, because he no longer read the news himself.

"Here's an interesting hot bulletin," she would say cheerfully in the tone one uses with the recently blinded. "Your friend Santos Roque is organizing a new charity to collect funds to help Cuban refugees resettle. It says here he denied any connection with the current election-year campaign by pointing out that most local Cubans are not citizens and could not vote for him in any case. And there's a short editorial about Church opposition to him."

"I must phone him," Mayoso said. He stared into space. "One of these days . . ."

Wrong item, Betsy decided. That news just made him feel more isolated from his troops. I'd better stay away from other local items; the new breed of tough kids coming back from New York to San Juan as skillful drug pushers; the feature stories about the internal sparring among Cuban refugee groups who fight one another to lead a new Cuban invasion.

International news might be safer. She scanned the columns by foreign correspondents. The new global television network was making Hollywood Boulevard, Fifth Avenue, Carnaby Street, the Champs-Élysées, Via Veneto and Main Street one continuous electronic promenade. The roll call of emigrating British scientists, now called the brain drain. A new Chinese Embassy in Paris.

Betsy finally found neutral ground under Society Happenings. "Ah, here's a cute story about all the new discothèques. Continuous music so loud you can't hear yourself think. Flashing lights to blind you. Partners you dance toward, not with." She stirred her tea absently. "The final triumph of solitary togetherness. Makes one feel senile, doesn't it?"

He did not answer. Her undertone ran her way, not his.

After breakfast, no one troubled Mayoso. Betsy or the maid simply brought a lunch tray to him out on the patio. There he retreated each day into a fan-backed woven chair in the shade of a white frangipani tree, staring out over the windy Atlantic distances. The sun's assault stopped at treetop height and the wavering branches juggled the light through a translucent viridescence. In the deep crushing quiet of tropic noon, the subtle summery fragrance of the frangipani blossoms wove itself sweetly through his silence as he sank onto his bed of nails.

His withdrawn brooding opened again Betsy's own never-healed wounds—her mother's death which had struck from nowhere, like Cristina's death. And her father, dissolved in alcohol, laid out in a dim back room with a soaked-in rancid smell. Oh, how different that dead stranger; no prince, no player, but a shriveled stranger whose slack dropped jaw was bound up with a cloth sling, grotesquely like herself as a youngster with the mumps. Arms folded over his shrunken chest, votive candles head and foot, from wax unto wax, R.I.P., where has my childhood's bright boasting Dad gone?

She had borrowed the clean pillow and sheet under him from a neighbor lady, and, as she recalled begging the white linen for her father's body, a young girl's shame and aloneness pierced her again.

Mayoso's pain was intolerable to her. She turned her back on him and wandered off among the poinsettias and hibiscus blossoms which hedged their gardens, escaping his grayness in the color of tulipán crimsons, lavender jacarandas, the saffron canarios and the buttercup clusters of a single wild cotton tree which blossomed only during the Lenten period. Everywhere through the splashes of sunlight, small birds the size of her thumb twittered shyly until the maid brought out to them little dishes of powdered sugar, guava juice and honey. Then they became bold, perching chummily on the glass rim while they bent their tiny rounded citrine bellies forward and dipped their beaks into the sweetness.

Mayoso surprised Betsy once by surfacing unexpectedly with a few words. "Your house is a paradise for those little reinitas."

She looked back over her shoulder. "Is that the Spanish name for them?"

He sat unmoving in the tall chair. "Sí. It means little queens. They're all over the island, searching for sweetness. And when they find it they take over the place as if they owned it."

She tried to keep him talking. "Reinitas? Did I prrronounce that r rrright? Spanish is really a poetic language, isn't it?"

"Most people say so," he said. "Death is such a next door neighbor for the Spanish. They grasp at poetry, music. Any illusion to color life or promise love."

She put down her armful of flowers on the glass-topped patio table and came over to sit beside him in the scented shade of the frangipani. "You know," she said in a low hurried voice, "I'm not ignoring how you feel, but I'm a terrible coward. I can't stand pain. There are some griefs you never get over, especially the ones from when you are young. You can't bear them again. Even in someone else. Do you know what I mean?"

He said nothing but turned his massive white head to look out at the sea again. Sun flecks bobbled over the patio as the wind stirred among the frangipani blossoms. He knew he would never again catch even their faintest perfume without feeling stabbed, but he could not bring himself to leave the nearness of this tree.

Without daily personal duties, without the folklore disciplines—nose to the grindstone, shoulder to the wheel, eye on the ball—he became isolated within the immensities of land and sea as he wandered through the honeycomb of light which spilled around the white frangipani tree. Migrant humming birds hovered and darted out of it. A yellow canario, brushed by a wingtip, trembled and reminded him of Cristina with a yellow flower in her hair, twirling from the lighted room of the hotel penthouse out to the darkness of the terrace.

Betsy spoke quickly; he might stop listening any moment. "Witt and I want you to stay with us here," she said. "We certainly don't want you going back to live by yourself in that hut up in the hills. But please don't think I'm running away if I leave for awhile to trek around the island with Witt."

He swiveled his big frame to face her. Her constant tantalizing shimmer of sexual snuggle was completely gone, as suddenly as she discarded an outworn dress. She seemed done with Gaelic decoys and her art of winsome girlish seductiveness. Now she spoke to him with a poised womanly calm and he could talk to her with an unguarded directness. "Of course you'll be running away, Betsy. We all run away, so why shouldn't you?"

"Oh," she said, caught unexpectedly by his concern for her. "There's always so much more depth to how we feel than we know ourselves. Isn't that so? Witt's somehow closer here on the island. He talks to me about what he's doing, about his expensive gamble on the experimental farm. Business. Things he never mentioned back home. Maybe I listen better, or maybe he wants to show me his muscles." She flashed her electric smile. "Anyway, one good pride deserves another."

"The Sommers are like small-scale kings, Betsy. This week's decisions by them are next month's pay envelopes and groceries for a good many people." He paused. They had never talked in this practical way before. "So if Witt's a king," he added, "you're the *reinita*."

She glanced across the patio at the small birds tippling in the honey. "I suppose you're right. I suppose I'm always flying around searching for sweetness and light."

"I didn't mean that," he said quietly. "I was only using the Spanish to mean just what the word says: little queen."

She's become more sensitive and considerate of Witt, he thought, and more generous toward me. She's stopped quoting poetry, and she doesn't pretend jolly Dublin absurdities anymore. The elaborate dark eye makeup to emphasize the green of her eyes is still there, but no longer theatrical. More of a woman, less a girl; yet, even though she thinks she understands my grief, she doesn't. We are not dancers discothèquing in solitary togetherness.

How could she know that grief alone could never paralyze me this way? Rage has exhausted me. A rage doubled by my barehanded helplessness, rage against needless human pain, the century's butcheries, against the rotting away of hope, the whoring of science. Rage against Filho who was responsible yet not responsible for Cristina's death. A fury that someone so young and blossoming with new life should lose her life without reason. All these crush me. Without hope, despair swaddles us like mummies. My bones have become brittle just when I should be working for the quick, not the dead. In Havana, Filho told me that he and I were men halfway between worlds. In Caracas, that angry priest, Möttl, warned me I was a temporary man. Halfway and temporary.

To wander among the wastes of a century? Merely to endure while the lights dim? Are we the new Spain, with Mao Tse-tung our new Columbus? To be beaten to exhaustion by men whose dynastic clocks run backward to so many less obvious forms of dying?

How like a god is man, he thought, only because he walks upright and laughs at himself. When I forget that, my rage is with myself. So, on your feet. You are not only what you think, but what you do. Up on your feet. Your ancestor Martí made big *pronunciamentos* that to witness crimes in silence is to become a partner in them. But for you, today, no rhetoric, no bugle calls. Only piece together a shaky crutch of courage to help you stand again and struggle.

More and more, Betsy began to travel with Witt as he surveyed the island for possible experimental farm acreage. She discovered the narrow back roads lined with umbrella-shaped poinciana trees, shady archways of red petals, air-hung gardens, and the blossoming lavender poui trees growing wild in the valleys. The more widely she explored the island with Witt, the more she sensed she was discovering the lost continent of herself.

She watched barefoot boys pinch tulipán buds to make them squirt like water pistols, while behind them someone's little brother lay on his back under a patient mother goat to hold her bag of milk while he nursed from it. He was Timmy's age. She missed her son, his tousled perpetual motion, his six-year-old bumptiousness. Timmy was staying with his Uncle David and Aunt Alice back home in New Haven and Betsy decided to phone him that evening just to hear his voice.

She asked Witt to take time off from his work. They were both caught off guard. He, because she had asked him; she, because he said yes. They hired Mayoso's friend, Tranquilino, to drive them around the Island. First they went to Mayoso's hilltop bohío to fetch some of his clothes. While Tranquilino went to tell Mayoso's neighbors he would be absent for some time, Witt found Nefertiti and Ché-Ché scrabbling at one another like simpletons, and fed them. Betsy rooted in Mayoso's sea chest and corner closet for the things he needed. Around her, the rough plank walls spoke of him; the bookshelves, the stacked medical journals, the note-covered table and the old-fashioned dip pen. A striped cotton shirt and frayed blue jeans hung from a nail; his thonged huaraches, upcurled at the toes, waited as if he had just stepped out of them. Mayoso's most important request was for the leather-bound notebook which had once belonged to his father. Betsy riffled through its pages. The faded Spanish handwriting dated a generation ago was undecipherable, and its looping arabesques had a mannered long-gone intricacy, somehow echoing the rituals of courtship, brutal privacies beside public gracefulness, the Moorish silk woven through the Spanish hairshirt.

On the way to La Parguera, Tranquilino parked the car in the shade and brought them pineapples from the spike-crowned rows which marched beside the road. Betsy had never tasted a field-ripened pineapple, sun-mellowed and body-warm, so juicy that her chin dripped the sugary liquid.

"*Mire!*" she said to Tranquilino. "Are they all so sweet?"

"Ah, señora, this kind they call the smooth cayenne. Maybe someplace I can find you what is called a red Spanish." He kissed his fingertips. "The red ones, *dulces labios.*"

"Sweet lips," Witt translated for Betsy. He kissed her stickily. "Hard to tell," he said, "whether you're a smooth cayenne or a red Spanish."

They drove for miles. White-painted roadside crosses marked the location of traffic fatalities. They skirted ox teams dragging unbelievable wagonloads of cut cane toward the puffing smokestack of the sugar *central*.

The afternoon heat shimmered hazily above the road, and Witt asked Tranquilino to stop at a roadside cantina. The men ordered cold India beer, and the owner lopped off the top of a coconut, still dripping from the icebox, so that Betsy could drink the chilled coconut milk. Several cane cutters leaned along a short mahogany bar, drinking beer with long-throated swallows, their shirts dark with sweat, fatigued, their machetes carried underarm or over the shoulder so the bare blades' cold metal could ease their scorched neck muscles.

Betsy asked Witt to translate the flower-hung sign over the doorway: *No aceptamos la entrada de persona de conducta dudosa. Evítenos un mal rato.*

"'Persons of doubtful character not permitted,'" he read aloud. "'Spare us a bad time.'"

Under a bunch of niño bananas, an automatic record-playing machine took its siesta, waiting for the nighttime trade. Betsy put a coin in the slot and pushed the selector button labeled *Ojos Verdes.*

As the mariachi music began, Tranquilino wiped his mouth with the back of his hand and said to Witt, "Señor, allow me to say that your wife knows how to pick a song."

Although Tranquilino had not intruded on Mayoso's mourning, he knew these Americanos were Mayoso's friends, therefore his friends, therefore the polite compliment was permissible. The cane cutters at the bar courteously avoided seeming to watch them.

"*Green eyes,*" Betsy sang with the music, "*those cool and limpid green eyes. . . .* Come on, Witt. Let's dance."

"Betts," he clowned, using the old musical comedy line, "I've a crack in my back, in my sacroiliac—" He pointed at the handlettered notice on the jukebox. "See? A warning."

In stumbling Spanish she tried to read, "*Este no es un templo pero—*"

"'This is not a temple,'" Witt read for her. "'But children come here and we do not permit exotic or immoral dancing.'" He lifted her off her feet, spun her around, then bent her backward. "Like that. Olé!"

"Debauched DeWitt—"

"Delovely, degreen eyes. Come wiz me to the Casbah."

The men at the bar applauded, they bowed, everyone smiled, and Tranquilino drove them off in their car with a flourish.

They sprawled in their hammocks after lunch, swam at night through phosphorescent waters which parted like velvet to each side, the darkness over them benevolent and rich with stars, their dawns gearing up efficiently with the rigging of Witt's fishing tackle. Betsy survived several entire mornings without recombing her hair. They trolled for deep-sea fish and Witt's reel spun, smoking with the spectacular leaps of acrobatic game-fish. He gaffed and boated a staggering catch that filled their locker with yellowfin tuna, wahoo, snappers, and a bluesilver marlin. They packed their biggest snapper in ice and shipped it back across the island to La Fortaleza for the Governor's dinner. Tranquilino simmered fish chowder for hours, surpassing any bouillabaisse. He pan-broiled fish which Betsy tenderly anointed with lemon and served on broad sea-grape leaves with long loaves of hot *pan sobao* just slid on wooden paddles out of the village baker's oven. She and Witt sampled the local topaz rum without any of their old flailings at one another about Betsy drinking too much, because now she drank very little.

Tranquilino sang *Lamento Borinqueño* for them and told them what a dirtpoor rotting place the island had been before the great Muñoz Marín had stumped through the hungry *barrios* and legislated and orated and uplifted even the unemployed *agregados* and *jíbaro* cane cutters to think with hope and *dignidad*. Tranquilino unsnarled for them the complicated guntoting politics of the Cuban splinter groups, each of whom claimed Mayoso Martí for leadership and labeled him the future Muñoz Marín of Cuba.

"From that hill where Mayoso lives," Tranquilino said, "he can see so far." With his forefinger he tapped his head. *"Very* far." Betsy understood now why Cristina had shouted to Mayoso in Caracas, "Go back! They need you!"

Witt and Tranquilino discovered that they had both served in Korea. Never before had Betsy heard Witt talk about what those years had been like.

Tranquilino showed them a recent picture of his family: two boys and two girls posing stiff-necked and unsmiling in their Sunday clothes for this serious photograph; his wife smiling a little to herself because only she knew she had just become pregnant.

The world of work dropped in upon them one day. The snub-nosed blue-and-white Sikorsky helicopter whirled in behind the pint-sized harbor hotel on an appointment schedule which Witt had completely forgotten. Within an hour they were on their way, airlifted with such vertical swiftness that, to Betsy, the harbor seemed to sink under the sea. So, she thought, this is how Witt hop-skip-jumps around the island to search for more dioscorea land. She watched the green folds and dips of land slide by below. Heights turn everything into the executive view. Even our hotel penthouse in Caracas changed the battle into a spectacular. How easy to look down at everything and see people as parts of landscapes to be leveled, bulldozed, cultivated. Thank heaven the Sommers immunized their sons against bigshot-itis, although under their New England just-plain-folks manner they think and act the way Mayoso described them—like small-scale kings.

General Moshe Edin and Witt's farm manager sat safety-belted in the rear seats. Betsy heard them comparing Israeli and Puerto Rican irrigation problems, the St. Thomas seawater desalting plant, plastic versus metal pipes, evaporation retardation techniques, while she and Witt sat separated by a narrow metal aisle under the clattering rotors. Witt sorted out in his lap the box of mail the helicopter pilot had brought and began scribbling notations on the margins. Watching him, reading snatches of his work, Betsy was astonished by how much he had to absorb and decide on: research budgets, plant expansion, stock options for executives, currency pricetag problems due to inflation of the cruzeiro in Brazil, patent laws in Italy, the installation by a private detective agency of electronic surveillance devices in a key laboratory, the arguments pro and con additional international expansion in Europe and South America, cost analyses for rebuilding the Caracas warehouse and leasing more experimental farm acreage.

She had motioned for him to lean toward her so she could talk to him without shouting loudly. "I never knew you were so smart, Witt."

He looked at her quickly to see if this was one of her flicking remarks, then reached out to put his hand on her shoulder and say, "I'm not. I'm just stubborn. I stay on top of things until they're settled. But that's a secret."

"I won't tell," she said, "if you don't."

From the bottom of the box, Witt passed two pieces of mail across the aisle to her: a letter from Timmy with a scrawl across the back of the envelope, MOM SEND ME A COCONUT; and an odd-looking package wrapped in brown grocery-bag paper, stamped *50¢ Postage Due,* addressed to H. R. H. Betsy M. Sommers, at her New Haven address.

Out of the package spilled a silk tie. Betsy recognized it as the one she had loaned Roone the day they had driven from New Haven to Southport. With it came a short note written on Metropolitan Hospital paper.

DEAR PAT,

As the hart panteth after the water brooks, this Brooks Brothers tie panteth after my heart. But no matter. While ties may bind, expensive property is cherished in your circles, yuk, yuk, so I'm returning this to demonstrate a solid property-respecting heart tucked beneath my larcenous exterior. Also here's a translated poetic Gaelic fragment just unearthed in Ireland, inscribed on a chamber pot used by Gypsy tinkers.

> There once was a girl named Betts,
> Who ran round in the nude crying Lets!
> Don't try to ape us
> Begged men of Priapus,
> You want us only as pets!

Yr Ob't Servant,
MICKY FINN (Mike to my friends)

Wild goatish laughter and breath-catching annoyance mingled in her.

A madman! Shrewd, snotty, too cute, and blackmailishly suggestive—all at once! Her heart swung painfully in her chest. Her eyes darted toward Witt; he was scowling over a memorandum. The next three seconds will decide, she thought superstitiously. If he looks up at me and asks to see the mail from home, this week's sunny pleasant communion will explode. But if he concentrates on his own work and notices nothing, that will be a sign. She slid the tie and the poem into her raffia purse, as if they were hand grenades from her private underground, her heart pounding with danger.

She pressed her shoulders back against the padded seat, trying to slow the uncomfortable rise and fall of her chest and the air hunger of an out-of-breath runner. Damn that Roone! If he thinks he can swindle me into forgetting! The way he said, *Little Miss Biddy married money and now she wants to scratch where it itches . . . you been begging for the big O. . . .* Hipster language, the naked underworld of the young. Roone must be the only all-American boy student who is neither all-American nor a boy. A disturber, a gypsy honest about his dishonesty, an attractive non-political anarchist unconventional enough to act completely conventional.

I'm going to stay as long as I can here on the island, she decided. A thousand miles from New Haven. Roone, for me an unknown breed of cat, a tigerish jungle cat, burning bright—she closed her eyes—against whom there is no defense because he comes from all directions at once.

The island's hills and valleys swept beneath them, creased and pleated, winking with small reservoirs, streaked with the silver-wire capillaries of streams. Irregular tufted blankets of sugar-cane fields and military files of pineapple plantations ended in the foothills of the cordillera. Small coffee-growing fincas perched on the upper slopes. The helicopter drifted lower. They were over the giant parabolic radio telescope in the mountains near Arecibo.

The pilot twisted toward Witt and her. He pointed downward. "Some beeg deesh, no?" he shouted proudly over the eggbeater noise. "Size of futbol field! Some construction, no? An' ten years ago, my family in that valley, we don' even have 'lectric light. Not a bulb, not a light. Can you believe? Now look!"

Witt nodded. The enormous steel-ribbed hammock of engineered mesh-work was suspended ingeniously from a circle of hilltops, hollow-boned as a bird, an unblinking cyclopean eye of radio astronomy. Betsy could see tiny figures of technicians gazing upward at their hovering mechanical dragonfly.

"When I consider," General Edin said through the overhead racket, "that cosmic soup bowl down there can pick up radio emissions from quasars which exploded a billion billion years ago . . ." He paused wonderingly, "What I mean to say—" Then he and Witt looked amused together.

Let them talk about the stars, Betsy prayed. Or irrigation. Or fishing. Just let them ignore me, because my voice is probably gone.

"Cosmology," Witt said over his shoulder, "she's really some big dish." He glanced at Betsy. "What's the matter, dear?"

She shook her head slightly and tried to smile.

"Your face is so pale, Betts. Ride getting too bumpy for you?"

She touched her bottom lip with her tongue, then managed to say, "I'm all right."

"We'll land any time you want us to."

"No, no—"

The pilot turned his head. "Okay, señor? Back to Cayey now?"

"Yes," Witt shouted back. "The big hydroponic farm first."

Something in Betsy's manner caught him uneasily. Yesterday he would have asked more carefully what was wrong. Today, memoranda piled, guests aboard, business to care for, he detoured his disquiet with conversation. "Next time David talks about juggling human chromosomes in a test tube," he said cheerfully to Betsy, "and making humans to order, well, I'm going to fly him down here alongside Mayoso. Give them a little perspective." He looked down at the giant parabola as they pivoted inland and gained altitude. Her face had changed. What was wrong?

Betsy pretended to doze owlishly as the helicopter swooped sideways and leveled off to skim above the east-west highway. The men talked loudly through the engine din, words with cabalistic sounds—quasars, implosions, plasma fusion, solar winds spewn from the sun to reach here only eight minutes ago, the Milky Way pinwheeling at the speed of light outward to—to where? Men, she thought. Always running away when there's some bloody work to do at home.

They spiraled down to the helicopter landing space, the pitch of their blades fanning so strongly that the nearby sugar-cane stalks bent like grass blades. The pilot cut the engine. Two men ran out of the mixing shed of the hydroponics farm to set a short metal ladder against the helicopter.

"Extraordinary," General Edin said as they disembarked. "That fantastic astronomic antenna is still with me. All that strange new space out there. Wouldn't have missed it, Mr. Sommers, though it does feel very good to get back to earth, what?"

"Very," Betsy said emphatically, as if he had asked her, not Witt.

The domestic clockwork of the Sommers' secluded house by the sea revolved around him, but Mayoso was indifferent to it. He groped in his sealed hermetic vigil, disliking his becalmed pointlessness, his embalmed deathwatch, the drifting leisureless leisure of being a prisoner of himself.

A subtle ticking clinical acumen warned him to stop his hypnotic staring over the final cliff edge. Beyond that edge there was nothing, but on this side was everything of life to be lived. Never mind the difficulties—Churchill's comment?—they speak for themselves. All the philosophies pawed over, all idols powerless since Abraham knocked off their heads; even the newspaper cartoon Betsy had showed him at breakfast was captioned: WE HAVE MET THE ENEMY AND THEY ARE US.

With the spinal effort of the first anthropoid he pulled himself erect. You bumbling big ape, he told himself. Pithecanthropus erectus out of your cave. Are you up? On your two feet? You judged yourself, sentenced yourself as prisoner. Now attempt the next step, most difficult step: to forgive yourself.

He stood alone at the edge of the patio, feeling strangely upright after so many chairbound days. Up and moving, he thought. And I'd better keep it that way. If I stay down, I'll go native, fattening beneath the surface like some fecund vine creeping back toward the green riot of jungle. There are jungle people, chaos lovers, cannibal looters of the world, library burners and freebooters as Neanderthal as pirates of the Spanish Main—but you? You are one of the builders, the settlers, the knowledge makers and pathfinders. Arriba!

He crossed the lawn, vaulted the seawall to the beach, and shaded his eyes against the burning white blaze of sun. As far as he could see, the outthrust bleached jawbone of beach curved for miles. In the distance was a forest of cranes, structural steel of the new hotels and condominium apartments being constructed; much farther, a silhouette jumble of taller buildings in San Juan. Below them, on this Atlantic side, slept the old cemetery of Santa Maria Magdalena.

Ah, Cristina, never to learn carefree laughter, love open without darkness.

The high mare's-tail sky was a horizon-to-horizon cyclorama traced by lacy parallels of military jet contrails. The sun hammered him. Sweat burst from his skin. He kicked off his huaraches, threw off his shirt, rolled his trousers to his knees and walked into the water. He curled his toes against the formless sand, so strangely warm underfoot while the water swirling around his ankles was so cool. The shallows burst with reflected light; with each step his foot broke a miniature watery sun into shivering splinters. Farther out, the ladder of light pierced the water, but dissolved in rippling soluble rungs descending from sight.

How many thousands of fathoms down the water must go, he thought. It covers the slopes of this undersea mountain on whose exposed crest I stand. How unimaginable such depths buried beneath this calm arrogant lying sea, this enemy sun.

Ah, Cristina, the sun would be a friend if you were here, the trickling sea would tell the truth. As naturally as waves we would meet in this crucible, surging together so completely that who is which and what fits where would melt and fuse us into lovemaking's unfathomable oneness. How you would have enjoyed this light cool lapping at warm skin, the tickling nibbles of little fish, the powdery arc of sand. You would not complicate it or complexicate it or pontificate it the way I do, but breathe it intuitively as air. You would be part of sea and sky and sand, a laughing love, warmly cool, coolly warm, an unknowing knower, not primitive but simply simple about the patches of water sharpened into edges as a moment's wind glances off it, the personal liptaste of salt, the frangipani scent rising toward the green hills, all the many air and water sounds of silence, fish-wife gulls, the shore patrol of frigate birds beating upwind, on this topmost tip of a sunken island. Along this shore you will be alive.

Alive? her calm sensible voice said.

In a way, yes. If the stonecutter does inspired work, then you can stand near where you grew up, and every time I see you there you will be alive in my mind.

Oh, she said, you should be first to remember never to worship graven images.

Not worshiping, he said quickly. Only a reminder. A remembrance of love freely given, but not shallow. Not an assault, but a sharing.

Aie *bendito,* she laughed. And you're the one who always made fun of gestures by Spaniards!

Well, he said, after all, in a way, that's what I am.

If you say so, she said. But I'm not so sure. Maybe forgetting would be better.

Ah, I used to think so, too, Cristina, but now I know better. There is never any forgetting. There is only remembering by night and not-remembering by day, but never any forgetting.

You forget the stonecutter can carve only what he knows best: the image of death: And you want him to make the image of life?

Yes, he said, but the stonecutter was not quite sure. He said even the greatest ancient Greek sculptors never tried to carve Eros and Thanatos in the same reliquary statue. I can only carve death, he said. What you say about life I understand, señor, but I do not know how to do it. You will have to accomplish that in your own soul. He had that tone of competence and humility the capable ones have. So I told him to do the best he could, but only make sure you were standing, not bent, eyes open, not closed, and your head held up with some dignity. Life near where you grew up by the sea. A still life.

How contradictory you are, she laughed. La dignidad was always such a joke with you. And your father before you. And now, just listen. Listen to yourself. *Mira!* How you contradict yourself.

Don't confuse me with logic, Cristina. If life is absurd, and death has no meaning, then we will confront such meaninglessness with dignity. We are men, something more than molecules, no? A feeling can have the reality of stone. In all our comings and goings we reach out and touch one another, two halves becoming one, and we can feel the greatness of life as we pass by. The ancient gods are gone. God is gone. And now the bitter thumbsucking God-damning must go too. Remember when we talked in the hotel and I said I believe a new kind of courage is needed?

So. Dignity.

Yes. What's the difference if I invent it only in my mind? What I feel is real. The meaning of your death is real for me. When the stonecutter finishes and we bring the likeness of you to the grave near the sea, we'll set you on that narrow space, but facing east and the dawn palings of every day. I would change places with you if I could, because this whole geometry of space is for you to be newly alive in, while I'm once again the worn survivor, a borrowed-time man who casts no shadow except over those he loves and dooms: father, mother, sister, fiancée, and now you. With my heart and my hands I work for life, but those I love have died. I fought the death pulse beating perpetually in the Spanish heart. I mocked it. I ignored it, analyzed and exorcised it, and I ended like some illiterate superstitious half-drunk penitent on his knees before idols, embracing the most terrible discovery: mortality.

An elegiac tolling followed him while he turned and plodded back up the beach, across the patio and into the cool shade of his room. His hands, with a will of their own, took down from the bookshelf his leather-bound notebook.

At the top of a fresh page he wrote: *To the living memory of Cristina María de la Concepción Bretand Pagán.*

He paused, holding his pen in midair, clothed again by the sun, the cool circlet around his ankles, the fathomless watery abyss.

"In the beginning," he wrote, *"there was a great void. Then the salty biologic waters parted and they saw one another at the same moment, simultaneously. The sea-swell rose and fell so that he sensed her more than saw her, and she knew that in the embryonic darkness he would come.*

"A hundred astronomic forces tugged at them; a thousand mythologies

of coupling and joining, a single lunar cycle, the great galactic wheel of the sun, microscopic carbon molecules which linked their chromosomes to ancient exploding stars, the ovum's tumbling passage, the spermatozoic thrust toward fusion.

"He felt his swimming strength falter. The fluid oceanic resistance, the saline sting as the tides of life swept across aeons against him. She was there, straight ahead, then as the sea fell away she was not.

"She felt herself drowning. The depths pulled her down, down, deeper, drowning. Ahead of her he was there, straight ahead, then he was not rising, falling, as the sea rose and fell, its salt balance identical with tears and blood.

"The endless night around them had no horizon, no dimension, no Northern Star. They were two, alone in time's great tunnel with no end, only a deep mindless drive toward coupling, joining, fusing, living.

"Within her she felt the electric spin and charge of life. To have lived this long only to die now without completion? Within him spun engines of subtle ancient chemistries, the genes of genesis, the chromosomes of creation. With all his last strength he struck against the pressing darkness, against the tugging meaninglessness that defied him to bring life-meaning to her and himself. Genetic immortality, the final triumph over somatic death—this was encoded in the coiled helical molecules which drove them toward one another.

"They carried within themselves primal genetic residues which came from a time before time began, before the great global seas rose greenly over all the land and then sank slowly back, before the earth's poles were reversed, before the terrestrial orbit around the sun lengthened and warped the astronomic day and the astronomic year. Toward one another, they carried the ultimate gift for which love was invented: Immortality.

"The liquid biologic world rose, lifting him forward, then fell away in a great sloping rush that brought them together suddenly with a drowning stranger's clutch, an embrace of embryonic lovers.

"There on the life-giving saline sea they gave one another life, each surrendering in utter faith to final partnership, molecule for molecule, atom for atom, life joining life, sperm joining ovum.

"On all the other indifferent solar planets the miracle went unattended. But here, now, unique and immortal on this voyaging planet, a new individual human had begun."

He had held the pen so tightly that his fingers felt cramped. He stared at the page without seeing it. In the beginning, he thought, was the Word, and the word was love. He flexed his fingers a moment, then signed at the bottom of the page his given name, which no one now used: DIONISIO.

16

IN HIS HIGH-CEILINGED office at La Fortaleza, overlooking San Juan Bay, Governor Santos Roque began cranking up his village-by-village campaign for the primary elections in May. He shut off five of his six telephones; only the hot line was left open for serious emergencies. Usually he left the details of his campaign to his assistants, but this year is different, he told himself. They've lost the lean and hungry drive which put us in power years ago. They tuck in their shirttails now, and they're embarrassed by the barefoot *jíbaro burra canción*, our old song, *Lamento Borinqueño*. They keep flattering me with anecdotes of my shatterproof popularity because they've become slack and fat with success. They should have been with me that night, years ago, when I sat with the President's staff in the Executive Wing of the White House, listening to the election returns radioed from Britain. Winston Churchill, iron-guts commander, heraldic lion rampant, striped-pants colonialist ripened into world statesman, drinker among drinkers of Scotch, chomping Havana Corona Coronas, Churchill the invincible, the noblest Roman of them all, dismissed by his own people in that election.

So, Santos Roque told himself, that election night you learned the best way to campaign is to run scared. He pushed himself impatiently out of his chair and said to his male secretary, "Repeat that, Jorí. The editorial from the San Juan *Star*."

Jorí lifted the tabloid-size newspaper. "The whole editorial, sir?"

"No. Just the point of it. The last line."

Jorí shifted the glasses on his nose and, in a selfconscious elocution student's voice read, "'The Church hierarchy is against Santos Roque, the man, because he is irreligious. Politically, it is against his being elected even one more time. But the Church is wise in the ways of men, patiently cementing communal bricks with theological mortar before openly challenging his widespread popularity.'"

The Governor halted in front of the French doors; sunny rectangles fell where the jalousie shutters were latched inward. This story of my widespread popularity only erodes my campaign by creating overconfidence. The noblest Roman of them all, sent down at his highest moment because the voters had decided in the electoral collegiality of their brains and their bellies and their balls that they wanted someone else.

Spring drifted humidly through the tall open door which faced the garden. He pulled off his coat and rolled his shirtsleeves up to the elbow.

Several *reinitas* darted into his office from the garden, then out again, their yellowish underbellies bobbling like lemons in the deeper green foliage. The golden oriole which nested in his chandelier capered along the mosaic fountain inlaid with the kneeling Lamb and Cross emblem of Ferdinand and Isabella.

Their Catholic Majesties' escutcheon also blazoned from the stained-glass window lighting the staircase up to Bishop Sosa's quarters in Bishopric House. The Powerhouse was the name given the remodeled three-hundred-year-old building by local reporters. I have to ensure my own power to guarantee that I'll never be reduced to climbing the Bishop's stairs to negotiate a truce. Murky paintings of martyrs line that staircase, holy men torn by lions, transfixed by arrows, welcoming death. If I lose this election, I'll send the bishop that *Time* cover portrait of me to join his art collection.

The first telephone call of the morning had come from Bishop Sosa. The call would have been comical if its purpose had not carried such serious implications. The bishop had diplomatically asked whether the employment dollars of the Sommers Pharmaceutical Company were worth the degradation of permitting company use of a local church name, Fátima, in a gratuitous insult on a condom label.

"I can't imagine," Santos Roque had said carefully to Bishop Sosa, "that DeWitt Sommers would be so stupid or so crass."

"I quite agree," the bishop had said. "But I've checked the facts myself. Father Gofredo Möttl, whom you may recall, is a very precise man—"

"Yes, he himself called it Teutonic precision—"

"He reported an unusual combination of circumstances to me. One of his parishioners, a Señora Dolores Valdez, saw Doctor Mayoso Martí with Mr. Sommers and two women in Caracas recently. As you yourself know, Doctor Mayoso had contemptuously ignored a formal appointment with Father Möttl in your own office."

"Mayoso may have had a reasonable reason for that—"

"He told Father Möttl he forgot it. He dismissed the Father's plea for cooperation. He expressed a vindictive hostility. When one recalls that he was once close to Castro—"

"Many liberal and democratic men were—"

"To be sure. All the same he may see Father Möttl as a barrier to his social ideas. This meeting Mr. Sommers at a resort hotel and this scandalous use of the name of Father Möttl's church. Father Möttl has reasonable reasons—to use your own phrase—for considering all these elements as more than isolated circumstances."

"The good padre must have the best intentions, Bishop—"

"I respect the accuracy of Father Möttl's reports. In lay terms he may appear overzealous, but he bears witness with utmost honesty."

"I've watched him on television. His language leans toward the, the incandescent."

"Shedding light is what sermons are for, Governor, *qué no?*"

"Light, yes. Blinding light, no."

"I hope you'll admit, Governor, there's a bit of glitter in the recent newspaper picture of you and Mrs. Marjorie Sommers, side by side, at Blair House. She is a lady who is, ah, shall we say, relentless in her anti-population enthusiasms."

"Oh Lord—"

Bishop Sosa chuckled. "Welcome back to the Church, Governor."

"If you've kept your sense of humor this far," Santos Roque said quickly, "let me arrange a small informal dinner so that you can chat with Sommers. Some distinguished foreign guests for window dressing, an Italian agronomist, an Israeli general, so there's nothing provocative for press speculations. How would that be? There's no need to make a big hullabaloo over a little misunderstanding."

"Father Gofredo would never agree with your estimate of size, Governor. I'll look forward to breaking bread with you."

"I promise you more than just loaves and fishes, Bishop."

"You're a magician politician." Bishop Sosa had sounded amused. "In politics, I've heard your first concern must be your image."

"No," Santos Roque had said, "your opponent."

From behind him, Jorí interrupted his recollection by saying, "At La Casa de las Almas, last night, our *espiritista* predicted victory for you, Governor. So there is nothing to worry about."

"Ah," the Governor said without turning from the open door. "Your *espiritista* prophesied victory for me last night, did she? So there's nothing to worry about."

"You wouldn't make fun of our fraternidad, Governor, if you would come out to one of our Santurce message sessions, for even one night."

"I'm not making fun of it, Jorí. I've read your panfletos. When I think of the number of people on this island who believe in your séances, then I really begin to worry."

"Governor," Jorí said earnestly, with missionary zeal, "just remember that the first Christian churches never held masses. They were really séances. Remember only one truth was revealed by God, that we all have a spiritual life."

"So," the Governor said, "from the revelation of truth by God, there now follows the revelation of my election victory by your *espiritista?*"

"Sir, you mustn't be so skeptical. She has a very impressive record of successful *trabajitos*. When she prescribes a *botánica*, every root and herb that goes with it is blessed."

"Right now, Jorí, the only *botánica* I want blessed is that experimental farm out in Cayey. If Sommers can grow the right kind of medicinal botanicals out there his company will bring a big payroll to this island. Wages for unskilled farm *jíbaro* labor, not just a handful of San Juaneros with college degrees. Por favor, ask your *espiritista* to bless the Sommers' *botánica* with the same sure success as my next election."

"I will, Governor." Jorí scribbled a quick note on his pad. "I'll do it tonight."

"Thank you, Jorí. Now back to the San Juan *Star*. You said that you had something more marked in the newspaper."

"Sí. There's an interview with Bishop Sosa on page two."

"Read it," the Governor said. He frowned at the crucifix-shaped hands of the antique Spanish grandfather clock tirelessly cogwheeling toward noon. Which of us is the lamb, he thought, and which bears the cross? Sosa is respected as one of the *periti* just back from Rome, rumored to be marked for a Vatican post, and Father Möttl is an ecclesiastical torpedo charged with Hispanic theology and only God knows what else. Señora Valdez? I've met her at receptions. One of those rich Cuban refugees who send their daughters to convent schools, their sons to Spain, and their money to Switzerland. Caramba, what the hell was all that about Mayoso being vindictive to Möttl? And that foolishness about the name Fátima? And it occurs to me that this sudden page-two interview Jorí is now reading must have been given out by the bishop yesterday, before he phoned me this morning.

"'The Commonwealth of Puerto Rico'"—Jorí's voice was droning pontifically—"'is fortunate to be a part of the great United States of America and, at the same time, to be a Roman Catholic island. The fastest growing and most prosperous Catholic community in the world is that of the United States. The largest single religious body in the country is Roman Catholic, with seventeen thousand churches, almost sixty thousand clergymen, about fifty thousand seminarians studying for the religious life, and a membership rapidly approaching fifty million souls—'"

"That's the first time," the Governor said to the office air, "that someone has tried to answer Stalin's question about how many divisions does the Pope have—" The Governor tilted his ear, waiting. Just over his head the golden oriole whirred into the office.

"'We can recognize that the so-called separation of Church and State, as our esteemed Governor phrases it, is only a red herring—'"

"Touché for the bishop. A neat *double entendre* in that *red—*"

"'There is no such thing as separation of Church and State to any man who believes in God,' Bishop Sosa told this interviewer firmly from behind his efficient modern desk in Bishopric House. 'The separation of Church and State is a shibboleth. I challenge anyone—'"

"Meaning me, of course—"

"'—to show me anything about the separation of Church and State in the Constitution. But the Constitution does state that this is a nation under God. How can there be a separation of Church and State unless we take the terrible step of turning our backs on God to become Communists or materialists exchanging our souls for a mess of pottage?'"

The Governor about-faced into the room. "Very good. Very good. Bishop Sosa is an intelligent man. But I'm no kneeling lamb, so the tactical question is: Will Möttl be his cross to bear, or mine?"

"Sir? I don't follow your thought—"

Santos Roque paced the room again without speaking. This gambit was too simple, and Bishop Sosa was not a simple man. If he made his opening moves on the separation of Church and State issue, he would lose. No, the bishop would have to do better than that. Perhaps I should be running more confidently, less scared, if these are the sort of pawns Bishop Sosa has.

He paused before another open doorway overlooking the stone perimeter walk of La Fortaleza and the steep fortress wall to the harbor. Beneath him was one of his favorite antiques, a bronze Spanish cannon almost four hundred years old named La Sibila. The feminine name was affectionate as the elaborate tooling along the gun barrel. The grandfathers of my grandfather brought that cannon here and they used it to fight off the English under Drake, and the French, the Dutch, so no one is going to drive me off this island now.

The golden oriole hidden in the chandelier chirped as the wind tinkled the glass pendants and wheeled out into the garden. The Governor pulled off his tie and opened his shirt collar. Once again, as he did every year at this time, he had refused to install air conditioning in the name of efficiency. Air conditioning meant closing the doors and windows. The birds would not flutter down to peck at the porcelain basket of sugar his wife kept filled at the end of the room or drink from the large glass dime-store ashtray on his telephone table. A low-speed quiet floor fan, sí. Air conditioning, no.

He felt the edgy unreasonable wind rise annoyingly as he worked. But he was a modern man without old-fashioned habits, no tapping of barometers, no worried scanning of the sky, so he interpreted his pulse of uneasiness as internal; a trickling anxiety because this was an election year and his confrontation with Bishop Sosa could not be delayed.

Outside, the garden colors dimmed, graying as a cloud shadow swam massively over and darkened the bright mosaic. The wind stiffened unexpectedly, whistling at the corner; the paired French doors of the office creaked on their hinges, then banged abruptly. Strange, he thought, feeling the faint mist a moment before rain splattered against the walls. Then, as the wind puffed again, his chandelier shivered and tinkled glassily. Jorí jumped up to close the doors on the far wall while the Governor hurried to the nearer doors. One of the chandelier *reinitas* fluttered upward with a small flourish, tilted toward the garden outside, and flew directly into the door the moment he closed it. She fell like a feathered stone to the tile floor.

"Aie, a bad omen," his secretary said.

The Governor stared down at the broken little bundle; she had held office in the chandelier so long. "Poor creature."

Jorí put his notebook on the desk. "I'll clean it up."

"No, no. Later. I'll lose my train of thought." He raised his voice. "And don't slide back into any morbid *espiritista* nonsense, you hear me? Your job is safe. A bad omen," he muttered. "Listen, Jorí, did you ever hear of the Sibylline Oracles in ancient times? You never did? Well, let me tell you, they were a bunch of female prophets who could foretell the future of Rome's destiny. No Roman general would start his campaign without consulting the sibyls. Well," he said, straightening, throwing back his shoulders, "before you talk to me about bad omens you'd better know that there's only one prophet on this island. Me. Not your *espiritista*. You hear me? You know that old bronze cannon we have out beyond the patio?"

"You mean the one with the name stamped on it, Governor?"

"Yes. Did you ever read the name, Jorí, my fine feathered superstitious friend?"

"No sir."

"The name of that cannon is La Sibila. Ah, ah, you're catching on? Mao Tse-tung once said that revolutions are born out of the cannon's mouth. But on this island we let the cannon rust so our people can fight through the ballot box. I want you to learn a little elementary political wisdom, Jorí. I don't want you to make a nutty superstitious mountain out of one sad little bird. I don't want you to go running over to your favorite *espiritista* and spread gloom in a public séance, an off-beat squib the reporters will surely pick up. You hear me?"

Jorí lowered his eyes and drew a small ectoplasmic doodle on his dictation pad. He's talking too much, Jorí thought, the way he always does when he's worried. He thinks I'm superstitious, but he's the one talking about a dead bird.

"Jorí," the Governor was saying, "I can tell by the look on your face you're getting the message. When you walk out of this office, when you take a coffee break with the staff, when you take notes for the election committee, when you stand up in Santurce tonight at one of your séance sessions, I want you to radiate confidence. As the one official prophet and oracle on this island, I want every district chairman, every municipal chairman, every Party member down to the smallest *barrio* to understand that Bishop Sosa and the hierarchy must not stampede them with Jesuitical *culipandeo*." He began pacing the office. "Put this down. Have it typed as a draft."

Jorí stopped doodling and sat up, alert. "Yes sir."

The Governor jabbed the air with his finger. "Point one: We are a middle-of-the-road Commonwealth in free association with the United States. Two: We reject the extreme left of Castro and the extreme right of Franco-type state religion influence. Three: Castro's argument that we cover the stink of capitalism with a perfumed colonialism may be a clever pun in Spanish—cologne, colonia—but the fact is that our people have more schools, more health clinics, more electric light, more food. The unaligned free small nations of the world send their people here to study our accomplishments, not to Cuba. The Latin American students and their teachers will do well to choose between the Cuban cannon and the Puerto Rican ballot box as instruments of social progress. Three: Catholics will have to make a choice between the traditional medieval wing of the Church and the liberal twentieth-century group. The eternal triangle of Latin America—Church at the apex, resting on a base of a privileged oligarchy and a privileged Army—does not exist on this island. We are living proof that Latin Americans can freely improve their lives in the twentieth century—"

"Governor, could you slow down just a little?"

The Governor ignored him; his voice had gone up, as if he were addressing a conference of backsliding political party chiefs. "I stake my entire political future on one belief: The left is the cannon's mouth offering apocalyptic revolution to wipe out starvation by wiping out men and women and children who oppose them. On the right, the pulpit offers two billion starving people pie in the sky. Cry now, pay later. In the middle of the road, this island—this barefoot poorhouse of the Caribbean of my childhood—has shown the world that Latins are able to industrialize by educating the people, by improving agriculture so that people have enough to eat, and by setting up sensible restraints against population growth so that starving babies don't crush us all."

He stopped his pacing in front of the tall antique Spanish pendulum clock and stared at it. "The time is now. A decision is here. This island is the fulcrum of a seesaw between hundreds of millions of people. No matter how traditional our emotions, only rational common sense will lead to survival in this century."

As he spoke, the long delicately made crucifix-shaped minute and hour hands reached twelve noon together as they had for centuries. The Governor frowned slightly, and then turned to his secretary. "The air is getting close, Jorí. Rain or not, open the doors."

As Jorí stood up, the Governor glanced at the crumpled feathered ball of the dead *reinita*. "And get somebody to bury the little bird in the garden."

17 FATHER GOFREDO MÖTTL met with his curates in the rectory of his parish La Virgen de Fátima. A memorandum had come from the Bishopric House Chancery directing all Catholic churches in the diocese to ring their bells simultaneously at eight o'clock as a sign of unity during the election campaign.

A pastoral letter to the Reverend Priests and the Faithful in general, to guide the thinking of parishioners in the coming primary elections for the governorship of the Commonwealth of Puerto Rico, was to be read from the pulpit on Friday. Members of the Christian Doctrine Brotherhood would make their annual Lenten procession carrying the life-sized crucified Christ past the Cathedral. From Father Möttl's own church, the marchers would carry their beautiful Madonna through the streets with her sky-blue, gold-bordered robes draped symbolically in black. The shellac tear droplets on her face had begun to discolor and crack. Father Möttl asked one of his curates, Father Leary, personally to see to it that when these tears were touched up a better grade of varnish was used.

Young Father Keenan Leary, the curate whom the parishioners called el Americano, was busy studying for his junior clergyman's examination. He looked up from his book at Father Möttl with a friendly smile, hoping to lighten the military precision of their conference across the rectory breakfast table. "Padre," he said to Father Möttl, "for our handful of real right-handers from the old sod, will you mind if I sneak in a green Mass on St. Patrick's Day?"

Father Möttl lowered his head, seeming to ponder this joking question seriously, communing with himself as if in prayer. How long, O Lord, he thought, will our brethren Irish clergy cling to the assurance they are the chosen people of God, supervisor of all other immigrants, and cast out anyone who questions this as blindly prejudiced or pagan freemasons or disrespectful atheists?

His silence was so prolonged that the young priest's cheeks flushed. Father Möttl raised his head at last, trying to convey simpático understanding but somehow sounding serious and a bit grim. "This is a Latin country. St. Patrick may have destroyed the druids and their pagan rites of spring, but should that justify last year's comedy of painting the street traffic markings in green? Or joining in parades held by the Ancient Order of Hibernians?"

"Padre," the young priest said, "I was only—"

"Yes, I know," Father Möttl said. "I recognize your commendable attempt at modifying the tone of our conference." His voice deepened into the organ tone he used for his weekly telecast, *Hour of Eternity*. "But let me remind you we are the world's only witness of the Passion and Death and Resurrection. I am aware of all the talk about *aggiornamento* and *apertura*, but I cannot bring myself to some so-called modernizations. You can charge me with obscurantism and rigid formalism, but"—he elevated his hand to emphasize each phrase—"but we are not performers. I will have no betrayals of our profound mysteries only to submit to the entertainment orientation of the present age."

"Padre—" the young curate began, then stopped. His entire face was red and his forehead shone with perspiration.

Father Möttl rotated his hand quickly into a gesture of *stop*. "No, no, Father," he said to the young priest. "Apologies are not necessary. You meant well. How effortless it is to have good intentions. Good intentions always seem so warmhearted, so praiseworthy, most dangerous when they are sincere."

"Padre," Father Leary tried to say, "I wasn't suggesting—"

Father Möttl's instruction swept into an oration. "I say to you that the smallest hairline crack in the fortress wall of faith—yes, yes, even with the best intentions—is the beginning of breaching the only protection our world has against the rising tide of godless secular materialism." His voice dropped but his pulpit tone remained intense. "No retreat! *No retreat!*" He paused, thinking: What can I say to a young curate who comes from one of those seminaries which permit Coke machines and mimeographed class notes and the ownership of personal radios and visiting back and forth between rooms and pseudodemocratic preoccupation with municipal sewage plants? Sophomoric apostles, buddy-buddy administrators, ordained gourmets and rare-book collectors who permit in the lobbies of their churches the sale of holy cards which have touched the picture of Our Lady of Help in Rome and were indulgenced, these indulgences purchasable at the nominal sum of fifteen cents for each card.

Oh my Lord, what has any of this to do with our solemn remembrances of the sufferings of Christ during that ancient Roman spring of Crucifixion and the eternal blessing of Victory over Death? He did not wash and kiss the feet of his brothers at the Last Supper and refuse a Caesar's pagan offering of clemency and stagger alone through agony for us all, only to have druidical cults creep back, in fluorescent crosses, bingo piety, hootenanny masses, apostolic real estate promoters, holy toastmasters and social workers of the order of Melchizedek. When will they learn, these new young priests with all their talk of cassocks being anachronistic and unhygienic, their dabbling with Freud's church of Vienna, their chatter about worldly politics and picket lines and the rescheduling of Vespers to allow seminary students to catch their favorite TV comedy program —when will they ever learn in their hearts that even the smallest deviation in sacred practice is a surrender, a backward step toward pagan religions of sticks and stones?

Father Leary stumbled to his feet uncomfortably. Hellfire for breakfast, heartburn for lunch. The day's practical agenda was still unsettled. "Padre," he said, humbled, "will you be meeting today with the Israeli general?"

Father Möttl's ear rejected the question. In his mind's eye he was hypnotized again by a young man on fire, his clothing ablaze, a burnt offering, an incredible martyrdom to godlessness. If they can kindle such a passion, he thought, then they have succeeded in raising an economic dogma to a religion. He stared at the curate. "I'm sorry. What did you say?"

"The Israeli general who's making courtesy calls on all the churches. Something about thanking Latin Americans for their support of admitting Israel to the United Nations."

"Israeli?"

"Yes. He brings each one a page of the Polyglot Bible." He was surprised by the change in Father Möttl's face. Interested? Fascinated? Father Leary tried harder. "Down at the Powerhouse they've mounted it on the Bishop's wall. A real humdinger of a museum piece. A passage from Genesis in parallel columns of Greek, Latin vulgate, and the Hebrew original."

"But," Father Möttl said haltingly, "the Polyglot Bible is in Spain. At Alcalá University. I've seen it there myself."

"Oh, these are color reproductions. Modern printing can do anything."

"A general?" Father Möttl repeated.

"Well, the scuttlebutt I hear is that the Israelis retire their top men young. The goodwill ambassador trip routine is supposed to break them into civilian life gently."

"An Israeli *general?* What was he doing in Spain?"

Father Leary shrugged. "Beats me. Arranging for all these Polyglot Bible gift pages, I suppose. After what the Inquisition did to a couple of hundred thousand Jews, this Bible thing makes a very forgiving sort of ecumenical gesture, don't you think?"

"Don't make the error," Father Möttl said in a tight voice, "of believing centuries of Protestant bigots who saw only sadism in the Inquisition. One of the few reservoirs of mercy in Europe and the only court of fair trials for the accused was the Holy Office of the Inquisition."

I surrender, Father Leary thought. He turns every word into a challenge. He's big on scholarly knowhow, but awfully small in how he shares it.

"Father Leary, why haven't I heard of this so-called goodwill visit before? My schedule can't be changed."

"You don't have time to roll out the carpet for him?"

"No," Father Möttl said hurriedly. "I can't. Bishop Sosa has asked me to hear confessions at the cathedral this morning. Two of our brothers are down with catarrhal *monga*. Will you greet him for me?"

"Certainly, certainly." Father Leary was grateful to escape from the bear trap which had snapped with his earlier joking reference to a green Mass. Saints, he thought, what if I'd opened my big yap about a Yiddish Sons of Erin party with green matzo-ball soup and stuffed kishke à la Killarney?"

Father Möttl was uncharacteristically grateful. "It's not asking too much for you to take the time?"

"Happy to do it," the young curate began to say impulsively, then held himself back from appearing boyishly enthusiastic. "Padre," he said, "I'll get here in time. I'll hurry a bit through my sick calls."

"Nothing serious I hope?" Father Möttl's voice was muted.

"No sir. Just the German measles virus the children have been picking up at school during the last month." A new peace offering occurred to Father Leary and he said more confidently, "If we could lock horns with the Governor Santos Roque and get construction funds for more parochial schools, all our crowding—"

"I agree with the thought," Father Möttl said in an abstracted way. "But I doubt we should be included in your suggestion about locking *horns*."

The young curate flushed again. He muttered, "If you'll excuse me, padre—" and escaped from the room.

The housekeeper came backward through the swinging kitchen door and then turned into the dining room with a large breakfast plate in each of her hands. "Eggs, ranchero style," she announced. "Just what you like, padre."

Father Möttl was hunched over the table, bent deeply into a question mark. He waved her away. "I'm not hungry—"

How overly clever they are, he thought. A handsome page, in color, from a precious Bible. They retired their generals as goodwill ambassadors. Civilians. Were they ambassadors of goodwill who spirited Eichmann out of Argentina, carrying scholarly theological gifts? He straightened himself painfully. "If anything urgent arises, I will be upstairs in my room."

He walked with effort toward the hallway, his sandals scuffing, treading other ground.

At midday, Father Möttl's housekeeper knocked lightly on the door to his room in the rectory. Before he could answer, she hurried in. She was a figure of perpetual mourning, dressed in black, black cotton stockings, black shoes with holes cut out on either side for her bunions. She inhaled and exhaled a never-ending penance, alert to any happening which might be a sign or warning from God. In her soul lay her parents, in Mexico, who had bought their coffins in advance and had slept in them side by side, like twin beds. Now she was a woman so scrupulous about trifles that she worried about having unpure thoughts whenever she inserted a key in a lock or took a bath. She brushed back the gray tangle of hair which had fallen over one eye.

"Perdóneme, padre," she said, "something urgent." She was still puffing from her trip up the stairs. "A letter for you. *Entrega inmediata.* Just now."

As he accepted the thin crackling envelope of the special-delivery letter from her, he saw the familiar stamps first, then the return address scribbled in crabbed minuscule writing into the upper corner. An immediate sensation of furious pity blazed through him. Of course! In the same time span, the Israeli and now this letter. More than a coincidence. I'm not a blind fool. He held his breath so long, his neck veins swelling against his collar, that the housekeeper fluttered her hands. "Padre, what's wrong? Bad news?" She crossed herself. "Aie, Dios mío, please not."

"Look!" Father Gofredo pointed stiffly at the stamps on the letter. His voice was choked, but he controlled himself. "If you can't read the country named on the stamps, at least you can try to recognize the picture on them!"

The housekeeper bent forward to peer at the mysteriously anger-causing stamps. "Generalísimo Franco," she said. "Each stamp," she added proudly, having solved the puzzle, "has his picture."

Father Gofredo slapped the letter against his other hand. "Spain! Spain!" he repeated tightly. "How many times have I told you that a letter from Spain with this tiny handwriting must never be brought to me?"

"But padre, special delivery—"

"It does not matter at what cost it comes. Only where it comes *from,* you understand?" He saw her clasp her hands to stop their trembling, and dropped his voice charitably. "Don't you remember the other letter like this?"

"Sí, padre. You didn't eat for two days."

"Gott im Himmel! My not eating means nothing! I have lived for weeks on Zwieback and schmierkäse! You don't remember my instructions when the previous letter came?"

"Sí, padre." She knew that whenever he lapsed into German expressions much emotion followed. "You tore up the letter and told me: No more. Don't bring me these letters again. Forgive me, padre, but when the postman said special delivery—"

He threw his hand upward. "Enough. I understand. The postal system excited you with the noises and hurry of the world. So, for me, and to help you remember"—he extended the innocent-looking but explosive letter to her—"you will go to the *barrio* post office today and tell the men to send this letter back to Spain."

"Sí, padre. I'm sorry—"

His voice rose again. "You will tell him to stamp this envelope with a rubber stamp that says the letter could not be delivered. Do you understand me?"

Her mouth was half open. To lie? She was proud of this flashing padre, his *embajadora* in the markets where other women told her he was a television star, but this of the return of a special-delivery letter sent via *correo aéreo* from Spain—even in the face of the padre's holy and inspired wisdom, it was forgivable to wonder about such actions. She nodded vigorously and took the obscurely evil letter he thrust toward her as if it were the messenger of obscenities. "Sí, sí, sí, I'll remember, padre."

"The rubber stamp?"

"Sí. The rubber stamp."

"The letter could not be delivered."

"But padre, if they say your name is on it—"

"Don't worry. You are not lying. The truth is simple. When the addressee does not accept a special-delivery letter, that letter cannot be delivered."

Her eyes fell. "Sí, padre." How firmly exact he was. Aie, what a stern one he must be in the confessional!

He saw the humbleness of her bent head and changed his tone. "Good. *Bitte*, go now. *Besten Dank!* I'll pray for you."

"Gracias, padre."

After she tiptoed out, he sat at his table creating isolation in his mind by lowering his eyelids. The Angelus summons rang from the belltower of La Virgen de Fátima. He should go downstairs for lunch, but he was not hungry. The hard constriction in his throat would remain for hours. Because of an Israeli visitor, because of the Spanish stamps, because of Franco's picture, because of the cramped return address . . . he shuffled along the dusty village streets of his boyhood again, through the noonday Spanish sun blaze, he heard the tense low voices of his parents in the next room, the careful door creaks of midnight with visitors who never stayed the night. He felt the pride of being first in school, always first, the fatherliness of his Jesuit schoolmaster who was his true father in a spiritual sense, which was the only sense, and the seminary, the shadowed arched corridors, the discovery of a beauty and a glory not of this earth; the clear sense of balanced payment for the sinning, punishment as a welcome penitence, the one time he had bent forward in shamed obedient humility as his bare buttocks were chastised because he had slept through the sacraments; the calm humility of ordination, the holy oil on his hands bound palms together with linen strips as the archbishop welcomed him solemnly into the profound mysteries and duties of priesthood, *Ego te absolvo*. How much rose up from that trinity of words!

De profundis clamavi, Domine.

Out of the depths, I beseech Thee, O Lord.

Israel. Jerusalem, city of a Hebrew carpenter, destiny's courtroom. Their bloodhounds of history tracked Eichmann down across oceans and continents.

In the confessional of my head, in the dark tangle of my brain cells, I have kept secret guilt a guilty secret.

I have consecrated my life to cancel out the guilts—whose guilts?

Balancing blood accounts only cries out for more blood, the arrogance of private spiritual bookkeeping. God never bargains. *If the world hate you, know you that it hath hated Me before you.*

All that exists, only thanks to a single cause, and this cause, which is the only power that exists through itself, is God.

I must see the bishop, be relieved of pastoral duties. I am exhausted, my balance is shaken. I need restoration to the Light. How else can I carry on Christ's work while I am nailed to this secret?

De profundis clamavi, Domine.

18

ONE DAY Betsy brought Tranquilino out to the patio, but Mayoso was not there.

"Señora," Tranquilino said, "I'll come back later. Maybe he still doesn't want to see anybody."

"Oh, no, he's much better now."

"A man's grief is private—" Tranquilino started to say, then stopped. He looked shy and uncomfortable in his lumpy suit, his starched white shirt divided by a clumsily knotted tie. Instead of his usual army fatigue cap with its broken visor, he was wearing his Sunday straw hat with a sweatstained band.

"He's much better," Betsy repeated. "He said he would like to see you."

They found Mayoso alone on the beach, hunched against the stone seawall. He hefted himself to his feet ponderously when he heard them scuffing toward him. "My friend," he said to Tranquilino. "*Qué más?*"

Tranquilino held out a wrapped box of cigars. "Here," he said stiffly. "Huevas still makes a few of these by hand, so I brought you some."

"All of a sudden," Mayoso said, "you're rich? The fish are jumping into your boat? Since when do you buy me cigars?"

Tranquilino pretended to become angry. "God's teeth! Don't think your size scares me." He shrugged. "When my boat was damaged who paid for the repairs? You did." Left hanging in the air was the thought: Now you're the one damaged. He turned to Betsy making her witness and judge. "He doweled the wood pegs for the gunwales. Would you believe it? That with a surgeon's hands, this hombre makes himself a carpenter? He even painted the eyes on the boat!"

Betsy tried a pale smile, uncertain about all this. "Eyes? On a boat?"

"For sure," Tranquilino said. He swept his arm outward, taking in the bay, the Atlantic, the world beyond. "When you fish, you look for something, no? You don't know what, which fish, but who can see down there? You sail over a lot of dark water. When you sail in the darkness, something has to help you see, no?"

"That's reasonable," Betsy said. She began to understand how these two different men had become fishing partners.

"Reasonable," Tranquilino said to Mayoso. "You heard the señora? Don't be stubborn, hombre. If you want to hand out one or two," Tranquilino said, "the first cigar can begin with me. Yesterday I learned from Elena I will be a father again. I wanted to tell you first."

Mayoso shook hands with him. "You old goat," he said. He pretended to throw a punch at Tranquilino, stopping his fist short. "*Qué macho.*"

"Elena says she wants you to be her doctor. Even if she has to wait all year."

Mayoso laughed out loud and Tranquilino pretended to cough into the bend of his elbow while he hid his grin.

"And Elena's feeling fine?" Mayoso asked.

"You know how women are, amigo. Backache, headache, left elbow, right elbow. New tastes—this time cinnamon sprinkled on *bacalaítos.*"

Mayoso explained to Betsy what Tranquilino had said and she shook his hand also. "Congratulations. I envy you and your wife."

"It is a mixed blessing," Tranquilino said. There was silence; then, unexpectedly, the two men stepped forward and embraced, a clumsy *abrazo.*

Praise be, Betsy thought, he's come out of his isolation cell, away from the shadowy brooding all day, the hypnotic watching of gulls' dawn patrol wheeling from nowhere to nowhere.

"This calls for a short snort," she said brightly, the trapdoor of her own barrenness dropping her toward bitch humor from the ould sod. "Increase and multiply, the law of life, my father used to announce over the potatoes and marge and chutney sauce. A baptismal bit of booze for the coming babe."

Tranquilino squinted questioningly at Mayoso. He was too polite to say that he did not savvy what she meant.

"A drink for congratulations," Mayoso explained, covering up for Betsy. "The real stuff. Not *cañita.*" He unwrapped the box of cigars.

Tranquilino glanced past him at Betsy. When she nodded encouragingly, as if to say: you're doing fine, keep going, he said, "Maybe tomorrow you'll come fishing with me?"

"And while we're fishing," Mayoso said, sifting the cigar box gently in the air, "maybe I'll let you try one or two of these cigars."

Tranquilino had come breathlessly to the house later the same week, in a taxi. Mayoso threw open the door as Tranquilino hurried up the flower-bordered path.

"What's wrong, Tranquilino? *Qué más?*"

"Elena. Aie *bendito.* Sick all night. *Qué fuego!*"

"Where is she now?"

Tranquilino looked feverish himself. "In the hospital. I left her only to come here." He shuffled apologetically. "To intrude at a time of sorrow—"

"Don't talk such foolishness. Didn't you ask me to be her doctor?"

"*Sí, si Dios quiere.*"

"Tell that taxi to go. Mrs. Sommers will let us take her car." He put a hand in his pocket and said lightly, so that he would not offend Tranquilino's pride or add to his shame of being obligated, "Those taxi meters run faster than a man can count, amigo. If you're temporarily short a dollar or two—"

"No, no." Tranquilino waved his hand. "I have enough."

"Then pay him and come inside. Did you have breakfast? Have a cup of *café con leche* while I get dressed. *Voy!*"

Betsy drove them to the hospital herself in the compact convertible Witt had rented for her. Mayoso, all legs, jackknifed himself into the rear seat while Tranquilino kept twisting back toward him with questions.

"You think Elena's eyes could be going?"

"What about her eyes?"

"On the way to the hospital she kept complaining the lights hurt her eyes."

"Was she able to walk?"

"*Sí,* but not by herself. Shaky, you know? Very shaky in the legs. You think it could be a miscarriage?"

As they went on talking, Mayoso reassuring Tranquilino without saying anything definite, Betsy watched him in the rearview mirror. Not only had he shaved and combed his hair, but also he had put on a fresh shirt, a tie, and a conservative suit like any conservative doctor going to make medical rounds in a hospital. In the sunlight, his mane of hair blazed whitely and he kept his head up, speaking carefully, listening sympathetically. Just, she thought, as a working doctor should.

The nurse at the entrance to the women's ward stopped them. "I'm sorry," she said, "but we can allow only two visitors."

"We have only two," Mayoso said. "I'm here to work."

"He is Doctor Mayoso Martí," Tranquilino explained proudly.

"Ah. Ah. Sí. I know the name. If you need anything, Doctor—"

Betsy sat down on the wooden bench in the hospital corridor. "I'll wait here." She envied the nurse, that calm tone of doing useful work.

Mayoso found Tranquilino's wife Elena lying flat on her bed with her eyes closed. Tranquilino bent over her. "Elena, I told you Doctor Mayoso would come."

Elena looked up cautiously, shielding her eyes from the window light with trembling fingers. "Oh it seemed like such a long time. It's my eyes. Mother of Mercy. I hope I don't have a tumor on the brain."

Out in the hall Betsy watched the clinical traffic with the appraisal of an experienced hospital volunteer worker. The same morning comings and goings must be happening in New Haven right now. Just drape me in that blue sack of a uniform, she thought, and I could be doing my Play Lady bit in the Pediatrics ward. Puppet plays and nursery stories. Goldilocks and the Three Bears: who's been sleeping in my bed? How exotic Roone would look here, in this hall filled with dark haired people, he with his blondness and *ojos azules*. Roone would be taking a coffee break at the Womb with a View, probably jabbering with that fantastic Gypsy creature, Volga. Oh that madman. His self-assurance, that morning in the kitchen. Too clever, too cheeky, too everything. Little Boy Blues go blow your horn someplace else. The lady is a lady after all. Not a one-night stand.

And David, this morning? In his lab, boiling water in a Pyrex flask over a Bunsen burner to make instant coffee? I wonder if David even knows about Mayoso's coffee trees and the little bohío out in the country. David's university world, the new breed of professors beginning to make or marry money, the playpen corners of We Intelligent Us, Damn the Dean, Washington Advisory Review Boards (review boards, Witt called them)—the world of *Wednesday? Whose Seminar Today?* David's world, all-knowing but ignorant of a Roone under the polite med student façade, or Roone's randy playmates, or Roone's anarchy. Roone, Roone, will the real Roone please stand up?

She was startled enough to jump, snapped back to the wooden bench in the hallway, when Mayoso sat down beside her.

"Well," he said, "Elena's got it, too. German measles."

"Oh, I'm so glad it's nothing more than one of those childhood diseases."

"Too bad Elena didn't have it as a child."

"Really?"

"It's not serious for her, but it is for her pregnancy. Did you ever have German measles?"

"That's a strange thing to ask."

"If you haven't had it, here's your chance to catch it."

"Thanks, but no thanks."

"Well," he said, "it's not as foolish as it sounds. Every woman should develop immunity to the disease by having one attack of it. The immunity protects the embryo later, when she becomes pregnant."

"You picked the right lady to talk to about immunity, Doctor Mayoso. I'm sperm-immune. Impregnable, remember?"

"Yes," he said, "of course I remember. Sperm-immune isn't a diagnosis. It's a description for laymen."

"Laywomen, too? Opportunity knocks you up but once?"

"Am I supposed to say ha-ha?"

"I'm sorry. My barfly sense of humor. But when you tell me I should catch measles—never-pregnant me—I laugh lest I cry."

"Betsy, never say die."

"Oh, please. I can't stand the medical buck-up-old-girl."

"You're young. So's Witt." He paused. "Maybe he'll come around to the artificial insemination donor idea. He's changed. We've all changed since Caracas."

"We have," she said quickly. "I know we have. It's almost like old times with Witt. Isn't it rotten the way it takes suffering to make living seem better?"

He clasped his big hands between his knees, opening and closing his fingers, silent. When he raised his head, his voice had the thoughtful professional tone which had returned this morning. He hoisted himself to his feet. "Good of you to give us a lift to the hospital. But I don't want to keep you waiting in an uncomfortable place."

"No no—" she began. He too thinks of me as only ornamental. Don't dismiss me. I can do *something*. "Really, I'm not uncomfortable. They also serve who sit and wait."

"I can take a taxi back home."

"I'd rather wait for you. Who's taking care of Tranquilino's children?"

"Elena's sister. I won't be more than half an hour. I want to talk to the clinical pathologist to doublecheck the lab work."

"No hurry," she said. "I like being useful." Her eyes met his. "I told you, we've all changed. I'm in no hurry."

Mayoso opened the door labeled: PATOLOGÍA. Inside, hospital laboratory technicians were sorting their metal test-tube racks of blood tests, urine jars, small cartons of stool samples. The pathologist who was director of the laboratory saw Mayoso lumbering down the aisle between the long lab benches and jumped up to meet him at the door of his glassed-in corner office.

"Oh, Mayoso! They told me you had disappeared!" He gave Mayoso an *abrazo,* clapping him on the shoulder and back. "Where the hell have you been?"

"Around," Mayoso said. What can I say, he thought: that I have endured a season in hell?

"Not around here. It's not like you to run away from a battle."

"A battle? Julio," Mayoso said, "I apologize. Forgive me. I don't know what battle you mean. I'm in a hurry about a patient."

"Don't give me that Yanqui hurry-up line," the pathologist said. "We do careful lab work here. If you hurry us our accuracy goes down."

"You're absolutely right, Julio. I don't want to burden your technicians."

"*Qué va?* Don't blame my technicians. It's you guys. You clinicians don't trust your own clinical diagnoses anymore. Every damn little everything has to come into my lab in the name of scientific accuracy."

"You're breaking my heart," Mayoso said. "That I should live to hear a pathologist complain about clinicians who want laboratory proof."

The pathologist threw up both arms, speechless in the face of injustice. Then, "Professor, what the hell is this *proof*? Because a reaction happens in a test tube, you think it is more true than if it happens in humans?"

"Julio, tomorrow I'll buy you a big philosophical drink and you can give me scientific hell. Today I'm in a hurry."

"Still rushing me? I'm cooped up here or in the autopsy room all day. So few clinicians walk in here on their own two feet to get my opinion face to face that you've shocked me a little bit."

"Listen, Julio, you caballero, before they throw you out of the pathologists' union for all your subversive talk, let me tell you I have a friend whose wife is a patient here. She's one or two months pregnant, admitted with a working diagnosis of German measles."

The pathologist raised his shoulders and gestured with his hands again. "So I just asked you—where were you during the battle?"

"Caramba! One of us must be off his rocker. I'm talking about a sick woman and you're talking about a battle."

The pathologist nodded briskly. "Sí. One hundred and forty-one cases of German measles in this hospital alone during the last few weeks. Just as a matter of scientific curiosity, these last couple of weeks, where the hell have you been hiding?"

Mayoso stared at him. "One hundred and forty-one cases?"

"In this hospital alone. Since when do you pull this kind of humor? Somebody at staff conference said you yourself reported the first cases. A school child, then his mother."

"Of course, of course . . ." Of course, he thought. That afternoon in the clinic before I left for Caracas.

"Mayoso, amnesia?" He tapped his forehead. "Senile memory. Alzheimer's disease? How is it possible you didn't know we have such an outbreak of German measles?"

"I've been away," Mayoso muttered. Explain that a season in hell is a solo trip, never a guided tour? Impossible. I never even read a newspaper. I must seem idiotic. "So you can run a twenty-four-hour test for my friend's wife? Her name is Mrs. Elena Díaz. Women's ward."

"You're really in a hurry? She's probably got a whole army of kids running around at home. She'll be glad to sneak a few days' rest in the hospital."

"Well," Mayoso said, "if the diagnosis is proved"—he raised one hand quickly—"excuse me, not *proved*, if the diagnosis is 95 per cent accurate, I will advise my friend and his wife to authorize a therapeutic abortion." He cocked an eye at the pathologist's face. "What's the matter, Julio? Did I say something?"

"Yes." The pathologist's eyes narrowed. "In this hospital you said a dirty word."

"Wait a minute, Julio. A *therapeutic* abortion."

"What the hell are you begging for trouble for? You want to get kicked off the visiting staff? Pretend you have the organized scientific brain of a pathologist. Look at it in a sequential way, step by step—"

"Julio, I know you mean well—"

"The front office will not give you an operating room. That's item one," Julio said, raising a finger. A second finger. "Item two. Even if you could get an operating room, the anesthetist will refuse to put the patient to sleep. Item three, the surgical nurse will not hand you a single instrument. Item four, the circulating nurse will not bring supplies to the O.R. Item five—"

"Julio, you said enough."

"Why bang your head against a stone wall? And lose your staff privileges? They'll all tell you the same thing. In every hospital."

"Then I'll do the operation in my policlínica."

"Right in your own office?"

"Yes. I have two small O.R.'s with a connecting scrub-up corridor. My nurse has had training in psychiatric social work. We do careful work-ups and keep good records. My young associate—do you know Pedro Llanos?—he was raised so strictly, choirboy, Opus Dei family. Now he's gone to the opposite extreme. He's antireligious. So he'll assist."

"Aie, amigo. I had heard a few whispers that you did therapeutic abortions. All the doctors are grateful—it's like research, somebody has to do it, no? But if you bring it out into the open they'll cut off your balls." Julio shook his head. "Like the Basque sheepherders." He clashed his teeth to illustrate the castration of a lamb by the most primitive method. "Zah! Doctors have no mercy with other doctors."

"*Mire*, Julio, I'm shaking with fear."

The pathologist held up one hand. "I know, hero. I know. I know. You're a hero. Very big *macho*. A descendant of Martí. A big guerrilla hero that fought in the mountains. But didn't anybody ever tell you that the difference between a hero and a martyr is very simple? The hero wins."

"To hell with heroes. Sometimes failures are hidden victories."

"Suit yourself." Julio hit the air again with his teeth. "Remember the lambs. Dumb animals. In this therapeutic abortion business, you cannot win."

"Julio, I don't care about winning. Put yourself in my shoes. What do I tell my friend? Do I say: Your wife has German measles and at this early stage of pregnancy the virus could cause a chronic disease in the embryo while it grows into an infant, so your child might be born with any one of a half-dozen serious diseases? But forget it, amigo. Do I say that? My friend is an honest uncomplicated man. Poor. Four kids to raise. An invalid child could wreck the family. When he asks me if I have the ability to stop this from happening, what do I tell him?"

"We feel for them, but what can we do? We didn't make the law. Our hands are tied. That's just what we told the last one hundred and forty-one cases."

"Cases? Julio, these are people. We take advantage of their tradition of resignation. But more and more, don't you see it all around you, don't they fight for a better life? Women today are like farmers today—plant or not. By deciding, not by blind accident."

"Your fashionable patients must enjoy your ideas," Julio said. "Planting. Farmers. Caramba!"

"You can make fun of unscientific clinicians like me, but how many times each week do I see a woman from the *barrios* who pushed a crochet hook up into her uterus and *perforated* it? The hemorrhages? Julio, don't shake your head, hombre—how many times in the emergency room of this hospital have I had to order one or two liters of blood when your blood bank supply was low? And the next day a heart patient or a cancer patient needed that same blood? You tell me, Julio, what happens inside you if you stand with your hands in your pockets while somebody in front of you just bleeds to death?"

"Listen," the pathologist said, "don't give me riddles. If I wanted impossible problems like that I would have been a clinician, not a laboratory man."

"Aie, Julio. Womb to tomb. No easy answers, ah?"

"You can say that again." The pathologist touched his arm. "Don't worry, we'll get the test on Señora Díaz. I'll phone you as quick as possible."

□ □ □

The next afternoon, while his wife Elena had a dilatation-and-curettage procedure, Tranquilino sat expressionless with his clasped hands dropped between his parted knees in the waiting room of Mayoso's policlínica.

Mayoso touched fire to a train of gunpowder. The next day four women came in complaining of German measles symptoms. By the end of the week, so many women came that there was no room in his office and they stood in line outside on the street. His clinic had the besieged look of a battalion aid station.

His nurse anesthetist glanced up at him. How worn he looks, she thought, but all she said was, "The patient is ready, Doctor. Pentothal for now?"

He nodded, and went to work with speed and precision. The vaginal speculum, the exposure of the cervix, the insertion of the most slender dilatation bougie, quickly replacing the number-nine Hegar with the next larger size and the next until the largest dilatation had opened the cervical canal wide enough so that he could slip the curved blade of the curette upward into the uterus.

"Nitrous oxide," he told the anesthetist. "Stop the Pitocin. Another half liter of the five per cent glucose." He worked quickly, not only because so many women were waiting in the corridor for their turn, but also because he had no hospital beds available. The patient would be kept under anesthesia the shortest possible time so that she could awaken and be taken back home later that same day.

Outside the small operating room the metal sunshade clattered again in a momentary whine of unseasonal wind. In the solemn silence of the little O.R. there was only the deepsleep blubbering of the patient's breathing and the strange thin screech as the curette raked through the lining of the uterus and reached the muscle wall tightened by Pitocin. His curette stroked back and forth, stroke by stroke, each overlapping the one before it to make sure none of the products of conception were left inside. A continuity ran from the tough uterine muscle and its soft gelatinous lining to the curving curette blade to his fingers, his wrist, his arm, his brain, so that just the right surgical counterbalance could be struck between making certain the uterus was emptied completely, yet guarding the uterine wall as a vessel for future life.

Without looking up he muttered into his gauze surgical face mask, "How is she?"

Marta Gómez, his nurse, said calmly, "Blood pressure and pulse steady."

"You can ease off," Mayoso said. "I'm almost finished."

With his curette blade he lifted out a curled tangle of tissue and tapped the blob into the sterile gauze square on the draped Mayo stand beside him. There lay an embryo the size of a grain of rice. He could see the pinpoint dots of the optic cups, visioning in his mind's eye the microscopic swarm of German measles viruses growing in these neural cells, the sickened cells shriveling instead of beautifully synchronizing into the specialized different parts: retina, vitreous, lens. Sickened cells, the beginning of glaucoma or cataracts. This was the sixth such embryo this morning and at least a dozen patients were waiting on the corridor benches.

His young assistant in the neighboring operating room had performed twice as many therapeutic abortions by a simple change in technique. Doctor Llanos used the slender vacuum aspiration apparatus reported by the Chinese in 1958, and brought to Europe by some Soviet medical Marco Polo. Now a Yugoslav institute in Ljubljana manufactured the equipment. The vacuum tube was like a slim soda-straw with an opening in the side of the tip instead of at its end. A suction pump and meter were attached flexibly to the long tube which the physician inserted and simply swept back and forth, vacuuming the interior of the uterus. Often no dilatation of the cervix was needed, and Mayoso's young colleague had assured him the method was safer than the curette blade because there was so much less loss of blood. But when Mayoso had heard the vacuum airhiss and had seen the globs of suctioned tissue and amniotic fluid spurting into the big glass collection jar, he had been—to his surprise— revolted. Illogically, unscientifically, blindly, superstitiously, emotionally, revolted.

The vacuum suction technique might actually be safer for the patient; faster for the heavy case loads; the surgical goal of detaching the embryo or fetus from its nidus in the uterus was the same as curettage; the suction tube was more—the sanctified modern word—*efficient*. But only a balanced dispassionate comparison could decide. The Yugoslavs had reported 742 cases without a single perforation of the wall of the uterus, but procedures of this importance needed thousands of reports to discover rare exceptions.

I regress ten generations of medicine when I react this way, he told himself, back to blood leeches and mumbo jumbo. A surgeon must remove whole organs when he must, but something about living cells groping toward combinations of combinations which might some future day be human—after all, mothers ill with German measles had a coin-spin chance, about fifty-fifty of having a normal baby—so some of these barely begun embryos and fetuses were healthy—ah, I'm looking over the cliff again into an awesome oceanic nothingness.

Each day I am uncomfortably reminded of people who live like animals in the jungle and think that because I do this, against the law, I am one of them. The sleazy man who said he would open his heart and his home for unwed mothers so that he and I could share the thousand dollars he was paid for each baby sold through the adoption black market. The woman with glossy straightened hair who called herself a marriage counselor so that she could find unhappy women who could be persuaded, by her counseling, that prearranged hotel-room meetings with tourists would fill their bodies, hearts, and pocketbooks with happiness.

For them to dare to approach me with such filth means that in their eyes a physician who performs abortions lives in some unnamed under-world, like a defrocked priest or a leper of the Dark Ages.

What a simple pleasant satisfaction it would be to practice the fashionable idea of medicine: seeing one patient at a time inside the narrow funnel of one's own specialty; contributing some time to teaching and to a few charity patients; but seeing mostly people who paid well. Ignoring the medically unfashionable ideas about prevention, about the health of populations, about the social and economic implications of malnutrition and all else which medical students sidestep because one-patient-at-a-time medicine is hard enough to learn without all the sticky questions of the world.

What's the answer? I don't know. Hippocrates and Maimonides and all the rest who came before me all took oaths to cure sickness if one could. And, if one could not, to treat the illness. And, if one could not, to make the patient comfortable as possible. That is what must be done. So back to work, hombre.

This patient, Anna Vega Pérez, had surprised him two days ago when he asked her the routine obstetrical question. "Your last menstrual period, señora, *la regla?*"

She had shrugged.

"A month ago, señora? Two months?"

"Much longer, Doctor."

"On your medical record here, señora, I see that you began your menstruation when you were eleven—*cuando tuvo su primera regla?*"

"Sí, sí. *Yo desarrollé* near eleven."

"And married at sixteen?"

"Sí, sí."

"*Y primera barriga,* your first pregnancy, señora?"

"I was seventeen, señor."

"A healthy baby?"

"Sí. Strong lungs—" she had paused, remembering—"like his papa. He is ten years old now."

"And since then, señora. How many pregnancies?"

She had folded one thumb and held up both hands. "Nine."

"In the last ten years you've had ten pregnancies?"

She had shrugged. "*Mire,* señor Doctor. What can I do?"

"Let me understand you, señora. Are you saying—I mean, you are not able to tell me when you had your last menstrual period because you have not had one in ten years?"

"I'm *encinta* all the time, Doctor. *Sabe?* Always with child, so my nature never comes. *No costumbre.* Not one in ten years."

With a rubber gloved finger he loosened the thumbscrew on the speculum, removed it and dropped it into the stainless-steel basin at his elbow. The ribbon of gauze accordion-pleated and packed into a solid tight tamponade. He stepped back, pulled off his rubber gloves, and dropped them into the basin beside the mound of crimson jelly.

Although his right wrist and fingers ached with fatigue, he knew this would disappear as he scrubbed them with the stiff surgical brush while washing up for the next D and C. But the deep hollow he carried, something beyond fatigue, could not be shaken off or scrubbed off. Hollow hatred of loss of life. But at least I'm functioning, he thought. He peeled off his surgical gown and dropped it inside the laundry hamper in the alcove where he scrubbed before going into the neighboring operating room. Without work that makes sense, a man shrivels. At least I'm a fireman fighting the fire and not the useless man I've been, lately.

Outside, the noontime going-home-to-lunch traffic crawled past Mayoso's policlínica. Señora Dolores Valdez del Sevillano sat annoyed behind the wheel of her Lincoln Continental. She was on her way to the Club de España, but at this rate she would never get there in time to choose her own bridge partners. She lighted a cigarette impatiently and discovered too late that she had lit the wrong end and was inhaling smoke from an ignited cork tip. Angrily she threw the cigarette out the window and noticed a long line of women standing patiently before the small medical office building of Mayoso's policlínica. Strange, she thought, like a supermercado.

She remembered some of the whispered stories she had heard at last week's retreat where she and her friends had met at a pleasant mountaintop *cursillo* to discuss establishing a Puerto Rican branch of the Spanish Opus Dei. Father Möttl had talked about the Sacerdotal Society of the Holy Cross and Opus Dei, and had explained that the Opus Dei was not a religious Order but rather an association of well-educated and influential persons seeking Christian perfection in their workaday lives.

Her husband had embarrassed her in front of Father Möttl by saying that he heard the Spanish Opus Dei referred to as a Holy Mafia, which engaged in blackmail, traffic in foreign exchange and import licenses, private dossiers on the intimate lives of everyone, and virtuous terrorism. Chaos, shouting, everyone upset. Father Möttl had been kind enough to speak to her privately, later on.

The door to Mayoso's policlínica opened and a woman came out leaning on the arm of a man. Several of the women waiting in the line spoke to the couple with a quiet seriousness which was noticeable even from across the street where Señora Valdez sat in her car.

The whispers must be true. Mayoso was performing the most criminal kind of illegal surgery. Her husband's accusation of the Opus Dei as a corruption of religion into power and big business was not only embarrassing, but stupid. This wholesale supermarket of death across the street, here was the real corruption. On impulse, Señora Valdez edged her big car out of the traffic lane into a parking space. How easy it would be to prove that the whispers were true. The bridge game could wait. She locked her car and strolled across the street feeling enlarged, uplifted, and took her place as if she were another worried woman at the end of the line.

19 FATHER MÖTTL SAT in the narrow wooden compartment of one of the cathedral confessionals. To his right and left were booths for the faithful, empty except for the wooden step on which the penitent could kneel, and the narrow wooden ledge, a shelf just beneath the confessional window on which men and women could lean their elbows while kneeling beneath their invisible burdens.

A dark maroon gold-fringed drape hung on a curtain rod before each of the three booths. Its bottom edge was cut on an angle so that the curtain was longest to the right and to the left, giving maximum privacy to the outer booth, but sloping upward to a peak before the center booth in which Father Möttl sat so that, from the outside, one could recognize the priest only from the shoulders down. Inside, by lowering his head just a little, Father Möttl could see between the gold fringes of the drape out to the lobby of the church where a large marble font of holy water stood.

He disliked this compromise design for a confessional, not quite closed, yet not quite open. Compromise was always a mistake. A confessional, he felt, should have proper doors, complete privacy, a contemplative darkness, a quiet unity in the sacred dialogue between priest and penitent invisible to one another through the small screen between them. The medieval church officials who had introduced darkness and latticework between priest and beautiful temptresses had been not only zealous, but wise.

On the other hand, he was willing to be as modern as anyone else, and hold group seminars which turned the personal confessional concept into a kind of liturgical meeting. His *cursillos* at several mountain fincas were always joined by men and women who sensed a need for meditative retreat under priestly guidance. The criticism that the *cursillistas* were always well-educated, well-dressed men and women, with the time and leisure to spend several days in the mountains, was part of the current irrational bias against those with the energy and intelligence to accomplish something in their lives. At the last organizational meeting of the Opus Dei his most faithful supporter, Señora Dolores Valdez del Sevillano, with her freethinker husband scowling beside her, had said with heartwarming sincerity: Faith makes no distinctions between the rich and the poor, either way.

He shifted uncomfortably on the oblong maroon-covered gold-edged foam-rubber cushion. He disapproved of its bouncy synthetic comfort in a duty which had nothing whatever to do with bodily comfort. These departures from tradition, someday we will pay dearly for them.

The air was close, the humid weather strangely unseasonal, his breviary stuck in his perspiring palm. The girl on the other side of the window grid stumbled after him in Spanish as he concluded with the Latin prayer *Misereatur tui omnipotens Deus . . .* , then, while sketching the final sign of the Cross in the air before him, he blessed her and dismissed her.

Through the little openings of the window which separated the confessional booths wafted a puff of air as the girl slid open her side of the maroon curtain to leave. With the air came another one of the remarkable parade of perfumes which seemed forever blended by equal parts of confessional sanctity and a primitive female need to talk privately to a man. Through the fringes of the curtain he watched the girl walk to the marble holy font to dip her fingers and cross herself. She wore one of the tall lacquered beehive coiffures which he had seen on most of the young women this year; as time-consuming and as useless, he thought, as the elaborate confections they put on wedding cakes.

He loosened the three-knotted cord of his Franciscan habit which made a sweaty belt as tight as the linen cincture which confined the alb, recalling spontaneously the vesting prayer: Gird me, O Lord, with the cincture of purity, for the cincture reminds us of the cord which bound Christ to the pillar when He was being scourged. Quench in my heart the fire of concupiscence, that the virtue of continence and chastity may abide in me.

Father Möttl took a deep breath and tightened his rope belt. The bishop had given him his duty as a confessor to provide a convenient bridge to the conference a half hour from now. Bishop Sosa did nothing casually, so the appointment must be an important one.

Even when he had awakened in the upstairs back bedroom of his rectory, he had been alert immediately with a sense of much to do before meeting the bishop and not enough time to do it. He had hurried, feeling that all was going well.

The day had begun so smoothly. Seven o'clock Mass sped by, the Ordinary, the Proper, remembering after the Epistle, Gospel, Offertory and the rest to offer today's holy day of obligation, the invocation of divine mercy in the Kyrie Eleison and the infinite tenderness of the Agnus Dei; the quick enumeration from the altar of the black-shawled women and the rare men scattered through the pews, the enlarged timeless calm as he heard his own voice . . . *Judica me Deus, et discerne causam meam de gente non sancta: ab homine iniquo et doloso erue me* . . . knowing this calmness because he devotedly wanted to be judged, to have his cause distinguished from the nation which was not holy, and to be delivered from unjust and deceitful men . . . later, the quiet Spanish pleas of his parishioners . . . *Bendecid, Señor Dios nuestro* . . . *recibe, Señor, las oraciones de los fieles* . . . they are *speaking*, Father Möttl thought gratefully, not mumbling mechanically as they did when I first came here to a church that had become a building, a place smelling of neglect and dirt, incense and worn varnish, melted votive candle wax, a place abandoned to elderly women, a place for death's sad triumph in Requiem Mass with the young coming rarely, only tiptoeing in for the quick just-in-case baptism of their infants. . . .

He had finished the morning's duties with just barely enough time to catch a ride into town to hear confessions at the cathedral during the last part of the morning, after which he was to meet the Bishop Sosa at Bishopric House.

A sound on the other side of the grating, and a new wave of some kind of perfume surely, inevitably, called Taboo or Forbidden or My Sin. He leaned his latticed ear slightly toward the pierced window and cleared his throat to indicate he was listening.

A woman's voice, of course. "Bless me, padre . . ."

He waited, but when her silence stretched out, he asked, "Sí? Sí?"

Her voice was low, halting. "I . . . have . . . sinned."

A mature voice, he thought. Stumbling. Some real difficulty, and during Lent. An alcoholic husband. Or, from the perfume, impure thoughts of adultery.

"You have sinned?" he repeated, encouraging her to go on. He wanted to loosen his belt again, then did something in his mind, which he had learned to do by prayer, so that he no longer felt the warmth, the belt, the down-pressing close air.

"Padre, I am *encinta*."

"Married?"

"Sí."

"By a priest in church?"

"Sí."

"Your husband—Catholic?"

"Sí, sí."

"This pregnancy comes from the union of you and your husband?"

"Sí, sí."

"Does your husband come to church? Take the sacraments?"

"No, padre. You know how it is with men."

"Men have duties, just as women do."

Her words came in a rush. "I do not want this child. I think about it. I can't sleep."

"Do you know what a serious thing you are saying?"

"Sí, padre."

"Do you really understand the teaching of the Church?" She did not answer him. In his cubicle the heat was oppressive. I must rise above this discomfort, he thought. Charitable, less blunt, a confessor not a judge. The hierarchy of Christ's Mystical Body is the humanity of each one of us on earth. Led into blindness, weak before passion and prone to sin, God grant me to hold fast to that, to show the world, to share the bread and wine with each passerby. Quietly he asked, "Did you vote in the last election?"

"Sí, padre."

"For Governor Santos Roque?"

"Sí, padre."

"How many children do you have?"

"Six."

"All baptized?"

"Sí, padre."

"All born in the hospital?"

"No, padre. The first two at home, with a *comadrona*, then a miscarriage, then the Governor built the hospital. My last four niños came in the hospital."

"The Governor did not build the hospital. The people and the taxes of the people built the hospital. Do you understand that?"

"Sí, padre."

"When the health department made clinics, did you go to the clinics?"

"Sí, padre."

"Did the health department clinic teach you birth control?"

"Sí, padre."

"What did they teach you?"

"They asked me: are you Catholic? I said I am a Catholic. A believer, they asked me. I am. Then we can only teach you the rhythm system, they said."

"Ah. You did this?"

"I did, but—" she stopped again.

"But—?"

"But mistakes happen, padre. I try to tell my husband how it is. He must hold on to himself. You want me to sleep on the floor? he shouts. What can I say? I think I hurt his *machismo*."

Sooner or later, Father Möttl thought, everything comes back to *machismo*. The same Latin man who wears a holy medal around his neck, even Castro wore one, this man fears a loss of *machismo*. If he comes to church, the only priest he respects is the backwoods renegade who lives in concubinage. They tell coarse jokes about seminary students—making a priest out of a man by dressing him like a girl and treating him like a boy. "Did your husband ever have religious instruction?"

"As a boy." In a rush, "He wants me to use the birth control."

"Does he know that God and Jesus Christ condemn birth control? Does he understand that the primary purpose of marriage is procreation and the education of offspring? Whether he is a churchgoer or not, the natural and divine law of God binds all human beings, members of the Church or not. Every carnal act from which human generation cannot follow is a vice against nature."

She blew her nose softly, but not until she spoke again did he realize she was crying. "It is not possible to talk to him, padre."

"Not even to reason with him?"

"Nothing. He is gone. He is gone from the island. He is someplace in Nueva York."

"If he abandoned you and your children he can be found. In the meantime arrangements can be made through your pastor for family help."

"It's more than that, padre. That's not what I came to confess."

"What is it then?"

"I—" She stopped and blew her nose again, then suddenly broke into muffled sobs, "It's not just his child that I carry under my heart, but I am sick."

"Sick? From a faithful review of your conscience?"

"My body, padre. I'm sick. My eyes. My head. Fever."

"Did you go to the health department clinic?"

"Sí, padre."

"Did they examine you? Take your temperature?"

"Sí, padre. The lady doctor said I have German measles."

"For certain? Fevers and headaches can come from many things. Bad water. Worry. A missing husband. Catarrh."

"They told me so, padre. They made a test from the blood."

"But German measles is a child's disease." Why must we call it *German?* he thought irritably. Forevermore, must innocent Germans suffer for the guilty, like the children of Israel after Herod, after Hitler? We took the lives of their infants for fertilizer, hacked off the hair of the mothers for mattress stuffing, salvaged gold and silver fillings from their father's teeth. Did we also take from them, without knowing it, their crown of thorns? "This measles," he said harshly, avoiding the word *German,* "lasts a few days like a cold in the nose, then gone."

"My neighbor upstairs in Apartamiento 20, she had these measles. Her niño brought it from school. As you say, padre, it was nothing. But it became something when her baby was born. You could see a milky thing in both eyes. It stopped him from seeing. Little white places in the middle of his eyes. I saw them."

"Cataracts?"

"I do not know the name, padre. But I see them in his eyes."

"God loves a blind child as much as one with clear vision. And so must his mother because of this greater opportunity to show her love. Just as the demands of Lent make you aware of our comforts before and after, so also is suffering the way in which we understand happiness on earth and life everlasting in Heaven. It was Christ who taught by word and example the sublimity of our sufferings and how agony can ennoble our character. Your neighbor's infant is destined for the eternal bliss of Heaven as much as any other infant."

"Padre—padre. I pray each night on my knees to La Virgen. But I cannot push out of my mind the wish to get rid of this child I carry."

"How can you say that? Not only God's Church, but even the ungodly government forbids what you say. I warn you that you are contemplating nothing less than murder."

"What can I do? What can I do?"

"You must do what you know. Pray to God who will surely give you

strength. Take the sacraments faithfully. Remember that the sorrow of
Holy Week ends with the joy of Resurrection. Do you understand what I
say to you?" When she did not answer he repeated, "Do you understand?
Do you understand your obligation?"

"Sí, padre."

"And can you say with a clear conscience that you are heartily sorry
for your sins?"

"It is hard, padre."

He suppressed a shudder. *It is hard.* The groan of women fleshed with
lust since Eve, unrepentant. *It is hard.* Woman, women. The Son of the
Father, did He avoid the Cross because it was hard? "You cannot step
aside from God's Commandments. In this time of Lent you have every
opportunity to review the sacraments frequently. And with deeper meaning than ever." He bent toward the little window between them, feeling
as if coming closer could help lift her. "If you are heartily sorry for your
sins—"

"I am, padre—"

"Then for your penance, say the Rosary daily for the remaining time
of Lent. Before you leave church today say ten Hail Marys while facing
the main altar, and pray for my intentions. Make a good act of contrition,
Misereatur tu omnipotens Deus—" and, as he prayed side by side with her
he slowed his words to let her know he was pacing the Latin to her halting
Spanish. He closed his eyes; with deep feeling he crossed the air before
him and said, "God bless you."

Fiat voluntas tua. He slumped unmoving in his cubicle, smelling the
warm trafficked boards and closed-in fusty sweat of the confessional, wiping the salty sting of perspiration away from his eyes reflectively. That was
crudely done, he thought. That was carpentry, a crude wooden jointing of
sacred beams, when you should have offered her delicate surgery, a dissecting exploration and suturing of wounds. But the scalpel in the right
hand can become a sword in the left, terrible, more terrible because it
masquerades as healing. Surgery, terrible surgery, and the letter from
Spain. No, backward. The letter from Spain and surgery. And an Israeli
general. All parallel lines come together someplace in the universe.

In the stern womb of the cubicle, hollow and darkened with holy
shadow, the brass-tongued words *German* and *surgery* tolled in his head.
Echoes. Voices. Boys' voices. Not for years had he heard them. He pressed
his hands over his ears, but the voices ravaged him again. A letter from
Spain, an Israeli official, the week of Golgotha, how was this possible, all
disconnected yet so interwoven, and the boys standing in the open trucks
came back, I am there, they are here, I am in the truck, they are in the
confessional, I shouting my name, screaming my name.

He wept. Oh my Master, how I understand as never before Thy aloneness in the Garden of tropical night, Thy most unbearably lonely aloneness which Thou didst bear for every one of us. In Thy love is grace, in
Thy sacrifice is strength. *Sine mente caput, vigiliis et inedia multa exhaus-
tum.*

I beseech Thee, here in this confessional, uncompassed and penitent
and utterly alone, out of the depths of my weakness I beg Thee: give me
strength, give me forgiveness.

The Angelus rang out from the cathedral belltower as Father Gofredo
Möttl stepped from the confessional booth. His appointment with the
bishop was for noon, and he believed in always being on time. Hurriedly
he faced the main altar, genuflected as he crossed himself, then turned so
swiftly toward the lobby doors that he bumped into a woman just coming
in from the bright sunshine.

Both of them stepped backwards, apologizing at the same time. In that
moment he decided that even if her carefully coiffed hair was local and
her swift instinctive courtesy Catholic, she was nevertheless Americano.

Her sleeveless lime green dress had an expensive tourist look and the
astonishing plastic apparatus she wore like a white bandage over her eyes
confirmed his judgment. Was she blind?

He realized he was gaping when she stepped out of the doorway shaft
of sunlight and pulled the plastic thing from her face. "Is something
wrong, Father?" she asked politely.

He saw that she had remarkable eyes, very much the same color as her
green dress.

"No," he said, "nothing wrong." The Angelus was midway and he disliked being late even by a minute. Before he could circle past her she
asked, "Father, which one is the famous tomb of Ponce de León?"

Her question was so unexpected that he had to stop to think a moment
and, as he did, she smiled intimately at him, as if they were two old
friends. "I'm really looking for the Fountain of Youth," she said, her red-
lipped smile widening. "But I suppose the tomb of the discoverer is as
close as I'll ever come to it."

He pointed across the intervening aisles and pews toward a side chapel.
"Over there, señora. In the south transept." He began to go but then, to
his own surprise turned back on impulse. "Señora?"

"My name is Mrs. Sommers, Father. My husband and I are living here
on the island temporarily."

"Señora Sommers, if I may ask—" That name. Pronunciation played tricks. Summers? Sommers? It sounds familiar. Irritation chafed him. I am never elaborately polite or faintly confused. Then why am I now?

She held up the white plastic thing she had worn over her eyes. "These?" she asked shrewdly. She laughed in an open pleased way, "Startling, aren't they? They're a new kind of French sunglasses."

He avoided looking at her, and concentrated carefully on the plastic thing. "Sunglasses? But they're solid plastic. How can you see?" Even the Madonna of the Calle San Jerónimo troubled men's dreams and disturbed their devotions. This woman possesses just such a beauty, but estranged by two green eyes like wasps.

"Oh," she said, lifting the glasses so he could see a thin green translucent stripe which ran horizontally across the opaque plastic, "you see out through this narrow green slit. The idea is that you can look out, but nobody can look in." She paused, her extravagant smile returned. "I bought them as a joke at Casa Caribe. They're called Boy Watchers."

"Toy watchers?"

"Boy. B as in boy. But they're no excuse for bumping into you."

He nodded sagely, their conversation was becoming feebleminded, and he had recovered his dignity. "I trust you will have a pleasant stay on the island, Mrs. Sommers."

"Thank you, Father. It's a beautiful island."

He gave her a very slight bow, then stepped around her and plunged out the door. Diagonally, down the street, was one of his favorite glazed-tile paintings of Saint Francis of Assisi. It had been fired long ago in Madrileño kilns and then fitted together skillfully about twelve feet above street level. The Poor Man of Assisi, humble patron saint of Father Möttl's own Order, kneeling in the ceramic square with a seraphic piety which embraced even birds and beasts, so worshipful of God's miracles of grass and trees that, while dying, he asked to be carried to a hill to see and bless for the last time the countryside of Assisi.

Möttl was definitely late, and half trotted up Calle Cristo. His sandals clapped so loudly on the rounded blue cobblestones which had come to the Island long ago as ballast from the Spanish Netherlands, that the high school students coming out of the walled wooden doorway of the Saint Thomas Aquinas School stopped to watch. The bishop must be in his office already, because his car was parked across the street from Bishopric House, recognizable by souvenir license plates which bore the initials SCV, Stato Città del Vaticano. The bishop had brought them back from the Vatican conference.

Father Möttl leaped up the street steps, strode through the cross-tiled shadowed lobby, past the metal grating and the pretty little Madonna on the far side with a vase of fresh flowers at her feet, and up the tiled staircase to the upper floor. An oval mirror was mounted on the landing beneath the stained-glass window of the Lamb and Cross of Ferdinand and Isabella; he saw himself reflected among the religious statues and sacred paintings of martyrdom which flanked the walls. He paused frowning at the mirrored picketpost in a brown belted robe, viewing himself distorted vertically and elongated by the curved glass, gaunt as an El Greco canvas. From downstairs all the Chancery sounds followed him: the laundry-tub thumps of rotating mimeograph machines, the toy machinegun clatter of typewriters, telephones ringing, the stacking of bundles of religious pamphlets, all the administrative paraphernalia which had led to tasteless cognomens—The Bishop's Powerhouse—and the special joke over the ecclesiastical grapevine which used the Vatican SCV license plate to make the Italian phrase: *Se Cristo Vedesse*. If Christ saw. Yes, Father Möttl thought, if He could see me now, He would say, as He had once said, *Take courage, I have overcome the world*. Someday, the whisper was, Bishop Sosa might move to Rome's Borgo Santo Spirito, an elected Superior General of the most powerful Order, the Society of Jesus. Bishop Sosa would then be the so-called Black Pope, General of tens of thousands of intellectual warriors with their own professed elite and much Order pride. Better, better, he thought, the gentle Francis of Assisi than the rowdy Basque knight-turned-priest, the Loyola of Montmartre.

Caution, Father Gofredo Möttl thought, that was the bishop's whole message the last time I saw him here before he sent me on the fruitless appointment to meet with Governor Santos Roque and the then missing Doctor Mayoso. As if caution could replace the militant thrust the times cry out for. What pharisaical heavyhandedness, to have sent me to La Fortaleza in a pretense of dignity, like a chargé d'affaires, but actually as a *dummkopf* errand boy who could later be either rebuked or praised, expended or supported, depending on the pragmatic political need of doing business with the Governor.

All the more to be criticized when a bishop who had been fed on unyielding traditionalism with his mother's milk, whose courage had been forged in Cuba, now became cautious, conciliatory, compromising, like the so-called liberal building bishops of the American cities.

Thou art a priest forever according to the order of Melchizedek. How can he have forgotten that the ministry must go beyond the offering of the Mass and the forgiving of sins to an apostolate fulfilling of the Church's proprietary witness by declaiming against the evils of society? *Regimini militantis ecclesiae.* For the Rule of the Church Militant. How can Bishop Sosa have forgotten his own Order's ratification?

The long strand of rope hanging from his robe swung against his right leg as he hurried. The bottom knot tapped him. The bottom knot on the

rope, below the two knots which symbolized poverty and chastity, symbolized obedience. This was the knot which every Franciscan was trained
to kiss on the cord of a Provincial Supervisor, while kneeling on one knee,
even before kissing the Superior's hand.

As he wheeled around a corner and came to the wide baroque doors
of the Bishop's study, he thought: Obedience I must offer him, under
penalty of sin, no matter how ill-advised or unjust he is. Bishop Sosa and
his Jesuit brothers knew by heart Saint Ignatius Loyola's *Spiritual Exercises*: To arrive at the truth in all things we ought always be ready to
believe that what seems to us white is black, if the hierarchical Church so
defines it.

But by my Crucified Master's pierced side, if the bishop tries to politic
me with his caution or silence me or blunt me into a—a—a boy watcher—
then duty compels me to remind him that I also have made a higher vow
of obedience, to God.

Father Gofredo Möttl stood for a moment before the dark paneled
archway whose doors, it struck him, were the counterpart of those in the
Governor's office. He tightened the belt which girded him, then knocked
strongly several times. From inside the study he heard a few sounds, then
the door was held open by Bishop Sosa himself.

Although rounded and short, the bishop looked solid and weatherbeaten
as oak inside the simple white cassock he wore. His cassock was fastened
with a newfangled zipper because the bishop disliked fumbling around
and losing time with a long row of little buttons. His blue amethyst ring
was not on his finger, Father Möttl saw. The newspaper story of the bishop
giving it and his jeweled pectoral cross to charity must be true.

"Padre Gofredo," the bishop said, sounding pleased to see him, "come
in, come in. Won't you sit down? Just take the pile of newspapers on the
chair and dump them on the floor."

"Thank you, Your Excellency." Father Möttl could not bring himself
to anything so disorderly as dumping anything on the floor, especially
such a mixed bag of the sacred and the secular. On the nearest window
ledge, he stacked the papers and books in an orderly sequence one by
one: a copy of this week's *L'Osservatore Romano*, today's *Wall Street
Journal* and Washington *Post*, the airmail edition of the Manchester
Guardian, a copy of *Time*, the weekly *Il Borghese*, a mail-order advertisement for a reprint from *The Crusader* called "Would Mary Approve
Present Bra Styles?," the front page of a recent copy of the *Daily Worker*
with a penciled circle around the headline: REBELLION OR REACTION?, the
textbook *Faith in Action*, Hume's *Catholic Church Music* and a copy of
the *People's Hymnal*.

He mistrusted the bishop's comfortable ease partly because the informality lacked episcopal dignity, but more because the friendliness had a nimble agility to oscillate between solemnity and smiles. I always feel off-balance with the bishop; he changes centuries as if they were hats: off comes the medieval skullcap, on goes the twentieth-century clergyman's fedora. He swings in and out of languages, from his native Estremudura speech to precise Castilian or canonical Latin, from literate French to American slang. Every one knew the bishop enjoyed vintage wines but few knew that his gift of jewels to the Bishops' Committee for Latin America had been anonymous until a religious paper printed the story. The bishop had never shown a symptom of Order pride; yet, when after three centuries the Jesuits' headquarters for the vice-province of the Antilles had left Havana, the bishop had made clear his determination to establish the Ministry headquarters in Puerto Rico.

Father Möttl took the cleared visitor's chair stiffly. What an irony, he thought, that the most militant Order of the Counter-Reformation should be ruled from a modern office of steel furniture, with no bookcases, and a random hodgepodge of printed matter, while a secular materialistic Governor in La Fortaleza had a grandee's office, once a Gobernador's throne room, filled with treasures of the Spain of Ferdinand and Isabella. The nonreligious Governor had one of the finest collections of sacred polychrome figures and devout primitive *santos,* while the ordained bishop had only a large wall-mounted uncanonical real estate map of the city with colored tacks to mark the new parochial schools under construction.

Bishop Sosa sat down heavily in his padded leather executive swivel chair. "That's a fine firm knock you have," he said. "Sounded like Martin Luther nailing his Points on the church door."

Already, Father Möttl thought, off-balance. "Your Excellency," he said, "how do you mean that?"

"As a jest, padre. Now don't frown so seriously. A bit of humor, better than a *digestif.* I don't have many chances, and when a scholarly colleague like you comes to visit, I'm able to let myself go a little."

"I understand, Your Excellency."

"Do you? You look so"—the bishop searched for the right word—"so preoccupied. Any difficulty I can help with?"

"Thank you, no."

The bishop studied Father Möttl's sharp intense face. A true anchorite, the Bishop thought. Burning with intensity. Austere and zealous. Troubled with sanctity. And so complex. Just when he seems as remote as an ancient saint seated atop a desert pillar, then one sees him warmly alive and close, on television. Those fervent eyes must see me as a fat friar, faintly gluttonous, and worldly. And I see him, not as a monk pledged to the gentle Saint Francis of Assisi but as militant as Saint Igna-

tius of Loyola. He hardly sits; he has the warrior's alert crouch, poised for
rebellion. Oh, the ancient authority-obedience conflict. I have no wish to
command him because what I plan to ask him to do should be done with
a willing heart, the labor of a brother. With his ascetic intensity, his
spiritual strength and skill in exhortation, he might go on to the widest
possible universal mission of salvation. But one step in the wrong evan-
gelical direction and he might end among the super-patriots, the lovers
of bans, the fawning tiara watchers, and naïvely superstitious fans of
Fátima. Therefore tread lightly, lightly, he told himself. Thoroughbreds
have the most need for a gentle hand. Sometimes the long way around is
the shortest way across.

Bishop Sosa picked up a spoon and pulled toward himself the cup of
consommé which had been set on his memo pad. "Can I offer you a bit
of nourishment, padre?"

Father Gofredo's chin rose a fraction. "Thank you, no, Your Excellency."

"It's very good. Our housekeeper's *specialité de la maison.*"

"I am fasting today, Excellency."

One up for him, the bishop thought. Straight is the way, but longer
than I thought, and I have that cornerstone ceremony and an official
dinner at La Fortaleza to get to today. But lightly, lightly. "Soup—" he
said. "You don't mind if I go ahead? I had no breakfast, and it's impossible
to eat those full-course meals La Fortaleza serves to visiting dignitaries."

Father Möttl looked interested for the first time. "La Fortaleza?"

"Yes. An Israeli technical mission. Ever since the Governor visited
Israel, he seems to believe both our countries have much in common.
Short on resources, long on brains." He waved his soupspoon. "But as I
was saying, soup has always been a basic for me."

Father Möttl watched the bishop's magical grand-piano smile appear.
Soup! What does the bishop want? he thought. What is he driving at?

"To men like us," the bishop was saying, "born in Spain—"

"I was born in Germany."

"Ah? But you grew up in Spain."

"Yes."

"Then you understand that bread and soup are the staff and bowl of
life." Casually he asked, "What province?"

"Galicia."

"Oh. I was born in Estremadura, and just as the name says, we had to
be extremely durable. Sometimes we lived on soup made from straw. I
believe that's why I felt a special affinity, during the Council in Rome,
for Pope John. One peasant boy to another, or are you among those who
feel there's too much *aggiornamento?*"

So, Father Möttl thought, he's sounding me out. Good. The time for caution and compromise is over. "Your Excellency," he said firmly, "I believe the only path to unity of the Church and the solidity of doctrine is to be traditional. When I hear talk of changing the liturgy from Latin into ordinary everyday speech it troubles me. When I read clerical support for contraceptive pills in an influential Jesuit magazine like *Mensaje*, it troubles me."

The bishop gave himself a spoonful of soup thoughtfully. The offer of food had been rejected. The bond of shared roots in Spanish soil had been contradicted—but lightly, lightly.

"Padre," the bishop went on, "I would like to share my thinking with you. You've been right several times, when I've been wrong. When you first suggested the radical idea to stop taking up Sunday collections I was against it. After all, who ever heard of such a thing? Who ever depended on an inside-out way of getting contributions? And yet, you were right. The contributions that came into your church increased—"

"They doubled, Your Excellency."

"So, you were right and I was wrong, padre. When the newspaper people and the television reporters came to see you, I was against such publicity. After all, you and I come from a Spanish background and tradition very different from the modern Paulist priests with their emphasis on communications with the secular world. But I was wrong again because your televised *Hour of Eternity* reaches thousands of people on this island—including Governor Santos Roque himself—who otherwise close their doors and their hearts to our mission."

Father Möttl lowered his eyes. Such frankness and open praise embarrassed him. He felt a genuine humility about his television sermons because it was so difficult for him to connect his standing in the studio, talking into the merciless glass eye of the squat metal television camera, with the people who later stopped him on the street, or who wrote him letters, as if his electronic image in a glass tube had been a personal discourse with him.

"Padre," Bishop Sosa said, "I've been examining my conscience. Understand, I'm sharing my doubts and my thinking with you. I'm not asking you to agree or to trouble your conscience with what may sound like little heresies. In Spain we were trained as a princely aristocracy, not as pastors to a freely choosing electorate. We were trained that it was more important to have a vision of ultimate mysteries than to be fed and clothed on earth."

"So I still believe—"

"And I respect your belief, padre. But I've just come from a meeting with the Papal Nuncio's staff in Santo Domingo. The Apostolic Delegate from Washington was there. The Fathers see us in Puerto Rico as a bridge between North and South America. A bridge under attack. Our fore-fathers came to the New World seeking gold. Their greed and cruelty were so great that not even the gentle Franciscans—men very much like yourself—could turn them aside. And today, as someone at the meeting said, South America has God but no gold. And the Protestants, who colonized North America to worship God as they chose, today have ended up with just the opposite. They have much gold, but little God." Bishop Sosa leaned forward, "This island is the bridge."

Father Möttl stared at him, astonished. No talk of caution? Compromise? Had the meeting with the Papal Nuncio in Santo Domingo restored the bishop's vision of the Church Militant?

"What I am saying, padre, is that we must not repeat the rigid tactics and princely pride of showing the Martin Luthers a mailed fist instead of an open hand."

Cautiously, without seeming to test the bishop, Father Möttl asked, "For example? At La Virgen de Fátima my work is pastoral from day to day, with baptism and confessions, visiting the sick and saying Mass. To think in such large geopolitical terms, Your Excellency—" He shrugged.

"Specifically," the bishop said, "specifically, we are under attack by Governor Santos Roque. We must adopt a new tactical flexibility. We must not respond as the traditional Catholic, infuriated by the slightest word of comment or criticism. The trap is to sound, as we often do, poverty-stricken and nagging when even barefoot peasants know how much property we own all over the world. Financial circles know the Vatican has a portfolio of almost six billion dollars in securities alone. When bigots spit out that we are the privilegentsia, the opium of the people, instead of locking the doors and closing the windows, we should prove the lie, celebrate and offer the Eucharist in terms they can understand."

"Your Excellency, in my television sermons I have tried—"

"The very people who watch you on television and admire you, the people whose children drop pennies in your offerings box, also drop their votes for Santos Roque in the ballot box. How can we solve that contradiction?"

"Is Your Excellency saying that I should change my sermons?"

"No, padre. I'm only sharing my thinking with you. I have been wrong when you have been right. In all humility, I simply suggest that you find a single issue in the daily lives of our people—the price of bread, the cost of clothing—those are poor examples but they illustrate the kind of specifics you yourself asked for."

"I see." How very clever he is, Father Möttl thought; under his bishop's fabric he wears the hairshirt of humility. If I complain his geopolitics is over my head, he turns it into proof that my theology is over the heads of my listeners. "I feel you are suggesting a new course of action for me, Your Excellency."

"Only in the sense that upon the bishop rests the responsibility of the continual formation of his priests. Only in the sense that I consult you. A bishop may have achieved the fullness of the priesthood but we share the episcopal ministry conferred through the Sacrament of Orders. After all, even the disciples of Christ went out two or three together. A hierarchy we must have, but we labor side by side in the same vineyard, defenders of the common good. You know, padre—and please, this is no criticism —there are dangers in spiritual loneliness. There are times when each of us in the heat of the day feels the fatigue of office and the cutting edge of bitterness and depression."

Father Möttl felt a new-found brotherhood with the bishop. His sincerity was unmistakable. Indeed, Christ's disciples had been sent two or three together so they might be mutually helpful. If only I could open my heart to him completely, tell him about those letters from Spain which tear me to pieces and make the saying of the word *Father* a torment no one understands. He lowered his head remembering Christ's invitation to the weary apostles: *Come aside to a desert place and rest awhile.* But in the desert where I live, Father Möttl thought, there is no rest, not because I am alone but because I bear another's guilt which can only be tolerated by a lifetime of expiation.

He raised his head. "Your Excellency, I believe it was Paul who said that He became all things to all men that he might save all."

The bishop nodded. "Yes, Paul. Very much to the point, padre, because of the talent you have shown. Paul the Apostle who could say of himself, For when I was free of all I made myself the servant of all, that I might win over many. Among Jews I was a Jew that I might win over the Jews. Padre, I believe you're the priest who can win over many."

Father Möttl lowered his eyes again. The reference to the Jews and the Israeli technical mission reminded him of the letters from Spain, the private cross he carried, and the heightening sense of mission he had been feeling now dropped.

"Padre?" Bishop Sosa's voice had an urgent edge. "You look very pale. Are you carrying your Lenten fast too far?"

Father Möttl shook his head. How could the bishop begin to know all my inner conflicts over one word: *Father?* He felt a soft touch on his shoulder and looked up. Bishop Sosa stood beside him.

"Padre," he said, "fasting and zeal are commendable but you need your strength to do God's work. Let me bring you a little soup." He put his hand on the younger man's shoulder for a moment. "Just sit quietly, I'll be right back." Without waiting for an answer the bishop walked quickly out of the room.

How decent he is, Father Möttl thought. Just when he seemed clever and shrewdly administrative, he changes and becomes an understanding brother. I resented his manipulating me to become a televised megaphone or a ventriloquist's puppet for his own words, but now I see that he means what he says. Apostles must go in twos and threes.

From the moment I saw that boy set himself on fire, that terrible moment in so unseemly a place for an ascetical martyrdom as the Hotel Laputa, then the confrontation with Doctor Mayoso in the lobby, and the killing in the streets of Caracas—all those events, I should have understood sooner, were the same message as the bishop's reminder to come down the steps from the altar, come down to where the people are.

The door opened. Bishop Sosa came in carrying a soup bowl on a small tray. "Nothing fancy," he said as if carrying bowls of soup were an everyday job for him. "Just enough to remind you that an army travels on its stomach." As he put the tray on Father Möttl's lap he said, "Go slow with the first spoonful, padre. It's hot. I had them heat it."

"Thank you, Your Excellency. I have had several thoughts—"

"Soup first, thoughts later." As he walked around his desk to sit down, Bishop Sosa said, "I'm sorry there's this urgency. With Lent here and Holy Week so soon, such a sacred time of the year, it's easy to forget that the following month will bring the primary election. Is that soup too hot?"

"No. It's just that I've had a sudden idea. A basic issue. A moral crisis for us, but as you said, Your Excellency, daily bread for everyone."

In the short distance that separated them the bishop's eyes measured him. "Before you say anything, padre, let me tell you that I realize you may have doubts about my sincerity concerning your freedom to speak. So I tell you that at this time tomorrow I'll be leaving the island for a meeting of the Bishops' Committee of the Spanish-speaking. I'll be gone a week or two, so you have my *nihil obstat,* so to speak, in advance."

"Your Excellency, I confess I did have some doubt—"

"Of course. Now finish your soup. Things won't seem quite so grim."

"Your Excellency," he said, remembering Doctor Mayoso's leonine face and his hair as white and wild as one of Michelangelo's doomed prophets, hearing again the woman's voice through the confessional screen, "the central issue is birth control."

The bishop threw up both hands. "Oh no! Not that one. Padre, you can scuttle my entire tactics. I refuse to do battle in the muddy ground of Church-State conflict. I refuse to give Governor Santos Roque this shibboleth issue. Padre, haven't any of your own parishioners made jokes about calendar contraception and Vatican roulette?"

"Your Excellency, a short while ago, a woman making her confession pointed my thoughts toward the real issue."

"The *real* issue?"

"Yes. The sacredness of life. Life is the divine image of God." He waited but the bishop said nothing, only tilted his head a little, listening carefully. "Your Excellency, the sacredness of life is the rock we stand on. How can we accept caution or compromise? We will make a moral error if we are practical, if we allow science to become the new golden calf to be worshiped with the people's taxes. Our world becomes a cinder in a journey to noplace around a sun that will grow cold and die."

"And the woman in the confessional who suggested to you the real issue?"

"She had her foot on the first rung of the ladder down to Hell. One side of that ladder, Your Excellency, are the tax-supported clinics built with the approval of Governor Santos Roque. Contraception is available to anyone who asks, even if the asker is an unmarried woman."

"But that's a funnel, padre, not a ladder."

"No, a ladder. It has a second side. The murder of humans, by the technique of abortion." Father Möttl stood as if speaking not to one man but to an audience. "Your Excellency, I'm not talking about back-alley abortions, or taxicab abortions." He pounded his two fists together softly. "I'm talking about a licensed physician. A clinic run openly, as if it were a legal business or factory." His voice was hoarse with anger. "A small assembly line of death."

"A doctor? A *medical* doctor?"

"A physician, Your Excellency. It's public knowledge. The government must be protecting him. Without the word of some higher-up, the police would close the doors of his clinic tomorrow and the medical society would cast him out."

"A higher-up?"

Father Möttl leaned forward to put his soup bowl and the tray precisely parallel to the edge of the desk. He set down the spoon neatly beside the plate.

"Are you suggesting," Bishop Sosa asked, "someone at La Fortaleza?"

"There is only one higher-up at La Fortaleza," Father Möttl said. "The Governor himself."

20

BETSY HESITATED UNCERTAINLY as she came out of the cathedral. A green slit of sunshine came through the plastic Boy Watchers, making an artificial twilight across her eyes. I feel like a kid let out of school, she thought. Footloose and fancy-free. If it weren't just a teeny bit lonely, I'd enjoy it. With Witt over in St. Thomas at the Dorothea Experimental Station, and Mayoso working all day like a surgical machine, and only myself to think about—well, this should be a vacation for me, but as they used to say in the old country, if I was goin' to Dublin I wouldn't start out from here.

Several men sitting on the shaded bench across the street ogled her as she stood on the cathedral steps in her sleeveless batik dress. Purposeful women marched past her toward some kind of child welfare office at the end of the steps, pregnant most of them, carrying a baby in their arms, with one or two children tagging along behind. Spit out a seed, Betsy thought, anywhere in the tropics, and it'll grab hold and sprout and grow. Except me. Except the one out of twenty like me, lethal to sperm, a hooting madman's joke in a world filled with women scared stiff of becoming pregnant, babies practically crawling out of that welfare clinic over there. And they look at me the way I might look at some kind of emerald in a jeweler's window.

Oh hell, what's all this whining? You've been doing great. You've been feeling fine. Healthy mind in a healthy body, and all that jazz. You should be ashamed of yourself, the world's your oyster. To get what you have, women would queue up for miles and hang themselves by their thumbs. But nobody's ever found the pearl in *your* oyster.

Damn everything. Just when I thought things were almost perfect, along comes little Miss Hormones, or what the hell ever it is that makes me feel like a longtail cat locked in a room full of rocking chairs.

Poor Mayoso. Witt and I *enjoy*, yes, that's the dirty word for it—being able to take him in and nurse and use him as the only fireplace where Witt and I warm our hands together. Witt began to be better in bed across the island in that little fishing village, and Lord knows I tried. I *tried*. But trying's all wrong, huffing and puffing when you should be taking off like a seabird and soaring.

Oh God, I didn't come to this cathedral of yours for dryasdust guidebook poking into dark corners after tombs, but only to pray for love to work at and some work to love doing. What's this wild thing I keep locked behind bars, so that Witt's decency and quietness and never making demands all turn upside down into dull flat stale unprofitable food I can never feed to the wild thing?

Through the pencil-line green slit she caught sight of one of the men across the street pointing at her. A private masculine joke was breaking up the boys. She decided to walk the other way, toward El Convento. A little lonely lunchie. A wee willie working lush-type lunch—no, no, let's not get maudlin and muddled now—maybe just one or two chilled poco coco-locos and a *plato frío,* a nice crab salad, a loaf of bread and thou beside me drinking poco coco-locos in the wilderness unless you prefer lime mist, just to match this lovely sleeveless little lime-mist nothing you're wearing to knock out everybody's goddam eye at twenty paces. Or something a bit more efficient, like maybe a Tía María y Amigo, if the maître d' can get you an amigo even though amigos are not on the menu and usually work at night.

My, my, she thought as she strode down the steps, moving lightly within her batik dress, feeling admired, watched, envied, lovely-legged, anonymous behind her *crazy* sunglasses, enjoying herself, disliking herself, happy to be free and unencumbered and without duties, but wandering lonely as a cloud.

As she crossed the street to El Convento she reminded herself: Never but *never* use the street entrance to a bar. A lady always enters a hotel through the front door and then enters the bar from the lobby, like a guest, not a lush.

Clever. Gee, hey Ma, looka me, genius.

No, genius is the infinite capacity for taking pains with self-punishment, and we were going to get off that kick, remember? To a restaurant we will go, ho-ho-ho, and order a sensible low-calorie *intelligent* lunch, with only a bit of a nip before, maybe something on the rocks.

Jesu, what a barbaric expression. On the rocks. I'm so old I can remember when that meant a wreck, a disaster, a crack-up. Now it's a people drink.

A half hour later, on her second lime mist—the coco loco would taste better, but I'll shoot myself before I drink out of a coconut with a plastic *straw.* Anyway, this lime looks better with this veddy soigné dress. Rum go, what? Men had it made. To be a man, and slightly tight, was forgivably being just a man. A soft answer turneth away a man's bar check. A man can stash away a bottle in the bottom desk drawer, just friendly-like. Or the corporate manager's genuwinecolored decorator-chosen walnut bar, just to keep the clients happy. The masculine invention of the executive lounge, the convention's off-the-lobby cash bar, ho-ho-ho and a bottle of rum, splice the mainbrace, one for the road and one to get ready and two to go. Three to make sure. Lissen I luv ya like a brother but business is business. The reflex office protectiveness closing in at midmorning around Harry Hangover. Milord's favorite saloon, liquid lunch, politely itemizing the credit-card monthly bar bill with a charitable *Cash pd. out* instead of *Beverage*.

Ah, she thought as the waiter brought her next—third? Who's counting—lime mist. Men. They've got it made. Laid. Paid. Women are the last unrecognized unsung no-civil-rights minority. Tote that barge, lift that bale, git a little drunk, baby, and you land in jail.

She held down a little giggle, because a lady sitting in a tropical patio restaurant, even if she's half hidden by greenery and masked under white plastic Boy Watchers, you've got to admit frankly, she'd look wee willy silly if she giggled out loud there all by her lonesome.

Made, laid, and paid. But just let a lady make a pass, and *bang*, she's a slut. You're even worse if you give 'em the good swivel-arsed heave-ho they want. And if their own wives squirrel around, they're nothing but whores. With passion you're a bum; without it, frigid Fanny. Always the great swinging extremes, you're either cold nun or hot nooky, a sweet sister or a scarlet sister. The giggling farce of it. Them and their stiff-ponged pole-vaulting over the smallest simple truth that women are just like people, including men, partners not slaveys, willing bouncing bosomy playmates if only they weren't treated like rifle targets, raised up to be dart boards, collected like show-off scalps to wow the boys down at the gym.

Oceans of mush, blood, laws, handy homelike hatreds and moonshine and poetic chiffonry, and all the while the little red rosebud of truth sits out in the open for any simpleton to see. Everybody knows, because the boys have penetrated the territory, and sold the bill of goods that the way to a man's heart is not through his heart. But who's dared to whisper that the way to a woman's womb *is*? Love, the mystic rose. Ah, sweet mystery of life, and how're yer bones t'day? How wisely we Celts bind up our wounds with mythologizing lingo. The talk, the talk, the great spooling-out bandages of talk. Praise the fine phrase, lads.

The maître d' was holding the menu in front of her face. Okay, she thought irritably, okay. I can take a hint. We're in this thing together, amigo. Nobody likes a woman lush, especially the woman lush.

She raised her glass toward him slightly, defiantly, but with a trace of explanatory embarrassment. "I'm drinking for the dead," she said. "Longest damn wake you ever saw."

His hinged waist bent slightly. "Señora." His expressive eyes pointed at the menu. "Today we have a very nice langosta. A half, nice and cold? A little mayonnaise for the lady? Asparagus? Maybe tomatoes and petits pois?"

Super-soberly. "Are there vitamins in lobster?"

"Tastes good, so what's the difference?"

She waved her finger at him. "Vitamins . . . are vital. Prevent liver trouble, cirrhosis. Vital for viscera. Viva vitamins!"

The hinged bow, the hinged smile. "Sí, señora. Lobster with vitamins. Yess?" The menu left her hands. Gone. Management frowns ecclesiastically on unaccompanied loco ladies unless they pay cash for a big tab and remember to vomit only in the ladies' room.

Betsy Mary, she told herself, you try the patience of angels. I cannot abide a *public* fool. In private, you can go to hell in a canoe. But in this striped-awning-patio chic restaurant, baby doll, you will suppress your infinite capacity to become sordid and gauche and panting and gaggling after whatever's forbidden. Not because the forbidden is so damned attractive, but only because it's *there*. You have the fine thing in you, so chin up, Missus DeWitt Delovely Sommers. Instead of showing your slip, show your profile.

I must look like a fool, sitting here all alone by the telephone, wearing this ridiculously cute Boy Watcher thing, but if I take it off, then the world moves in through thine eyes, the windows of thy soul, and plays *Ojos Verdes* and here and there some peeping Tom girl-watching from a shady bench, takes a guess that I feel bruised, isolated. Then there's panic in the streets. A private openness, or an open privacy, is my best bet. Correction. My best Betsy.

Over the hum of luncheon voices came a familiar laugh from the opposite end of the patio. She barely managed not to turn. It could not possibly be—but when the unrestrained laugh broke out a second time, free, released, footloose and freewheeling, clear and fancy-free, she twisted in her chair and peered through the thin green slit, furious with herself, wretched to be so needful, embarrassed at the instantaneous speedup of her heartbeat—*Roone?*

No, of course not. A crowd of dark-haired islanders at the far table, two of them standing in a slouched way so they could embrace the person to each side, but no familiar blond head, no curious contrast between the standard advertised clean-cut look and the nonstandard never-advertised dirty mouth. Memories' leg irons worn from long ago and the handcuffs of now while he twirls freedom's key.

David was fond of saying that the wish was father to the fantasy, which was a typically medical lordly kind of remark, and only went to show that the Sommers thought that the world was their oyster even if Witt never got the pearl. She felt her mood swing toward stability. Her pulse slowed and common sense came when the waiter put the garnished plate of cold lobster before her. Cold lobster and hot pants as the heart panteth after the water brooks. Praise be, he's not here. He's a thousand miles away, hot stuff buried cold in the ground, and I can have my massas in the cold cold lobster in peace. Nothing like the Nobel piece prize. She picked up her fork. Then, as the laugh boomed out again, she dropped it. The fork clattered off the table. The waiter hurried over with a clean fork.

As she lifted her head to say "Gracias," she saw Roone.

There he was across the patio. His almost ashen hair, his eyes, his vaga-bond face.

My astonished heart. What in God's world is he doing here on the island? What if he sees me? What if he *doesn't?*

The noisy group left their table and wound among the umbrella-shaded chairs in twos and threes yakking as they headed for the door. Behind Roone, Betsy recognized Volga and Tabac. Volga's hair was piled up in an elaborate lacquered beehive, the spitting image of toasted almond glamour in a tight white-knit suit. Tabac carried a long cigar cocked in an upward angle between his teeth like a caricature of a gunman from an old gangster movie. As Roone was about to pass her table, Betsy thrust out her foot. He tripped and almost sprawled on the patio.

"Son of a bitch!" He caught his balance by grasping a chair. As he swung toward her, half snarling, she lifted the masking Boy Watchers off her face and gave him her most dazzling smile. "Doctor Livingstone, I presume?"

□ □ □

Only later could she try to create some sane order in her head, the way she might tidy up and straighten a room after an all-night party, or awak-ening after a distorted realistic dream and asking: What is it? Why?

The hardest part was to explain to herself how her intentions, so cool, so intelligently decided, had collapsed into a pile of jackstraws at the touch of a finger. Was it the unexpected low comedy of bumping into one another, the hail-fellow manner of lonesome tourists greeting one another in Paris or Rome? But they were not tourists. She was a busy woman, run-ning a household of more than ordinarily busy men, and Roone was certainly not lonesome, not with his favorite million-miles-from-med-school playmate, Volga, all but massaging him in public.

The anger, she decided later. Under her surprise, under the *toujours gai* feeling she got from Roone, under the delightfully youthful to-hell-with-the-humdrum-world, far down under all that, she told herself, I wanted to punish him. The anger. Tit for tat. Unfortunate phrase, un-couth but true. You, buddy boy, were cruel enough that day in Southport, boasting you always mislaid things. The time had come to take you down a peg, my boy, because I'm not the frantic lovestarved kitten that I was with Mason that seventeenish aagh summer in Atlanta. Not grateful or awed by your standardized homogenized tom-turkey muscle strut. You're up against a lady liontamer now, cool and capable, savvy about animal stunts for boys with a tiger in the tank. You want a li'l tasty tidbit, buster? Well, you just beg for it, up on your hind legs, beg now, good boy, *good* boy, until I decide when to slip off the leash. The bigshot talk of making a big killing with Tabac in some kind of crap game, the shrewd run-along-now-and-play to get rid of them all. Uh-uh, no score, buster. Distasteful. The faint gypsy-tinker cockiness, the blue-eyed boyish hard-on eagerness—much better.

But she could not tidy up the clutter in her head any more than she could sweep the ocean off the beach with a housewifely broom.

Just as she had known—expected? wanted?—he had come from all sides at once. The wide, canopied Spanish bed had fooled her with a phony aristocracy; the hotel room filled with enough Castilian reproductions to make her feel otherworldly, on a separate island from ordinariness, the atmosphere as artificial as candlelight and just as gracious.

But he had homed in without even the faintest pretense of preliminaries, no bother with dexterity, the high-topped overwhelming roar-rushing wave of fearful delight lifting her and then its downsucking rollercoaster undertow drowning her, the world churning behind her shut eyes more darkly underwater-green-tinted than the private darkness inside her Boy Watchers, this boy, this watcher, this tender fury, this straddling hair-yanked-back, legs widened half throttled no chance to breathe never-felt savage assault without a single decent graceful thee-and-me two-to-tango fitting trying moving together, but only the bony aim and ramrod thrust through her, his spiking her through the bed, the floor, through the civilized crust of the world into the blinding volcano's center where daylight words *stop stop stop* meant nothing, *oh God God* meant nothing, *oh Roone please please I can't* meant nothing, impact and recoil and bruising, legs circling like frantic embracing clutching arms, until the dark center of no-word sounds, sounds alone, the deepest cave where she had seen herself crouch, there now she trembled infuriated because she would beat him at this life-and-death wrestling match, beat back with all her bucking body the single-muscled sword he valued so much, make him—him? and who else?—feel as incomplete unfinished lost unworthy as she had felt, but the tremors came alive of themselves, explosion, I'll *die*, nameless nerves bombarding her position of half-suicide half-attack, the hailstorm of thunder in her ears, no longer crushed because passive earth cannot be crushed, no longer violated because where laws are not then no violation can be invented, not pained because in the ape-core of the brain stem which recognizes only *happening right now* there is no pain, only the long down-sloping to

storm ended.

Suddenly as begun.

Sprawled sweat-drenched across the sheets.

Childhood. Shoulders pressed back against the cottage wall under the thatched roof overhead, storm past, in the after-quiet only the slow drip of rainwater droplets.

Ahhhh. This stretched-out sweet dreamsleep, this whatever it is, *is*, this acceptance of languid soft-as-Christmas-pudding complete wellbeing. Why did people hurry and scurry and worry themselves halfway into graves when this was so peacefully peaceful? Poor people, the whole last lot of them. To lie like this, to sleep. Ah, the rub's the thing. Conscience of the king. *Reinitas'* rounded bellies, dipping into honey.

She slept. One minute. Ten minutes. No minutes.

His mock devil face. "What class."

"Noble piece prize?"

He scrunched his face into an exaggeratedly deprecating snout. "You show talent, kid. Little more practice, daily workout, maybe you can make the big leagues."

"I'll fetch you a terrible clout for that cheap sort of talk," she said. "You think life is a four-letter word."

"Not in Gaelic, Pat."

Am I all that Irishy again? she thought. Give the girl a chuck under the chin, fling her over your shoulder like a fireman, strip off her clothes and public gloss—and little Betsy Mary peeks out between her fingers?

There was so much about him she did not understand: his presto alaka-zam magic-mirror change from student breadcrusts in New Haven to this room-service plush resort hotel, the offhand doubletalk references to a big deal, the story of a borrowed student-rate half-fare air ticket for the spring holiday. Vaguely she recalled, now it seemed years ago in New Haven, hadn't there been some jabber about Volga and Cuban refugees in Port Everglades, and Tabac, obviously a streetcorner hoodlum, talk—of what? What had they talked about, that day in New Haven, in that anti-people coded jargon? Drugs? Joy-joy on the moon? No, I don't understand, Betsy thought. I don't even *want* to, and I don't care if I ever do.

She telephoned her house from the hotel, wriggling her bare toes in the carpet and enjoying talking sensible wifely details with her maid at home while she watched herself in a smoky antique mirror, a naked nymph, hair tumbled, green-eyed as a mad captured queen: "Sí, leave some beer and sandwiches in the *nevera* for Doctor Mayoso, he'll be home very hungry and very late. You're sure no long-distance *telefonema* from Mr. Sommers in St. Thomas? Don't keep dinner for me. I'll eat with friends in town and I'm not sure when I'll—"

"You," Roone said, "who would ever in his right reverend mind imagine you—*you*—Mrs. Teacozy? You ought to sell tickets. What a cool performance!"

She dropped the phone back into its cradle and pretended to measure the way he lay spread-eagled on his back. Then, with a scrambling serpentine movement, she stretched herself on top of him and bit his mouth. "Now," she said, "I'm on top."

"Upsadaisy for you."

"You were, oh I'll tell you—"

"Tell me, pretty maiden—"

"You were un-be-liev-able, Roone."

"Flattery will get you nowhere, except"—he moved his hands cunningly —"right here—"

She rocked herself lightly, using her entire body like a hand stroking his warmth. "I never knew it was possible."

"Skyrockets?"

She kissed him. "Don't ask."

"The dark side of the moon?"

"And stars. You were *marv*elous."

"Roone and Sons. Our motto: We Aim to Please."

"You're an idiot."

"Sons? Did I say *sons*? Are you on pills?"

"Uh-uh."

"Dutch cap? *Something*?"

She bit the tip of his chin. "Secret weapon. I'm sperm-immune." Said lightly. Just right. Said out loud.

He lifted her face away from his to look into her eyes. "You're what, Lady Doctor? Lawdy, who's been teaching you them big words?"

"Bet you never heard of it."

"Of course I have. Immunity to sperm—that's like an allergy, spelled backward. But you've got a kid."

"Adopted." She nodded. "Timmy was adopted by us. I've never ever been pregnant. I never ever can be. A pitless peach. A seedless cherry."

"I'll be damned—"

"You are." She lapped the tip of his nose wetly. "You are." She grasped his ears like jug handles. "Wasn't I marvelous?"

"A bomb. You knocked the fillings right outa my teeth. You?"

She tried to talk his way. "Head-on collision."

"And you with no seat belt. No chastity belt."

She bit his bottom lip again; so hard, this time, it bled.

A crude charcoal pit had been hollowed out in the beach sand and above it the speared roast pig was kept turning by one of the guests at Tabac's party. A rectangle of corrugated tin lay propped up on its long side as a windbreak; behind it the man who turned the spit glistened with sweat as if he himself were being roasted. He stopped to make himself a cigarette, tapping the tobacco along the thin paper, rolling it and licking the edge to seal it. His eyes were like his little tobacco pouch, half-closed, small pursestring bags. He wiped his forehead in his elbow while looking up at Betsy. "You like the"—he inhaled deeply—"smell, señora?"

"I'm *starv*ing."

"You try my *guasacaca sauce*"—he kissed his fingertips—"aie, mother of saints." His wrinkled earthen eyes, unfogged by manners, unimpressed by accent, dress, status, read her openly. "When you hungry, hard to wait, qué no?"

Lord love a duck, she thought, turning away. That *hungry*. Is this afternoon printed all over me like some sexpot headline? Small trembles keep running through my head. I should hide behind the plastic Boy Watchers, because my eyes always give me away. They've even mariachi'd that *Ojos Verdes* song about my eyes, natch. But I can't help that unconscious slippery slide from the sensual to the salacious. I want people to see only a cool poised woman in a sleeveless lime batik sheath, flawless makeup. Señora Diarmada.

The pleasantly exhausted slackness I've been coddling in myself is gone and, as if Roone had stropped and sharpened all my hungers, Señor Rotisserie there guessed right. I really *am* starving. I left that stupid cold lobster sitting on the restaurant table; the understanding between us had been so instantaneous and fierce there didn't seem to be a minute to lose.

A man wearing a starched white guayabera shirt pumped away with his accordion and several couples in the crowd fell into a conga line to snake after him down the beach.

Roone came up holding paper cups. Tabac, directly behind him, balanced a jug on his bare shoulder. Tabac filled only half her cup, then stopped and sniffed. "Caramba!" He leaned toward the roasting pit and breathed in deeply. "Smell that *lechón asado*? Straight from the back kitchen of heaven."

Roone juggled the paper cups. "Fill it up, *atómico*. This banana *cañita* comes without taxes, so don't try to cheat the management."

Tabac appealed to Betsy. "My party, and he's already a management. You like my party?"

"You were very nice to invite me, Tabac."

"Any fren of my partner Roone." He waved his arm to include his several dozen guests. "Not fancy. No Condado Beach. Be a *jíbaro*. Take off your shoes."

"I already have," Betsy said. She scuffed the warm sand. "See?"

Roone held up his cup of rum. "And this takes off your skull."

Tabac swung his jug just enough to splatter Roone with rum. "You wanna drink tomat juice? Stay home."

A quartet of guitarists had begun to tune their instruments by ear while their friends set up a small circle of drums around a cleared space on the beach. One of Tabac's helpers was using his jug of *cañita* to swoosh more rum over all the girls.

"Where's Volga?" Roone asked. For a moment Betsy hated him.

"Oh, man, she's one sore dame at you, Roone. She stayed in hotel. I toll her, don't be a horse's ass. We made a big score, be happy! I says, so Roone meets a fren from home? So he takes a siesta to say hello?"

"That's what you said, huh? You speak only broken English? Broken by two years in the States?"

Tabac gave himself a long resentful swig from his jug and wiped his mouth. "All afternoon, pal. Thass some big hello, ah?"

Roone reached out and grasped a button on Tabac's shirt, then, with a wrist-snapping jerk, tore it off. "Keep talking, *pachuco*. Keep your big fat mouth flapping in the breeze, man, I'll make sure you lose all your buttons."

Again Tabac appealed to Betsy. "*Mire*. Does a partner talk like this to a partner?"

"I'll partner you into an early grave," Roone said. "I'll shove you into a Coke machine with a dime. You'll come out nothing but bubbles."

"He's crazy," Tabac said to Betsy. "He's the most crazy American I ever saw. We make a big score, it's a big party time to be happy"—he pointed to a table some of the women had set up, itemizing with little jabs—"roas chick, niños, mangoes, chicharones, *sierra en escabeche*. You like cocktail *de frutas*? Maybe *pollo* club sandwich?"

"Mine host," Roone said. "Will you stop being so goddamned hospitable and trying so hard?"

Tabac gestured with both hands, indicating the entire beach. "It's my house. She's my guest," he said.

Because he sounded as if he meant it, Betsy came to his rescue. The guitarists had begun to play softly, so she asked him, "That song, what does it say? What are they singing?"

"Harr to tell," Tabac said sullenly.

"Come on," Roone said. "Don't be a sorehead. I didn't mean to hurt your dignidad. I apologize, partner." He raised his paper cup and tossed down the *cañita.*

"You," Tabac said watching him, "you have a soul of a real *atómico.*"

"Muchas gracias, partner. I apologized, so now it's your turn. Tell the lady what the song says."

Tabac shrugged. "Somethin you don unnerstan, Roone."

"Try me for size, partner."

"Please," Betsy said. "It sounds so pretty."

"They sing, señora, it's Criolla antigua. Ol' song, you know what I mean—it's how love breaks open the heart." He listened as the musicians went on. "Love is why the angels lean down to look at lovers."

"Ah," she said. Her discovery this afternoon was not her discovery at all. Other prospectors had found the hidden places before her. An embrace of simpático lifted in her—the *cañita?* on an empty stomach?—an understanding that all these strangers were not strangers at all, but passengers on the same ship, hungry for the same food. Even Tabac, with his li'l brown jug, was back on his native island where he could feel like a man, a successful man who could invite his friends to a big celebration. King for a night. No longer the nickel-and-dime hoodlum, uneasy in Americano streets of office buildings and business talk and diploma'd jobs, but *el pato macho,* top banana, yesterday's barefoot *jíbaro* now Mr. Big, buying untaxed bootleg *cañita* and inviting his friends and his friends' friends to bring their guitars and drums to his party.

Somebody was spouting poetry, *calabó y bambú, bambú y calabó,* using a doomed declamatory voice over the drums' monotonous baticum borrowed from candomblé and macumba rituals.

Betsy turned her back on the performer to listen to the guitarists, caught up by their low-key flamenco interlacery. To her, they plucked from their dreamlyric music laments worldly people will not confess, arabic threnodies of love wasted, Andalusian yearning for gracefulness in courtship, a basso continuo of remorse for wrongs done, the laughterless Hispanic contradictions of piety and sensuality, unworldly love and worldly violence.

"Hey, beautiful dreamer."

She frowned at him for his interruption. "What's the matter?"

"You."

"What's the matter with me?"

"You're paying too much attention to the *músicos.*"

"But those guys are great. Really great."

"Great," he said slowly, "is not a word for spectator sports. You have to be in it, doing it, not just watching or listening. I mean you really have to be hot-dogging it before anything can be great."

"Hot-dogging?"

"That's surfing, the real skin-to-skin kind."

"You surf?"

"All over. From Tijuana Sloughs to Surfrider beach at Malibu before it got mobbed by the squares. From Canaveral all the way up to Gilgo on Long Island."

"Is that why you've been watching the water?"

"Well, there've been some big *bomboaras* out there."

"Say that again? Slower."

"Australian. The big waves that break outside of the normal surf line." He stood up, grinning. "Leave off this last lamentful music and I'll show you some real hot-dogging. Watch, luv."

She looked up at him. "But you don't have a surfboard!"

"Betsy, you want to be a spectator and holler great? I'm gonna show you a little body surfing."

"*Body* surfing?"

He raised both fists to thump his chest like Tarzan in the movies. "Body surfing," he said, "is the only pure religious form. There's nothing between you and the sea. No board, no surf mat, no skimmer. Just you and the ocean. Like it's getting born again."

She heard the ocean now, threading out between the party noises. The hump and crash of waves along the entire crescent of the shore seemed louder than before. She put her hand on his arm. "But it looks so hard—"

He grinned again. "Know what the swingers say? If it ain't hard, lady, it ain't good."

"I'm serious. Those waves look awfully big. Threatening, I mean."

"That's the whole idea, Betts."

"But without a board, Roone—what if you go under?"

"I've been trying to tell you, that's the whole idea. The surfer and the sea. No boards, no broads, no nothing. If you take away danger, you might just as soon spend your time mooching around, playing pinochle in your underwear."

She tightened her fingers. "It sounds *mad*." She came closer and dropped her voice. "Why do you do it?"

He put one finger in the center of her forehead and slowly traced it down to the tip of her nose, then across her lips. "Ssh," he said. "It's a secret. I do it because I'm afraid of it. So I have to go out and beat it."

"Please," she said. "I mean really. I'll ignore the músicos. Please don't go out there to beat it just for me."

"For me, dreamer." He began to turn away, then swung back. "Just watch. See—the trick is to pick up a big wave at the steepest unbroken point. That's where your slide starts. If you catch it, your body lifts and planes and shoots for the beach like a goddam arrow out of a hundred-pound bow."

"But what if you don't?"

"You never don't. You *do*."

She watched him go alone in the water, casting a long shadow toward her as he splashed toward the horizontal setting sun. The unexpected freakish wind had freshened and the lapping wavelets had risen, the new waves sharpened at their edges by the stiff breeze as they ran harder and stronger into shore.

Roone stood for a moment, waist-deep in water, putting on yellow rubber swim fins, just long enough for Betsy to think: He's a crazy show-off. Anybody who would swim out there to the reef and try bodysurfing back into shore must be crazy. Several hundred yards out the waves looked twenty feet high, greenish white where the light struck them; a submarine darkness shadowed their shore side. They rose, hung, rose again, rode in over the reef, cresting, curling upward, up and over, and then, with the sound of a thousand leather whips, cracked down for the final run across the bay. And Roone would use his body as a surfboard in *that*?

She shaded her eyes against the operatic dying of an incredible fireball sun out there beyond the flamestreaked blaze of horizon. Properly Wagnerian, she thought. Tristan playing Valkyrie in a skimpy bathing suit. She could see that he must be a powerful swimmer by the impressively muscular rise and fall of his arms and the propeller wake of his kick. How stupid, she thought contemptuously, to go to all that trouble out there and purposely risk your life, just for the sensation. Why? One man against the elements? The danger? An exhibition of courage for the fair lady on the shore? No, she decided. It's for himself, just as he said. As he swims out toward all those crashing tons of water he must be feeling what I felt when we left the patio restaurant and went upstairs holding hands in the elevator, to his hotel room. The speeded pulse, the light-headed feeling of *soon soon this is it*, and then the raw turning vortex that spins you higher and higher before the crest lifts you and throws you down drowning gasping, struggling for the surface hungry for air until you come back up to reality, drenched, exhausted, and at peace.

If you have to explain it, she thought, it's no good. But what else would drive him out there along the edge of darkness under this tropical hellfire sunset? He was far enough out now so that as he turned to face the shore his blond head seemed no more than a bobbing ball drowned in torch-light.

Most of the guests lined up along the beach now. The musicians had stopped and were watching him, saying nothing or making the kind of short remarks, she thought, people make when they watch a man about to jump from a bridge. Beside her, Tabac was explaining that the danger was that Roone could not ride on a wave like a board surfer but would have to ride in the breaker. It all sounded as if Roone would be drowning, surrounded by tons of seawater moving at express-train speed.

"There he goes!"

Her heart pounded as she saw Roone rise and fling his finned feet upward in a jackknifing dive beneath an incoming breaker, priming himself to come up at exactly the right moment to enter the womb of the huge wall of water, letting it lift him to its shoulder as he stroked diagonally— *there!* The gray-green water monster had a human speck in it, roaring in, growing higher, cresting, white soup all along its top, cresting higher, sucking its belly inward as its outer edge changed from a balled fist into a great open claw tearing at the beach.

And Roone was alive in it, angled skywest and twisting, shooting the curl. Betsy could make out almost his entire body for a split second before the whole ocean came down on him with the slam of metal doors.

"Caramba!" said Tabac fearfully beside her. "Muss be a million ton water hittin bottom."

She spotted a jumble of yellow flippers, then he disappeared again with a spinning whirlpool motion, much closer now, his head surfacing just as a secondary breaker smashed down on him and he disappeared again. After a long sickening moment he shot out of a sloping trough, surrounded by flying white bubbles, pursued and pounded by more tons of seawater, but leveling now, planing, rocketing into shore. People shouting, Tabac running beside her into the water as the water tumbled him again, brawling with him, then threw him out of the wave into the shallows.

He drifted face downward like a corpse, but when she and Tabac reached him and grabbed him beneath the arms, he shook them off and tried to stand up. He stumbled, caught at her heavily, then straightened. His cheekbone and nose and shoulder had been sandpapered raw and bled down across his body. His jaw hung slack as his chest kept heaving for oxygen.

She wanted to embrace him and strike him, hold him and curse him, wipe his wounds and boil him in oil. He bent down toward her, still gasping, their faces on fire with the last of the sun, then put one arm across her shoulders, like an honorably wounded warrior who bestows his need for help as a distinction on his helper.

"How was it out there?" Tabac asked. "Good?"

"Crazy, man, crazy." Roone tightened his arm around Betsy and looked down at her with a victorious twisted smile. Like a man confessing about another woman he repeated to her, "Crazy."

□ □ □

"Wasn't there a song once," Betsy asked, "called 'I've Got You Under My Skin'?"

Roone ran his fingernail cunningly down her side. "Like the skin you're in."

"Cole Porter, wasn't it? And the other one, 'Mad About the Boy'?"

"No, that was no-no-Noel Coward."

They laughed together. To him, she thought, the world is all burlesque, very different from my cloudy lakes and lonely peat bogs. "'That Old Black Magic.' Wasn't that a great song?"

"What's this all of a sudden about songs?" He leaned across her and twirled his tongue in the dimpled hollow of her navel. She giggled and tried to sit up but he pushed her back "You want to play disc jockey?" he said. "Song titles? You be a longplay disc, let me be the jockey."

"Funny thing about song titles," she said. "They're almost like poetry to me. They say all the things we can't say by just talking."

"Just talking, what time will your husband be home tonight?"

She put one hand under her neck and with a single upsweeping gesture threw all her hair in a dark shower across her face. "I'm not sure."

"You're not sure?"

"No, I'm not. I'm gambling he won't be back until tomorrow." She tried to smile, but her mouth felt wounded. He had been close to ruthless in his pleasures. "Witt's busy. Over in St. Thomas, they're nursing his precious dioscorea seedlings for him. So he comes and he goes."

He parted her hair. "You getting careless?"

"Maybe. But don't worry." She touched the tip of his scraped nose. "I've lit a candle to Saint Thomas."

"Mad about the boy?"

"Maybe."

"That old black magic?"

She ran both her open hands up the broadening muscles of his chest until her fingers met at his throat and ringed his neck. She pulled him toward her until he gave her a comic kiss through the screen of her hair. With a quick heave she sat upright and pushed him back down against the pillow. She had come back to his room at the hotel convinced that she could be warm yet cool, tranquil and tender, lead him lightly wherever she wanted by a faintly maternal maturity. But, as always, his bawdy un-expectedness, his shifts from insolence to gaiety—even the way he saw right through the haughty labyrinth at whose center she hid to protect herself—swept aside her pretenses.

He had bought her a unique bracelet made of six linked little nautical flags. "They spell K-U-Z-I-G-Y," he had said while he fitted it around her wrist. "And from one sailor to another, that's my message to you, Skipper."

She had rotated her wrist so that the little yachting signal flags dangled back and forth. "I surrender, Captain. What's the message?"

"International code. Permission Requested to Lay Alongside."

"To hell with alongside," she had laughed. "You're more welcome aboard, matey."

She remembered the miniature gold roulette wheel Witt had found for her at Van Cleef & Arpels: its jeweled spinner pointed to tiny French phrases for *I love you . . . very much . . . not at all . . . madly*. She and Witt had been married only a short time, money was still unfamiliar religious stuff to her, and her first thought was: this one gold trinket could have paid for a decent funeral for my father. "What a silly gambler's toy!" she had said to Witt. She never wore it.

The recollection flashed through her so strongly that tears came to her eyes, making her vision spiky with colors; with her eyes closed, she put her hands on Roone's cheeks and kissed him hard.

With him, she forgot everything else. This total forgetfulness was part of his attraction, she knew, like being on a boat where no one can reach you by phone. She parodied the Cole Porter song: "You're the top, you're the tower of Pisa, you're the top, my Milk of Amnesia . . ."—and they had both held their noses and roared.

Like a beggar on horseback she enjoyed coming into this room of heavy somber Spanish furniture and flaunting her natural nudity against its stern grandiose antiquity. As soon as the heavy door closed, Roone pinned her against it, holding her there with his mouth welded over hers until she was breathless, then watched her kick off her shoes so nimbly that they sailed across the room, peeling his shirt while she threw her dress over one chair, her bra and stockings over another. The majestic four-poster canopied bed was an island outside time. In it, he had a practiced kiss-biting that made her arch her back and roll sideways until he forced her flat again.

She fought him but urged him on, wrestling him aside but then changing to straddle him, rounding and turning and sprawling until nothing in the world mattered except this.

21 For the Governor's dinner party, La Fortaleza disguised its massive fortress appearance for the night. Lights had been strung along the drive; in the foliage, torchlamps were cleverly concealed among palm branches. Behind scrollwork iron gateways twice taller than a man, the whitewashed façade stood splendid with dignity, all pageantry and historical pomp. But the citadel and the sentry box at the Pasaje de la Beata Madre gate could not be camouflaged by the flowers which hung everywhere like colorfilled parasols, nor mellowed by the timeless splashing of the mosaic fountain of Ferdinand and Isabella. Beyond the chiaroscuro of festooned blossoms and the afterglow of mock tangerine moons, archaic donjon stones led to the curving sentry walk overlooking the Bay of San Juan, a walk walled by embrasures through which siege cannons aimed commandingly at the harbor.

As Witt and Betsy and Mayoso drove up to the Governor's dinner party, Mayoso said thoughtfully, half speaking to himself, "This is a perfect picture of the Governor's mind." He waved one hand at the hidden lights, the lucent colors pooled along the driveway, the solid bulk of La Fortaleza against the tropic night. "Everywhere you look," he said, "you see complexity."

Betsy rested her hand lingeringly on Mayoso's arm. "My, the good doctor looks positively *dashing*. Rented suit. Black tie. Just like downtown."

"This collar's choking me," Mayoso said.

Witt interrupted. "Save the mutual admiration, fellas. Won't we be late for this informally formal dinner?"

"Now, now," Betsy said. "We mustn't get anxious and be vulgarly on time just because there're a few bucks invested here."

"Oh hell, Betts—" Witt said, surprised by the tetchy crustiness in his voice. He felt tired and vaguely irritable without reason. His meetings at the U.S. Department of Agriculture's Dorothea Station on St. Thomas had gone well. He had returned to San Juan feeling pleasantly reassured about his dioscorea experimental farm investment and immediately stumbled over a suddenly changed Betsy. Voice, stride, words, all changed back to her earlier manner. The same flushcheeked enlarged-pupil brightness, the conversational darting and swooping, the same chainsmoking anybody-got-a-match? Even her fine-bodied walk had reverted to a lithe model's nervous unsettled prowl. And—oddest of all—she now repeated an hour-to-hour concern about Timmy's health and loneliness that was forcing her to plan going home to New Haven. As soon as possible. The island was *divine*—she had gone back to using and pronouncing divine that way —but fun and games and selfcentered enjoyment should not come between a young boy and his mother. So, while Witt got the local show on the road, like the whole bit, man, the Caracas warehouse thing and the experimental farm jazz, she was going back to New Haven on the company plane tomorrow. Some student vacationer from Yale, somebody who did part-time lab work for David, would be hitchhiking a plane ride back home, okay?

I wonder, Witt thought, if she's afraid she might start her old chugalug with local rum? With deliberately random irrelevance, he said, "This Fortaleza party is too political for my taste. Seems the Governor is having a rough time these days."

Mayoso eased the collar of his dress shirt beneath his Adam's apple. "Rough time?"

"He told me that yesterday the police caught a boat off Vieques loaded with weapons from Cuba. The guns were supposed to be delivered to the Nacionalistas here on the Island. When you think of his tough election campaign coming up, the splinter parties, the Cuban refugees fighting each other about how to fight Castro, then add all the Church opposition —well, the Governor's chair gets hotter every day."

Betsy stopped short just before they entered the bright foyer. Roone, she had been thinking: Where are you this minute? With that Gypsy girl? She turned to Mayoso with a show of spontaneous wifely admiration. "Y'know, I'm just beginning to discover how much important information Witt carries around in the back pocket of his britches."

She had said it convincingly, but Witt explored her face unconvinced. Her involvement in the bitterness and difficulties of the last several weeks had cut away her little poses, her actressy pretenses. Was she sliding back into her make-believe? The Irish brogue was real enough when she was being real, but one never knew when it was just put on. Or why.

Two uniformed guards pushed open the massive doors to La Fortaleza's Hall of Governors and they went in, together but alone.

After dinner, some of the guests went outside to the breezeswept private patio off the dining room for coffee and brandy. Others remained inside La Fortaleza, drifting through the Governor's rooms filled with polychrome *santos*, panels of fifteenth-century retablos, intricate Hispano-moresco carvings and ecclesiastical tapestries; a mirror chamber of Spain's golden moment. The only exceptions were the paintings in the Hall of

Governors which centered around the Renaissance-looking portrait of the first great governor, Luis Muñoz Marín.

Mayoso was tapped on the shoulder by Jorí, Governor Santos Roque's aide. "Doctor," Jorí said with a conspiratorial whisper, "as you go by the Governor's study, will you please wait in there for him? He wants to see you privately. Bueno?"

"Sí." What was this hocus-pocus all about?

Outside, on the patio, the unseasonal wind had strengthened. Above the party, the canopy of trees caught each gust, ballooning like underlit sails, their upper branches creaking with the sound of a ship's rigging. White-jacketed men on the Governor's domestic staff went from guest to guest with an ivory inlaid mahogany humidor.

Witt was able to glimpse through the rose trellis the little patio where Betsy was flanked by her military honor guard. Even at this distance he could admire her fragile slim figurine quality in her long evening dress. Those two gung-ho generals are probably convinced she's just a mere slip of a girl sipping a wee dram as her first drink of the evening. Little do they know she has a hollow leg. They could never guess her ability to drink with both fists, and they'll probably end up under the table while she's just warming up. He noticed she was charming the Israeli general, very much the tactful wife of an executive who knows her husband might have to see this man on official business at some time in the future. He appreciated her not bothering with her usual catch-me-if-you-can act, and he had seen her listening really seriously before dinner when General Edin had said, in his underplayed way, "We retire our top generals very young, in their early forties, so I'm planning a whole new civilian career. I'm going to organize an ecumenical world congress of all the branches of Judaism—create a new spiritual unity by getting everyone to agree to forgive the Christians their bloodthirsty behavior over the last two thousand years."

Witt had heard Betsy laugh with complete delight. Who but my Irish wife, he had thought admiringly, could soften up a paratrooper general to indulge in such conversational kidding?

In his private enclosure of darkness behind the trellis Witt contemplated Betsy with a mixture of objectivity and embarrassment, as if snooping through a peephole. The night was becoming to her; she somehow wrapped all the staged prettiness around herself with the casual lovely drape of silk. She had always joked about her being one of the night people; he had learned she said what she meant most seriously in a deceptively half-humorous pitter-patter way. But the day people count too, he thought. When I told her the night people are gay children riding piggyback on the day people, hiding their distaste of grubbing for food and clothing and shelter, she had said, No.

We keep singing incandescent midnight songs, she said, to head off the trash collection of morning, the headline deliveries of doom, the baggy-eyed stumble toward monotony—*tonight*, now! that's what we night people sing in our songs, she said. Later is no damn good.

I'm just beginning to decipher her mirror code, everything reversed; pretending she's a pleasure-seeker while she's unhappy or defenseless. Poetic exaggeration and old country irony for armor. Her wild flights of fancy aren't supposed to be taken at face value—I've learned that much. She's a talker and a quoter from generations back, and so much like the bright hills and shining water of Dingle Bay that I feel all the rest of the world could be damn well lost for her.

During the last few weeks something of our early days had come back. I'd begun to think she was growing up, becoming selfassured enough to enjoy all that we have and let the rest go by. If she could keep her footing stable, the way she's talking now to those two military men—an intelligent woman talking with intelligent men, without swapping fake dollhouse seductions in return for driblets of flattery. She's been interested—until tonight—in what we've been doing, an ally. It would be better if she stayed here on the island with me instead of going back home to New Haven. But I can't hold her caged.

Knocking around the island with me, seeing all the sweat and expense going into the experimental farm, she'd just begun to get an idea of the brass-tacks profit-and-loss problems I have to live with every day. The more we get away from the power scrimmage, the possessiveness, the I-want-it-my-way, the sooner she'll be able to drop anchor and get her bearings.

He took a deep breath, surfacing for air after so long underwater, almost convincing himself, hopeful.

He heard a woman's heels approaching—Betsy's counterfeit party voice saying airily, "My, how I admire those sabra girl soldiers of yours, General. I'm an awful creampuff, myself. Even if we declared war against men, I'd be a conscientious objector!"—then she and General Edin came strolling around the corner of the rose hedge. In the translucence of the tree-hung lanterns, she was enameled theatrically by shadow and light, an artful queen on a tropical stage.

Very beautiful, Witt thought. Maybe we can meet each other halfway. I might be able to learn to play her game of yé-yé like the night people if she'll only make a try at being one of the day people.

The Governor cornered Mayoso in his leathery secluded study. "Mayoso," he said, "about this therapeutic abortion business—"

"It's no business, believe me."

"Apologies, my friend. Let me come straight to the point."

"*En garde.*"

"No, don't take that attitude, Mayoso. We're not fencing. We're not dueling. We both just happen to be in some hot water."

"I'm used to the heat."

"So am I," the Governor said. "But the Legislature granted you, a Martí, a special lifetime license for your job. But every four years I have to go back to the voters to get mine renewed." A shutter in the window of the study banged, and the Governor got up to latch it.

When he came back, Mayoso said, "You got me and my friends out of Caracas. This is my first chance to thank you."

"This is my first chance to tell you how sorry I was when Witt told me about your loss. I know what it's like because I've had it too, and I've never gotten over it." He sat down heavily and then added, "I should have come to see you—"

"I know how the political grind keeps you busy—"

"Much worse this year than ever before. I could have telephoned you, Mayoso, but every time I picked up that expressionless plastic phone—"

"I sneaked a look at your office. Your chess set—"

"It's *your* set, Mayoso—"

"All right. Our chess set. It's getting dusty."

"I'll get after the housekeeper."

"Maybe," Mayoso said, "we should just start using it again."

The Governor did not respond, but only knocked the ashes of his cigar into the ashtray beside him and said nothing. The ashtray had been the gift of a recent Greek technical mission on the island. It was a small silver human skull with an inscription in Greek letters around its base: *Know Thyself.* Aie, the Governor thought, all is vanity and a striving after wind. Betancourt was a refugee on this island and went back to Venezuela as President. Juan Bosch was a refugee here, and went back to Santo Domingo as President. Let the Caribbean tides change, and this man Mayoso may go back home to become President and a political colleague. But more than that, he is a man of honor and my friend. Worse, while he is recovering from one blow, I have to strike him another.

"We're old friends," Governor Roque said, "so we can talk man to man. Jorí tells me that someone in the Medical Society has filed charges against you with the Medical Ethics Committee."

"I heard it as a rumor." Mayoso shrugged. "Maybe it's a fact."

"It's a fact that one of my police commissioners was in this afternoon to raise hell about you. I can understand that, but I can't understand why Bishop Sosa telephoned to cancel his coming to dinner tonight but requested an urgent office appointment tomorrow before he flies off to the Bishops' Committee for the Spanish-speaking."

"And it's a fact," Mayoso said, "that this is an election year."

"And, as our television padre, the Reverend Gofredo Möttl, warned me—an election year in a Catholic country."

"So?"

"Nothing to say?"

Mayoso shrugged again. "Governor, on this island, you've got all the pawns, the castles, the knights, and the bishops."

"But you, the gynecologist, you're in the center of the board with the Queen."

"The Queen?"

"In this country, Mayoso, there are thousands of women voters. That makes them Queen."

"You mean the women's votes can make or break this election?"

Santos Roque took the cigar out of his mouth. "Exactly. The women are mostly practicing devout Catholics. My opponents tell them I'm anti-Catholic—"

"But everybody knows that's foolishness, Governor. Your accomplishments in maternal and child health, in liberal labor legislation—"

The Governor stabbed his cigar in the air toward Mayoso. "Yesterday. All yesterday's accomplishments. I thought I was solid enough to raise the complicated question of taxing business income of Church institutions —not hospitals or schools, but garages, radio stations, property not related to religious practice. I knew the risk I was taking. I knew, with our traditional weakness for living the past, the old ladies would start printing stories about the Mexican revolution. Priests shot in cellars, nuns raped, churches desecrated. I was willing to risk a one-front battle."

"But these therapeutic abortions I'm doing open up a second front?"

"Yes. Linking you to me is an attack from the rear. This is the first year I'm running scared."

"You shouldn't be. The women who hold the vote know what you did for them yesterday and what I'm doing for them today."

"Mayoso, you've never had to face pastoral letters read from the pulpit, threats of excommunication, thunder from Sinai. It's one thing for you to provide an illegal medical facility that serves the people privately. Your own colleagues are among the first to send you patients, no? While you're small and discreet you're like a sanitation department, like a sewage plant everybody needs. But no one wants it next to his own front door. Now, there's nothing small or private. You're becoming a public issue. I personally had to beg the local editors not to run pictures of the line of ladies and the traffic jam of cars parked around your office and clinic." He slapped the arm of his chair. "When the mudslinging starts, everybody ducks under cover. Give me the names of three physicians who are your best friends, then tell me, tell me honestly, if any one of them—just *one*, not more—would step forward in your behalf if a medical ethics committee or a court of law nails you."

"You never know, Governor. Doctors are the last of the rugged individualists."

"Yes, but only inside the club. Only inside, not outside. The doctors are churchgoers—and once you're excommunicated, they'll drop you from the club. You'll write your prescriptions in sand. You'll be a leper. No colleague would touch you for risk of being called unclean himself." He went on in a lowered voice. "You don't have to look at me like that. I don't condemn you. I admire your guts. Look, you're here tonight, an honored guest in my house."

"Because you didn't want me to come here for a daytime appointment?"

"That's a low blow. Aie, the sickness has begun already, Mayoso. When men of goodwill mistrust one another, they end by walking the plank one by one. The oversimplification of motives, the half-truth, the sticky compromises one uses to plug the leaks so the boat won't sink. To hell with the election. When I say you're an honored guest, I mean it personally."

"But politics is you scratch the people's back and they'll scratch yours. You can't be personal. There is still the election."

"Yes. There is still the election."

"You're putting me on a tough spot—"

"Let's say I've moved over to make room for you to join me."

"Governor, it should be unnecessary for me to say I don't want to give your opponents more ammunition. But I—"

"Don't but, Mayoso. Don't be as narrow as all the other experts I have to listen to! Don't you think there's more to getting the people on this island enough food and clothing and decent schools—there's more in the world than your ladies with their big bellies?"

"You're right, Governor. But all that starts inside those bellies. You and your elections and your taxes and your budgets and your traffic problems and your schools—they all begin in just one place."

"Dios, what am I? Some ancient body-worshiping Greek who wants to leave all blemished children out to die in the mountain snow? You think I don't know there are exceptional women who would rather have a child under all the risks in the world, who can love and raise a child who's half blind or with a bad heart—but that's one woman in a hundred. What about the other ninety-nine?"

"We've got to change the laws so that individual parents can make these decisions for themselves."

"Mayoso, now you make sense. There's a local chapter of Marjorie Sommers' L.I.V.E. organization and they're lobbying every day."

"But win or lose, Governor. A change in the law is years away. Imagine if you were one of those women I've been talking about."

"Mayoso, I want you to stop making me an insensitive robot. I have a wife and children and grandchildren. I can feel for these women patients of yours as much as you can. But I'm in the middle of a war. You were in Caracas—multiply it by a hundred all over Latin America. We're supposed to be a successful example of a small backward poverty-stricken, disease-ridden, Church-dominated country that is making a better life for people inside a democratic constitutional framework. And my Sybilline oracle warns me that you're leading me straight into another Dreyfus case."

"Ah, no—"

"Yes! It's bigger than me or the election. The newest smear slogan—copulation, sí; population, no—if that catches on, it could tear the country in half."

"You ask me not to make you a robot. Well, don't make me one. I don't have oracles, so I just do the best I can from day to day. Governor, you may as well know this now, I won't stop. A woman in the first few months of her pregnancy who has German measles has a right to understand the risks against the child she will produce. If she doesn't want the risks, so be it. She should have the right to end the pregnancy."

"So stubborn?"

"Not stubborn. The need of the patient is the only rule. Sometimes that means brain surgery or amputation. Or a therapeutic abortion. One decides very carefully, one patient at a time. But you—you have to think in terms of millions."

The Governor smoked thoughtfully for a few minutes. His cigar ash fell unnoticed on his vest. In a different voice he said, "*Compadre,* you think I've become corrupted with power?"

"So far, no. Power is part of life. It's all in how you use it."

"To use it I need scientific facts. Let me ask you the question I asked the Secretary of Health at our staff conference this morning. How long would you estimate this German measles epidemic to continue?"

"I don't know. There's a mathematical up-and-down in epidemiology—"

"I can't add two and two, Mayoso—"

"Well, the basic idea for infectious or communicable diseases is this:

At some point, more than half the people who are susceptible to the disease will have caught it, so the number of people left vulnerable starts to drop off."

"Are we on the downward slope of this curve of infection yet?"

"Ask your Secretary of Health. He can get an answer from his biostatisticians in fairly short order."

"All right, I will. Maybe this problem has just about burned itself out and that will be that. In the meantime, we need to build some stopgap popular support for you. A bronze bust of José Martí is going to be unveiled in Santurce this week. I want you to take my place and make the official speech. Will you? All the Cuban refugee groups will be there. It's a natural occasion for a descendant of Martí to demonstrate unofficial above-the-battle leadership."

"Not so fast. Lots of the refugees are sore at me because I won't contribute any more money for weapons. The warhawks may try to stop me from making a speech."

"Nobody can stop you from anything, except me. And even I haven't done very well at it. If the German measles epidemic ends itself, that will be rain from heaven. But heaven only helps those who help themselves, and I'm the right man in the right place at the right time. At the high tide of my life I refuse to be cast up on shore." Santos Roque's cigar had gone out. "Will you listen to compromise?"

"That depends."

"Then never mind. I'm not bargaining with you, Mayoso. I'm telling you. Because you're an honest man, you're operating openly as no criminal would dare. If you were sensible, you'd stop the therapeutic abortions."

"I've already told you. To stop would be a brutality."

"Then you'll have to stand alone. I find that a painful thing to say. I can't protect you openly, but I'll do nothing to stop you until one of two possibilities is reached." Santos Roque hesitated. "For all our sakes, Mayoso, I hope the epidemic ends very soon. That's the first possibility. But the second is the political lid blowing off. A five-alarm fire. Then, *compadre*, you'll have to run, not walk, to the nearest exit."

□ □ □

After clinic hours, Mayoso told his nurse and his surgical assistant that he would close the office himself as soon as he finished dictating the surgical record of the final operation of the afternoon.

"We put in a long day today," his nurse said. "Aie, Dios mío, I can't wait to get home and soak my poor old feet."

After she left, Dr. Llanos, Mayoso's assistant, said quietly while changing into street clothes, "Soak our heads, that's what you and I ought to do."

Mayoso stretched mightily, dog-tired in every muscle, and reached behind himself to rub his knuckles up and down his weary back. "Combat fatigue?"

"Fatigue, no. Combat, sí. Every night I get telephone calls. Some are anonymous. They just say something filthy, then slam down the phone. The other calls are my friends calling to warn me that the Medical Society is just waiting to skin us alive."

Mayoso stopped rubbing his back. "For a few more weeks, the Medical Society won't touch us—"

"I know, I know, your family name, you're famous, the Legislature passed that special bill to license you—"

"No," Mayoso said, "the medical ethics committee knows how many doctors are thankful their patients can come to trained men like us instead of some psychologically sick butcher. No, don't worry about them. The religious doctors will shout, but the others will keep busy looking the other way. And as for the anonymous telephone calls—" He shrugged.

He picked up the microphone of his dictation machine and began his final surgical note. After a moment, he heard Dr. Llanos say in the corridor, "I'm sorry, but our offices are closed now."

A man's voice became insistent. Mayoso pulled himself to his feet, worn out after twelve hours of operating, and went to his office door. Two men were talking to Dr. Llanos in the darkened corridor. They looked vaguely familiar.

"Ah!" said the taller man. "Doctor Mayoso! You remember us?" He clapped the shorter man beside him on the shoulder. "You remember Mateo? *Carajo*, you took a bullet out of his neck. Pain of Christ! That night, near Miami, remember? I'm Tomás, the skipper."

Mateo came forward and shook Mayoso's hand. "Buenos días, Doctor."

"Qué pasa? How are you feeling, Mateo? *Está como coco?"*

Mateo straightened his head. "Thanks to you, I'm here. No more rubberneck when a cute *polla* walks by, but I'm here."

"You look different, Tomás," Mayoso said to the taller man. "Last time I saw you weren't you wearing a scuba diving suit?"

"God's teeth, that was some night," the skipper said. He turned to Dr. Llanos. "See, I told you Doctor Mayoso would remember us."

Dr. Llanos shook his head apologetically. "Sorry. Doctor Mayoso has many friends. Well," he said to Mayoso, "I'll be saying goodnight. See you in the morning."

The two Cuban underground men followed Mayoso into his office and, with the solemnity of an official delegation, took chairs facing his desk. Mayoso hung up his white clinical coat. "If you gentlemen can wait until I change—?"

Tomás, the skipper, raised a large meaty hand. "A bloody shirt is nothing to us, Doctor."

A gust of wind threw a handful of gravel against the window. Mateo twitched slightly in his chair and Tomás grinned widely. "See, Doctor? He's still jumpy."

"Hey, Tomás," Mateo said, "you got a big mouth."

The automatic suppression of fatigue by years of habit helped Mayoso say professionally, "You look fine, Mateo. No more pain in the neck, ah?"

Mateo began to answer but the skipper held up his hand. "Still some pain. That's why we came here."

"But Doctor Martínez in Miami was supposed to take over," Mayoso said. "You came all this distance?"

The skipper nodded. "From Miami to here by jet is not exactly a slow boat to China." He chuckled loudly.

This skipper, Tomás, Mayoso thought, he laughs too loud at his own joke. "We came for the big political rally in Santurce tomorrow," Tomás said. "Men are coming from all over, New York, Ybor City, Panama, Caracas, Miami. You'd be surprised how many people are coming."

"Good," Mayoso said. He sat down behind his desk. "To make a speech about José Martí to maybe a dozen kids playing hookey from school, I'd feel like the rear end of a horse. I'm glad to hear people are getting together."

"Tomás—" Mateo began to say.

The skipper stopped him by raising his hand again. "I told you before, Mateo. Let me do the talking."

Mayoso became more wakeful, alert. "Something wrong?"

Tomás grinned broadly with a mouthful of teeth. "Nothing, nothing, nothing. *Todo va a salir bien.* Nothing wrong." He scraped a pack of cigarettes from his pocket, offered it around, then lifted a cigarette directly from the pack with his lips. He scratched his thumbnail against a wooden match and made a seaman's cupped windbreak of his hands as he lighted it. He inhaled deeply, holding his head back, but did not bother to blow out the smoke; it curled from his nose and mouth as he began to speak. "Nothing wrong, Doctor. Only we're broke. Busted. *Escándalo!* A navy, flat on our ass on the beach." He leaned forward. "I don't mean just us two personally. I mean our junta. Two years to build a nautical commando team, and now we don't have even a two-day supply of fuel for the boat." He drew lengthily on his cigarette again, and once more the smoke boiled from his mouth as he spoke. "You got a big operation going here. We counted more than a hundred women in the last three days."

"But," Mayoso said slowly, "didn't you say you just came from Miami?"

Tomás ignored his question. "In Miami," he said through his cloud of smoke, "they told us you stopped your contributions."

"I stopped paying for weapons. But the same amount of money still goes to the Refugee Committee."

The telephone beside him rang. Mayoso pressed the receiver closer to his ear as he recognized Dr. Llanos' voice. "Can you talk freely?"

"Señora," Mayoso said carefully, wide-awake now, "the office is closed."

"Those two hombres looked like trouble to me," Dr. Llanos' voice said. "I just remembered that I saw them in the waiting room yesterday. I don't want to stick my nose in if you—"

"Sí, sí," Mayoso said with professional expansiveness. "But, Señora, the sooner you make your appointment to come in, the sooner your problem can be solved."

"Shall I call the police?"

"Your husband is welcome to come in with you, señora," Mayoso said, "but no need for him to lose time from work. You should come in as soon as possible, even by yourself. Delay does not help in this condition."

"I'll be right over."

"Bueno, señora. Something serious, naturally the sooner you call the nurse for an appointment, the better." He hung up the phone and swiveled back politely to face the two Cubans.

"Busy business," Tomás said. "Surgical appointments all the time. Figure maybe five hundred dollars for each appointment, no?"

"People pay what they can," Mayoso said. "Some pay five dollars, ten dollars. Some pay nothing."

"But you," Tomás said evenly, "you have to pay something. Not nothing. Something for patriotism. A couple of thousand to start."

"Did you come from the Committee in Miami? Do you have some kind of authorization for this?"

"The best," Tomás said. He raised his hand and closed his fingers into a tight fist.

Mayoso glanced at Mateo. The small man hunched his shoulders forward and turned his head to look at the wall. Now Mayoso could see the long scar on his neck; a neat, difficult job, but perhaps too long. He turned back affably to the skipper. If I can keep him talking until Dr. Llanos gets here. "You fighting me," he asked Tomás, "or Fidel Castro?"

"Don't talk stupid, Doctor. Maybe you play both sides, red and black, ah? You sounded funny to me that night on the boat. In Miami, we hear talk you were in Caracas, but not on Committee business. What's in Caracas? Who knows? Fidelistas? Lay some eggs? You make a mint from dames that got knocked up, but you don't want to share the loot to help the fight." He stood up. "You make dirty money. You should be glad to give it to a clean fight, no?"

Mayoso slid open his desk drawer. "Will you take a check?" He reached inside the drawer.

"No," Tomás said. "No checks. Only cash."

"We don't keep much cash in the office. The nurse makes deposits each evening."

"I told you!" Mateo said. The small man sat shaking in his chair. "I told you, big mouth!"

Tomás whirled toward him and shouted, "Shut up!"

When Tomás turned back, Mayoso was already on his feet, holding the long letter opener from the drawer in his desk like a dagger.

Tomás' eyes tensed. "Caramba! More cutting?"

"It's up to you, Tomás." Watch his eyes, he warned himself. These waterfront brawlers move fast once they spot an opening.

Tomás shifted his weight, undecided on strategy: to swing, to rush, bargain, bluff, or vault over the desk. Each idea, Mayoso could see, came and went in Tomás' eyes. He felt his knees crouch slightly, ready to move in any direction. Don't count on the blade of the letter opener for more than a damaging thrust. Avoid letting this Tomás close in, he cautioned himself; he has the long powerful arms of a gorilla. Something snapped within him: sweat poured out over his body; his palms became so oily that he had to shorten his hold on the letter opener. A stab at the chest, he thought, or a slash at the throat? No second chance.

Quietly, without moving, Tomás said through his teeth, "Mateo—"

Don't look sideways, Mayoso reminded himself. If the little guy comes from the side, kick the desk chair at him. This Tomás has the muscles, but I have the height, a weapon, and a resistance they never expected.

He saw Tomás drop his shoulder for a lunge. "Try it!" Mayoso growled. "Try it! You'll get a knife in your throat. I've handled tougher babies than you in prison."

Tomás straightened slowly, a careful aboriginal feint of compromise, never taking his eyes off the blade Mayoso pointed toward him. "Mateo," Tomás grunted hoarsely. "Come around this side. Not the chair side. This side."

Mateo did not move. "No," he said in a low frightened voice.

"You yellow son of a bitch!"

Suddenly the little man, Mateo, crumpled forward in the chair making gagging sounds, his head bending toward his knees as he retched, then retched again, gushing his vomit across the floor.

"You goddam ladyfinger, you!" Tomás shouted. For a split second his eyes swerved sideways. Mayoso instantly daggered the metal blade across the desk. Tomás flung up his elbow protectively and the blade tip caught his sleeve and sliced a red stripe down his forearm.

A primitive antagonism poured through Mayoso: a sweatstreaked luxury of unbottling all his furies, the uncomplicated pleasure of fighting one of the apes who shambled the world like men.

Tomás took his jacket off slowly, holding Mayoso with his eyes all the while, breathing hard now. He wrapped his jacket around his left forearm, weaving slightly, clearly ready to go over to the attack. He thrust forward his padded forearm and, as Mayoso's blade flashed by, tried to clamp Mayoso's swinging wrist by a fast hooked grasp. The blow grazed Mayoso's wrist bone so hard that he felt a glancing pain. Before he could recover his balance, Tomás threw the heavy marble-base desk pen at him. It caught Mayoso above the left eye; a gush of blood began immediately.

Tomás was across the desk now, partly vaulting it so that his feet came toward Mayoso first as Mayoso fell back against the wall with blood glazing his left eye, half blinding him. Mayoso slid sideways, ducked under a round-house swing, and kicked upward as hard as he could. He missed the man's groin but got his knee, throwing him back so hard that Tomás lurched and fell into the desk chair with a choked scream. Mayoso attacked awkwardly with his blade, but the jacket-padded guard arm snagged it, tangled it, and snapped it out of his sweating palm. He caught Tomás across the jawbone with a reaching-out clubbing blow, but the desk chair rolled back as if Tomás had only been shoved.

Tomás shot himself forward and Mayoso felt a slamming pain slide across the blood on his face. He managed to retreat, but before he could gather himself to rush in, a ham-fisted right hook clubbed his forehead and forced him to reel back again. He staggered, twisting himself away, then, as Tomás charged him, lowered his head to butt Tomás squarely on the nose. Tomás toppled over, screaming, his hands clapped over his face so that Mayoso could straighten and before Tomás could bring his guard up, Mayoso threw all his weight into a right hand, a left, a long looping right swing that knocked Tomás sprawling into the wall. Mayoso pounced on him, growling like an animal, and they wrestled down to the floor together, with Tomás desperately trying to avoid the ramming weight of Mayoso's lunge. He jerked sideways, but Mayoso had him by the throat with one hand, while with the other he began slapping him as hard as he could.

Blood streaming over his left eye made a rippling partial blindness which infuriated him, dripping like red grease on his hands so that his fingers slid on Tomás' neck. Useless attack on me, caveman's cunning.

I'll kill him. This bucking ape, weakening in spasms, all the bullying ape-men of the world, every apemuscled madness that killed the mind's growth toward human humane oneness. I'll kill him.

With his ungloved surgeon's fingers, slippery with his own blood, he methodically beat Tomás' head against the floor, sickened, sickened by himself, by the need to kill another to survive himself, animal grunting in a room stinking with vomit, threatened from every side as this Tomás had threatened him by men who wanted to control women like farm animals, killing again now in his own medical office after having learned that killing only brings more killing until the Cristinas are shot down and children stumble blinded with phosphorus grenades. No more killing. But I'll kill him.

The pulling at his arms—Mateo?—the shouting, the labored sandpapery breathing, nothing reached him, the end of the road cliff-edge over into the bottomless nothing, his head butting aside the hands tearing at him . . .

Until darkness.

22 FROM INSIDE THE glass-walled control booth of the television studio the director of the *Hour of Eternity* program turned on his intercom. "Father Möttl," his voice boomed out of the wall speaker, "three minutes to air time."

Father Gofredo Möttl raised his head from the manuscript pages of his speech, shielding his eyes against the studio lights as he squinted at the control booth. Behind him the large projected color picture of a cathedral rose window was focused to form a background; it threw vivid chromatic hues on the television technicians as they rolled their heavy squat TV cameras into final position.

"Father Möttl," the director's voice boomed again, "number-one camera on your right, will handle the closeup shots. So your eye contact with that camera has to be socko. On the monitor screen in here, Father, you look like Hamlet. 'To be or not to be.'"

This is ridiculous, Father Möttl thought. I am not an actor. That voice of his, enlarged by the loudspeaker, is not a voice from a tabernacle but only that of a knowledgeable technical person sitting in front of three TV monitor screens. But he raised his chin and attempted a small benedictory expression.

He watched the unstoppable red hand of the big studio clock sweep inexorably toward the moment his sermon would begin. With this sermon, we trumpet a call to arms, the Church Militant.

He did not see the getready lights winking on the big cameras facing him nor the director's arm raised to give the cue, but listened only to the buzz of recalled voices: *These are called Boy Watchers. . . . There's an Israeli general visiting . . . goodwill ambassador. . . .* What was he doing in Spain? *. . . Israeli . . . in Spain? . . .* The anointment of the bishop's pontifical glance *. . . soup first thoughts later, that gets into the deepest theological waters . . . are you suggesting someone at La Fortaleza? . . .* The stony pillar of Mayoso in the lobby of that Caracas hotel *. . . you and I are in different centuries . . .* the woman's confessional whisper, *I cannot push out of my mind the wish to get rid of this child that I carry. . . .*

As the studio clock's red hand swept toward the remorseless second when he must begin to speak, he wanted to blurt out: Stop! I need more time for purification, for a penitence which can never end. Certain actions in my past leave in my conscience a torture of errors which cannot be overcome.

Make me, Master, he prayed, Thy rod and staff this Holy Week, not cautious, not shrewd or politically expedient, but as humble and open-hearted as those simple innocent men of Assisi. I am not worthy. *Fiat voluntas tua!* This robe has become a shroud. This room, filled with pagans, a place of final solitude, a hill of crosses surrounded by uncaring men bearing ladders and lances, a circle of thorns and Thy sponge of gall and vinegar.

Snake-eye cue lights glittered coldly on the cameras. The director's arm curved down at him like a scythe. Into battle! A bell tolled in his mind. His voice launched itself from him as if he spoke from the steps of a cathedral.

"A massacre of the innocents has begun among us.

"When, *when*, my brothers and sisters in Christ, shall we finally begin to heal the wounds of Him who mounted the Cross for us? A slaughter of the unborn has begun among us. As the fall of pebbles begins an ava-lanche, so this barbarism in the name of science can destroy us all. The souls of unborn children go down in darkness unbaptized. Those of us who stand aside and only watch, those of us who mock and scorn and see only the destruction of the material body, those of us who err or sin by omission or commission must once more open our hearts to the message of love, else our souls will suffer through loss of Grace.

"As was written in Matthew, there is no need to fear those who kill the body but have no means of killing the soul. Fear him more who has the power to ruin body and soul in Hell.

"The penalty of sin is the return from dust unto dust. The reward of Grace is life everlasting.

"We have been cast forth from Paradise, our generation has tasted a bitter gall to its bottom dregs, and once again a snake offers us, in the name of science, fruit from the tree of knowledge.

"The wise men in synod, the gowned and capped doctors of knowledge, have told us and told us again that new life must be limited because there are too many people in the world. Once they told us to use leeches and beat ourselves for our ills—and now, believe me, my brethren—for I have spent this week reading books by the demographers and biochemists and sociologists and doctors of the healing art of medicine who will no longer heal—and now, as once these doctors purged and leeched us, so now they make us fewer by their instruments and their unthinking rationality.

"Have Hitler and his Übermenschen won their war after all? They, too, persuaded us with lies so big, repeated so often, that we lay down in graves and called it bed. They too talked of science, reason, excess population which must be removed. We—I—who shared that time of terror know a penitence which never ends.

"To you, Lilith or Eve—you, the woman who permits her body to be entered with a surgical instrument of death—I say to you that you are despoiled and ravished, slave of your own carnality, prostituting yourself for the payment of material things at the price of your immortal life.

"If you lend your body to the destruction of life within you, the murder of that one life is different only by a few taps upon an adding machine from Hitler's murders—for what may begin as killing of your one child can become the taking of the next step, the killing of the aged, the incurably ill, and the next step, and the next.

"How simple, once you have killed a child within you, to kill those already born! How simple, as it was under Hitler, to register children with mental or physical defects, for the establishment of the Reich Committee for the Registration of Mentally Retarded Persons, to attend a medical staff meeting at Tiergarten Strasse 4 in Berlin, the headquarters of the Reichsführung S.S.—to decide that all such children as the doctors choose must be put to sleep. Humanely? Of course. Efficiently? To be sure. And what is more humane or efficient than setting up safeguards against personal judgments?

"And so the doctors of that rational scientific land set up the kind of jury which we are told could be set up among us now to judge which woman is aborted and which woman is not. So the T. S. 4 Project, as S.S. headquarters came to call it, appointed a jury of three doctors to review the little cards which came into Berlin reporting children with mental and physical defects. As a humane and efficient extra safeguard, the three doctors were told they must be unanimous. All must agree, humanely, efficiently, before a child could be taken from his parents' home, before the administrative symbol of death could be marked on his report card. And that symbol, my brethren, was a cross."

He held up his own crucifix. In the televised closeup his hand was trembling.

"Terrible, you say? Terrible?"

His voice dropped. "No, my brethren. Only a beginning. Beginnings are never terrible. Beginnings are always only one step, in the name of an ideal, be it the *Führerprinzip* or population control.

"But how easy it is to take the next step. And when Hitler's war came, did not these same humane doctors take off their white coats and put on their uniforms as a patriotic duty? But was it patriotism or duty which motivated the infamous Doctor Mengele to meet each trainload of prisoners at the unloading dock of Auschwitz? The friendly physician, attentive to the needs of the children and the aged. Friendly, smiling. A twist of his thumb, right or left, sent the ablebodied men and women to slave labor, and the children under fourteen and the aged and the sick to the right, where they entered within the hour a purgatory whose flames we feel even now. Childhood braids clipped for mattresses. Dental fillings melted down, some thirty kilograms of gold each day. Their ashes scattered in a fallout which has poisoned us to the marrow more profoundly than the radioactive dust from our mid-century bombs. Our hearts recoil. Our ears close. Who can imagine monstrosities? But the gradual escalation of killing must be clear to us.

"The minds on Tiergarten Strasse 4 which exterminated three thousand children as a humane measure easily became the minds which accepted Auschwitz.

"If you turn your eyes and ears away from this, during this Holy Week, you turn away from a Mother bent over her executed Son across her knees, the Mater Dolorosa in every one of us."

Father Möttl paused and covered his face with one faltering hand. His silence was so prolonged the television cameraman glanced back at the control booth; but the director only sat there, paralyzed.

Father Möttl lowered his hand and said very quietly, almost conversationally, as if to a friend, "My brethren, once again we have been told there must be fewer people. But we have been hearing this for hundreds of years, since Malthus preached his doctrine. Too many people, Malthus said. But Malthus never dreamt that a monk named Mendel would discover the basis of modern genetics, and from the science of genetics would come the scientific production of new foods which now make North American agriculture so bountiful that it can feed not only the entire United States, but also one out of every twenty persons in Africa, Latin America and non-Communist Asia.

"How simple to condemn the unborn millions never to see the light of God's day! How much more difficult—but how close within reach!—lies the answer that once more we must provide moral direction to scientific research. More food can come from better seed strains, chemicals to fight pests and plant diseases, fertilizers, farm machinery, the return of wasteland into productive agriculture. And if agriculture cannot feed us, let us turn to chemistry. Do you remember when our families made their own soap from natural fats? But the soap with which you washed your hands today was almost surely completely synthetic. Remember when agriculture provided natural animal fibers to be cut and spun and woven into our clothes? Today, more than likely it is that you wear clothing made of chemical synthetics. Modern chemistry can pump oil out of Venezuela's Lake Maracaibo and turn it into high-grade edible protein—the protein two out of three of the world's people need.

"There still remains those five-sevenths of the earth's surface covered by the oceans. The ocean beds, my friends, the millions of square miles beneath the sea which lie outside the jurisdiction of any state, contain food resources beyond all human imagination. We have not only the parable of the loaves and fishes to guide us, but the knowledge that fish can be raised, just as we raise sheep and cattle, and that our increasing ability to live below water means we can farm the seaweed, the kelp, the plankton, which, combined, could feed hundreds of millions.

"Instead of destroying births let us bake bread!

"As long ago as ancient pagan Rome, the philosopher Seneca said that 'A hungry people listens not to reason, nor cares for justice, nor is bent by any prayer.' There is the terrible arithmetic which adds up to godlessness and world chaos—one, hunger; two, hopelessness; three, anger. Oh, my brethren—cannot this arithmetic become the one-two-three of reason, justice and prayer? Cannot science offer us more than the shutting off of life?

"Life, my brethren, life is sacred. If you think not, may Heaven help you, for you have taken the first step to join Doctor Josef Mengele on that platform in Auschwitz. The well-educated cultured scientific physician at Auschwitz who flicked his thumb left or right like some omnipotent pagan god, that man was but a child when compared with the new power over human life which is coming out of our laboratories. The techniques for the artificial insemination of pedigreed cattle have now become the accepted techniques for the artificial insemination of women.

"Imagine the spectacle of a nation dreaming of supermen and super-women—capable of removing the fertilized ova from dozens of women and growing them in litters, transporting the embryos elsewhere, trans-planting them, so that finally women would give birth to offspring not their own!

"Fever? Fantasy? Only one generation ago, were not such men as Mengele—slaughter factories such as Auschwitz—dismissed as fantastic nightmares?

"Control over life, my brethren, is the sacred prerogative of God, and God alone! Once the vessel of human life is entered, even in the name of medicine, a human created in the image of God becomes a mere physical thing—and, once it is a *thing*, how many men of power will stand on how many platforms, flicking their thumbs from left to right, telling themselves all the while that they do so in the name of some greater good, some patri-otic duty, some improvement of the race, some materialistic goal in which clipped hair becomes war matériel, dental fillings become gold, and slave labor turns back Caesar's clock two thousand years to Caesar's Jerusalem?

"These are terrible things. I want to forget them just as you want to forget—I beg you to forgive me for this reminder—but what begins as a line of women standing before an abortion clinic can end with an army of women treated as slave resources of some superstate. From the flame of a single burning match to a roaring forest fire is not so far a distance!

"Ponder this, my brethren, this Holy Week as you look up at the Father of us all. As you weep with our Holy Mother. Pray that the scientific im-moralists and anti-moralists will cease and desist in their terrible destruc-tion of human life. Let us mount a new crusade!

"Remember that Our Blessed Lord said 'He that is not with Me is against Me.' Forgiveness, charity—tolerance for our enemies—but a brave intol-erance for the nightmares the men of science bring us in the name of healing. We remember that Herod, in ancient Israel, massacred the inno-cents at Bethlehem—but who remembers that Herod also murdered his own wife? For just such sins, for the sins of all of us, did Our Lord offer up His body this Holy Week so that you and I and every one of us might know the everlasting bliss of Grace and immortality.

"The wicked flee when no one pursueth—but now the time has come for spiritual pursuit and moral action—truly a new crusade!"

23 "WELL," BETSY SAID with the cheery brightness one uses with the sick, "you look very distinguished with that turban bandage over one eye."

"Thanks," Mayoso said. Her bright hard chatter is back, he thought, as if she cannot decide who or what to be. "It's hard to believe you're going home to New Haven."

"I know," Betsy said, "so much has happened."

Mayoso sat up straighter in the hospital bed and fixed his one unbandaged eye on Witt. "Please give my love to your mother and father and to David and his wife."

"Betsy can do that," Witt said. "I'm staying here."

"Now, Witt," Betsy interrupted very quickly, "you promised to turn this experimental farm project over to somebody else as soon as possible."

"I'd fly back to New Haven with you today," Witt said, "but how in the world can I just turn my back on the size of investment we've made in dioscorea plant production?"

"I know. I'm not nagging you about it, dear. I know you have to stay as long as you're needed here."

"By the way," Witt asked, "where's the kid?"

"The kid?"

"Didn't you say there was some medical student who worked in David's lab? Somebody on Easter vacation here who wanted to catch a fast ride home?"

"Oh," Betsy said, "oh yes." A fast ride home, she thought. Roone would appreciate that phrase. "He's waiting for us to pick him up at the hotel." To illustrate Roone's total unimportance, not worth discussing, she said to Mayoso, "You're the one who should be coming back to New Haven with me."

"Thanks, but no, Betsy. You and Witt have already been more than kind."

"You're too big to be shy," Betsy said. "In New Haven we can feed you and fatten you up with something a lot better than hospital food."

"How soon can you get up and move around?" Witt asked. "How soon will your eye heal?"

Mayoso spread his hands. "Soon. Not a day or two, but soon." He did not want to explain to them that his facial injury had left the inner lining of his left eye with a diffuse inflammation called uveitis. The inflammation might or might not become a syndrome ironically called sympathetic uveitis, in which the inflammation progressed to the other eye. This could not be known for several weeks. No one clearly understood why a disease in one eye, following a perforating injury, should sometimes spread to the other eye weeks or months later. Many ophthalmologists, his own eye doctor had told him, practiced preventive enucleation. "If we enucleate the inflamed eye within two weeks after injury," his eye doctor had said, "we completely prevent the disease from spreading or developing in the good eye."

"One glass eye, like a banker?" Mayoso had asked. "A one-eyed surgeon?"

"Better than a blind one," the eye doctor had said. "That's a brutal thing to say, but it's true. Think it over."

Mayoso had been thinking it over. Each day and each night he lay in his hospital bed thinking it over. He had few interruptions, for his friend Tranquilino had stationed himself on a wooden chair beside his door to keep away from him all the curious people who had heard about Father Möttl's television sermon and wanted to see Satan in the flesh.

In the middle of the night he found himself awakening at the slightest sound, turning on his bed lamp to test his good eye for the blurring, or photosensitivity, or tenderness, that would signal the spread of the disease. Patients had often told him they could hardly believe some brutally serious illness had singled them out; now he knew what they meant.

A blind guitarist often played in the open courtyard of the hospital below his window. He had lain flat on the bed, one eye bandaged, listening to the Spanish voice within the instrument, remembering Cristina dancing that night and her ancient reticence, her stoic acceptance of all things human.

That afternoon he told his eye doctor he would gamble. He would not permit his right eye to be removed because, injury or not, no foreign body had been left within it, the inflammation had not spread backward to his retina, and, after so many gambles in one's life, this would be one more. His eye doctor had nodded understandingly, clearly a man who disagreed with that most difficult of patients—another doctor—but was moved by his patient's wishes.

"I had a long talk with David on the phone last night," Witt was saying, "and we both want to offer you a deal. Want to hear it?"

"*Mire,*" Mayoso said, "here it comes. The turn of the screw."

"Both David and I need help, and you've got the knowhow."

"I can't leave the island," Mayoso said. "There's too much left undone."

"Listen to Witt," Betsy said, "and don't be a mule."

"Is that what they teach hospital volunteers now? To talk like that to sick patients?"

They all laughed, and Witt said, "You see how it's all in the family? A family fight even before we begin. You want to hear the deal or don't you?"

"Go ahead, Witt."

"Well, Sommers Pharmaceuticals has a big load of clinical testing of the hormone yield from these dioscorea plants. Some doctor is going to have to run those tests. And David's research is busting out all over. Fantastic stuff—" He checked himself. "Quite good, really."

"Come back to New Haven," Betsy said. "You can stay with us—we'd love to have you, wouldn't we, Witt? To Dad and Mother, well, your coming back to Connecticut would be like the return of the prodigal."

"How generous you all are."

"Generous, hell!" Betsy said. "We're so filthy rich we can do anything we want that's legal!"

"Now listen," Witt said, "how am I going to turn Sommers into a publicly owned corporation if you go around ranting like that?"

"I'll think about it," Mayoso said.

"You won't," Witt said. "I know you, now. You're a tough hombre. Nothing impresses you anymore except some kind of wallop."

Betsy stood up. "Witt!" She went over to Mayoso and kissed him on the side of his face which was not bandaged. "Don't listen to the old meanie."

"He's right," Mayoso said. "A bang on the nose is impressive."

"Sure, I'm right. Santos Roque told me just this morning you're *mucho macho.*"

"So," Mayoso said, "you and the Governor talked about me this morning?"

"Frankly, yes. That speech by Father Möttl over television went off like a bomb. The wire services picked it up. International TV has been running video clips via communication satellites. You're a junior-grade Dr. Mengele from Auschwitz."

"I know, I know," Mayoso said. "But I can lie here in a hospital bed, while Santos Roque has to face the fireworks."

"He asked me to bring you a confidential message."

"A message?"

"Yes. I left it just outside the door with Tranquilino." While he walked out of the room, Mayoso turned his head to look at Betsy, puzzled, but she had swung away with her nervous whippet stride to stand at the window, jabbing a cigarette in her mouth as she stood there, flicking her lighter over and over again. Witt came back into the room carrying a large package wrapped in brown paper.

Mayoso stared at him. "Is this the message?"

"Yes." Witt put the package at the foot of Mayoso's bed very carefully. "It's your chess set."

"No letter? Just the chess set?"

"No letter. Just your chess set."

"That's all? He didn't say something?"

"He said you and he had talked about a five-alarm fire that night during his dinner party. He said you would understand."

Betsy said furiously, "That civilized son of a bitch!"

"No, no, no," Mayoso protested. "What can he do? You have to understand. He needs all the strength he can get for this coming election. A platform he can stand on. I'm like a broken leg." His single eye dropped to the chess set. "When there is too much to say, silence becomes a message, ah?"

"Oh balls! Pardon my French, but Santos Roque's being rotten."

"What's all that supposed to be?" Witt asked. "Celtic French for gee whiz?"

"You know damn well what I mean! Instead of being careful and businesslike, why don't you just say what you know is true? That Santos Roque has thrown out an old friend without a sign of feeling!"

"It's not that way at all, Betts—"

Speaking at the same time as Witt, Mayoso said, "Betsy, you don't understand—"

"You two are the ones who don't understand! You never just let loose on your feelings, do you? Always the long balanced view, the men of measured merriment—"

"Betts—"

"Oh hell, don't be sweet and reasonable now, Witt. You'll make me feel guilty for talking up a great storm—"

"Betts," Witt said patiently, "if you'll just let me get a word in edgewise—"

"Edgewise! Get it in any way you damn please, but get it while it's hot!"

Witt began again. "Betts, when you have a lot of power over people, what they earn, how they live, you have to keep cool every time you get hot."

"Oh," Betsy said, "as long as I draw breath, may God spare me that kind of topsy-turvy power."

"Pretty comfortable," Witt said coldly. "But who's taking care of the store while you're busy being so free, so gallant and so gay?"

Betsy walked toward Mayoso. "Forgive me. Really. I shouldn't be sounding off like this. We came just to say hasta luego, and I swear I won't open me big mush again. And with you just sitting there like some great clunk of a Cyclops and not saying a word."

How tense and stormy she is, Mayoso thought. What's happening to her? "Cyclops' neighbor was a lady named Circe," Mayoso said. "Quite a girl."

"Betts and I didn't mean to get you caught in our domestic meat-grinder," Witt said. "Even I try to keep my big mush out of them."

She talks too fast and Witt talks too slow, Mayoso thought. Maybe that was one of the attractions between them when they first met.

Betsy leaned forward and kissed Mayoso's cheek, bringing him a gossamer expensive scent. "I won't say goodbye, you monster. Witt will be home in a few weeks and I expect to see you marching in our door beside him."

"He will, he will," Witt said. "The epidemic of German measles is just about over—no fooling, don't look at me like that, Mayoso. Front page, this morning. Only one case reported in the last three days. And, if you promise not to squirm while I make the incision, Santos Roque would be perfectly happy to see you take a sabbatical leave until after the election, obviously. And David badly needs an associate in his research." He came around the end of the bed. "We really need your help."

"And," Betsy said, "it'll be spring in New Haven before another week crawls over the garden wall."

"We'll see, we'll see—"

"Don't give me fickle talk. Just say yes and come. Home is where you hang your harp, y'know."

"If I come," Mayoso said with a crooked smile on the unbandaged side of his face, "I'll bring my harp."

The wide door to the hospital room swung open and Father Möttl came in. Conversation broke off; Witt and Betsy and Mayoso stared at him, the sudden intruder whose skin-drawn face framed two live coals, his eyes. He dropped his head in a fleeting formal bob, a kind of bow, and said to Mayoso, "I was paying a last visit to one of my parishioners on the floor below. His family told me you were here."

Mayoso rubbed the stubble of his unshaven chin with the back of his hand, puzzled. "Sí, sí. I'm very much here." He held a hand toward Betsy. "Let me introduce my friends. This is Mrs. Betsy Sommers."

"We have met before," Father Möttl said.

Betsy was surprised. "Have we?"

"Weren't you the lady in the cathedral wearing the Boy Watchers?"

"Boy Watchers?" Witt sounded skeptical.

"Oh, you know, Witt, those silly white plastic things. Father, this is my husband, DeWitt Sommers."

Witt put out his hand, but finessed it downward when Father Möttl said, "I cannot shake hands with you, Señor Sommers. Without the patience of angels, I cannot pretend even common courtesy."

"That Fatima business?" Intuitively, Witt became tactful and business-like. "I believe you and Bishop Sosa misunderstood our use of an old trademark. I've squared it away by agreeing to change the name on all our local packaging. I may not be an ally, Father, but I'm not an enemy."

"Of course." Möttl seemed agreeably surprised by Witt's lack of Yanqui bigshotism. "My own errors are teaching me that none of us are fated to be enemies. Perhaps we are all victims of the same war. Each of us in his own way." His watchfire eyes swiveled to Betsy. "I assume you are Catholic, señora."

"More than that. A whole broth of Irish."

"Ah. A potent combination. I've visited Maynooth, so I distinctly remember a beautiful land, pious as Spain. If your husband and your doctor friend cannot understand me, at least you can."

"Yes. Yes, how well I can. The San Juan television station rebroadcast a video tape of your sermon last night—"

Her off-center tone made Witt step toward her.

"Ah—?" Father Möttl had caught the aroused tone in her words.

"—and watching you, Father," Betsy said, mounting fluently, "I remembered how troubled and bullied Catholic women are. How lost in mythology you are that you can tell women how to live and die like medieval martyrs."

"Betsy!" Her outburst amazed Witt. Buttonhole a priest so bluntly?

"No!" she flashed. "Look at Mayoso. Look at all that's happened. I knocked against a childhood filled with that whole bill of goods—Father Knows Best. The whole swindle that God gave men dominion over women."

Father Möttl suppressed an imperceptible avenging smile, making it clear that he pardoned her rancor and that he would not descend to hand-to-hand combat. "Señora, our Lord depended on His Mother for His birth. Mary presented him at the Temple for the prediction of the Cross, and announced his public life at the marriage feast of Cana. Without her Immaculate Heart we would not have his Sacred Heart. In Christ, there is no more male and female, but we are all one person."

"Ah, that familiar theological hairsplitting—"

Möttl's bony face sharpened. "Hairsplitting? If you were knit closer to the faith, señora, you would recall the reminders that happiness requires twoness, never oneness. Surely as"—his penetrating eyes caught her change in expression, the salt in her wound—"as a loving wife and mother you must know that." The pain in her face was so apparent that he lifted one hand apologetically and said, "But forgive me; I don't mean to remind you of catechism." He glanced at Mayoso. "I came to—"

"Heal the sick?" asked Mayoso with muffled anger. "Raise the dead? Cast out devils?"

"Our company plane is standing by, waiting," Witt said.

"And we still have another passenger to pick up. We'll be running along."

"Please—" Möttl started to say.

"We were just leaving when you came in." She gave Mayoso a feathery brush of a kiss. "Don't go hiding yourself away again in that hilltop bohío. With jets, we're only a buzz or two away."

"And we'd better start buzzing," Witt said. "Pronto."

Betsy made a little kiss in the air before her, and answered Mayoso's brief wave with one of her own, then she and Witt left without speaking to Father Möttl.

The priest's eyes followed them until the door closed. "Mrs. Sommers is a troubled person," he said to Mayoso.

Mayoso's eye held him. "Victims," Mayoso said, "of the same war. Each in his own way. Close quote."

"But I meant that sincerely, Doctor."

Mayoso's eye glared. "You mean everything sincerely. Every zealot, every fanatic, is sincere. You drive your sincerity over people's lives like a bulldozer."

Möttl held his hand out to indicate Mayoso's bandaged face. "I never intended injury to you."

"You called for a crusade."

"A moral crusade, not physical violence." In a voice just above a whisper, Möttl asked, "Is it true that your left eye is blinded?"

"No. Injured."

"Will it heal?"

"Only God knows," Mayoso said. "But as usual, He isn't telling anyone."

"I'll pray that your sight is restored." His fervent voice dropped again. "I feel responsible."

"The eye injury was Cuban political gangsterism, not religious conflict."

"Truly?"

"It's a fact in police records. So spare yourself this one guilt."

"You're generous to tell me so."

"Don't credit me with being generous. I wish you were a fool or a faker instead of a man with a deadly combination of intelligence, Hispanic otherworldliness, *a más no poder,* and absolute unselfquestioning sincerity. Men such as you must have brought hemlock to Socrates."

"You may be a pagan, Doctor, but you are not Socrates. I may be blinded by sincere zeal, but I did not come to bring you hemlock."

"Of course not. I've already been knocked out of battle. I've been told as much as to get off this island."

Möttl nodded as if he were comparing notes. "The same for me. I have been told to expect a transfer to Rome."

"Congratulations. Proof of your accomplishment."

"Yes. To everyone but me. To me, proof of defeat. You see how close our positions are?"

"Your reasoning, Father, is too complicated for me. When you finished with the holy Viaticum downstairs, you came up to see me just to tell me our positions are close? What next—you'll defy gravity?"

"I came," Möttl said, "for many reasons." He passed his hand absently across his face as if his eye, not Mayoso's, were bandaged. "I came because of what has happened to you."

"No," Mayoso said quietly. "You came because something has happened to you."

The hollows in Möttl's cheeks deepened. "Yes. Yes, now that I hear it said, yes, that's true. All my life I have fought against the temptation of despair. I always felt confident that I could pass on to men and women the passion of God through the sacraments. Now, this Holy Week, I find myself not capable of making an act of contrition. In the face of death downstairs, it came to me like a sign and a wonder: that just as you are a physician, half blinded, I am a metaphysician, half paralyzed. Instead of peace and gentleness, I am tormented by self-doubts and haunted by memory."

"Ah, memory. Puts iron in a man's soul, I know."

"You must feel as isolated as I do," Möttl said.

"That's a strange thing to say. We're opposites."

"No, we are both strangers in our own country."

Mayoso's single eye measured Möttl carefully. "What happened? Some crack-up? What memory haunts you? What did you come to tell me?"

"Tell you? No, *ask* you. I came to ask you for forgiveness."

"But I am only a physician, not a metaphysician."

"But you have hope."

"Yes." Mayoso gestured toward the chair beside his bed. "Sit down. You're wobbling."

"Thank you, no. I would rather stand."

"Does suffering mean so much to you?"

"Yes. I'm not an especially good Franciscan, and I reach for union with the agony of Christ."

"If you're without hope, you'll find what you're looking for. Human isolation can be as bad as the crucifixion of Saint Peter."

"He was crucified upside down."

Mayoso looked at Möttl's shadowed face, the sharp ascetic cheekbones, the driven eyes. "Pick up your victory. Go to Rome. For you, Rome will be better than some remote Spanish noplace. Faith is made in Rome and believed elsewhere."

"You say that so harshly."

"No, philosophically. Every Roman alley has a secret Spanish name: Street of Disillusion. Walk around. You'll learn something about a position which you delude yourself is close to mine."

"For me, Rome—not Paris—is the world's city of lights."

"Then Rome will never show you the Italian darkness. As a guardian of the deposit of faith, you can ignore the fact that for every one of almost a million Italians born each year there is another aborted secretly, because not even therapeutic abortions are permitted in Italy. Your favorite target, the doctor-killer, won't be as convenient a target, because every Saturday night about ten thousand women pick up a knitting needle, a crochet hook, a tire gauge, a pencil, or the handle of a wooden cooking spoon and go through all the wretchedness and agony of unwanted motherhood."

"How do I know that's the truth?"

"You don't. But investigate. All of Europe will listen to you on television when you preach that Saturday night is not only the night of love, the night when women's bodies—which you teach are the temple of the Holy Ghost—are treated as often as not like looted liquor stores. You think of Sunday morning as church time, a time for Mass, don't you? You blind yourself against the ten thousand Italian women who wait for Saturday night to attack themselves inside because the next day is Sunday, and somebody else will be at home to take care of the other children while they go to the hospital for antibiotics and blood transfusions and a little surgery. Or, maybe, an autopsy, because five hundred women out of every ten thousand do not live through Sunday. You can sit there in your Roman confession box—Betsy Sommers was right—teaching women submission. You can nail yourself to your own private cross if you want to, but do you know how many millions more you are crucifying alongside you?"

Father Möttl clasped his hands together so tightly his fingers whitened as he raised them to strike the center of his forehead. "Enough," he said. "The depths and mysteries of faith are beyond you."

"Oh, no, it's my turn to sermonize now. A hundred years ago, men like you, men of all religions just like you, attacked doctors for using anesthesia for women in childbirth. God meant women to bring forth life in pain, they said, and then went home to Sunday dinner. People fought inoculation against disease because doctors were interfering with nature. They're still fighting, some of them, against the giving of blood transfusions. You can tell the Italians need to catch up. Maybe they began modern medicine in Padua and Salerno five hundred years ago, no? But they still treat their biggest problem, too many people, as a medieval one with a Machiavellian form of hushed-up mass murder."

"Mass murder—" Möttl's knotted fingers were pressed against his lips so hard that Mayoso could barely make out what he said. "We both use the same word."

"You accused me publicly," Mayoso said. "I'm accusing you privately. That's why the victory is yours."

"Mass murder . . ." Möttl dropped his chin almost to his chest and closed his eyes. "That's what I thought of last night as we drove up that dark country road to your bohío. A pillar of fire by night, a cloud of smoke by day."

Mayoso stiffened. "*Qué más?* My bohío. What are you talking about?"

Father Möttl raised his head. "They burned your house, your library. They burned your bohío to the ground last night."

"My bohío? All my books—?"

"I was told about it too late. My driver hurried, but we were lost twice on the country roads. I got there too late."

"It must have been planned. Religious vigilantes—*bandidos. Canaille.*"

"Even your pets, the bird and the monkey, killed."

"Both of them?"

"Yes, I got there too late. Believe me, I tried. I tried to save some of your books, but the unseasonable wind kept spreading the fire." Astonished, Möttl watched Mayoso force himself back against the metal bedstead, his big chest rocking with a silent painful charade of unweeping laughter.

"Aie, aie," Mayoso managed to say, as he pressed both hands over his eye bandage, "this stupid jiggling is bad for my eye." With his head back, his neck corded, speaking into the hollow of his hands, he said, "When they came to Freud in London and told him the Nazis had burned his library, he said: We're making progress. A few hundred years back they would have burned me."

A sign, Möttl thought. His mentioning the Nazis. How similar our thoughts are! When I saw those flames last night, the bodies of Mayoso's pets thrown into them, I remembered the crematorium chimneys of Auschwitz, pillars of fire all night, clouds of human smoke all day. Even the gusts of air blowing stinking ashes reminded me of the stench in the wind coming across those Volhynian steppes.

"What a weird joke," Mayoso was saying, "that your television sermon compared me with the Nazis."

"Let me explain that—"

"Don't bother. I think you ought to go."

"No, please—"

"We've said enough. We're both hanging upside down. We both contradict ourselves. I have hope, but in Caracas I had a vision of an apocalypse, the world burning down with hunger riots. And you say you're haunted by torments, yet you dream messianic visions of God's kingdom on earth."

"Oh my friend, my friend!" Father Möttl twisted his hands. "If only you could see as clearly as I do where your distorted idealism leads to!"

"Spare me from your evangelism and pulpit authority—"

"No pulpit, believe me! I know. I *know!* There are physicians in Germany today who participated in Action T-4. In the name of Nazi idealism they destroyed retarded children. And all the while believing in their *Menschlichkeit!*"

"What does that mean?"

"Their humaneness."

Mayoso saw again in his mind Señora Dolores Valdez sitting beside him in the airplane flying to Caracas. *My confessor,* she had said, *he was raised in Spain but he's German.* "You were born in Germany, Father. Isn't that right?"

"Yes! Believe me, I know what I'm talking about. I remember things from my childhood during the war—" He stopped and grasped the knotted cord hanging at his side, trying to control himself. I've carried this secret darkness since then, he thought. From my secret sins cleanse me, O Lord, and from those of others spare Thy servant. If they shall have no dominion over me, then I shall be without spot, and I shall be cleansed from the greatest sin. Aloud he said, "How often I remember the lament from Ecclesiasticus, 'The children will complain of an ungodly father, because for his sake they are in reproach.'"

"But you were only a child—"

"What I remember from my childhood, and what I learned later, those things I cannot separate in my mind. Give us the child until he is six. The Jesuits discovered that."

"How old were you when you moved from Germany to Spain?"

"About twelve." Möttl began to pace back and forth, talking excitedly, a hemorrhage of words.

A small German boy with not a word of Spanish coming for his first day into the whitewashed schoolroom filled with watching faces of unfamiliar children, the long dusty mile down the rutted road from home to the town church where he had learned to pray with the other children: *Infundan en nosotros, o Señor Jesús, tus Santos Misterios un fervor divino.* Their Spanish sibilants blending together, so different from the glottal German his father and mother still spoke at home, a language which made him feel helpless and small in the dark lying on his narrow cot while they argued in the next room. Later, Latin had come to mean size and stature through its enduring words, while his parents' language brought back only his childhood bedroom in Birkenau, a room dimmed by a thick cloud of smoke each day and by night filled with a frightening glow from flames shooting so high out of the red brick chimney of Krema No. 1 that even the lightning rods fastened to the bricks were bent crooked by the never-ending heat. The wonderment, to a young boy, of deluxe civilian cars, during a war, painted with the symbol of the International Red Cross to disguise the delivery of cans of Zyklon B gas to the four Kremas. Spain had not existed for that small boy then, and Spain and that barbed-wire camp were connected only years later, when he was a seminary student and learned of the forty thousand Spanish refugees from Franco who had been rounded up in France and sent to work in the Nazi quarries to build Mathausen where they went down into darkness—this at a time when at his home there were always Dutch chocolates, Danish hams, and bottles of Polish cumin brandy for the visiting Oberscharführer.

The Ukrainian servant who spent each evening polishing his father's soft high boots with Glissando while listening to the Grossdeutscher Rundfunk. Not until his seminary days in Spain had he woven together the many separate threads. He had learned *for a father's good repute or ill, a son must go proudly or hang his head.*

"You would be surprised what a twelve-year-old boy remembers," Möttl said. "The personal equation between a man's suffering and the sufferance of Christ belong in the confessional, but an Israeli general visiting here, a man said to have been recently in Spain, and the sight of your burning library, force me to confess this—"

"Not to me," Mayoso said. "I remember enough of my Catholic upbringing to know that confession is concerned with wrong intentions and sinful deeds. A boy of twelve—"

"Ha, Mayoso, I'm talking about good intentions and idealistic deeds. Sincerity, you called it. A boy's invincible mythological heroes, Siegfried and Barbarossa. My heroic father suffered shame because he believed his country had been betrayed at Versailles. In his boyhood he had been taught *Nie wieder Krieg*. Never again war."

"You are not your father," Mayoso said.

"Yes," Möttl answered quickly, "but in the prelude to Easter, Jesus said to Annas: the Father and I are One. And how many times I have scanned Ecclesiasticus: 'The children will complain of an ungodly father, because for his sake they are in reproach.' "

"Don't expect me to match your Biblical exercises—"

"You prefer your own guidelines, Doctor Mayoso? That a mass murder of infants is the last Final Solution?"

"Now listen to me, Father. Let's settle this difference between your ancient idea that an embryo is human and my knowledge of modern embryology."

"My telling you of the Third Reich—that's how modern is my ancient theology. Even in the fourth century Saint Basil was faced with arguments like yours about formed and unformed life. Today, just as in the time of Augustine and Aquinas, the living process of *becoming* human means that your curette blade kills a life."

"Let me tell you something. I'm reluctant to do therapeutic abortions. Surgery is a confession of failure of preventive medicine, just as the surgical removal of a peptic ulcer is the failure of medicine to have prevented it from forming in the first place. There is no mass murder, because as much as I respect the idea that a sperm fertilizing an ovum carries the greatest mysteries of life, I refuse to consider that combination of cells as a human being."

"You believe that—sincerely—do you, Doctor Mayoso?"

"Of course I do."

"Then you can understand how a modern German doctor who served with the Spanish Blue Division in the first Russian winter fighting of Sychevka, a man who saw his own men die with frostbitten bare feet inside summer boots—ah, he knew what suffering was!—this man who perhaps believed that a breakthrough discovery of some new pain-relieving drug could mean promotion to Obersturmbannführer and rotation back home. So he believed logically and patriotically he could try out a new drug, like S.E.E., by immediate testing on live prisoners. Women's legs cracked open in the name of experimental surgery, prisoner-doctors spared so they could help with the dissecting and autopsies, always with professional pride in doing good work regardless of hairsplitting moral complications. After all, Zyklon A gas was manufactured by I. G. Farben as a disinfectant, but Zyklon B—a minor alphabetical difference?—was classified *geheimmittel* to keep the secret of assembly-line exterminations."

"Aie, to open again the barbaric wound of the century?"

"Yes, because all my life I have shrunk from this as you shrink now! I wanted to pour all this out to my own bishop, but my tongue froze! But the violence and the burning have melted it. When I read of Spanish police making a bloody attack on a protest march of priests in Barcelona, the wheel of history has turned full circle. This is Lent, very soon the Passion. What better time to remember?"

To remember a skinny boy of twelve standing in the *Blockführerstube*, waiting while the sergeant went to telephone someone. Over there, only a hundred yards away, beyond the electrified fence and the barbed wire, he watched hundreds of boys like himself lined up in the January snow. Shivering, on command they had stripped themselves naked. Many were weeping and helping one another as they were whipped up steps into open military trucks, packed together, skeletal, shaven-headed, while women beyond the next line of barbed wire crowded to watch in dumb horror as the trucks ground over the frozen slush toward the tall red brick chimneys of the crematorium. The young children shook with terror, but the older boys cried out their names to the watching women, to the icy world of January air, their mothers' names, so that word might reach some woman someplace, some slave of the Teutons who would bend down in mute agony at what men had done to her son.

Mayoso could say nothing. Möttl spoke to the glass window, staring outside, reliving it. When he turned back into the room his eyes were wet. "Am I to keep silent? Or do I speak during Holy Week? Stand up and speak as Bishop Galen spoke up in Münster? Or Father Maximilian spoke up in Auschwitz? There is a German proverb that the devil lives in details. Each historical detail is one more rung on the ladder down to Hell, and you must be convinced the ladder begins with the first step!"

"I'm beginning to understand you," Mayoso said. "I see how all this is mixed together in your mind."

"You understand? When I heard about the women lined up outside your clinic—"

"I understand. There's no need to torture yourself now. I know very well how memories of childhood—sisters, brothers, mother—"

"Not my mother. During the war, she ate the liver sausage, the delicacies, legs of pork in aspic, jellied eels, the chocolate and biscuits, like a Michaelmas fair—special food available only to Nazi Party *Bonzen* when others were starving—but never did she lift one hand against another. Later, in Spain, she worked her knuckles to the bone to make a home for us. Our family quarters were behind an export firm that was really a front for the underground S.S. escape station on the route to Madrid."

"And now you sound more completely Spanish than a Spaniard."

"Spain saved my life by making me over into a Spaniard. How can I keep silent while in our own holy Catholic Spain even *los grises*—the security police—turn their backs when the ex-S.S. men set up an underground escape route through Madrid to Latin America? An ex-S.S. doctor who thinks an Israeli team is on his trail because he was a member of the Eichmann Kommando only has to contact the nearest underground post, usually a travel agency or an export-import firm. The Organisation der S.S. Angehöriger takes over. The name means the S.S. Family, but the code name is ODESSA. The money comes from concentration-camp gold, now banked in Switzerland. And the ex-S.S. scientists, every *Todesvogel*, every ex-bird of death, running for his life, disappears across borders until he reaches Copacabana Beach in Rio. Or the Mar del Plata of the Argentine, or Gezirah Club in Cairo." With ferocity he added, "The same money paid for a fine gold chalice, the traditional gift to a newly ordained priest. I—I threw it at my father's feet."

"All this time you've been talking"—he saw Möttl cringe—"about your own father?"

Father Möttl could hardly speak. "He . . . writes me . . . begging letters from Spain. Save him from Israeli agents." Möttl flung his hanging sleeve upward across his face, sobbing. "*In Nomine Dei* . . . an Auschwitz physician . . . Oberstarzt Ludwig Billroth Möttl. My father."

Mayoso raised one hand as if to touch the priest in a communion of pity, but in his mind he thought, *El que se mete a Rendentor sale crucificado.* He who plays the Redeemer ends up crucified.

24

"BETTS," Witt said as their taxi maneuvered into the bumper-to-bumper traffic stream, "if you don't mind my saying so—"

"I do. I do mind your saying so. I know every word you're going to say. As usual, my fault, my most grievous fault."

"Hell, Betts, no fault. But Mayoso's battles—you can't fight those for him."

"If he ever needed friends—"

"Sure, but don't put yourself into his skin. You see this scar on my scalp from the Korea days?—well, Mayoso's got scars like this all over him. Inside and outside. We're members of the new invisible Foreign Legion, guys who served time in military or political prison camps and survived. We didn't have a faith like Catholicism or Communism for a life raft, so we had to sink or swim alone. You get to know the bottom of the barrel very intimately that way." He stopped short, and absentmindedly scratched the side of his head where the scar was. "So don't worry about Mayoso. He'll survive."

"But Witt, to see a big man like that bundled into a dinky hospital bed —and then that Roman candle sizzling in like a firecracker—"

"Betts, you took off on a skyrocket of your own. Actually, you just sounded sore about things in your own life."

"Did I? Was I really so self-centered?"

He put his hand over hers. "I didn't like your making a fuss, Betts, but I admired your frankness. I don't very often hear you saying what you really think."

"Well, that's what I thought." He weakens me when he's thoughtful and understanding this way. It's easier for me when he wears his public corporate face and uses business lingo. She turned to him impulsively. "Oh, Witt, why do you have to pretend you're a hardheaded executive every time you do something generous?"

"Because I don't trust charity. It implies one is strong and the other is weak. Mayoso would be doing David a favor by teaming up with him in New Haven, as well as the other way around. Couldn't you see by his face that he knows it's a good idea for him to get off the island? Leave the rest to me, okay?"

"Okay okay okay—"

"Betts, you sound wound up as a clock—"

"I do? Maybe you even know what makes me tick?"

"To hell with that. What makes you chime?"

For the first time that morning she felt assured enough to laugh, cheered by the look of relief which crossed Witt's eyes, and pleased that she was able to steady her jitters about Witt meeting Roone.

The taxi ground in low gear over cobblestone streets, snaking through traffic thicker than they had ever seen. Black flags and streamers seemed to be everywhere. Many of the cars, including their own taxi, flew black ribbons from their radio aerials. On both sides of the street, windows and doorways were hung with black crepe. The sidewalks were jammed with clusters of families, many dressed all in black, congregating in tribal groups moving toward the cathedral.

Two blocks from Roone's hotel, their driver spotted a space marked NO PARKING and angled into it so sharply that his wheels rode up on the curb. "Wait for you here," he said to Witt. "Okay?"

"But the hotel's down there."

"Señor, see all this people? So many, no? Who can go? The hotel is on the calle from the cathedral to the Iglesia de San José." As if explaining why he had stopped so far from the hotel he added in a guidebook sing-song, "Oldes' church—*la más antigua*—in the New World, señor, señora. Statue of Ponce de León, melted down from cannons, statue *metálico*."

"Maybe we need a cannon to shoot us out to the airport," Witt said. "We've got a plane waiting to take off."

The driver made a face of resignation, then surrender. "Not possible, señor. To make war on a religious procession? We fry in hell, no? And your plane is private"—his mouth widened upward into a melon slice—"so it will not leave before the boss come, no?"

"No," Witt said. He got out of the car, saying over his shoulder, "Wait here, Betts. I'll squeeze my way down."

"Take it easy, dear. When delay is inevitable, relax and enjoy it"—she imitated the universal inflection—"no?" She slid across the seat, holding her narrow skirt expertly so that she could swing her legs out after him.

"Where are you going, Betts?"

"With you. You've never met the boy, and I have. Somebody has to recognize him." She shook his elbow indulgently. "Relax, señor. A private plane. They don't take off without the boss."

They let the mass of people press them forward, working their way gradually toward the hotel. From the opposite direction, coming down the slope from Plaza de San José, the leading host of a Lenten procession was shuffling this way to the slow sepulchral rattattoo of a drum corps.

Betsy and Witt wormed their way carefully through the spectators crowded on the hotel steps; then, in the lobby, Betsy spotted Roone near the mail desk, talking with Tabac and Volga. She could see that Volga kept interrupting, and, with each phrase, tugging Roone's tie downward as if it were a pull chain which turned him on or off.

Preferably off, she thought. They mustn't meet Witt. I couldn't swing that, she thought, feeling her mouth get dry. The way-out jive talk they use, their secret passwords to thumb noses at the world, and Volga sure to ask some bitchy question about Roone or the beach picnic or some equally captivating bedtime story. Desperately, she stood on tiptoe and tried to call above the heads of the people pressing around her, "Roone!" When his head turned, she waved her arm.

Nearby, Witt asked, "Is that the boy?"

"Yes." Mad about the boy. An out-of-date song by no-no-Noel Coward. With relief, Betsy saw Roone wave back, turn to shake hands with Tabac, then lean toward Volga, probably saying goodbye in some out-of-sight unmentionable way. Young beast, she thought.

On Calle Cristo the processional drumbeat was closer now. Murmurs rippled through the throng as two lengthy religious floats came closer, borne aloft by human centipedes of stevedore bearers, all members of *cofradías,* religious brotherhoods. The first *paso,* mounted in the center of the float and surrounded by flowers, was a lifesize figure of Christ crucified so realistically that blood seemed to stream from his forehead and hands and feet. As if God walked alive through their midst, people on both sides of the moving statue knelt and crossed themselves. The figure swayed and tilted slightly; the *costaleros'* disembodied legs and feet had halted. On cue—"Unnh-ah!"—the men underneath the canopy of the float hefted their traditional burden to the opposite shoulder, and the statue leveled.

Roone had edged himself into the cramped space beside Witt. As the crowd crushed into the arm's-length space separating them, Betsy watched, crumbling, while Witt introduced himself in an artificially hearty older-man's way. "I see you haven't wasted any time making friends on the island."

"Well, sir—" Roone's courteous bit, deference verging on softsoap— "just getting the lay of the land."

Roone's deadpan eyes nudged her across the people surrounding them, his sign language with the trace of ridicule she knew so well. Our immediate bridge of intangibles, though boxed apart in this noise; only yesterday the silences between our echo soundings, sailing that cushioned broadbeamed bed. Her inward eye saw herself stretched out so clearly that she was startled by an unexpected voice behind her shoulder: "Mrs. Sommers?"

The Israeli general, Moshe Edin, smiling beneath the handlebar brushwork of his blond military mustache. "I've been admiring your profile instead of the procession," he said matter-of-factly, without flattery.

"Mmm," she said, shifting her attention away from Roone, unable to keep the annoyance out of her voice. "I know. Wedgwood."

"No. Goya."

She recognized the joke—not only that a Spanish painter was appropriate to everything around them, but also, from her Chicago days, the recollection that "goya" was the Yiddish word for a Gentile woman. Humorists, she thought. I'm surrounded by humorists this morning. Two can play this game. She cupped her hand over her mouth and stage-whispered, "What's a nice Israeli boy like you doing in a joint like this?"

The fanned-out lines around his eyes puckered. He motioned toward the procession. "This only dramatizes a nice Israeli boy entering Jerusalem. But I actually live there."

"Touché." Maybe if I concentrate on him, instead of breaking my neck trying to hear any ruckus Roone might kick up with Witt, I'll manage to survive.

A trumpet sounded. Beneath the platform of the Faith, the *costaleros* rubbed their dripping faces with their handkerchief sweatbands, and braced their shoulders penitentially; the many-legged *cofradía* shuffled forward to the drumbeat again. Now Betsy saw that the drums were draped in black, a black cloth shrouded the base of the Cross, and Judas, crouched and evil behind the Cross, wore a black cloak. A barefoot priest followed the elevated platform, a four-cornered canopy held aloft over him, its maroon velvet and gold tasseled fringes crisscrossed by more black bunting.

"Odd," General Edin said beside her. "Everyone's flying black flags. Unusual. I rather suppose it's some sort of *protesta*."

Directly in front of them a woman clasped her hands, praying brokenly in Spanish, and went down on her knees. Throughout the crowd, other women knelt, bowing their heads, and soon men began to join them.

"What's happening?" Betsy whispered to the General.

"Women are saying what unbearable agony, what terrible pain." He motioned his head toward the second platform on which was mounted a lifesize statue of Mary, Our Lady of Bitter Sorrow. A length of black monk's cloth had been drawn around her like a tent, covering her gold-embroidered blue velvet robe and its intricately jeweled designs. "Amazing," General Edin murmured. "I've seen many *pasos*, but never anything like this. Not in black."

He turned to a dignified white-haired man beside him and began to question the man in a low voice.

Into Betsy's view, behind the tall float of the Virgin Mary, marched a double file of children. They were all girls, very young, no more than three or four, so small that they had been hidden from sight until they were almost opposite her. Except for a few little girls in the black habit of the Sisters of Saint Joseph, they were dressed entirely in white, as if ready for Communion; and, as she had once seen in Italy, each child wore half-opened white gauze angel wings. With an eerie somberness, each carried a small black box, narrow as a miniature coffin. Betsy's skin prickled; the macabre effect was funereal. Her mother's pine plank casket surfaced, dug up by reverie, then lowered itself into the grave of better-to-forget.

Again the trumpet sounded briefly, the procession halted. An old man groaned, "The wounded heart of María Purísima. To suffer so." Another man, stronger, saying, "Espléndido!" as he applauded softly, almost soundlessly, the aesthetic pinnacle of portraying death.

Gunfire crackled from the second-story balconies of the houses overlooking the *paso* of Christ and Judas. Betsy jumped and grasped General Edin's arm. Caracas revolution, *here*? Here? Edin turned away from the man he was questioning. "Blanks," he said. The crackle of gunfire was

irregular now, but across the street, a young boy on an elaborately carved
balcony aimed a submachinegun and fired downward in short unwavering
bursts. Her throat tightened. The angelic little girls in purest white carrying toy black coffins, and now this kindergarten marksman with a toy
machinegun?

"Blanks. My dear lady, don't be frightened. They kill Judas every year
this way. Each kills his own personal Judas. We all have one, you know.
But this year's Judas is different. This year more people may have more
venial and mortal sins they want to dump on his head." He raised his voice
slightly as the gunfire volume doubled and people in the crowd cheered
wildly. "This year, the dignified chap just informed me, Judas is a doctor."

"A *doctor?*"

"Yes. Some sort of a crusade against abortions on the island. Like ancient Jerusalem, a massacre of the innocents."

"The black—"

"And the shoebox coffins carried by the little future mothers." He took
her arm as she closed her eyes. "Easy does it, Mrs. Sommers. Suffering is
always realistic among Latin people, always has been. That statue of Cristo
de la Expiración, Christ Expiring, that's about as close to real bleeding
as can be."

Bleeding, she thought behind her eyelids. Mayoso.

She heard General Edin murmur, and opened her eyes. What now?

From around the corner had come a new *cofradía,* each penitent carrying a tall lighted candle and robed in black to the ground, all shoulder
to shoulder, an inquisitorial phalanx grotesquely reminiscent of darker
ages; each wore a three-foot pointed hood which entirely masked his face
except for the two round staring holes tunneling into unblinking wounded
black eyes. The white-haired man beside General Edin spoke very quietly
to him, then General Edin said close to Betsy's ear, "The Opus Dei—
bloody scary, what?"

Their masked anonymity, their threatening hooded concealment; the
expiatory gunshots at Judas; the dead march of little angels carrying toy
coffins to a funereal drumbeat; the bowed and weeping women crying out
almost hysterically to the Holy Cross; a hundred resonances from her own
girlhood making of good confessions, the white world of Communion; the
vein of fear that Roone's voice might say something outrageous to Witt;
Mayoso bigger than life with his great shoulders immobilized against the
bed, his lion's head in that tragicomic slanted turban of bandages while
contemplating the possibility of blindness with his remaining eye. And the
humid crowd compression, the weight of sun, the heat shimmering in back
of her eyes . . .

To faint is ridiculous. Damn you, she told herself fiercely, pull up your damn ladyjane socks and fly right. Hear? But her heart had stopped, breathing was impossible, tiny shivers of tension ran through her legs. She wanted to throw open her arms to them all, the tiny girls in white, the boy with the machinegun, the Israeli general who really lived in Jerusalem; and to Witt, Witt who listened patiently and spoke patiently and angered her so much because he never became angry enough to make her feel comfortable when she struck out at him.

When a woman several steps in front of her threw out begging hands toward the statue of Mary crying "Madre del Perpetuo Socorro!" Betsy clasped her hands so tightly that her rings bit into her flesh.

If I close my eyes long enough I can open them in New Haven. I'm glad to leave all this bizarre worship of dying in the midst of the sun-drenched greens, blues, palm fronds, *reinitas*, church bells, blue cobblestones four hundred years old, guitars, pig roasts, Hispanic manners smooth as patent leather, the whole picturesque travel-poster rumba-rhythm colorfulness that covers the squalor and misery of a woman begging at the kitchen door of a Caracas hotel, and a medieval sin sense more skeletal than any maiden aunt wrapped in rosary beads and paisley shawls creeping up the stony path of Saint Patrick's on skinned bleeding knees.

Jorí came in with a gold-tooled leather portfolio which he unfolded on the Governor's desk. Santos Roque was lost in thought, listening to the crowd noises pulsing through the open windows of La Fortaleza. In his line of sight were two highbacked regal chairs, but, between them, no chess set stood on the game table.

Jorí straightened; he recognized these moods but said tentatively, "Ramey Base telephoned, Governor."

To exile Mayoso, Santos Roque thought. Aie, what bitterness.

"They'll have your jet ready about 1830."

Santos Roque was not listening. The eruption of funeral drapery decided for me, he thought. *Una protesta*, like a political black plague infecting the streets.

"The Resident Commissioner will meet you. A helicopter will take you directly to the White House grounds. Señora Marjorie Sommers will meet you in the East Room. The Pablo Casals musicale for the new Mexican Ambassador will begin about 2130."

Santos Roque lifted his head. "Jorí, Jorí, what's all this military precision? We'll never be on time with this windy loco weather."

"Governor, Ramey Base Weather says the storm center has veered away from us. Toward Cuba, the way Hurricane Betsy did."

"They're up to the C's now, aren't they? Hurricane Castro or Cuba should be the name with this change in direction."

"Governor," Jorí said unsmilingly, "weather regulations use only feminine names. This one is Hurricane Carmen." Why was the Governor staring at the empty chess table? "Governor, in five minutes you're scheduled for a swearing-in ceremony."

Through the sunlit murmurous distance came a wave of human ululation from Calle Cristo. The Governor rested both hands on his freighted desk, then pushed himself upward to his feet. "Don't hurry me, Jorí, I'm feeling my age this morning."

The semicircle of flags of all the Latin American nations in the Organization of American States rippled and snapped in the wind flurries sweeping across San Juan's International Airport.

From the front seat of the taxi, Roone said, "Three hours. We could have made better time by walking."

The driver beside him shook his head. "On a day like today, señor, three hours is like—" and he snapped his fingers. "I'm not so religious. But when you see that Padre Möttl on TV you know that faith is a good thing for people."

"You have faith," Witt said, not quite making a question of it.

The driver glanced back shrewdly. "Oh no, señor." He took one hand off the steering wheel and used it to tap the left side of his chest. "The Spanish heart is very complicated, sabe?"

Men, Betsy thought, always convinced that any taxi driver is vox populi. Witt should know better.

She had strained to measure each nuance as Witt and Roone chatted all the way to the airport, until, finally, she was reassured that Witt sounded exactly like a busy company executive with a great many problems on his mind making polite conversation with a clean-cut intelligent medical student who did some kind of research with his brother.

On the airport highway, Roone had said to Witt, using his shy-sounding all-American-boy voice, "Your brother, Mr. Sommers, is the most dedicated doctor I've worked with in the hospital."

"Is he? I've always liked my brother, but somehow I never thought of him as being dedicated. The word usually means bright people working for coolie wages, the way I've heard it."

"I appreciate your letting me hitchhike home on your plane, Mr. Sommers," Roone said. "Flying airplane steerage class is strictly for birds."

"No trouble at all, Mr. Roone. I'm sure that Doctor Sommers will be happy to have you back at work in the lab on time. When you graduate, will you go on with your research with my brother?"

"No, sir. Internship first."

"Oh? In New Haven?"

"I'm not quite sure yet," Roone said carefully.

A lie, Betsy thought. The National Intern Matching Program ended last month. He knows he's going to Los Angeles, but he won't say.

Roone twisted himself in his seat and gave Witt his ingratiating boyish grin. "But I plan to stay in obstetrics and gynecology. I've even got my sign painted: PHONE OUR OFFICE ANY HOUR. WE DELIVER."

"You stole that from my brother."

"Well, the obstetricians have to know all the jokes. There's even one universal prescription."

"I'll bite only because my company makes a living from doctors' prescriptions. What is it?"

"Take each night before retiring, shake well before using, and stay out of bed for a week."

Man-to-man laughter, the three of them. Oh Witt, she thought, can't you see this is his way of making fun of you? I was proud of you when you stood up against me and said I was wrong. Angry-sounding or not, I was proud of you for fighting back. With a rush of protectiveness, she thought: Don't let this boy trip you up. Don't let that respectful *sir* bit fool you for a minute. She slid her hand under Witt's elbow and tightened it in a small embrace. He glanced at her, surprised and disarmed, immediately appeased about her going home without him.

But when the taxi stopped and he hitched himself forward to reach for his wallet, Betsy caught Roone watching her between his long half-closed eyelashes, his *love that skin you're in* look. An instant sensation warmed the skin of her thighs, his entrances and exits.

Call us any time. We deliver.

If I close my eyes long enough, she told herself again, I can open them back home in New Haven.

BOOK VI

CONNECTICUT:
Come All Ye Fair
and Tender Ladies

25 I'm LATE *I'm late for an important date, said the White Rabbit to Alice.*

Or maybe I'm just getting nervous in the service. When a grown woman can't even count up to twenty-eight without using her fingers and her toes . . .

Betsy navigated her spiral-bound appointment calendar across her dressing table. It came each year from Marjorie Sommers with a note on U.N. stationery praising the charming illustrations by international artists who contributed their work to the Children's Fund. Actually, it was Marjorie's diplomatic way of hinting to Witt's raggle-taggle wife who, after all, had not had terribly many advantages or opportunities to learn, that time and hour run, and wait for no man.

The merry month of May. Hard to believe. The elastic band of time stretching out and snapping back; but on the calendar time's a one-way street with the rigid forward march of a picket fence. May? April's Easter week in San Juan seemed just yesterday—how can I be so far into May?

My darling bud of May, stop your gibbering and count. Ignore the little calendar notations for Timmy's Parents Day at school, the hospital volunteer days and the red circle for my birthday and our big family party at the beach house in Southport. Just count twenty-eight days. But dammit, I've forgotten whether you start counting on the first day of your period or do you begin the day after your last day, or what? I've always been regular as a clock and now, all of a sudden, just because I think I'm a few days late, all of a sudden I have to learn monthly arithmetic again.

If I'm pregnant, Betsy thought, Marjorie will celebrate by doing cart wheels from U.N. headquarters in New York all the way up the road to Connecticut. My, what a marvelous blast-off into space that would be! All of us dancing around the Maypole because Betsy, sterile barren sperm-immune drink-too-much wild-and-woolly Betsy finally brought forth a small miracle. A darling bud of May.

So, the calendar. I'm late I'm late for an important date. Even Alice, David's wife, will be happy because their two children will have two cousins, Timmy and—. And? A boy? A girl? No matter. Just a fine fat bouncing babe in the candy-striped nursery that had been Timmy's only a few years ago: the soapy clutching of a wee sprite's unbelievably tiny hands and feet slithering and splashing in the bathinette; that special towel-rubbed smell of health as you smooth baby talc over a cherub's pink rump; that lovely sensual silly bliss of a well-fed baby just as his eyelids slide down with sleep.

Oh, Mary Mary quite contrary, you should be scared stiff instead of glad.

She poured herself another finger—third? fourth?—of the Japanese Scotch-type Scotch she had bought at the hole-in-the-wall liquor store next door to the Womb with a View. You had to drink a fair amount to really tie on to its special flavor; I think I've tied on because I've drunk—drank? —a fair amount. Marjorie Sommers' tactful fund-raising United Nations calendar labeled May is not going to buffalo *this* darling bud. Who may or may not be budding. Far far better to bud than never to have budded at all, said Mary Mary quite contrary to Madam Butterfly. A little sobriety if you please. This Japanese Tokyo-tippling it strictly sayonara.

The indistinct sound of the back door, slammed hard enough to wake the dead, reached all the way up to her bedroom. Timmy was home from school. If he doesn't stop in the kitchen for a glass of milk and something, she thought, he'll come bursting in here armed with crayons and mimeographed notices pinned on his shirt about some Parent-Teachers Association teatalkytime in the school gymnasium tonight.

On your feet, buddy. Budding invisibly. So far. Maybe.

But no maybe about Timmy's thundering little hoofs prancing up the stairs to waltz in with a big frecklenosed smackeroo kiss-hello for his mommy. And here's dear old tipsy Mom aromatically alcoholic as Neary's Pub. So off to the john we go, my fair lady, to brush our pearly white teeth and hide away this plastic bottle of sayonara-type mouthwash and chew some Madam Butterfly Sen-sen.

She examined herself hazily and speculatively in the bathroom mirror, expecting tragic grief lines, a brave spartan mask, and was surprised to catch herself with an inward smile classified top-secret. I hope it's true. I'd rather be pregnant than President. To hell with counting and calendars. I'll just wait. Is there a woman with heart so hard that never unto herself has said: Wherefore art thou, late period? I really hope I'm late for this important date.

And if I am, I'll have to convince Witt. Me, the artful dodger. Get hot, Witt ol' buckaroo, and he turns on his electric blanket. But after all the years of trying he'll be delighted, especially if I've done my homework like a very good girl. Love is an inside job. The counting and calendar bit will be just proof. Just stick to a few convincing half-truths. Simple. Every woman learns how at her mother's bent knee. It'll be champagne corks, a big family thing, show biz. You're *on!*

I should be scared, but I'm not, said Mary quite contrary. So it's rub-a-dub-dub on those perfect rows of teeth and pull yourself together, mother.

With a bittersweet tinge of astonishment she had decided several weeks
ago she had reached a headlined and footnoted place called: in love. The
phrase about parting being such sweet sorrow was textbookishly familiar;
but now the words became real, a black-and-blues fracture. Each time she
edged closer to Roone she felt premonitions of goodbye. His complete
unawareness of it, his offhand remarks about graduating and leaving
New Haven, gave their meetings—for her—an unbearable poignancy.
Why, I'll be in my *forties*—the age of saints and suicides—when he's a
young doctor just up to thirty-five!

This time scale became her daily almanac, the weather of her feelings,
the entire barometer of their stormy or sunny weathers.

Sunshine was when he simply stroked a fingertip along the back of her
neck, or when he strummed his naked muscled ribs like guitar strings,
singing with bathtub solo exaggeration *Black buh-lack black izz the color
of myyy trueluve's hay-air,* or reached for her with a grasping hungry
primitiveness, overpowering, both exhilarating and frightening, close to
assault.

Rains sliced coldly when he would mutter, "Keerist, lay the hell off
for a while, can't you? I've got to study sometime, goddammit!" Or, "Why
do we have to eat now? Because your Van Cleef wristwatch says so? Can't
you just latch onto the simple idea of eating whenever you get hungry?"
Fraying tempers had always upset her, even as a child, so she invented a
defensive maneuver, the doing of small tasks—such as washing his heap
of dirty socks—useful for him, an act of contrition for her.

Winter descended when he would calmly and icily analyze her, the
dental probe touching, touching, poking until *there,* right there, that's
where the decay is and must be drilled out. "Upper-class slumming," he
would say with a pretense of thoughtfulness which was actually taunting.
"That's the name of your game, Ladyjane. You can't get your kicks
unless the phallus is forbidden, can you? But you're not the Pepsi generation. You're too late. Why don't you form one of those Comstock
public-decency committees so you can play around in your sandbox with
ickypoo indecency? Give yourself an honest-to-God feeling of spiritual
and brassiere uplift? Ward off evil thoughts with something highly ritualized, like scratching your navel and repeating *Om mani padme hum?*
Write a letter to Advice to the Lovelorn. Sign it, *Lonely Heart.*"

She would lift both hands self-protectively, shelterless. "Please. Please
don't get . . . *mean.*"

"But this is therapeutic, Mother Goose. This is for your own good. Puts

the id in kid. If money won't bandage the sore spots, Mrs. Grundy, then"
—raising one ministerial finger—"only the tuh-ruth can set you free."

She would look around his cellar room for some intangible escape, opening and closing the insulated picnic chest he used as a refrigerator.
"Where'd you hide it?" she would ask. "I left it here yesterday—"

"Seek and ye shall find, kiddy," he would say without moving. "O
Magdalene, on this li'l ol' road to Damascus of thine, what seekest thou?"

"There was half a bottle of Suntory in here yesterday—"

Her mention of the Japanese Scotch changed him instantly. "Ah so?
Betsy-san wish kowtow for riddle drinkie?"

Driven beyond endurance, her eyes shining with furious tears, she
snarled, "No, damn you, you animal! Just a cup of kindness!" Then, just
as he began to speak, she said exactly the words she knew he would
ridicule her with: "Yes! For auld lang syne!"—and, miraculously, the ice
broke, the sun returned, as they both dissolved into maniacal laughter by
their own partnership in banality.

She had risked asking him, "Something has to mean *something* to you."

"The good life. Mine."

"Seriously."

"My serious military deferment."

"Aren't you in the active Reserve?"

"No. Radioactive."

"Some joke."

He snapped a military salute off his brow. "Yes sir, Colonel Cheesecake. You want my name, rank, and horsepower?"

"My, you do need basic training, don't you?"

"New wine, Colonel. Too tart for the older set. Needs aging."

"Say—maybe forty years before corking?"

"I can be corked right now."

"Have your cheesecake and drink it, too?"

"Why not? One highball, one oddball. Better'n no balls at all."

"I'm serious."

"I'm Roone, yé-yé."

"*Something* has to count!"

With one finger, he had curled the tendrils of hair on the warm curve of
her neck. "Face up to it, Queen Victoria. Nothing counts."

"Nothing?"

"Nothing."

"Just like that? Nothing? No one?"

"Yup. Nothing."

"You have to believe something."

He pulled his eye corners into slants. "Confucius believe like so: other men's wives are best. Missy lady have Chinee yen play with poor hon'able Wun Hung Lo?" He released his eyes. "Don't let my inscrutable Oriental smile fool you. I'm very scrutable. And so to bed."

"Not so fast, Confucius. Honorable man can get to be pretty damn monotonous."

"Me? A wandering minstrel?"

"Maybe even a thing of shreds and tatters?"

"Hoo-ha. Gilbert and Sullivan, yet. A lucky strike for Scotland Yard: you've found me out. You stuck in your thumb and pulled out a bum. Honorable bum from Forbidden City."

"Pass me my cigarettes."

"You smoke too much, Mistress Mary. While I parse nursery rhymes you make air pollution. Awfully sticky wicket."

"Stiff upper lip, choom." He always stings and snares my wordiness into these playground name-calling skull-butting contests. The skin game. "As vices go, smoking's minor, Doctor."

"Pretty minor, that exclusive sayonara sake club you're in. All it takes is a bottle to join."

"Takes a member to know a member, Doctor. And I don't mean Tea for Two."

"Behold: my stern Iron Maiden." He clawed the air and snorted like a movie monster. "Aggh. And me with iron-poor blood."

His relentless shaggy burlesque inevitably needled her into "Oh shut up! Just stop the blarney for one blessed minute."

"Only one minute for contemplation, girls. We'll gnaw the bones of penance. Bedtime at nine, girls, then home by midnight." He mimicked her slips into Dublin lingo. "Oh, now, don't go lookin' at a man so tense and all stormy. I've got a set of factory-equipped marbles. I'm ready to roll."

She had stood up. "Roone." Go home, she told herself. Go now. I will arise and go now, and go to Innisfree. "Your vulgarity, sometimes—"

"Okay, no marbles. We can play with my tinker toy."

"See what I mean? You need basic training. Toilet training."

Now he became demonic. "Hurt feelings, Evangeline? Your bleeding-madras heart all blurry from too much laundering?"

"I can't stand cruelty. I—I get sick."

"You need a hobby. Not hubby—hobby."

"I heard you the first time."

"Some brave new employment, Betts. A nighttime thing where you can howl, go mad, offer sacrifice." He snapped his fingers commandingly. "I've got it. For bored broads who want thrills and chills. A Pop-Op art gallery. Hang the painters beside their paintings."

"To hell with you. You're impossible. I'm going home."

He pulled her down beside him. "Let's not be the lonesome abandoned bride tonight." He had rocked her head back and bitten her earlobe delicately. As he began to kiss her she veered away from anger and let herself drift; calmer, directionless. Needfully, she slid her arms around him, her open hands pressing against his hard back as if the room were spinning.

The best of times were his slow pluckings of love music, she his instrument; his strumming of chords, the quick erotic fingering of tightening strings, the faint shiver of expectation and fear as the musician played wildly. Just beyond this wildness could be only a discordant madness. Always, afterward, she asked in a little-girl voice she hated herself for using, "Was I all right?"

His favorite answer was the word he had picked up in Puerto Rico as a cutting machete of two-edged praise: "Olé!"

Everything changed; her eye and ear sharpened so that flower colors, children's voices, became more vivid. A word, a phrase overheard from the next booth at the Womb with a View, at times became symbolic, oracular. She thawed herself near the watchfires of his eyes; his bare chest had a radiant warmth as if he stored heat. When they lay silently intertwined, the blowtorch of his mouth mercifully closed off, they breathed together so easily that small sounds said more than words.

She walked queenly, with a brave straight back, not her former nervous whippet stride. When they successfully avoided verbal scuffles, her face in the mirror became secret-smiling, innocent and poetic, less careful and more responsive, less pale and more clear-skinned. So, she told herself, surprised, this is the love fed with apples. I always knew it was there, around the corner and under a tree. Her body's promise brushed her pulsebeat now, a central sensory core in all the vague happy expansions which wove drowsy textures through each day.

Nights were better, not the fools' daytime scurry but explorations of the dark side of the moon. Like a novice wife anxious to keep her alcoholic husband company, she wised up to Roone's jargon of narcotic meanings hidden in bland songs in which *mother's little helper* might mean pep pills, and *straight shooter on the mainline* was junkie talk for the injection of heroin directly into a vein at the risk of heart stoppage. She learned the ropes about *taking a trip around the world with a travel agent*, which Tabac—now back in New Haven from San Juan—had told her meant scoring a home run with a dame while you both were in orbit, full of LSD. She learned the ins and outs of the elaborate shifting scale of what was cool or square; who made the scene and who goofed it; which jelly roll got turned on horse and cooled it like it's goin' outa style, and which Johnnycake got stoned like there's no more tomorrow.

Lunching across the table from him in the hospital cafeteria was play-acting fun while they pretended they did not know one another. Their secret password, "Saturday? This Must Be Love!" Hours of patient diplomatic negotiations with the fearsome Mrs. Crotty, Director of Volunteers, ended in victory; Betsy matched her hours as a hospital Play Lady with Roone's occasional free time.

During the weeks before Witt returned from San Juan she saw Roone every day and, once, gambled on a whole weekend at the shore anchorage of Mystic. A hootenanny of New England folk songs was held on a schooner deck, so authentically nostalgic it was televised coast to coast and via communications satellite to Eurovision as genuine cultural Americana.

In their motel room, that night, Roone had parodied the nasal twang of "You Got the Hottest Gun in Buckaroo Town." She enjoyed this kind of scornful clowning; he could make a monkey of anyone. Except me, she had thought. As long as I'm not the victim.

To share his contempts was to share his gypsy tinker's freedom, to shed her conventional airless mummy wrappings and outflank all those he dismissed as caricatured daytime dullards; elderly Squares, academic Nit-pickers, la-de-da Do-gooders, rich retired Senior Citizens, militant Tax-payers and their warhawk Washington Speechmakers, pussyfooting White Rockers and hotfooted Black Rockers, overmortgaged carpoolish Sub-urbanites, and all the rest of his labyrinthine warplans Order of Battle against The Enemy. Weeks ago she had protested, "But without them, you couldn't exist!" He had thrown back, "They exist. I live. *Cogito ergo sum.*" The Latin meaning was unsure, but the tiny hellfire flare behind his eyes was unmistakable. She had decided against being a booed referee between him and the world, and to join his guerrilla band.

A new kind of affection for him quickened in her. To be so young, spontaneous, innocent and knowing at the same time. Mellowed by affection, they had made love all night, partners instead of antagonists.

In the morning's paling light he had crept silently out of bed, disappeared, then padded back into the room to awaken her from her loose-limbed careless sleep with a kiss on the nose. "Good morning, teaspoon." Beside her was a sacramental devotion: reverential incense of strong tea, a burnt offering of toast. "I'm starving!"

He sat on the floor enjoying her licentious hunger.

During their quiet ride home, hunched beside her in the car without his usual demonology of contempt, picking abstractedly and gravely at his old steel-bodied guitar, he mused over troubadour ballads such as "Black Is the Color of My True Love's Hair." His pastoral poetizing captured her. Never before had he broken through the sonic barrier of his invisible furies. She had never seen him caress the fretted fingerboard as if considering the many meanings of music, softening the downward runs, thrumming the bass with a held-back reticence, taking off on melodic improvisations, robber rhythms that broke musical laws; then, from way out, riding back to town with modulated harmonies, voicing a brooding understanding of human pain and loss. Betsy recognized gratefully how far this musical introspection was from his usual savage falsetto gimmickry.

"Oh, I like that sound."

"That's motown. That's downtown sound."

"No, that's people sound."

"Soul music. Gospel. Really righteous, sister."

"Don't spoil it."

"This is how I swing a fado."

"Fado?"

"Portuguese blues. Sadness and sin. Very Edith Piaf-y but with some African slave song in it."

"I never heard it in the Caribbean."

"Of course not. Too much education and television. Fados are the music of the illiterate poor. I should be playing it on a guitarra, one of those Portuguese musicmongers with six double strings that carries the melody instead of strumming the rhythm."

Betsy secretly enjoyed his animal ability to lose himself completely in whatever he was feeling at the moment, discovering he had some hurts as deeply buried as her own. I'd love to ask him to play some of the old Irish ballads, but that might trigger an eruption of corrosive Dublin schmaltz.

For a moment, unexpectedly, his longlashed blue eyes met hers; not clever now, no flamepoints behind them, but smoky with dreaming. "You like?" he asked. "You capisc'?"

"I like. I capisc'."

"Something grandioso, fortissimo, or maybe pianissimo?"

"Arrivederci Roma."

"Ciao." His fingers drummed the hollow body of his instrument. "Maybe Home Sweet Home?"

She backed away from that. "Save the refrigerated American cheese. You tasted a lot of flavor in that groovy fado."

"Betsy, that's not groovy. A fado has one foot in a bucket of blood and the other on some pirate's island."

"Where do *you* want to go?"

"I never know till I get there. Hey, my ravenhaired enchanted beauty, you look great."

She had sieved her hair through her fingers and loosened it to the wind. "I feel great." She indicated his guitar by dropping her chin. "Play it, don't talk it."

Much as he orchestrated his acrobatic vocabulary and cocky gallows humor, his music became a put-on bravura heel-tapping display of arpeggios and trick runs and grace notes. "This drag you?"—then, after a carefully composed silence, rippled into an undulating movement enriched by feeling, piling up passages with a counterpoint of moods, melodic and anarchic, upgoing until he skylarked into the upper harmonies. She glimpsed a moment of beauty, precious and transient.

This kind of music entranced her, serious and playful, a green space between divided darks. The dissonance between the melody and the chords, he had told her, was because he kept searching for a note that wasn't there.

She had brightened when he had refused to let her pay for anything during their weekend in Mystic. He had spent his own money giving her an aura of being collegiate, a surfer's wahine. She could not imagine how his odd jobs left him with enough spending money. Once or twice in the Womb with a View, she thought she had seen Tabac slip Roone what may or may not have been money. It had nothing to do with anything, so she ignored it. To be young was to be poor, just as she had been most of her life. Even now she carried only pocket money, almost as if to play poor was her passport to the country of the young. Cash, Witt had said, was worse than useless; it only meant your credit was no good.

With Witt not yet home, the half-empty bed seemed broad as a bandstand. Witt's silent bedroom slippers crouched empty in the closet, waiting watchfully.

If ever Witt knew the fantastic arrangements and risks I take to see Roone, here and there and everywhere. People are wrong who say that the husband is the last to know, because Witt will never know. Witt believes completely that I accept unquestioningly all the taboos of social propriety and that any man who might interest me could only come from our own circle of friends. Witt would never be concerned about the summer country club lifeguard, or the tennis instructor; he'd be more thoughtful about the traditional best friend who might take me to dinner so I wouldn't be lonely while Witt was in San Juan. Uncomplaining loyalty to my volunteer schedule at the hospital will impress him when he comes home, I know. To Witt, someone like Roone is as unimaginable as a lover as his being struck by a meteorite in Siberia.

Witt could never imagine what an instrument of torture a telephone could be when it did not ring, the dizzy sense of danger when being kissed publicly, the thousand years of woman songs and man stories about the world well lost for love.

At first with Roone, she had not been sure whether she should be offended or amused by their charade of Lady Chatterley and the gamekeeper. She was baffled that he should be so scientifically erudite but so militantly primitive about history, food, furniture, art, literature, or any of what she considered to be civilization's accomplishments. Finally she decided that his careless blond good looks and his swagger were in the English tradition of the gentlemen rakes who tempered their cruelties with elegance and their excesses with taste. After that, he seemed twice as much fun.

When Roone was busy at the hospital, or studying for his final examinations, she felt isolated and caged in her own home. The couple who worked for her ran the house so efficiently and quietly that half a day could go by without a word. She filled the time by sitting cross-legged beside the hi-fi set, listening repeatedly to "Come All Ye Fair and Tender Ladies," a recording she had bought in Mystic. She was desolated and captured by the throat-full-of-tears, the hoarse vocal catch of a fado, a woman's voice singing huskily, *"Come all ye fair and tender ladies, take warning how you court young men,"* and two male minstrels adding their voices over the muted strings: *"They're like the stars of a summer's morning, first they appear and then they're gone . . ."*

A summer's morning star had no place in Witt's astronomy. Oh, those sensible rational Sommers! But what good was sense when you had no compass, no rudder, no Northern Star to steer by, but only the magnetic touch of another's warm skin. Other than love, really, what else was there?

Even Roone had mocked her about this. "When you start looking for love, you're really a lost lovely lady, you really are, Isolde. *Liebestod*. That's your theme song."

"I'm up. Don't make me try to touch bottom."

"Betsy, you don't even know your ass from your elbow about our modern existential angst. You're one of the walking wounded in a dead-letter post office, and you don't even know you're a casualty."

Oh the bold, sassy vulgar talk! Juvenile, tough, and plain English, all at the same time. Sometimes his deliberate pretense that only what her mother called country language described the real fundamentals of human life would amuse her, like watching a small boy trick-ride a big bicycle, no hands. Other times she was a little shocked; no, that wasn't true, a *lot* shocked, but no *de*cently sophisticated person would dare admit such naïveté. The forbidden *was* exciting, he had made a shrewd hit. She had been impressed because he had paused for a moment in his muscular swagger to lift a corner hiding the true intellectual underneath; and intellectual men were always, finally, vulnerable.

I may be able to teach him ordinary human tenderness. He has none. He fears it. And without tenderness I'll be what I am, what I've been, something *used*. Used and ashamed. I must teach him *thee* and *me*.

A desperation began to choke her, a sudden glimpse of chasm between her favorite four-letter word and his. Hers was *love*.

Oh, she thought, raised like a ninny, I was, for sure. Now, how the unblushing body betrays. She covered her eyes with one elbow, trying to bestow her hope elsewhere while her body, too, told its lie.

Afterward, he slept the athletic dreamless sleep of the old indifferent young. She felt herself contemplating maternally his closed defenseless eyelids, groping and fumbling between barbed contradictions in herself. He'll never know why he needs me: because he doubts his own courage.

In the tender pressing darkness in his basement room, surrounded by rumpled worn shirts wadded and thrown in a corner, jazz recordings, piles of back issues of *Metronome* and *Downbeat*, white wool socks hung unwashed on a plastic cord between two cellar pipes, and heavy medical textbooks stacked on the floor beside his sleeping bag, she smiled gently at his statuesque sleeping face.

You great big hunk of forbidden. You beautiful ball-bearing bastard, she thought, and smiled to herself in the dark. I've learned from him. He's my teacher, and I'm his ever-lovin' student body.

I'm glad he's becoming vulnerable. Even a little jealous. He doesn't like the way I tool around town in my car with the top down: "Just begging for applause, honey chile, like some high school kid." But there was no truth to be found in that.

She knew just what she looked like, the green Jag, her green scarf wound around her head and trailing out behind her fluttering in the breeze like a lancer's battle-gallop pennant. And when men drove up beside her open car at street intersections, waiting for the traffic light to change, she would look carefully straight ahead to prove to herself Roone was wrong. She did not challenge men. She did *nothing*.

If a man leaned toward her to ask, "How many miles you get to a

gallon in that car?" she would turn slowly and casually and say, "Enough."
Just one word, without expression, unless he happened to be young and
goodlooking; then she would find herself smiling across the small space
between the cars and saying, "Enough, thank you." The traffic light would
change and she would expertly shift gears, revving the engine, letting the
green Jaguar walk away from the crowd, her green scarf whipping backward.

She yawned and stretched with feline luxury on the sleeping bag next
to Roone.

How simple lovemaking could be, if you just relaxed and didn't fight it.
In flagrante delicto, Witt's lawyer, Terrence, would probably call it. But I
call it a creature comfort a damn sight more heartwarming than patrician
indoor sports: Witt's father who scratched away in his book-lined study at
a never-ending manuscript while the noblest Roman of them all, Marjorie, hustled and bustled at the United Nations, or organized more
local chapters of L.I.V.E. Always pushing hard for Life Intelligence
Vigor and Efficiency. And David, in his warm little womb of a laboratory, so calm and sane and rational, while Witt wheeled his cogs and
cogged his wheels in a clockwork of profit-and-loss reports, and, as he was
fond of saying, taking care of the store. How much better to dally luxuri-
antly on a randy sleeping bag in a basement room more satisfying than
any ivory pleasure boat in Kashmir. Every room with a view needs a womb
with a view; she pinched her nostrils tightly to keep herself from laughing
out loud and waking Roone.

Roone always slept whenever and wherever he could. Two nights before Witt came home, Betsy had found Roone slumped comfortably in
the bucket seat of her car.

She had worked very late on the Pediatrics ward to decorate the playroom before the visit of a group of British pediatricians the next day. Oh
Lord, she thought, as her high heels clicked hurriedly down the marble
steps of the hospital, unnaturally loud in the quiet midnight air of May, he
might even be gone. Automatically she began fumbling in her cluttered
purse for a cigarette and her elusive lighter.

Betsy cut across the hospital parking lot, zigzagging between the spaced
cars of the night shift. She thought she glimpsed a man watching her, but
then the pale glimmer of face behind the window of a dark auto was
gone. She shivered slightly and ran up to the side of her car.

While she looked down at his sleeping Apollo head, she felt the familiar
blade of his beauty—he hated the word—turn inside her.

"Come all ye fair and tender ladies," the mountain minstrels sang on the

radio, *"and lock your heart in a box of golden . . ."* Their voices wept, diminuendo, and died out slowly.

The radio music stopped and the announcer began to speak but Roone still did not move. *Every woman deserves one bum in her life, and I'm yours.* My vagabond god. Impulsively she bent through the open window and kissed his open mouth.

His lips began to stir warmly and she began to use her quick darting tongue. He bit it. She stepped back, clapping one hand over her mouth. "You devil," she said. "You dog. That hurts."

By straightening his legs he pushed himself higher in the leather seat, looking up at her through the open window, completely and immediately awake. "Where the hell have you been, Mother Sommers?"

"No, Roone. No names."

"You attacked me first. A sexual assault."

"If you don't know the difference between attack and affection, Roone—"

"It's all aggression. Nature, spelled backwards—" his voice imitated a ponderous radio commercial—"to keep you *regular*, after thirty-five."

She laughed. This tone was better. The other had been too close to the truth. "All right, Doctor. Save it for the clinic." She walked quickly around the car and slid in under the driver's wheel. She pulled at the twisted edge of her raised skirt, but he reached out one hand to stop her.

"Don't be coy, Betsy. With legs like that, you can lay 'em in the aisles."

"I'm receiving your message, Sigmund, loud and clear."

"I know you with that hootchy-kootchy smile. All you want to do is bite my left earlobe, the only left earlobe I've got."

"What else can a lady do in a bucket seat?"

"Bucket," he said. "You bought the car, Betsy. Cockpit, joystick, and all. Now live in it."

"Well then, let's go over to your bed of roses." As she opened her purse and took out a cigarette, he said, "No. I've got a pathology lab deadline."

"Mind if I smoke?" Then quickly, speaking in exact unison with him, with the practiced timing of a comedy team, they added: "Ah don' care if you *burn.*"

She held the cigarette up to see if this was one of those rare symbolic times he would light it for her. He didn't. If bad manners were as fashionable now as good manners used to be, he was the height of fashion.

She thought of Roone's story of how the best mustangs were broken to the bridle. "Our American cowpokes, why, they'd jump on the horse's back and ride him till the man got thrown. Or the bronc got busted. The Mexicans had lots of time, mañana, so they just slowly starved the horse and beat it into the bridle. The Indians, they were funny. They'd tie the bronc so he couldn't jump and hurt himself. Then they'd stroke him, talk this easy kind of horse talk till he got used to the touch and the voice, and then they'd just mount him and ride away." "And you," Betsy had said, "use the American way?"

Remembering, she pushed the dashboard cigarette lighter in so hard she hurt her thumb.

"Well?" He sounded angry.

"Well what?"

"What the hell kept you so long—playing Peter Pan with the night shift?"

"Sorry. I hurried."

He tapped the round face of the dashboard clock. "You're late. I've got that unfinished autopsy dissection to report first thing in the morning."

She looked across the small space between them, the air suddenly charged, the radio playing quietly, the faint dashboard light from below catching the planes and angles of his face. How will I tell him? Two more days before Witt comes home. How will I tell him?

He's talking too loud, she realized. He forever pretends nothing matters, but this time something does. Good. Very good. Let him feel a little agony of doubt for once, the way he's made me feel it a hundred times. As he would say: play it cool. No sweat.

She leaned forward with the cigarette in her lips, pretending to wait for the dashboard lighter to pop back.

"And your last night on the town. Day after tomorrow your husband comes home."

A mindreader? No, he must have heard the news from David, in the lab. She pulled out the lighter and aimed it waveringly at her cigarette. Cunning boy.

"So, like the warmhearted ever-lovin' girl you are, you used up the evening fussing and farting around your Play Lady playpen."

He lifted the lighter out of her fingers—"Your hand is too shaky for surgery, Miss Nightingale"—and rammed it back into its dashboard socket.

"Tough guy," she said. "You think you've got the hottest gun in buckaroo town."

He leaned toward her and put his hand on her exposed leg and slid his fingers up to where the stocking ended. She forced herself to sit still. Damn the treason of skin.

"This isn't like you, Betsy. Playing cat and mouse while the peasants beg for bread. You get some sadistic slam bang if I have to sing for my supper?" He lifted his hand and leaned back in his seat. He made a gesture with his bent thumb, a quick upward thrust of a fishhook under his jaw. "Okay, you hooked me. But don't keep me hanging, Betsy."

"Roone, must you always have the first word, the last word, and all the words in between?" Oh God, how I hate these fights.

Until this moment she had honestly planned to tell him that even with Witt home, even with Mayoso coming back to Connecticut and her feeling obliged to help Mayoso find a place to live near the hospital, somehow she would manage to see him and meet him until he graduated. But now she said angrily, "Here we are, cats and dogs, and you leaving in June for California. All the way out to California, just for an internship."

"No. Just for the beaches and the surfing."

"And I'll never see you again." She felt the familiar rush of tears behind her eyes, furious with herself because she always cried so easily. She reached into her purse for a handkerchief. "I'm sorry. Tonight I'm on a weeping jag. I know how you hate for me to cry."

"You're crying for you, Betsy. A long time ago I decided not to cry for me." He jerked his head toward her. "The lady is shocked. The world is full of piss and vinegar, and the shocked lady runs a temperature."

"I do." She put one hand to her cheek. "My face feels hot."

"You travel in strange places, lady, you catch strange fevers."

"You're not a strange place, Roone."

"The hell I'm not. You don't know what's real as rocks, Betsy. You love slumming, you and your sense of sin, and the more you sense it the more you love it, baby doll."

"Stop it. Please. Don't be so angry. I can't stand it. You know how I love you."

"God Almighty. You say it like a lovely lady to her hubby helping her dry the dishes. 'Dear, I'm going to be a mother.' Go ahead, cry."

"When you start this kind of crazy talk—"

His eyes narrowed. "You're downtown now, madam. No grass and trees and pretty flowers downtown, in the stone jungle." He grinned wickedly. "No Cub Scouts. No Den Mothers. Low life, high prices."

"You're absolutely crazy."

With one movement he opened the car door, swung out, and slammed the door behind him. She pitched toward his side of the car frantically. "Roone—"

He thrust his head into the open window space. "I'm crazy? The hydrogen bomb is sane? A billion megabucks to shoot a man to the moon is sane?" He slapped one hand on the door. "Kee-rist! Stop the whole cockamamie world. I'm getting off."

As he walked away she scrambled out to run after him, snagging her stockings as her knee scraped the door. He did not stop until she caught his arm.

"Roone! My God. You can't just walk away like this. You'll kill me."

"Let go, Betsy. I've got an autopsy exam tomorrow, first thing, and I can't be sitting with you playing tea and sympathy." When she tightened her fingers he put his hand over them. "Betsy, it's late and you're so beat you don't even know which end is up. Go home. I absolutely have to study."

"I'll sit next to you. I won't make a sound. I'll wash your whole pile of socks."

"I'm not going home. This exam is a practical, with cadavers."

"I feel like a cadaver. Why can't I sit next to one? If you walk away like this, I won't see you for days, I'll go mad counting minutes."

"I'll see you around. I'll help you finish painting your playroom mural while Mrs. Crotty snoops around us."

"That's not enough. I'm in love with you in too many places. In the cafeteria. In the Emergency Room. Upstairs near the O.P.D. Everyplace we've ever met this last month. Let me come with you."

In the dark, his eyes thumbed over her. "And you call *me* crazy?" He laughed. "Let's go."

As they plunged side by side into the underground tunnel system which connected all the buildings of the large medical center, the somnambulistic citizens of the night-shift hospital world clattered past them with rolling metal racks of intravenous fluids and specially wrapped sterile instrument trays from Central Supply. The night electrician strode by, carrying a large Stillson wrench.

Overhead the large delivery tubes hissed as a patient's record rolled in a special carton shot by compressed air toward a nurse's station. Although the exposed steam pipes were wrapped with layers of insulation, a Death Valley heat radiated into the tunnel. Betsy felt faint as she hurried beside Roone, her staccato heels echoing hollowly. Like sleepwalkers, they said nothing, both keeping careful armistice faces. An intern hunched by, sleepy-eyed, stethoscope dangling from one pocket, neurology hammer and ophthalmoscope handle bulging in another. He lifted a fatigued hand. "Hi, Roone. How you doin', boy?"

"Okay, man. How's life in surgery?"

"Patients fine. Me, I'm dyin'."

"See ya."

"See ya."

They turned a corner and almost bumped into three student nurses in starched uniforms, neat and tidy as new dolls. A flurry of greetings filled the tunnel as Roone stopped.

Betsy stepped carefully to one side, separating herself, trying to push away the downrush of feeling old, never young again despite the open car, the green scarf, the youthful lover. She caught the curious—contemptuous?—glance of one of the student nurses, and immediately straightened her shoulders and lifted her chin. The girls wore no makeup other than a trace of lipstick. No eyeshadow, no eye liner, no highlighted cheekbones. Betsy felt painted, gaudy, what was delicately called *un certain âge*. The sagging tear in her stocking was no longer a private combat wound but a public frumpy sloppiness. She stood apart, smoldering, listening to their glib young chatter.

"Come on over to the cafeteria for a coffee break, Roone."

"Can't, honeychile."

"You're up late for a young fellow, Doctor."

"Look who's talkin'! Don't you know this is the hour before dawn when all the little hens lay and the big cocks crow? You should be tucked in bed."

All three girls laughed delightedly and moved off. One turned and called, "Keep kissable, Doctor."

Roone took Betsy's elbow. "Don't look like that. They're just a coupla sweet kids."

"Especially the one in the middle. The kissable one."

"Oh, I've helped her with her anatomy exams a few times, that's all."

"I could tell it was anatomy. Especially the bones and muscles of the female pelvis."

"All right, all right. So I gave her a quick bang or two. What the hell's the difference?"

He stalked away from her and once again she trotted after him, this time on fire. In silence they strode along together to another bend in the tunnel and a locked door. Roone took out a bunch of keys. "This is the only way into the back of the cadaver storage room."

"You really meant cadavers, didn't you? I thought you were making it up to get rid of me."

He unlocked the door, and a wave of cool chemical-smelling air passed them invisibly. "Watch your step." He closed the heavy insulated door carefully behind them. Except for the crack of light beneath the wide metal-sheathed door, they were in total darkness. A lofty hollow echo enlarged each footstep.

"Don't move," Roone said. "We've been working on bodies here all week and there're gut buckets all over the floor."

She stood rigidly, her face doubly hot in the chill room. Roone and those student nurses. *You should be in bed now. Keep kissable. What's the difference?* She heard him tap his way cautiously in the darkness. "No lights?" she managed to say. She could not recognize her own voice.

"I'm trying to find the small night-light. It won't show under the door."

The cadaverous darkness closed in around her, an uncoffined void without beginning or end, a terrifying night of the soul with no human voice, no companion for the journey. "Roone—" she began to say, then caught her breath as the night-light of the morgue went on. Lodged level by level in a floor-to-ceiling pipeframe catafalque, cadavers lay stately and enduring in the naked confident sleep of contributors to science. Two hung suspended on sloping tables in the corner, attached by tubes to bottles of fluid above them. A wall sign read NO SMOKING above a glass catacomb of instruments.

Her mother's bareboned funeral. Her father, the threadbare prince of players, weeping beside her. *Best I could do, Betts.* And the hearse driver: *Jasus. Better than being put to bed with a shovel in potter's field.*

The wake. *In the midst of death we are in life. And you, prince with no clean sheet in the house to shroud you decently, was your last stage like this, without applause?*

She felt the deadhouse floor rock slightly under her feet and covered her eyes with one hand. "Roone. Please. The light."

He laughed in his throat, misunderstanding her completely, and casually turned off the light. When he reached her in the great dark, she clung to him so fiercely that he whispered, "Baby, you're on fire. What a little jealousy will do . . ."

She found herself going down on her knees, as in prayer. Down, down, she thought in a fevered charity, unwilling because this was purgatory, willing because she had him locked as the young girls never could; willing, unwilling, unwilling but willing until they stretched out and his hands began their familiar exorcism and she abandoned herself mindlessly, gratefully, for companionship, any kind, anywhere, for the long journey.

The sound of weeping awakened her. A quiet faraway sobbing. Someone who had been hurt and had given up hope. She listened for a moment, wondering who it could be, until she realized she was lying on the white field of carpet beside her bed, curled up, her clenched fist against her lips to stifle her own muffled crying.

By holding the edge of the bed, she managed to pull herself up painfully to a sitting position. The muscles in her neck and back ached from having slept on the floor, and there was a tightened soreness in her hips, between her thighs. Roone, she thought suddenly, remembering in a rush.

She let her head fall against the blue silk coverlet beside her, beginning to cry again, rubbing her burning forehead against the satiny smoothness. Alone, alone. The trapdoor of love. Your feelings bound like wrists roped by an executioner. Your eyes blinded by the hood. Your heart pounding with wanting and not wanting. Wanting to end the unbearable waiting, wanting to body-surf the foaming wave's crest to an oblivion beyond hurt. Not wanting to lose the promise of a companion for the journey, the lost landscape of another earlier time. Someone's Dublin lilt in elegiac sing-song:

> *I only know that summer sang in me*
> *A little while, that in me sings no more.*

Downstairs, distantly, Betsy heard the telephone ring once, then stop. Roone? Calling to apologize? She sat up, wiping her eyes with the back of her hand. With more strength now, she raised herself beside the bed, surprised again to find it smooth and unused.

Roone must be calling to apologize. The feeling of trampled shabbiness in her body; he must have it, too. He must have finished that important autopsy examination and gotten one of those morning-after realizations of how awful he had been. He must have realized she had been strung tight as a guitar string and that he had abused her beyond forgiveness. Oh no, no, not *beyond*. No one should ever be *beyond*. Forgiveness should be a final refuge, never beyond anyone.

A wave of shame swept over her, drowning her, and she slid to her knees, folding her hands together as her mother had taught her in that snug sheltered time.

Oh my God, she thought, trying to remember the words of the act of contrition, I am sorry for having offended Thee. I detest all my sins because I dread the loss of Heaven and because they offend Thee, who art all-good, deserving of all my love.

All my love. How many times she had written quick little notes to push under the door of Roone's basement room: *Sorry to miss you, darling. I've been thinking of you all day. See you in the hospital tomorrow. All my love. Betsy.*

She looked down and saw that she was still wearing her garter belt and stockings. One stocking a nylon ruin. I'm mad, she thought with savage perception. What's happened to me? My stupid alcoholic moonlight-and-roses. I'm a fool. A stark-raving-mad fool who can't tell left from right, a raw screwing from, from—her mind rummaged for a word that would mean tenderness and passion and trust, but somehow no word was there. This must stop, she thought with fury. I detest all my sins because the price tag is too high. To stagger in here last night, fumbling dazedly for the bedroom light switch, feeling ravished and gutted and barely able to reach the bathroom bowl before the burning upsurge of vomit. To crawl, crawl, head drooping and swaying with a great looping vertigo amid spinning walls, to crawl across the miles of carpet of this delicately silken bedroom world, slipping sideways, clutching crazily at air, as if the floor were quicksand, bottomless and frightening.

For a time Witt had taken the fright away. When he had been repatriated from the North Korean prison camp after the Panmunjom settlement, he had stopped off in Chicago on his way home to Connecticut and had telephoned her. She had been modeling at Marshall Field's then, and she took Witt's call standing in her stocking feet in the models' dressing room, wearing a slip, just as she did now.

"This is DeWitt Sommers," the voice on the telephone had said. "Your husband was in my company when we were hit at the Chosin Reservoir. I was with him when he died in prison. I promised him I'd see you and give you the silver I.D. wristband you gave him."

She had stood there with the telephone, instantly cold-fingered, aware only of the incongruity of the haute-couture workshop she was in, the oddly comic feeling that she wasn't dressed properly for this kind of military telephone call about a boy-husband she had met at a USO dance and had married two weeks before he left for Korea. Those two weeks were misremembered now, a strange teenage smudge she could hardly decipher, and somehow words like *husband* and *widow* could not be applied to a girl not yet twenty who would in ten minutes saunter out on high heels into a fashion show, enameled, glittering. Her mother had taught her such respect for ladylike politeness that she did as she always did, which was to ignore her wish to say *no* to DeWitt, and, instead, to do the Right Thing. She wanted to say: Keep the silver I.D. bracelet. Wrong address. I don't live there anymore.

She had met Witt that evening, after persuading the dress buyer to let her borrow one of the sample Balenciaga dresses; black, high-waisted in the Empire style, simple, with a price tag like it was human. The buyer had used her two most religious adjectives about the dress: it was important, and, on Betsy honey, stunning. Whoever Mister Special is, the buyer had said, you'll knock him dead. You'll *kill* him.

If I'm supposed to be in mourning, Betsy had thought, I'd better wear some of that *ravissant* black underwear, everything elegantly sorrowful, even the fine white handkerchief with the delicate black edging.

She had expected DeWitt to be stiff, a correct cardboard soldier, not a tall thin man with a zigzag head scar showing through the close-cropped military haircut, with a crooked grin and no apparent idea of the value of money. She had never before seen money used as casually and usefully as knives and forks. Within the first hour she realized he was intelligent, literate, amusing, a bit rusty and humble about what was new in the

United States. This, and his gaunt look of suffering, made him even more attractive. She decided she would have him.

Conversational exploration first. Zero in on what interested him most, encourage him to talk about it while she rested her chin charmingly in her hand and listened to him with apparent fascination.

Then, she knew, there would be the gargle of drinks, the dim grotto lighting, the quick superficial intimacies. ("Really? You like shish kebob too?"), and the evening's pile of jackstraws would grow until a single light push would tumble them into bed. And the pretty confusion on the rumpled bedsheets of morning. ("How could I let myself go like that? Must have had one for the road and one for the bed! Mind if I use your toothbrush?")

Nowhere near Christmas, but Witt had been a surprise package.

He had given her the silver I.D. bracelet, and had asked her if she wanted to hear what had happened in North Korea, between Yudam-ni, Toktong Pass on the breakout to Frozen Chosin. "No, please don't," she had said. "Telling can't change anything."

Much later, after they were married, Witt had told her how his misunderstandings about her had impressed him. "There you were, with your black hair parted in the middle, and that very neat black dress—"

("Very *neat!*" She had exploded into laughter. "At those prices?")

"—and hardly a speck of makeup. And the honesty to say you didn't want me to talk about Korea. And the way you talked about yourself, without stopping, as if nobody had ever listened to you before—"

("I was telling you my secret," she had said. "I was lonely. Really all alone.")

"—and the way you went scrounging through your dinky little apartment refrigerator for some food so we wouldn't have to go out. The steak you grilled over the fireplace coals, and the baked potatoes, and those cold tomatoes you sliced all lopsided—"

("And later," she had said, "when I started to cry and you put your arm around me—")

"—and the delicate, unhappy way you said no when I tried to move toward the bedroom that night, and the next night, and the next—"

("Ho," she had said, "my period had started, *swoosh*, just like that. That afternoon. I'm usually on time each month like a clock, but that night, of all nights!")

"—and I was impressed. Here was classic beauty. Virtuous young widow in black. Good taste. Simple dignity."

Witt had not left Chicago for three weeks. Four months later they were married in Trinity Episcopal Church, in Southport, Connecticut. Oh Mother, Mother, and Daddy there in the shadowed corners, look at me in the mirror there. Did you *ever?* That's *me!* The dream of a dress flown in from Dior, the orchestra flown up from the Caribbean, and my heart flown in air express from Chicago to heaven.

We're on deck again, arriving in America, but now I'm the Statue of Liberty.

She got to her feet slowly, her head clanging strangely, the faint far-off sound of a bell on the moon. That elevator-going-down feeling in the stomach. She fussed with her heirloom gold marriage band, twisting and untwisting it. Those first words of the matrimonial sacrament.

Versicle: Our help is in the name of the Lord.

Response: Who made Heaven and earth.

Versicle: O Lord, hear my prayer.

Response: And let my cry come unto Thee.

There I go again, she thought, like the child they used to warn: Pray to God and make a good confession.

She tilted the window's white shutter blades, welcoming the oblique ladder of sun across the bedroom carpet.

Mary was my confirmation name, I chose it myself, and names are very special for Catholics. I wanted to be like Mary. Pale, lovely, transcendent. Cool beauty on a pedestal. Blessed above all women. Mary, Mary, quite contrary, I was. Marry in the Church with a boy who flew off to Korea after two weeks. Leave the Church for DeWitt. Ah now, girl, apostates never die. They just fade away.

Her black brassiere lay on the floor, empty, deflated, one strap torn, with the saving grace of the ridiculous. Roone's derisive voice: "The Peter Pansy look? Kee-rist! With removable push-up pads for that new boyish rounded line. Jee-suzz!"

She picked up the bra and dropped it on her dressing table.

("Oh Betsy child," her blackhaired mother used to say, "don't think a few glad rags will give you *charm*. Charm is only kindness nicely done, child, not make-believe.")

Mother, Mother, a part of her grieved for a moment, if you'd lived to see me grow up, if Daddy hadn't shut himself up in the back room of that dreary Chicago tenement apartment, from then on I was always so alone, then maybe I would have been like you and believe in kindness nicely done, not make-believe.

26 *Mire,* MAYOSO THOUGHT, the more things change in New Haven the more they're the same. He scanned the other six people seated expectantly around the scarred oval table in Dr. Benjamin Sommers' conference room. The quietly conversational air was—what? Audience before the curtain rises? Waiting room for fathers in the obstetrical wing? No, more the climate of a courtroom just before the judge enters.

Edwina Hawthorne tiptoed around the table laying out seven yellow pads and seven sharpened pencils as if this gathering were an administrative hospital meeting, not the bark before the bite.

The hospital Administrator, Dr. Anthony Hale Douglass, who always felt chilled by the winds of decision when caught at a crossroads position, was in no hurry to begin. He marked time disarmingly with Mr. James Stacy, the district attorney, by jovial reminiscences about neutral local topics: the tragic disappearance of the open trolley cars everyone used to ride on Saturdays out to the Yale Bowl games; the high cost of programming the hospital's computer; his curatorship of the collection of colonial snuffboxes, first assembled by his grandfather for the Boston Society for the Diffusion of Useful Knowledge; the deplorable loss of generations of effort when Yale-in-China got swallowed by the Red Dragon. A dogma-eat-dogma country, the new China.

David Sommers and his father showed no outward concern. They spoke to one another sparingly, low-voiced and unheard, as if they were in church. Marjorie Sommers concentrated on her leather-bound memo book, efficiently ticking off items, referring occasionally to a memorandum she extracted from the Dunhill ladies' attaché case before her.

"Before we start," Edwina Hawthorne announced, "who's for coffee and who's for tea? Milk, anyone?"

Seven people, Mayoso thought. Magic in that number, once. Alchemists and wizards changed lead to gold beneath cabalistic sevens. Our golden boy there, the district attorney, has the untarnished metallic smile and self-confident spellbinder's gleam.

Question, Mr. Stacy, if the Court please: Is all this morning's wonder-work to transmute me, the lead one, into 24 orthodox karats? Or just to melt me down the hospital's academic drain?

Marjorie Sommers bent across the conference table toward him to stage whisper, "Before I forget, when Betsy drives you down tonight for the party, make sure you don't mention our family birthday gift. It's supposed to be a complete surprise."

He nodded. Marjorie had taken time out of her busy official schedule on the Population Council to drive up from New York to New Haven this morning to plant her flag next to mine; simply by being in the same room beside me she's making it clear to the district attorney that she'll interpret any attack upon me as an attack upon her. How generous and thoughtful of her, because the district attorney's request for a meeting would ordinarily have been handled as a four-cornered triangle. Three corners occupied by the tweeded Dr. Douglass, by the sharkskinned district attorney, and by labcoated me. In the fourth, invisible, was public opinion.

For the Sommers to have shown up in force beside me so soon after my return to New Haven was an act of great affection, because they all fear patronizing generosity. They've seen how often the use of checkbooks as a conscience made those who were helped feel weak, shamed, ready to pay back with fury their clumsy benefactors. No, they'll jump into the trench beside me and pretend we've all met for no other purpose than the family birthday celebration for Betsy.

The birthday party for Betsy at the beach house in Southport was the reason Marjorie had given Dr. Anthony Hale Douglass for her being in New Haven. She had known the hospital Administrator as a boy in Miss Whipple's Class Dansant and still called him Doug. He called her Marjie, a cartoon nickname which she disliked but never mentioned.

"Doug," she had said to Dr. Douglass on the telephone two hours ago, "I've just called the Governor in Hartford and dragged the poor man to the phone about this young district attorney who's nailing together this, ah, Salem witchcraft trial with Mayoso."

"Marjie—"

"Of course, the Governor's a rural Republican, and Mister Stacy is a city Democrat, the elections come November are up for grabs, but even taking that into account, it's an old old story—don't you think, Doug?— of a bright and aggressive young politician on the make. Why else would a busy District Attorney like Mr. Stacy go out of his way to ask for this conference?"

"Marjie," Dr. Douglass had said on the phone, "we local yokels don't all travel in the upper rarefied atmosphere of the U.N. and the White House. City Hall is what I live with. Welfare, Aid to Dependent Children, old folks' hospital bills, you know? So, to me, this D.A. walks softly and carries one hell of a big stick."

"Local government by stick?"

"Come off it, Marjie. Jim Stacy could've kicked David in the teeth on our last go-'round. David was abusing the privilege of research beds. We would've lost our luggage in annual donations if Jim Stacy hadn't been a gentleman—"

"Until he becomes top dog, Doug. Then watch out."

"Fair's fair. He's sincerely doing his job. Asking for this meeting—why, he's just being courteous to Doctor Mayoso."

"Oh pooh," Marjorie said. "I've fought these professional knights in shining armor all over Connecticut. Every time we opened up a L.I.V.E. maternal health clinic, one of these legal fellows would mount his curb-stone patriotism and come charging hellbent for election down Main Street. Surrounded, of course, by reporters and television cameras."

"Marjie, you sound awfully *l'état c'est moi*. Your L.I.V.E. maternal health clinics were against state law—"

"And it took us ten long years too long to change it! Connecticut's the last state in the Union to strike out all that nineteenth-century prohibition against birth control. Why pick on Mayoso now?"

"I hope you won't be annoyed if I say this quite bluntly, Marjie, even though I'm an admirer of your maternal health orations—"

"No, speak up. Why's he after Mayoso? Tell me. I won't be annoyed." Of course I won't, she decided. I'll be furious.

Edwina Hawthorne served around the conference table from an English rolling tea cart: not the usual academic disposable cups, Mayoso noticed, but Dr. Douglass' best china; each cup bore the university's heraldic shield and its dual language motto in Latin and Hebrew: *Light and Truth.*

If the district attorney sheds some light, Mayoso thought, and I stick to the truth, we can drop these academic pretenses. This is a council of war.

Years ago, when I was a chief resident in this hospital, when Dr. Benjamin Sommers presented me with this handsome captain's chair with the University of Havana's seal engraved on the back, we all used to stumble wearily down to Oak Street for hot kosher corned-beef sandwiches and fist-size mugs of coffee. No tea carts, then. The spindrift of memory: Oak Street gone, all the crowded friendly unsanitary delicatessens and second-hand-book stores bulldozed away. Gone, so many people, so many years, yet here I am back in the same conference-room chair, across the table from the same Dr. Benjamin Nathaniel Sommers. David with the same eager undergraduate look, the same Yale swimming team crewcut; Marjorie still a crusader, blue-eyed and vigorous, flicking off the years like brushing lint from her sleeve.

An hour ago, in the hospital elevator, on their way up to the conference room, Marjorie had taken Mayoso's elbow and pointed toward the steel wall. There was a notice recruiting applicants to the Peace Corps to teach rural South American children how to read, write, use sanitary facilities, and eat life-sustaining foods. Some Spanish or Portuguese speaking ability required, of course. "More raindrops in the desert," she said, then repeated, "raindrops in the desert."

Mayoso recalled Filho's intense statistics, that day at Pirate's Bay on Grand Cayman Island. "There are so many South Americans," he said noncommittally.

"But only one kind of hunger, I'm sure." She paused and then said squarely, "When I heard about what happened to you in Caracas, I wanted to sit right down and just pour out all I felt in a letter. But I couldn't. Too much to say. You know?"

"Yes." Marjorie was so directly matter-of-fact, yet her sons were so hesitant and oblique about expressing their feelings. How had that happened? Benjamin Sommers' reserved low-key self-deprecating manner? ("Never understood Witt's going into business," his scholarly form of ironic humor went, "until I read Sophocles, the physician-playwright. Fellow who wrote *Oedipus Rex*.") Witt and David repaid their father's affection by becoming his friends, his audience, even his allies in practical jokes such as telling the *Time* researcher for a cover story on Marjorie that her greatest boast was she had never made a dinner-table-seating protocol error at her innumerable U.N. parties. Betsy, Mayoso thought, must have believed she was marrying into a dynasty. Actually, they're a clan.

"Betsy and Witt," Marjorie was saying, "told me your friend—I'm sorry, what was her name?—"

"Cristina." Dancing that night, a canario blossom in her Indio hair.

"—that she was an unusually warm and very pretty girl."

"Yes." Gunfire. Going down on her knees on the sidewalk, hit, genuflecting to rebuilt Aztec altars, human sacrifice.

"They said you were having a memorial sculpted for her."

"Not for now, I'm afraid. The stonecutter in San Juan is a devout man, and he caught enough of the anti-Mayoso hysteria to refuse to finish the statue."

"Oh." She drew her breath in, a fractional spartan sharing of his feeling. "That, too? On top of everything else? I saw Santos Roque in Mexico City last week—he feels politically secure enough to leave the island now —he told me that he still wakes up at night thinking of what he had to do to you."

"He did what he had to do. I'm glad it worked."

"Oh, it worked both ways. The bishop—what was his name?"

"Bishop Sosa."

"Yes, Sosa. Transferred to Rome. A promotion, I believe. And he took along as his secretary that television volcano—"

"Father Gofredo Möttl."

"What an unusual name! Well, with them gone, with you gone, Santos Roque came out blooming like roses. A balanced middle-of-the-roader, everybody said. He won the most smashing plurality in the primary elections he's ever gotten."

"Checkmate."

"Did you say—checkmate?"

"Yes. A private joke he and I had."

Her savvy eyes made a shrewd inventory of his expression, but she asked no more questions. They stood side by side in the elevator, separated by continents, history, experience, silently staring at the Peace Corps notice.

The cliché is true, Mayoso thought. A man's character is his fate. Like the Sommers, stand up in public and do what must be done.

The elevator slowed to a stop and the doors opened mechanically. As they stepped into the corridor, Marjorie said, "Well, at least your eye patch makes you look very *pour le mérite*. Like one of the dueling German corps."

"Out of style, Marjorie. The modern German duel is between generations."

"Well, a distinguished grandee. A magnifico."

"I'll be happy to look less distinguished when this summer comes. When my eye is healed, I can be measured for visual acuity accurately, and get new glasses."

"Glasses? Heavens, all wrong for you. All wrong. Keep the elegant patch."

"To do surgery? Even to carry out some of the procedures in David's lab, a man needs binocular vision."

"Don't be silly. Hire an assistant, but keep the eye patch. Remember, in the country of the blind, a one-eyed man is king."

"Grandees, kings. Marjorie, you're one hell of a democrat."

She had put her hand on his arm to stop him in the corridor. "Even with only one eye working full-time, I'm sure you've noticed the change in Betsy."

"Yes—"

"Bright-eyed and bushy-tailed, don't you think? Betsy, slogging through her first Caribbean business trip with Witt—that sounds silly, doesn't it?— I mean, seeing all the work and worry that goes into an investment like that dioscorea experimental farm. I think her island stay must have made a difference."

"That could be—"

"Oh, Mayoso the Magnifico. So careful, so discreet. You son of a grandee! A difference in her head would make a difference in bed, wouldn't it?"

"Marjorie. Head, bed, why do so many Americanos say things in rhyming words? Television commercials, or what?"

The laugh lines around her eyes fanned out. "Such discretion! What an ambassador!" As they walked to meet Dr. Benjamin Sommers and David in the conference room she said, "Take my advice. Keep that eye patch."

"If I may hazard a guess," Dr. Anthony Hale Douglass drawled, "we've got our little quorum and can get to business." He angled his head to look down the oval table past the district attorney and Edwina's tea service, trying to catch Benjamin Sommers' eye. "Doctor Sommers, inasmuch as this conference room is your sanctum sanctorum, and you're, so to speak, the senior officer present—may I nominate you to chair this meeting?"

Dr. Benjamin Nathaniel Sommers checked an eyebrow at his wife and son, an expressionless message circuited among them, then he aimed a second appraisal at the bright vigilant face of the district attorney who sat diagonally across the table. By the time he answered Dr. Douglass it was clear that he had reservations. "I'm just a hospital trustee, Doug. One of the front men. You're the one who really runs the place, so why don't you skipper this clambake?"

Dr. Douglass fanned out a quick left-right glance, modestly assuring himself he had a unanimous mandate, then reached for an amused tone. "Perhaps we're being just a bit too formal about all this. After all"—his amusement enlarged—"Doctor Mayoso isn't on trial here. This is supposed to be an opportunity for mutual communication. Would you disabuse me of any misunderstanding, Mr. District Attorney, if I misconstrue the question?"

"No, Doctor. You're one hundred per cent correct. My job in this town is to be a keeper of the peace. Even though there's a time and place under our adversary system to slug things out in a court of law, my whole aim and endeavor on this beautiful spring morning is purely and simply to reach a meeting of minds."

"Hear, hear," Dr. Douglass said. "Good kickoff, Jim."

"Law enforcement is no picnic. Especially"—the district attorney smiled tolerantly—"in this world of sinners. And it's twice as hard for a prosecutor, because we're in the public eye so much."

"I'm not sure I follow you," Dr. Benjamin Sommers said quietly. "Talk of a meeting of minds suggests some earlier disagreement. Phrases like 'law enforcement' suggest some preceding crime. And if it's twice as hard to be a prosecutor, there must be clever criminals in the neighborhood.

What you suggest seems more important than what you actually say."

Dr. Anthony Hale Douglass looked down on the university emblem on his china cup, pained. The district attorney's shoulders straightened with the experienced recognition of a traditional courtly adversary.

"Doctor Sommers," he said, "criminal law lost a great trial attorney when you went into medicine."

"Well," Benjamin Sommers said calmly, "somehow I never got ambitious to be Attorney General, or Governor. But almost fifty years in obstetrics and gynecology teaches a man to beware of the right hand which giveth while the left hand taketh away."

Everyone laughed, and Mayoso said to the district attorney, "Mr. Stacy, you wanted to talk to me, didn't you?"

"Yes, that was the original idea. Doctor Douglass, if I can have the floor for a minute or two more to make my position clear—"

"Certainly, certainly." He rested, less threatened. The show was on the road with no grinding of gears.

"I happen to hold a J.D. degree, that's Doctor of Jurisprudence, and I mention that item not to pin any medals on myself—I've lost too much money at church bingo to believe anything comes easy—but I'd like to present my case in medical terms, so to speak."

So to speak, Marjorie thought, and closed her eyes lightly. So to speak. And speak and speak until Jimmy goes marching to Hartford, then to Washington, the whole flag-waving distance.

"So, as one sort of doctor, to use a medical analogy, a district attorney's job is like being a medical doctor in the emergency room. Night and day, it never stops because our civilized society is not very civilized nor sociable."

"Don't be so cynical," Dr. Benjamin Sommers murmured. "Leads to peptic ulcers."

"With all due respect to your fifty years in medicine, I doubt that any sheltered person can imagine the bums and beasts, the muggers and rapists, the crooked nice people and the nice crooked people I have to examine and cross-examine and play father confessor to."

"Confession? I thought your job was to seek out and prosecute."

"I plead innocent to that, sir. I like to indulge myself in the belief that I practice law like preventive medicine. The Public Health Department chlorinates the water and immunizes the kids, doesn't it? Preventing is better than curing, my doctor friends—and some of my best friends are doctors—tell me. When I ran for public office, I made a holy vow to practice preventive law."

"So to speak," Marjorie said, opening her eyes.

"Mrs. Sommers, I stand second to no one in this community in my respect for you—the way you sign a blank check to this hospital every year to cover the annual deficit, no, please don't shake your head, it's just one of those public secrets."

"Doug," Marjorie said, "much as I admire the handsome use of the English language by the city's senior legal officer, would I be out of order if I asked one simple Quakerish question?"

"Depends, Marjorie."

Edwina Hawthorne smelled smoke and interrupted with great genteelness. "More tea, anyone?"

No one heard her because Marjorie was asking very firmly, "Just exactly what is the problem here? With no crime, no criminal, and no disagreement on which our sheltered minds have to meet—"

"On the contrary, Mrs. Sommers! When I said preventive law, I meant it. Sometime back, when I was still assistant district attorney, I had occasion to meet your son— If you recall that meeting, Doctor Sommers?"

David stared back at Jim Stacy without expression. "Word for word."

"Preventive law, that's all our discussion was. The law of the State of Connecticut is explicit and definite in extending its protection of human life, including the unborn child in the womb. Your use of administrative subterfuge—I mean your research beds used to get around hospital regulations—was skating over thin ice. Close to criminal liability."

Marjorie whispered to her husband, "Ben, why isn't our lawyer here?"

"I phoned Terrence's office," Benjamin Sommers whispered back, "but his secretary said Terrence was in New York with Witt. Some kind of Italian patent law blow up."

"Fatta la legge, trovato l'inganno."

"Make a law—?"

"And find a way around it. I'll phone Terrence later."

"This community can rest assured so long as I'm D.A. that the laws applicable to criminal abortions will not be subverted, contravened, monkeyed with, fish fried, or just plain broken."

"We gave our promise to you, Jim," Doctor Douglass volunteered rapidly, nodding gravely at David who stared blankly back at him, "and we've kept our promise. The first few women we had to turn away caused several fairly messy situations, but we had expected a few bumps on the road, and"—he began speaking more hastily as he spotted blue flames rising in Marjorie's eyes—"the word has gone out over the supermarket circuit. Any lady who wants to break the law is just wasting her time when she comes here expecting us to be an accomplice to criminal abortion. There'll be no hanky-panky in my hospital."

"As a trustee," Benjamin Sommers said quietly, "a representative of the public to maintain this as a nonprofit charitable and educational institution, your saying 'my hospital' is more enthusiastic than it is accurate, Doug."

David hitched his chair forward and cleared his throat. "Can I put in two cents' worth on that education idea? I have to live with the medical students. Every day we talk a good game. Let's take the high road, we say. But every day the students see us taking the low road. They see us set up a hospital committee for therapeutic abortions. Then they watch us twist ourselves trying to meet the state law that the operation must be necessary to preserve the mother's life or that of the unborn child. And even when the patient meets the standards of the committee, the students see doctors back away from having their names attached on the surgical schedule to cases like that because they're scared stiff of the dirtiest label in medicine: abortionist. The students hear rumors that there's a hospital quota for therapeutic abortions, but nobody would dream of putting quotas on appendectomies or heart surgery or even biopsies." He leaned toward Dr. Douglass. "You ought to listen to them in the student lounge sometime."

"David, if you knew how complex and difficult hospital administration has become—"

"Of course, that's why I'm telling you this. The students say that the only difference between a clean therapeutic abortion and a dirty one is money. Somewhere between, say, two hundred or two thousand dollars. Maybe half of the unmarried people they know are having intercourse, and they know that Connecticut law has made a public crime of the religious doctrine that this is a private sin."

"My office prosecutes the sinners, not the sin—"

"Then, let's look at the sinners. In their obstetrics classes the students learn statistics showing that maybe nine out of ten illegal abortions are performed on married women." He leaned back in his chair, then added, "You should have heard them when they read about the college girl who was arrested for a crime on the statute books of Connecticut—'the secret delivery of a bastard.'"

"Yes, I remember. One of my colleagues prosecuted. But, if you don't mind my being frank, I didn't come here to plead the case for our laws. They're on the books, and it's my job to enforce them."

"You came to talk to me," Mayoso said.

"Yes, quite frankly, I did."

"And," Mayoso added, "when you talk about just doing your job, you're using what's been elevated to a slogan. What good is professional pride without ethical boundary lines?"

"I'll ignore that, Doctor Mayoso, in the interest of courtesy and improving our communications." His smile became flat-lipped. "In my book, for you to use the word ethical is immoral hypocrisy."

"This is outrageous!" Marjorie's voice was actually shaking. "For Doctor Mayoso to accept an invitation to come here to New Haven, to take a faculty post as a research professor, and to be accused of crimes in the *future!*" She shook her head. "Blackmail."

"No, Mrs. Sommers. Preventive law. I've been assured by Doctor Douglass that Doctor Mayoso's research position does not give him staff privileges to admit patients to this hospital."

David and Doctor Douglass spoke at the same time. "Now just a minute—" David interrupted but the hospital Administrator's voice rose smoothly over him. "Let's clarify that item, shall we? Doctor Mayoso's position permits him to admit special patients for research study."

"But the signature on the hospital admission sheet," the district attorney said, "has to be the signature of a doctor on the clinical staff, right?"

"Welcome to New England," Marjorie said across the table to Mayoso. "Cradle of the Revolution and sweet land of liberty. Why don't you just chuck it and come to work with me at the United Nations?"

"Marjorie," her husband said pleasantly, "just don't go barging down the Nile."

The door to the conference room opened narrowly, and one of David's young laboratory technicians leaned through the space to motion to Mayoso. "Telephone, Doctor."

"Later, please."

"It's long distance."

"Perhaps you'd better take it," Dr. Douglass said with the extra courtesy he extended to those whom he had injured. "We'll wait for you. I'll make sure nobody says anything important until you come back."

Mayoso followed the technician across the corridor. "Sir," she said, "you can take the call in Doctor Sommers' study if you want a little privacy."

Dr. Benjamin Sommers' study, just a step off David's laboratory, was walled completely by books, an old rolltop desk near the window, world-weary leather chairs, bronze heads of Semmelweiss and Freud, signed photographs of all his former residents whose brass nameplates marked their chairs in the conference room across the hall. A rack of pipes, a box of wooden kitchen matches; a dog-eared pile of yellow manuscript of the book he was writing crowded the telephone to a corner of his desk.

"Doctor Mayoso speaking."

"Go ahead, New York," the long distance operator said.

"Mayoso? Witt. I hope I'm not interrupting you too badly—"

"No, no—"

"I've been trying to reach Betsy," Witt was saying, "but she's not home.

I'm going to be late as the devil for her birthday party in Southport tonight."

"Too bad. There's going to be a special surprise, Marjorie says."

"Oh? You mean that painting of Timmy? Mother commissioned it
while Betsy and I were in the Caribbean."

"Yes."

"Betsy's driving you down to Southport, isn't she?"

"That's what she said this morning."

"Is Mother there in New Haven?"

"Very much so."

"On that district attorney thing?"

"Yes. The Sommers clan make good allies."

"Dammit. I should be there, too. Of all days for me to get shafted by
a messy situation! Look, now that I've reached you, will you explain to
Betsy that I tried to phone her? As soon as I get my office debugged I'll
be along for her party."

"De-what?"

"We had a kettle of fish here, research stealing, industrial espionage,
whatever you want to call it. Terrence persuaded me to call in a spy-by-
night electronic firm to nail the crooks. Today, just by accident, I discovered that my own car and my own office were bugged, too. I'm so damn
mad I can't even spit. Fantastic gall. Who'd believe it?"

"I would, Witt. Snooping corrupts, and absolute snooping corrupts absolutely."

"Explain the whole nutty mishmash to Betsy on your way down to
Southport, will you? I've got to stay right here, until I personally make
sure every damn little microphone and gizmo and tape recorder is thrown
out. Do you know if Betsy will be taking Timmy down to Southport with
you?"

"David said that Alice took Timmy along with his two children to
the Barnum Museum in Bridgeport. They'll drive down to Southport
later."

"Good. Old-fashioned family get-togethers don't come every day. I promised Timmy a box kite, so I'll bring it along. Hasta luego."

"Hasta luego."

When he returned to the conference room he sensed immediately a
change for the worse. The tea-party pretenses were gone; the air was
abraded with anger. Instead of the neat circumference of evenly spaced
people, chairs had been moved, pushed back at crooked angles, a twisted
uncomfortable grouping. The district attorney was flushed, talking at
Marjorie in an oratorical way.

"And if you could have been with me this morning, Mrs. Sommers, you might ease up on your sport of trying to beat the devil with his own tail. You have to see a twenty-two-year-old girl stretched out on a marble slab with a falsified death certificate. Acute cardiac failure, it says. In fact it was a bungled abortion with a catheter." Stacy's voice was husked with anger. "The abortionist got away with it because he runs a phony nursing home as a front. Half of his patients are young ladies too far along in pregnancy to fool with, so this neighborly fellow and his partner, a friendly unethical attorney, specialize in housing these girls, room, board and floor mop, until they have the baby. The infant is sold through blackmarket adoption channels. The girls all sign legal consent forms, so everything's inside the letter of the law." Stacy clenched a fist. "Legal. The wrath of God will surely get them, but what can the law do when public leaders like you—"

"When Doctor Mayoso—" Marjorie began to say, but Mayoso interrupted her.

"Thanks, Marjorie, but I'd better speak up at this point."

"Amen to that, Doctor!" the district attorney said immediately. "You tend to your job and I'll tend to mine. But let me tell all of you something —you people live in a very cozy separate world from mine. Here," he added, pulling a magazine from his briefcase and throwing it open on the table, "here's the kind of so-called drug companies I have to deal with!"

He pointed at a half-page advertisement with a headline PERIOD LATE? DOCTOR'S PRESCRIPTION TYPE MEDICATION WILL RELIEVE YOU IN MIND AND BODY! SEND NO MONEY! PAY POSTMAN WHEN YOUR MEDICATION ARRIVES IN PLAIN WRAPPER! YOUR SUPPLY MAILED SAME DAY YOUR HURRY-UP ORDER ARRIVES! WHY SUFFER OR BECOME FRANTIC? WRITE NOW! RIGHT NOW!

"You aren't suggesting that Sommers Pharmaceuticals—"

"No, Doctor Sommers, what I'm suggesting is that this kind of garbage couldn't exist without some kind of crooked doctor in on it. A doctor who knows that nobody has yet invented a substance you can swallow which will abort an early pregnancy without extremely hazardous or fatal effects. A guy who knows that not one woman in a thousand believes that simple fact."

A teacup clattered. "How awful," Edwina Hawthorne spoke under her breath, but the district attorney wheeled toward her.

"Awful? You don't know what awful is until you see that young lady on the marble slab with a fake death certificate. And the butcher who did it goes free."

"Free?"

"Yes, ma'am. Legally there is no abortion if there was no pregnancy." He put the knuckles of both his hands on the table and bent toward her as if she were a hostile courtroom witness. "Isn't that a star-spangled kissoff? The young lady wasn't even pregnant! Missed her period. Just scared witless." When Marjorie Sommers raised her chin abruptly to say something, he swung to her with a sensual narrative enjoyment, star of his own drama. "Believe me, I'd like to take you for a short stroll through some of our not exactly ethical drugstores. You can buy nifty sticks of slippery elm. It's squashed-together tree bark, dehydrated, loaded with germs. There's ergot, with a nice chance of poisoning, which also goes for quinine and castor oil and tansy tea and, worst of all—correct me if I'm wrong, Doctor Mayoso—good old double-barreled Spanish fly that the swingers think is an aphrodisiac, and their girl friends think has a glamorous foreign abortive magic. Like the famous English Mrs. Seagraves Pills or dried seaweed pencils that used to come in from Germany and a half a dozen other European countries." He looked from one to the other. "You don't have to stare at me as if I'm the one with dirty hands. You doctors can have everybody smiling and feeling nice all over just by talking about newborn babies and happy childbirth. But just let an officer of the law mention, just *mention*, the whole abortion underground, and all of a sudden people look at us like pigeon guano, or maybe worse. You'd think that we were the butchers."

"You are," Marjorie Sommers said calmly. "Men have been making your precious laws for a long time, not women. They've even convinced women that abortions are just one more of a long list of difficulties a woman is supposed to learn to live with."

"Mrs. Sommers, forgive me if I sound rude, but I came here to speak to the hospital administrator and Doctor Mayoso—"

"Never mind that, Mr. Stacy. Doctor Mayoso and Doctor Douglass are here every day. You can talk to them anytime. But I'm here only this morning, and I want to tell you that all your horror stories only convict your own barbaric laws, not the crazed frightened women who go through desperate humiliations you never mentioned because you don't even know about them. Do you think women enjoy being swindled and hounded and medically excommunicated? Do you think any woman can go through terrors that smash everything she learned as a girl, all her dreams of motherhood, and then ever look at the world in the same way again? Do you?"

"Marjie, if you'll allow me to call this meeting to order—"

"Doug, I hear these things every week from South America or Arabia. But to hear them in my own hometown—!"

"Doctor Mayoso," Jim Stacy said, "you haven't said a word."

David broke in. "This is becoming a kangaroo court. He doesn't have to say anything."

"I do, David. Marjorie, I have to agree with almost everything Mr. Stacy has said."

"Mayoso!"

"I do. Even when you throw out the criminals and the butchers and the chemicals and the probes, even when you just look at physicians who are full-time abortionists, you'll probably find a sick twisted man."

"Well, I'll be god-damned!" the district attorney stared at Mayoso. "D'you mean that?"

"Of course. But now the academic people, I mean university people no one can seduce with prestige or buy for money—and here's where I agree with you, Marjorie—they have to challenge the laws in an honest open way."

"Frankly"—Dr. Douglass' voice was honed with finesse—"now that I see the dimensions of both sides of this thing"—he zeroed in on Mayoso— "I'd like to make myself abundantly clear: this hospital is definitely not, and I repeat, not, in the business of challenging state law or becoming a test case."

Mayoso's white mane turned toward him with a massive leonine dignity. "I'm a guest in your house, Doctor Douglass. Understand, please, I have a great mistrust of martyrs. And I'm not in the test-case business, myself."

Without inflection, Jim Stacy asked, "Just what business are you in, Doctor Mayoso?"

Mayoso frowned slightly, then got up with a slow thoughtful solemnity. For him, the meeting was over. He looked at Jim Stacy, then through him. "Personal insults solve nothing. But I'll tell you this much. Medicine has only two businesses. To relieve suffering and to discover new knowledge. I'm in both of them."

"This new knowledge, Doctor"—the district attorney shifted his feet slightly to include David in the widening arc of his smile—"this gee-whiz research, doesn't that include experiments on human beings?"

"Oh, for Pete's sake!" David Sommers wagged one hand in the air as if wiping away any objections the young lawyer might make. "Wait a minute, wait a minute, I've sat here determined not to let you get under my skin, but now—!"

Dr. Douglass interrupted. "We have the most carefully arrived at controls." He nodded to reassure the D.A. that he understood that no layman could fairly be expected to understand. "No patient in this hospital, not while I'm here, will ever have anything done which is not in his benefit or which does not have his complete understanding and approval."

"You say *his*, Doug. What about *hers*? The ladies? Do they understand what you're doing?" Jim Stacy came back to David and Mayoso again.

"Isn't it a fact that right across the hall, right now, you have a human fetus growing in an artificial womb, a stainless-steel monstrosity with glass portholes? Just like the ones they have in Russia?"

David grasped the conference table edge before him, as if to push himself up, but his father put a hand on his shoulder. "Yes," Benjamin Sommers said, "and it was my idea in the first place. And the Russians are working on it for the same reason we are—to be able to save the lives of prematurely aborted fetuses—miscarriages, if you'd rather call them that."

"But these children, Doctor Sommers—"

"They aren't children."

"They're *alive*, aren't they, Doctor?"

"Of course."

"And these living humans die in that steel chamber after a couple of days, don't they?"

"They live longer and longer," David said wearily. "We've been able to carry them up to three days. Maybe someday we can carry them to full term development, just like normal nine-month newborns."

"And your women patients actually cooperate?" Mr. Stacy shifted from skepticism to incredulity. "With full and complete knowledge and consent?"

"Of course. Each fetus was separated from its mother only because she had a miscarriage."

"And what about your experiments to fertilize human female ova with male sperm? Haven't you done that and nursed the resulting human embryo along for a month or two? Until you decide, like God, to just throw the switch?"

"Good Lord!" David exploded. "Why don't you just call the reporters and television people in without all this cat-and-mouse routine?"

"Your holier-than-thou doesn't impress me one little bit, Doctor. It's only because I don't prosecute you under statutes forbidding the willful taking of life that you can play God with the most sacred thing there is!" Again, his unexpected flank attack. "And, as usual, Doctor Mayoso is not talking."

Mayoso, who had remained standing, measured the forceful young lawyer with his eyes, sensing a mind so misunderstanding, threatened, fearful, that it must take refuge in making sure that everyone shared the common-sense certainty that the world was flat. He pushed his fists into the shallow pockets of his white laboratory coat. "Playing God? You've said that twice, Mr. Stacy. You picked the wrong men, because every day we are reminded of how small and weak our knowledge is. As for the uncomfortable thought of our medical equipment—lots of people feel uncomfortable even thinking of getting an injection or having a tooth pulled. Our artificial womb across the hall is made out of stainless steel only because it holds oxygen under a pressure of two hundred pounds per square inch. If the mother could have carried the fetus to a full-term normal birth herself, that machine would not be there. And just ask Doctor Douglass how many other machines his overworked budget has to carry each year—artificial kidneys, electronic pacemakers for hearts that have stopped." His eyes never left the attorney's face. "I refuse to give you the satisfaction of calling you a flatheaded anti-intellectual ambitious public official. I give you the benefit of the doubt—"

"Hah, thanks!"

"Because I share with you, Mr. Stacy, the same puzzlement I get myself sometimes. Why are we doing this? The word motive is a good court-room word, isn't it? Boys will be boys—do our motives come from peep-holes? A chance to fool around with so many females? The adolescent snicker while scribbling graffiti on washroom walls? Is something wrong with us as men? Under these white coats, are we unconsciously monsters who hated our mothers? Now wait, let me finish. You began this, but let me finish. You asked what business I'm in. Research only happens when people see a big need. The researcher may only be curious, like Leonardo da Vinci or Darwin. Or maybe practical, like Pasteur. But the public test is whether or not we are humane. Out in the open where our colleagues can see us. Whether our patients benefit—or, at least, are not harmed—by what we investigate. What frightens you is that science is power to you. Isn't that it—power? If you're worried about power, so am I. I come from a culture of medieval coercion, religious, political—the power of coercion as the basic idea to channel our human future. Here, in the state of Connecticut, the New England of history, I see again the same fist in the same glove."

"When the people vote—"

"Mr. Stacy, voting gets harder as the questions get bigger, no? At least we, in this medical research that worries you, we are asking ourselves these questions, maybe confused and humble, but searching—"

"For the first time, I'm receiving you loud and clear—"

"Loud maybe, but not clear. To be clear you have to start being a real keeper of the peace. You said you were a Doctor of Jurisprudence, a doctor of preventive law. What have you and the law done about dealing with the human consequences of human biological advances? If a woman pa-tient accepts artificial insemination from a donor, is she an adulteress? Some judges have said so. They have ruled the children illegitimate. What will City Hall record about such a person? His father, or his mother, or his citizenship? How is he to think of himself when he is grown and learns of his origin? What about inheritance, wills, descendants? No answers will come from professional pride in just doing a job. In the end, far down the road, the Nazis taught us something: *that* philosophy leads to concentration camp doctors delivering babies with every modern aseptic technique, professionally skillful, then sending mother and infant off to the ovens." With an undertone of weariness, compassion, a kind of sorrowful anger, he looked deeply and hopefully at the attorney. "You, before anyone, see every day how we all carry a germ of that Nazi stuff—"

"More or less—"

"So, Mr. Stacy, all decisions are not professional chess problems, agreed? All boil down to moral and ethical choices."

"Well, I'm glad to hear you—"

"Don't be glad to hear me. Don't insult me with politeness. You came here to have a polite fight, to warn a notorious criminal that he would be kicked out of town if he did not keep his hands clean, ah?"

"If you want to put it that way—"

"I don't want to fight City Hall, or you, or anybody. You're a busy man. We're all busy people. Already we've talked too much. Enough, no?"

Jim Stacy's face muscles were knotting as he picked up the magazine advertisement from the table and dropped it into his briefcase and tugged the zipper fastener around it. Finally, as everyone watched him in silence, he made an inclination at the waist, the beginning of a bow to the hospital Administrator. "Well, Doctor Douglass, many thanks for your cooperation. No need to drag things out."

"The State versus Mayoso rests its case?"

"Now, now, Mrs. Sommers, that's no way to talk. Contrary to popular belief, or hotshot television, the last thing in the world that any D.A. wants is trouble. As for you, Doctor Mayoso, after hearing so much about you, I'm glad to get the straight scoop from you in person. I'm satisfied that we understand one another, Doctor."

"I'm sure we do."

"Well, now that we've got the trolley on the tracks, I'd better hop back downtown to the snake pit. Goodbye. It's been a pleasure and a privilege."

27 "So-so. MOSTLY so."
"You can do better than that. Today's my birthday and I'm not taking back talk from *any*body."
"Happy birthday. Happy happy birthday."

"It's been that all day—just wait till I tell you! Are you ready to turn your back on this lab and go go go? We'll be late getting to Southport."

Mayoso pulled a high metal stool out from beneath the laboratory table and patted it. "Make yourself at home, Betsy. I'll be with you in a minute. Sit down."

"I'm no mountain climber. To get all the way up on that lab stool with this tight skirt? And these heels?" She frowned at him. "What's the matter with you, amigo?" She put a hand to her forehead and wiggled two fingers. "My antennae detect a few vibrations."

"Aie, since this morning I've been asking myself: Do I look like a threat to the peace and dignity of the People of the Sovereign State of Connecticut?"

"What a question! Does Macy's tell Gimbels?" She made a comedienne's skit of hitching her skirt higher and mounting the lab stool.

"Your Macy's reminds me—Witt called from the New York office." Mayoso explained about Witt's being late for the dinner party.

"Oh hell. And I rushed home and fought my way into this girdle just to wear this new dress for him." Betsy gave the seat of the lab stool an experimental twist, then a faster merry-go-round spin. Mayoso's laboratory rotated past her. The room had Roone in it, invisibly. *I wish I could ask him which corner Roone works in when he's here.* The acid-proof bench tops cluttered with glassware were a part of Roone's world she did not share. The gleaming precision balances under their dustproof glass covers, the Leitz research microscope in the corner set up for photographic copying, the refrigerated analytical ultracentrifuge anchored in the far corner on its special platform. "*Round and round I go,*" she sang, "*down and down I go, like a leaf that's caught in the tide—*"

She braked herself to a stop. "Woo! Dizzy." *I'm a wee high. He'll spot it, especially if I keep singing about that old black magic called love. Talk about* him. "Discover any world-shaking discoveries today?" Suddenly she giggled. "*I* did!"

I've discovered, Mayoso thought swiftly, still reverberating with the district attorney's siege, *that jungles grow everywhere. Not just in Caracas or San Juan, but also in New Haven, Connecticut.* "My discovery for today," he answered her, "is that whoever put you together knew a thing or two about anatomy."

She grasped the metal seat and leaned back a little so that she could swing up both her legs, outstretched, ankles touching. "Not bad. Mrs. Crotty, the volunteer ladies' boss, won't let me wear high heels with my volunteer's uniform. Not by the hair of her chinny chin chin." She lowered her legs slowly and grinned across the room at him while he hung up his white laboratory coat. "You know, I'm awfully glad we never became lovers."

"Now Betsy, all of a sudden, where did that come from?"

"I mean it. Everything's so much more comfortable this way. Easier. Friendlier."

He slid into his suit coat. "If you'd been at the meeting with the district attorney today, you'd know what a butcher I really am."

"*You?* Loyal, courageous, brave, and all those other Boy Scout things I can't remember. You? What did he say?"

"I'll tell you in the car. Do you want me to drive?"

She wagged her finger at him, closing one eye with exaggerated shrewdness as she pushed herself off the lab stool. "Smarty pants. You think I've had a drink or two too much, don't you?"

Now he was sure of it. "Have you? You sound as if you're feeling no pain."

"None, thank you, Doctor. Just a wee drop of pick-me-up after a long hard day."

He switched off the room lights and waited for her at the door as she came toward him with her own particular way of walking, as if she were being photographed stepping out of a sunken tub. "Birthdays are not supposed to be long and hard, Betsy. Didn't you know?" Even in the twilight dimness of the darkened laboratory he could see her face change.

"I'm pregnant," she said. She reached out and checked his hand. "No, don't turn the lights back on."

He lifted her hand and kissed the back of it. "*Qué milagro!* No back talk from me. Really a happy birthday, isn't it?" This must have been the real surprise both Marjorie and Witt had mentioned.

As if she were reading his mind, she said quietly, "I haven't told anybody yet. A missed period isn't exactly a sure thing, is it?"

He looked down at her. All the merry-go-round bravado was gone from her voice. "Betsy—do you really want to stand here in the dark?"

She shook her head, almost a childlike gesture the way she did it.

"Here," she said, handing him her car keys, "you drive."

They sat side by side without speaking, Mayoso concentrating on the highspeed traffic and files of Diesel trucks making their smokeplumed run from Boston to New York. She smoked lazily, her head back on the seat, curled there with the lassitude of a dozing cat. Mayoso had closed the convertible top before they had started so that the wind would not drown them out; she missed the familiar whipping roar of the airstream past her fluttering green chiffon scarf.

He told her briefly how the district attorney had boxed him in at the hospital, and how the Sommers had stood up for him. She hardly heard him. The Sommers. Marjorie would always find Problems to attack, just as her mother had found lampposts to chain herself to for the suffragette movement. And Witt would go right on being his grandfather, but in a company jet and a debugged office. That isn't being fair to them, I know it isn't, but on one of the most important days of my life I shouldn't have to persuade Alice and her children and Timmy to visit the Barnum Museum in Bridgeport just so that I can make a clever excuse for leaving town to find some doctor who doesn't know me from a hole in the ground and who'll tell me whether the pregnancy tests said yes or no. I should be able to be happy, in the natural way that a woman should feel happy, without having to fake all the gay noises of a little black sheep who'd lost her way and can now be welcomed back into the bosom of the flock.

Through the twisting upcurl of cigarette smoke, she watched the Connecticut shoreline slide by. The water of Long Island Sound glittered metallically in the near distance, notched by the white sails of a squadron of Lightning-class sloops tacking toward Port Washington. That goofy but touching nautical bracelet of miniature yachting flags Roone had bought her in San Juan. K-U-Z-I-G-Y. Permission Requested To Lay Alongside. That shackup artist! Praise be he'll graduate and be gone soon. Go west, young man, go west. Take your California internship and bodysurf into a solid-gold girl-studded success. Best he'll never know if I am or I'm not pregnant. A boy who knows none of the persuasions of grief or the making of one's own penance.

The industrial clutter of smokestacks which marked the marshy shore of Bridgeport marched past. Something about Bridgeport stirred her memory. Witt? That day at the County Courthouse on that ironically named Golden Hill Street? No, something else. The strange doctor's office on Main Street?

That day Roone rode in this car beside me, the birthday that was not his birthday at all. His saying: ask me no questions, I tell only lies. Laughing is the only truth left around. The tollbooth man remarking it was a real nice day for a ride, and Roone's suppressed snarl: Yeah, if the Chinese don't drop a bomb on New York.

Sitting right here, that cornball guitar in the back seat like the beard and sandals crowd, with that lunatic jabber of his: *Truth or Falsies. War in Heaven, the ovaries against the testicles* . . .

A choked laugh unexpectedly caught inside, as if she had swallowed a peach pit. She coughed, then coughed again so hard Mayoso began to steer at an angle into the slower-moving right-hand lane. "Want me to stop?"

She patted her chest. "I'm—I'm—really, nothing—" She gave him her unfailing sideways smile to reassure him, anything to stop him from becoming concerned or doctorish, because a buried remembrance had been unearthed in a rush. Roone, Main Street, brass-knuckle talk. *You're the slickest booby-trapped manhole on Main Street . . . DeWitt's out of the saddle now and you're on a muddy track, right? . . .*

A connoisseur of degradation, you are, Ladyjane. Marjorie Sommers raises Japanese orchids in her greenhouse, while Betsy Sommers raises hell in her hothouse. Floral offerings accepted, the darling buds of May. You, lying there in your birthday suit like some gift box, just to wrap your foolgirl ribbons around his Maypole. My schoolboy travel agent, one-way ticket to outer space, wheeling senses and a swooning darkness. War in Heaven. Shot down in flames.

"You're so quiet, Betsy."

All quiet on the western front. "Saving my strength."

"That rainy Sunday feeling?"

"How'd you guess?"

"People get it on birthdays, Betsy."

"Not people. Ladies."

"Some of my best friends are people." What's wrong, he wondered. She had seemed delighted with her news—but now what?

She kicked her shoes off and tucked her feet beneath her as she twisted sideways in the seat to talk to him. In the sports car cockpit he bulked enormous, his white thatch almost scraping the cartop. With his eyes on the road, his head unmoving, he looked sculptured in profile.

She put one hand lightly on his big shoulder. "I need some medical information. Just how reliable are pregnancy tests?"

"They differ. Which did you have?"

"Some chemical thing." She snorted. "The be-a-dear and pee in the pan."

"Whose lab did the test?"

She told him about going to the doctor in Bridgeport, using an assumed name, her embarrassment about not having enough money to pay either the doctor or the laboratory because she never carried a checkbook or any amount more than cigarette money. She barely managed to tell it as an amusing anecdote. The penniless rich lady.

"You've got an honest face, Betsy. Any doctor would trust you." But I don't, not quite, he thought. Why drive twenty miles to Bridgeport for a pregnancy test that could be done in New Haven, right down the hallway from David's lab? She must have been very unsure of herself—after all, I myself told her that it could be many years before she might become pregnant. *If* pregnant is what she is.

He began to say, "If you don't mind a suggestion—"

"Oh—oh. That tone. Here comes Moses carrying the tablets down from Mt. Sinai."

"Well, the first commandment in obstetrical practice is to make sure the lady is really pregnant before you tell her so."

"That's what the doctor in Bridgeport said. I told him I had to be absolutely positively sure. But when I didn't even have the money for the first test—"

"But all you have to do is breathe one word to Witt. He'll build you a lab, or buy you one or anything you like."

"I know. I must sound stark raving, but—I can't quite explain it—I don't want to lift him up and then drop him. I want to be absolutely sure before I say a word."

She sounded too pat, almost rehearsed. He occupied himself with steering into the narrow space made by concrete platforms and stopped to pay the uniformed toll collector. As the car picked up speed again, she said, "You think I'm being unfair to Witt—I mean not making him a partner in this—don't you?"

"Only you can decide when to tell Witt. You're being very sensible to wait for a second test to confirm the first."

"What's that, the second commandment?"

"No. Just a veteran warhorse who knows that people feel what they feel, and do what they do. Handing out opinions about wives and husbands—" He shook his head slightly and did not finish.

She stretched her legs out before her, rubbing them while wiggling her toes. "Poor circulation. I must be getting old." There was an intimacy of the enclosed space. Thank God I can count on Mayoso. If I ask him not to, he won't say a word to Witt. All I need now is a little hap-hap-happy talk, the birthday girl, a quick wraparound hug from Timmy that's-a-my-boy, the cute piping voices of Alice and David's two darling kids, some appreciative ahhhing over the centerpiece Marjorie is sure to have concocted from her Japanese mountain orchids, all followed by a sweet wifely understandingness when Witt huffs and puffs in late and apologetic and bearing some impossibly expensive gift.

If the second test comes out positive, I'll tell Witt. He'll be so deliriously happy that we can start again at year one. After that, brace yourself, Betsy Mary. You'll be on candid camera, taking curtain calls, applause and cheers and every eye on you, all the warmth and wealth and protectiveness of family around the proud mother-to-be.

All I have to do is not lose my nerve or panic. Witt's been home long enough now so that a practiced innocence has become second nature. Just follow the advice to maybe-pregnant ladies printed on the top of every mayonnaise jar: *Keep Cool But Do Not Freeze.*

With a sense of confidence and power, almost debonair, she said, "You won't mention this to Witt?"

"Of course not."

"Just as soon as the second test, and I'm surely sure—"

"Of course."

Southport, the highway exit ramp sloping toward Trinity Episcopal Church. Greening elms lofty, their upper branches filled with sundown light. Pequot Street thawed by spring, a picture postcard perspective of white clapboard houses with latched-back shutters, green lawns bordered by white gothic fences with pickets of alternating heights; the fey touristy coyness of two polka-dot-painted circus horses hoofing their pedestals at the entrance to a dress shop; a municipal Ford pickup truck parked at the sidewalk which led to the one-story tan-brick green-tile-roofed Pequot School. The driver of the truck was opening the birdhouse-size glass door of the Public Notices box. Probably a warning to renew dog licenses on time, or the repairing of the Harbor Road. Vital village issues. Under a gilt Federal eagle flanked by boxy carriage lanterns, the Nathan Hale Gift Shoppe framed a single white-haired woman customer suspended daintily amid the pewter candlesticks, Paul Revere teapots, and quaintly printed copies of Ye Olde Guide Booke of Colonial Connecticut.

The local pace is just right, Betsy thought. I've been rattling in circles like a revolving door. Easy does it, Ladyjane. Nobody's gotten excited around here since the British landed up the coast to burn New Haven, and that was a wee bit before my time. If Witt's warehouses burn down in Caracas again, I'll watch this time through the bloodless glass windows of a TV set. I need a slow calm restrained happiness—just the feeling I'd have if men didn't make such a messy complicated can of worms out of a straightforward pleasant happening, simple and biological as the leaves budding on all these elms and oak trees. If only we were honest enough, or sophisticated enough, or maybe primitive enough, for me to tell Witt this, I could explain I've known all along, deep down, that Roone doesn't really count. He'll be gone so soon. Nothing needs to change in our lives except for the better.

Mayoso made an effort to ease his grip on the steering wheel; his hands had tightened the moment they had curved off the expressway down into the town and had passed Trinity Church where Betsy and Witt had been married. That time so long ago, that innocent time before disaster, barely to be recalled: a young Cuban doctor training at Yale, captured by this cool New England world so different from the sun-drenched Caribbean islands. The aromatic press of apple cider as autumn lengthened the leafy guardian spaciousness of elm-crowned shadows. The churchly Sunday mornings, Sunday Family Service and Church School at 9:15 A.M., sensible plainspoken hours in a church so different from those in his tropic world; a church with no enforced humble approach up any steep steps of stone, no tortured sacred martyrs dying in effigy, no stage, no drama, no blaze of golden rococo angels and cherubim, a church four-square on-the-level grass with commonplace white paint and a spired finger pointing skyward with a stern uncompromising no-nonsense which, at first, slightly chilled him.

Those Sunday mornings with the Sommers *familia* who, in almost the Biblical phrase, took him in because he was a stranger in their land. Tranquil Sunday mornings, belled booked and candled, a stroll of church-goers. Witt's bride Betsy acknowledged by the townspeople as just the spicy pinch of pepper the Sommers clam chowder needed. The right sort of newcomer was welcome; the Sommers' money wasn't all that old, not like the old old money up in Boston, stolid bankers who banked on God each Sunday and on the sea trade the rest of the week. Money from the Chinese tea-and-opium-trade days, money from the slave-trade, sugar, spice and rum days.

How wise the Sommers, Mayoso thought; let the Sunday strollers make snide jokes about Marjorie's L.I.V.E.—the organization did have a holy-roller tambourine rattle to its name—but the Sommers believed with their no-nonsense plainspoken church in Life, Intelligence, Vigor and Energy.

The harbor harmony of this village. The Sommers could have retreated to this easygoing complacent isolation to become bystanders and specta-tors, like the Manchu mandarins who contemplated carved jade tigers and the tiny aesthetic feet of their concubines while the Boxer Rebellion exploded outside the walls of their Peking palaces.

Beside him, Betsy said, "Here we are."

The golden sea-horse weather vane above the stately white house was turning mystically to point their way. Timmy and his two cousins were playing croquet on the lawn.

Mayoso swung the Jag between the posts marking the long curving driveway to the Sommers house. Timmy threw down his croquet mallet to come racing across the lawn toward the car.

Betsy's heart rose with pleasure as she scrambled out to meet him. From inside the car Mayoso's voice said, "Feeling better now?"

She twisted her head to glance back at him. "You bet your sweet life I am."

No. I'm betting *my* sweet life that I am.

□ □ □

Her happiness might be a fresh-minted coin. She turned it over, then like a collector over again, enjoying just the feel of it. The second tests had seemed to take so long, but they were completed now and the days of waiting and nights of sleeplessness were over. Finished, she thought, and positively positive. And now this purr of a car can buzz up the highway to New Haven twice as fast as Mayoso drove it past here the other day.

A surreal laxity folded around her, the gold coin put away because happiness ought not to be examined or handled too long. The jealous gods had their ways of reminding you of that. More enduring, below the belly-button, was this begotten rhythmic delicate manufacture of new life. Really divinely incredible when you up and thought about it, even the faint nippling tension as if the babymouthed rooting hunger for nursing had begun.

How could I ever have envied men as the moguls and maharajas of the earth? They have nothing to compare with this blossoming feeling of roots trunk branches greening outward, nested with lights, at oneness with the groundswell of seasons.

At home, in her own driveway, she pressed the knob on her dashboard, enjoying the tiny omnipotence of the radio-controlled robot garage doors opening at her command. The station wagon was parked inside the garage: Either the Barretts had not gone shopping or Timmy was home from school—no, it was too early in the afternoon for that—or something domestic and tiresome, such as a service call for the automatic laundry machine, had kept them home.

Not until she was partway up the flagstone path to the house, her heels tapping with a pleasant going-places sound, that she thought, maybe Witt's home. About once a year, when things at the office were especially good or especially bad, he came home to make a longer evening and an earlier night of it. Poor Witt. Everyone thought his international comings and goings were so jet-setty and pizzazzy, but no one knew about his patent problems in Italy or the warehouses burned down in Caracas or the tropical storms that could flood a two-million-dollar experimental farm into a mud puddle.

As she ran lightly up the house steps a moment's fear pricked her. Witt was nobody's fool. His lifetime family training in restraint was deceptive:

he could be penetrating, knowing. Ah, for God's sake! Today's a sunny day, a day for optimism. Any rattle of suspicion in Witt's mind will be drowned out by holiday fireworks when we celebrate a child after so many barren years.

She aimed the housekey straight into the door lock, pleased with her steady hand. Bull's-eye! That fine Dublin motto: do what ye like, so long's ye say the right thing. Witt *needed* good news! What better news than this? His coming late to the birthday party in Southport the other night had been a bit scary, sort of the play's the thing wherein we'll catch the conscience of the king. But everything had gone smooth as silk and satin. Timmy's portrait had been the nicest birthday surprise in years. And the flawless strand of pearls Witt gave me, vulnerable as I was when he walked in, hadn't been half as much the crumb of comfort as his birthday kiss and his remembering to bring Timmy the promised box kite.

The house was so silent that she paused in the kitchen, almost an intruder in the hush. She crossed the foyer and had her foot on the first carpeted step going upstairs before she turned back. There was no spill of light from the west windows of the library. The vertical linen jalousies should be tilted, not closed. At this time of day the filtered afternoon sun always gave the cushioned affable room a shadowless illumination. Not until she was across the soundless V'Soske library carpet and had her hand on the window hardware did she notice Witt. He was slouched at the far end of the library couch, isolated by the undersea dimness.

My prophetic soul. That once-a-year look of the company pressure cooker. Washington or Rome or San Juan? Or a bucket of money down the drain on that experimental farm? No wonder he'd been exchanging a jabber of legalisms on the phone with Terrence so late last night.

"Leave the blinds closed," Witt said tonelessly.

Now that her eyes were adapting to the faint light, she could see an unfamiliar hard set to his mouth. The open attaché case at his feet, the clumsy spill of papers on the floor, Witt scrootched down in a corner—even the jumbo tumbler of a drink on the table beside him—bankruptcy? Impossible. The Sommers are too big. A business loss might be bad, but not fatal.

Be bright, cheerful, *listening*, really listening to him, whatever it is. Wine with dinner, no tablecloth so a pair of candles can reflect warmly on the heartwood of his grandfather's table. Then my good news. His troubles first. Out of the way. Then the jaunty good word. Easy's done it before. Do it again.

She nodded at his drink. "Don't mind if I take a drop myself."

"You do that."

"What've you been belting for a nightcap this afternoon?"

"Just leaning into a little something. None of that coffin-varnish cookin' sherry, by God."

"Witt, I keep *that* locked up with the Mothersill's and Irish Mist."

"Well, this stuff is fairly misty. You must've been feeling domestic while I was in San Juan. You sure bought yourself some really decent jugs of booze." He waved one hand grandly. "Tell me, hostess, before I get a cutting edge on—is this your bar car or the champagne flight or just a neighborhood married man's saloon?"

Witt's toping voice and the untidy scatter of business papers were very unlike him. But easy does it. "Hangover heaven, sir. Sommers' rum-runners, but liquor is quicker."

"Sa-a-ay, you're a real crowd pleaser, Betts."

"If you pitch 'em," she bubbled, still trying hard, "I'll catch 'em."

"Spitball curves? Foul balls? One home run at a time?"

"One's a drink"—she smiled with genuine intimacy—"but two's company."

"Two's company. And three sheets in the wind, decks awash. Right?" Clank of ice cubes. A long bottoms-up swallow.

The decanter trembled in her hand. Fingertips cold, not quite so steady now. Witt, repeating words? Mimicking and mocking were Roone's line, not Witt's. She inserted the glass stopper with a trace of shakiness, afraid she might drop it, then set the decanter back on the tray carefully. She braced herself to turn around to face him. "Well, cheers." She saluted him with her glass, raised it to her lips, then stopped. He had not moved. She motioned with her glass again and said as offhandedly as possible, "No cheers?"

"For what?"

"Aren't you drinking?"

"No. I spill most of it."

"Wasting twelve-year-old truth serum? Shame on you." She sat down on the matching couch which faced his across the coffee table and crossed her legs, almost posing, chin line up, shoulders high. "Nice to see the man of the house home early for a change."

"Things got gravelly, so I cut out early. Shame on me. The loneliness of the long-distance company president."

"No, seriously, Witt. We can have a really slow lazy dinner. Timmy'll probably bend your ear about assembling that man-size box kite."

Easy, she reminded herself. See things his way. Think executive, sweet. That business-is-business bit only burns a hole in your gut. Just keep your eyes on home sweet home. Let the control tower talk you down through the foggy Irish mist to a safe landing.

"The kite," he said, in a veiled monotone. "Timmy's due home from school soon, isn't he?"

"Any old time now. Depends on how far the kids have to push the school bus." She finished her drink and kept herself from getting another. Better to just keep up this slow massaging sort of talk about children, home, dinner. The trend, friend, is up. Her taut muscles slackened. To be so understanding of his needs, especially when he was way down like this. When you sorrow, Daddy always quoted, all Ireland's at your side. No matter what Witt's company trouble is, we'll end only by feeling closer. Relieved, she piloted the silver cigarette box over to herself.

Abruptly, he raised his glass. "Hurricane Betsy," he announced.

Her cigarette snapped between her fingers, scattering tobacco. "Witt!" she protested. That strange unhealthy timbre in his voice. "Look what you've made me do." Takes effort. But hold your voice as level as you can. Let's have no more jittery spills of tobacco shreds. A light and easy manner, that's the ticket. Not defensive. Chipper. "Unaccustomed as you are to public speaking, dear, you ought to hoist a warning flag with each drink. That toast may have been funny the first time we heard it in Puerto Rico, but let's face it, dear—"

"Shut up."

A cold clap of silence. She stared at him. "*What?*" Immediate indignation swelled in her throat.

"Shut up. You and your gift of gab. You talk too goddam much."

Barfly cuffing—from Witt? The arrested moment expanded into a plunge through a bad dream's darkness, clutching out for handholds of smoke, a downrush of panic. Nervous breakdown? Brain tumor? The tops of tall trees always sickened first. Someone who must be herself was swallowing, scrunching up her eyes with puzzled amusement at his moon-shine sense of humor, proudly managing to laugh gamely along the border between annoyed tolerance and sympathetic understanding. Tense husbands had been known to growl at their wives before.

"*Grrr* yourself." She lifted herself to her feet with the fluid grace he admired, her stance was still part model, chin still up, shoulders well back, but her voice all domestic concern and efficiency. "Hungry as a bear and crocked as a hoot owl, that's what you sound like to me."

"For Chrisake, stop acting!" His rasp jarred her. She sat down as if pushed. "For once, Betts, just one time in your eloquent life can you stop the wisecracks and blather and behave like a grown-up woman?"

She pretended to misunderstand him and raised her eyebrows pityingly. "Oh? I never got *that* complaint before." She did not mean to challenge his husbandly pride, and asked, more sharply than she intended, "How would you know? Maybe if you can pull yourself together—"

"I'm sober as a judge."

"Then if you'll condescend to tell me—"

"My God, there you go again! That phony tongue! Anybody who pretends as much as you do, I swear, ends up being what she pretended. And you've ended up like some goddam wind-up doll that walks and talks and says mama!"

With great dignity, not outraged or irritated, but merely with the patient understanding of an adult allowing a child's temper tantrum to run its course, she said evenly, "Don't explain what's eating you, dear. Just let me guess."

"You're usually one dandy little guesser, Betsy, so why don't you?"

This was her chance. "Yes I can!" she said, exasperated. "This touchy irritability. Putting everybody's teeth on edge. I knew it would happen when Terrence kept you up talking business hours past midnight. Not enough sleep—"

"That's all I need? More sleep?"

"Yes. A healthy mind in a healthy body—simple as that, Witt. What could be so earthshaking that Terrence had to nag you at home?"

"Just a breach-of-contract suit, that's all. A two-bit electronics private eye claims that my canceling their contract is an expensive black eye. Maybe lethal."

"Couldn't Terrence—?"

"They insisted on a heavyweight match with me. Today. Tough operators. Sandpaper guts. Very put-up-or-shut-up."

Relief flooded through her. "Now, really, Witt. Couldn't you have gotten all that out a bit sooner?"

Men. Treating business the way women treat love, putting their whole hearts in it. All or nothing at all. Praise be to Saint Vitus and all the other twitchy saints, Witt's spat the damn trouble out. "After they bugged your office without permission, you had every right—"

"Betsy," he said wearily, holding his forehead with one hand, "they bugged everything in sight. The ladies' room. The laundry. The broom closet, for all I know." His voice cracked. "They even bugged your car."

"*My* car?"

"They goddam well did. When you sign up with us, Mr. Sommers, we by God do a job—that's what the boss man proudly pronounced in my office today. The professional-pride sales pitch."

"But *my* car?" My *car*? And where else? Her mind skittered in all directions at once. Car? Telephoto cameras? Telephone? I've heard about telephones . . .

Witt bent clumsily—toward his shoes?—no, to turn the attaché case toward her. Cradled in its enclosed foam padding sat a lifeless tape recorder. Her heart ballooned painfully. Witt stabbed at a switch and the tape began to rotate. Only an electronic hissing scratched out at first—thank God! Wrong button. He's erased the magnetic tape. An unreasoning hope flared: This whole ghastly nightmare, this divorce detective muck on our shoes, it can be wiped off, cleaned off, everything made as good as new.

But when the music began to play faintly, sounding tinny in the small speaker of the tape recorder, she recognized the betrayal instantly. That woman's smoky contralto. *"Come all ye fair and tender ladies . . ."*

Then a man and woman talking, hard to understand. A woman's laughter.

Then Roone. *"Don't be coy, Betsy. With legs like that you can lay 'em in the aisles. . . ."*

"What else can a lady do in a bucket seat?"

"Bucket. You bought the car, Betsy. . . . Now live in it."

Incredible. Out of that—that metal toy as mindless as an open razor—came someone who sounded just like her, but disembodied, saying, *"Well then, let's go over to your bed of roses. . . ."*

Witt was talking again, using the same impassive monotone, his words garbled with the tape recording of two bodyless actors rehearsing a no no Noel Cowardish sort of—

"If we don't show proper appreciation of this considerable accomplishment with a certified check, the boss man plans to keep the original tape recording. Maybe even play it for new clients. Sort of a salesman's sample."

"Tough guy," her own voice was saying. *"You think you've got the hottest gun in buckaroo town."*

"Bragging's half the fun, isn't it?"

She shrank. Oh God, this mechanical peeping Tom? Lunatic comedy, not two harried people sitting side by side in a car, but a scratchy copy of an original tape recording of a his-and-hers amateur theatrical.

As if he were reading her mind, Witt tapped the attaché case with the toe of his shoe. "Hard to believe, isn't it?" His ragged gruffness disguised his hope she could explain the whole idiotic thing.

"You don't know what's real as rocks, Betsy. . . ."

"Please. Don't be so angry. I can't stand it. You know how I love you. . . ."

"Stop it, Witt! Shut that thing off! If you're going to believe some trumped-up blackmail of some—some gangster—against the word of your own wife, some clever cruel stunt just to hold a gun up against your ribs—"

"Me, I'm holding the gun." Gently he added, "Against my own head. I okayed the original deal." He shook his head. "Baited my own booby trap. Spy now, pay later." He breathed out a long sighing sound. "Snooping corrupts and absolute snooping corrupts absolutely."

She had never seen him like this. How could he sit there with his skin off, invisibly chained by a nerveless control, unable to break through the gothic picket fence of his upbringing? His suppressed suffering was painful, his stoic matter-of-factness infuriating. She jumped to her feet. "Go ahead! Your wife gets framed and you just sit there making clever remarks!" Confront him. Keep it up, something told her as she heard herself spin out denials, explanations, indignant accusations of notorious detective blackmail, commercial trickery. "Witt, I swear to you, I *swear*, listen to me—"

Oh holy Mother of Sorrows, why doesn't Mrs. Barrett come in to interrupt me to ask about dinner? Or Timmy bounce in from school? Any kind of armistice, a pause to breathe in, anything . . .

"You're downtown now, madam. No grass and trees and pretty flowers downtown, in the stone jungle. No Cub Scouts. No Den Mothers. . . ."

If only Witt would burst with uncontrollable grief or violence, shout curses, strangle me—not this smoldering bottled-up Sommers self-control I've always hated in him. She took a few shaky steps toward the machine and kicked as hard as she could. The pointed toe of her shoe tore a hole in the plastic cover of the case, but the machine went on playing relentlessly.

Witt peered up at her, nodding. "That's how I felt. But this is only a copy. There are more tapes. There's one of you telling Mayoso you're pregnant."

She put the back of her hand up against her mouth, trembling, but unable to weep for the loss of all the glad news she had wanted to bring him. This brainless guilty shivering had to stop. Those unyielding inherited eyes of his. If only he could feel a decent moment's pity for me, just hold out his hand—but Witt was holding himself together rigidly; even his eyes were rigid and bruised with pain. His thin disguise of judicial poise was flaking off.

She stumbled back to the couch and almost fell into it, still shuddering convulsively. "I am, Witt. I'm pregnant." Part of her mind watched with horror as waves of hysteria foamed upward in her head, her neck arched backward, her mouth quivering against her pressing closed fist. "I—I—" She lowered both her hands and spread all ten fingers, fingertips touching, across her lower abdomen as if she were nine months' pregnant. "I—we finally did it."

He doesn't believe a word I say. What else does he know? Thank God I never mentioned Roone's name! He's just a voice on a tape. The brooding thunderhead of Witt's face, a gathering storm. A pitying sense of what he must have gone through these last few hours tore through her. "It's yours. I swear to God." She did not know that she was wringing her hands as she moved toward him, a begging wish that all this would vanish, if only he would understand that life itself was all that counted. Not inseminations or test tubes or syringes or clinical invasions, but only life itself. With that one seed of acceptance, life would flower.

"Yours, Witt," she repeated, believing it herself now, trusting that if she repeated it while believing it herself she could still convince him. "That wonderful week—remember?—fishing together at La Paguera, all those nights on the island—"

His hand shot up like a guillotine. The downstroke spun her backward. No, he couldn't actually be hitting. Not *Witt*. This cringing recoil—me?

"All those nights on the island!" He was seething furiously.

No, this didn't happen to sensible intelligent people. To flinch back against a wall of books, the tongue taste of blood, the military obscenities reeling out of his mouth while he stomped on the tape recorder with heel-smashing thoroughness, methodical and total. Anger erupted from her. "Hit me again, why don't you? Big brave Witt. The man who takes care of the store. Go ahead, you big brave Sommers bastard, hit me again!" She was screaming hysterically now. "You don't give a shit about me! All you care about is who pays the Sommers bills and bugs your bigshot office and your blueblood fucking pride!"

He stood before her, legs wide apart as a drunken sailor, his fists clenching and unclenching, a twisted murderous hate in his face so terrible that her own pain dissolved.

"You and your bastard," he was spitting out chokily. "Get out before I kill you." They stood at arm's length, crouched like caged animals in mid-combat, breathing hoarsely in the serene upholstered room.

The front doorbell chimed, startling as a gunshot. Then jangled again. Muffled, "Hey, Mom!" The parental world rushed in between them, leaving them staring at one another, pale, ashamed, grieved; two mourners looking into the same grave. The doorbell bonged out its two-toned chime again.

With automatic domesticity, Betsy said, "Mrs. Barrett will get it."

"She's gone." His chest was heaving.

"But the station wagon in the garage—"

"She took her own car. I told her not to come back until dinnertime."

She wiped her mouth and tugged frantically at her dress to straighten it as she stumbled across the rug-covered miles to the foyer, feeling weak-kneed and undefended, a tumult of rage, despair, Timmy, the desperate need to be practical.

"Hey, Mom!" His small impatient boy's face, one hand waving a large sheet of kindergarten creativity he couldn't wait to show her. "I was ringing and ringing," he accused her. She kneeled to embrace him, a downpour of horror submerging her with a vision of what would happen now, the walls of her throat closing with the needless pain this child, and the child inside, would face.

All the comforts of home, this motel. A home away from home. That nice-looking well-dressed woman in the bathroom mirror is reassuringly me. Ah, there's my sweet slip of a girl. My wild Irish rose.

With both hands she pushed back the dark heap of her disordered hair, watching the woman in the mirror do the same. Oh, what a fragile vulnerable face. What porcelain slenderness, with Wedgwood bluegreen eyes shining from the damaged shadow of makeup. And that unexpected tiny uplift at the corners of the lovely mouth, the Gioconda smile that makes men ask: What are you hiding? What's your secret?

Nothing resembling the hysterical woman steering blindly through traffic, but with sense enough to stop and fix her lipstick and comb her hair before walking into the fluorescent motel office, straight up to the shrouded eyes of the clerk at the desk, ignoring his frank stare of vulgar appreciation. Jerk off, you ratty jerk, she had thought while unhesitatingly signing the guest card *Cristina Mayoso* and saying with aristocratic firmness, "A quiet back room, please. I'm an awfully light sleeper."

His septic pawing grin, hard as nails. "Nothin' but, in this establishment, ma'm. Every room's for light sleepers. Need a hand with your luggage?"

"No, thank you."

"Pays to travel light."

Let me be brief, she thought. Drop dead.

"Here's your key, ma'm. Last room, second row back. Real quiet."

As soon as she had locked the door behind her she had torn open the paper bag. Tabac had bought it for her.

("If this stuff is Japanese," he had asked, "how the hell can they call it Scotch?")

The first gulp hit her stomach so burningly she doubled over, gasping and shuddering. To this, to this low measure, drinking straight from the bottle? Ladyjane, that's not becoming. Must be a drinking glass in the john, wrapped in a waxy little cover that reads SANITIZED FOR YOU.

Which it did. But a curving kiss of someone's lipstick still on the glass. Yesterday's thirst. Saturday's child.

Beside the bathroom mirror was a boxy contraption, a six-inch shelf

with two plastic cups, and a decal label: COURTESY COFFEE. PRESS BUT-
TON.

Oh yes. A sanitized sign of the times, good for all occasions. Press Button.

Drinking Scotch from a *cup,* for crisake, like back in speakeasy days.
Leave a kiss in the cup and I-eye will pledge with mine.

The lady, the nicely groomed lady in the mirror made a small salute
to her, refined and understated, nothing operatic or contrived or heavy-
breathing or thespian . . .

(There he lay stretched out, the prince of players, votive candles head
and foot and his silenced-forever slack jaw bound with a cloth, not a
penny or a clean sheet for a decent funeral . . .)

So the mirror says you might be penniless but you handled the situation with Tabac with all the casual command of Marjorie Sommers telling
her gardener: *Weed out that row* . . . and always, reflexively, adding
the New England *please* as if he could accept or refuse with an independent spirit.

Independent *spirits.* Cup fulla Scotchy. Joke, no?

"You kiddin?" Tabac had asked while they sat across from one another
in a booth at the Womb with a View.

"Hell of a thing to kid about, amigo."

"You soun different. Know that? How you gonna drive that green bomb
if you get cockeyed on ready-mix?"

"Tabac, you never ask your hostess questions in a respectable saloon.
I invited you here, so you're my guest."

He had crossed his arms on the table before him and had edged toward
her to whisper, "You figure it's so easy to fix up a l'il party like that?"

"Oh, come on now. Who's fooling who? You're a big operator."

He had leaned back against the wall of the booth, his arms still folded
across his chest, conveying to her that her request was very difficult but
possible, maybe, if she persuaded him right.

"You and Volga, you both have connections."

"Volga's still shacked up in San Juan. She's pissed off at Roone."

"Let's leave Roone out of this."

"Okay by me."

She had flapped one hand to indicate the rest of the room. "You know
every nurse and intern who comes in here. Big educations and small
change in the pocket, right?"

"Right. Money talks."

"You do the talking, Tabac. You know exactly how to do it."

"Maybe. Maybe. What kind of money you talkin about?"

"I don't have any money."

He wheezed with appreciation. *"Coño!* I like that. You? Widda green Jag on the street outside? People live on what rich ladies call no money."

She slid her pocketbook across the table. "See for yourself. Go ahead, open it." She had tilted her glass to her mouth, seeing him darkly through the wet bottom. Men. Monsters. All of them.

He snapped the purse shut and pushed it back across the table toward her. "Nickles and dimes. A five and two lousy ones."

"Seven's a lucky number, amigo."

"Listen. No money, you're dead."

"Don't kill me with kindness, Tabac."

"Hah. You soun just like Roone."

Her clenched fist had come down on the table between them, startling them both. "I swear to you, Tabac. One word to him and it's no payoff for you."

He flicked his fingernails across her purse. What an admirable naturalness of contempt, she had thought.

"No what, señora? You gotta put you money where you mout is."

"And these"—she was twisting her rings off her finger so impulsively that her knuckle was skinned—"you know what these are worth?"

"The rock looks like maybe twenny G's. Too big. Looks hot. Who can fence it, cut it up, take a chance on some *bandito?"* He shook his head. "The rock is trouble."

Her insides dropped.

He hefted her wedding band in his palm while something tore apart in her. "Nice heavy gold piece. Gold is nice. It melts."

"Now you're talking, amigo." Her heart started to beat again. "What do we do next?"

"No me apure."

"Tell me!"

Tabac had explained about the Sans Souci Motel so readily that she had immediately realized he knew the ropes.

"But first," she said, "I want you to go next door to the liquor store and buy me a bottle of Suntory."

He had tossed her ring lightly in the air, caught it, then slipped it into his pocket. He reached for her bag and took out the five and two ones without asking her for them.

"Be my guest," she said.

He was robbing her openly. But I'm walking a crooked mile, she thought, on his one-way street. "Tell them to put the bottle in a plain paper bag—please." She felt plundered and violated.

She had sat in the booth waiting for him, her shoulders stiff and aching, numbly observing herself dissolve away. And yet, even gold melts.

The lady in the mirror jumped, startled, as someone knocked firmly on the motel room door. Plastic clatter as the cup fell into the washbasin, giving her a fleck of drenched amusement because it was a Courtesy Cup and someone was knock-knock-knocking on yonder Ladyjane's door, loud enough to wake up that baboon at the desk.

Oh Holy Mother pray for me now and at the hour of my death.

"Coming, coming," she croaked huskily as she staggered uphill toward the stupid door, making all that noise in this quiet room for light sleepers. Walk a crooked mile.

Turning the lock was a task; her hands weak as wet paper. Unwanted help had come. Survival, release from exposure and shame so unbearable there was no name she knew for such bondage.

Lock. Click. There. Finally. Doorknob. Smile a crooked smile, hostess. Barely managing to shuffle backward as the door was pushed open roughly.

"Oh God," she said. "Roone."

Dreams wavered like this, a milky veil. The downrushing ski slope of a whirling snowstorm dream, launched into a flailing white windstream, out out way out, no turning back, earth below curving roundly away, a whirlpool of spectators, uncaring faces staring up at her flying green chiffon scarf.

Dream? Had she dreamed the innocent-looking canvas bag, his rubbery surgical equipment? His slamming her wedding ring down on the bedside table, snarling, "You horse's ass! You want to *ruin* us *both*?"

Her pity for him, a dream? His cornered trapped eyes. Don't lose your cool, luv. Honestly, don't worry about about me, my frightened child.

"Betsy, I'm sorry, this might hurt—"

"Don't worry about me."

Ahhhh. . . .

Rootless, dispossessed, unattached. All this grotesque manhandling so much like the postures of love, so exactly so, so diabolically different. A bed of sodden newspapers, naked on headlines of riot, bleeding on editorials, two's company, three soiled sheets in the wind. Bladder collapsing, decks awash. Sow the wind, reap your bed and lie in it. Soaked on a paper winding sheet and no clean sheet of decent linen in the house for my prince of players. Mother, not even making a lap to lay my head in? No one can live alone, so I cannot live.

A dream that he had said, "Goddam. It's too late to get more gauze packing. Hear me? Don't get up or move around. I'll come back in the morning, first thing, hear? Drink some more of this."

A cup of kindness. Leave a kiss in the cup.

Spent, drained, hollow. Late morning sun burning through the windows into her flaming face. A pounding sick headache.

"Whoo-*whee!* Lady, what happened to *you?*"

A woman? Her eyes focused through a glaze of pain. A spectator, staring? Betsy tried to lift her head from the pillow but fell back, dizzy, flushed with heat. Hangover hell.

"My, my! Lady, maybe I should call the front desk, huh?"

The motel maid, holding a broom. All eyes. Like Roone, scared stiff. How . . . odd. No, no desk. Where had the long night gone? "What—what time is it?" Did I dream he'd be back?

"Almos' twelve noon. That's checkout time. Oh-oh—"

"Bleeding?" Roone. Where in the name of God are you? I'm on fire.

"Oh, my. Looks bad. Lemme call the front desk, ma'm—"

"No. Please. No."

"Lady, I seen 'em all, but you look mighty sick to me. Lemme take a feel you head."

A cup of kindness. "Thank you."

"Oh, honey, you *hot!* You burnin' with fever."

"Please—could I have a drink?"

"Sure, honey."

And the warmhearted spectator brought water in a plastic Courtesy Cup. "Honey, you jus' stay put. Front desk'll get you a doctor."

"No, no. My own."

"You from in town? Family doctor?"

A feverish burbling laugh over *family* and *doctor* choked her. The intolerable captivity of aloneness was closing down again. Effort to speak. "Phone Metro—Metropolitan—"

"Metropolitan Hospital?"

"Doctor—" Her brain spun. Doctor *who?* Then, turning her face to the wall in surrender to final shame, she said mutely, "Doctor Mayoso."

BOOK VII

WORLD:
Behold This
Dreamer Cometh

28 "MRS. SOMMERS," the judge said, looking down at Betsy standing beside a police matron, "the law requires me to advise you that you are presumed to be innocent of the charge against you until there is reasonable proof of your guilt. You may, still at this time, choose to be tried by a jury if you so desire. What are your wishes?"

"I wish to have a jury," she answered in a low voice.

"You may speak or not, as you choose," he continued. "And if you do not choose to speak this fact shall have no significance in the disposition of the case. You may be seated. Doctor Dionisio Mayoso Martí? Doctor Benjamin Nathaniel Sommers? If you gentlemen will step forward to the Bench . . ."

The late morning sun fell across two American flags whose varnished wooden staffs were crossed above a round, indifferent electric wall clock. The early sun streaked with brightness the chromium water carafe and the bronze nameplate on the judge's bench: JUDGE BRENDAN BOYNE LE-HANE. On the far wall the glass of two framed parchments threw back the light so opaquely that their printed words could not be read.

The first framed parchment enclosed the *Judicial Oath;* the second, the *Oath of Admission to the Bar.* On both oaths, the initial gothic capital letters were drawn elaborately by hand within red squares of color to give the appearance of medieval illuminated manuscript pages.

An out-of-date calendar for the three months of June-July-August, head-lined DAILY LEGAL NEWS, loitered on the wall beside the ornate parch-ments. Near it, the potbellied bailiff stepped heavily from behind his desk to ask the detective lieutenant beside him, "Too friggin' cold in here, ain't it, Charlie? Maybe I should shut off the air conditioner?"

"It'll get hotter, pal," the detective lieutenant said. "Just wait till they get that baby doll's cute ass up on the witness stand. That Mrs. Sommers hotter'n a two-dollar pistol."

"You got a dirty mind, Charlie," the bailiff said. "Just one idea all the time."

"Yeah. Money," the court reporter said casually as he folded the con-tinuous stenotype transcript paper into its oblong metal tray. He cracked his knuckles, then folded his morning newspaper—whose main headline was DEADLOCK OR WEDLOCK: JUDGE TO RULE ON DEFENSE ACTION—to the back page, where the crossword puzzle was printed. Court would be called into session within a few minutes. Reporters and cameramen swarmed around the three defendants and their attorneys.

"She looks awful lonesome," the bailiff remarked to the detective lieutenant. "Everybody's talkin' to somebody, but she's not talkin' to nobody."

The detective lieutenant stared across the room at Betsy Sommers. Her smallness and isolation in the noisy room had built a walled enclosure of emptiness around her. "I seen 'em before," he said. "Only one thing they do right."

"Listen to the big lootenant. Sore 'cause he can't get his flag up over half-mast."

"Don't be a goddam fool," the detective said. "I arrested her. It's an open-and-shut case."

"You got money that says so?"

"I never bet on my own cases."

"This Judge Lehane, Lieutenant, he's a great one for surprises."

"Wipe the egg off your face. How many surprises can there be when Exhibit A's a motel register signed Cristina Mayoso? Or Mayoso's statement that he surgically cleaned her out? Or the old doctor's signature on the hospital admission chart? This barbecue is strictly an open-and-shut case. I seen 'em before. A doctor knocks up his girl friend, cha cha cha. Then they play doctor in a motel room."

"Then why did the old man, this Benjamin Sommers, put his signature on the hospital operating papers?"

"You know something? With a dumb question like that, it's a good thing you got a city job. The old man loved her like a daughter. And this Mayoso guy, listen, he was almost like one of the old man's sons. You wanna bet the judge'll take one look at three people who broke the eleventh Commandment—"

"Don't ask me to count so high—"

"Thou shalt not embarrass thy class by getting caught screwing. We dug up enough evidence to give Jimmy Stacy the ammunition to blast 'em."

"Man, who needs enemies? You sound mean today."

"I feel mean today. I don't like what they did. Neither does the law."

In the tight clump of reporters, the legal team around the district attorney was good-humored, talkative, winning players between halves at a big football game.

"Mr. District Attorney," the Manchester *Guardian* asked, "is it true that you will run for Governor in the next election?"

"First things first. I'm just holding a solemn high pontifical press conference," Stacy answered calmly. "This case is far too demanding for me to even think of the future."

"Bull," said a voice quietly in the rear, immediately drowned out as the district attorney warmed to his theme.

"Life begins at forty—you're as familiar with that philosophy as I am, gentlemen"—then, with a quick apologetic smile—"and ladies. I don't mind saying I happen to be forty and that it's been a pretty full life up to now." The pretty woman from *Life* seemed to be listening to him with interest so he became expansive. "You big-city fellas have probably never seen the desk of a small-town D.A. like me. I doubt it's the sort of desk my learned colleagues of the defense have in their private offices—my desk is just a combat veteran in the wars of human nature."

"Mr. District Attorney," a voice began, but James Stacy rolled on, ignoring the questioner and speaking directly to the girl from *Life*. "On my desk I've got the three wise monkeys, and, in all humility, I say to you that these humble little desk ornaments summarize better than I can the tradition and mission of my office."

"Bull," the voice in the rear repeated.

"The evil we see does not blind us to the vision of Grace."

At the back of the group of reporters the voice mumbled, "Here we go again. Blast off for the state capital!"

"The evil we hear we subject to the most vigorous investigation because the law is the backbone of our civilization." Even the deputy attorneys on his staff, who knew this speech by heart, stopped whispering among themselves with his new reading of it.

"The evil we do," James Stacy went on, "we do with love in our hearts and malice toward none."

"Trial by newspaper," muttered the voice in the rear.

"So if I interpret your question correctly, sir, you are asking me if I lust for the powers of office and rewards of rank. How could I, when right here, the town where I've been raised from babe to altarboy, to the people's choice, as their huntsman of the wolf and protector of the lamb, as the balance between the informers and reformers, the man who stands between the innocent wronged and the guilty wrongdoer—in a word, as father-confessor for all the people, regardless of race, creed, or color—what more could a man ask? What man could ask a better assignment from his friends and neighbors than this?"

The girl from *Life* was smiling as he finished and he was sure this was admiration.

"What, *bitte*, please, sir," the correspondent from *Der Spiegel* said in accented English, "is the significance of what the judge will later make a ruling on?"

"A good question," the district attorney said vigorously. "You don't want a long legal pseudo answer I'm sure. Am I talking too fast for you?" He smiled broadly—"mein Herr?"

"No. No. Zank you," *Der Spiegel* said.

"And," the district attorney added, "I'd be the last one to encourage a trial of the defendants in the papers while their case is *sub judice.* So I'll put it to you short and sweet. The judge's ruling will decide whether or not to try the defendants as three separate individuals or as a combined group. It means that the defendants, willy-nilly, will sink or swim separately or together."

At Betsy Sommers' table the Bridgeport *Post* reporter, taking advantage of his local friendship with Betsy's defense attorney, asked, "Norty, would you say a ruling by Judge Lehane against camera coverage of the trial will hurt or help your client? She's pretty photogenic."

Norton Fletcher lifted himself slightly onto his toes to glance significantly toward the district attorney, then rocked back on his heels. He evaded the question to slant his answer. "Well, sir, if any of us with an ounce or two of ham, or ha, ha, a pound or two of political ambition, had any ideas of playing a TV-type lawyer in a courtroom drama, well, I can only express my anticipation that the judge will fix that sort of publicity wagon for keeps. My client is a woman in distress, not photogenic. We seek only justice from the Court, not oratorical quasi-semi-nonpolitical appearances on TV!"

"Mr. Fletcher," the New York *Times* said. He sounded tired. He had gotten this assignment late and had driven up to Connecticut in a hurry, without breakfast. "Mr. Fletcher, the judge will rule on motion by the defense for the two doctors to separate their trial from Mrs. Sommers'. A separate trial would hurt your client's case, wouldn't it?"

Norton Fletcher slid his fingers into his bottom vest pockets but, just as he began to answer the *Times,* a woman reporter leaned over Betsy and began questioning her at the same time. "Please," Norton Fletcher said hurriedly, "Mrs. Sommers is fatigued and she has no comment. If you'll please address your questions to me, I'll do my level best to answer them."

Betsy had cloistered herself in the uncomfortable armless wooden chair all morning, completely still, as if she were meditating under a vow of silence in the crowded room. Her face and lips were waxen, expressionless as a mask.

Some festering self-punishing pride kept her from confessing to anyone she was paralyzed with fear. Yesterday, the last day she had been free to come and go, her lawyer had brought her to the courthouse to review the indictment. As the taxi had chugged up Golden Hill Street, her attorney, the public defender, had been telling her that her decision to go to jail during the trial rather than stay out on bail would earn her public sympathy; then, as the taxi stopped before the courthouse, a small crowd surged down the granite steps and had blocked her way out of the taxi.

Women, some with children, had pressed forward first. Betsy saw an older woman with lips drawn back as if she had hurried here hungrily without taking time to put in her teeth. The younger women were snarling with indignation at her reported freedoms, pleasures, beauty, money, men, sexual depravity incarnate.

"The bitch," she heard them repeating as she had thrown on dark glasses with trembling hands and had clung to her lawyer while his voice had risen angrily: "Please! Please! Let us through!"

Adolescent boys with shamed concupiscent faces, red with acne, held cameras upside down, arm's length above their heads, to snap her picture. The older men hung back, instinctively masking any daytime disclosure of their empty hallway bedrooms and their night sweats.

Betsy was incredulous at the sight of four young men in the uniform of the American Nazi Party who were strutting in a line beyond the wooden pickets' barrier—each man's thumb hooked Hitler-style over his belt buckle, a swastika armband on his sleeve—wearing Prussian faces under chin-strapped military caps, each carrying a placard reading: JEWS WANT CHRISTIAN BIRTH CONTROL.

Several policemen came out to push open a path. She was determined not to flinch or show fear in the face of such brutishness, but, uncontrollably, shrank back into the taxi.

Now, in the courtroom, voices rose and fell around her: "Hey, look this way!" "Pssst, Betsy, up here!" "Just one more shot, Mrs. Sommers!" But none of them reached her any more than distant rain splattering against a sealed window.

Every few minutes, with the unthinking regularity of a tic, she had unclasped her hands to pick up her attorney's ballpoint pen. On the ruled yellow legal-size notepad before her she had drawn a small circle inside a precise larger one. Within her cocoon of silence, she had added a third inked circle within the first two.

Her careful geometry of circular enclosures grew smaller, narrowing down to a pinpoint center of gravity, dead center.

Mayoso sat about six feet away from Betsy. The table surface before him was heaped with a strapped and buckled yeomanry of briefcases, the file folders and yellow legal pads of the attorneys representing him and Dr. Benjamin Sommers.

The morning had begun on the left foot. He regretted letting Terrence stand there begging the judge to separate his trial from Betsy's. All morning, as Terrence had pleaded persuasively, he had felt guilty and uncomfortable. Betsy had no way of knowing that he was not trying to scuttle or drown her but only letting his lawyers follow their best professional judgment.

Terrence had warned him, "Everybody in court will be figuring Ben Sommers is somebody, Betsy's nobody, and Mayoso's the fall guy. Our strategy's obvious. We've got to separate you and Doctor Sommers from her."

Terrence's two assistant trial attorneys flanked him. They had pushed themselves back from the table and were leaning toward one another just behind Mayoso's chair to confer in low voices.

"With all the pickets and demonstrators and local-yokel spear carriers outside," one of the assistant attorneys was saying, "and the mob crowding in here with cameras, I'm beginning to consider falling back on Section 1443, Title 28, of the U. S. Code. That way we might remove our case from Connecticut jurisdiction into a Federal court."

Mayoso felt honed and sharpened. All their law, he thought, pivots on one belief: that there must be order in the universe. But there is only chaos. Order is man-made. Is this order?

"Well, Doctor Mayoso, I'll tell you frankly," the educated voice of one of his attorneys broke in: "*If the judge denies our motion to separate your trial from Betsy's—let's face it, that will not help us at all.*"

"Yes," Mayoso said. Chaos, not order. Benjamin Sommers, there—Samson, blinded and humiliated between the temple pillars, the stone roof falling.

"This is going to be an adversary trial in the old tradition," his second attorney said. "Accusations and antagonisms." He sniffed. "Smell it in the air?"

Mayoso did not answer. Chaos. His right hand clenched into so tight a fist that even his trimmed, short surgeon's fingernails dug into his palm.

"You seem a little out of touch, Doctor Mayoso," Terrence said. "I'm not at all confident you're really listening."

"I am, Terrence." That letter to David, written in the plane en route to Caracas: *We're like mountain climbers, all roped together.* The sentence spun gyroscopically in his mind, stationary, yet spinning. We? Who are *we*?

All these people who brutalize themselves and us by treating this trial as games and circuses? The Father Möttls of the world, bailing frantically and fighting off secular sharks? The Filhos, using sticks and carrots, hunger and dogma, to tunnel beneath continents? The Santos Roques, prisoners of their own followers, experts at eating half a loaf, satisfied by the possible? Marjorie there behind the rail, convinced that reason could marry self-interest and then practice family planning? Benjamin Sommers, a courageous mandarin, willing to leave his palace walls and sign hospital admission papers and a surgical chart in the teeth of Dr. Douglass? For Benjamin Sommers the Ice Age is closing in, civilization's fires faltering in caves, while a glacier of legal cannibalism grinds over us all. David, protected and sequestered as a monastery monk in the Dark Ages, bitter now that the winds of the world are blowing burning ashes into his laboratory. Witt, hobbling on a crutch of success that fails to help him walk.

Occasionally, as the morning intricately unwound, he had glanced at Witt, behind the rail beside Marjorie; and at Betsy, sitting there at the next table with her hands in her lap, white-knuckled, fingers locked, her newly cut dark helmet of hair bowed slightly. She isn't posing. If she were, she could never have captured the Raphael line: the marble stillness of a Renaissance angel cast down, long past weeping.

From where he sat, he could see Witt staring at her across the cautious air between them until her stone profile moved; a counterfeit serenity. Her ambushed eyes had emerged bright as a blade to meet Witt's, sword against shield.

Witt had been watching Betsy, seeing her in his memory, feeling her monogrammed scented towel in his hand as he had wiped the wet shining slope of her back and then had kissed the nape of her neck.

"Coward," Betsy had said years ago. "Taking a lady from the rear."

"All's fair, Betts," Witt had said, "in love or war."

She had made her voice deep, imitating the omnipotent salutation of a news broadcaster. "This . . . is . . . war." Then she had turned and kissed the tip of his nose. Their tumbling April time. The wild encounter, her damp hair tossed loose as dark spray. But it had not been love, Witt thought. Her snappy comebacks and banter were her only truths. All's fair, but not in love. Just in war.

Here in court she had none of her usual eye makeup. On her lips no lipstick, not even to pretend courage to herself. A trim dark blue suit, not the favorite battle armor he knew she would prefer: her green Chanel with tiny gold-chain links bound into the pocket edges, the matched

T-strap sandals which Frattegiana on the Via Sistina made for her with special four-inch heels. Not even earrings. The newspaper wire services had gleefully reported as cynicism what had been her own kind of bravado: "I don't *always* put a dab of Haig and Haig pinch on my earlobes. Only *sometimes*. For an interesting evening."

The faultless makeup he had seen her concentrate on so intensely, the dressing-room séance, the mirror tricks from her days as a model, the pointed sable brush to outline her lips, the ceramic flawlessness of a Wedgwood cameo, all this was gone.

Her hair was her penance. She had always carried with her, everywhere, the amulet of beliefs about grooming her mother had bound to her bones, the hairbrushing magic of at least one hundred strokes each night. The public gloss, black beneath her green scarf. Now she had cut her hair short. Pretending again? He watched her warily. Acting the repentant anchorite? No, he decided. The tribal tyranny had cast her out, a leper without staff or begging bowl. He knew how deeply she dreaded the shroud of isolation. He felt a cold pity twist in his gut.

In front of him, Betsy turned in her uncomfortable wooden courtroom chair and was getting up. Witt swung to his feet and stepped forward, bumping into the spectators' wooden rail, sensing only the iron months dividing them.

"Betts," he said softly as she moved slowly from the defendant's table.

Betsy turned to Witt slowly, with that unique way of looking into his eyes steadily, as if they were alone. Her pale gaunt stillness was startlingly unlike her.

"Betts," Witt said quickly. "I want to help you."

Her eyes slid past him to his mother, who was folding and refolding a linen square of handkerchief.

Now a fragile cobweb sifted over her isolated face and she began to turn away from him. Only a pulse leapt suddenly in the column of her neck. He reached across the rail quickly and touched her arm, rebuffed by the muscle's tautness beneath her sleeve. Again, the cold twisted within him.

I outloved her, he had been thinking all morning as he sat watching her back. I outloved her and that excess could never cure the mortal sickness of being a beautiful woman. I never knew it then, but I must have believed the reverse twist of the most motheaten lie of all: the love of a good man will change a woman. Oh God, he thought in pain, I loved you with everything I had. And you were dying of beauty.

Now, bending uncomfortably across the wooden rail of the courtroom, he thought: I must have been so cocksure we could come together as lastingly as sun and air, until the inevitable cold rains came. A thin flicker of hatred against his pity, leaving him dry-mouthed.

"Betts," he said, tasting his own begging like vomit, "let me put up your bail. Let me get you out of this—this cuspidor."

The reporters had spotted them and the rapid-fire cameras had begun circling around them, glassily hawkeyed, their automatic shutters making little reptilian hisses, capturing on film two human cardboard cutouts.

Witt hardly noticed the photographers. He was caught by his pain, by her terrible isolation, and by the wiry tension his fingertips had sensed in her rigid arm. The tiny recoil from his touch was another stab.

"I don't need bail," she said tonelessly. "You're very kind."

"Betts, you can't live in a prison cell like some kind of animal."

"Why not? I've been arrested for a crime. Or two. Or maybe three." Her bitter-lemons smile. "Three's a lucky number."

"But you're allowed bail. A couple of bucks and you're out."

"Oh, how you remind me, Witt," she said in a sudden breathless rush. "How I used to believe your beautiful money would be the key that opened all the doors. Love and Money, Thy Magic Spell Is Everywhere."

"Talk sense."

"I know what you're talking about, Witt. But you don't. You've never been a criminal even in your *head*, Witt. You don't even *know* what you're talking about."

"I'm talking about getting you out. Getting you more than one public-defender lawyer. Getting you a staff, a law firm, not just one man appointed by the court." He dropped his voice. "Timmy wants to see you, but I don't want a boy his age to visit his mother in some goddam cage, behind bars."

She closed her eyes. For a moment he thought he had reached her, that she might weep for their public nakedness, for their son, for herself and for him, and the unbearable loss of love.

"Betts," he said, humiliated that he could think only of the barest words to bridge the wooden rail, "I want to help. Let me help you fight this thing."

Her eyelids opened. She had no tears. He recognized her dry unblinking stare for what it was: the hermit gaze of an outcast who saw ahead a burning desert, an empty landscape no one else could see.

"Fight back?" she repeated. "After my mother died I thought a man, my father, would help me fight back. He didn't. Then I thought another man, a man I married, maybe he'd help me fight back. You. But you didn't help me."

"Betts—"

"I'm just plain no damned good, Witt. So let go. Don't try to hold on. Just let go."

Her lawyer left the district attorney's garrulous circle and came up to the defendant's table behind her. He whistled *Bésame Mucho* silently between his clenched teeth as he rearranged the chairs with the manner of a thoughtful host. "Mrs. Sommers—" he said, and frowned imperiously across the wooden rail at DeWitt Sommers. The bigshot Sommers guy musta laid her like a rug, he thought, but by golly, she's my client now. His judicial frown deepened.

Betsy nodded to him slowly, then said quietly, "You always played it smart, Witt. Let go."

He gripped the wooden rail between them with both his hands. "I can't, Betts."

Her bluegreen eyes, their dark pupils enormous now, held his. "I always wanted you to let go, Witt. But no man knows how to do that. It kills them."

"It's killing me right now."

"Well," she said, "maybe we can have a His and Hers funeral."

Upstairs in the judge's courthouse chambers, Judge Lehane's male secretary pressed the plastic *Hold* button on his telephone and spoke over his shoulder to the judge. "Overseas operator calling again, Judge. Poor girl's been telephoning in from San Juan all morning."

"Tell the operator to call back in ten minutes. This happens to be my first chance since this morning to empty my bladder."

The judge turned away from the tall window overlooking Golden Hill Street. He had been watching a lengthy chain of pickets confined to a long marching oval by the wooden sawhorse barricades set up by the police. The pickets were dressed in Halloween costumes, tight black sheaths with spooky white skeletons painted in bold outline on them. Their tall placards read JUDGMENT NOT WHITEWASH FOR BABY KILLERS.

In the judge's lavatory a window had been left open a few inches. Through it the judge could hear the rhythmic beeping of auto horns. Since early this morning the long line of antique cars had been parked bumper to bumper along Golden Hill Street in front of the courthouse. He had recognized three or four of the tall awkward vehicles from his boyhood: a Model T with brass headlights and foldback windshield; a chain-driven open-seater that looked like a pioneer Mercedes; even a Detroit Electric of long ago with overstuffed chairs, cut-glass flower vases and fringed silk curtains. He remembered the whitehaired maiden ladies who called the electric cars *juicers* and drove them sedately clutching the steering tiller bar while pretending to look neither right nor left.

Behind each steering wheel of the antique cavalcade before the courthouse, the judge had seen a woman driver wearing the floppy widebrimmed motoring hat of 1910 tied on with a long silk scarf knotted in a big bow under her chin. Each auto carried a bumper sticker in bold print: A CHILD PLANNED FOR IS A CHILD CARED FOR.

As the judge's dark official sedan had driven slowly past the lineup of costumed lady drivers this morning, the women had recognized him and had begun squeezing the rubber bulbs of their antique motoring horns, filling the air with a hoarse foghorn croaking.

"People," his driver had said. "They're funnier than anybody, Judge."

"What in the world do they think they're doing?"

"The World War Two V-for-Victory code in Europe."

Judge Lehane had looked back through the rear window of his sedan as it swung into his courthouse parking space. A sign above the first antique car read: L.I.V.E.

Now, in the lavatory of his own chambers, he washed his hands slowly, without hurrying. As the water foamed over his hands, Judge Lehane decided he was in no hurry to hear what Governor Santos Roque had to say. It was perilously close to impropriety to take a call from the Governor under this morning's circumstances, but both he and the Governor knew enough of the law to be careful.

The judge shook the drops off his wet hands into the washbasin while looking into the wall mirror. He was surprised to see himself so tightjawed.

You've got to be the best damn judge of the law you know how, he told himself. The old bromide, *the eyes of the world are on you,* was now a simple fact. Television cameras poking through your court like X-ray tubes. People playing at Truth and Consequences halfway around the world.

They'll pick the flesh from your bones. They'll leave what's left to the buzzards. Pickets in Halloween costumes. Skeletons. Antique cars in the suffragette tradition. Next, they'll begin chaining themselves to the courthouse flagpole, I suppose.

He began to dry his hands carefully on one of the efficient modern paper towels he disliked, then remembered to reach for his own linen towel on his own glass-rod hanger. The learning of Judge Learned Hand. Brandeis and the social usage of a living law. And Judge Woolsey's memorable line: *It must be remembered that his locale was Celtic and his season spring.* Here in Connecticut the season is hellish.

Oh Lord, why here and now, with me on this bench?

A criminal trial, the judge thought, is really not a very efficient way of finding out what happened. Betsy Sommers appeared to be truthful.

Then why the constant sense of skillful lying? Not lying, exactly, but an avoidance of truth. Not her words, but her silences, told lies. Was she protecting the two doctors? Or someone else, some shadowy unknown person or persons? And for the state—what was the yardstick of justice? Mercy? Punishment? A ritual, a carnival for men and women bored by the repetitive and monotonous tasks of an industrial civilization? Should the defendants be considered pioneers of some brave new kind of world, praised, then released?

Last night he had stood before a massed wall of books in the upstairs study of his house in the Black Rock section of Bridgeport. From the hill where the house stood he could see past the boat club, to Seaside Park beyond it and the farther stretches of Long Island Sound.

He had tilted his head back to peer carefully through his half-moon reading glasses, tapping each volume as he moved along the bookshelf. He had been looking for the *United States Law Week* which contained two decisions by the Supreme Court. Curious, he had thought, that the justices should have handed down rulings in the same week on two such different questions, and now both are tied together in my own courtroom. Justice John Harlan's dissent leaves the door ajar for less obtrusive indoor television equipment in the future to creep back into the courtroom. But for now, he had thought, my closing the door in Bridgeport is on the side of the judicial angels.

He had found the volume which included the second ruling he wanted to review, the Supreme Court's seven-to-two decision to strike down the anti-birth-control statutes of Connecticut. Slowly he read a sentence in Justice Hugo Black's dissent: "I like my privacy as well as the next one, but I am nevertheless compelled to admit that government has a right to invade it unless prohibited by some specific Constitutional provision."

And Justice Potter Stewart's dissent: "We are not asked in this case whether we think this law is unwise, or even asinine. We are asked to hold that it violates the United States Constitution. And that I cannot do."

The judge had raised his head and looked unseeingly over the tops of his half-moon glasses out the window. The dark glass surface of Long Island Sound was dotted by ships' lights; the ferryboat to Port Washington, nighttime fishermen, yachts churning north toward the jazz festival at Newport or the Quaker cobblestones of Nantucket, a cargo vessel headed for the long reaches of the open Atlantic.

. . . *whether we think this law is unwise* . . . *and that I cannot do.*

Judge Brendan Boyne Lehane straightened slightly as he glanced curiously at himself in the lavatory mirror, then he went back into his leathery chambers to accept the call from Governor Santos Roque.

He picked up the phone as his secretary released the *Hold* button. I recall him now. We met at a dinner party in New Haven when he was the distinguished lecturer on international relations.

"Hello," he said into the phone. "Judge Lehane here."

"Judge," Governor Santos Roque said over the telephone heartily, "how are you feeling?"

"Well, Governor, I can't complain. Other than a touch of the hemorrhoids which are the occupational hazards of sedentary judges and psychiatrists, I really can't complain."

Their use of titles was not accidental. In New Haven, at the evening's convivial end they had reached *Brendan* and *Cándido*, but the Governor's office in San Juan and the judge's chambers in Bridgeport were far from the hail-fellow-well-met camaraderie.

"Over television," Governor Santos Roque said, "there seems to be quite a hullabaloo up there in Bridgeport."

The judge swung his highbacked leather chair to face the window overlooking the street. The pickets in skeleton costume were still marching. "Ah," he said, "they're fairly orderly. We have to expect a trial like this one to be a lightning rod for any crackpot who wants to make thunder."

"I've been informed that Mrs. Sommers' counsel has moved for a change of venue." When Judge Lehane grunted noncommittally, the Governor added quickly, "If I ask any improper questions please don't hesitate to overrule me."

"There's nothing improper," Judge Lehane said firmly, "in my telling a governor the plain facts already out on every radio and TV news broadcast. Connecticut's a pretty small place. Whether the defendants could get a trial more fair elsewhere in the same state—well, I'll be making my ruling on that later this morning. After all, the defendants are very prominent people. The Sommers family is equally well-known everywhere in Connecticut."

"An understatement, Judge! Please understand that I'm ready to fly up there on a moment's notice to appear as a character witness in behalf of Doctor Mayoso."

"Thank you, Governor," Judge Lehane said slowly. Santos Roque was getting too close to the line.

"What I don't understand, Judge, is why Mr. Stacy and the prosecution staff have decided on such extraordinary charges. Isn't the criminal abortion charge enough? Why are they pushing for a homicide conviction?"

Judge Lehane swiveled his leather chair back and forth through a short impatient arc. This conversation was at a crossroads. Had the Governor deliberately led him here, guile disguised as official information-seeking? Was this actually a spontaneous and proper concern about a citizen of the Commonwealth of Puerto Rico? There must have been some discussion with Washington.

He gripped the telephone more tightly and said, "I cannot take the slightest judicial notice of what you've said, Governor. Your abortion-homicide statement is not quite accurate."

"I'll be most grateful if you'd share a little accuracy with me, Judge. I'm on a hot seat."

"The legal complexities, Governor—"

"Exactly, Judge—but I'm holding out my hand. Please don't rap my knuckles."

"We can discuss only what's on public record—"

"Of course, Judge. Of course." The Governor's voice changed. "I must say, Brendan, an ambitious D.A. is understandable. But Mr. James Stacy's running too hard for Governor. The knight in shining armor, with about half the voters in the state Catholic. It sounds like old Ireland—the Catholic knights and the Protestant dragons. Stacy's charging these people with homicide—that's the opposite side of the Protestant bigotry in North Ireland!"

"Governor," Judge Lehane said firmly, ignoring the Brendan, "when the jury is impaneled, they will decide from the facts if I continue as presiding judge. We have a fair adversary system, not an inquisition. The defendants are represented by competent counsel."

"Certainly, certainly. But the judge decides the law. You must have, at the pretrial attorneys' hearing in your chambers."

"I did."

"Those were oral motions, arguments, and rebuttals, weren't they, Judge?"

"Yes, oral. Naturally, there is no jury present during procedural discussions. Juries need facts, and procedural arguments and rebuttals can be rather misleading. But most of it's part of the public record, Governor. I directed our court stenographer to record the motions of the attorneys on both sides. I've placed my reasoning and findings on record because of the possibly grave precedents which may be established."

"If your reasoning's on the public record, Judge—"

"Well, the pretrial hearing was fairly blunt and to the point. . . ."

During the pretrial in the judge's chambers the district attorney had been blunt about his moral certainty in accusing the defendants of homicide.

"Your Honor," the district attorney, James Stacy, said, "I make no dis-

tinction between law and morals. Morality gives life its value, and law is
the cement that keeps our houses upright and in order. I will present evidence that Doctor Mayoso's hand held and used an instrument which removed a fetus from the womb of Betsy Sommers. Even in an operating
room, that is premeditated, planned, calculated, scientific murder." He
faced Terrence, senior defense attorney for the two doctors, and Betsy
Sommers' defense attorney, Norton Fletcher, with the authoritative assurance of a military surgeon who must cut and cause bleeding to help win
a war.

Terrence raised his head sharply. "Your Honor—I thought we had
agreed that theology has no place in this trial."

"It's unavoidable, Terrence," Jim Stacy said. "Thou shalt not kill.
That's basic. Rock-bottom. And about five thousand women are killed by
abortionists in the United States every year. The Ten Commandments
were written on the hearts of men before they were written into codes of
law."

"Please, Jimmy," Terrence said, "don't waste all that on me. Save it for
the jury."

"I agree," Betsy Sommers' lawyer said quickly in a high unsure voice.
"Theology isn't law."

James Stacy ignored the younger man and concentrated his calm deliberate smile on the older lawyer. "Terrence, with your reputation as a
bona fide law-school scholar—"

Terrence shook his head. "Jim, let's square this philosophy thing away
right now. We were both parochial school kids and left-handed. You
want to drag in the Church? Natural law? Aristotle? The state as a natural
and good institution, so it must promote virtue?"

"I knew you'd know about it, Terrence. Do *you* want to dig back to
Augustus? After all, everybody knows your client's a real buff on ancient
Rome—and you'll say your law is Augustan? D'you want to say in court
the state is basically evil, based on the fall of man? Needed to check vice
but not much else? Maximum individuality in a minimum state? That's
basically the Protestant pluralistic tradition, isn't it?"

Judge Lehane tapped his desk lightly. "Gentlemen, this display of eru-
dition is glittering, but all that glitters is not et cetera." The three attorneys seated across from his desk in a semicircle smiled—more broadly,
the judge noted, than the witticism warranted. "All individuals, religious
or not, look to the law to enforce morality and social behavior."

"Your Honor," Terrence said, "the district attorney has said in effect
that he believes my client should be exposed to the death penalty! The
removal of a spoonful of protoplasm, before life or quickening is felt, is
considered murder only in theology, not law."

"Your Honor," Jim Stacy said, "I'd like to cooperate on moving matters along. The counselor's argument is that law and theologically determined morals, or natural law, are separate. Sir, I submit that is human disaster! Some of the finest German jurists have pointed out that Hitler came to power by law. He stayed in power by law. By law, he removed more than a spoonful of protoplasm—"

Terrence was on his feet, pale with anger. "Your Honor—"

"By law," Jim Stacy said loudly. "Those same German jurists now say they have changed to a moral theory of the basics of law."

"Please be seated, Mr. Terrence."

Terrence sat down, muttering, "Hitler, homicide—Jim, you're chewing up all the scenery for the voting crowd in the balcony."

"Mr. Terrence," Judge Lehane said, "I'll have to hold you in contempt if you continue to impugn the motives of the district attorney."

"I apologize, Your Honor. I'm beginning to realize he means every word he says."

"I accept the apology," Stacy said. "I want to make it clear how hard I'm trying to be guided by Connecticut law, not my personal beliefs. For example, I've dropped the first degree homicide charge against Doctor Benjamin Sommers. The state's charge against him is homicide in the second degree—"

"Your Honor," Terrence interrupted quickly, "abortion is a separate crime—"

"Let Mr. Stacy finish—"

"—and abortion," Stacy said. "The charge of homicide is brought to vindicate the rights of the unborn child. The charge of criminal abortion is in behalf of the state. Mrs. Sommers is charged as an accessory before the fact in both the voluntary manslaughter charge and the abortion."

"Your Honor," Terrence said. "To be scrupulous in duty is one thing, but I submit the district attorney is being punitive—"

"I'm guided by the very law you've just been emphasizing, Terrence. The three clients have been extraordinarily punitive to the state by not cooperating in our investigation. If they have nothing to hide, why their strange total silence?"

"Your Honor," Terrence said quickly, "the code of silence regarding a patient's private life has been part of medicine for two thousand years."

"May I add," Betsy's attorney, Norton Fletcher, threw in quickly, "that my client's silence is within her rights—"

"She was hostile and uncooperative with the police, even before counsel entered the picture—"

"I repeat, punitive, Your Honor," Terrence said carefully. "Now, Jim, stay put. Let me finish. I have no wish to sweep a justifiable contention

under any rug of privilege, Your Honor. Criminal abortion rubs every one
of us the wrong way. The word alone does it. When perhaps a million
women a year risk death to break a law, we find that the law almost
everywhere—here, England, Europe—treats the woman as the victim, not
the criminal."

"England, Mr. Terrence?" Judge Lehane pointed at the stack of law
volumes piled on his corner worktable. "The Offense Against the Person
Act in England is one of the most severe in the world. A consenting
mother may be sentenced to imprisonment for life."

"But in practice, Your Honor must know that the woman is not prosecuted at all. And similarly in the United States. The English-speaking
peoples do not make the woman a defendant."

"Of course," Stacy said. "The police and D.A. need the woman to give
evidence against the abortionist. And as for those million women—does a
satisfied customer ever file a complaint?"

"Your Honor," Betsy's young attorney said, "may I join my colleague
in suggesting the district attorney is being punitive?" He held up a sheaf
of papers. "Here are some supporting statements taken from the writings
of Dr. Benjamin Nathaniel Sommers—"

The judge pursed his lips. "They may be surplusage, if not actually
irrelevant—"

"Your Honor, they are most relevant. Doctor Benjamin Sommers is my
client's father-in-law. They were very close. His words may be said to
represent her own if she could speak with medical knowledge."

"What are these writings?"

"A guest editorial in the *New England Journal of Medicine*, Your
Honor."

"I don't see the direction you're taking—"

"I speak to the point of asking judicial notice of the degree of Mr. District Attorney's charge. I agree with my colleague's description, 'punitive.'"

Jim Stacy turned the beam of a patient, faintly patronizing smile on the
young attorney. "If the writings are not lengthy, Your Honor, I confess
some interest of my own."

"No more than a few sentences."

Judge Lehane nodded. "All right, Mr. Fletcher."

"'Illegal abortion is one of the great public and private health problems
here at home as well as abroad. To neglect it will not solve it. A tiny fraction of our interest and expense on outer space, if only directed to the
most profound of inner spaces—the human womb—could erase the silent
cowardice of my medical colleagues and the backward inhumanity of
my citizen neighbors overnight.'" In the quiet, the young lawyer looked
from one to the other. His voice had wavered for a split second and he

glanced up anxiously to see if this intelligent manly conference, in this tall paneled room of dark mahogany and leather volumes, could be somehow touched. "The key word, Your Honor," he said in a deeper voice, "which emphasizes the hypothesis of punitiveness, is 'inhumanity.'"

" 'Illegal' is the key word," the district attorney said calmly.

Judge Lehane ran his fingers along the edge of his desk, then, with his thought framed, tapped his fingers twice. "The Court is familiar with the judicial reluctance to convict a woman in such circumstances. New York statutes follow English law—a pregnant woman who commits or attempts abortion upon herself is guilty. Other states exempt her. In some states, the consenting mother is an accomplice. In others, not."

"Nevertheless, Your Honor," Terrence said quickly, "the prosecution gains a great advantage—even when the woman is not held as an accomplice—because her testimony to the occurrence need not be corroborated."

"The advantage," Stacy said, "is society's. Precisely because the woman is almost never prosecuted. Your Honor, we now have in criminal abortion just about the only crime for which the perpetrator, the woman, is not punished. Your Honor, wherever we look, at home or abroad, we find a low rate of prosecutions, and an even lower rate of convictions. And—" his voice hardened—"even with conviction, most punishments are hardly enough to deter future crime. Actually, Your Honor, the defense has the advantage. The abortionist always claims someone else did the job and that he operated later only to save life."

"Your Honor," Terrence said, "could the District Attorney be enjoined to use a less pejorative term than abortionist? My client is a licensed surgeon."

"The law," Stacy said, "makes no distinction between a back-alley midwife with a knitting needle and a medical practitioner with a curette blade."

"Agreed. But let each one be referred to by name or profession. Please don't cover both with the blanket term: abortionist. My client's surgical activities were a normal legal part of his medical school faculty and hospital duties. Doctor Mayoso found a very sick woman, in high fever, in shock with blood loss, and quite literally saved Betsy Sommers' life. There was no crime here, hence my motion for dismissal."

Stacy raised his head. "A crime is what the Legislature says it is. These were crimes."

"Your Honor," Betsy's lawyer said, "the preponderance of information from Betsy Sommers is that she did not know with finality and certainty that she was pregnant. Her only criterion was the absence or delay of the menstrual period. Without the knowledge of pregnancy before the action charged, there can be no premeditation or accessory action to a crime. I also move to dismiss."

Judge Lehane swung forward in his big leather chair. "Gentlemen, I thank you for a more scholarly presentation than those I usually hear in these chambers—albeit a trifle heated for a moment. The opinions and conclusions of this court touch such basic human matters that I've directed the court stenographer to record our pretrial deliberations as part of the trial record in the event you should later seek higher review."

He clasped his hands so tightly the district attorney and the two defense attorneys could see his fingertips blanch from their side of his desk. "The motion to dismiss cannot be granted. This case cannot be dismissed. I don't see Doctor Benjamin Sommers or Doctor Mayoso relieved of legal responsibility. Doctor Sommers signed Mrs. Sommers into the hospital, and Doctor Mayoso did the surgery. The doctrine *mens rea* cannot be applied here. Even if one assumes a good intention—even so, a good intention would not erase a criminal act. Sufficient proof already exists of an action which requires jury decision as to criminality or not, and if so, to what degree. Abortion is legal under Connecticut law only if necessary to preserve the life of the mother or child. My review disclosed no reported cases in which the accused has claimed the procedure was necessary to save the life of a fetus of six or eight weeks' gestation." The judge paused. "Necessity. Necessity to preserve the life of the mother. That's the legal pivot."

He leaned back and looked at the district attorney. "In many states the burden of proof that there was such necessity rests with the state. Connecticut is such a state."

He drummed his fingers lightly on the edge of his desk, as if on piano keys. "The district attorney will agree he has insisted on an unusual stepwise climb in the gravity and degree of his charges. First, the woman in a criminal abortion case, if living, is rarely brought into court. Second, the person accused of performing an illegal abortion is usually charged with that separate crime only, even in harsh circumstances such as when the woman operated on has died. Third, to charge the woman and the two alleged perpetrators with manslaughter raises some very basic questions. Your criteria, Mr. Stacy, may set up very far-reaching precedents."

"Your Honor," Stacy said slowly and patiently, "to do otherwise would undermine public faith. The eminence of these individuals cannot appear to provide immunity. The legal issues touch the constitutionality of statutes in every state. I contend that constitutional guidelines are becoming more and more blurred. If the courts interpret current social mores rather than law, then we will be forced to accept the current hypocrisy." He looked at Terrence as he went on. "We cannot have one law for the rich, the powerful, the educated"—he turned directly to Betsy's lawyer—"or one for the beautiful, the charming, the gay. Once we crack the law, where does the breakage stop? It's like saying a woman's only a tiny bit pregnant. Your Honor"—he leaned forward and closed his hands weightily on his knees—"the entire direction of recent courts has been to enlarge the rights of life to include the right of the unborn child within the womb."

Terrence held his fingertips to his temple. "Your Honor," he said with an almost whispering patience, "there was no child. There was only the embryonic protoplasm. The law too easily confuses the words fertilized ovum with zygote, embryo, fetus, and living child. The distinction between a jelly-like mass of cells and a formed human is critical."

"What there was," Judge Lehane said, "will be a matter for expert testimony, judicial interpretation, and jury decision." He paused, seeing the boundary he must cross, then asked in a flat austere voice, "In the light of these on-the-record arguments and opinions, Mr. Stacy, do you wish to persist in your original charges against the defendants?"

James Stacy took a long breath and spoke as he exhaled, "Yes, Your Honor, I most certainly do. A human being was deliberately killed. That's homicide, sir."

What the judge did not know, and could not tell Governor Santos Roque, was that Terrence had walked to the elevator with Jim Stacy and Norton Fletcher in complete silence. The two older men had nodded goodbye to young Norton Fletcher like two grown dogs to a puppy.

"Why wait for the elevator?" Fletcher had said. "I take the stairs all the time." He had patted his belly—"Good for what ails you"—and clattered off, two steps at a time.

Suddenly Terrence turned to Stacy and burst out, "Jim, you're crucifying two fine people!"

Jim Stacy's steady never-failing smile stopped. "Even though you're not basically a trial lawyer, Terrence, I've always respected you, personally and professionally. But I won't stand still for that kind of talk."

"It's so plain, Jim! I tried to warn you by calling your approach punitive—"

"*Warn* me! Did you, now?"

"Oh, hell, Jim, don't look as if I'm threatening you. But Jim, I swear, even if we have to drum up a campaign, house to house, door to door, for signatures to petition the Court—"

"You don't call that threatening? Who would bankroll an expensive campaign like that? You? Look, you're all shook up."

"You can say that again—"

"Terrence, the Sommers' retainers and fees keep you and your law firm eating high on the hog—"

"Jim, this personally slanted vendetta has to stop."

"Then why don't you advise those two doctors to make Betsy Sommers speak up and stop the accusation? Why the long guilty silence?"

"You know as well as I do that silence isn't—"

"This time it is! And don't call me punitive. Or use words like vendetta. D'you hear?" Jim Stacy lowered his voice. "My guts are just as sensitive to human suffering as your guts, Terrence. Or the high *and* mighty Sommers family. Two weeks ago, right in this courthouse building, I cross-examined a smooth slick bastard who ran an abortion mill like it was an assembly line. Cabdrivers. Codes. Answering-service intermediaries. Cab picks up the girl on an unlighted streetcorner at night, lights out, no license plate numbers to be seen. Collect the cash payment first. Then throw the girl on the floor under a blanket with a cotton wad of chloroform over her face. Take the girl groggy into a motel she could never identify, use ergot, packing, forceps, any damn thing, then throw her out on her bleeding ass in front of some hospital emergency room and scoot over to the next job in a different place. If the girl succeeded in getting rid of the pregnancy, she won't talk. She's satisfied. The dissatisfied ones are dead."

He pointed at Terrence. "You don't like the facts of life? The shit piss and corruption of daily life the way the poor live it?"

Terrence gauged him cautiously. Any answer was hit-or-miss. Stacy's genuine anger, his crusading public service, honor helpless before thieves, was understandable now. As a low-pressure feeler Terrence said, "Jim, we were raised on the dictum: If you got facts, pound 'em. If you haven't, pound the table. You're pounding the table."

"Wait now. Just wait. Let me pound the facts. When the court recessed for lunch, what do you think that slick bastard did? From just twelve noon to two P.M.? He waltzed out of here, walked over two blocks downtown to an office building with lots of people coming and going, zipped up an elevator to an office, aborted an unmarried secretary in the toilet off an empty executive suite, a working girl without a rich husband and a big house and a Jaguar convertible like Betsy Sommers. And then the bastard came back by two P.M. for the afternoon court session." He paused. "In his hurry, he perforated the wall of the uterus, which, Terrence, is notoriously soft and mushy in pregnancy. The girl lay on the toilet floor bleeding and she never called for help. They never do. Women actually die of shame, I swear. She just bled to death while the abortionist sat in court beside his lawyer and the charges against him were dismissed for lack of evidence. And to you I'm just the night-school graduate bucking for public office who comes in to clean up."

"Jim," Terrence said, "I apologize for my outburst. I mean that. And for your information, Mr. Stacy, I worked my way through law school myself. The legal work I do for Mrs. Sommers' L.I.V.E. maternal health clinic—Jim, I do that free."

"But you also represent the Sommers companies, Terrence. They manufacture more condoms per day—ever see all those electronically tested condoms stand up under checkout pressure like Coxey's Army of erections? So one hand washes another, wouldn't you say?"

"You make that a fairly dirty inference, Jim—"

"You were the first to attack, Terrence. I'm just doing my janitor's job. You brought up a house-to-house, door-to-door campaign. You said punitive. You said vendetta."

"I've apologized—"

"That's not good enough, Terrence. Crap apologies like that may sound okay across the teacups in that cozy little half-million-dollar cottage the Sommers have on the Southport beach—but you swung on me first, Terrence." He aimed a mock punch at Terrence's solar plexus and stopped midair as Terrence flinched instinctively. "And I've never lost a fight, legal or illegal."

"You will this one. Careers don't get built by tearing down fine people."

"Fine people? Did you say fine people? Ever watch how Betsy Sommers crosses her legs? I hear tell you're very big with the girls down Washington way. Or didn't you ever have time in your lucrative practice to learn how to spot a hooker?"

"She's a lady, Jim—"

"And how. All woman. And she won't let you forget it, not for one hard-on minute. Hell, it's obvious. First, one son, then tripped up father. It's practically Biblical. She screwed the first one down, and now she's screwed the second one up. And what a boyfriend for a girl with an overheated crack—a tropical gynecologist! One quick surgical flip of the wrist, and presto, now you see it, now you don't. No pregnancy, no problem. And off we go to the Caribbean as the sun sets in chilly Connecticut." He waved both hands in the air as if blocking objections. "You don't have to look like you're eating crud. There's nothing vulgar. It's how we all get born, remember? She had her fun, right? You're naturally and charitably blinded by your friendship with the Sommers." He poked Terrence's elbow. "Otherwise, I'll bet you'd be fighting like hell's fire right here next to me."

"Jim, I'm only reminding you that to use the police power of the state against a private life—"

"Oh, come off it, Counselor. Come down off that cloud. That tighthole *Law Review* tone. Come down where all the rest of us live, Terrence. You know perfectly well a state needs police power. You know the exercise of that power can't make personal or private exceptions. Why, for the love of God, with exceptions, I could be asked to ignore every purveyor of pornographic literature on the grounds that he contributes to the Orphans' Home!"

"Jim, I'm only asking you to draw reasonable distinctions between the decent world and the underworld—"

"At last we agree. I'll shake on that. That's exactly my position. To draw distinctions. To draw the line. I'll make a deal—I'll take you to the coroner's office next time there's some nice lady stretched out on the slab. The cold facts, Terrence. Then I'll ask you, friend: Where would you draw the line?"

When Terrence did not answer, Jim Stacy marked an invisible boundary in the air beside him and said wearily, "I'm drawing it here, right now."

"I appreciate very much, Judge, your willingness to go into the—"

"It's all in the public record, Governor. And I appreciate your willingness to fly up here from San Juan, and your interest in the welfare of one of your most famous constituents." Try that on for size, he thought. "I'm going to have to conclude this conversation, Governor. I'm due downstairs in court."

"Thank you again. I've made a few notes so that I can call him right back."

"Him?"

"The Vice President."

"Oh."

"If you feel like a vacation, Judge, when this is over, we'd welcome your visiting us down here in Puerto Rico. Adiós, Judge."

"Goodbye, Governor." He set the telephone down slowly. From outside came the faint sound of the auto horns blowing their hoarse V for Victory. We'll see, he thought.

□ □ □

Judge Brendan Lehane presiding.

"Motion by counsel for Doctor Benjamin Nathaniel Sommers and Doctor Dionisio Mayoso Martí that their trial be separated from a trial jointly with Mrs. Elizabeth Mary Sommers is denied.

"Motion by counsel for Mrs. Elizabeth Mary Sommers for a change of venue is predicted on counsel's affidavit that a fair trial cannot be held for Mrs. Elizabeth Sommers in Fairfield County Courthouse in the city of Bridgeport. This change-of-venue motion will be held in abeyance until it is determined whether a fair and impartial jury can be selected.

"Motion by counsel for Mrs. Elizabeth Sommers that all cameras and sound-recording equipment be removed has been taken under advisement by the Court. There is a clear continuity of argument in support of such a motion in Canon 35 of the American Bar Association, and in Rule 11 of the United States Senate. More fundamental are Federal Constitutional guarantees against invasion of privacy and of fair trial, and Connecticut statutes to a similar effect. Motion by counsel for Mrs. Sommers is granted.

"A detailed journal entry will be provided to the news media. Anyone found in violation will be cited summarily in contempt of court.

"The Court is committed to the public right for open transactions of justice. The Court is mindful that human reproduction and contraception and abortion are timeless questions of universal concern, morally and medically as well as legally. The Court is also aware of journalists who have come thousands of miles from other continents, who are unfamiliar with our legal system, and are temporary guests of the United States.

"Nevertheless, this Court, and the jury to be impaneled, must weigh only the grave charges against the three defendants under the laws of the State of Connecticut which grip the taproot of life.

"Only the facts of innocence or the facts and degrees of guilt can be determined. Not the social conduct nor sexual morality of American women. Not the ethical code of American medicine. Not the effect upon matters of state and foreign policy pending in the Congress. Not the religious nor financial nor international implications of medical research on human reproduction. The law and the doctrine of *stare decisis* are the only grounds on which the Court must stand.

"Neither the shouting and tumult and picketing in the streets outside this courtroom nor the cameras whose presence changes human behavior will be allowed to enter here. The profound hazard of inflammatory intrusion will not be permitted to influence the jury when their deliberations begin. Jammed corridors and blocked fire exits will be cleared. This is neither a spectacle nor a forum nor a town meeting of the world. It is a court of law.

"On this protocol the Court will proceed. We will now recess until one-thirty this afternoon.

"Court recessed."

In the immobile moment during the double tap of the judge's gavel, the entire court remained motionless and suspended.

The defendants, each seated at a separate table in the well of the courtroom, stared upward at the judge. Mayoso frowned at the judge, puzzled over the meaning he knew must lie between the rotund magisterial lines of unfamiliar legal language. Benjamin Sommers looked over his shoulder at the first row behind the mahogany rail. Marjorie sat there, joined elbow to elbow between Witt and David. Marjorie's letter to the President resigning from the United Nations Population Council had been in the morning papers, alongside thumbnail biographies of David and Witt. They held themselves carefully upright and unyielding.

"What sanctimonious hypocrites Americans are," the London *Sunday Telegraph* whispered to the *Christian Science Monitor*. "Everything the judge says the trial is not, it is."

"Don't sell Old Ironsides short," the *Christian Science Monitor* said. "New Englanders consider him a chip off Plymouth Rock!"

"Oh hell," one of Doctor Sommers' junior attorneys whispered to his legal colleague beside him. "Now the sweet young thing catches a free ride on our backs. What'll Terrence do now?"

Benjamin Sommers' senior defense attorney, Terrence, stopped polishing his glasses and glanced with blank annoyance at his two assistants. Experienced criminal trial lawyers, both of them. They knew as well as he what a legal wallop the judge's ruling was to his clients. Now Betsy Sommers' lawyer could hitch her broken wagon to Dr. Benjamin Sommers' rising star. But Terrence wanted no one on his staff ever to show either elation or dismay. "Lose a battle, maybe," he said, "but we'll win the war."

Norton Fletcher, defense attorney for Betsy Sommers, had been admiring the agreeable symmetry of his client's legs until the significance of the judge's ruling struck him. He leaned back, forgetting dignity, and tried to keep his spreading grin within modest bonds.

The gavel tapped twice, the second rap nailing down the first, and a soft universal exhalation arose from the crowded ranks of spectators. Everyone had been certain that the old ironsided Yankee judge would rule favorably for old ironsided Dr. Benjamin Nathaniel Sommers, but now the trial was up for grabs. They had witnessed that justice was not an ugly Bridgeport courthouse built way back God only knew when, not a political crap game with a cozy loyalty for the first families. The judge had unsheathed justice like a naked sword. Most of them had come to witness the embarrassment of Dr. Benjamin Sommers and enjoy the warm flush of forgiving him. After all, the man in the hospital operating room who had actually done the abortion was the big Cuban doctor. If Benjamin Sommers had been foolish enough to admit the woman into the hospital over his signature, then assisted more or less—what the hell, she must have been like a daughter to an old man who had only sons.

The woman, who was too darn good-looking for her own good, well, she'd had her fun, and probably with that Cuban doctor. Now, surprisingly, the judge had ruled in a way which lifted her sins to the more easily forgivable level of the doctors' mistakes.

At the long scuffed-oak press tables, and the new shiny extra table, the foreign reporters conferred in whispers about in-depth interpretation.

"*Mire*," the Buenos Aires *La Prensa* correspondent said to the Caracas *El Tiempo*. "How the hell can I file a story with the basic issue being a philosophy of life?"

"Don't," the *El Tiempo* man answered in Spanish. "For us, Mayoso is the lead. He's the only one who doesn't think we come from banana republics with popcorn revolutions. If they freeze him here in this cold country, we'll catch pneumonia in Latin America."

"Wonder how that dignified ol' coot Terrence will handle this one," the Bridgeport *Post* reporter said to the Hartford *Courant* man. As local newspapermen, they were relaxed, superior to the visiting firemen, confident of their command of every detail of local color and their pressroom friendships with courthouse officials. They left the deep-think and background social analyses to the big-city crowd from New York, Washington, and several foreign capitals.

"The corporation of trustees at Yale is not going to like this," the New Haven *Register* legman said. "Old school ties aren't supposed to get knotted around a dame with fame."

The tensely coiled silence of the courtroom was unsprung. People jumped up, some stretching and yawning, loud talk released everywhere, others shuffling along the aisles of wooden benches, gesturing with surprise and excitement. The jockeying for position in the spectators' line had been worth the wait.

The television men wrestled with their cables as skillfully as snake handlers. When they darkened their big Fresnel lamps, the courtroom returned to shadowy strips of light stenciled by the slanted oblongs of morning sun. Newspaper and magazine cameramen at the press table pawed through their leather equipment cases for high-speed lenses and films for their last chance at courtroom shooting.

Each began to document his own choice of objective photographic coverage: Betsy Sommers, mostly. Caught in profile, or preferably from a low angle to emphasize her legs crossed high above the knee in the carefully trained posture of an actress, the short skirt riding up, legs close together. Beyond the cameramen and press corps stretched invisible hierarchies, staff and line, rewrite men ("JUDGE RULES AGAINST DOCTORS' SEPARATE

TRIAL"), editorial writers ("When medical scientists of high repute in high places . . ."), columnists ("Below the obvious surface of a criminal trial, more complex issues require analysis . . ."), beat-the-competition commentators (Flash! Word just in from that Connecticut trial! The judge has just ruled . . ."), bureau chiefs ("I want a balanced story, Joe, until the evidence gets dirty or legally tricky. Pick up the big names, then drop 'em. . . .").

On the blocked-off street outside the courthouse, the BBC Third Programme documentary crew had set up their No. 1 camera's zoom lens to cover the courthouse, the street turmoil, the antique autos and pickets. No. 2 was trained for the moment on the TV engineer who wore earphones and watched the screen of his own monitor set.

"Andover," he said to the bespectacled director beside him. "Eurovision satellite systems operational and clear."

The director pulled off his glasses and raised one hand as a signal to the program narrator who faced the camera from across the street. "Stand by. Stand by, please. Stand by."

"Eurovision link with Fucino and Prague now operational and clear. Tape rolling, five seconds to air time—four, three, two, one." The director's arm came down, and the test-pattern picture on his monitor screen changed to the narrator standing in an open street before the courthouse. The narrator spoke conversationally, very person-to-person, with an Oxbridge accent, directly into the camera's intimate eye.

"World Edition. Alistair Duguid reporting from Bridgeport, Connecticut, U.S.A. We bring you the third dimension behind the headlines, a report in depth, a weekly on-the-spot editorial page, from the New World to the Old via communications satellite. Today's report: The Lady and the Tiger . . . Showcase or Showdown?

"In this courthouse behind me, one of the fifty sovereign states of the United States, the State of Connecticut, has placed on trial two men and a woman. Also on trial is a point of view about men and women, the nature of human reproduction, and the relations between nations, although none of these is charged in the indictment. Presiding Judge Lehane has particularly said such subjects do not belong in his courtroom. The state can charge crimes only to people, not social forces. In this case the people are Doctor Dionisio Mayoso Martí, Doctor Benjamin Nathaniel Sommers and Mrs. Elizabeth Sommers. Mrs. Sommers is known to all here, in this nation of nicknames, as Betsy.

"Perhaps one can best understand the brouhaha of the doctors' and Betsy Sommers' trial by recalling unique trials in one's own country in which part of the nation was on trial invisibly alongside the defendant.

"Recall the Dreyfus trial, in which the French General Staff was the invisible antagonist and protagonist.

"Recall l'affaire Profumo-Keeler, in London, in which the Establishment found itself pilloried. The Fascist and Nazi show trials of Matteotti in Rome and Dimitrov and Torgler in Berlin, which so early showed the Fascist and Nazi governments and judicial systems for what they were. The Tukhachevsky trial in Moscow under Stalin.

"With a bit of historical imagination, one can see other *social* trials, if I may use that term, other ghosts walking those worn steps behind me. The Scopes trial some forty years ago, in which not only a schoolteacher was on trial, but also Darwin's theory of evolution in conflict with a fundamentalist interpretation of the Bible. Also, in some of the harsher statements about Doctor Mayoso and his research on human reproduction, one hears an echo from the Place de la Concord of the Revolution.

"So the courthouse behind me is a lens to focus America, that is to say, the America which is an offspring of all of Europe, and as the Yanks say, and then some. The laws here in the U.S.A. are Hebrew, Greek, Roman, British, Napoleonic, and uniquely American, quite in that historic order.

"You see, then, our Old World and the New are here fused in ways of life and codes of law which will—in days to come—deeply affect the jury inside the courthouse in ways they may hardly consider consciously. The world of northern Europe, the world of the terrible religious wars of the Reformation, the world of Protestantism, led directly to the laws of Connecticut governing man-woman doctor-patient relationships which the two doctors and Betsy Sommers are charged with having offended by an act of homicide. The world also insists on sitting as a jury. It sends these pickets and demonstrators you see in the background to Golden Hill Street outside the county courthouse. . . .

"And here, as our camera comes round, you see what Judge Lehane called the tumult and the shouting. . . . These pickets in expressive skeleton costumes . . . these antique cars . . . and—here—a few platoons of easygoing small-town policemen, who, unlike those in New York, London, Paris, Rome, any European capital, have had little cause to practice riot control . . . and there, at the bottom of this hilly street, named, curiously, Golden Hill Street—'steeper,' as Betsy Sommers, who is devoted, perhaps addicted, to literary allusions, said last week, 'steeper than the Via Dolorosa'—there at the bottom of Golden Hill Street is none other than Main Street, one more of America's ten thousand Main Streets . . . somewhat like our many High Streets at home . . . or the Karl Marx Streets of Eastern Europe and China. . . ."

Aie, Mayoso, Filho thought, on their street of gold, they'll pile more faggots for your auto-da-fé. Karl Marx Street would be a better address than Golden Hill, hombre.

Without taking his Pharaoh eyes from the television set in the Delegates' Lounge of the U.N., Filho set a Montecristo cigar firmly between his teeth. The morning's news from Havana was encouraging. Even though the Chinese had reneged on their promise to buy two million tons of sugar, a disaster equal to the damage of the last hurricane, the Soviet negotiators had just signed a deal for the lot at prices pegged high enough to barter for Soviet-bloc capital goods.

As he took the first long draw on his cigar, Filho said in his mind to the British narrator on the television screen: Is this your famous intelligent Third Programme? To show the visual symptoms for dramatic effect, but never the disease underneath?

Aie, Mayoso, I warned you. Pity, the fatal disease which killed even God.

At Los Angelenos Mercy Hospital, Dr. Gerald Roone was being paged by Emergency. He was in the men's room, carefully and precisely tearing to bits a letter from Betsy. She had addressed it to him at the medical school, with neither a signature nor a return address to identify the sender, and the school had forwarded it to him at the hospital. She had written only two words: *Don't worry*.

He flushed the toilet and watched the paper fragments circle faster and faster and then plunge downward into the plumbing, out of sight.

You said it, mother, he thought. Step down, next witness.

Then he heard himself being paged and swung easily and silently out of the room on his white rubber-soled shoes. Another day, another dirty shirt.

Rafael de Jesús Cándido Santos Roque, Governor of the Commonwealth of Puerto Rico, looked over the tortoiseshell rims of his scalloped half-glasses at a television set Jorí had wheeled into his big office.

"Jorí," the Governor said, "don't we know that Englishman from someplace?"

"Sí, sí," his aide said. "He was here with a camera crew last year. They did a program called 'Caribbean Crossroad: Left, Right, or in the Middle?'"

"Oh yes. That interview in the garden next to the mosaic table." Alistair Duguid had asked him the impossible: to predict the revolutionary potentials of Latin American countries. The Governor had paused, pretending to think hard, but had been captured by the colored mosaic inlay, 1492. What a year that must have been. The change in popes, the Moslem scimitar across the Mediterranean, Columbus under sail toward the outer edge of the known world. And this bright young man wants me to prophesy for his TV cameras the future of a volcano?

Several blips of swift color winged into his office and flickered past the chandelier. The *reinitas* skimmed around his walls, then pivoted wildly out another window. Below him, in the lush foliage of the garden, the fountain spurted gently, a serene splashing sound.

That long-distance telephone discussion with Judge Lehane, Santos Roque thought, a circle going nowhere except to return to its starting point. That rockbound Yankee reserve. It was all that I could do not to remind him that Tacitus warned long ago against exchanging the oppression of tyrants for the oppression of laws.

Less than a mile from where Governor Santos Roque sat watching his television set in La Fortaleza, the long green combers came foaming toward the Santa Rosa Gate to the shore of the Santa María Magdalena cemetery. Tranquilino came whenever he could, usually on Sunday afternoons, to put a fresh flower in the vase above Cristina's grave. It was understandable, but mournful, that the stonecutter had refused to finish the statue. Ah, one bears with God.

The bonging bronze community of five hundred bells clanged across the limpid air of Rome, scattering flocks of *rondini*. They spiraled upward above the olive trees into the sienna-colored Sabine hills, pivoting on their wingtips over urine-stained Trastevere squalors, the burnt-umber palazzi of exquisite corruption and elegant cruelties, wheeling past seminarians clopping along in sandals past the Communist offices on Via delle Botteghe Oscure, swooping over the two-by-two hand-in-hand columns of uniformed little girls shepherded by nuns over early-rising *negozianti*, skimming above Moses brooding massively in a dark corner of San Pietro in Vincoli and the stone woman in the Basilica of St. Peter bent heartbroken above the carved body of her dead son.

But the clangor of the bells hardly penetrated the damp narrow mausoleums dug into the grottoes of the lower Vatican basilica or the lofty colonnaded travertine passageways lined with blank-eyed Roman portrait busts in niches; the murals crowded over ornate walls and domed ceilings with painted pale martyrs, adoring kneeling saints, muscular prancing satyrs carrying Bacchus as a lustful cherub through the pomp and grandeur of Renaissance forests.

Within the red damask motion-picture projection room of the Vatican no one heard the bells. The television program from America, from the strangely named place called Bridgeport, Connecticut, had been recorded on videotape, and was now being projected on a screen.

Three men sat erectly in the highbacked baroque gilt-and-red Genoa velvet chairs, two in priestly garb, the third a layman. There was a shadowed anonymity in the room, for they could only barely see one another in the spillover from the light beam of the videotape projector. Much of what was on the screen did not interest them, so they held their conclave sotto voce, ignoring parts of the recorded narrative sound track of Alistair Duguid in remote Connecticut.

Bishop Sosa's eyes closed with patient ex cathedra tolerance. He had gained weight in Rome, and, even at rest, the surge of his breathing was visible. "A parochial trial," he said. "A suburban matron and two physicians. Not every burning matchstick is a bonfire, Father Möttl." He opened his eyes and glanced at his secretary. "Not so, Father? You disagree?"

"But this is much bigger than an American imbroglio, Excellency. I'm convinced this is only one more arena which engages the lifeblood of the Church around the world."

"You are *engagé*, Father. You and I bring an understandable intensity to Doctor Mayoso and his apostate ideas."

The layman, an editor from *L'Osservatore Romano*, spoke for the first time. "The woman is also an apostate."

"Not—" Father Möttl started to say.

"An Irish apostate never lets go," Bishop Sosa said. "They may become violently anticlerical, but you'll find him—or her—in church each year on Holy Thursday and Good Friday. They remember the anti-Catholic penal laws of old British rule, and how they welcomed the Jansenist teaching at the seminary of Maynooth—"

"Excellency—" Father Möttl interrupted politely.

"I know, Father, I know. The Jesuits denounced them as Calvinistic. And the Jansenists attacked my Order for granting absolution from sin too leniently. But that must be the legendary and historic past from which the Sommers woman came, the keel of her vessel—of which she probably knows nothing while she believes she steers with the loose rudder of free will."

"The sensational branch of the press," Luigi said, "has made her very complicated, *la femme fatale, la femme inoubliable,* a suburban Cleopatra."

Father Möttl raised his head. "Actually, she looks like a pretty and rather sweet child."

"You *know* her, Father?"

"We met. She asked me for directions in the cathedral of San Juan." He decided against saying more.

Luigi referred to a file of clippings. "The newspapers report that very little of her education was religious. Most of her education is personal, much of it from very wide but indiscriminate reading. Like many who teach themselves at public libraries, she is forever quoting." Luigi put aside the file. "One can psychologize: Is she showing intelligence or a highly motivated memory? Or only indulging in a schoolgirl performance to replace her missing parents and confessor with guiding precepts from books?"

On the screen, as the conversation paused, Alistair Duguid could be heard saying, "Every culture has and has had its own idea of how rigid or how elastic this control of sexuality should be. The extremes run from no control all the way to very rigid control. Either extreme knocks the world flat on its axis. . . ."

"That's a pun in English, isn't it?" Luigi asked, leaning across the arm of his chair toward the bishop.

Bishop Sosa sat still, watching the British narrator on the projection screen. "No control or very rigid control. Luigi," he added imperturbably, swiveling toward the editor. "May I suggest a brief mention for our short-wave wireless. Not the people, but the issues. Perhaps an editorial, too?"

"*Prego,* Excellency. But we have a feature story already worked up."

"Along what lines, Luigi?"

"Along Sons of Italy lines. That one cannot travel from New York to Bridgeport, or New Haven, Connecticut, without riding over tracks put down by Italian immigrants to New England—"

"*Bene.* Historical. Factual. Mediterranean Catholicism woven into the American fabric. The ancient Hebraic lex talionis softened by charity and humility." He pointed at the screen. "But this? The inheritance of the harsh New England ministers. The Cotton Mathers. The Comstock laws —all derived historically from the puritanical Pilgrims, not from Catholic doctrine. These emotional distractions cannot blind the Church from the longest view of the nature of man. The Pope's words were *in signum legationis divinae—*"

"Pope—?" Luigi reached for his notepad.

"Pius XII followed the encyclical of Pius XI on marriage, *Casti Con-*

nubii, saying it was as valid today as it was yesterday, and it will be the same tomorrow and always."

"Tomorrow and always?" Father Möttl's question startled even himself.

"Are you surprised? That to the Church a century is like an hour? Not the secular here and now, but for all times, *semper tradita?* We reject the whole legacy of secularism, from Darwin onward."

"Excellency," Möttl said, "the trial is cast in secular form, but it's a holy contest."

"As important as all that? The glow of understanding in one editorial by Luigi is more profound than the glare of sensationalism."

"Excellency, we are all on trial. We should take a position."

"Father, I'm always mindful of your strongly held positions—"

"May I suggest even more? A cable, *molto urgente,* to the Papal nuncio in Washington requesting an observer at the trial?"

"Father, you say you've met the woman?"

Father Möttl recognized the bishop's gambit. "Mrs. Sommers is estranged from the official Church, but she may find herself so in good faith. In good faith she is still within the Church if she is of good conscience and subjectively inculpable before God."

"What is intrinsically wrong, Father, you know as well as I do, cannot become right because of an existential situation. Ends never justify means. My regret is that this trial should have widened into a whirlpool in which all men see all manner of things. The Church has been presented as a medieval monolith, crushing two helpless men and a woman. That is unequivocally not so."

"Excellency, thanks to the opportunities you have given me, I see these people differently than I did in Puerto Rico. From this room I can see German Catholicism struggling toward a less dogmatic theology, the French toward less nationalism, and the Spanish genius changing from speculation to social action. From this elevation, if we fail to give united witness in this trial, we harm ourselves with the Catholics among the most loyal and generous to Rome, the Americans."

"In my editorial I can sketch in our *pou sto,* the place we stand on—"

"Sketchy editorials are not enough, Luigi! We'll sound like Curia autocrats spraying a bonfire with a perfumed atomizer of holy water. As foolish as chaplains who push Holy Communion through a pigeonhole to the nuns so they won't be contaminated by the sight of anyone but themselves." Möttl twisted toward Bishop Sosa. "What is science but an act of faith without reverence and victory without triumph? When the Americans compare us with science, they picture a sleepy giant puttering between novenas and beeswax candles. In the Latin American countries we have a defensive besieged position because most of us have retreated into past glories. We dine off china, collect rents and dividends, and share the property and protocols of dictatorships."

Bishop Sosa held himself with a brooding immobility. "I thought," he said gravely, "Rome would temper you as conservatively as it has me. But the opposite has happened."

"Excellency, between us there can be no conservative and no liberal. There is only the importance of recognizing more changes in the last five years than in the five centuries since St. Peter's was begun."

"There is virtue in what you say, Father, but after two thousand years of upheaval and catastrophes the accumulated wisdom of the Church avoids hubbub and diocesan heroics and shields itself from errors and imprudence. We've seen too many sins of commission."

"Excellency, there are also sins of omission. We change only with understanding. Else you would not permit me to oppose your thoughts so freely, no? To have spoken out this way five centuries ago would have meant having the skin cut from my hands and lips to wipe out the ordination of holy oils before my execution. Yet, here we sit today, and you permit me this privilege."

"Only because you have employed your time so humbly and so austerely with pastoral concerns and the corporal works of mercy. Also—and you must not quote me, Luigi—I have been deeply impressed by a statement by Cardinal Suenens. When he saw not a single woman among the laity invited to our ecumenical sessions, he said, 'We are ignoring half of humanity.'"

Luigi held out both his hands, as if begging Möttl for reason. "Father, what do you want us to do? Take sides with the people on trial?"

"We don't presume we are angels. We should not cast them out as devils."

"An *abortionist?*" Luigi stared at the bishop for support, aghast. "*Gesù!*"

"Father," Bishop Sosa said, "you cannot mean that—"

"Excellency, do I have the right to withhold water from a man dying of thirst? Do we have the right *not* to intercede if an act of intervention saves both life and soul? This storm over the pill—artificial or natural? Yet artificial respiration saves a drowning man. Do we shrink from using it because it is artificial and not a natural intervention?"

"You move too fast for me—"

"Only because speed is part of our times. Everything *immediatamente*. Excellency, I have read in textbooks, all this week, that when the male sperm fertilizes the ovum, the chromosomes shared in that meeting contain in their molecules the entire blueprint of a new life from then on. That new life has sacred rights, but the biological process, as a process, should have none. To understand this means reconsidering the Church's position on abortion, especially if the mother's life is in danger."

"Father, our spiritual task is to elevate the Church to a peak of moral authority, *urbi et orbi*, which she has not held since the Middle Ages. There must be better ways of reconciling continuity with change than an eruptive crisis in religious authority."

"Excellency," Möttl said hoarsely, "that explosion is already upon us. My eyes are opening. We're attacked for arrogance, and I see I myself have been guilty. I proclaimed anathema from the rooftops instead of listening to the suffering in all those confessional voices."

Bishop Sosa stood up abruptly, casting the looming stately shadow of his head and shoulders on the videotape screen. "I've seen enough. Please remain seated. Luigi, an editorial? *Bene*." He inclined his head toward Möttl. "Father, it is by neglecting small things, not big ones, that we fall away little by little. Mental sobriety compels me to ask for an aide-mémoire of your sentiments first thing tomorrow morning."

In the *archivio* of Extraordinary Ecclesiastic Affairs of the Vatican's State Secretariat the shelves were stacked with boxes, edge to edge, laid neatly as bricks, each labeled in Italian with a name of one of the world's countries. Father Möttl hunched over the small airweight Swiss typewriter in his lap, typing clumsily, baffled by the impossibility of summarizing his views in an aide-mémoire for Bishop Sosa.

He stared blankly out across the vaulting apse dimmed by the gray hairnet of light strung over St. Peter's Square, hardly seeing the enormous world-encircling embrace of Bernini's marble colonnades or the majestic apostolic statues on the basilica who were as meditative as he was. From anathema to a beginning of understanding, a long hard road. Rome, Mayoso had said in the hospital, will never show you the Italian darkness: for each one born, another is aborted in hiding. Now I know his terrible statistics are right.

The College of the Propaganda Fide was outlined darkly against the sky at the extremity of Janiculum. The east bank of the Tiber was underlined by shadow, the liquid curve still hazy between Ponte Umberto and Ponte Mazzini. The whole crowded swarm of Rome winged like a flight of arrows toward him—the stony Appian Way outstretched past the Caelian Hill, the emerging mountains of Tivoli, and Via Aurelia running to the sea. Domes, belfries, monuments, ruins, towers, chapels, basilicas, cathedrals—the tawny external splendor lay stretched in slumber, muscular and potent as a lion.

Time everlasting, a fragment of Dante's vision of infinity. He lowered his eyes to human scale.

A letter to Mayoso, he thought; *logos,* a word of humaneness. But how unwise that would be. Yet, change from anathema to understanding. How unexpectedly kind Mayoso had become, that day in his hospital room. Perhaps a cable directly to the court. Wise or unwise—a humane word.

Some workmen on bicycles rode slowly into the square from Via della Conciliazione. Soon they would be chipping, scraping, brushing away the thousand-layered years from mausoleums and sarcophagi in the lowermost sacred grottoes of the second Christian century near the Scala Braschi of the Sacristry. An international flotilla of barefoot seminarians drifted across the square, their loose cassocks billowing like sails in the dawn breeze, the scarlet German cassocks, the Greek blue, the Scottish purple. Only the Americans and Irish wore somber brown and black. Once, so long ago, Möttl thought, I was like any one of them, repeating the same jests that the Society of Jesus was a monarchy limited only by the incompetence of their superiors and the insubordination of their subjects. Now, even as an adopted Roman, may God protect me from such corrosive cynicism.

Dawn was slipping down the timeless Roman streets. He rolled up the page in the typewriter and stared wearily at its oversimplifications. No aide-mémoire could focus medieval parallels with today: the believing-but-questioning Renaissance world which praised Greek antiquity, warred in new lands beyond the seas, baptized souls and sold papal indulgences, worshiped God and hated men. He took a deep breath, loosened his collar, and fitted a fresh sheet into the typewriter. In a burst of rattling keys he typed: "A woman and two men are charged with homicide. To view their trial as parochial and temporary, as we once did the trial of Galileo, is a serious mistake. They are a Galilean telescope, so to speak, through which to view a constellation of societies historically circling around a single sun: the divinity of life in mankind. Our position . . ."

His fingers stopped on the keys. Our position? From anathema to understanding—the century's seesaw across a razor edge. Slowly he crumpled the sheet in his hand and threw it into the tooled Florentine wastebasket at his feet. Oh, Lord, he thought, where does logic end, doubt begin, and faith overcome?

29 In the empty well of the courtroom the three men huddled in a cluster of attorneys' chairs. A mahogany silence imprisoned them, a ponderous indoor quiet scattered only by the wallclock's insistence, hushed by the dusty air of the law's temple.

Mayoso slipped on his new glasses, tugged them off, folded them away, fidgeting after hours of passivity; only patience and common sense will do, he warned himself. This enacts an orderly process, apparently rational. Its irrational origin is not apparent: the idea that men must decide the uses of women. We breathe that notion in and out as uncritically and mechanically as fish bubbling salt water through their gills.

Terrence ran one hand over the flawlessly parallel comb tracks of his freshly barbered hair. He kept his head down, his long yellow pad of notes balanced on his knee, scanning them line by line with lively cynical intelligent eyes as he repeatedly tapped the eraser of his pencil against his teeth.

David coughed once, then, as if he had broken some vow of silence, cleared his throat, hard.

Mayoso saw that David had a cool remote look of distaste; a distrustful man keeping up appearances despite wretched odds.

With everyone else gone to lunch, the courtroom's massive encircling bulk held an expectant temporary quality: a coliseum between combats just after the fallen gladiators have been hooked and dragged feet first across the blooded sand; the brief pause before the next act, when the lions would come.

"Didn't you say," Mayoso asked Terrence, "you wanted us to have a family conference?"

"Yes, I did. But the Sommers have dodged me. Marjorie wanted Witt to stay with her until we join them for lunch." Terrence's pencil tapped his teeth once more, then paused in midair. "And against my considered judgment, Benjamin Sommers has taken himself upstairs to get permission to visit Betsy in her cell." He blinked gravely. "So David has kindly consented to represent the family."

David's kind consent, Mayoso thought, from the chafed look of him, has the arm-twisted appearance of a very silent and very reluctant representative. The cancer of distrust. Now is the hard time. We should be together, but we're apart. Even the solid Sommers family is broken into individual fragments, uncommunicative, going their separate ways. Whenever David's troubled eyes flicked by with a show of sightless vacancy, Mayoso detected a buried pain in them. Blind, Mayoso thought, at blaze of noon. He wants to be a bystander at this wreck, not one of the trapped victims. David kept shifting his spectator gaze across the room to the wooden bench where he and Witt had flanked Marjorie all morning.

He's terrified of losing his self-control, Mayoso decided. He actually considers this representing his family a deed of courage. A backbone of solid jello. Now I've found out how he faces a hard decision. He looks it square in the eye, then chickens out. He'll never forgive me this discovery, nor I him. Our brotherhood is splintered; no worse enemy than such a former friend. Under our uneasy alliance smolders civil war, the worst kind.

"Doctor Mayoso." Terrence had an edge of faintly vexed formality. "Would you mind if I speak to you straight from the shoulder? After all, you're almost one of the Sommers family—"

"Of course. They're the only family I have, one might say."

"Exactly, exactly. That's why I've got to be blunt. I had hoped we could take advantage of a Connecticut law, Section 54-196, which provides that any person who assists, abets, counsels, causes, hires, or commands another to commit any offense may be prosecuted and punished as if he were the principal offender." At *principal offender* Mayoso's head snapped up quickly. Terrence put his fingertips together and went on smoothly. "My strategy of making Betsy a separate principal backfired this morning. The judge bushwhacked us by lumping her together with you and Benjamin—"

"Well, after all, we're all in this together, aren't we?"

"To laymen, yes. To an attorney, no. The legal tactic was to separate Betsy. Keep her off to one side. As an isolated principal she could be the lightning rod—"

Mayoso bristled. "By herself?"

"Let me explain, Mayoso—"

"You said lightning rod. Isolated. To stand alone? A sacrificial offering?"

"Only temporarily," Terrence said uncomfortably. "In no time at all, almost immediately, her lawyer could enter an appeal for mitigation."

"I don't know what that means. Except, maybe, dragging Betsy through more jails."

"She's the one who's stubborn about that unnecessary kind of self-punishment. Her reasoning escapes me."

"She doesn't reason, Terrence. To understand her, use your imagination."

Terrence bent forward and rapped Mayoso's knee with the pencil as if

calling a dull pupil to attention. "Look. You may be standing on a trapdoor, but don't pull a hood over your eyes. Look at the facts, not Betsy's
imagination. In a criminal case like this we don't have a lawsuit—we have
a fact suit. Facts, facts. Brief, material, and relevant. The rule of law,
opinions, fancy technical reasoning"—he waved his hand—"that's television blarney. The judge wants facts. The jury will want more facts."

"I gave the police plenty of facts."

Terrence pointed his pencil at Mayoso. "But what did you leave out?"
When Mayoso didn't answer, Terrence added softly, "Mayoso, I've just
reread your statement to the police. There are two big factual gaps the
state's attorney is sure to focus on." Mayoso's face hardened. Terrence
stared at him impatiently. "You know what's waiting for you if we lose
this?"

"Sí, sí. You have explained about that—"

"Not a persecuted patriot, not a secretly imprisoned Cuban political
prisoner. This time you'd be a public criminal—"

"You explained. You explained."

"I'm obliged to be candid, Mayoso. Don't be a nebbish. Don't count on
appeals. Very frankly, we could appeal a criminal conviction up through
the state appellate courts, up to the Supreme Court, and still lose. You'd
literally be a man without a country."

"I know, Terrence. I know. Like the history book stories. The boy stood
on the burning deck."

"This is one hell of an inappropriate time to joke!"

"I apologize. But all this, the strange people out on Golden Hill Street,
the legal language, this courthouse which is becoming our world—all a
little unreal to me, surrealistic, because this is not the whole world."

"If you refuse to think seriously of yourself while withholding important
facts, at least think of the Sommers."

Mayoso kept half an eye on David. "I have." David was a fact.

"Marjorie. You've seen her—chin up, but eyes down. Witt—didn't you see
him this morning?—on his knees, a beggar. The public degradation of Benjamin Sommers, a man who's been like a father to you."

"Terrence," Mayoso said, "I feel all this more than you can know. I
don't need reminders."

Terrence flushed. "Frankly, you worry the bejasus out of me. How can
I represent you if you won't open up?" He jabbed the air between them
with his pencil. "Facts. The first big gap in your signed statement—just
what happened in that motel room?"

"I don't know what happened. I was never there." The cancer was
spreading. He looked from Terrence to David and back again. "Both of
you. You both think I was the one who made Betsy pregnant. You think

I tried to abort her in that motel room. That's what you both think? All the family? Marjorie, Witt? Even Ben? I swear in the name of my lost family, I was never there."

Mayoso saw David's face pale. Terrence became cunning, guarded. "No one's ever said one single solitary word of such an accusation, Mayoso."

"True. I haven't heard David say a single word."

"He's not on trial, Mayoso. You are."

So this was why Terrence had forced David's kind consent to this three-man meeting. To protect Marjorie and Ben and Witt. To set apart Betsy as a decoy. To pressure me. Aie, civil war. There could be no victors, only casualties.

Terrence tapped the notes on his yellow legal pad. "The transcript of your statement to the police has a second hole in it. What happened in the Emergency ward when the ambulance brought Betsy to the hospital? Wasn't Betsy able to talk?"

"Hardly."

"Remember, Mayoso, the state has witnesses. Nurses. The surgical resident in charge of the Emergency ward, Doctor Greene. He'll have to testify you sent him out of the examining room. Until Benjamin came, that left you and Betsy alone."

"Doctor Greene left," Mayoso said with restraint, "because he refused to admit her to the hospital."

"Of course. The state can put Doctor Anthony Hale Douglass on the stand to prove Doctor Greene was only obeying his instructions about such cases." Terrence twisted awkwardly in the wooden chair to face David. "Doctor Douglass had made that a hospital rule, hadn't he, David?"

David winced and began to cough. He nodded his head, meaning yes, trying to speak but unable to stop his coughing.

Mayoso viewed him as from a distance. What did it matter if David couldn't talk? What he said didn't count; only what he did. And David had done nothing. Not a thing. That bitter unforgettable unmentionable fact must be knotted inside David's guts—that, and his quarrel with Mayoso. Civil war. And now there was no enemy like a former friend because of what Mayoso had done, and what David had not done, that day in the hospital.

▢ ▢ ▢

"Where the hell are you?" David had asked over the telephone that day.

"In the Emergency ward. *Mire*, I'm talking through the switchboard, so discretion, okay?"

"Mayoso, I'm with Witt—a family thing. I can't leave now."

Mayoso had glanced down at Betsy lying motionless on the examining table, leaden as a corpse under the green surgical drape. Even with the very small injection of morphine Dr. Greene had given her, she appeared in a deep anesthetic sleep. Her sunken eyes had rolled upward, as if gazing into the roof of her skull. Greene had left the blood-pressure cuff wrapped around her upper arm for continuous monitoring; it made a wide black mourning band. On the floor lay the glass slivers of the clinical thermometer; in one muscle spasm, Betsy had bitten through it.

Mayoso turned his back to the door of the small treatment room to shield his voice from the corridor. "I've got a patient here in critical condition, David. Incomplete septic abortion. She needs lab work, blood typed, cross-matched, surgery. She should be admitted pronto, but I can't sign her in."

"Isn't Doctor Greene there? He's the surgical resident in charge. Talk to him."

"I have. He agrees she's sick, but that's all. To him this is one more common nuisance."

"I remember. Greene's a tough resident to convince." David's voice changed. "Wait. Hold just a second—"

David must have put his hand over the telephone because Mayoso had just barely been able to make out his saying, muffled, "Witt! Put that damn bottle away!"—then the change in timbre as his hurried voice came back to the line. "Mayoso, I'm sorry, but I've got to stay with Witt—"

"David, I can't explain too much. Trust my judgment. You must come down here right away."

"I just told you—"

"David, this patient is bleeding steadily. Septic endotoxin shock. Blood pressure practically out of sight—I need your signature, we need an operating room—take my word for it."

Mayoso had never heard David lose his temper before. "Your word! You promised to stay away from clinical practice! Especially this sort! If you're not there to teach or do clinical research, what's your crazy compulsion to fuss with these women?"

"I was called—an emergency. David, we're wasting precious time—"

"If you want to go over Greene's head on a surgical emergency, call one of the senior surgical men! You can't take risks with this patient, hear me?"

"Dios mío!" Mayoso pressed the phone mouthpiece directly against his lips to whisper fiercely, "David, this is *Betsy*." For a moment he thought the telephone connection was broken; there was no sound except the clatter of passersby in the corridor outside the door. Beside him, the green drape heightened Betsy's clammy translucent pallor. "David, did you hear me?"

"I heard you! But you haven't heard Witt!" David was shouting with a baffled choking resentment. "You don't know what she's done to him!" His voice dropped. "He's touching bottom. I can't leave him."

"If you tell him Betsy's sick, he'll come with you—"

"He won't. She left him, yesterday. He's not the father—"

"He's not the father?"

"You heard me. She's left him."

"*Jesús!* I don't understand what's going on. I only see her right here. Witt will have to understand how sick she is. The least she needs is curettage, David. She's spiking quite a fever. I'll start fluids and oxytocin I.V., some blood and antibiotics, and stay with her to get the lab work started. Just come down long enough to sign her into surgery."

"Get it through your head—I'm not coming!"

"David, stop ranting and raving. You're a doctor, not a hanging judge."

"You want to get tough? Get tough with her."

"David, stop blabbering, just *come.*"

"You damn fool, she'll ruin you, just like Witt. You're asking me to be a criminal. My God, they could take away your name and mine! We'd be prison numbers for years! Take away our medical license. Our citizenship."

"David, tell anybody the circumstances—tell Witt—she's a critically sick woman. Without good blood pressure, with so much infection in the uterus, she may need total hysterectomy. Do you hear? You know what losing her uterus can mean for Betsy? And Witt? You hear me?"

David's tormented voice boomed furiously from the earpiece, boiling, out of control. "Since when is this *your* problem? Why are *you* so goddam concerned?"

"We're her only brothers, David."

"Come over here, goddammit, and try telling that to *my* brother!"

"You've got to feel for her as much as you always did—"

"Me? I feel just like Witt. She put a gun to the back of his head and pulled the trigger. I hate her guts. She deserves to die."

"You son of a bitch. If you won't sign her in, I'll get a doctor who's a man." Over the telephone Mayoso heard David begin to cough, choking with it.

In the courtroom, sitting beside Terrence, David wiped his lips with his handkerchief. "Sorry." His husky rasp reminded Mayoso of the throttled bubbling from a throat-wounded soldier's open windpipe; it was painful to hear. "Little upper respiratory thing I can't seem to shake off." David cleared his throat noisily.

"Doctor Greene was following hospital policy," Terrence repeated. "A fact, Mayoso?"

"Yes." The hoarseness of his own voice surprised him. Remembering the struggle with David over the Emergency ward phone had speeded his pulse rate as if they had just finished snarling. Aie, Dios mío. This is only a taste of what will come on the witness stand . . . and the truth shall make you free . . . but anything about David's betrayal could not be said, not ever, not to anyone. Neither Betsy nor the Sommers must ever hear it. Make an end to civil war, family vendettas. Each of us has done enough harm to the other. Our offenses against the state have already been paid. Standing trial will be only a tightening of thumbscrews, while all the ancient urges to appease the totemic gods by sacrificing a maiden will poison the courtroom. Ah, change the laws, change them, and even then we will still need to learn how to live with one another. Civilization moves by hunger and love, but the hungry multiply, while everywhere we distort love. How can I ever again hide away in my hilltop bohío? From now on I will have to live on the Main Street of the world where the people are who make the laws, break them, make the mistrustful motions of love and break one another.

In the thickening ugly silence Terrence said quietly, "Mayoso, I won't pursue this line of questioning about your relationship with Betsy."

"That's wise, very wise."

"But be ready for the state's attorney. With the facts."

"There are no brief, material, or relevant *facts* about Betsy and me," Mayoso growled wearily, knowing no one believed him.

Terrence tugged at one earlobe and screwed up his eyes, tilting back his head to consult the ceiling. "I've got an idea. Just a thin wedge of an idea—"

David interrupted. "If your idea includes my father, drop it. He's had more than he can take already."

"David, your father's the traditional good Samaritan, and everybody knows it. Jim Stacy knows it. I can assure you Mr. Stacy has no wish, personal or political, to make himself look the villain by hounding a dignified and well-known doctor in his aging years."

"Then," Mayoso said, "it boils down to Betsy and me."

"When the heat's on, yes. The opening wedge of my idea for you is the pair of cables Jim Stacy received today. Character references for you."

"*Character* references? Cables?"

"Cross my heart. I was just as surprised when he showed them to me. Stacy was very much impressed by the caliber of men willing to speak up in your behalf. Governor Santos Roque. Also, and this carried weight, some priest writing from the Vatican. Better than a bushel basketful of fan mail. Casts you in a new light, for Stacy."

"But he's cast himself as the Lord's avenging angel. You make him sound reasonable."

"My theory," Terrence said, with a shrewd appreciative narrowing of his eyes, "is that Stacy pegged his charges at a punitive height so that he could lower the charges charitably at the right time. He can punish and forgive. That way he wins the affection of both sides."

"Is that possible?"

Terrence sighed. "He's a bright, aggressive, ambitious man. Anything is possible. Why would he show me those two cables?"

"You mean he wants to make a deal?"

"No, no. Nothing as crude as that. But he sees the handwriting of public opinion on the wall. In the newspapers. On the television. The reporters have written you up as a refugee leader. An oddball, but a humanitarian."

"So. It's Betsy the crowd wants."

Terrence tapped his teeth again with the end of the pencil. "Let me show you something." He reached under his chair to pull out a newspaper which had been folded to frame a large two-part picture. "This must have been taken the day Betsy was bound over to the grand jury."

Mayoso squinted at the double photograph. In the left half, Betsy had been caught approaching a picket outside the courthouse. Her face was twisted sideways, incredulous and startled by his large overhead sign which read: SHE EATETH AND WIPETH HER MOUTH AND SAITH I HAVE DONE NO WICKEDNESS.

The neighboring half of the newspaper picture showed the reverse side of the picket's placard: LUST NOT AFTER HER BEAUTY IN THINE HEART, NEITHER LET HER TAKE THEE WITH HER EYELIDS.

Mayoso frowned at the photograph. After thousands of years, still the same angers. Women had to be either mothers superior, giving uncarnal virgin births, or the opposite extreme, wanton daughters of Eve. "Either nuns or whores," Mayoso muttered, "never just plain ordinary people."

"Some very plain but extraordinary ladies," Terrence said harshly, "are this minute competing outside. One group is passing around mimeographed do-it-yourself abortion instructions while across the street another dame hands out free bumper stickers that say KILL A COMMIE FOR CHRIST."

Mayoso began to fold the newspaper, then suddenly tore it full length and dropped it on the floor.

Terrence tipped back in his wooden chair. "I'm afraid that about sums it up. Jezebel. Bathsheba. But with this morning's cables backing you in the public record and a little cooperation from you on the witness stand, we can make you a saint by comparison."

"Oh? Sell Betsy to buy me? I'm the humanitarian, am I?"

"Wait. Stop right there. My responsibility is to win your case, but you can't win Betsy's. We've got to show you're well-meaning, but taken in. You can't afford the slightest appearance of being her accomplice or champion."

"That's like putting her in solitary—"

"That's like common sense. What the hell do I have to do, petition and plead and coax you on my rheumatic knees?"

"Stacy showed you those cables for a reason—"

"Maybe. You're the boy on the burning deck. Maybe with a little dignified mooching and schnorring and sniffing around we can turn the tide your way, Mayoso."

"What in God's name do you want me to do?"

"In your own name, cooperate."

"You mean ignore her?"

"Completely. Don't even say hello. Don't visit her. Don't write. Don't nod. Nothing."

"Aie, you too?" Mayoso said softly. "After we isolate her, which of us will cast the first stone?"

The turnkey unlocked the door to Betsy's cell with much clattering of metal, then walked away without a word as the police matron inside swung the bars open to admit Dr. Benjamin Nathaniel Sommers.

Betsy stood up to meet him. On the floor beside her was a plastic lunch tray of untouched food. "Hello, Dad," she said.

"Hello, Betsy." Dr. Sommers stepped sideways with a dignified politeness so that the police matron could close the barred door. "Thank you." He was thinner. His suit bagged slightly, but he carried his old bones erectly, his face surprisingly clear except for a faintly puzzled expression, as if he had mislaid a gold-headed cane in the cell. "I'm sorry to interrupt your lunch," he said to the police matron.

"That's okay, Doctor Sommers. Sheriff's office said you and Doctor Mayoso can visit with Court permission, but I'm not allowed to leave you folks alone."

"I understand. Judge Lehane and the sheriff have been very courteous." He held up a cardboard box. "This has been examined already by the turnkey. Do you want to look inside, too?"

"No need. A famous man like you don't sneak stuff in and out. Here, Doctor, please have my chair."

"Thank you. One of the many pleasures at my age is being able to let younger ladies offer a chair and to accept without embarrassment."

The network of wrinkles around his eyes deepened as he turned to Betsy. They looked at one another, then she stepped forward and put her head against his shoulder. He put one arm around her and they stood without speaking.

"Oh Dad," she said, muffled. "This is one more time I feel like crying."

"We've all got plenty to weep for, Betts."

She took a deep breath and sat down abruptly on the cot behind her. "I can't. My eyes feel covered with sand."

He pulled up the wooden chair to face her so closely that their knees almost touched. "You have a mild conjunctivitis. I can see it from here."

"I stay awake all night."

"That's the bottom of the world."

"My mother used to say: 'Be a sundial girl. Just count the sunny hours.' She really believed in nonsense like that."

He tapped the cardboard box on his knees. "I heard you weren't eating, so I brought you a bit of a bite."

"Thank you, but I'm just never hungry anymore."

From behind him, the matron said, "Doesn't touch a thing, Doctor. Honestly! Just tea. English tea and Irish tea and Chinese tea. Tea, tea, tea—nobody can live on just *tea*, can they?"

"Indeed not." Very casually Benjamin Sommers lifted his cardboard box toward Betsy. "Not exactly Fortnum and Mason, but some interesting samplers in here."

The police matron in the corner giggled.

Betsy took the box carefully, as if it were gift-wrapped. "For you, darling, I'd eat stones. Oh my, where'd you ever find this very very thin rye? And paté-filled prunes for dessert!" She lowered her head abruptly, resting her hands over the box, biting her lip.

"It's—" he hesitated uncertainly, then brightened. "Great stuff for snake-bites."

She raised her chin and tried smiling at him. "Ah, it's the tempter in you, Dad."

"If you're trying to flatter an old man, Betts, don't waste your strength. I completely understand and agree with Sophocles' comment: At last, the fires have gone out." He pointed at the napkin inside the box. "Irish linen, I'll have you know."

"Oh, you Yankees! You still believe the Irish have a secret society, or something."

"Not secret, just something."

She spread the napkin on her knees and unwrapped one of the small sandwiches. "Um. I'd forgotten what it's like to be filthy rich."

He moved his head in a short arc, inspecting the cell, the caged ceiling lights, the seatless toilet. "Very plain accommodations. Not much space."

"Enough. Two graves wide, grave and a half high."

"That's a heartwarming description, Betts."

She kept her face as straight as his. "Notice that busy locker-room smell?"

"I've been trying very hard to convince myself that my first cranial nerve would become accustomed to the olfactory stimuli."

"You can't scare me with big medical words. Under that halo there's the same old-fashioned high-button-shoes devil."

"I confess—" he began, then stopped. The word was all wrong. Their whole make-believe that he was a gentleman caller dropping in for a social visit was destroyed by the legalistic sound of *confess*.

"Scientifically," she said, "I've wondered. Urine, that's what I thought it was. You know, that human universal something that clings to all public facilities. But it's more goaty than that."

"Modern luncheon chitchat?" Doctor Sommers asked mildly. "Or just medical hardnosed humor?"

"You're right, Dad. Let's keep it clean."

"It's sweat, that smell," the police matron volunteered from the corner. "Over in the Misdemeanor Block it's paraldehyde for the drunks. In Armed Robbery and Missing Persons it's carbolic on the floor. But up here in Felony it's mostly sweat. People sweat like pigs in here."

"That's what I mean, Dad. The locker room of a losing team."

"Nothing's lost, Betts." Without changing his conversational level-headed tone he added, "We'll go up the line all the way to the Supreme Court if we have to."

"At the state capital?"

"No, Washington."

"Mother would just enjoy a tea party in the capital, now, wouldn't she? Have the White House folks drop in just for laughs."

He decided against mentioning anything about Marjorie's resignation from the U.N. Population Council. "You've been reading the wrong Washington columnists."

"Marjorie must be angry you came here. I don't mean this harshly, but does she even know you're here?"

"Of course. I have no secrets from my wife or my sons."

"And David? Does he know you were coming here?"

"Yes. And Witt, of course. Both my sons approved."

"A mistake, Dad. You're awfully sweet, but the newspapers will say you've turned against your own family."

"You know I haven't. And Marjorie and David and Witt know it. Mayoso and I know it. Who else counts?"

"What the legal gentlemen call the People. Two graves wide. That crowd on the street outside. The People versus me. They want the lady for burning."

"But why should the lady be so cooperative? Why should you, all by your lonesome, force yourself to pay the piper?"

"No piper, dear. Just kettledrums and reversed boots." Through the open barred window came a growl of sounds from Golden Hill Street. "Pavane for a dead princess, played by the Stella Maris Club for Fallen Ladies. The Ancient Order of Hibernians will remember me with black shamrocks on my stone." She paused, then whispered, "I'm talking too much. Witt told me I pretended all the time. I must be wound up like a clock. Oh, Dad." She sighed. "Poor Witt. He must think I hate him."

"No." Benjamin Sommers hesitated. "Worse. He's sure you're ill. Exhausted. That you don't care about him or Timmy."

"Oh God." Her mouth trembled. "Timmy's in Southport? With David's kids?"

"Yes. Until school opens."

"Witt asked you to come, didn't he, Dad?"

"I'd have come anyway, you know that."

"I know. Poor Witt. Always an early bird trapped with a night owl."

"Well, I'll admit that Witt did react a bit to your refusing bail. I'm not trying to make your decisions for you, Betts—but with bail you could be out of here. And that young lawyer of yours! He can't command the staff facilities he needs, the things you should have! You need a whole law firm. Where can a public defender from the Legal Aid Society get that? And your legal young man is so obviously using the newspaper hullabaloo for his own private public relations. It's natural to be ambitious, but I think—"

In a low voice she interrupted. "But I love to help ambitious young men."

Benjamin Sommers cleared his throat. "There's another sandwich in here, Betts."

"Thank you, dear, no. I don't want to keep you in this hole an extra minute."

"What kind of talk is that?" the police matron asked. "With all this publicity, they just dressed up the joint. Cretonne curtains in the corridor. Two nice potted rubber plants."

Betsy began to laugh strangely. Her shoulders shook uncontrollably as

she held her hand over her mouth, gasping, "Rub-rub-"—her voice quavered—"rubber . . ." The matron looked startled as Betsy went off again,
choking with laughter, so beside herself that Benjamin Sommers' façade of
nonchalance cracked. He put one hand on her shoulder.

"Betts—"

"I'm sorry. I'm sorry, Dad—I just remembered explaining how rubber
plants got potted." Her voice broke. "In Caracas. To Mayoso."

"He's waiting down at the desk. He wants to see you."

"Oh, no. Please. I can't. I've done him too much harm."

"Betsy, we all love you. Don't you see? We've all been—a bit insensitive.
But each of us has his own way. Timmy. David and I. Witt. Mayoso, too."
He got to his feet slowly, more bent than when he had come. She stood
up to face him as he said, "We all want to help you."

"None of you can. You're all too close."

"Well, I can understand that, Betts."

"And what have I ever brought to the family—?"

He grasped both her elbows. "You brought us all the poetry and pepper
and salt we didn't have. We all still need you." His fingers had begun to
tremble. Awkwardly, he released her arms, but she raised her hands
quickly to grasp his.

"My dear, my dear," he said brokenly, "your hands are like ice."

She lifted his two hands in hers, hiding her face in them. "In here, people sweat." For the first time she began to weep.

Mayoso's visit was shorter. He had decided to ignore Terrence's instructions about her. I can't become shrewd and inhuman in the name of survival; that would mean simply surviving with one's own corruption. But
Terrence was right about her self-imposed sentence. She's exiled herself,
he thought, seeing her without pretenses, the corners of her eyes and
mouth splintered by exhaustion. "Betsy, only you have all the answers.
They'll ask you questions that can make you or break you."

After a moment, she asked, "What can I say?"

"You have such a funny little not-caring look on your face."

"Oh, you know how scatterbrained I am. I was just remembering our
tête-à-tête at the hotel in Caracas. My getting sozzled while explaining
how rubber plants get potted."

"I don't remember." Caracas? That far-off revolution of hunger. Perhaps Betsy's revolution, just as biological and explosive and widespread,
was a different branch on the same tree of life. He saw the expectant rise
of her heavily curved black eyebrows; she wanted him to remember a
broken thread. He shook his head. "No, I can't remember." Cristina, I do.

Closer to the taproot of the lifetree, twirling barefoot from dark into light. Into dark.

Her expression changed, contained within itself again. "It's too foolish to matter." But you listened, Mayoso, she told herself. You won't want to listen to me again.

"All I remember is your laughing and saying: All our wars are merry and all our songs are sad."

She dropped her head, then raised it slowly. "And I keep having a nightmare. You, coming into the Emergency Room the way I always think of you—Moses down from Sinai in a white coat." She put one hand over her mouth and spoke through her fingers. "Your . . . talking to David on the phone . . ."

"My God, I thought that morphine shot had put you to sleep."

"My head was all dopey and foggy. But I can remember your voice, not the words, your begging him. And his saying no."

"He didn't say no. He—"

"Oh please. Don't bother lying." She pretended her old smile. "I'm down, maybe, but never out. Even asleep"—she raised her hands to tap both sides of her forehead—"those temple bells keep ringing."

"You have to understand. David's never had disaster insurance. Where could he ever learn to live through a hurricane? You have to forgive him."

"No, I'm the one who needs it. But people don't forgive, do they? Because they don't forget."

"You want me to be hopeless? Didn't you just tell me—down, but never out?"

"Yes, Father. Yes, yes, yes."

I deserve that, he thought. "I don't mean to sound so paternal."

"But you do. I always liked you for that, and disliked it very much. From now on I don't want you to worry yourself about me."

"If I do, it's not as a father. To me you appear almost numb. I worry because I know what jail does. The *reinitas,* remember them on the island? They can't be caged. Jails, the loss of privacy—I remember how one withdraws inside, hiding, not caring. The secret of survival is to care."

"You're afraid I won't help you and Dad?"

"We'll manage. I'm afraid you won't help *you.*"

"My lawyer said that Dad won't get more than a slap on the wrist, especially if the hospital trustees and Doctor Douglass back him up."

"Yes, that's possible."

"So everything's twisted around to point to you, isn't it?"

"Not me alone, Betsy. Also you."

"Never mind about me. Any crime was mine, not yours."

"Betsy, no crime. You and I are not criminals."

"You want me to learn how to whistle in the dark?"

"Don't whistle. Just think. Without self-pity, without shame. We should see ourselves as victims, not criminals. Out of millions of people, lightning struck us. . . . You look as if you don't believe me."

She shook her head, not trusting herself to speak. I used to respect his lofty, slightly formal way of expressing himself in English, but I don't anymore. He has that elevated self-energizing tone of compulsive fighters for lost causes. Maybe he gives himself courage to keep fighting by making big talk. For me, I need small talk. A child, a hug at the door and a hot cup of tea.

"Betsy, listen. We're criminals only under horse-and-buggy law maybe a hundred years old. Two hundred years ago a ten-year-old boy who stole a loaf of bread in London was hanged as a criminal. What's criminal and what's not—it depends on who and where and when. Even in Switzerland, what's illegal in one canton has become legal in the next."

What was he saying? She found it hard to concentrate.

"Laws are being changed," he said encouragingly, trying to penetrate her shut-in aloofness. "Everywhere. Marjorie just told us at lunch. The whole Atlantic world is shifting. Criminal code treatment about abortion and pregnancy is being rewritten. There's new health legislation. England, Netherlands, Italy, France—all changing. If they can change, so can the State of Connecticut. We are not criminals."

He's way out, Betsy thought. Way way out. His doctorish reassurance. As artificially good-cheersy as a plastic Christmas tree. "That certainly sounds like lunch with Marjorie. China, Europe. Dishing out global Welt-politik with the soup."

"All right. Drop global. Let's stick to us. If you'll agree we are not criminals—"

"Oh, Mayoso, I *feel* criminal. I'd feel better if you just hauled off and whacked me. After what I've done to you, I can't bear your still trying to help me—"

"But I've done as much for strangers—"

"Why, *why?*"

"Aie, I do what I do for a hundred reasons."

"Please don't try to make me feel better by pretending—"

"I'm not. Nothing we do is an isolated action. It's many things, no? Maybe a memorial to everyone near me I've lost. I want my life to mean something."

"But my life means nothing."

She really believes that, he thought. The frantic grapple of a drowning swimmer who drags under her rescuer. She's really convinced the hand-made beliefs her mother knitted with Irish yarns are old worn-out worthless rags, and her new beliefs must come off the readymade bargain rack —that new love is a brief banging, the matched isolations of passing strangers, new drip-dry synthetic feelings woven to be laundered and drycleaned for another binge or brawl of a party next Saturday night. Viva right now. *Toujours gai.* She really believes she's discovered a new freedom in slavishly raising and lowering her bed behavior like her hemline. But what to say? I'm down, but not out, and I have no more to offer but friendship, and every woman knows that's only a smudged copy of love. He managed to say, "Betsy, your life means a great deal."

"It's easier for you to pontificate. You're a man. A strong one. It's easier for you."

"No, it's hard for me, too. Don't men have feelings? You think their tears are not so salty as a woman's? Don't I dream of having Cristina alive? Doing some satisfying medical work? A house with children—"

"When I think of how your bohío was burned—"

"Better to think of how hot this trial will be. Anyone can build a new bohío, no? But only you can build your case in court. No dreaming of the bones." He put his hand under her chin to lift it. "Look at me. Listen."

Her old quiver of a grin, but lopsided. "I'm no listener, remember? I'm a talker."

He dropped his hand. "Then talk. Tell me. Better yet, tell your lawyer. But come out of your shell."

"I'd rather talk about you."

"You said: don't worry about me. I say the same, but I can prove to you why." He made his voice brisk. "With evidence, the hospital records —infection, fever, shock, hemorrhage—Terrence hopes he can prove I did legal surgery. It's legal to abort to save life."

"You did. Don't worry. I'll tell the judge and the jury and that whole pickety mob outside."

"But think ahead, Betsy. When Mr. Stacy asks you if you or someone else attempted criminal abortion in that motel room—"

"How could I? How? I was stoned. They didn't find a single instrument or anything else in the room. Just a sick woman upchucking like a slob and having a very rough miscarriage."

"Is that it, Betsy?"

"That's it."

"Then Mr. Stacy will ask you: Why did you sign the motel register Cristina Mayoso?"

In her cell, Betsy lay on her iron bunk with her ankles crossed. She was smoking, drawing so deeply on her cigarette that its ashen tip glowed red. She stared straight ahead, hypnotized by the ribbon of smoke spooling into the motionless dank air. Slowly she blew out between her tight lips a long thin streamer of smoke, ignoring the flakes of gray ash which fell softly on her.

In Biblical times adultery came first, then you got stoned. Today it's the other way around. The love bit. Why didn't they tell me the swindle it actually is?

The matron had Scotch-taped on the wall a picture sent to her by Timmy. On the rough sketch paper he had crayoned a kindergarten Madonna ikon of affection: a large oval head, two long uneven green eyes, and a wavering black waterfall of hair, all sloping to the right because he was left-handed. And—a detail which filled her eyes with tears—an upturned smiling red mouth. For a moment, buoyed by a flood of tenderness, life made sense, there was hope in purgatory. When the matron unfolded Timmy's drawing Betsy had tried, as she always did when she felt vulnerable and moved, to say something light, humorous. Saturday's child, she had tried to say, but her voice had failed. Now, musing over her portrait through half-closed eyes, she decided: If I die, he'll hardly remember me when he's grown.

As she lifted the cigarette mechanically to her parched mouth she was surrounded by a companionship of shadows. How often she had lain just like this, flat, spent, ankles crossed primly, gazing upward in the dark, asking Roone beside her: Can you reach the cigarettes? After the anarchy of sexual encounter there was always so little to say. Conversational intimacies with a spent man, a sprawling stranger, was blind woman's buff, a clumsy fingertip touching in the dark to round out fragments of another. To yawn "What time is it getting to be?" somehow sounded as mercantile as the appointment book of a professional call girl. Most important was not to show too much feeling. But under the cool, luv, wasn't there the dream that a silent circle in the forest might be stumbled into, a sweet innocence restored? All that hurrying and scurrying and looking under rocks—what Mayoso had once called the genital search—for what? For what? To brood over a child's crayon drawing of what he had lost? To lie here looking upward, but really downward, in the gathering dark?

A prayer from childhood filtered through her. Hail Holy Queen, Mother of Mercy, our life, our sweetness and our hope. To Thee do we cry, poor banished children of Eve. . . .

She ground her cigarette into the floor. Why pray, with no one to listen?

Why did I sign my name as Cristina Mayoso? Not to injure him, as Mayoso believes. It was envy. Envy of the calm companionable assurance of someone young, dancing, loved; one who knows it and sees a road ahead. But for me a long long trail awinding to this tomb.

Dead end.

30 *THIS WORN LEATHER notebook my father left me is the last of the wine. He and all my loved ones survive in it, which must mean that I do, too. Last night and today have been a doomsday time without end.*

Women are heroic against death, but cowards who cannot face shame. This was clear to all of us: courtroom spectators, judge, attorneys for prosecution and defense, the Sommers family, even the street pickets; all of us today were hushed and hurled in upon one another by her little folding of her hands to sleep, a shared disaster. We were like air-raid victims picking our way among the ruins and rubble of what only yesterday had been an open beautiful city.

Yesterday we were modern, which is to say bright as stainless steel, clever as computers, stunned with the exhaustion of dragging our lengthening chains toward mirages, promised lands which retreat just beyond our fingertips, addicted to private narcotic nourishments to numb us against the greatest overhanging public terror—ourselves. Private hallucinations are madness. Is the sharing of public hallucinations sanity? Tonight, her mirror throws our reflections back upon us.

With the news of her death, our oldest communal deceit died: that we in the Western world believed and lived by the laws and moral guidings and ethical habits of our fathers' fathers. Her death stripped us all naked, and we goggled at ourselves for what we are, stunned by our cunning face of cruelty painted as justice, our burned-out eyes blinded by the hellfire of Guernica and Coventry and Rotterdam and Leningrad and Dresden and Hiroshima, our mouths opened to cry havoc but astonished into silence by astronautical discoveries of a New World, the islands of Columbus revisited. One uncommon woman, one statistically common act, did this to us.

Her afterimage sat in her empty courtroom chair, a ghost at the feast, more real in her death than her inked pictures in newspapers or her phosphorescent glitter on television—the hallucinations offering up for sacrifice a dream-raked glamour girl. Her death made her real: the pretty one who tried to earn love by becoming a love-thing, plundered like some emerald-eyed temple figurine, isolated as a death-cell prisoner condemned by codes, complexities, authorities; to her, invisibles.

All our separated guilts briefly flowed together, an unspoken pact: If you don't say it aloud, I won't. The substitutes for human sacrifice—lambs, ears of corn, wafers and wine, money and anxiety—no longer appease the moloch furnace-mouthed god inside us, and in her death, as in the others of my inner and outer life, I recognize how our jaded senses are discarding substitutes for the real thing.

I was her friend. As someone who loved her, as a physician, I should have recognized her fixed smile when I saw her last, as the tetanic defiant risus of the angry brave ones, the lockjawed useless fury and courage her kinsman must have worn when they propped up his litter in the execution yard at Kilmainham. Gaiety has long been used as a ritual against terror, and I should have recognized her singsong talk and poetic tambourines for what they were: cymbals and gongs and firecrackers to drive away devils.

I tell myself I am no more guilty of this than I am guilty of Auschwitz. Just as the Nazis were directly responsible, this act was directly hers, not mine. And yet and yet and yet . . . the efficient killing of millions, the clumsy suicide of one . . . we know, and I know, this need not have been.

We who loved her are, in the emotion-fearing modern way, less than mourners: we are survivors. Witt is shattered by this blow she has struck him; his family shares his muted agony over hers. I envy their pain, for my decades' scars cover nerve endings woodenly and mechanize my skills as a survivor. I bandage my guilt, I splint my fractures, by understanding the joy she must have felt to know she could bear life.

Genesis without joy had been her childhood mold, and joy without genesis was the pleasure-seeking perfumed air she breathed in her playing at a grown-up world. Half child, half woman, she sailed our deep waters with no compass for true north; the ocean must have seemed an endless fearful place, a flat world, easy to fall off.

The prosecutor tiptoed past her empty courtroom chair—he had wanted to punish her, her body, her shy but haughty-seeming beauty, her careless privileges and primal human pleasures . . . but he did not want to kill her.

The subduing effect of her act, or the humanizing unity of heartbreak, perhaps the orgiastic release it gave them, dampened even the pickets in the street when the Sommers and I came out of the courthouse. Strange, the dead are better persuaders than the living. Every one of us knew she had carried immortality in her womb; now we were mortal fugitives because she was dead.

I could not drive off in their car, with the Sommers. I wanted to be by myself. Once more I walked down the short slope of Golden Hill Street and, at the corner, entered the stream of people hurrying along the endless artery of Main Street.